I0831131

Tales of the Wanderer

Volume One

Garrett Robinson

TALES OF THE WANDERER VOLUME ONE

Garrett Robinson

The author greatly appreciates you taking the time to read his work. Please leave a review wherever you bought the book or on Goodreads.com.

Interior Design: Legacy Books, Inc.
Publisher: Legacy Books, Inc.
Editors: Karen Conlin, Cassie Dean
Cover Artist: Sarayu Ruangvesh

1. Fantasy - Epic 2. Fantasy - Dark 3. Fantasy - General

First Edition

Published by Legacy Books

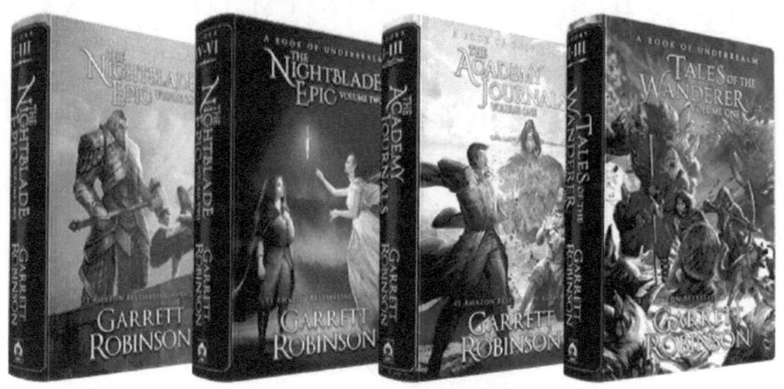

GET MORE

Legacy Books is home to the very best that fantasy has to offer.

Join our email alerts list, and we'll send word whenever we release a new book. You'll receive exclusive updates and see behind the scenes as we create them.

(You'll also learn the secret that makes great fantasy books, *great.*)

Interested? Visit this link:

Underrealm.net/Join

THE BOOKS OF UNDERREALM

THE NIGHTBLADE EPIC
NIGHTBLADE
MYSTIC
DARKFIRE
SHADEBORN
WEREMAGE
YERRIN

THE ACADEMY JOURNALS
THE ALCHEMIST'S TOUCH
THE MINDMAGE'S WRATH
THE FIREMAGE'S VENGEANCE

THE TALES OF THE WANDERER
BLOOD LUST
STONE HEART
HELL SKIN

THE TENTH KINGDOM
A CLOAK OF RED

RISE OF THE NECROMANCER
QUEST

THE CHRONICLES OF UNDERREALM
COLLECTION ONE

THE BOOKS OF UNDERREALM

CHRONOLOGICAL ORDER

NIGHTBLADE
MYSTIC
DARKFIRE
SHADEBORN
BLOOD LUST
THE ALCHEMIST'S TOUCH
WEREMAGE
THE MINDMAGE'S WRATH
STONE HEART
THE FIREMAGE'S VENGEANCE
HELL SKIN
YERRIN
QUEST
A CLOAK OF RED
THE CHRONICLES OF UNDERREALM

CONTENTS

CONTENTS

CONTENTS

CONTENTS

CONTENTS

CONTENTS

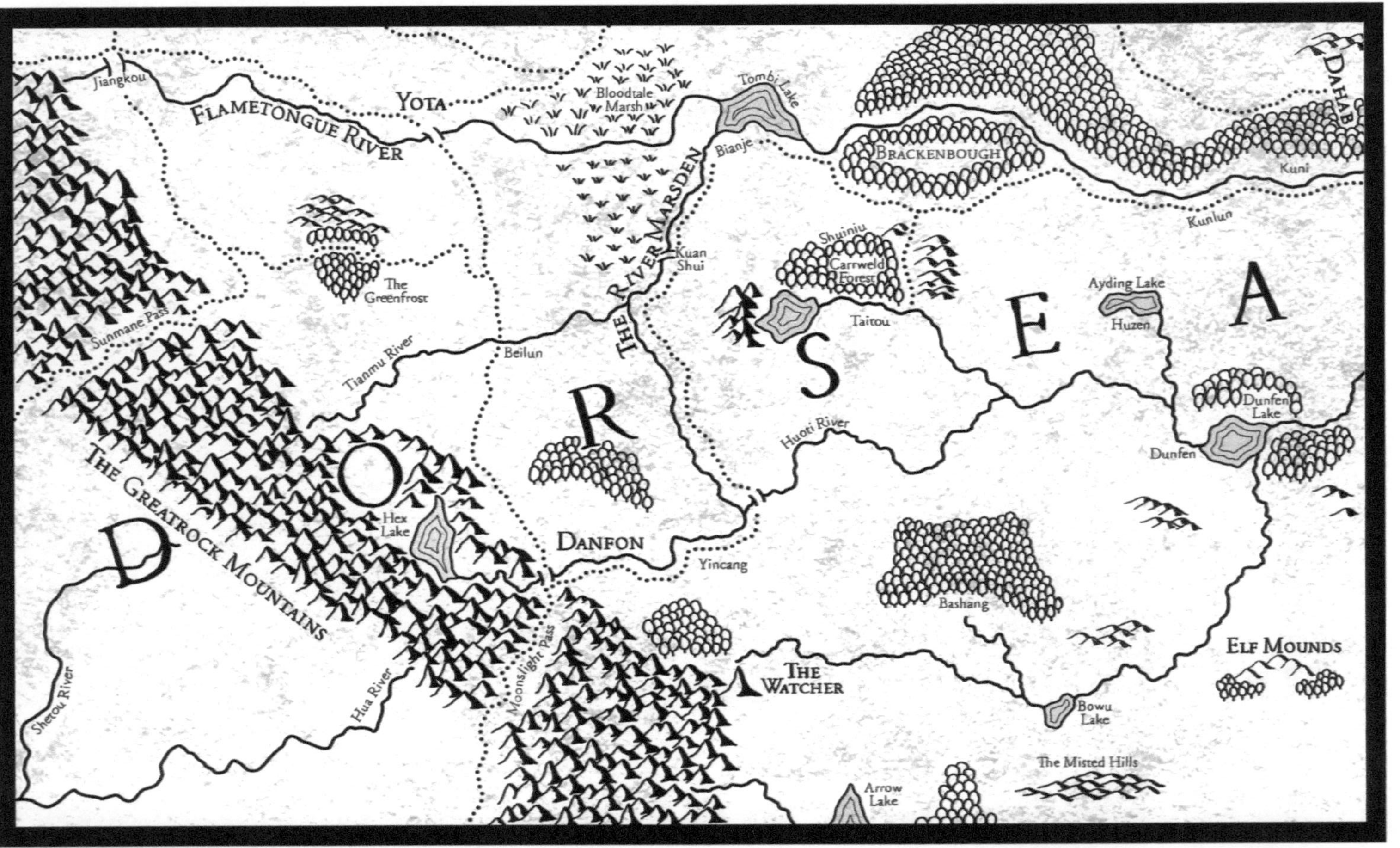

Jiangkou
Flametongue River
Yota
Bloodtale Marsh
Tombi Lake
Brackenbough
Dahab
Kuni
Kunlun
Bianje
The River Marsden
Kuan Shui
Shuiniu
Carrweld Forest
The Greenfrost
Sunmane Pass
Tianmu River
Beilun
Taitou
Ayding Lake
Huzen
D
O
R
S
E
A
Dunfen Lake
Dunfen
Huoti River
Hex Lake
The Greatrock Mountains
Danfon
Yincang
Bashang
Elf Mounds
The Watcher
Moonslight Pass
Hua River
Sherou River
Bowu Lake
The Misted Hills
Arrow Lake

This book is for my family, the ones in my life who have helped me be the person I want to be, and who have kept me safe and sane enough to achieve that.

It is for the wild, untempered community I have found in this world, who love unreservedly and constantly strive to better themselves and each other.

And it is for everyone who has taken even a few steps in Underrealm. We have wandered farther than I thought we would, but I've enjoyed every league.

This ending is not the end, but it is one that's come at just the right time.

Tales of the Wanderer
Volume One

Garrett Robinson

Blood Lust

BEING BOOK ONE
OF THE FIRST VOLUME

OF THE
TALES OF THE WANDERER

ONE

Sun had long ago decided that she would rather be adventurous than sensible. That was why she was wandering the streets of a small Dorsean town in the middle of the night. She had not heard the town's name; she rather doubted anyone in her parents' retinue had bothered to learn it. They had passed through a dozen towns just like it, and they would pass through a dozen more before the end of their journey.

She did not look forward to that end. But then, it had never mattered to her parents what Sun wanted. She was the daughter of a noble family, and she was expected to do as she was told—at least until she herself became the head of her house. That was the cruel joke of a noble's fate. It came in two halves: for the first half, they were utterly subservient; and then one day, the second half began, and everyone else became subservient to them.

Sun wanted nothing to do with any of it. After nineteen years, she no longer had a child's enjoyment of a noble's life. She was old enough to know where it would lead.

It had been over two weeks ago that Sun had first snuck out of the camp, and she had repeated the venture in each new town along the way. Mother never noticed. Even Sun's personal guards had been surprisingly easy to avoid. But the royal procession had been on the road for weeks now, and Sun guessed that the endless journey made everyone weary.

Not often did Sun ask herself just *why* she kept slipping away from the others. She had a vague sense that she was searching for something, but she had no idea what it might be. And so she told herself she only wanted an adventure.

Most of the time, that was easy to believe.

As she strolled the streets, she kept a cautious eye out for any signs of black and gold uniforms—the colors of her house—but saw nothing. She herself had carefully chosen a cloak of muted blue and skins trimmed in the same color. Too, she had worn sturdy traveling boots that would withstand the mud, for the streets of the town were soaked.

Free to wander the town as she wished, she found herself unsure of what to do. At this late hour, there were no shops open. The streets were nearly empty, and the few passersby moved quickly with their heads down against the chill. There were no children playing outside.

Only the taverns were still open. Sun paused in her walk, staring at an open door. Through it poured firelight and voices that floated on the air half-heard, like Elves murmuring in the mist. That thought made her shiver, and she pulled her fine cloak tighter around her shoulders.

Dare she enter? Sun looked uneasily down the street in both directions. She had not gone drinking in any of the other towns. Yes, it would be an adventure, but visiting a tavern in a faraway kingdom might be a bit too risky, even for her. She was no stranger to ale or mead, but she always drank in her family's home, where a host of soldiers were on hand to ensure her safety. She did not have enough coin in her pocket to be worth killing for, but a thief would not know that until it was too late. Then again, mayhap she was safer inside the tavern than out here on the street.

Black and gold flashed at the edge of her vision, and Sun's blood froze.

Two guards in the uniform of her house were walking down the street towards her. At first Sun feared they were hunting for her, but she saw at once that that was not the case. They moved slowly, chatting amiably with each other, clearly off duty. All the same, they would soon pass by, and they could not fail to recognize her.

Sun turned and darted around the edge of a nearby building—and crashed straight into a red leather breastplate.

"Oof!" grunted the armor's wearer—a reedy man half a head taller than Sun. Sun felt a chill as she recognized his red armor: the mark of a constable.

"Sorry!" cried Sun. She spun around him and made to run past—but the constable's hand closed on her cloak.

"Here now," growled the man. "What are you doing skulking about this—"

Before she could think, Sun reacted with instincts honed by her family's master at arms. She spun her arm around the constable's, trapping his wrist in her elbow and then striking his forearm with rigid fingers. The constable cried out and released her cloak, and then Sun was running through the night.

"Sorry!" she cried again, this time hearing the desperation in her own voice.

Dark below, she thought in a panic. *What was I thinking?*

The answer, of course, was that she had *not* been thinking. But the constable would not care about that. And if her family's guards followed their duty—which they would—they would come running to see what this commotion was about. That meant at least three people were chasing her now, in a strange town far from home.

Her stomach lurched as she thought of being dragged back to her parents. For a mad moment, she wanted to keep running, beyond the town's borders and into the countryside, and never return.

But that was foolish. She would have her adventure, and then of course she would go back.

She turned a corner and reached a low wooden bridge over a river fifteen paces wide, running through the center of the town. Sun took two steps onto the bridge before she thought better of it. She seized the railing and leaped over the side, coming down on the soft bank at the water's edge. Crouching, Sun pressed herself back against a wooden piling, her ears pricked.

Heavy boots came pounding down the street. They thundered across the bridge. Sun heard three pairs of them. Her family guards *had* heard the noise, then, and now they were helping the constable in his chase. But all three of them ran straight across the bridge without pause. Sun heard "She went this way!" in the constable's gruff voice. And then the street faded to silence.

Sun breathed a long sigh of relief. Holding the bridge for support, she clambered up the muddy bank to the street. She wiped off the mud as best she could, looking down at herself with a smirk on her face.

"You went looking for an adventure," she told herself. "And you found one, even if it was nothing very grand."

And then, past the far end of the bridge, her family's guards skidded into view. It seemed they had grown suspicious and doubled back. One of them thrust out a finger towards Sun.

"You!" she cried. "Stop!"

Sun declined to obey. As she ran back around the next corner, she thanked the sky for her wisdom in not wearing her regular cloak. The guard had not recognized her from so far away—she certainly would not have referred to Sun as "you" if she had known who she was.

A strange feeling suddenly came over her. She skidded to a halt and tried to identify it. Then she realized—she had been here before. She was back in front of the tavern where she had first seen the guards.

She looked back over her shoulder. The guards were still out of sight, but their footsteps neared with every passing moment. She had no time to think.

Sun darted inside the tavern.

TWO

IMMEDIATELY IT FELT AS THOUGH A SOFT, GENTLE BLANKET HAD wrapped around her. The room was warm from twin fireplaces, but just as heartening was the low murmur of voices, filling the air with the cheer of good company. Most wore the simple clothing of Dorsean farmers and traders, with ballooning trousers and shirts that billowed at the shoulders, then gathered into tight sleeves running from elbow to wrist. Sun's supple leathers were strikingly out of place.

She had stood in the doorway for a long moment now, and people were looking at her. Drawing her cloak tight, she picked her way between the tables. The furniture was clean but worn with age, a reflection of the tavern itself: faded, but warm; old, but enticingly fresh to her eyes. Conversations were friendly but subdued, and the patrons sat straight, their elbows collected, their posture considered. It was quite different from the drinking halls of Dulmun, where revelers lounged in whatever position they wished, some sitting on or splayed across tables, and more often than not, a fight in one of the corners surrounded by cheering onlookers.

Despite the difference from home—or mayhap because of it—Sun felt a powerful excitement stealing over her. It was as though she was in a skald's tale, and every new face a character within it. The room felt like a place where anything could happen, where adventures lurked, waiting for someone to come and get them started.

And then Sun found a man in the corner who stood out among the rest. He was of an age that could certainly have been called venerable, but at the same time he seemed utterly uninterested in veneration. Contrary to the posture of those around him, this man had kicked his chair back to lean against the wall, and one leg was flung across the seat of the chair beside him. In his left hand he held a mug of beer, and his right arm was concealed beneath an old brown cloak that had seen many leagues and much hard use.

Sun stopped in the middle of the room, studying the old man—and she realized rather immediately that he was studying her in return. That intrigued her, but strangely, it did not frighten her.

And then she remembered that a constable and two of her family's guards were chasing her, and fear came crashing back into her mind. She darted a look over her shoulder.

The old man put down his mug and curled his fingers to beckon her. Seeing no better choice, Sun moved to stand across the table from him.

"Put this on." The old man reached into a bag sitting at his feet and pulled out a worn brown cloak, shoving it towards her. His voice was deep, and it grated with age, but it had a pleasant, almost musical quality. Sun briefly thought she would like to hear him sing.

She took the cloak and wrapped it around her shoulders over the blue one, sinking into the chair across from the old man. It was not a moment too soon. Behind her, the tavern door crashed open. Sun knew better than to turn around and look. She huddled under the hood of the cloak—it smelled like sweat and ale, but not in an unpleasant way.

Across from her, the old man's keen eyes swung back and forth, observing the front door without staring too long. "A constable," he muttered. "Alone. Do not turn around."

Sun wanted to tell him that she was not an idiot, but she kept her mouth shut. Instead of turning to look at the constable, she watched the barman. He was a portly fellow, with a bald pate above a fringe of hair that stuck out almost a handbreadth in all directions. As Sun watched, he did a very curious thing. He looked at the front door—presumably at the constable—and then he turned to look at where Sun sat with the old man. But rather than alert the constable to Sun's presence, he only looked at the old man, twisted his mouth, and then shook his head as if to say without words, *Not this again.*

"Tunsha," called the constable from the front door. "A girl in a blue cloak is running about. Have you seen her?"

The barman looked towards the front door again. Then, as if deep in thought, he rapped a silver ring on his finger twice against the bar. It rang out loud in the silence that had fallen since the constable came in.

"Not in here," said the barman. His gaze did not waver.

The constable hesitated a moment, and Sun feared she was lost. But then: "Send for me if you do."

The tavern's front door swung shut. Sun released a sigh. The tavern filled with voices again, the patrons resuming conversations as if the constable had never appeared.

"He knocked to tell the others," said the old man in a quiet voice. "When he hit his ring on the bar, I mean. He let the others know not to contradict him, even though most of them noted you when you came in."

"And they listened?" said Sun. "Why?"

"Because this is that sort of place."

Sun took that to mean *a place where people hide from the law.* And yet, she felt just as safe as when she had first entered. But it did not seem wise to remain.

"I thank you for your help, but I should leave you to your night," she said.

"It might not be wise to leave so soon," said the old man. "The constable will remain nearby for some time, I wager. Wait at least a little while."

"I . . . suppose," said Sun, settling back in her chair. She studied the old man again. He was eyeing her fine leathers, and Sun knew he could tell they were not Dorsean. He himself wore a brown tunic under a dark leather vest, and baggy pantaloons that were out of style here. Neither did his face have a Dorsean look. His skin was almost as pale as a Heddan's, but with a tone and features that suggested Calentin ancestry. Weather and travel had stained every bit of him, particularly his cloak. Sun felt that this was a man who could be very, very dangerous when he wished to be. Yet there was nothing about him that seemed unfriendly, and despite his unusual urging that she remain in the tavern, she did not fear any ill intent from him.

"You look like someone who is looking for something," said the man.

"And what do I look like I am looking for?" said Sun.

"That is less clear," he said. "Though I would not say it is something material. Sometimes we strive hardest for the things that we can only feel on the inside—an adventure, a tale, the thrill of love."

An adventure. "You . . . are not wrong."

He smirked. "I notice that you do not say if I am right."

Lifting his hand, he beckoned to the barman, who nodded and reached for a mug. But Sun had noticed something else. When the old man had waved, his cloak had fallen back slightly. She had thought his right arm concealed beneath his cloak, but now she saw that it ended in a stump just above the elbow. Something about that twinged in Sun's mind. But it was like a thought remembered from a dream, and before she could chase it down, a heavy girl in a faded yellow dress came with a mug of beer. She placed it before Sun and smiled.

"Eight slivers, dear."

"I have it," said the old man, reaching into a pocket.

"No, please," said Sun, grasping for her coin purse. "I can pay for—"

"Of course you can, with clothes like that," said the old man. "But you are a guest here, and I insist. It is my pleasure to share what I have." He produced the copper pieces and placed them in the barmaid's hand.

"Thank you." Sun turned to the barmaid. "And thank you as well."

"Of course, love." The barmaid winked and left. Sun felt blood rushing into her cheeks.

"Have a sip," said the old man. "It is a decent enough brew."

Sun sipped at the beer and found it good. Better than she had expected from a tavern in such a small town, though she still preferred the mead of home.

"That *is* pleasant," she said. "Thank you."

"And even better after a long day on the road," said the old man. Sun must have looked surprised, for he smiled. "Your boots are muddy, and as I said, it is clear you are not from this place."

He did not ask where she *was* from, for which she was grateful, though the question seemed to hang unspoken in the air between them. Slowly she drank another swig of beer.

"The second sip is better," she said. "I imagine the third will be more so."

The old man snorted and leaned forwards. "I love Tunsha dearly, and so I ask you not to repeat my words, but his brew is hardly the best I have ever had. In my youth I knew a woman who could brew the best ale in all of Underrealm."

Sun nodded politely. But again she was struck by a strange feeling—a sense that she was missing something obvious. It was disconcerting. She had never been in this place—why should she expect anything here to be familiar?

As the old man kicked his chair back to lean against the wall again, she studied him more closely. He kept saying how *she* was a stranger in this town, and yet she realized suddenly that he, too, had recently traveled here. His chin bore several days of beard, and his long-worn clothes spoke plainly of travel—not to mention the second, stained cloak which she herself wore over her blue one. And mayhap most telling of all was his money. He had paid for her drink as if it was nothing, and Sun had heard many coins in his purse. Only someone traveling, and traveling a long way, would bear that much coin while looking so shabby.

Then Sun noticed something curious: despite his single arm, there was an unstrung bow leaning on the wall behind him. Sun knew bows, and this was one of the finest she had ever seen. It had certainly been crafted in Calentin, and she had already noticed signs of that kingdom in his features.

Her thoughts came crashing together with the force of an ocean gale. Sun's mouth fell open and went dry all at once, and her fingers clenched upon the mug of beer.

The old man noticed her reaction, and his eyes glinted.

"Yes?" he said amicably.

"You . . . you are Albern. Of the family Telfer."

The old man took a long pull from his mug, returned it to the table, and wiped some foam from his upper lip. "Now, what would make you say such a thing?"

"Your bow. Your face. Your . . . your arm. Forgive me if I am mistaken, but . . ."

He cocked his head. "But do the tales not say that Albern of the family Telfer lived a very long time ago?"

"Not *that* long ago," said Sun. "And none of the tales say that he has died yet."

The old man's smile widened. "Then I suppose there is some worth in them. You have guessed aright."

"But . . . but you . . ." Sun gestured vaguely, having no idea what to do with her hands. "You . . . you fought in the War of the Necromancer, and—and in everything that happened afterwards. You—" Sun's voice fell almost to a whisper. "You walked alongside the Wanderer."

She thought his eyes went a little sad at that. But he answered only, "Take another drink."

Sun did so, downing quite a bit more than she had intended. It struck her gut, and a heady feeling crept into her skull. "I . . . what are you doing here?" she said finally.

Albern only gave her the same sad look. "I did walk beside the Wanderer, as you said. And it is her beer I praised so highly. Is that how you guessed?"

"That was part of it."

"To think that legends of her ale survive to this day." Albern shook his head. "I would give much to taste it now. Those were the days when Mag was happiest—when she lived in Northwood, and ran her inn, and loved her husband well."

Sun gave a start. "Her husband?"

Albern raised his brows. "You know of her ale, but not of Sten?"

"I had never . . . they say she was not a lover."

"They would be more correct to say she was not a bedder," said Albern. "But love? Oh, yes. She loved Sten. And I suppose it is not altogether surprising that he should have faded away from her story. She would hate that he did. Yet talespinners often focus only on the choicest gems in their own treasure. They have not the jeweler's touch, and so they discard the mountings that make the gems shine brighter still."

Sun did not know quite what to make of these words. She tried for a moment to think of an answer, but when she could not, she took another sip of beer instead.

"But now we are unequal," said Albern. "You know who I am, but I know nothing about you."

"What do you want to know?" asked Sun, her pulse skipping.

"Your name, for one thing."

"It is Sun." It felt strange not to give her family name. Her tongue wanted to say it by reflex, and she had to restrain it from doing so.

If the look in Albern's eyes was any indication, he had noticed her omission. But his tone remained kindly. "Do not worry. In this place, you are only yourself. You are not whatever person you left in the street outside."

It was a pleasant thought, that she had left her past at the door like a coat. But she did not entirely believe it. She felt a need to steer the conversation away from her identity, and she had a perfect excuse.

"Is it true what they said about the Wanderer? About the way she fought? All those things she did?" Again her voice dropped almost to a whisper. "Is it true what they say about how you lost your arm?"

Albern smiled. "That is a pile of questions all at once. You know, I imagine, that if I were to tell you all the stories you ask about, we would be here for months?"

"I know that," said Sun quickly. "But . . . but could you tell me the important parts, at least?"

He studied her more closely still, and Sun felt that he was seeing more than her face, more than her fine clothing. She felt understood in a way that she rarely had before, truly seen in a way that no one in Dulmun had ever made her feel.

"The important parts," murmured Albern, and it was as though he was talking to himself. "Yes, I suppose you might need to hear the important parts." Then he spoke in a normal tone of voice again. "But I think the important parts are quite different from what you believe them to be. I will tell you a story if you wish, but not the story of my arm. Not tonight."

Sun could not help the crestfallen look upon her face. "Why not?"

"Stories may belong to whoever knows them, but these are more mine than most," said Albern, smirking a little. "I do not mind sharing some of my adventures with you—but only if you will listen to the ones I choose. Do we have a deal?"

It was not such a bad thing, Sun supposed. Knowing what she did about Albern and the Wanderer, even a simpler tale was bound to be exciting. And the beer *was* good. Glumly, she nodded.

Albern motioned to the barman again—Sun had not even realized her mug was empty—and waited for two more beers to be brought out. When the drinks had been set down on the table, Albern leaned his chair forwards, drank deep, and waited for Sun to do the same.

"Very well, Sun of No Name. These are the tales of the Wanderer."

THREE

I WAS NOT YOUNG WHEN THIS STORY BEGAN, BUT I WAS YOUNGER, AT least. This was decades ago, and though my temples were just starting to grey, I was still hale.

In those days I lived in the town of Strapa, but I had been hired to guide a party of travelers through the Greatrocks. Leading the party—at the end of our journey, not the beginning—was Loren of the family Nelda. Have you ever heard of the Nightblade? That was her. Then there was the girl Annis, of the family Yerrin, and Gem of the family Noctis—no blood kin of Loren's, yet closer to her than siblings. There was also the wizard, Xain but . . . well, he was less than cheery company.

And there was one other who set out with us from Strapa. But I would rather not speak of him now, for no story should begin on a note of tragedy.

I guided them all through the Greatrocks, across long leagues and through great dangers. We had some dark times in those mountains, and some good ones—both victory and defeat, though not in equal measure.

What you care about is that at the end of the journey—the end of *that* journey, at least—we rode down from the Greatrocks and into the town of Northwood. Our hearts were heavy, but our steps were light. To me, riding into Northwood was like visiting an old friend. I had dwelled there for some time. And Mag lived there. Mag, who would one day be called the Wanderer, and to whom legend had already given other names—first among them, the Uncut Lady. Mag, the mercenary, the barmaid, the wife. Mag, my dearest and oldest companion.

How long had it been since I visited her last? I do not remember now. Too long, I am certain. It is often that way when two people part after their youth. We made plans, we promised we would not lose touch, we thought we would always remain close. Such promises are always made in earnest, but the world usually works to break them, and so it was with us. It had been years since we had seen each other, and though we sometimes sent letters, even those had become more infrequent.

Mag and Sten had built their inn with some help from the townsfolk. It had a second floor, which was unusual in Northwood, but very necessary; Mag's skill with brewing was well known, and she had many visitors from both near and far. But despite its size, the building did not seem to loom over you when you approached. Rather, it stood with welcoming arms spread wide, like an old woman greeting her grandchildren as they come to visit. Sten had fashioned a large sign to hang over the front door; upon it, a great rock thrust out of the land, waves and wind crashing against it.

"The Lee Shore," I said. "And does it not feel like one after those mountains?"

We were eager for rest, so after tending to our horses, I pushed open the door and led our little party inside. Once through the door, I stopped to soak in the feel of the place. It was a sunny day outside, but I felt like I had found a warm hearth in the middle of a blizzard. I imagine you appreciate the atmosphere of this tavern where we are now. The Lee Shore was superior in every way you can imagine.

There behind the counter stood Mag. A figure of legend, though she did not look it at the moment. Her hair was held back by a string, and her arms were streaked with grease and dirt and sweat. But she had washed her face and hands, and as we entered she was scrubbing a glass clean.

She looked up suddenly, and our eyes met from across the room. Her expression broke into a smile that warmed me to the depths of my heart.

"Now there is a face this place has missed for far too long," she called out. "Come here, you great lummox!"

I suppose I should tell you how I met Mag. It was not long after I reached adulthood. I had left my home looking for freedom and an adventure. Great skill at archery had been drilled into me by my family's masters at arms, and my sword work was passable. So when I found a mercenary company that was recruiting, I submitted myself to their trials.

They were called the Upangan Blades, and they were a good lot—for mercenaries, you understand. There were no evil soldiers among their ranks, at least, and they had a code of honor. They treated each other well, and did as little as they could to make others' lives worse than they had to be. It had earned them a good reputation, which I knew even in my homeland, and that reputation meant they were never hired by cruel or vicious kings. That suited me just fine. As it happened, they were in their homeland of Feldemar at the time, and I happened to be passing by.

The master at arms was a hard-bitten woman—I imagine I shall tell you more of her later—and she did not look upon me very favorably. I fear I made rather a fool of myself when they asked to see me ride in plate. But they let me show them my bowcraft, and the head of the company happened to pass by while I was shooting. My acceptance was assured after that.

Still, they had a long period of training for all new recruits, and the master at arms tried her best to break us. We worked hard from sunup to beyond sundown. Many did not withstand the trials, but fled home in disgrace. It was not a pleasant time, but it hardened me for a future that was often even less pleasant.

And then, shortly after I joined the Blades, Mag arrived. My sergeant was a man named Victon, and he called me to him one day while I was in the middle of sparring practice. Mag stood beside him.

"Albern," he said, "we have fresh blood today, and you will see to her arrangements."

"Yes, sir," I said.

I stepped forwards, and Mag and I clasped wrists.

"Well met," said Mag.

"And you. Let me show you the first and most important thing you must know in the Blades, or so they have told me. Latrine duty."

Victon smiled and shook his head. "I will take my leave."

Mag watched him go. "He seems to have heard a private joke in your words. I imagine you make the newest recruits dig the latrines?"

"Nothing so unfair." I fished into my pocket and drew forth a copper sliver. "A thousand decisions must be made every day, and a soldier has no time for arguing. When we must choose between two things, and both choices are equal, we let fate decide. Now—head or moons?"

I flicked the sliver into the air. "Head," said Mag.

The coin came up. The face of Andriana stared up at me.

"Congratulations," I said. "You get to dig the latrines."

Mag scowled. "I said heads."

"And your sign came up. We did not specify if you got to choose who dug the latrines, or if you had to do it yourself." I clapped her on the shoulder. "Here is your second lesson as a sellsword: when you gamble, make sure the other person is not stacking the odds in their favor."

"Now *that* is a lesson I will take to heart."

"Fear not," I said. "It is your first day, and so I will be generous and help you dig."

"I suppose I shall take it," she said, smiling, "since you should be doing it on your own."

I decided that I liked her. After we dug the latrines, I took care of the other little details of her indoctrination, showing her around the camp and introducing her to those who would call themselves her superiors—though as we would soon learn, that was only in name.

FOUR

ALBERN COCKED HIS HEAD. "DO YOU KNOW WHY THEY CALLED MAG the Uncut Lady?"

The question seemed to come from nowhere. "I . . . do not think so," said Sun. "I know they call her the Wanderer because of the way you two crisscrossed all the nine kingdoms."

"Yes, but she was called the Uncut Lady long before that," said Albern.

"I always assumed she could not be touched in battle, and so had never been cut."

Albern smiled. "You are not wrong."

Sun grinned back. "I notice that you do not say if I am right."

He gave a great laugh at that. "Oh, well done. You speak the truth of Mag's name, but you understate the matter. Let me tell you another, smaller tale that will explain further. It happened at the end of Mag's second day with the company. As you know, sparring is sweaty, dirty work. It was common for the recruits to go and bathe in the river Sky-tongue at least once every few days. Some recruits were more modest than others, and they would find places to bathe alone. But most of us stayed together, stripping down to our skins and flinging ourselves into the water."

Albern paused for a moment as he saw color rising in Sun's cheeks. "Ah. You would have been one to bathe alone, I suppose? I do not need to tell you this story if it makes you uncomfortable."

Sun shook her head. "I am not uncomfortable, and I would not have bathed alone. Just because I have never done it before does not mean I would be . . . squeamish."

He hesitated only a moment before nodding. "Very well. Then, with your permission, I will continue."

"Please," said Sun.

"Well, we were all young, then, and blood flowed in our veins. Recruits often stole glances at each other from time to time—though there is nothing very lovely about bathing, truth be told. But in any case, I got a better look at Mag than most. I will not dwell overmuch on the details. Suffice it to say that she had a fine body. Exquisitely muscled and strong and . . . well, she was worth glancing at, let us say."

Sun's blush deepened, and Albern gave her another smile. "Are you sure you do not want me to stop? I had nearly forgotten about the proclivities of noble children."

"Oh, please," said Sun. "I am not some trembling son of Selvan. I am fine."

"Well, then. It was quite some time before I noticed the oddest thing of all about Mag. She had no scars. None at all. Not on her body, her arms or legs. Not even her hands."

"That makes sense, considering how well she could fight," said Sun.

Albern frowned. "It does *not* make sense. No matter how skilled a fighter may be when they learn warcraft, they still have to *learn* it. And everyone, when they are learning to fight, gets injured. Training accidents are common. Your opponent is trying to strike you with a blade. No matter how blunted it is, no matter how padded your training armor, at some point, everyone spills a little blood. You yourself have scars on your hands that do not look like they came from a cooking accident."

Sun frowned and looked down at a few tiny ridges on her knuckles. "That? That was no injury, only a blister from the back of my shield."

"I knew that before I mentioned it," said Albern. "Yet what I am trying to tell you is that Mag did not have even that much of a mark upon her. Her skin was perfect. Flawless."

He paused, looking at Sun, who suddenly realized her eyes were wide and her mouth was hanging open slightly. Albern nodded.

"Yes. Do you understand now? Can you begin to glimpse Mag's prowess? How skilled do you have to be—how *naturally* talented, I mean—to avoid *any* wound at all, even early in life? Even when you are first training to use a blade, or fight with soldiers by your side? And as time went on, we got to see Mag train—if you could call it training. Privately, I thought it was more of a demonstration that she was the best among us, and we were unworthy to march beside her. Not that she ever lorded it over us. But no one could touch her, no matter how many opponents they put against her in the practice ring.

"That was the beginning of her legend—right there, in the Upangan Blades. How could she be real? Think beyond her skill with a blade. How could she have avoided *any* cuts her whole life, even on her hands and knees as a child, running amid mud and rocks and scaling to the tops of trees?"

"It . . . it does not seem possible," breathed Sun.

Albern slapped his hand lightly on the table. "And yet, there it was," he said. "The evidence of it was plain—it lay right before our eyes. The Uncut Lady. I came up with that name myself, by the way."

Sun felt herself entirely caught up in the wonder of it. But then the tavern's door opened, and there came the sound of new voices. Sun glanced behind her—and felt her blood freeze.

There in the doorway stood the two guards from earlier, the ones from her family. They looked about the place, and for a frightful moment Sun thought they were still searching for her. But they stood relaxed and lazy, and when they saw an empty table on the other side of the room, they moved towards it.

They were not here for Sun, but only to get a drink. Although her pulse seemed to resume after a long moment of holding its breath, Sun still felt herself far too exposed. She glanced back at Albern, whose eyes had widened slightly.

"I take it you do not want those women to see you," he said. "As with the constable."

"You are correct."

"Then ignore them, and talk with me as if we have been conversing all night."

"If you will promise to keep an eye on them for me."

"Of course."

Sun sighed. "Very well. Tell me what happened in Northwood."

A shadow passed over Albern's face. "Many things, and nearly all of them dark. But it did not start out that way."

FIVE

When we arrived to her inn, I asked Mag to let me pay for the food and lodging of my friends. She understood at once. I had never done so before, and she could see the pain in my eyes when I asked it of her. By those signs, Mag knew we had come to her on an evil road. She never troubled Loren or her friends to pay for their lodgings, and when, in the end, I tried to pay her, she refused me, too.

Loren met an old friend in Mag's common room—a boy named Chet. They went off on their own, and the rest of us ate and talked and simply rested after a journey that had gone on far too long. Shortly after the sun set, I encouraged the party to ready for bed.

I myself did not go to sleep right away, but stayed up to speak with Mag and Sten. It had been years, after all, and I was eager to hear how they had been getting on. Mag and I could never have been lovers, but she and Sten could never have been anything else. You could see it in the way they looked at each other, the little touches on the arm or shoulder when they would speak. They would share smiles that turned into private moments between the two of them, and never mind the fact that I was sitting right there.

First I told them all that had happened to our party in the Greatrocks—of how we had ridden north through the mountain pass, and had been attacked by harpies and satyrs, and had found a growing darkness in an old fortress. Those matters had to do with the Necromancer, though of course we did not know that at the time.

"How under the sky did you get involved in all this, Albern?" said Mag. "I thought you longed for peace and quiet in Strapa."

"I did. But even Strapa is less quiet than it used to be, and less peaceful," I told her. "Has word of Wellmont reached you yet, this far north?"

Sten waved his hand vaguely. "Rumors. Some Dorsean border squabble."

"It is a bit more than that, I am afraid," I said. "I did not witness the battle, but Loren and her friends did. Dorsea seems intent on bringing the city down to its foundations."

"Why?" said Mag. "Surely they cannot think the High King would let that stand."

Sten snorted. "Who understands Dorseans?"

"Well, first I heard of Wellmont, and that weighed on me," I said. "And then that girl Loren strode into my bowyery. When I saw her and her companion, I felt . . . I do not know precisely what I felt, but I knew I had to go with her. There was something about her—and the man she came in with, but mostly her—that told me something *important* was going on. Something I could not ignore. And besides, their road north brought me here to visit you."

Mag raised her eyebrows. "Though you almost got yourself killed along the way. That would somewhat have diminished the pleasure of your company."

I gave her a half-bow from my seat. "I am pleased to hear you value it enough not to want to lose it."

That made all of us chuckle, and we spent a moment or two enjoying Mag's ale in silence. As an aside, whatever tales you have heard about her brew cannot do it justice. It was sweeter than honey, and as bracing as a bear's roar. She would chill some kegs of it in the river, and then it was like drinking a draft of gold pouring from the peaks of mountains. Other times she would serve it from barrels kept in a storehouse, and then it was like pouring the warmth of a good hearth directly into your gut. There are stories of people who have killed each other for a barrel of it. Those stories are not true, but they could be.

"So you took a Mystic and three children into the mountains," said Mag, sighing. "And you thought it would be a lark—a pleasant jaunt, after too many years standing still."

"I had no reason to think otherwise," I said. "And of course, that was before I found out about our fifth, unwilling party member."

Xain walked into the room at that moment, as perfectly timed as if he had waited, listening, until he heard me speak of him. Most people know a few tales of Xain of the family Forredar, once a savior of the Lord Prince, once a dean of the Academy for Wizards, and all the other titles he acquired. But in that room, at that time, he looked far from impressive. He was thin and sickly, and his hair had become sparse upon his scalp. He suffered from a sickness, then, though that is too long a story to tell now. He would have walked right by us, had I not spoken just as he passed.

"Can you not sleep, Xain?"

He paused for the space of a few heartbeats, his arms wrapped tight around himself despite the room's warmth, and surveyed us with shadowed eyes that glittered. Then he pulled out a chair and sat—but suddenly he went rigid, looking uncertainly at us.

"May I sit?"

"Of course," said Mag, ever the gracious host.

"Thank you," said Xain, sinking back into the chair and relaxing—at least somewhat.

Mag turned back to me. "You said that something bigger is going on. What, exactly?"

I suddenly regretted mentioning it. There was a curious light in Mag's eyes, an interest she could not hide. I did not want to further stoke that fire. A darkness *was* gathering, it was true—as we know now, in these later years, all too well. But I feared that if I made it plain to her, it might pull her away from Northwood, the place where she had finally settled down with Sten—and thus, found happiness. Mag deserved that happiness more than most people I had met in my travels.

But while I hesitated, Xain did not. He knew nothing of my reason for secrecy, of course, and so he spoke before I could think of an answer that would forestall any more of Mag's questions.

"You have been telling them of the Greatrocks?" he asked me. "*Something bigger* hardly begins to describe it. We found an ancient enemy in the mountains. An enemy of the Mystics, I mean. Our friend and leader, Jordel, perished trying to stop them. Now that he has fallen, it is up to the rest of us to warn Underrealm. I do not know everything, and I cannot say everything I do know. But we stand on the brink of a great conflict. The Mystics must be alerted, and the sooner the better."

"Then where are you bound?" said Mag. "The Mystics have no stronghold here, and I do not know of any who currently dwell in the city. Will you ride for Cabrus?"

"They make for Ammon," I cut in. Xain looked surprised, and I shrugged. "Did you think I was not paying attention? You and Loren did not take much trouble to conceal the plans you made."

Mag frowned. "You say 'they' as though you do not mean to go with them."

"That is because I do not, as I told them already."

"And we understand that choice," said Xain. "I would do the same, were I in your shoes." But though he spoke the words easily enough, he did not meet my gaze.

"Then what?" said Sten, frowning at me over the mug of ale he had just begun to raise. "Will you stay here?"

"For a time, yes," I said. "It has been too long since we saw each other last. But after a while, I will ride home for Strapa. I have had enough of wandering for a good long while, I think."

Mag did not seem to think very highly of this plan—or of me, in that moment, if I am being honest. She did not scowl, exactly, but I could see a flash of anger in her eyes. "It seems to me that Loren and the others need help. Will you not aid them?"

"I do not mean to, no," I said. "I am not beholden to anyone. They hired me to bring them here to Northwood and nothing more."

Before, I had felt certain about my decision. But I cannot deny I felt a small bit of guilt as I answered. Yet I was sure that I was doing the right thing, even if I had my qualms.

In our youth, Mag and I had been mercenaries, fighting on battlefields across all the nine kingdoms. A mercenary's life is not for everyone, and it is especially deadly to those who have a place they call home. A king's soldiers are different—they fight *for* their home, and that is what gives them strength. But in a sellsword company, such a soldier is death to have beside you on the battlefield. They will be the first to break at any sign of trouble. I thought I had learned a lesson in the Greatrocks. I thought my days of far-ranging adventure were behind me, and that I had become a man with a home, a man who would wander no more.

What a fool I was.

Xain did not say anything, but he avoided my gaze as he took a sip of his ale. I wondered what was going on behind his dark eyes—whether he was thinking of what I had confessed to Loren. That secret was too painful to think about then, and certainly nothing I wanted to tell Mag. But if Xain was indeed thinking such thoughts, he kept them to himself, for which I was grateful.

Mag did not speak, either, but she was less adept at hiding her feelings. She fell into a silence full of thought, taking many long pulls at her ale.

Sten, sensing the sudden discomfort at the table, tried to pick up where the conversation had left off, asking me about matters of small importance. I answered him easily enough, and we carried on that way until Xain, wearying, at last excused himself to go to bed.

When he had gone, Mag put down her mug and fixed me with a look. I steeled myself, for I feared she meant to reprimand me. But when I met her gaze, she smiled.

"How would you like to go to the Reeve?"

I balked. "Now? Tonight?"

"Yes, of course," she said. "The moons are right for it, and the sky is clear. Sten and I went just a few days ago, and it was perfect. We meant to go again tonight, even before you arrived."

"If we all go, who will watch the inn?"

Sten waved a hand. "My wife still has reputation enough to keep filching fingers from our stores and our coin. We step out fairly often, especially at night."

"I . . ." My voice trailed off, and I shook my head with a smile. When had I become such an old worrywart? I took a deep breath and released it, and suddenly it felt like we were young again, like we had just come here to Northwood together for the first time.

"I would like nothing more in all the world."

Mag led us out through Northwood's south gate. The city had no reason to close them at night, for the land was untroubled in those days. The guards waved to us as we passed, and then they returned to their game of Moons. The country beyond the wall was open and beautiful, the farms well tended, though of course they were now deserted. A wide road cut in straight lines through the fields, turning with the borders of each farm, but always at perfect angles—and always taking us farther south, in the end. We were on foot, and so the journey took us a little longer than it would have otherwise, but in less than an hour we had reached the Reeve.

I do not know for certain, but I would guess it got its name because it used to be a place of official business. It was easy to see it as a place to deliver solemn proclamations. The Reeve was a large hill, and though it was not really all that tall, it was impressive. There was something in the shape of it that gave a sense of eminence, of importance. If Mag's tavern was a kindly grandmother, the Reeve was an old man, wizened but still hale, his arms folded as he considered you, judging your worth with eyes still sharp with wit.

A footpath cut back and forth across its eastern slope. We climbed it to the top, which was flat but surrounded with large boulders. The boulders looked natural—certainly they had not been cut by any human tools—but they stood about the edge of the hill like a crown, as perfectly spaced as if they had been put there. Mayhap it was something done by ancient humanity, a relic of the time before time. Mayhap that was where the hill had received its name, as well. I did not know.

But I did know what had been buried at the top of the Reeve.

My eyes strayed to the patch of dirt as we passed it. There was no sign it had ever been disturbed—but then, it had been many years since a spade had last touched it. I shivered, though the night was warm. Sten avoided looking at the site altogether, and his beard twitched with a frown as we walked by it. Mag did not seem to pay any attention, either. But I knew her well. I looked closely, and I could see her fingers flexing, anxious to grip something.

"Come, my fine boys," she said suddenly, startling us both in the silence. "Show me you have not grown too old to be useful."

She crouched and sprang, landing on a narrow ledge halfway up one of the huge boulders at the edge of the clearing. It was a leap I could not have made two decades ago, and I had no hope of it now.

"I am afraid we are both useless next to you, and always have been," I told her. "But could you help two decrepit old men make the climb?"

Mag laughed loud at that, and she lowered a hand. Sten seized it, and she levered him up to the ledge beside her. I was next, and each of them took one of my hands to pull me up. I was momentarily shocked by the strength of Mag's pull, though I should not have been. When you looked at Sten, you thought he was a man who *should* be able to lift you off your feet. Mag did not project the same strength, for all her plentiful wiry muscle. And indeed, when it came to sheer strength, Sten outmatched her. But Mag understood something about the way the world worked, and the way the human body worked within it. She knew how to twist, where to bend, and how to leverage every ounce of her strength into something much greater. It came naturally to her, as natural as a tiger stalking the jungles of Feldemar.

But as I said, they pulled me to the ledge beside them. Then Mag made another leap, and then she hauled us up again after her. It was like a game to her, and she urged us to move faster with each climb. Soon we had reached the top of the boulder, where there was plenty of room for all three of us to lie down beside each other. Mag lay in the middle, and Sten beside her with his head close to hers—but I was on Mag's other side, and I lay with my feet near her head. Sten and I breathed heavily with exertion, but Mag's chest rose and fell steadily.

"You were right," I told them. "The moons are perfect."

Sten pointed. "The sisters are returning home. Enalyn leads the way, urging Merida to hasten her steps."

"Enalyn may find that her home looks different than when she left it."

The words came out without my even thinking them, and they surprised me as much as they evidently surprised Mag and Sten. Both of them raised their heads to look at me.

"You are very thoughtful tonight, and very dour," said Mag. "I gave you ale to fix that."

"Mayhap you are losing your touch, brewmaster." We all three laughed, for that was a plain lie. "No, you are right. I . . . suppose I was thinking of Loren."

"Were you." The words seemed inquisitive, but Mag did not speak them as a question.

"If she returns to her home, she will certainly find it different than she left it," said Sten. "What a long road that child has ridden."

And has yet to ride, I thought. But this time I managed to keep the words to myself.

"Speaking of riding," said Mag. "Do you think we ought to worry about that boy Chet?"

"Sky above, Mag," said Sten. He actually sounded embarrassed.

I laughed aloud. "Though you might have put it more delicately—no, I do not think we need to worry."

"Loren seemed distressed after they spoke," said Mag.

"Likely he brought bad news of home," I said. "But he seemed a good sort, if mayhap a bit foolish. But putting Chet aside, I have faith in Loren. She can care for herself, even if he is of ill intent—though as I said, I doubt it."

"As you say," said Mag. There was a long moment's silence, and then she spoke again. "You do not think we need to tell her of silphium, do you?"

Sten groaned. "If you wish to have children, can we do it the usual way, rather than leaping straight into parenting two people who are very nearly adults?"

Mag slapped his shoulder, and Sten winced. "I am only teasing. Well, *mostly* teasing."

"She has always been this way," I said. "Quite a number of new recruits suddenly found themselves with a mother in their own mercenary company. And once she latched on to one of them—"

"Latched?" said Mag indignantly. "You make me sound like a leech."

"I might not have used that word, but you are not wrong to."

Quick as a flash, Mag leaped to her knees and shoved me. My head slipped over the edge of the boulder, and I was only kept from falling off by Mag herself, for she had seized me by the knees.

"Take it back," she said mildly.

"Mag!" I cried. "If I fall I will break my neck!"

"You will bruise at worst," she said mildly. "You have fallen from here before—on previous occasions when you refused to apologize for your rudeness."

"Mag!" She did not reply. "Sten!"

"You are on your own, I am afraid," said Sten.

"I think I feel my grip slipping," said Mag, whose fingers had not budged whatsoever. "You had best hurry."

"I am sorry," I said through clenched teeth.

"For?"

"For calling you a leech."

"Which I am not."

"Which you are not."

Mag yanked, and I flew back atop the boulder to land in a heap. "There now," she said, dusting off her hands—I did not miss the implication that I was unclean. "Was that so difficult?"

"It is not very fair of you to treat your friends this way," I said. "If every argument comes to a scuffle in the end, no one will countermand you, since they know they will end up losing."

"But that is just the point," said Mag, settling herself down next to Sten again and clasping his hand. "Who wants to be argued with?"

I thrust out a finger at her and opened my mouth, ready to go on. But Sten caught my gaze in the moonslight, and he grinned while shaking his head. "Leave it," he said, chuckling. "Tell us how things have been for you in Strapa."

He was right, of course. I was not going to defeat Mag in our verbal sparring, any more than I could have done if we had had training weapons in hand. Huffing, I lay down again, crossing my arms over my chest. "Very well," I said. "I will have you both know, however, that I am entirely disgruntled."

"I will keep it foremost in my thoughts," said Mag.

And despite my words, my soul was filled with joy. It *was* just like the old days, and my love for my friends had not waned in the slightest. For the first time in years, I felt like I was home—more so than I had ever felt in Strapa.

SIX

Now, none of us knew it, but far away, another three friends had gathered in council—though their aims were much crueler than ours.

The southern arm of the Greatrocks serves as the western border of the kingdom of Selvan. But north of the Birchwood Forest, there is a spur that juts out into northeastern Dorsea, and at the end of that spur is a peak they call the Watcher. And at the base of the Watcher, in the council room of a great and long-forgotten fortress, three people were deep in a conversation that would bring disaster down upon me, and Mag, and everyone in Northwood.

First was Kaita, a weremage and a Shade. She had skin the color of burnished walnut and Calentin ancestry plain in her features, and she wore her black hair in a long braid down her back. Across from her was Tagata, a Shadeborn woman whose name is, thankfully, not widely known. And at the head of the table was Rogan of the Shadeborn, imposing and terrible. I can see by the look on your face that I need say no more about him.

These were the days before the Necromancer and the Lifemage had revealed themselves and done battle. The Shades still lurked in secret across the nine kingdoms, and none knew of their designs—none save for me and my friends, and we knew precious little. The Mystics had long been an arm of the King's law, and they dealt with crimes beyond the norm—with rogue wizards, especially. The Shades were their mirror, dressed in blue and grey instead of red, and as far as we could see, intent on toppling all the nine thrones of Underrealm.

So Rogan, Tagata, and Kaita were hatching whatever secret plots they were busy with, when a heavy pounding came at the door of their council chamber.

Rogan's thick, shaggy locks swung as he looked up at the door, frowning. "Come."

The door flew open, and a Shade ran into the room. Her blue cloak was muddy and soaked with rain, and her black hair was bedraggled and wild. She ran to the head of the table and knelt by Rogan's chair.

"Rogan," she gasped. "I bring word. Dire news."

He looked at her, unsmiling but not angry, either. With one great hand he took her shoulder and pulled her to her feet. "Come, Nian. Be seated. However troubling your words, you can take a moment to rest before you give them, unless there is an enemy pounding at our gates this very moment. But if there were, I think I would have heard of it sooner."

Nian looked at the others, obviously unsure. Rogan smiled and waved his hand at Tagata.

"Come, sister. Make room for her."

"Of course," said Tagata, abandoning her seat at once and motioning Nian into it.

Kaita watched the proceedings silently, her right hand toying idly with her black braid. It grated her to see Nian seated at the table across from her, but by now she was well familiar with the eccentricities of Rogan and the other Shadeborn.

Nian sat silently for a moment, still clearly uncertain. But when Rogan moved to pour wine for her, she tried to stop him, horrified.

"Please, I can do it."

Rogan forestalled her with a raised hand. "You forget your place, as well as my own. I have no more authority than I am granted by our father. I am no king, thinking myself superior to those who serve me. We are all of us siblings, partners in a great cause."

Nian seemed taken aback by the words. Kaita doubted the woman fully understood them. Rogan finished pouring her cup and handed it to her, and Nian took a great swallow of the wine.

"Thank you," she said breathlessly. Her eyes, when she turned them upon Rogan again, were full of a fervent respect that bordered on worship.

"Of course," said Rogan. "Now. What brought you here with such urgency?"

"There has been an attack," said Nian. "In the Greatrocks."

The air in the council chamber seemed to freeze. Rogan's brow furrowed at once. "An attack? By the satyrs? Or have we lost control of the harpies again?"

Nian shivered. "Not by the beasts. Mystics."

Rogan and Tagata sat bolt upright, and each gripped the arms of their chair with pale knuckles. Even Kaita could not pretend to be aloof any longer.

"Mystics? In the Greatrocks?" said Tagata. "How did they know about our stronghold there?"

"We do not know," said Nian. "There were not many of them—only half a dozen."

"Dark take them," growled Tagata. "Rogan, what are we to do? If the Mystics—"

"There is more, my lord—Rogan, I mean," stammered Nian. She looked as though she would rather do anything in the world than say her next words. "There was a battle, and Trisken . . . Trisken fell."

The room went deathly still. Kaita straightened in her chair, staring at Nian in wonder. Rogan leaned forwards over the table, as if trying to bore through Nian's skull with his gaze alone.

"What do you mean, he fell?" demanded Rogan. "He is Shadeborn."

Nian's voice was like the squeak of a reluctant hinge. "He is dead, my lord. They killed him, and he did not rise again."

Rogan slammed his fist on the table with a cry. Tagata gave an anguished roar and kicked her chair away. It struck the wall, one of its legs snapping off. She went to the wall and seized her greatsword, smashing it into a cabinet without bothering to unsheathe it. The cabinet shattered to kindling, scattering books and scrolls across the room.

For her part, Kaita felt as though the stone floor beneath her had become as shifting and unstable as water. Who could kill a Shadeborn? How was it even possible? The Lord had made them invincible. He had all but promised that his favored children would live on forever.

Slowly, Rogan sank back into his chair. He sagged into it, covering his face with one hand. Tears streamed from beneath his fingers, running into his thick black beard. Tagata stood facing away from them all, her shoulders heaving, and Kaita suspected she was weeping as well. She fell abruptly to her knees, head bowed over her sword hilt as its tip rested on the stone floor.

"Death as my witness," whispered Tagata, "I will kill the ones who did this."

That seemed to bring Rogan back to himself. He uncovered his face and looked upon her, his eyes still brimming with tears. "We will, sister," he said. "I swear to you, we will do it together."

They seemed to have entirely forgotten Nian and Kaita in their grief. The messenger looked terrified, quaking in her seat, and her fair skin had gone even paler. Rogan noticed, and he forced a bitter smile.

"I am sorry for our lack of restraint, Nian. Trisken was . . ." His voice thickened, and he paused for a moment. "Trisken was with me almost since the beginning. He trained Tagata. This is an evil day."

"It is, my lord," whispered Nian.

Rogan shook his head slowly. "I told you. None of that. There is but one Lord, and he is your father as well as mine. We are all equal before his kindness."

Tagata turned back towards the rest of them, hastily scrubbing at her face with the back of her hand. She strode over beside Nian's chair and put a hand on the woman's shoulder. Nian jumped with fright. But Tagata pulled her gently to her feet and wrapped her in an embrace.

"You have ridden hard to bring us ill news. It could not have been easy. Thank you."

Slowly, Nian returned the embrace. She began to quiver, as if she, too, was finally relinquishing her grip on emotions she had long kept within—as though Tagata's massive frame gave her the strength she needed to let go.

"I could have done no differently," said Nian. "It was my duty."

"And doing one's duty is worthy of the highest honor," said Rogan.

"Fetch yourself another chair, Tagata. Let us all be seated and discuss what is to be done."

Tagata gently held Nian's cheek for a moment before finally pulling away. She took another chair from further down the table and brought it next to Nian's before sitting down. Rogan shifted his chair closer to the table and leaned forwards, his shoulders hunched.

"What more do we know, Nian? Can you tell us anything about these Mystics?"

"We did not recognize all of them. But we know the party was led by Jordel of the family Adair."

Another shock went through the room, though far less explosive than the last. There was not a Shade alive who did not know that name.

"Jordel?" said Rogan. "That is ill news."

Kaita slapped the arm of her chair. "Why did you not mention Jordel from the beginning?"

Nian quailed, but Rogan raised a palm towards Kaita to pacify her. "We hardly gave her the chance, after she told us of Trisken's fall."

Kaita looked grudgingly away, tugging at her braid again.

"How could Jordel have found us?" Tagata asked Rogan. "Our agents have worked tirelessly to keep him and Kal off our trail. Hewal sent no word of this whatsoever."

"Jordel has been away from Hewal for some time, and our ability to guide him has lessened the longer he has pursued Xain," said Rogan. "But as for your question, there are two possible answers. The first and far more troubling possibility is that they have been aware of us for some time, and somehow they have kept that knowledge from us. But I do not think that is the case. If they had meant to assault us—or even to investigate and gather more information—they would have come here, and not to Trisken's stronghold. The other possibility is that they knew nothing of us at all, and that pure happenstance brought Jordel's party to our doorstep."

"That seems so unlikely as to be impossible," said Tagata.

"Yet it may be true," said Nian. "For I have still more to say. Jordel died in battle with Trisken."

"Ha!" barked Tagata. "And good riddance. Darkness take him."

But Rogan did not seem to share her elation. "That is good, I suppose," he said slowly. "But what else, Nian? For I sense that you still have more to tell us."

"We did not recognize all of Jordel's party, but we recognized some of them," said Nian. "The Nightblade was with him, as was the wizard Xain, and the children who have been with the Nightblade as long as we have known of her. But they had with them someone new—a guide from the town of Strapa. He is a Calentin archer, unknown to us. It is he who led them into Northwood."

Kaita went rigid in her chair.

"A Calentin archer?" she blurted out, interrupting Rogan's next question.

The rest of them paused. Nian and Tagata frowned, but Rogan looked searchingly at her.

"What is it, Kaita?"

She did not answer him at once, but kept her attention on Nian. "Where did he take them when they reached Northwood?"

Nian looked confused. "We . . . have not learned that yet."

"But how do you know?" asked Sun.

Albern paused and cocked his head. "What?"

"How do you know all this?" said Sun. "You were not there. Yet you are telling me the tale as if you were in the room."

Albern smiled. "Of course I was not there. But it has been many years since then. In that time I learned much of what happened, and I guessed at even more."

Sun shook her head and straightened in her seat. "But . . . but why, then, do you not simply tell me what happened? You are making it part of the story—the words they spoke, this woman Tagata's fit of rage, that other woman Nian and her terror at delivering the message. You cannot possibly know it really happened that way."

Albern gave a low chuckle and sipped at his beer. "Ah, I understand. You are looking for a story you can *believe.*"

"Of . . . of course I am!" said Sun, scowling.

"Then I am afraid you will never find what you seek," said Albern. "If you believe every story you hear, you shall live a false life. The same may happen if you believe *any* story you hear. But if you put your faith in the right tales—if you *choose* to believe in them, seeing how they may be useful—there is no limit to what they can teach you."

His words hardly registered. Sun had a vague feeling she had been betrayed, as though she had come upon some beggar who tricked her into a game of chance that she had no hope of winning. "So your stories are lies, then."

"Lies? Oh no," said Albern. "But even the craftiest storyteller knows better than to trust every word coming out of their own mouth, for they know a story is simply something to be learned from."

Sun could not help herself: she scoffed. "You cannot honestly think that is true. History is a story, too. But what good would history books be, if their authors simply made them up as they went along?"

"Historians are often the greatest liars of all," said Albern. "I have read their tomes. I have seen their version of events that I myself lived through. They were far less trustworthy than I am, and far less accurate, I can assure you. But history is only a story that most people have chosen to believe in, without thinking they made such a choice. Like any tale, we use it to shape the future in the way we want, and darkness take anyone who wants otherwise."

Though Sun had been ready with a retort, those words made her pause in confusion. Albern's words had the sound of a deep wisdom, yet she could not understand them. And something in her still rebelled at the thought of hearing a story that even the teller did not believe.

Albern studied her, and a small smile tugged at the corner of his mouth, as though he could read her thoughts and found them amusing. He gave her a moment longer to think before speaking again.

"Should I go on?"

Sun nodded, though she was uncertain if she truly wanted to hear more.

Kaita rose and paced back and forth in the council chamber, her mind working. And as her thoughts spun faster and faster in circles, a blind rage began to build inside her, and it grew until it was like a wildfire ripping across her skin.

"Kaita," said Rogan. "What is it?"

"The archer is Albern," said Kaita, meeting his gaze. "It must be. And he is bringing them—Loren and the others—he is bringing them to Mag."

Rogan paused, lifting his chin slightly as he regarded her. Nian and Tagata still looked lost, but in Rogan's eyes there was a deep understanding.

Kaita strode to the table and slapped her hands down, leaning forwards intently. "Let me go to Northwood. I will . . . I will deliver justice for Trisken, and for all our siblings who fell in the Greatrocks."

"Kaita," said Rogan quietly. "I love you like all our siblings, and with that love comes a profound respect. Return that respect to me, I beg you, and do not lie to me. You do not wish to go to Northwood to deliver justice, but to extract vengeance—and not for Trisken, but for yourself."

Kaita faltered only a moment. "And what of it? I have followed your orders for a long time, because you thought me too weak to seek out my revenge. But the time has come, Rogan. And it will mean the same thing, in the end. I have waited so long."

Rogan spoke quietly. "I know you have. And I have never thought you weak. But that is not the plan." Kaita began to flare with anger, but he spoke again quickly. "The time for lurking in the shadows has ended."

Tagata looked taken aback, her scars appearing even whiter as a flush crept up her skin. "What do you mean?"

"I have had many words with our father of late," said Rogan. "Now I must bring him news of Trisken, but I do not think that will change his mind. In fact, I think it will make him even more resolute. We cannot yet declare ourselves openly, but our period of subterfuge and intrigue is over. The time has come for war. We will strike from the shadows, as we always have—but we will strike with blades and arrows, and no longer with secrets."

The effect on all of them was immediate. Nian looked at Rogan in wonder, her eyes shining. Kaita's hand tightened on the back of her chair, and Tagata seized her greatsword again, as if she meant to march off to battle at once.

"Brother," whispered Tagata. "Are you saying. . . ?"

"Yes," said Rogan. "Nian, you have ridden far and long, but I must ask you to deliver yet another message. Rouse the captains. Order the troops to ready themselves. We make for war, and Northwood will be the first to fall before our might."

"And I will have my vengeance," said Kaita, her eyes shining.

Rogan fixed her with a look. "I do not think so," he said.

She flared with anger. "Rogan, you cannot expect—"

"Unless I am very much mistaken," he said, "Northwood will not be the end of your shadowed road. But you may try, Kaita, so long as it does not interfere with the battle. I only give you one command: stay alive. Our father needs all of us, now more than ever."

Kaita scoffed. "You worry for my safety? It is our enemies who should be worried."

Rogan sighed. "Then you may have your vengeance."

SEVEN

Now, on that same night, near the Dorsean town of Lan Shui west of the Greatrocks, a dark evening had come.

A woman named Zhanu lived on a farm just a few spans beyond the walls of Lan Shui. Zhanu was a veteran of the Dorsean army and had fought in the king's wars. Then, one day, she had retired with much honor and a gift of the king's gold, and she had settled near the town where she had been born. In the years since, she had taken a wife named Shu, who had died old and happy, and had mothered three children, all of whom had grown and left Lan Shui to live their own lives elsewhere. Now Zhanu lived alone on her farm, working the land each day and visiting the town's taverns each night.

Except that recently, she had not been visiting the taverns. Like everyone who dwelled outside the town's walls, she had been spending her nights locked up in her own home, a weapon near at hand.

Zhanu stumped about her house, ensuring the windows were closed and shuttered and the front door was tightly secured. She grumbled as she fidgeted with the lock. It was new, having been added only a few days ago by a blacksmith from Lan Shui. Never in her life had Zhanu felt the need for a lock on her door. Lan Shui had never been that sort of town.

"All the nine lands going to darkness," she muttered. Zhanu had taken to talking to herself sometime in the last few years, and though she despised the habit, she could not seem to break it.

A single candle burned in the main room of her house. Zhanu lifted it and brought it into her bedroom, the only other room in the house, and nothing very grand. She had never felt the need for fancy lodgings—truthfully, even two rooms in her house seemed a bit grandiose to her. But her wife had insisted.

Zhanu set the candle on her bedside table, stripped down to her underclothes, and crawled beneath her thick blanket. It had been a long day in the fields, and she looked forward to a good night's rest. She snuffed out the candle and closed her eyes.

Not quite an hour later, they snapped open as something scratched on her roof.

Skritch, skritch.

She lay perfectly still in her bed, her whole body tense, waiting.

Skritch, skritch.

The sound had moved. Whatever was making the scratching, it was moving from the rear of the house towards the front.

Come for me, have you? thought Zhanu. *Well, you will find no frail old victim here.*

Zhanu slid from her bed, moving as quietly as possible. She lifted her sword from its place on the wall, trying to remain as silent as she could, and crept into the house's front room.

Skritch.

The scratching sound came again, but this time it seemed to cut itself off abruptly. Zhanu paused a step away from the door, listening.

There came a soft *thump,* like something landing on the ground outside. Whatever was making the noise had leaped down from the roof.

Zhanu stole to the wall just beside the door. She gripped her sword in both hands, holding it ready to swing.

All was silent for a long moment.

KROOM

The window behind Zhanu exploded inwards, showering the room with splinters.

With an old soldier's instincts, she whirled and stabbed out with her sword. There was a sharp *shunk* as it slid deep into flesh.

Zhanu froze, staring at her intruder in horror.

The creature would have been as tall as she was if it stood upright, but it was hunched over on all fours. Its skin was pallid white, mottled with light grey, and it wore no clothing at all. Its long, thick limbs ended in claws as long as her hands, and its wide, red mouth was rimmed with sharp teeth designed for ripping and tearing into flesh. It had long, pointed ears, like an Elf's.

Zhanu had buried her sword in its chest halfway to the hilt. Her thrust had been pure reflex. Yet the creature stared at her, and its yellowing eyes were filled with hate, not pain.

"What in the dark—"

Zhanu's words cut off as the creature struck her a heavy backhanded blow. She flew through the air before crashing hard into the wooden floor. Nothing broke, but she bit her own tongue hard enough that she tasted blood.

She pushed herself up on her elbows just in time to see the creature seize the sword by the hilt and drag it out of its own flesh. It hissed with discomfort, but the wound did not seem to slow it at all. And as Zhanu watched, the skin and the flesh beneath began to stitch together, until soon there was no sign there had been a wound there at all.

The creature threw the sword past Zhanu. The steel sank into the wall and stuck there, quivering. Zhanu tried to push herself away, but the creature stalked towards her on all fours, its shredded ears twitching, a rasping hiss sounding from its throat.

"Dark take you," said Zhanu. "Shu is waiting for me anyways."

She spat, and the bloody spittle struck the floor just in front of the creature. It stopped in its advance for only a moment, stooping to lick up the spit.

A hungry gleam came into its eyes. It leaped for her, and Zhanu knew nothing more.

Constable Yue of the family Baolan was summoned to Zhanu's farm the next day.

One of her neighbors had not seen her in the fields that morning and had gone to investigate. Once he had seen the horror inside her house, he had run straight to Lan Shui and found Yue in the constables' station. Even as a dark foreboding seized her, she summoned Ashta and Sinshi, the town's other two constables, and set out for the farm with them in tow.

Yue had no illusions about what she would find. Zhanu's neighbor had been too afraid to describe what he saw, but it was not the first such grisly murder she had investigated in the last few weeks. Zhanu's home looked just as she expected it to. The window beside the door had been broken open by something attacking from outside the house. The front door was still closed and locked; Zhanu's neighbor had not been able to open it, and had looked in through the smashed window. The constables forced the door open, and inside they found a scene all too similar to others they had seen recently. Zhanu's corpse lay in the corner, her head propped up against the wall, her eyes staring sightlessly at them. Her sunburnt skin was unusually pale. There was blood on the floor and on the wall, but not nearly as much as one would have expected, considering how the woman's throat had been torn open.

"Again," said Sinshi, averting his eyes. "Sergeant, is it the—"

"The creature," said Yue. "Yes."

She winced at her own unwillingness to name the thing. It was a foolish superstition. But then, Yue had been born and raised in Lan Shui. She had no illusions that she was anything other than the simple child of a small town, and among such folk, superstition died hard. It was her opinion that such traditions had been started for a reason, and she would not change them unless she, too, had a reason.

"Should we send another messenger, Sergeant?" said Ashta.

Yue looked at her. "Would you go, if I asked you to?"

Ashta and Sinshi both grew visibly paler, and Sinshi swallowed hard. But Ashta lifted her chin. "I would."

"As would I," said Sinshi, his voice shaking.

"Then the two of you are idiotic, if brave," said Yue. "I would not send you even if you begged me to, because you would die—just like the last two. And if I do not send one of you because I do not think you would survive, I have no right to ask another of the townsfolk to go."

"What do we do, then?" said Sinshi, voice thick with despair.

"I wish my answer were otherwise," said Yue. "But we have to keep waiting. I have not sent a report to Bertram for three weeks now—nor the Mystics, for that matter. The king's collectors have received no taxes. That cannot go on forever without prompting an investigation. We may not be able to leave the town, but that does not mean others cannot come here."

"That could take weeks," said Ashta. "And the attacks are coming more—"

"Do you think I do not know that?" snapped Yue. "We have warned the townsfolk, and we have warned the farmers. Many have retreated inside the walls, but others are more foolish—like poor Zhanu here, may she rest in the dark. When you have been a constable for a while longer, you, too, may learn that you cannot protect everyone from themselves."

Sinshi stared at his feet now, chagrined. But Ashta still held her sergeant's gaze. "I have been thinking—"

"When did this start?" said Yue, raising an eyebrow.

Ashta heard the joke in her tone and pressed on. "I have been thinking. No one has tried riding east. A messenger could reach the Greatrocks in less than a day. Before nightfall."

"And where do you think the creature is coming from?" said Yue. "It is far more likely to have its home in the mountains than in the western spur. And even if I am wrong, and a messenger made it deep into the mountains, they would never survive. Satyrs are plentiful there, and harpies, and other, worse things that humans have never named. I have thought of all of this, constable."

At last Ashta averted her eyes, joining Sinshi in his awkward discomfort. "As you say, Sergeant," she muttered. "We will remove the body, and burn her."

"I will write a letter to her eldest son, so that we may send it when the road is safe again," said Sinshi. "He is in Bertram."

"Good. Do it quickly, and return to the station when you are through. And do not despair." Yue looked through the shattered window at the world beyond—too bright for such a solemn day. Too sunny.

"Someone will come. Eventually."

And she was right, though she would not know it for some days yet.

EIGHT

Of course, we in Northwood knew nothing of all these dark events, and so our lives went on quite uninterrupted.

I had thought that Loren and Xain would be eager to leave the city and make their way east. But for some reason I did not know, they remained in Northwood for some time. Loren spent long hours walking in the woods with Chet, the children helped Mag around the inn, and Xain skulked about the place as he recovered from his illness.

Others have asked me, and I have often wondered, why we all did not feel a greater urgency. We had defeated a great evil in the mountains, but we had not wiped it out. I have been called foolish for being so lax about our situation. And indeed, with the benefit of hindsight, I was foolish. But what I said earlier, about stories, and believing them, is never more true than when speaking of the story we live day to day. And we are always prone to believe that which we think will make our lives easier. I thought, as I am sure Loren did, that having defeated our enemy, we would be free from them for a time. After all, they had been hidden in the shadows for so long—why would they reveal themselves now?

That was our notion, anyway. And so, for my part, I spent much time revisiting my old haunts in Northwood and the lands around it. I visited old friends in the town, for of course I knew more people than only Mag and Sten. There was Len, a distant cousin of Sten's. He was a somewhat shifty fellow, and he often got into trouble with the constables after being found with small valuables that did not belong to him in the strictest sense—or in any other sense, truth be told. But he was always a joy to play Moons with, as long as you did not wager any money against the outcome, for he was both bad at the game and a poor loser. And there was old Elsie, who had been wizened and wrinkled even when I first came to Northwood with Mag. Now she could barely walk, even with her stick, and yet she did not let that stop her from managing her farm, from which came the best butter and cheeses that could be found for a hundred leagues. She had hired hands to help her with the milking and the mucking, for that was quite beyond her, but she oversaw all their goings-on with a sharp eye and an unwavering attention to detail.

One day, over an afternoon snack and more than one cup of wine, Elsie and I fell to talking about Mag. She had long been friends with Mag and Sten, of course, and in the midst of all our talk—Elsie's being mostly gossip—she said something that troubled me, and upon which I thought often afterwards.

"It shall lead to trouble, you see if I am wrong."

"What shall?" I asked, cocking my head.

"You. Mag. All this." Hefting her stick, she swung it around generally at our surroundings, so that I had to duck to keep from being brained. "She has been sitting still too long."

"Not as long as you."

"Hah!" barked Elsie. "Peace and quiet are meant for some folk. Folk like me. Not for your kind, or Mag's."

That made me smile. "And what, pray tell, is our kind? What makes us less deserving of the rest you enjoy?"

"I said your kind, *or* Mag's." Elsie took a sip of wine and a large bite of cheese before continuing around a full mouth. "You are neither of you alike, and neither of you is meant for stillness. And what is this talk of deserving? Deserving has nothing to do with it. A silly notion, if ever I have heard one. It is something inside you that is different, not anything you have done. All the important things about us are on the inside. And what is in you has never been in me. I never was a mercenary, you will notice."

"I shudder to imagine it," I told her. "Any enemy would have thrown down their arms in terror upon seeing you across the battlefield."

"Why do you think I never took up the life?"

I laughed, and she chuckled, and our conversation turned down another path that was not important, and which I cannot remember. But though I did not show it, my thoughts grew heavy, and they remained so for a long while.

Mayhap I could not stop thinking of her words because they echoed what I myself had come to fear.

The day came at last when Loren decided to leave Northwood. Xain had been growing more and more impatient the longer they delayed. At last he had had stern words with Loren, well outside the inn and away from the rest of us. I did not know what he said, but when he and Loren returned that night, Loren told us she meant to leave—the next day, if she could possibly manage it.

I have thought often, in the years since, what might have been different if she had made her decision just one day earlier. It is useless to consider such things, of course, and yet our minds will not let us be sensible at all times.

But just like that, our spell of inaction vanished. Mag broke into furious activity at once. That night, though Loren and her party went to bed early, Mag and Sten stayed up late into the night, listing what supplies the children would need, and where they could find them for the best price. The next morning, we went over the needed supplies with Loren and Xain. They agreed to all of it, and they gave us their heartfelt thanks for our help.

Mag waved a hand. "Do not be silly. We are old hands at long campaign roads. It would almost have been cruel of us not to share some of our expertise."

"I will take care of procuring everything," I told them. "I know the town, and if indeed you wish to leave before sundown, you will need to purchase everything quickly."

"Mayhap I will come with you," said Sten. "You shall have to carry a great deal, and your arms are scrawny."

"With shoulders like yours, you could say that to anyone, oaf." I slapped his broad arm. "But I would welcome your aid."

"One of us should help," said Loren quickly. "Let me send Chet."

"You will need Chet's help more than we will," I said. "Be ready to go by the time we get back."

Loren sighed. "Very well. Here." She pulled a few gold weights from her purse and put them in my hand. "Will that be enough?"

"It will. Go see to the horses." As soon as she had left, I turned to Mag and handed over the gold. "Sneak these into her saddlebags, will you?"

"Of course," said Mag.

Sten and I went about our task quickly, and before long we had returned to the Lee Shore with food and many skins of water, as well as new blankets and bedrolls. With the help of Xain and the children, we packed these as well as we could and distributed them between the saddlebags of the horses. Before long, Loren and Chet came to eat with the rest of us.

"I have fetched as many provisions as I thought the horses could carry," I told her. "It should see you at least halfway through Dorsea, though you shall need to stop for more supplies at some point."

"We will stop as rarely as we can afford," said Xain. "The fewer people who mark our passing, the better."

"Once you are deep into Dorsea, I think the danger shall lessen. In the south their kingdom is preoccupied with the war, and in the north they remain as untroubled as ever at the goings-on of the nine lands."

The boy, Gem, suddenly looked past my shoulder and frowned.

"Who is that man there?" asked Gem.

What could have told me that Gem had seen the first sign of a disaster that would shape not only his life, not only Loren's, but mine, for years to come?

I turned and looked.

At the bar stood Len—Sten's distant cousin I mentioned before. He and Mag spoke in hushed, hurried tones. Mag caught my eye and tossed her head at me. I went to her, and Loren came with me.

"Len, tell them," said Mag.

Len pinched his nose and sniffed. "There is a man. He is wandering about the city, searching for a girl in a black cloak."

You know, of course, that the Nightblade always wore a fine black cloak as one of her hallmarks. There was no doubt in our minds: this man, whoever he was, sought Loren. And I could think of no innocent reason why a stranger would come seeking for her here in Northwood.

Len read the reaction in our expressions. "Aye, that is what I thought when I heard," he said. "Black cloak and remarkable green eyes, he asked for. Used that word, remarkable. Calls himself Rogan."

Kaita followed Rogan through Northwood. Her fingers twitched, desiring to pull at her braid, but it was done up in a bun now. She and Rogan were not dressed in Shade colors. Kaita had on a dark skirt, easy to discard, over grey trousers and a fitted tunic of homespun white cloth with yellow trim. Rogan wore a plain outfit appropriate for a farmer or street vendor. But there was no hiding the sheer magnitude of him, nor the fact that, despite being unarmed, he looked and moved like a weapon. Everyone who saw him seemed afraid—as well they should have been.

"I know where the Lee Shore is," said Kaita. "Let me go off and find it."

"Not yet, please, Kaita," said Rogan. "Before you strike, Loren must see me. That is very important."

"Why?" growled Kaita. "And why did you not mention this when we were making our plans?"

"Our plan was for you to accompany me," said Rogan. "I did not know you needed a reason, else I would have given it. Loren must see me because she must tell the High King and the Lord Prince about me."

He kept speaking to passersby as they went, asking after a girl "with a black cloak and remarkable green eyes." Everyone they spoke to claimed not to have seen her, but Kaita suspected many of them were lying. They looked upon Rogan with fear and distrust, and she had the feeling none of them would have revealed Loren's location even if they knew it.

But of course, they did not truly need to ask where Loren was. She would be at the Lee Shore. Mag's inn.

Kaita itched for the coming fight. She even considered slipping away from Rogan and going to the Lee Shore despite his wishes. The last time she had fought Mag, she had been foolish. She had tried to overpower the woman with sheer strength, but Mag was simply too fast. Kaita had learned. She was ready at last.

And then she saw us.

Mag and I had accompanied Loren into Northwood to see Rogan for ourselves. We came around a corner and froze stock still, our eyes fixed on him. I have told you already how fearsome and deadly he looked, and you must have heard stories of him before. So transfixed were we by the sight of him, we did not even notice Kaita standing at his elbow—not that I would have recognized her if I had seen her.

After a few moments, I pulled Loren back, and we retreated into the crowd again. Kaita jerked forwards, one hand outstretched and the other groping for Rogan's arm.

"There!" she cried, pointing. "The girl is with them!"

Rogan's gaze followed her outstretched finger. For one brief moment, he and Loren looked into each other's eyes. And then we were gone.

"Perfect," said Rogan, grinning. "She has seen me, and she knows the fear of my presence."

"Then I am free to go after them?" said Kaita.

"Not yet."

Kaita seized his arm and pulled him around to face her. "What do you mean? That is why I am here."

"I said you were free to seek vengeance, as long as it does not interfere with the battle. I need you to fly west of here and order the attack. Then you may seek out Mag."

She wanted to refuse him. She wanted to tell him to order the attack himself. But she knew, too, how much longer that would take, and what that might do to his plans. He had been there for her in some of the darkest times of her life. And despite her unfair words, he had never treated her as anything less than an equal. She could not refuse him this small service.

Still, she did not have to enjoy it. With a frustrated growl, she cast off her loose cloak. Then, right in the middle of the street, she turned. Her eyes filled with brilliant light, drawing the gaze of many in the crowd. They recoiled as her body shrank, her well-fitted clothes sinking into her skin, which soon erupted in black feathers.

In just a moment, it was done. A raven launched itself from the ground at Rogan's feet. Kaita wheeled once in the air. Rogan stood looking up at her, a grateful smile on his handsome features. The townsfolk around him looked somewhat disquieted, even offended, for of course it is not generally considered polite to so brazenly use magic in a public place. But they paid little more attention to Kaita than that.

Fools, she thought. *Useless fools. They do not even see their own approaching doom.*

She turned and flapped hard, shooting west through the sky.

I will bring it to them. And then I will burn down the Lee Shore and kill everyone within.

NINE

Mag, Loren, and I ran back to the inn as fast as we could. Loren and her friends had to leave immediately. I went with her to the stables to ready their horses, while Mag excused herself for a moment, taking Sten with her. Together they went to their room in the Lee Shore, though Sten followed his wife with a mystified expression.

"What is it?" he asked as she closed the door behind them both.

"Danger," said Mag. She went to the bed and flipped it up on its side, scattering pillows across the floor. "I do not know how great the threat is, but from the fear in Albern's voice, it is considerable. The children and the wizard must leave at once, and we are going to protect them."

"What?" said Sten, frowning at the mess she had made. "Protect them from who?"

"I do not know that either, save that his name is Rogan." Mag knelt, seizing the lock of a chest that had been concealed beneath the bed and fishing in her pocket for its key. "You heard Albern speak of the ones he fought in the mountains. I believe they have come here, though I do not know how many."

Sten fell on his knees beside her and took her shoulders, turning her towards him. Mag paused in her hurried movements, looking him in the eye.

"You mean to fight," he said.

"If need be," said Mag.

"It has been a long time since you picked up a blade."

She smiled. "I only wish I had time to go to the Reeve."

His eyes darkened. "You promised," he said. "You swore to me."

"It was a joke. A poor one." The words sounded weak even in her own ears.

Sten looked into her eyes a moment more, letting her see that he did not believe her. But then he squeezed her shoulders, and from his breast pocket he produced the key she had been searching for.

"You always leave it somewhere," he grumbled.

"Thank you," said Mag, taking the key. "Look after the inn."

"Now *that* was a poor joke," said Sten. "I am coming with you, of course."

For the first time in a long while, Mag's face filled with fear. "Sten, you should stay and—"

"I certainly will not," said Sten. "If the children must be seen to safety, then I am coming, too."

"Sten," she pleaded. "If it comes to a fight, I would rather not have you involved."

"You will have to bear it, unless you mean to stay here with me."

"It will be more dangerous for me if I have to worry about you."

Sten laughed, his shoulders shaking. "Do you jest? You and I both know you will be in no danger, whatever may happen."

"But you will," said Mag. "Sten, please—"

"Albern is going. That wizard is going. Even those children are riding by Loren's side. I want to help, Mag. We belong to each other, but you do not own me."

Mag's fingers clenched around the key. But after a silent moment, she bowed her head. "Of course not," she said. Her voice had become quite small and frightened—very different from her usual strong, matronly tone. "But if anything were to—"

The blast of a horn cut the air. Mag's head jerked up, and Sten met her gaze. The horn faded away, to be replaced with the tolling of a bell.

"An attack," said Sten.

"Yes," said Mag.

"We should go."

"Very well."

Mag's hands quivered slightly as she unlocked the chest and threw it open. Inside were two swords and two shields. She handed one each to Sten before taking up her own. Together they stood, and Mag gave her blade two quick swings.

"It has been some time," she said.

"I wish it were twice as long," replied Sten. "Quickly. The others will be in the stables."

They rushed downstairs. On the threshold of the common room, Mag paused. The customers were stirring, looking around anxiously as the bell continued to toll. The front door of the inn burst open, revealing a woman whose face was a mask of panic.

"An army!" she cried. "An army has marched out of the Greatrocks! They have the west gate, and they are killing everyone they can get their hands on!"

A great tumult burst out in the room, terror rising like a tide. But even as everyone rose to their feet and looked about, trying to decide what to do, Mag raised two fingers to her lips and gave a sharp whistle. The common room fell silent as all eyes turned to her.

"Foes attack Northwood," she said. "If you can fight, fetch your weapons. If you cannot, find a good place to hide yourselves and your families. But whatever you do, do it quickly, for they will not wait for you to decide. Go!"

The last word cracked like a whip. Her customers jerked where they stood and then began moving with purpose. Mag nodded to Sten, and they made their way to the stables.

When they threw open the wide double doors, Loren and I whirled, drawing our weapons. We relaxed as we recognized them—but then Loren balked at the sight of their swords and shields.

"The city is under siege," said Mag. "We shall see you safely beyond the walls."

"You should go back inside," said Loren. "Wait until we have gone. They will pursue us beyond the city and leave Northwood in peace."

"That I doubt," said Mag. "There is already killing in the streets. And you have no time to convince me otherwise. Mount your horses. Quickly."

Before Loren could argue, I took her arm and urged her towards the saddle of her horse, Midnight. "You are nearly a match for Mag in stubbornness, girl, but not quite. Heed her."

Loren clearly did not like it, but she did as I asked. We rode out, with Mag and Sten on foot, walking to either side of Loren like an honor guard.

We hoped to reach the north gate before the Shades could, but that hope proved to be in vain. We could not avoid the fighting in the streets. Dread and horror came over me as I saw the Shades in battle against the people of Northwood. The attackers were trained soldiers, well armed and armored. The people of Northwood were hardy, but most of them fought with simple clubs and farm tools. Some few of them had old weapons, heirlooms of ancestors who had once fought in the king's army, and there were a few constables among their number trying to organize a defense. But they never had a chance.

It pained me to see Northwood burn. I could only imagine how it felt to Mag and Sten. I watched them as we moved. Mag's eyes darted everywhere, her sword arm twitching occasionally as if aching to be used. We had not yet entered battle, but I knew what would happen when we did. It filled me with the same feeling I had had on the Reeve—that curious mix of trepidation and excitement. But I knew Sten must be filled with dread of it.

Two spans away from the north gate, it happened at last. We came to an open square, and there we found the largest battle we had seen yet. The people of Northwood had assembled into some attempt at rank and file, and they outnumbered the Shades. But though some of the Shades had fallen in the fighting, their victims' corpses outnumbered them three to one.

Mag stopped dead, and I felt the mounting tension inside her vanish. Sten saw it, too, and his jaw clenched as if with pain.

She closed her eyes and took a deep breath, rolling her shoulders.

When she opened her eyes again, something was gone from inside them. It was as though a fire inside her had been hidden behind a heavy black curtain.

I had seen it too many times not to know what would happen next, and I will not lie to you: excitement filled me to see it. But looking into Sten's eyes, I saw his heart break.

"No use," said Mag. "It will be a fight."

Her voice had become a chilling monotone, flat and lifeless. I could see the effect of it on the children, who had only known her for a few days, and had only seen her act motherly. They looked at her as though she were a stranger. I drew an arrow and spoke to Loren and the others.

"Stay behind Mag and Sten. Stay your blades unless you have no other choice, for they will try to seize them and pull you down. Now, charge!"

And Mag did. The battle-lust had taken her. She had seen her fellow citizens cut down without cause, without justice or mercy. Her town burned around her. It filled her with a rage that was white-hot and utterly merciless, and Mag intended to douse that rage in blood, forging it into a weapon against which no one could hope to stand.

The Shades did not see her coming until it was too late. In a heartbeat she had plunged into the thick of them. Even when they closed in and tried to surround her, they could not pierce her defense. Her shield moved just as quickly as her blade, blocking every attack. Then Sten was behind her, guarding her flanks even though she did not need it. He was a fine fighter in his own right, but he battled to survive, to keep the blades of his foes at bay. Mag fought to kill, to destroy, to cast her foes into the darkness from which there is no escape.

I played my part, of course, loosing arrows as fast as I could—and though I dislike boasting, that was quite fast indeed. I chose my targets carefully, bringing down Shades as close to Sten as I could while being careful not to endanger him. Had there been a hundred warriors like the three of us that day, I do not mind saying that Northwood might not have fallen.

The first fight was over quickly. The remaining Shades turned tail and ran. They had not planned to face determined fighters who knew their way around city warfare. Mag watched them go. She must have wanted to chase them, but the children still needed her protection.

She turned to Loren. Blood had spattered her face. When she spoke, there were flecks of it on her teeth.

"On," she growled. "Do not stop moving, not even for a moment."

Loren and the others obeyed, though I could see in their eyes that they were now almost as frightened of Mag as they were of the Shades. We pushed for the north gate. Twice more we met Shades in battle, and twice Mag massacred them until the rest fled in terror.

I had almost forgotten. The long years since our time as mercenaries had dulled my memories of Mag's battle-trance, the thrill and the terror of it. Thrilling because I felt nothing could stand against us with Mag on our side. Terrifying because when you stand shoulder-to-shoulder with such blood lust, it is impossible not to imagine what would happen if it were turned on you, instead.

Two more turns in the street brought us within sight of the north gate. But there we stopped, for the way was barred. The Shades had already encircled the city. Ranks of them were marching through the gate, swords bared and shields up. It was an army—a far, far greater number than we had seen in the Greatrocks.

"There are so many," breathed Loren.

"Surely not even Mag can defeat them all," said Gem, his voice small and squeaking. "Albern . . . what do we do?"

I hesitated. The boy was not wrong. Mag was the best fighter I had ever seen or heard of in legend. Yet even she could not defeat an entire army on her own. I looked at her. She had stopped in her tracks. *Surely,* I thought, *surely even her thirst for battle is not enough to draw her into a fight against so many foes.*

Loren gripped her reins, pulling them to the right. "Come. Mayhap they have not reached the eastern gate yet. We can try to—"

"They will have reached it," said Mag. She turned to the rest of us, and there was no trace of a smile on her lips. "Come now, little children. Do you fear so few of them? Come with me, and you shall reach the Birchwood. I swear it."

I heard the words. But I heard what she left unsaid as well. Mag had said the children would reach the Birchwood.

She had said nothing of herself.

Fear gripped me.

"Mag!" I cried.

It was too late. She turned and charged straight into the midst of her enemies, her blood-soaked blade held aloft. Sten did not hesitate, but plunged into the fray just behind her.

Fury filled me then, and though they were not to blame, I turned it on the children. Loren had taken a vow not to kill. She would be no help to us in this fight.

"Make use of those bows on your backs, or give me your arrows, but do not stand here idle while she risks her life for yours."

And so saying, I spurred my mount onwards behind Mag and Sten.

It can be hard to tell a story of your own exploits without sounding prideful, particularly when you accomplish something especially noteworthy. Let it sound like pride, then, when I say that my bow sang a mighty anthem of death that day. I fought like I had never fought for any mercenary company I had served in. This was no warfare for mere coin. For the first time since I had met her, I feared that Mag might fall in battle, and I swore I would not let it happen unless I had perished first. When the Shades got too close, I drew my sword and hacked them down. And I fired arrows as fast as heartbeats, slaying any Shade who dared approach my friend.

Mag, for her part, fought with all the glory and fury that legends have built up around her. Others have been called "one who walks with death," but Mag was death's master on that day. My friend was gone, and a merciless killer had taken her place. She was the Uncut Lady. She was death made beautiful. No matter how many she felled, her strikes never slowed. Her foes could not pierce her defenses, not even when they surrounded her, for Sten was behind her. Back to back they fought, Sten the bulwark and Mag the striking serpent. And I was the vengeful stormcloud that rained death on any Shade who threatened to break their guard.

"Albern!"

Loren's scream pierced the chaos, and I wheeled in my saddle. She sat there with bow in hand, her already pale face Elf-white with fear. But her finger was outthrust, pointing north.

I looked, and I saw what Loren had spotted. The Shades, seeking to kill Mag, had drawn to one side of the wide street. There was an open corridor on the other side, and it led straight to the north gate.

For one moment, hope swelled in my breast. We could escape. We could ride hard before the Shades noticed, and we could reach freedom.

But then I turned back to the battle and saw Mag surrounded by her foes.

We could escape. But she never could.

And then Sten slipped.

TEN

WHEN THEY TELL TALES OF BATTLE, THEY NEVER TELL YOU THAT THE deadliest threats are often the most mundane. There are a thousand details in any fight, and the least glamorous are often ignored in songs and stories—like the way a person shits and pisses after you kill them, their bowels and bladder voided as their bodies slacken.

Other details are less crude, but even more vital in the heart of a fight. One is the way that blood soaks the ground. It turns dirt to sticking, sucking mud, or makes a city street slick as a greased board.

Sten knew it. He was never a mercenary, but he had done his fair share of fighting. He tried to compensate, keeping his stance low and wide to keep balance. But Mag had spilled enough blood to bathe in. It was only a matter of time before it became too much.

A blade crashed down on his shield. The shield held, but Sten lost his footing, falling to one knee.

The weapon came around again, flashing in the sun. Sten's head jerked back.

For a moment, I thought he had dodged the blow. And then the skin of his throat parted, and blood poured from the wound.

I felt many things all at once, but three stand out to me now: a surging wave of anger; a heart-wrenching sadness for my kind, gentle friend.

And a rising wave of terror. Terror for Mag, and terror of her.

She did not see Sten at first, for he had stood behind her. She must have thought he merely lost his balance. With her shield arm she reached back, trying to pull him up.

He fell on his back instead, and his blood splashed across the street. And Mag saw him.

I will never forget the way she screamed. I can hear it now, as clear in my mind as it was in my ears then. We had been all across the nine kingdoms together. We had faced many dangers, lost many friends. But I had never heard her make a sound like the one that ripped from her throat then. It was like the scream of a banshee that strikes the listener dead in the night. It was the sound of a storm ready to break the world. If a host of Elves had gathered and proclaimed the doom of all humanity, they would not have frightened me more.

The Shades fell back from her, their spirit broken for a moment in dismay. But Mag did not let them retreat.

Before her scream had ended, she was killing again. But her movements had lost their methodical beauty of a moment ago. Now she plunged headlong into the fray. When Mag entered her battle-trance, she was cold, emotionless. But now she had removed the leash from her fury, and it burned like darkfire. Now she took no care to guard herself. She sought only to kill. Though she moved too fast to follow easily, I saw blood on her skin that I was certain did not belong to her foes. She would never escape from the midst of that press.

Beside me, Loren kicked her horse to leap into the fighting. I saw a wild light in her eyes. Mayhap she was ready to kill at last, or mayhap she thought she could help Mag escape the melee somehow. But I barked a command before she could.

"No! Fly, while you still can!"

She met my gaze, and I could see the anguish shining through the brilliant green of her eyes. I looked past her to Xain. He gave me a grim look and a slow nod before taking Loren's arm.

"Fly," he said. "Remember Jordel."

Tears streamed into Annis' eyes, but Loren did not weep. After only a moment's pause, she took her quiver from her hip and threw it to me. I caught it and looked upon them all—for the last time, or so I believed. I loved them in that moment, even Xain. We had passed through much peril together, and I hated that it should all come to this in the end. But I thought, at the same time, that there was something very right about it. They had ridden together before I had met them, and they would ride on together after I died. It had been my fault, after all, that we had taken that cursed road through the Greatrocks that had led to Jordel's doom. If Loren and her friends did indeed survive, then mayhap my own death was only fair.

We all think we are the heroes of our own story. But I realized suddenly that I was only a passing figure in a tale that had been about others all along.

I rode for the battle, rode for Mag. And out of the corner of my eye, I saw Loren and the others ride off. They passed the Shades and reached the gate, vanishing out of sight. It was a comfort, if a cold one. No matter what happened to Mag and me now, they were safe. They would warn Underrealm, and evil would be defeated.

Of course, back then, I believed that such a thing was possible.

All my arrows were gone before I reached the Shades' ranks. I fought with my sword from horseback, but then they killed my horse. I managed to jump clear of it as it collapsed. I took Sten's place at Mag's side, and together we forged a path of blood into the Shades' ranks.

And then a chorus of cries broke out behind us. The Shades froze, looking over our shoulders at something to my rear. I risked a look back.

A mass of Northwood citizens poured from the streets and alleys. The people of Northwood had rallied, and they were coming to our aid. There were at least two hundreds of them, and though they held no weapons more frightening than a pitchfork, their eyes were alight with fury, and their screams of rage curdled the blood.

Despite everything, I managed a smile.

They slammed into the Shades. Now it was something close to a fair fight. They had not expected such a fierce battle, that much was certain. And Mag was still there, still cutting them down, covered in blood, the thrill of battle keeping her on her feet.

It was not long before the Shades turned and fled—not forever, I knew, but the respite was most welcome. I fell to one knee right there in the street, planting the point of my sword on the cobblestones and resting my brow on clasped hands over the hilt as I gasped for breath. Mag was on her feet, and darkness take her, she did not even seem winded.

And then I heard a faint croak, and a hand scrabbled at my boot. I looked down, and my eyes flew wide.

It was Sten's hand. His eyes were pained, and his whole front was covered in blood. But somehow, defying all expectation, he was still alive.

"Mag!"

She looked as if she had been contemplating running after the Shades, but she turned at once at the sound of my scream. When she saw Sten lying there, the color drained from her cheeks. Her battle-trance passed in an instant, and she dropped her blade and shield to the cobblestones. Falling to her knees beside him, she grasped one of his hands in one of hers, and pressed the other hard on the wound in his neck.

"Sten, Sten, my love," she pleaded. "Stay here. Stay with me."

"Healer!" I roared. Everyone within earshot turned to look at me, and I gestured at them frantically. "Healer! Now! Sten is alive!"

One of them, a young, bearded man named Taron, managed to gather his wits. "The medica! She is not far. I will be right back!"

He darted off down the street, leaving me thunderstruck. A medica, here in Northwood? That was a stroke of fortune I could hardly have imagined. But Mag had not even looked up—Sten had to survive until help could come, and even then it might be too late.

"Hold on, friend," I said, gripping Sten's shoulder. I ripped off my cloak and gave it to Mag so that she could press it over the wound on his neck. "We are getting you help. We will not let you go so easily."

Sten huffed through his nose, and a choked sound slipped between his teeth.

"Be silent," said Mag. "Trying to talk will make it worse."

Sten ignored her. He gripped her arm in a bloodied hand and met her gaze. I could not tell you, even now, what passed between them in that moment. When two souls are bonded as theirs were, many things can be said without words.

"I will not let you go," whispered Mag, her voice shaking with grief. Tears dripped from the end of her nose to splash on his cheek. "Not though the Elves themselves should demand it."

He gave another grim huff through his nose.

"There!" I turned at Taron's shout to see him dashing across the cobblestones towards us. Behind him he pulled a younger woman with dark skin and long hair that she had tied back in a tail. Her hands and clothes were stained with a great deal of blood, but her gaze was steady, and as she knelt by Sten's side, she was as calm as if this were a king's garden.

"The throat?" she asked.

"Yes," said Mag. "We thought it was fatal at first, but it must not have been too deep." Sten growled, and despite everything, Mag smiled at him. "You know what I mean."

"I will count to four," said the medica. "Then you must pull away the cloak. This will hurt. One. Two. Three. Four!"

Sten's whole body went rigid as Mag pulled away her hand. The medica's fingers clutched his skin at once, and he tried to seize her wrists by reflex. Mag and I held his hands away, and the medica's eyes began to glow. Beneath her fingers, I saw Sten's flesh start to flow like water. He tried to scream, but only a gurgle came out.

"Try to be silent," said the medica sharply. "It will only be worse."

Sten's guttural sounds cut off, but his eyes were wide and wild. They locked on Mag's, and she lifted his twitching hand to kiss the back of it.

"Almost, my love," she said. "Hold on."

The flesh stitched itself together, sealing the wound. As an ander man, I knew more about medicas than most. This was not true healing—no wizard had that gift. This would only keep Sten from bleeding to death while his body fixed itself from the inside. But as the medica's eyes stopped glowing and she pulled her hands away, Sten's limbs relaxed, and he gave a deep sigh through his nose.

"It is done," she said. "He is not out of danger yet, but—"

A flash of movement. I saw it from the corner of my eye, and a lifetime of instinct took over.

"Down!" I cried. I dove out of the way, seizing Mag and the medica and taking them with me.

A flash of brown fur streaked through the air where Mag had been a moment before. It landed on Sten's chest. I heard the biting *shunk* of claws sinking into flesh and looked up, horrorstruck.

I recognized the creature at once—yet at the same time, I could not understand it. It was a great cat, the sort one finds in the mountains, larger than a man and with teeth and claws like daggers. This one had a white tail. But what on earth was it doing here in the midst of this battle?

All this passed through my mind in an instant. But before my thoughts could spin themselves into a conclusion, I heard Sten groan, and I realized what had happened. The creature had pounced on us, but I had pulled us out of the way. It had missed us and struck Sten instead. Its razor-sharp claws had pierced his chest many times over.

For a moment, Sten's fingers grasped for the mountain cat's throat. And then his whole body slackened as he died—truly this time, his sightless eyes staring into a sky streaked with the smoke of burning buildings.

"No," said Mag. Not a scream this time. No battle-lust protected her from the pain now. She had dropped all her defenses, and nothing stood between her and her grief, no bulwark against the sharp, crushing reality. Sten was gone. This time he would not return.

"No," said Mag again. She rose to her feet, and her hands curled to fists at her sides. Her sword was nowhere to be seen, but she did not seem to care. The mountain cat growled at her.

"No," she cried, and she ran for the beast, even as I scrambled to my feet, even as I went after her, tried to drag her back.

"No!" she shouted, as the cat roared and leaped for her. She stepped to the side, but her hand flashed like a knife. Rigid fingers struck the cat in the eye, and it yowled in pain. I barely scrambled out of the way in time as it sailed past.

"No!" she screamed, and flung herself at the beast. It had curled its neck and was pawing at the eye she had struck. Her heavy boot caught it in the jaw, and as its head came up, her hands struck twice, thrice more. I saw blood gush from a wound in its other eye, and as it staggered back, one of its nostrils gaped where she had ripped it open. Mag tried to press the attack, but the beast yowled and leaped back out of reach.

And then its eyes began to glow.

That struck all of us motionless, Mag and the medica and all the onlookers, and me as well. As we watched, the cat's form began to change, to shift and melt. It was the transformation of a weremage, and in a moment, there she was. A woman, not much older than I was, with nut-brown skin and dark hair worn in a short braid. She had on tight-fitting trousers of grey and a white shirt with yellow trim. Blood still ran from one of her eyes, which continued to glow as she tried to heal the injury.

"Sow!" she screamed, staggering back away from Mag. "You feckless sow!"

Mag did not answer, but merely stooped to pick up a fallen pitchfork. She crouched, readying to leap after the woman. But then there came a great roaring on the air, and another contingent of Shades burst out from between two buildings, rushing to support their master. For the weremage was their master, of that I had no doubt.

"Kill her!" cried the weremage, thrusting a finger towards Mag. "Kill them both!" But rather than help them, she turned and vanished into the press. I saw another flash of light from her eyes, and in an instant she had become a raven. It wheeled up into the sky, heading west towards the Greatrock Mountains.

For the second time, I saw Mag alone amid her enemies. My sword lay on the ground nearby. I scooped it up and launched myself towards the fight with a battle-cry.

Before I could even strike one of them, a club crashed into my temple. I fell into blackness and knew nothing more.

ELEVEN

"Are you all right?"

Sun blinked. "What?"

"Your eyes," said Albern.

Raising a hand to her cheek, Sun found it wet. She did not know when she had begun weeping. The tears had come slow and silent, wending their way down her face.

"I am fine," she said, scrubbing at her eyes with the back of a hand.

"We could enjoy silence for a moment," said Albern. "I do not mean to distress you."

"It seemed so unfair," said Sun, keeping her voice low for fear it might betray her and break. "For you and Mag to think Sten would live, only for that witch to . . . Sten did not even want to be there."

"None of us did," said Albern quietly. "That is sometimes the way of it. You find yourself somewhere you never thought you would be, and great tragedy or great fortune befalls you, unlooked-for. And then, too, things are not always what they seem. Sten was hardly the first friend I lost that way. I had a friend who I saw struck down on a battlefield in Wavemount, but he lingered on for three more days. One of my captains in the Ruby Crowns took a scratch on his cheek from an arrow. He laughed at the time, and led us to victory. The wound became infected, and he died a month later. Then there was young Bowtin, a foolish boy I met in Dulmun. He fell from a ship into the Great Bay during a sea-battle, and we thought him drowned. We mourned him and moved on—and then we met him in a Dorsean tavern two months later, for he had fought his way to shore and survived. Loren, our friend who rode from Northwood? She thought us dead in that battle. She mourned us for a long while. Our deaths helped shape her life for a good deal of time afterwards—and then she discovered that we had never died in the first place. Life and death are never so clean as we imagine them to be, especially when it comes to those we love. And they have not moved."

Sun frowned. "What?"

"Your friends in the corner," said Albern. "You keep glancing at them as I speak, as if you are afraid they are watching you, or looking for you. But they have not moved since they arrived."

"I know. Is that not odd?" Sun scowled into her beer and took another sip. "They have not even risen to relieve themselves."

"Nor have you."

Sun glared at him. "I would, but I am afraid they will take notice of me."

"I can take you outside if you wish," said Albern. "But if I do, you will have to move when I tell you to, and do exactly as I say."

Sun blinked. "What?"

"I can take you outside. In fact, I think I should."

She did not understand, but his words were earnest, and his eyes held no trace of a joke. "I . . . yes."

Albern lifted his hand, and Sun noticed for the first time that he wore a silver ring on the middle finger of his left hand. It bore a symbol she had never seen before, and it was part of no tale about Albern that she had ever heard.

Curling his knuckles, Albern rapped twice on the wooden table—just as the barman had done earlier in the night. Then, whispering, "Come," he abruptly stood and strode through the back door, snatching his bow up as he went.

Sun dared not glance at the guards in the corner as she leaped to her feet and followed him, but she guessed they must have noticed the commotion. She hid her face under the hood of her borrowed cloak and tried to get through the door as quickly as she could.

In the brisk night air, Albern stood with his face raised to the moonslight. He looked as if he was listening for something, or mayhap sniffing the air. But when Sun emerged into view, he turned at once and smiled at her.

"You will have to make a bit of a climb," he said. "But if I can do it with one arm, I am confident you can do it with two."

So saying, he jumped atop a small crate beside the tavern's back door. From there he took a large step up another two that were stacked atop each other. Sun saw that a pile of crates, which she had thought were stacked at random, actually formed a little mountain leading up to the edge of the tavern's roof, and Albern was scaling it like a satyr.

She hurried to follow him, and soon they had both reached the solid ceramic shingles. There was a little platform there, with two piles of soft cushions. Albern kicked off his mud-covered boots with some difficulty and sank down on one of the cushion piles, and after a moment's hesitation, Sun took her place on the other.

"What is this—" Sun began, but Albern shushed her and pointed down at the ground.

Sun watched as the two guards from her parents' retinue burst out the back door of the tavern. They stopped in the alley, searching left and right. One of them spoke, and the words drifted up to Sun and Albern on the rooftop.

"Where did she go?"

"I do not know. She vanished."

"Our lord will have our heads."

"Not if we find her. Split up. And if you see that useless constable, enlist him into the hunt."

They ran off, one to the left and one to the right, and soon they were lost from view.

"They knew!" hissed Sun, who feared to speak too loudly.

"They did," said Albern.

"They followed me to the tavern!"

"So it seems."

"My parents sent them," said Sun. "Curse them. I thought I had snuck out without detection."

"Our parents often like to let us think we are alone and independent, but they watch us more closely than they allow us to see. Royal children especially."

That drew Sun's attention. "Not royal," she said.

Albern smiled. "Noble, then."

She turned her gaze from him. "You have not asked why I am hiding."

"That is your business," said Albern. "It has nothing to do with me, unless you wish it to."

"What if I am a criminal?" said Sun. "I could be a thief or a murderer."

Albern chuckled. "Those women are guards. Retainers of a noble family, or mayhap hired hands to protect a merchant's caravan. If you were on the run, you would not be afraid of them, but of redbacks."

Sun frowned. "What?"

"Forgive me," said Albern. "It is not a polite term. Constables with their red armor, and Mystics with their crimson cloaks—those who fear the King's law call them redbacks, collectively."

"And how would you know that?" said Sun.

He grinned at her. "I, too, could be a thief or a murderer."

That forced a laugh from her, though she quickly hushed it and threw another nervous look at the street below. "The stories say many things about you, but they say nothing about being a criminal."

"I suppose they are not entirely worthless, then," said Albern with a smile.

Sun chuckled.

"If you still need to relieve yourself, climb down and do it quickly," said Albern. "That shed built against the back wall is an outhouse. I will wait here."

Sun nodded and did as he suggested. After she had climbed back up and settled herself on her pile of cushions again, she looked at him expectantly and waited for him to go on.

Then she nearly jumped out of her skin at a loud *thunk* behind them.

She tensed, ready to run—but then a hidden panel swung up from the rooftop. The barmaid from earlier climbed halfway up through the hole, and in her hand was a tray with two full mugs of beer.

"I am glad you found your way here safely," she said to Albern. She put the tray with the mugs on the roof between the two piles of cushions. "Anything else? Some food, mayhap?"

"None for me, thank you, Morled," said Albern. "Sun?"

"No, thank you," said Sun, who suddenly found her fingernails very interesting as a flush crept into her cheeks.

The barmaid only smiled at her. "Sun. A lovely name." She leaned over and planted a quick kiss on Sun's cheek. "Bear no worries tonight. No one here will let you fall into the hands of the constables—or anyone else who looks for you."

With a final bright smile, she retreated back through the roof hatch into the tavern. It was quite a little while before Sun realized she was frozen staring at the hatch, one hand gently touching her cheek where she could still feel the warmth of Morled's lips.

"Have another sip," said Albern. The moonslight was not bright enough to show it, but Sun could hear the smile in his voice.

"Yes, thank you," said Sun distractedly. She seized the mug and drained half of it in a single pull.

"You are clever," said Albern. "If you finish it quickly, she will have to come back."

"I—that is not why I—"

Albern's smile widened and turned into a grin. "I know."

"Does your injury still pain you?"

He frowned. "What?"

"Your injury. The blow that knocked you unconscious in Northwood. Does it still hurt you?"

Albern raised the stump of his right arm. "This one does, on occasion. But the knock on the head I took in Northwood . . . no, that does not pain me any longer."

"And Mag?" said Sun. "Her injuries—were they very bad?"

Albern's mouth twisted. "Mag suffered greatly at Northwood. But her hurts were of the mind, not the body."

Sun frowned. "I thought you said—"

"I said I thought I saw her injured," said Albern. "In the thick of battle, I was sure of it. But war turns a mind to madness. Soldiers often think they see things that never happened. It is one reason you must be very wary of believing stories—and war stories in particular."

"Do you mean they did not hurt her, even in Northwood?" said Sun. "Even in the press of all those Shades?"

"They hurt her," said Albern quietly. "They hurt her more deeply than she had ever been hurt in her life. But she was Mag. She was good at getting back up and carrying on. We both were, then. And Kaita, the weremage, had always been good at it."

Even as I lay unconscious on the ground, Kaita was winging her way west over Northwood as it burned.

Unarmed, she thought. *She beat me unarmed.*

Again.

Beyond the city's western outskirts, she found Rogan in council with his captains. They had gathered atop a hillock, from which they could observe most of Northwood and the progress of their troops through the city. Kaita landed and resumed her human form. Once he saw her growing out of the bird's shape, Rogan bid his captains away with a wave of his hand and went to speak to her alone.

"I need more troops," said Kaita. "I know where Mag is, but I need more to overwhelm her."

"We cannot spare them," said Rogan.

"Rogan—"

"We cannot spare them, Kaita," said Rogan. "I must ride north after Loren, and I must take many of our siblings with me. And I need you to lead the rest of them back to the Watcher."

"No!" cried Kaita. "Mag is still in there! She defeated me, but I must try again. Who knows when I will get another chance?"

Rogan tilted his head and looked upon her with a kindly expression. "What happened?"

Kaita scowled. "She . . . she was too fast. I had taken the form of a mountain lion, but she still outmatched me." She did not mention that Mag had done it unarmed. She spat. "At least I killed her steer of a husband."

"Sten is dead?" said Rogan.

"He is, and darkness take him."

Much to Kaita's annoyance, Rogan's lips twisted in a soft smile. "I told you that I did not think you were destined to defeat her this day, Kaita."

"You did," said Kaita, avoiding his gaze. "And how did you know that?"

"I have some of our father's sight, though I cannot see as far as he can," said Rogan. "Do not despair. I have made you promises, and I intend to keep them."

"You promised I would defeat her," said Kaita. "How do you mean for that to happen while I am leading your army to the—"

"Your army as much as mine," said Rogan, his tone betraying a rare note of admonishment. "And I have changed my mind. You will lead our siblings into the Greatrocks, but you will not take them to the Watcher. When they turn north, you should continue west. Make sure you leave a trail they can follow. I have been led to believe that Albern is an excellent tracker."

"I suppose," said Kaita through gritted teeth. "And where would you have me lead them?"

"To where it all began. Between the two of you."

Kaita's eyes shot wide. "Home."

"Yes. And not just for your own personal reasons. I need to send a trusted captain there to hurry things along. For some time now, I did not know who it would be. Now the answer is obvious. I trust no one more than you. Lead Albern and Mag there, and help our siblings accomplish their mission. You can claim your vengeance at the same time."

Kaita stepped towards him and smiled. "Yes, this . . . this is better. This is far better. Sky above, Rogan, why did you not tell me this was your aim in the first place? I would have done as you asked."

Rogan shook his head. "This was not my plan. Many things are not clear to me until it is time. Even an hour ago, I would never have considered it. I am sorry, Kaita. It frustrates me as much as you."

Many emotions warred within her. But her fear was still nearly as strong as her excitement. She shook her head slowly—not in refusal, but in thought.

"If I do this," she said, "I want a guarantee. I may need more strength than I currently have."

"You are strong beyond—"

"That is not what I mean," said Kaita. "I want a guarantee, Rogan. If I do this, and yet I cannot take my revenge alone, I want our father to grant me the power he has long denied me."

Rogan's eyes narrowed, filling with . . . not fear, but something akin to it. "That is too dangerous."

"I am no simpleton."

"The risks—"

"The risk to me, and to my mission, is also great," said Kaita. "Promise me, Rogan."

Rogan sighed. "Kaita, if things go ill, we will have to—"

"I know."

"I have no wish to see you harmed."

Her expression softened. "I know that, too." She went to him then, and she laid her head against his chest. "Whatever you may think of me, I am our father's child. My heart is true. But I need this."

"Then you shall have it," said Rogan. His tree-trunk arm wrapped around her shoulders. "If you cannot vanquish her alone, you will have every power our father can grant you. And I only hope neither of us has cause to regret it."

"Thank you," Kaita whispered into his chest. Then she drew back, out of his reach, and looked up into his eyes. "Go after Loren. Bring our father's vengeance to those who call themselves our rulers."

"I will. May death stay its hand from you."

Kaita smirked. "I would wish you the same, but in your case, death has no choice. I will contact you when I can."

Rogan gave her a final smile and left. Kaita took a moment to gather herself before finding the captains to order the retreat.

TWELVE

I WOKE WITH A SPLITTING HEADACHE TO FIND ELSIE KNEELING OVER me, bathing my face with warm water.

"Mag," I groaned.

"You are alive," she said, her brows rising. "The healers told me so, but I did not believe them. Neither would you, if you could see yourself."

"Mag," I repeated. I tried to lift my head, but a spike of pain nearly drove me senseless again. I fought to remain conscious. "Where is she?" I whispered.

"Puttering about the place," said Elsie. She rose and went to fetch me water from a bucket by the wall.

"Alive?"

"No, she died, but that has not stopped her. Of course she is alive, you dolt."

I let myself relax, at least a little. "Everyone else?" I said. Each word came with great effort. "How many survived?"

Elsie's brisk demeanor seemed to fade away. She looked over at me, and for a moment her eyes sparkled with tears. "Not enough. Though I suppose each one is a blessing."

She had been there when I first fought to defend Northwood against invaders all those years ago. I could see from the sadness on her face that this time was far, far worse.

"I am sorry," I said.

Her resolve returned at once, and she turned back to the water, ladling a cup full of it. "You should not be. You fought like a champion. Not as well as Mag, of course, or she would be lying here and you would be the one walking around. But you did all right, I suppose."

That forced a weak chuckle out of me, and with it, I felt a bit better. Strength had been creeping back into my limbs. I tried to lift my head again, and this time the pain was not so bad.

"No," said Elsie at once, coming towards me. "You are to stay—"

"I want to see the town," I told her firmly. "And I need to see Mag."

Before she could reach me, I sat up, and I gently batted away her hands when she tried to push me back down. Despite her protests, I rose from the straw pallet where I had been laid.

It was not till then that I realized I was in the common room of the Lee Shore. Mag's inn could not have looked more different. All the tables had been cleared out, and the floor was covered with four rows of pallets holding the wounded. Healers and helpers moved down the line, providing more pillows, fetching water, and seeing to their patients' needs.

"Are these all who remain?" I said as I fought painfully to my feet.

Though she clucked her tongue at me, Elsie at last abandoned her attempts to force me back to bed. She took an arm and helped me rise to my feet. "Of course not," she said. "Every tavern and inn throughout Northwood has been turned into a sickroom. Those that were not burned down in the attack, anyway."

"Help me to the door," I said.

"You mean to go *outside?"* she said, horrified.

"I told you I need to see Mag. If she is not in here, then yes, I need to go outside."

Elsie glared up at me and did not budge. "I am not sure how else to tell you this, and I do not understand why I have to, but: *you nearly died, you great idiot."*

I smiled at her. "I am no stranger to injury. I will be fine."

"No stranger indeed. You seem well acquainted with head injuries in particular." But she sighed and moved forwards, helping me hobble towards the inn's front door. With her help, I pushed it open.

And there was Mag.

She stood across the street, leaning against the building opposite. Her head was tilted back, resting against the wall, and her eyes were closed. Dirt covered her face, her arms, every scrap of her clothing. A great deal of blood was mixed in with it. But as I looked closely, I could see that none of it was hers. There were no rents in her skin, no angry red wounds. Not even a scratch.

I stood there for a long moment, staring at her, entirely dumbfounded. And as I stared, Mag opened her eyes and looked at me. A small smile tugged at her lips.

"Mag," I said. "You are alive."

"Albern," she said. "You are up. That is good, I suppose."

Gone from her voice was the lifeless, heartless monotone of her battle-trance. This was the Mag who was my friend, who did not mercilessly cut down her enemies, but who provided beds and food and rest to a band of children who had come down out of the mountains with her old mercenary companion.

I walked towards her. Elsie tried to help me, but I had almost forgotten her, and I pulled away from her grip. The pain in my body, even in my head, was forgotten. I went to Mag and put my hand on her shoulder.

"I am sorry, Mag," I said. "Sky above, I am so sorry."

Mag shrugged. "It was not your fault, nor mine. Blame the ones who did this." She gestured vaguely at the town. "Something is happening, Albern. If that was not clear to both of us before, it should be now. It is bigger than either of us, bigger than poor Loren and her friends. All we can do is try to weather the storm and pull the ones we love through it with us." She turned her gaze away, looking into the blood-soaked mud of the street. "And sometimes fail."

"Mag—"

"Leave it," she said. There was just a hint of sharpness in her tone, enough to make me obey.

After a long moment, I spoke again. "Before I went down, I saw you surrounded. I thought I saw you wounded."

That seemed to bring her out of the darkness her thoughts had cast her into. For a moment she smiled, and it was like we were on the campaign trail again, trading boasts around a campfire. She stepped forwards and held out her arms. "They did surround me. I fought my way free. Do you see any wounds?"

I did not. I sighed. "You are frightening sometimes, Mag."

"Only sometimes?"

"But . . . but then what happened?" I pressed. "How did we drive them away from Northwood, in the end?"

Mag frowned. "I have only an answer that is both poor and troubling. I do not know that we *did* drive them away. They simply turned and marched into the mountains. No one knows why."

My jaw clenched. "I would like an answer. And I would like them to answer for other things as well."

"As would I," said Mag. "But now that you have risen, many things need tending to—and one of them, in particular, was not one I wished to tend to until you were awake."

My shoulders sagged. "Sten."

She had cleaned him already. I helped her wrap him in cloth. But when I moved to lift him, she shook her head.

"I will take him," she said, and her expression brooked no argument.

She lifted him into her arms. Now, Mag had always been strong and well-muscled, but Sten was a large man. She was breathing hard before she reached the southern gate, and her steps began to falter before we were a span away from the walls. But she did not stop, not even once, and despite her staggering, she never seemed close to dropping him.

Near the bottom of the Reeve, she laid him down at last. She had prepared the place in advance, and a neat pile of wood lay there to receive him. His final resting place. I could not help but think of how Loren and I had buried Jordel in the mountains. I had not known him nearly as long as Sten, and I had loved him less well—but not by much.

"Too many," I said quietly.

"Too many," agreed Mag.

She struck flint and steel upon the heaps of dry branches, and they caught with little effort. We stood back, watching as the flames licked higher. The wood burned bright, and soon it caught upon the cloth we had wrapped Sten in.

I sang, then. I have been told I have a fair enough voice, though I did not think it sounded well in that moment, for my words were thick with tears. But I had learned a number of songs in my travels, and many of them were songs of mourning, for this was not the first time I had lost a friend.

To all of you, come all of you
No tarrying, I call to you
The darkness calls, the fall of you
It bids you come to rest

It welcomes you, and all of us
The years will pass, the fall of us
And you below, will call to us
And bid us go to rest

The wind is cold, and hollow too
All joy has passed, and sorrow too
The children weep, and follow too
They bid you come to rest

Now mourn no more, and we as well
Sit by the fire, and heed as well
One day they call for me as well
And bid me go to rest

"Will he truly rest, do you think?" said Mag.

"No one knows the darkness," I told her.

"I asked what you think."

"I hope so. He deserved it. More than either of us, at least."

"Truly said."

Her frame was steady, but I could see her hands shaking. I put my hand on her shoulder for a moment and then took it away. We stood a long, silent vigil, watching as the fires burned away the last evidence of my friend and her husband.

When the flames were only coals and the last of the drifting smoke was nearly out of sight over the trees, Mag turned to me.

"Will you come with me?"

I looked at her in surprise. "Where?"

"Atop the Reeve."

A thrill coursed through my heart. "Mag . . ."

"Something has weighed on me ever since the battle," she said. "I did not know exactly what it was. It was like a sense that I should be doing something, but I do not know what. Do you feel the same?"

"I do," I said. "What *would* you do, if you could?"

"Only one thing," she said. "Kill the weremage."

The words hit me like lightning. I straightened, balling my hands to fists at my sides.

"Yes."

Mag's eyes blazed with fire. "I want to find her. Wherever she may have run to. Wherever she may be hiding. And I want to end her."

"As do I."

Mag balled her right hand into a fist and slammed it into her hand. "Then let us do it. Come with me. Let us have vengeance for Sten."

"She will be nearly impossible to track down," I pointed out. "We do not know where she has gone."

"I have nothing better to do with my time," said Mag.

"Even when we find her, she could very well have an army at her back."

"Let them try to stand before us," said Mag. "Will you come?"

I grinned and thrust out my hand. "Even if we must ride into the darkness below."

Mag seized my wrist and pulled me into an embrace. My head, still tender, swam for a moment, but I held her. Finally, I gently pushed her back to hold her at arm's length.

"We will need horses."

"There are some in my stables," she said. "Come with me to the top of the Reeve, and then we will fetch them."

"And then into the Birchwood."

It was as if a cold snap rushed through the air, piercing us both in an instant. I felt the thrill inside me vanish even as I saw it disappear from Mag's eyes.

"The Birchwood?" said Mag. "Why the Birchwood?"

"To go after Loren, of course," I said. "Wherever this weremage has gone, she will come into conflict with Loren in the end. And she and the others will need our help, in any case."

"The weremage went west," said Mag.

"And who knows where she turned, after she entered the mountains?" I said.

"I do not know, but the mountains are the best place to start."

"But Loren—"

"The way she and the children rode from here, I doubt we could catch them even if we wanted to."

"We could try."

Mag frowned for a moment—but then her expression softened. "Latrine duty," she said. She pulled a copper sliver from a pocket. "I say heads."

"We are not new recruits," I told her. "This is not—"

"I say heads, Albern."

I sighed. Half a chance was better than none—better, indeed, than an argument I knew might not end. Any soldier knows the virtue of a firm, clean decision—even if it is a poor one. "Very well."

Mag flipped the coin. I think I knew, even as it flashed in the air, what the result would be. She flipped it onto the back of her other hand, looked at it, and smiled.

"West."

THIRTEEN

Mag led me unswervingly up the Reeve. I had to take its sloping path carefully, for I was still tender. But it was not long before we stood on the flat top. The boulders around us now loomed like old, wizened councilors, bearing witness to some grim business of their king.

Mag went to one of them and crawled underneath it. She emerged with an old spade and pickaxe. They looked as though they had been there for many years, untouched. A bit of the wood had rotted, but for the most part they were still solid. She took the spade and dug into the ground—the flat patch of earth that I had watched so closely last time, that Sten had tried to avoid completely. The soil was hard, but Mag attacked it with fury, and it broke before her onslaught. I wanted to take the pickaxe and help her, but I withheld myself.

A pace below the surface, Mag's spade struck hard rock. She dug the hole wider until it was big enough for her to stand in, and then she fetched the pickaxe. She made no remarks about the fact that I did not aid her. As when she had carried Sten to his pyre, there was an unspoken agreement that this was something she had to do alone.

Mag attacked the stone, and it shattered before her. Shards of rock flew from each blow, but Mag hardly seemed to notice.

At last she broke through. Beneath the stone were two bundles, wrapped in oiled leather to protect them from the elements. One was long and thin, the other wide and flat. Mag lifted them out and placed them on the ground outside the hole, then climbed out after them. With steady hands and a reverent bearing, she unwrapped them.

A spear, a shield, and a shirt of scale mail came out. Without pausing for even a heartbeat, Mag took them up and began to clean from them any traces of dirt.

I had not seen that spear in years. Sten had made her bury it here. It was part of the promises she had made to him when the two of them wed.

These were not the heirlooms of Mag, tavern owner and brewmaster. These were the arms of Mag, the Uncut Lady, the most feared warrior in the nine lands. These were for a quest where only death waited at the end. But not Mag's death, I was certain.

I was certain of so much, back then.

Mag had been fierce from the day we met. With any blade in her hand, she was a living weapon. But with that spear and a good shield, she was a walking incarnation of death.

Still I said nothing. I only waited. When she had finished her task, she rose to her feet and donned the mail. She gripped the straps of the shield and hefted the spear, giving it a few experimental thrusts.

As though she needs to practice, I thought. *As though she does not remember how it feels in her hands. As though she and the spear are not two parts of a whole.*

It was not often that my fear of Mag eclipsed my love of her, but I feared her then, for just a moment.

And then she looked at me. "Time for the horses," she said.

We walked back to Northwood, Mag now clad in her armor. When we reached the Lee Shore, I fetched my bow, my sword, and my travel pack before meeting Mag in the stables. They had remained largely untouched during the battle, and the masters of several of the horses had perished in the fighting. Mag went to one of them, a large mare of light grey, and began to saddle her. My horse had died in the battle, so I went to one of the other stalls, where a tall roan gelding snorted at me.

"That one has something of a temper," said Mag.

"Coming from you, that says something," I replied. But I ignored her warning and fetched a saddle from the wall. The gelding stamped a hoof when I stepped up beside him, but I clicked my tongue at him.

"Easy, fool," I told him in gentle tones. "If you throw me, I will butcher you for the townspeople to eat."

He gave me no more trouble as I made him ready to ride, almost as if he understood the words. Mag led the way out of the stable, where we mounted. The gelding shied at once, shaking himself lightly as he felt my weight on his back. But I kept my balance. My family had owned many horses, and I had learned to deal with all sorts of them.

"I am not going anywhere," I said, as the horse began to calm. "You had best get used to it."

"Indeed, it is hardly possible to get rid of him," Mag told the horse. "I have tried." Our gazes met, and I smiled.

As if it understood her, the gelding settled down, though he gave a disgruntled snort. Mag's mare nickered, and I was reminded of one of Elsie's disapproving *harrumphs.*

"Lead on," I told Mag.

She guided her horse over next to mine, holding my gaze. "Thank you, Albern," she said quietly. "For all your many years of friendship, and for your company on this road. It is going to be a long one, and it will grow dark before the end. Yet I would have no one else beside me."

"Nor I."

She nodded, and then she nudged her horse. We rode west out of Northwood, breaking into a canter as soon as we passed the western gate.

High above, far too high to hear, a harsh croak sounded as a raven circled and flew towards the mountains.

The raven sped on, far faster than our steeds. It rode the warm currents of air, drifting through the lazy smoke of the last fires in Northwood, fires soon to be extinguished as the people left their homes forever. Before too long, it winged its way over the peaks of the eastern Greatrocks.

In the valley on the other side, a small party of riders waited, clothed in blue and grey. The raven descended towards them in wide, sweeping circles. When it was less than a span above them, one of the riders took notice of it. He was a large man, with shoulders like cornerstones and a thick, bristling beard. His name was Ertu.

The raven landed on the ground before the man, and its eyes glowed. Kaita emerged from its form and stepped forwards. The man handed her the reins of her horse.

"They are coming," she said.

"I am glad to hear it," said Ertu. "All this waiting grates upon me."

Kaita frowned sharply at him as she climbed into the saddle. "You serve at our father's pleasure."

"Of course," said Ertu. "I will always obey him. But I am free to wish I was with the rest of our siblings."

"So long as it is only a wish," said Kaita. "Their march north went as planned?"

"As far as we know, yes," said Ertu. Then, curiously, he nudged his horse, walking it closer to hers, and he held her gaze as he went on in a quieter voice. "Some of our furred friends have been watching us for the past few days."

Kaita almost looked over her shoulder, but she restrained herself at the last moment. She knew he meant the satyrs. "Have they caused trouble?"

"They have not. I think they want to know why the six of us have been left behind when all the rest of our force has ridden on."

"They will find out soon," said Kaita. "We are to ride west. I am going to Lan Shui—and so are the rest of you, but after a stop along the way. The satyr elders have not heard from us since Trisken's fall. Father wishes for you to visit them and deliver his . . . displeasure."

Ertu's beard jumped as his lips twisted in disgust. "I have visited the satyrs once. I do not relish the idea of repeating the experience. They are foul-smelling creatures."

"Father has—"

He shook his head to cut her off. "Sky above, Kaita, I have not refused your orders. I am only grousing. Father deserves our obedience, but you act as though we are supposed to be his unquestioning slaves."

Kaita steeled herself. Even after so many years, she was unused to the way the Shades conducted themselves, the way they treated each other. But then, Kaita had been raised in far different circumstances.

“Of course not,” she said at last. “Forgive me. The changing . . . it tires me.”

“I imagine,” said Ertu graciously. “Fear not. You will be able to rest well, now—or at least, as well as one can when on the road. Let us set out, for the glory of our father.”

He turned in his saddle and motioned for the riders to set off. They went west at an easy walk, and Kaita fell into line with the rest of them, her thoughts uneasy.

FOURTEEN

"So she was following you," said Sun.

"Leading us," said Albern. "But you have the idea."

"Why did she wait? I am certain the people of Northwood guarded against another attack, but you left Northwood. Did she not think to wait until you were sleeping, and creep into your camp, and kill you in the night?"

"I am certain she thought of it," said Albern. "But we always set a watch. And I think she well remembered the injuries Mag had given her. But I could not tell you for certain. Many things I know about what Kaita thought in those days, but not everything."

"And how do you know this, again?" said Sun.

Albern smiled at her. "That is another story entirely, and not one I intend to tell you tonight."

"What about the two of you?" said Sun. "You knew you were after a weremage. Were you not frightened? I would suspect every shadow. Any beast could have been the weremage, or anyone you met on the road."

"They could have been," said Albern. "But remember that we

thought we were chasing the weremage—we did not know her name, then—and that she was fleeing with the Shades across the kingdom. We did not know we were being led. Not until much later."

Albern stared into his mug of beer for a long moment, his brow furrowed and his lips pursed. Sun studied him. The tale had thrilled her, she had to admit. When he had spoken of riding off from the Reeve, she had felt a sudden desire to rise to her feet and start a journey at once—though she knew not where. Yet the same words that had excited her were obviously disturbing to Albern. She waited in respectful silence, not wanting to agitate him further.

And then, all of a sudden, he drained the rest of his mug and rose to his feet. "Well, I have to be taking care of something."

Sun drew back, blinking. But before she could answer, Albern took up his bow and climbed rapidly down from the rooftop. He reached the ground and passed around the corner of the tavern without so much as a backwards glance.

It was another long moment before Sun thought of standing up. She stood there, staring stupidly down at the empty alley behind the building, until she realized he was not coming back.

Not knowing what else to do, Sun clambered down after him and ran around to the front of the building. Albern stood by a horse that had been tethered to a pole. It was already saddled, and he was checking its straps.

Anxiously, Sun approached the old man from behind. "Albern?"

"Hm? Yes?" said Albern. He glanced back at her and gave a brief smile before raising one foot to the stirrup. With impressive grace considering his age and his single arm, he vaulted into the saddle and took up the reins.

"Where . . . where are you going?" said Sun. The question seemed too obvious to need to be put into words, but she felt as driftless as an unmoored ship.

"I have an errand to take care of," said Albern, looking down at her. Then he seemed to notice her expression for the first time, and he smiled. "Forgive me for not mentioning it sooner, but I had rather hoped you would come with me."

"But . . . but where?" said Sun.

"Oh, this errand is not too far away," said Albern.

This errand? The wording was not lost on her. Nervously, Sun glanced both ways down the street. Two of her family's guards were searching for her even now. She thought of her mother and father, of their caravan beyond the bounds of the town.

"But I need to be getting back soon," whispered Sun. She had meant to say it aloud, to say it to Albern. But she spoke quietly, as if to herself, and Albern did not answer.

She *did* need to get back. Her family expected her. She was supposed to ride on with them tomorrow. On to their final destination, there to remain for a time before returning home. And before long, they would take her somewhere else, and then somewhere else. All part of a plan, a great dance that had always been determined for her, the steps laid out before she had first set foot on the floor.

Sun turned back, looking up at Albern. "You will keep telling the story if I come with you?"

Albern's smile widened. "Until the tale's true end."

Her pulse raced. Her breath seemed to catch in her throat, and she was not sure she could feel her fingers. But she stepped up next to Albern's horse, and as he nudged it to a walk, Sun followed.

She expected Albern to continue the tale immediately, but as they left the town heading south and passed into open country, still he remained silent. He only made gentle noises to the horse as he nudged it one way or another. Sun gave the steed another glance, half expecting to see the roan gelding from his tale. But that was ridiculous, of course. That had been decades ago. This horse was a deep chestnut brown.

"What are you thinking, child?"

Sun had been thinking many things, but none seemed like the right answer. So she asked him the question that had not left her mind, despite his reassurances. "Did all of this *really* happen?"

Albern cocked his head. "I told you already that stories are—"

"—Are meant to be learned from, yes," said Sun. "I understand, but . . . how can you expect me to take it to heart, to learn from it, if I do not know for certain that it even took place as you say it did?"

Albern looked at her askance. "Do you think *I* am certain of how it happened?"

"I . . . what?" said Sun, frowning up at him. "Of course you are. You lived it."

"Hm," said Albern. "I see the lesson still has not taken root. Let me ask you this, then. Tonight you told me your name, but you left out your family name. Do you know if that answer was true or not?"

"Of course I do," said Sun. "I knew what the truth was, though I did not speak it."

"Mayhap. Or mayhap, in crafting a lie, you struck upon a deeper truth."

She frowned. "I do not understand."

"Do you really think you are still the noble daughter who first entered that tavern?" Albern chuckled. "I doubt she would have gone scarpering off with a decrepit, one-armed man. Those sound like the actions of a girl with no family, the actions of Sun of No Name."

This was almost too much. Sun's thoughts spun, and her feelings gave her no peace. She had often wished she was not a daughter of the family Valgun, but she *was.* Was she not?

Her parents' guards must have reported that she had gone missing by now. She knew there would be consequences, and that they would be worse the longer she remained away. Yet she was not returning to her family, but traipsing off with an old man, simply because he was telling her a good story.

That did *not,* in fact, seem very like something Sun of the family Valgun would do.

Her mind whirled, and she felt that strange, unmoored feeling again.

"Why are you telling me all this, about Northwood and the rest of it?" she asked. "Why will you not tell me what happened to your arm, or what happened to Mag?"

"Because you *want* to hear one story, Sun, but you *need* to hear another," said Albern. "Any talespinner must seek a balance. He must tell the listener what they *need* to hear, but tell it well enough that the audience is willing to stay and listen, no matter what they demanded in the first place. Do you think, when your Dulmish king brings a skald into her court, that she merely searches out the one with the best voice? No, not if she is wise. She seeks the skald who will tell her the stories she most needs told, even—mayhap especially—when she does not want to hear them."

"So you think you know better than me what story I need to hear?" said Sun. "You are just like my parents, and that is no compliment."

"I think I do, yes," said Albern mildly. "But if I judge correctly, I am different from your parents in one important respect: if you do not wish to take my advice, I will not force it upon you. You are free to go at any time—or, if you wish, you can simply ask me to stop telling the tale, and we can talk of other things."

"You compare yourself to a skald," said Sun. "Yet if a king demands a tale, her skald will tell it if he is a true servant."

Albern's eyes flashed as he looked at her, and for the first time he appeared truly angry. "You vastly misjudge us both if you call me a servant and yourself my king."

Hot blood rushed into her cheeks. "I am sorry. I did not mean it like that."

He held her gaze for a long moment. But then the hostility in his expression faded somewhat. "No, I suppose you did not. It is clear to me—forgive me for saying so—but I would guess you have little opportunity to exercise your skill at argument. I would wager that people in your life have been of two kinds: those who obey you, and those who *you* must obey without question."

"Is it so obvious?"

"As obvious as the fact you come from Dulmun. You walk like you wear a crown, and those leathers of yours are hardly Dorsean, nor are they the garb of a poor commoner. I knew nothing about you when you stepped through the door of that tavern, but you told me much in the way you moved and spoke. And you are avoiding my point."

Sun still did not wish to look at him, for her cheeks still burned with shame at the way she had spoken to him before. "What point is that?"

He fixed her with a look. "I am trying to tell you the story you need, Sun of the family Valgun. Yes, I know your family name as well. I think I know what you need to hear, and I am certain I know how badly you need to hear it. But I am trying, also, to make it a tale worth your time. Have I done a good enough job so far? Do you want to hear more?"

Sun felt many things. She was frightened, uncertain, and more than a little apprehensive about the shadowed wilderness they now rode through.

But above all of that, when she looked deep into her own heart, she had to admit one thing: she *did* want to hear what happened next.

"Yes," she said quietly. Then, louder, "Yes. Tell me. Please."

FIFTEEN

I TOLD YOU OF MAG FETCHING HER SPEAR FROM THE REEVE. YOU should know something of that spear, before I continue the tale.

You had heard, before I told you, of Mag's prowess in battle. But whatever you have heard, and however well I myself describe it, all tales are inadequate. Never have I seen or heard of such a master when it comes to combat. Her mastery extended to any weapon—in the battle of Northwood, she fought with a sword, you remember—but she became truly terrifying when her spear was in her hands.

I was with her when she got that spear, as it happens. We were in the western reaches of Dulmun. I had persuaded her to join the Silver Stirrups for a time, and that company had been summoned there for . . . sky above, I cannot remember. We were there for months, yet I cannot remember the conflict that brought us. Yet I remember every detail of the moment Mag found her spear. It is often that way when we age, and our memory begins to fail us.

The two of us had been given a day's leave, and we were spending it in Vaksom, the city that sprang up around the warlight Arod. It was my first time visiting Dulmun, and I found myself uncomfortable—

meaning no offense. To an outsider, your people appear quick not only to laugh, but also to anger, and they almost seem to enjoy settling disagreements with their fists. It left me feeling on edge.

But Mag seemed curiously at home in Vaksom. It was strange to see the way she looked at everything, as if she was trying to solve a mystery. Her head was cocked and her eyes were narrowed, and it seemed that half-hidden thoughts swirled around each other in her mind.

"What is it, Mag?" I asked her. "You look pleased to be here, and at the same time confused."

"I suppose both are true," she said. "There is something familiar about this place, though I have never been here that I recall."

"Mayhap you came here as a child?" I said.

"Mayhap," she murmured.

Suddenly she stopped dead in the street, staring at a shop. I looked it over. It seemed to be the shop of a bladesmith, but a far grander one than I had ever seen. Two stories tall it stood. Its front windows were open, and in them were displayed blades of the highest quality. I saw swords, daggers, and spears, but also many strange weapons that I had never seen the like of. Too, I had never seen a smithy with someone standing guard, but there was one here—a large brute of a man with horribly scarred hands.

"You have good taste," I told Mag. "But I think your eyes are larger than your purse. Sellswords such as us could not bring the custom a place like this demands."

Mag did not appear to hear me. She only stepped towards the shop's door. As she approached, the guard barred her way and held up a hand.

"Stay yourself," he said, his voice rumbling like an ocean wave. "What business do you have here?"

"What sort of business do you expect?" said Mag. "I wish to buy a weapon."

The guard eyed her up and down. "You are no customer of this place. Begone."

"You do not know how much coin I am carrying," countered Mag.

"You could not carry enough coin on your whole person, and since you do not have a pack horse behind you—"

"Friend," I said quickly. "You are a hired sword like us, are you not?"

The guard's mouth twisted. "Not like you."

I spread my hands wide, giving him a friendly smile. "Oh, not a mercenary, certainly. But we all have something in common: we are paid to fight. You have a greater appreciation for the art of battle than most people could imagine—as do we. And my friend here is special. I swear to you that you have never seen her like in combat."

The guard arched an eyebrow as he looked down at Mag, who stood a good two heads shorter than he. "If you mean to intimidate me, you are not doing a good job."

"Not at all," I said. "But when someone ascends to her lofty heights of skill, they gain a rarefied taste for weapons of war. You may be right: we may not have enough coin to afford your master's astonishing wares. But can you not understand a desire to simply see them? Let her at least have the dream of fighting with such tools of war, though they may be fit only for the nobility who pay our wages."

His expression did not change a whit, and I thought my words had been for nothing—and, too, I feared that Mag might escalate matters, for that was a bad habit of hers in those days. But after a moment the guard drew aside, waving an admonishing finger at both of us.

"Disturb nothing," he said. "Touch nothing. And do not approach my master if she does not speak to you first."

"You have our word," I said, nodding my thanks and ushering Mag into the shop.

"I could have taken him," Mag muttered once we were safely away from the man.

"I know you could have," I said. "But it might have put a damper on our experience here. Now you can peruse the weapons without worrying about constables showing up."

It is customary for shopkeepers to put their finest wares on display in the windows, using them to draw in customers. But I could hardly have said the weapons in the window were any better than the ones we found inside. Every new blade I saw seemed to be the finest I had ever beheld, until I saw the next one. I am and have always been an archer first and foremost, but I know my way around a sword, and I found myself transfixed by those on display. They were made in the Dulmun fashion—longer and heavier than those in Calentin—but that did not prevent me from appreciating their quality.

After a moment I looked up and realized that Mag and I had become separated. I sought her out quickly, as I still did not trust her not to make trouble if anyone should bother her. I found her standing before a display of spears. The weapons were arranged in racks that held half a dozen each. These were no long infantry spears, meant for fighting in formation, and which are usually much taller than the soldiers that wield them. These were Dulmish dueling spears. If you have never seen one, they can appear a bit strange. They are usually only a little taller than the shoulder—just long enough to serve as a walking stick, not so long that they are burdensome for long journeys. Their spearheads are larger than those of infantry spears, and they have long edges so that they can be used to slice and cut, not just to pierce. There are smaller, curved blades just behind the head, almost like a hilt, that you can use to entrap and entangle the weapon of your opponent.

I had never seen anyone wield such a spear before—after all, most of the battles I had seen had been formation fighting. It struck me as curious that Mag was so transfixed by the weapons, for I had had no inkling that she knew how to use them.

"Mag?" I said, for she did not appear to have seen me. "What is it?"

"These spears," she muttered, and it sounded almost as if she was talking to herself. "I . . . I almost remember."

"Remember what?"

She only shook her head. And then came a voice from close by, startling both of us out of our thoughts.

"It is rare to have someone lavish so much attention on my spears."

Mag and I turned quickly. Before us stood the woman who I knew must be the master of this shop. She was of medium height, but as broad as a barn. Her arms, like any good blacksmith's, were thicker than my thighs, and her torso had several more layers of weight over thick muscles. The back of her hair was done up in a tail, but the front cascaded like the wings of a crow wrapped around her moon-shaped face. Over her shoulder, I saw the door guard surveying us, his face stern but impassive.

"Do we have the honor of addressing the owner of this fine establishment?" I said, speaking just loud enough that I hoped the guard could hear my courtesy.

"You do," said the smith. "Smedda of the family Stalhert is my name."

"I am Albern of the family Telfer," I told her, placing a hand over my heart. "And this is Mag."

Smedda cocked her head. "Sellswords, I suppose. What brings you to my shop?"

"Why, only the desire to gaze upon your incomparable wares," I said.

"Flattering," said Smedda. "I am not in the habit of entertaining those who wish to peruse and not to buy, but courteous words can go far in changing my mind. I imagine you did much the same to Bronhil at the door, or he would not have let you in."

"We impressed upon your noblest and most loyal servant," I said, projecting my voice in Bronhil's direction with all my might, "that our appreciation for your work was nearly limitless. Truly, your purse must overflow with wealth from grateful patrons."

"Only one patron, really," said Smedda. "King Lannolf, of the family Valgun. Once I secured his custom, it is rare to find anyone else who can match the coin my wares fetch."

I had two curious sensations at the same time: I felt as though the walls were pressing in upon me, and at the same time it was as if I had shrunk to the size of a mouse, and the shop had become incomprehensibly vast. I gasped suddenly, realizing that I had forgotten to breathe for the space of several long heartbeats.

"You are King Lannolf's armorer," I said, my voice a mouse's squeak. Mag had stopped paying attention to the conversation and was looking at the spears again. I smacked her hard between the shoulder blades, trying to get her to turn around. She ignored me.

"I am one of his smiths," said Smedda. "He has others. And I rarely attempt armor. It is not my passion, and therefore my work is not as good as it could be. But when it comes to weapons: yes, I arm the king, and all his kin, and anyone else who catches his favor or fancy. And I am well rewarded for it."

At once I dropped into a deep bow. I noticed that Mag still seemed to be paying no attention to what we were saying, and I smacked her again. "It is our deepest honor to be in your presence."

"I can tell," said Smedda, eyeing Mag, who had not stirred despite my actions. "May I ask why you are so—"

"What do you call them?" said Mag, turning suddenly and pointing at the spears. "I have never . . . that is, I do not recall ever seeing spears like this before."

"They are rare, even here in Dulmun, and I have seen them nowhere else," said Smedda. She stepped past Mag and lifted one of the spears from its rack, lowering it and running her fingers along its length. "They are called spontoons. Meant for a single fighter, not for soldiers in formation, but then you can tell that. Nobles today rarely seek them out, for they are not considered 'fashionable'—which just goes to show you how useless fashion is. If two fighters of equal skill face each other, one with a sword and one with a spontoon, I would bet half my considerable fortune on the one with the spear, every time."

"They are a weapon of Dulmun?" said Mag, as though she had not heard anything Smedda had said after that.

"They are," said Smedda. "The skill of their making was passed to me by my master, whose family has dwelled here since the time of Roth. As I said, I have never seen them in any of the other kingdoms, and I have visited all of them." She cocked her head again and regarded Mag carefully. "Would you like to feel it in your hands?"

"Yes," said Mag at once.

"Mag," I said, "are you sure that is wise? If you were to damage it in any way—"

"Do not worry," said Smedda. "I will not hold you accountable. There is a light in your friend's eyes, and I wish to see what it might illuminate. I have a small yard in back of my shop. Choose whichever spear you wish, and meet me there."

She set off for the back of the building at once, leaving Mag alone to choose her spear in peace. But Mag hardly seemed to need the privacy—she scarcely glanced at the rack before selecting one of the spears. Its haft was somewhat thicker than the others, its head a bit broader and a bit shorter.

Mostly, I noticed that it looked to be the most expensive spear on the rack. Mag had that habit, too—walking into any shop and choosing among its wares at random, she would inevitably gravitate towards the priciest item in the place.

But that thought fled my mind as Mag handled the spear. She tossed it lightly from hand to hand, and then she spun it on either side of her like a staff. The movement was natural and fluid. That was hardly a surprise, for I had seen Mag with all sorts of weaponry, and she was always formidable. But I could tell at once that this was different. The spear had become part of her almost from the moment she laid her hand upon it. Thunder did not crash in the sky, but it felt like it should have. A shaft of sunlight did not pierce through a high window to illuminate her, but it felt less like something that had not happened, and more like something that *should* have happened, but which the sky had forgotten about.

Silently I followed her out the back door into the yard. Smedda waited there—and to my great shock, she had thrown on a set of light padded armor, and in her hands was a blunted training spear of the same kind as Mag's.

"That looks good in your hands," said Smedda, nodding towards Mag's weapon.

"It feels . . . familiar," said Mag.

"I thought you said you had never seen such a weapon before," said Smedda.

"Not that I remember," said Mag. "Yet holding this one feels like embracing an old friend."

Smedda nodded slowly. "I have seen such things before, though rarely. Come. Let us spar, and we shall see what you can do with it."

A pit formed in my stomach. "I am not sure that is wise," I said at once, stepping between the two of them. "Mayhap you should let me face off against Mag." Thoughts raced through my mind of the unimaginable wrath we would bring down on ourselves if Mag were to injure the king of Dulmun's personal bladesmith.

"Afraid she will hurt me, are you?" said Smedda, and she laughed. "Do not be a fool. You know your friend better than I do, but even I can see that that blade will not kiss my skin unless she means it to—and she does not mean it to. Do you, girl?"

"I swear I will do you no harm," said Mag solemnly, gripping the spear in both hands and taking a wide stance. Then she smirked. "No lasting harm, that is."

"That is the spirit," said Smedda, grinning. "Now, let me see what you can—"

And then suddenly she was on her back, the tip of Mag's spear a fingersbreadth away from her throat.

"What—" gasped Smedda. Her face scrunched up, for all the world as though she was searching for a distant memory. "You tripped me."

"Yes," said Mag. She put up her spear and lowered a hand to help Smedda rise. "Your reaction almost saved you, but it was just a tad too slow."

"A tad?" said Smedda, frowning. "I did not even know what had happened until it was done."

"Is the spear all right?" I said, leaning forwards and peering at it.

"You stop that," said Smedda, glaring at me and holding up a finger, like a grandmother scolding her progeny. "No warrior can fight while worrying about the state of the blade in their hands. No matter a weapon's value, no matter its heritage, when you fight with it, it has only one purpose: to be a tool with which you enact your will." She turned back to Mag. "If you would indulge me: I would like to try attacking you and see how you defend yourself. One of the great strengths of a spontoon is its use for protection as well as for aggression."

"Of course," said Mag. "Whenever you wish."

"First," said Smedda, going to the side of the yard. From the wall she pulled a battered practice shield, tossing it to Mag. "Use that. It is imperfectly balanced, but it should serve for this purpose."

Mag began to slip her left arm through the straps—and Smedda struck before she was finished. But even the moment's distraction did not matter. Mag's shield was like a wall guarding her from harm, and wherever it could not protect her, the haft of the spear came in to block Smedda's swipes and turn her jabs. Mag danced around Smedda's every blow, barely even stepping back to avoid them.

I felt then, as I would go on to feel many, many times, the sheer awe of seeing Mag with that spear in her hand. She had already been a peerless warrior in my estimation. But in that moment—though I did not quite know it—she was taking her first steps on the road that would turn her into a legend.

After a short while of sparring, Mag finally turned the tables. Rather than blocking Smedda's thrust, she caught the spear between her own and the shield, and then twisted to flip it out of Smedda's hands. Finally, almost as an afterthought, she flipped the spear around and jabbed the butt of it hard into Smedda's belly. All Smedda's breath left her in a rush, and she fell on her rear on the sandy yard.

"My apologies," said Mag. "Instinct took over. You understand, of course."

"Of course," said Smedda ruefully, holding up a hand for Mag to help her again. "Well, that settles it. You have to buy that spear."

"What?" I said. "She could not possibly afford it. You said your prices—"

"Are considerable," said Smedda. "And I cannot give you the spear for free. I have a reputation to uphold, and no warrior values a weapon they did not pay for—in gold, or in blood."

"I would value this spear," said Mag fervently.

Smedda grinned. "I imagine that is true. It belongs with you, and you with it. Therefore I will let you buy it for two hundreds of weights."

Even as my guts turned a somersault, Mag said, "Done."

"Mag!" I said. "That is more than either of us will earn in a year. If you paid for nothing else, if you avoided all costs for—"

"I may be green, but hardly any more so than you. I know full well what I am doing." Mag sighed and removed her shield, then held the spear out to Smedda. "I will return when I can. Please, hold it for me."

"I will hold it, but not for long," said Smedda. "Before I can allow you to take it, it must be enchanted."

Behind Smedda's back, I threw my hands into the air and tried to mouth "No!" to Mag. Enchantment was a service provided only by wizards trained at the Academy, and it was fantastically expensive, beyond the reckoning of anyone but royalty. Mag did not even glance at me, but only nodded at Smedda.

"And how much will that be?" said Mag.

Smedda waved a hand. "The enchantments are simple. They will protect the blade from wear and keep the haft from breaking. The spear will not be wreathed in magical flame or anything so ridiculous. I have a shipment bound for the Academy next week already, and I will include the spear with the rest of them, for the same cost."

I froze, my hands in midair where I had been trying to gesture to Mag that she should abandon this foolish idea. Now I cocked my head. Two hundreds of weights was already a bargain, even if Mag could not afford it. But with enchantment at no extra charge . . . that changed the nature of the deal considerably. I doubted if I could have resisted such an offer, and I knew Mag would never be able to.

"Done and done," said Mag. "I imagine I can write you here, as I acquire the funds I will need before I can retrieve the spear?"

"I told you already, I will not hold the spear that long," said Smedda. "You two are with the Silver Stirrups, yes? They will be in Dulmun for at least another half-year. Before you leave the kingdom, come and retrieve the spear. You can send me your payment later, or even in parts, as you are paid."

Still behind Smedda's back, I grabbed great fistfuls of my own hair, my face filled with delight as I looked at Mag. For her part, she seemed utterly thunderstruck, and it was a moment before she spoke.

"That is generous," said Mag.

"I can afford to be generous," said Smedda. "I do not know if you have heard, but I serve King Lannolf. I trust you to send the payment when you can; only a great fool would try to cheat the king's own bladesmith, and you are not a great fool."

"You still extend a great deal of trust," said Mag. Where a moment ago she had sounded so self-assured that it annoyed me, now she seemed full of doubt. I almost thought she would refuse the deal. "The spear could be lost, or I could die in—"

"Ha!" barked Smedda—a single shout of laughter that I suspected was meant more to shut Mag up than to express mirth. "Girl, I *just* fought you. You, dying before you are able to pay me? You jest, and poorly."

Mag seemed at last to be overwhelmed. She sank to one knee in the sand of the yard and bowed her head towards Smedda.

"Thank you," she said softly. "You do me a far greater honor than I deserve, and I will not forget it."

"I expect you shall not," said Smedda. "But you honor me as well. Any smith has only one wish: to see their creations used well. King Lannolf and his kin are fine warriors, but when was the last time they went to war? The blades I make for them languish in training yards, or in fine halls where they are used as decoration. Fah! When you take this spear from me, you will take it and use it the way it was meant to be used. I could ask for nothing more."

Mag knelt there for a moment, silent, looking at the spear in her hand. In her eyes was some trouble, or some deep thought, at which I could not begin to guess. But it seemed clear the spear was more than a weapon to her.

I almost remember, she had said before, when I first found her looking at it.

But remembered what?

We left the shop soon after, and two months later we returned for the spear. Mag carried it ever afterwards, and it became part of her legend.

She never told me what she had almost remembered—not for many, many long years, anyway.

SIXTEEN

After leaving Northwood, we rode into the Greatrocks together, traveling up the same path I had used to come down out of them. It had taken me six days when I rode with Loren. Now, we took the journey more slowly, for I was still tender from the battle. I slept long each night, setting camp as soon as night fell and often rising hours after the sun. It was ten days before Mag and I got very deep into the mountains.

It surprised me how easily we both fell into old routines. There are little tricks one learns after years spent on campaign trails—the best way to unfurl and repack a bedroll, the tricks of choosing a campsite, the skill of falling asleep quickly and waking up with speed. It came somewhat more easily to me, for I had ridden a long trail just a few weeks ago, guiding Loren through the mountains. But though Mag had not left Northwood in years, she picked up our routine just as quickly as I had.

Though we rode as fast as we could with my tender condition, we kept a wary eye out in case of attack. Yet we saw no sign of the Shades, nor of any other creature, save for an occasional rabbit or game bird fit for hunting. The satyrs and harpies avoided us entirely—until we entered their territory at last.

In the middle of the tenth day, we came to the Shade stronghold in the mountains. Then, for the first time, I ordered Mag to slow. We approached the fortress slowly and with stealth. If the Shades were to stop anywhere in the Greatrocks, it would be here.

Leaving the horses behind us, we crawled up a steep slope that brought us to a lesser peak overlooking the fortress. We crawled on our bellies for the last few paces, poking our heads over the edge of the land to peer down.

There it sat: the stronghold about which I now had so many evil memories. It crouched on a rock platform like a lurking, malicious spider. There was a chasm below its eastern wall, and a stone bridge reached across the gap. It was mayhap seven paces wide and had only low stone walls for railings. It was from that bridge that Jordel had fallen to his doom, though he brought a great foe into the darkness with him. Barely visible from where we lay in the grass, I could see the long stone ramp that led down from the stronghold's west wall, falling away to the valley far below.

The stronghold itself, however, looked empty. I saw no signs of motion within, nor was there any indication that anyone had been there recently. From what I could see, it looked as though the Shades had passed straight through the fortress without stopping.

"No one there," said Mag.

"Not that we can see," I said. "We must still be cautious."

"When have I ever been incautious?"

"Always. Every time, everywhere."

"They had too many soldiers for them all to be hiding within those walls," she said, ignoring my answer. "Not even if all of them were clustered together and standing as close as lovers."

"Yet they may have left behind a rearguard," I said. "I do not mean to say we have to inspect the whole fortress. But when we pass through it, let us be careful."

She crawled back down the slope and away from the ridge. I followed her back to the horses, and together we rode out across the narrow stone bridge towards the stronghold. I paused for a moment in the middle of the span, looking at the low stone wall that rimmed it. Xain had used fire to burn words into the stone there, a eulogy for Jordel. But Mag did not notice, and she pressed on without stopping. I hurried to catch up with her.

The eastern gate stood open, as did the western gate on the other side. The wide courtyard within the walls was just as empty as it had appeared from the outside. The only thing to be found was some hay scattered about the place, floating and scraping along the ground in the mountain wind. Mag stopped in the middle of the yard and dismounted. I did the same. She looked about, brows raised.

"A good fortress," she said. "The walls are strong."

"Yet not infallible," I said.

"Hm," she said. "No walls are infallible. No enemy beyond reach."

I grinned. "Do you speak of the Shades, or the weremage?"

Mag smirked. "There appears to be no one here. We should ride on. But hold a moment. You have a loose strap."

She stepped up, fiddling with my saddle. I stared at her. My straps were tight, and we both knew it. Once she drew close, she spoke in a low voice.

"There are satyrs watching us. On the rocky slopes above the walls. Fetch something from my saddlebags. It will give you an excuse to look."

I went to the other side of her horse and unbuckled one of the pouches hanging from the saddle. My eyes slid up the side of the mountain that towered over us. Tiny flashes of movement caught my gaze as satyrs ducked back out of sight. I took out a waterskin and brought it back to Mag.

"There are several of them," I said, handing her the water skin. "But they do not seem interested in troubling us. Likely they are only keeping watch. We are past the border of their homeland, after all."

Mag took a small swig of water and handed it to me. As I drank, she murmured, "They will have seen where the Shades went. We should ask them."

I pursed my lips and put the stopper back in the waterskin. "Agreed. But try not to kill them, will you?"

She arched an eyebrow. "I thought they gave you a great deal of trouble when last you came this way."

"They did, at the orders of their elders," I said. "And their elders are under the sway of another."

"The Shades?"

"Whoever leads the Shades," I said. "The satyrs spoke of a Lord."

"Satyrs have no lords."

"No, they do not. To hear them speak of one worried me more than anything else we found in these mountains."

"That is little concern of ours now. But let us get our hands on one of them, and we will have some answers about the weremage."

I finished pretending to dig through her saddlebags and returned to my horse. "And I will have them answer for other things as well."

We mounted again and rode through the western gate, down the long stone ramp into the valley. I found no good excuse to look back at the satyrs shadowing us, but every so often I would hear the soft clatter of hooves on the rocks high above. They were still there.

I knew we had to lure them into open lands, as far from any slopes as possible. Satyrs can nearly fly up a mountainside, and they could rain arrows down on us. But on open ground, they were no more nimble than a human. Only there would we have any chance of taking one of them alive.

To tell the truth, and despite my words to Mag, I found myself filled with anger that almost defied reason. Yes, the satyrs had only acted upon the directions of their leaders. But they had still nearly gotten me killed, along with all of my friends. That was not easy to forgive, though I was trying. After all, satyrs are not quite beasts, but neither are they quite human.

Not far from the bottom of the stone ramp was a small cluster of trees, a little wood that bent and huddled over the thin stream that ran through the middle of the valley. I led Mag towards it. The satyrs would think we were merely watering ourselves and the horses. But if they tried to approach us among the trees, we would be able to take them by surprise.

Though it was not very late in the day, the sun had already hidden itself behind the tips of the western mountains above. Dismounting, we ducked in among the shadows of the trunks, quickly losing ourselves among the trees. Once we were a good distance in, I stopped Mag and drew her against the side of an old beech tree. Together we looked back in the direction we had come.

There were the satyrs. They were making an attempt at stealth, but they were not used to it on such open terrain. They approached the trees warily, darting between brush and rocks with their awkward, loping gait. I counted six of them. Not an inconsiderable group, but against Mag and me they stood little chance.

"Let us tether the horses," I said. "We do not want them to run off during the fight." The beasts were already nickering nervously, for the satyrs had approached from upwind. My gelding eyed me as though trying to plan the right time to bolt.

We lashed the horses to a tree deeper in the wood and then returned to the beech tree. The satyrs were creeping between the trunks now, heads darting nervously back and forth in search of us. I had my bow in hand, and Mag had her spear and shield. We waited in total silence, listening as the creatures came closer.

Mag nudged me with her spear, and we sprang.

I fired two arrows in quick succession. One satyr went down with a shaft in its leg, another with fletching sticking out of its arm. Mag swung her spear in an arc, slamming the flat side of the spearhead into the temple of a third. It fell with a pathetic bleat. The other creatures screamed in fear, but they did not flee. They leaped towards us, flailing with clubs and short stone axes.

I got off one more shot, and another satyr fell with an arrow in its shoulder. Then they were too close, and I had to draw my sword. But there were only two left, and Mag and I made quick work of them. Mag blocked one blow with her shield before piercing her foe's thigh with her spear. I backed up step by step, warding off my foe's club with wide sweeps of my sword, until Mag came around behind her and slammed her shield into the back of the creature's head. It fell to the ground, senseless.

Looking up, I saw the other satyrs fleeing for their lives. The ones with leg wounds limped away, while the ones with maimed arms fled in great, bounding leaps. The first satyr Mag had downed had regained its senses, and it stumbled out of the woods, swaying as if drunk. That left only the creature on the ground before us now.

"Rope," said Mag. I nodded and went to my gelding, fetching a coil from one of the saddlebags.

SEVENTEEN

LONG BEFORE THE SATYR AWOKE, WE HAD HER BOUND TO A TREE A FEW paces from the river. We had set up a campsite for the night. When the sun fell, we started a small fire. I knew its light might be visible through the trees, but that worried me little. The satyrs were few in this part of the mountains, and they seemed to be even fewer since the Shades had passed through.

After a while our captive stirred, her head lolling back and forth before snapping up. One of her horns had a large chip near the top of its curve. She bleated angrily at us, but she winced with pain even as she did it.

"Hello," I said. "We have some questions."

"Die, human," hissed the satyr.

"No, I am afraid that is not the answer we are looking for," I said. "A weremage passed through these mountains, leading the humans who fled west from Northwood. What do you know of her?"

The satyr looked away. "I know nothing of what you speak."

"Come now," I said. "You speak the human tongue well. That tells me you are wise. Surely you have heard which way she and her friends went."

"I know better than to speak to you." The satyr tried to spit at me, but the gobbet fell short, landing on the ground by my feet.

"Let us start with something simpler," I said. "What is your name?"

She glared at me and said nothing.

"I shall tell you ours, if you wish," I said. "This is Mag. And I am Albern, of the family Telfer."

She only scowled harder. "I know your name, human. You tricked Tiglak. You made him betray us."

"I did no such thing," I replied. "I spared Tiglak's life in exchange for safe passage."

"He had no right," said the satyr. "The elders punished him for his cowardice."

That made me angry. I had known Tiglak for a long time. I am afraid I cannot say we were friends, but I respected him, and I like to think he respected me.

"He was both brave and honorable," I said. "Yet he knew I could kill him if I wished, and he hoped his elders might be more merciful. He could have fled into the mountains in shame, but he returned, courageously, and faced their judgement. It is not my fault, nor his, that they were cruel in that judgement. I ask again: what is your name?"

She tossed her head, but some of the fury in her eyes had died. I guessed that she, too, thought better of Tiglak than she was trying to lead us to believe. "Greto," she said at last.

"Greto," I said. "Do you see? That was not so hard."

"Now, Greto," said Mag. "As we have said, we require more answers. What can you tell us about the weremage?"

Greto's eyes burned with fury. "Your ugly human words are meaningless."

"Ah, I forgot," I said. "A weremage is a shape-changer. A human wizard who can take other forms."

"Pah," said Greto. "Your wizards are nothing to us. I know nothing of any skin-shifter."

"What of the Shades?" said Mag. "Which way did they go?"

Greto's dumbfounded look was too perfect to be false. "The what?"

"The humans who wear blue and grey," I said. "They are called Shades, and they passed through the mountains. Where did they go?"

A hunted look came over Greto's face, and she dropped her gaze to the ground. "I do not know."

"You are an awful liar," observed Mag. She lifted her spear and placed the tip gently on Greto's shoulder. "I thought we were past the point where you would try to deceive us."

Another snarl broke out on Greto's face, but she relented. "They went north through the mountains. We did not follow them past the next bend in the valley floor. But a small party of them left the others."

"And went where?" I said.

"West, towards our home," said Greto.

Mag and I tensed in the same instant. "Are they still there?" said Mag. "Are they there *now?*"

"I have been away for several days," said Greto, sounding like nothing so much as a plaintive child. "I do not know."

"Was there a woman with them?" said Mag. "Skin the color of a satyr horn, and black braided hair?"

Greto sneered. "All humans look like humans to—"

Faster than blinking, Mag turned the spear so that the edge of it was pressed to Greto's throat.

"Yes!" cried Greto. "Yes, the woman went west, into our lands!"

"Why would she go there?" I asked. "I know from experience that you are not kind to trespassers."

"Sometimes they—the Shades—they visit our elders. They speak with them, delivering messages and directions from the Lord."

"Is that where the weremage is going?"

"I do not know." Greto's eyes widened as Mag pushed the spearpoint forwards, just a hair. "I do not know! I swear it! She may be!" she bleated.

Mag dropped the spearpoint to the ground. Greto relaxed for a moment.

"My apologies," said Mag.

Greto looked confused until Mag brought the butt of the spear spinning around and slammed it into the satyr's face. Her head crashed back against the tree with a *thud* and then lolled forwards.

"West," I said.

"Yes," said Mag.

"The western mountains are deep in satyr territory—in the very heart of their home."

Mag shrugged. "We have already said we will march into the middle of the Shades' forces if need be. The satyrs cannot be worse."

"They are not more fearsome," I said with a sigh. "But neither do they bear as much blame as the Shades for what has befallen us. I hope you will bear that in mind."

Her expression softened. "Of course I will. And I do not think they bear any great love for our enemies. If we remove the Shades from their homeland, they may even be grateful."

I gave a short, barking laugh. "You have much to learn about satyrs. If the weremage aims to speak with them, she will seek out their elders. Humans are forbidden from even seeing elders, on pain of death."

"Yet it seems the Shades visit them on occasion."

"Traditions may change," I said with a shrug. "Yet I doubt we will be afforded the same courtesy. We should be ready for a fight."

She grinned. "Have you ever known me to be otherwise? We should rest now and set off early tomorrow. I will take the first watch."

She went to the edge of the camp and sat on a low, moss-covered rock there. I went to unfurl my bedroll, trepidation in my heart. Mag was a peerless warrior, but we meant to march straight into the homes of creatures who had little love for us. I feared that if things went horribly wrong, even Mag's considerable skills might not be enough to keep her alive. And if the Uncut Lady could not escape her doom, what hope did I have to save her?

EIGHTEEN

The next day, Kaita rode west out of the Greatrocks with her party of six Shades. In the mountains' western foothills, she stopped her horse and turned to the soldiers accompanying her.

"And now we part," she said. "Once you have finished with the satyrs, return to the Watcher. You should find Tagata there, for Rogan will be in Dorsea by now."

"Very well," said Ertu, his beard twitching as he frowned. "And can you make the journey to Lan Shui unaided?"

"You need not worry for me," said Kaita.

"Yet I may if I wish," said Ertu. "That demon woman from Northwood is chasing you, not us."

"I can look after myself," said Kaita.

"I hope that is true," said Ertu. He extended a hand. Kaita grasped his wrist firmly, and they shook. "Fare well, until we meet again. Until life ends."

"Until life ends."

He turned and rode away, and the rest of the Shades accompanied him. Kaita did not ride on, but sat watching them for a moment. She had joined the Shades many years ago. She loved Rogan, as he loved her. But Rogan's affection extended to all who wore the deathly livery, and in that he was different from Kaita. The Shadeborn, like Tagata—and Trisken, death keep him—were one thing. But Kaita could never muster any great love for the rank and file soldiers like the ones riding away now, half of whom served for love of coin and not from belief.

Yet Ertu believed. Yet Kaita disdained him, and she did not know why.

She sighed as the last blue cloak vanished around a fold in the land. Turning her horse, she struck out for Lan Shui. She had to reach it before nightfall, or she would lose her horse.

Lan Shui is no great burg. A mere pinpoint on a map compared to Bertram farther west, and not even so big as Northwood used to be. It sits near the place where the Blackwind River comes tumbling out of the Greatrocks. There are many beautiful falls in that area, and it gives Lan Shui a chilled and often-misted air—which is excellent for tales and for atmosphere, but horrible for wooden buildings, which often warp and rot. "Rich as a carpenter in Lan Shui" was once a saying in those parts, and it might still be.

Despite its proximity to Bertram, which is the second-largest city in Dorsea and was once that kingdom's capital, Lan Shui is a quiet, uneventful place, for it is bordered on the west by a sharp and insurmountable spur in the land, as though the Greatrocks were kicking up one last time before letting the earth lie flat. That spur cannot be traveled across, but must be ridden around, and that adds half a week to any journey between Lan Shui and the King's road.

In other words, it is the perfect sort of town for one to go to when they wish to avoid being found.

Kaita approached in the afternoon, careful to wait out of sight in a small wood just visible from the town. Soon a young man, hardly more than a boy, came to her amid the trees. He had a sallow face and bulging eyes.

"You are she?"

"If by 'she' you mean a servant of our father, then yes," said Kaita. "Are you not supposed to ask me for a password?"

He avoided her gaze. "I . . . forgot it."

"Fool," spat Kaita. "What if I were one of our enemies? You still do not know that I am not. We do not play at some child's game."

"Of course," mumbled the boy. "I am sorry."

Her nostrils flared. "Sorry" would not save them from the King's law if it sniffed them out in this town. "I care little for your apologies. Can you get me within the walls?"

The boy ducked his head. "I can. No one will see you. My name is Pantu, by the way."

"I do not remember asking for your name. Get moving."

He took the reins of her horse and set off, and Kaita followed. First he took her to a part of the eastern wall that was out of sight of any gate, and then he led her along it until they reached the south entrance. No guards stood there to watch them enter.

"That was simple," said Kaita. "I could have done it myself."

"The constables and guards are much preoccupied during the day," said Pantu. His voice grew hushed as he continued. "And besides, only the night is dangerous now."

Kaita gave a grim smile.

They moved wordlessly after that, passing through the streets until they reached an old, abandoned-looking building near the center of the town. A woman came to take their horses without having to be called. After they made sure no one was nearby to see, Kaita followed Pantu into the home, where they both threw back their hoods.

The front room was wide and low. In the back wall was set a stone hearth with no fire, and around it sat three people in thick wooden chairs. They turned as one to see Kaita and her companion standing in the doorway, and all three of them shot to their feet at once. One of them, a brawny woman with her grey hair in a braid, took a step forwards and looked at Kaita with joy.

"Kaita," she said. "At last."

"Happy to see me, Dellek?" said Kaita, giving her a wry smile.

"Always." Dellek came and embraced her. "Ever since we received word you were coming, I have eagerly awaited your arrival. Some of us—including myself—wanted very much to join the rest of you in Northwood."

"There were more than enough of us to do what needed to be done," said Kaita. "Now, let me see how you have progressed in your work for our father."

Dellek nodded and led her deeper into the house. In the back room, she opened the secret door, revealing a dank stone staircase leading into the earth. After Dellek lit a torch, Kaita followed her down the steps. Dellek held the torch high as they descended, and Kaita kept a hand on the wall to steady herself. The stone beneath her feet was slippery.

A wide chamber opened up before them. The walls had been formed by alchemists, and were lined with smooth ridges. High above, the wooden ceiling looked incredibly fragile compared to the thick rock walls, and between the boards, minute shafts of sunlight pierced the shadows, occasionally blocked as someone above walked across them.

But Kaita's gaze was drawn immediately to the massive cauldron in the center of the room. It was more than two paces across, and shallow, and a black liquid bubbled within it, hardly illuminated by the many torches on the walls. Three Shades stood in the room, tending the cauldron nervously, careful not to touch it. They looked briefly up at the newcomers, but when Dellek gave them a nod, they returned to their tasks.

Kaita could feel the power emanating from the room. The smell was heady, powerful, intoxicating—even a bit overwhelming. For an instant, she had the mad desire to cup her hands and drink of the liquid. The magic within her bristled, sensing the energy that saturated the air. It filled her with exhilaration, anxiety, and anger in equal measure.

She knelt to look beneath the cauldron. The flames were well tended and did not quite reach the iron bottom of the cauldron. She could feel the vicious heat of them, though they were small and she was well over a pace away. Standing, she turned to Dellek.

"You are being wary not to stoke the flames too high?"

"Of course," said Dellek.

"And it is having the desired effect?"

Dellek gave a grim smile and tossed her grey braid back over her shoulder. "Indeed, it is far more effective than we had dreamed it would be."

"Very well," said Kaita. "Let us return upstairs. I must speak with you privately."

Dellek took her back up into the house, and then she climbed another staircase to take her to the second floor. The largest bedroom had a small antechamber, and within it were two chairs and a small table with some wine. Dellek poured them both a cup and gestured for Kaita to sit.

"Well?" she said. "Ever since I knew you were coming, I have wondered what this was all about."

"I am being pursued," said Kaita. "By a woman from Northwood named Mag and her companion, whose name is Albern."

"Pursued?" said Dellek, arching an eyebrow. "I imagine you must not want them dead, then, or you would have used your magic."

I want them dead more than you can believe, thought Kaita. But she nodded, as though Dellek had the right of it. "I am leading them home."

Dellek went very still, and her eyes widened. "Really?"

"Yes," said Kaita. "And I need them to know that that is where I am running to. But Dellek—they must *not* learn about anything else the Shades are doing here. Albern is a master tracker, and I came through the mountains with a party of six horse. He will have a trail leading him to Lan Shui. But I need one of your people to give them the next part of the trail."

Dellek pursed her lips, running a finger along the edge of her wine cup. "Interesting. There are a few here who I can trust to—"

Kaita stopped her by putting a hand on her arm. "That might not be wise. This woman . . . Mag . . ." She almost winced as she remembered the pain of Mag's strikes. "She is a killer. Whoever gives her this information could very well die."

Dellek's mouth twisted. "Say no more, then. I will send that boy Pantu, the one who brought you into the city today. He knows nothing of the underground chamber, and he is little more than a nuisance, anyway. Completely useless."

That drew a small smile from Kaita. This was one reason she and Dellek got along so well. Dellek understood that, whatever Rogan might say, not *everyone* was worthy. Not everyone was useful. Rogan would not approve of such a course of action, but he would never know.

"Excellent," said Kaita. "I will remain here to ensure everything goes well."

Dellek drained the rest of her wine and stood. "It will. And now, let me get you arranged in a chamber. I imagine you could use a long sleep."

As if the words were a spell, exhaustion came crashing down on Kaita. She had been on the road for a week, and had not had a proper rest since the battle of Northwood. “I could,” said Kaita, getting to her feet. “Thank you, Dellek.”

All is well, she thought, as Dellek led her to a small bedchamber and she began to undress herself. *Come to me, my prey. Find me in Lan Shui.*

NINETEEN

After our night's rest, we released Greto. Before we loosened the rope that held her to the tree, I fixed her with a hard look.

"We will release you now," I told her. "You are free to go your own way, as long as you leave us alone. We will not trouble you again, and I hope we can expect the same courtesy."

She merely spat in response. At least she did not seem to be aiming for me, this time.

"I thought you might say something like that," I told her. "But before you decide to run home and tell your clan what transpired here today, I would bid you to remember Tiglak. He, too, thought he could rely on the mercy of your elders."

Her eyes filled with fear at that, and I was satisfied. I untied her, and she bounded away south, in the same direction her fellows had run after our fight the day before.

"Do you really think she will leave us be?" said Mag.

"I know no reason why she should not," I replied. "She may stalk us as she did before, but she will only see us heading west, and she knows we are chasing the weremage. She would never guess that we mean to find the satyr elders and threaten them, because, of course, that is an incredibly idiotic course of action."

Mag gave an easy smile and began to fetch food to break our fast. "Then we will have the element of surprise."

I laughed and helped her prepare the meal. As we ate, I began to form a plan. I had some vague idea of where the satyrs were—many treks through the mountains had brought me to their borders, so I knew the edges of the lands, at least. Most of their homes were in the western end of the mountain range. They had dwellings in the caves there, which they had connected with a series of tunnels so that they could travel through the mountains with relative ease. But satyrs did not naturally dwell within the earth except when they denned to birth and raise their children. More often, they were to be found in the open air, leaping from slope to slope and across all the flatlands along the valley.

Therefore I guided Mag west, across the valley floor and into the mountains on the other side. There were no roads or paths in this part of the mountains, but we did not need them. The trail of the Shades was plain before us. Hundreds of feet had trampled the ground, so that it was churned and muddy, like a farmer's field laid open and ready for fresh planting. Sometimes groups of bootprints would break off from the rest, turning north or south and away from the main march.

And then, on the second day, the army's tracks turned and headed north, deep into the mountains. But the tracks of a smaller party carried on west from the spot. They were few—mayhap a half dozen, no more. We stopped on the spot and ate our midday meal, enjoying the warm sun above, and then pressed on as soon as we had finished.

I continued to lead Mag west, until we came to the end of the valley and the beginning of the mountains again. There we found a wide road leading up into the peaks. It was bordered by perilous drops in places, but wide and firm enough to provide no great danger. I had never traveled this road before, but in past years I had espied it from afar. I guessed that it was no construct of some long-gone king, as the Shade stronghold had been. This track was not paved at all, but had been worn into the ground by many feet—or, more likely, many hooves. It looked like an animal track that had been adopted by the satyrs, who would not have cared how steep it was or how high the drops on the side. It branched often, but I always led Mag on the most well-worn routes. Those, I hoped, would take us to the heart of the satyrs' domain. The side tracks would likely lead to smaller camps and settlements throughout the mountains, or mayhap even into the heart of the cave system the satyrs had built.

The horses did not seem to enjoy the journey much. They had some difficulty on the steeper parts of the road, and on occasion I had to find another way around, a gentler slope that would allow us to circle back to the main path.

I should have been reassured by the absence of any satyrs watching us, but I found myself growing more and more perturbed as we pressed on. We had passed the borders of their lands already. All my experience told me they should have attacked us long ago. But there was no sign of them. I could not fathom it, though I spent much thought on it during the day when we rode and during the night when I stood watch. I could understand if the bulk of them had retreated farther into their caves and mountains when the Shades had passed this way. But their patrols should have increased. Instead they had vanished entirely.

It was the third day after we had left the valley floor that I finally spotted signs of the satyrs again. We came around a bend in the path to find ourselves suddenly standing in plain view of one of their villages. It was little more than a glorified camp, with a few huts built of wood and mud, along with caves in the mountainside where I guessed most of them dwelled. Several campfires could be seen on the ground outside the dwellings, but none of them were lit. The place had been abandoned.

"Where did they go?" said Mag.

"I wish I knew," I said. "Let us hope they are only hiding from the Shades."

We looked through the huts and poked our heads into the caves. The satyrs were not hiding—they had abandoned their homes. All their supplies and tools were gone. Though that seemed an ominous sign, it actually eased my mind somewhat. It meant they had had time to plan their departure, and had not been driven to flee in terror. I had harbored half-formed fears of some great force sweeping through the mountains, driving these creatures before it. But whatever had prompted them to go, they had had some forewarning.

Still, I did not feel comfortable making camp in their village, so we found a flat shelf not much farther along on which to stay the night. I was especially dour as we laid out our bedrolls that evening, and Mag could not help but notice.

"Your frown will freeze on your face soon," she remarked.

"I like the look of things less and less the farther we go," I said.

"Yet our way has been easy so far."

"Easy, yet troubling. Do you not wonder what drove all the satyrs out of this region?"

She shrugged. "You are the guide, not I."

"I *am* the guide," I grumbled, "and a wise woman listens to her guide when he says something is wrong."

Mag chuckled at that. Then she pointed over her head at the horses. "What are you going to name your gelding, by the by? Bad luck cannot be far off if you continue to ride him nameless."

"You think I am not already overwhelmed with bad luck? I am by your side, am I not?"

A rock came flying, striking me right between my legs. I gasped and rolled on my side, clutching myself as I fought a wave of nausea.

"You have not chosen a name, then?" she said innocently. "Come, Albern, you know you tempt fate."

"Dorsean superstition," I wheezed.

"If you have not noticed, we are in Dorsea, or near enough to it," she retorted. "Some guide you are, forgetting which kingdom you are in."

I blinked away the last of my tears. "Very well," I said grumpily. "I shall call him Foolhoof, if it pleases you."

She raised her brows. "I cannot say that it does."

"And your mare? You have not named her, either."

"Oh, but I did," said Mag. "She is called Mist."

I snorted. "Mist. You are like Loren, naming her black horse Midnight. No imagination at all."

"Midnight *is* a foolish name," said Mag, smirking.

"She is a child with dreams of being a legend," I said, waving a hand. "What do you expect? Sky above, she calls herself the Nightblade."

Mag laughed. "Still, you wound me. Mist is a better name by far."

"I think you made it up on the spot," I retorted. "If you named her before this very moment, I will eat my bow."

"You have caught me," said Mag, bowing her head.

"You see? And you had the gall to say I tempted fate. What tragedy will your destiny heap upon you for such a transgression?"

The smile on her face died at once. "I think it has given me quite enough already," she said, in a horribly forced attempt at nonchalance.

I cursed myself for my foolish words. Yes, we had remembered many of our old habits from our mercenary days. But I had forgotten that campfire talk was supposed to steer away from bad fortune, and especially the grief of the near past.

The rest of our conversation that night was stilted and awkward, and I was grateful when I finally rolled myself in blankets to sleep.

Far, far away, in the woods northwest of Lan Shui, a creature stalked through the woods.

Through the trees, it could see the soft glow of firelight shining through the windows of a human home. And even through the walls, it could smell its prey inside. There were several of them—enough to feed on for days.

The creature knew that would not sate its deeper, stronger hunger. But it was enough for now.

It came out of the woods and stalked forwards, approaching the house's front door. Each motion was virtually silent. The smell of the humans in the house was nearly overwhelming. It ran a black tongue along its browning teeth.

Suddenly there came the sound of padded feet inside the house, and a snuffling. Then a low, rumbling growl.

A surge of hate and hunger ripped through the creature. A dog. It had been so focused on its emptiness and the smell of the humans, it had missed the scent of the dog.

Careless.

It tried to step back, away from the house. But its broken claw caught on the ground, and it stumbled.

Inside the house, the dog's growls turned to full-throated barking. Chairs scraped against a wooden floor as the humans stirred.

"Oku?" said one of the prey. "What is it?"

The creature screeched with impatience and lunged, bursting through the front door into the house. Inside, the prey shot to their feet. They had weapons close at hand, and they seized them. Standing before them was the dog: a large wolfhound almost a pace in height, brown with black spots in its fur.

The creature screamed in hatred and hunger.

Snarling furiously, the dog launched itself at the creature. But a wild swipe staved the beast off, and it slunk back, favoring a light gash in its left flank. The prey drew closer to each other and took a step forwards.

"Liu!" cried one of them. "Run into the woods! Take Oku!"

"Mama!"

The creature's eyes shifted. Behind the three larger prey, one of their offspring stood at the back of the room, cowering in terror. Its eyes were wide, and palpable fear radiated from it.

"Go!" cried another of the prey—young, but nowhere near as young as the child. "Oku, tiss!"

The wolfhound bounded towards the child, taking his tunic in its teeth and tugging. Reluctantly, the child rose to its feet and scurried for the house's back door, vanishing into the night. The creature dismissed it at once. It had been a tiny thing, and there were three full-sized prey still in the house—not enough to completely satisfy the hunger, but enough to stave it off for days.

Roaring in fury, it leaped and sank its claws into its first victim.

TWENTY

The day after we camped near the empty satyr town, we reached the crest of the western Greatrocks. Then, for the first time, I took us off the most well-worn path and up one of the side routes that climbed south, riding even higher into the peaks. South, because that was the direction of the heart of satyr territory, at least as far as I was aware. If we meant to find the elders, I was confident we would find them there.

It was not long before we started to come upon more satyr encampments and villages. These were less populated than I had imagined they would be, but they were not entirely abandoned. I spent almost half an hour scouting the first one we came upon. Many satyrs moved from building to building, but from what I could tell, there were no fighters in the village, only children and those caring for them. The warriors were elsewhere. I guessed we would find them with the elders. That was not an entirely comforting prospect.

When I had inspected the village to my satisfaction, I returned to Mag. "We must hide the horses somewhere and leave them," I said. "If we bring them any farther, they will certainly alert the satyrs to our presence."

"There are no woods this high up to hide them from view," said Mag.

"We need a cave," I said. "The satyrs do not dwell in all of them, nor are all of them connected. We should be able to find an empty one without too much trouble."

And that proved to be true; in less than an hour of searching, we found just what we needed. The cave was too shallow for the satyrs to have bothered with, but more than deep enough to conceal our horses. We hobbled them and tethered them to a rock that thrust up out of the ground. Foolhoof tossed his head as I wrapped his reins around the stone, and I gave him a reproachful look.

"Do not even think of chewing your way free," I told him. "I will find you if you do."

"Mist would never think of doing such a thing," said Mag haughtily.

I shook my head and led her from the cave.

Without the horses, it was easy to slip past the first satyr village, and the second. We passed them every few spans now, clusters of crude buildings built onto whatever flat ground was available on those high slopes. Occasionally the villages had a sentry posted nearby, but they were easy to bypass. They appeared to be weaker members of their kind, satyrs with missing or twisted limbs, and they leaned heavily on their weapons.

Always we found our way back to the main path, and now I began to notice markings upon it. They were not the prints of cloven hooves, but of heavy boots. Other humans.

"Look," I told Mag, pointing at the tracks. "It seems we are not too late. We might find our foe at the end of this road."

"I am right more often than you give me credit for," said Mag. "Let us hurry. The weremage could be dead before the day's end."

We were neither of us wont to bloodthirst, but hunting a foe will quicken anyone's pulse. We pressed on faster. Yet despite our speed, it was early evening before we found what we sought. To our right, the sun was setting in a display that was as beautiful as it was fiery. It painted the ground in hues of red and gold, and the scant clouds in the sky blazed like the fires of war. But the light had not yet faded when we came upon a great gathering of satyrs, and I had to be quick to rush

Mag behind cover before we were spotted. Together we crouched behind a boulder shaped like a black, broken tooth.

On what appeared to be the top of the highest mountain for many leagues, a great circular space had been trodden flat by what looked like centuries' worth of satyr hooves. Upon that space were now gathered mayhap two scores of satyr warriors, wearing wooden shields on their arms and hefting axes and clubs. They stood in a half-ring two rows deep, all their attention fixed on the center of the circle. There sat ten carved stone chairs, though only eight of them were occupied. The satyrs upon those chairs were old, wizened, and grey of fur, and I knew we had found the elders of the clan.

But almost immediately, my attention went from the elders to the humans who stood before them. They numbered six, and they wore clothing of blue and grey. The Shades were here, just as Greto had said they would be.

"Can you see the weremage?" whispered Mag.

"I cannot," I said. "Not from here. We must get closer. I want to be certain before we attack."

"Very well." Now that we were here, I found myself quite reluctant to draw any closer to the satyrs. But my desire to find the weremage overpowered my caution, as did my curiosity. I wanted to know what the Shades were saying that put such fear in the faces of the satyr elders.

We left the cover of the rock and crept along a slope that fell away from the platform. We were careful to keep ourselves concealed, but it hardly seemed necessary. No one, neither the Shades nor the satyrs, looked away from what was going on. At last, when we were only a score of paces away, I bade Mag to hide again, for now we could clearly make out the Shades' words. Again we ducked out of sight, each of us poking one eye into view to see what was going on.

"—after you killed the messenger?" one of the Shades—a burly man with a thick, bristling beard—was saying. At first I dismissed him, searching only for the weremage. Then my better sense caught up with me, and I realized the weremage might very well have changed her appearance. Though why would she do so, when she had no idea we were watching her?

The elder in the center of the row shifted in her stone chair and bleated an answer in the satyrs' tongue. I spoke but a little of their language and did not understand her, but there was a clear defensive tone in her voice, like a child who had been caught in wrongdoing and was inventing an outlandish tale to excuse it.

An elder at the end of the row spoke in the common tongue. "Elder Seko says: Tiglak's debt was paid. Then we drove the humans towards you. We have told you this already."

"But what you have *not* told us," growled the Shade, "is why you did not tell us of these interlopers."

More bleating from Seko, and then the translator spoke again. "Elder Seko says: the Lord never said to tell you. He said not to let any humans pass through the valley and live."

The Shade thrust a finger towards the center elder. "Which is exactly what you did!"

The translator quivered at the anger in his voice, but now one of the other elders spoke. He was not quite so hoary as the first, and there was a clear current of anger in his words. The translator looked uncomfortable, but after a sharp reproach from the elder, she spoke. "Elder Hagan says: we allowed nothing," she said, her voice shaking. "We brought them to you. You allowed them to escape, not us."

I looked at Mag behind our rock. "We were right on that count, it seems."

"Never mind that," said Mag. "I cannot see the Shades clearly enough to tell if the weremage is among their number."

"What of the leader?" I said. "Satyrs respect only strength and size. She would have better luck speaking to them as a large warrior than in her natural form. You saw how slight she was."

Mag frowned. "So it could be her, but how can we know?"

Before I could answer, something happened in the circle. The Shades seemed to have had enough of the satyrs' arguments. Their leader raised his hand, palm pointing towards the elders, and the circle fell quiet.

"Enough," said the Shade. "The Lord is tired of your excuses. There will be payment in blood. Two of you may present yourselves, or we can make the choice for you."

My stomach turned. The elders cowered in their seats, and as they did so, I glanced at the two empty stone chairs. Did I see bloodstains on the rock, or was it my imagination? Had this Lord already demanded such a sacrifice once in the past?

Elder Seko looked at the others. They chattered back and forth in their own tongue for a moment, with Seko sounding increasingly desperate. Finally, Elder Hagan shot to standing and barked a series of short, loud words. The rest of them fell silent.

Slowly, Elder Seko stood from her chair. Beside her, another elder, almost as grey and wizened, stood as well. Together the two of them stepped towards the Shades.

"The two oldest," I muttered.

The Shade leader stepped forwards. He held up a hand—and then his eyes began to glow. My heart did a somersault, thinking of the weremage—but then just as quickly, it sank into my stomach. Elder Seko gasped and clutched at her throat. Slowly, a finger's width at a time, she rose into the air.

"You are servants of the Lord," intoned the Shade. "As are we. And he does not brook failure."

"He is a mindmage," I said. "He is not who we seek."

"He will kill them," said Mag. Her voice had taken on the lifeless monotone of her battle-trance.

"I am not certain that it would be wise to—oh, sky save us," I said, for Mag had leaped out over the top of the slope. She sprang forwards, shield raised and spear held high.

Mag was among the Shades before they knew what was happening. From five paces away she threw her spear. It impaled the Shade mindmage through the chest. He froze, staring at her weapon as the glow died in his eyes. His magic fell away, and Elder Seko fell gasping to the ground.

Before the Shade had started to fall, Mag seized her spear and kicked him away, ripping the weapon from his torso. She had killed another of the Shades before the rest could react. I loosed two arrows, each taking a Shade in the head. They fell like puppets with cut strings. Two stood, but not once Mag reached them. One managed to get his sword out—Mag batted it aside with her spearhead before it sliced around in a wide arc and laid his throat open. The other leaped towards Mag with raised blade, but I fired another arrow. It took the Shade in the chest, and she fell to one knee, wheezing. She looked up just in time to take Mag's spear in the neck. Her body fell to the floor, her hands jerking as they tried to reach for her throat. She died before managing it.

It was over almost before the half-ring of satyr warriors realized what was happening. But once they saw the corpses on the floor, they raised their weapons with angry brays, smashing the weapons against their shields in a violent cacophony. Mag fell into a fighting crouch, her shield up and her spear ready to strike. I nocked another arrow, but did not draw.

"Enough!" I cried. "It is over."

Elder Seko had risen by now, helped to her feet by the other satyr who had offered himself in sacrifice. She spoke in anger and fright using the satyrs' language. I frowned at her and then looked over at the translator. The translator shook worse than ever, but she tried to compose herself as she spoke.

"Elder Seko says: it is not over," she whimpered. "Who are you? Why have you done this?"

I arched an eyebrow. "We have saved the lives of two of your elders. You do not sound particularly grateful."

The elders might not have deigned to speak the human tongue, but they seemed to understand it well enough, for the oldest one screamed a reply without waiting for my words to be translated. The translator swallowed hard. "Elder Seko says: you are no servants of the Lord. This was not his will. His retribution will fall upon all of us now, and it will be swift and merciless."

"Then I suggest you stop obeying this Lord, whoever he may be," said Mag. Elder Seko drew up straight and raised a hand. The half-ring of satyrs edged forwards, but Mag stood firm. "I would not do that, if I were you. It will only result in a pile of satyr corpses to go along with these human ones."

I gritted my teeth. Mag did not know the nuances of speaking to these creatures. Threats rarely worked unless one had a satyr utterly at their mercy. The satyrs might have been in such a position, in truth, but they could not know that—they only saw a normal human woman, and would know nothing of Mag's skill.

"We saved your elders," I said loudly, trying to draw attention to myself and away from Mag. "Two of your most venerable and wisest leaders would have died if we had not intervened. That ought to earn us at least a moment's clemency."

Elder Hagan, who had interjected before, brayed a response. The translator spoke quickly. "Yet now all our lives are in danger. What are two lives compared to the whole clan?"

"Do you think the Lord would have stopped there?" I pointed to the elders' stone chairs. "Two of your seats are already empty. What would have stopped the Lord from killing the rest of you, if it pleased him?"

There was a long moment of dead silence. The satyr warriors were looking between each other and the elders now. Hagan looked furious, but Seko studied us, frowning but not quite hostile. At last she spoke in a slow voice, and the translator hastened to relay her words.

"Elder Seko says: who are you?"

"I am Albern of the family Telfer," I said. "This is Mag, the Uncut Lady, the greatest warrior in the nine kingdoms."

Mag gave me a wry look. But as the translator spoke my words in the satyr tongue, a low, angry rumble ripped through the satyr warriors. Quickly I realized my mistake.

"The greatest *human* warrior," I corrected. "We would never presume to question the might of your own brave fighters."

"Elder Seko says: your name is known to us, Albern," said the translator. "You turned the mind of Tiglak, our warrior. We punished him for his leniency towards you."

Anger blossomed in my heart at those words. I had met Tiglak more than once in my travels through the mountains, and more than once he had taken up arms against me. But he had not been bloodthirsty, and he had been an honorable warrior, in his way.

"I knew Tiglak," I said. "And I never tried to turn him, nor would he have let me. He was a faithful servant of Skal, the holy mother between the moons, and I know she honors him in the sky."

Elder Hagan erupted in a series of furious screams, but Seko silenced him with a raised and gnarled hand. She looked at me with an expression I could not read. Understanding? Curiosity? From what I knew of the satyrs, I was certain she had never been in the presence of a human who spoke of Skal with true knowledge. That is a deep secret of the satyrs, and one no outsider could learn of easily.

After a moment's pause, she spoke again. "Elder Seko says: I am Elder Seko," said the translator. "What do you seek here, Albern?"

"We are looking for a wizard," said Mag. "A skin-shifter. In her human form, she is short and slim, with horn-colored skin and black, braided hair. Have you seen her here?"

Seko looked displeased as she shifted her focus to Mag. "Elder Seko says: we have seen many humans who serve the Lord," said the translator.

Before Mag could answer, I stepped in. She would care little for the Lord, but his agents had already tried to kill me, and I had had questions ever since. Besides, I thought, I still might find Loren one day, and she would want to know. "Who is this Lord? What is he? Some have said he is not human, and I believe it, for I know the wise elders would never serve a human."

The elders raised their chins with pride at that, and one or two of them bleated quietly. Seko spoke through the translator. "Elder Seko says: he has appeared only to us who sit in the stone seats. His form is unknown."

"But when he appeared, how did he look?" I pressed.

"Elder Seko says: he was a form all in white, cloaked in mist and light—as terrible as an Elf, but speaking words we could hear."

I shuddered at that. Even a fleeting thought that the Lord might be an Elf was enough to make me want to run and hide in the deepest hole I could find, never to emerge.

"Enough of the Lord," said Mag. "The weremage. Have you seen her?"

Seko stamped a hoof and bleated. Soon the translator said, "Elder Seko says: how are we to know? You are humans. Humans look like humans."

Mag had enough sense not to point her spear at Seko, but it seemed a near thing. She slammed the butt of it on the rocky ground, and the satyr warriors shifted uneasily around us. "I have told you what she looks like. Surely some of you have seen her."

The elders seemed displeased. Mag's insistence was not far away from calling them liars. I stepped close to her and spoke in a voice I hoped was too low to be overheard.

"If she never performed magic in front of them, they may not know who she is."

Mag gave a frustrated growl. "I had not thought of that. Then what should we do?"

Before I could answer, Seko suddenly spoke more loudly and rapidly than before. My pulse skipped, and I looked to the translator. But she said nothing. Then, behind us, the warriors began muttering to each other. It took me a moment to realize the truth: Seko had not been speaking to us at all, but had been addressing her clan directly.

After some hurried conversation, one of the satyr warriors stepped forwards. He was large for a satyr, almost as big as Tiglak had been, and he rolled his shoulders as he answered whatever question Seko had put to him. Now Seko turned to the translator and spoke. The translator nodded and relayed the words.

"Our scouts have seen the woman you seek," she said. "She left the mountains heading west, and went to a village there. It stands near the place where the southern river of the Great Spearhead leaves the mountains."

"Thank you," said Mag, nodding to Seko. The elder inclined her head.

"Elder Seko," I said. "I have only one more question. How did the Lord first come to you? How long ago was it?"

Seko snorted, her nostrils flaring. "Elder Seko says: we have no more answers for you."

My breath had grown quick, and I tried to calm myself. "The Lord has caused great suffering in the human kingdoms," I pressed. "In this, we share your—"

Seko cut me off without waiting for the translator, and the translator relayed her words as soon as they were spoken. "Human worries are nothing to us. You have saved two lives, and we have answered more than two questions already. Leave now, and remember our generosity and kindness."

Though my nerves felt grated almost to the root, I knew better than to try to press her any further. Instead I took a step back and bowed low.

"Of course," I said. "Thank you, Elder Seko. We will never forget your mercy or your lenience."

Mercifully, Mag managed not to laugh, though she had to cough to hide it. I tossed my head at her, and we walked away from the circle of satyrs. I did not look back until we were well out of sight, though I imagined I could feel the satyrs' eyes boring into my back long afterwards.

TWENTY-ONE

Mag and I came riding down out of the mountains some days later.

Elder Seko had said the weremage went to a village near the southern river of the Great Spearhead. I thought long on those words, and soon I thought I had an answer to them. I remembered Dorsea well enough, for I had often campaigned there, and I remembered how the Blackwind River came down out of the Greatrocks to join the Bluewater, forming a sort of spearhead in the land. I knew there was a town there, though I did not recall the name of it. And so it was in that direction that I guided Mag, and soon brought her to the outskirts of Lan Shui.

It looked a sizable town to us. Not a large city, certainly, but big enough to lose people in. It was built around the river, and I guessed that they used it for trade and for travel. Farmlands were laid out beyond the town proper for leagues in every direction. But as we drew closer, I began to notice that some farms seemed abandoned. About half the fields had no one working in them, and the crops, though mature, were untended.

But I did not remark upon it at first, for Mag seemed to be in a poor mood. As we drew closer to the town, I thought I understood why. Though the homes were clearly of Dorsean make, and the people here wore Dorsean clothing, it was impossible not to see the similarities between this town and Northwood. And when thinking of Northwood, it was impossible not to think of Sten.

"Do you know why the river is called the Blackwind?" I asked her, trying to pull her from such thoughts.

Her head jerked around, as if she had forgotten I was there and was surprised to hear me speak. "What? No."

"It is the twin river of the Bluewater farther north, and they join at the city of Bertram to form the Fanrong," I said. "In the days of the Sunmane, one of her generals—a man named Torben—came through what would be called the Moonslight Pass into Dorsea's western reaches. His army was low on rations and water after the pass, where they had been attacked many times by satyrs, who were in those days more plentiful. They followed the Greatrocks south until they reached the river and the fertile lands that surrounded it. Torben named the river then, for as he said: 'It shone in midday's light like the purest sapphire, though I valued it more highly than gemstones, for instead of wealth, it brought my soldiers life.'

"His army camped around the river for one week, resting. At last they continued their journey south, seeking for the end of the Greatrocks and what might lay beyond them. Soon they arrived here and found this second river, and Torben called it the Blackwind."

My words cut off suddenly, more suddenly than I had intended, for in the middle of the tale, I had remembered its ending. Torben had called it the Blackwind because when his army came to it, they were attacked by a greater host of satyrs than they had yet faced, and there was a great swarm of imps as well. In the fighting, Torben's son had been killed, and so he had named the river as a curse. That was not the sort of story I thought it would be best for Mag to hear just then.

She did not seem to notice the strange way I had cut the tale short, for her eyes were on the town's gates ahead. I followed her gaze and saw why. The gates were almost fully closed, and in front of them stood three constables with less than friendly expressions.

"Trouble, do you think?" said Mag.

"I doubt it. It is not unusual for a town to be wary of strangers, especially this close to the mountains, where there are many perils." But we both knew that was not entirely true. There was no war near here, and so there was no reason for this town to be wary of anything except satyrs and harpies, neither of which would be hampered a whit by a closed gate.

We spoke no further word as we approached the constables, and for their part, they made no move and said nothing as we pulled to a stop before them.

"Hail, friends," I said in a cheery voice. "We beg your leave to enter this town—and, too, we ask its name, for we have never been here before."

One of the constables stood a pace ahead of the others, and the white stripe on her red leather armor marked her as a sergeant. Beneath her red helmet was a shock of bristling yellow hair. I guessed she stood a head taller than me, and half a head over Mag, and she had muscled limbs as impressive as her height. Now she stepped forwards, crossing her arms, and spoke.

"You stand at the gate of Lan Shui. Who are you, and where did you come from?"

"I am Mag, and my friend is Albern of the family Telfer," said Mag. "And we have little business here. We need a place to rest and refresh ourselves before making our way to the road that will take us to the Western Sea."

"Then why are you not on the King's road?" said the constable.

Her words made me frown. It was a reasonable enough question, but the tone behind it was strange—almost desperate. Something was wrong here. I thought again of the untended farms we had just passed.

"There is no great urgency to our journey," I put in. "The King's road would have taken us to Bertram more quickly, it is true, but that would have put many more days between us and a bed to sleep in. You have nothing to fear from us. We are merely weary travelers who have just passed west through the Greatrocks."

That did not have quite the desired effect. The constable sagged, passing a hand over her eyes. "You are from Selvan."

I glanced at Mag, confused. Dorsea and Selvan were fighting in Wellmont, but we were so far north that it should not have mattered.

"Yet we are all citizens of Underrealm. I am a man of Calentin, and Mag here is Dorsean."

I pointed at Mag, who tensed. It was true that she had come from Dorsea before I met her, but at the same time, I was not telling the whole truth. Despite her sudden despondency, the constable seemed to notice Mag's reaction, and her frown deepened.

Before she could ask another probing question, I spoke again. "My apologies, but this conversation is rather hard to keep up when you have not told us who you are. We gave you our own names freely enough—may we know yours, as a matter of courtesy?"

The constable's mouth twisted. "I am Constable Yue of the family Baolan," she said at last. "You have told me your destination, but not your business. Why are you traveling west?"

"Why, to visit Mag's family," I said. "And I thank you for your courtesy, Constable Baolan."

"Family, is it?" said Yue, who seemed to have ignored my second statement. "The two of you are wed, then?"

"Not at all," I said. "We are merely friends traveling together."

"Well-armed travelers," Yue pointed out.

"And would you go riding through the Greatrocks without a weapon?" said Mag. It was not exactly what you would call a polite question, but I was relieved that she did not let any anger show in her voice. And to my delight, Yue smiled at the question, though she quickly hid it.

"I suppose I would not," said Yue. She pulled off her helmet and swiped a hand through her bristling yellow hair. "Enter, then, travelers. Keep to yourselves while you are here, and stay indoors after nightfall. And before you leave Lan Shui, come and speak with me."

"Are we not free to—" I began.

"You are free to do whatever you wish," said Yue, scowling at me. "But if you have a lick of sense, you will come and speak with me before you leave my town. Is that understood?"

"Of course," I said quickly, raising a hand to pacify her.

"One question before we go," said Mag. "A traveler may have arrived here ahead of us—a woman with nut-brown skin and—"

"No travelers have arrived here," said Yue. "Not for many days."

"Constable, if I may," I said. "It sounds as though there is some trouble here. Is it anything we can help with?"

Yue's scowl deepened. "That is my business. Keep to your own. And heed my words."

"Of course," I said at once, nodding. "Can you recommend an inn for us?"

"If you have coin to spend, find the Sunspear," said Yue. "If you do not, the Stag's Sty will be easier on your purse, and they do not have too many fleas."

"A stellar recommendation," I said. "Fare well, constable."

She turned and nodded to the others, who heaved the gate open for us to ride through.

TWENTY-TWO

I WAS MORE ALERT NOW THAN EVER, AND AS I RODE THROUGH LAN Shui, I tried to take stock of the town. Though the wall was poorly kept up, it was manned, with several archers pacing its length. But though the guards looked alert and wary, they were few. It would have been easy to slip past them unnoticed, if that was the aim. It gave the air that this town was wary and watchful, but was unused to being either.

Armored soldiers walked the town's streets as well, but they wore neither the king's livery nor the red armor of constables. I guessed they were locals, pressed into service to guard the town. But against what? Had the Shades passed this way? Or had some rumor of their coming reached these people? I could think of no other threat that would have put them so on edge. But I saw some people weeping in doorways and in alleys, clearly in mourning.

"What has happened here?" I said, hardly meaning to speak the words aloud.

"In many places across Dorsea may be found the consequences of war," said Mag.

"Yet Dorsea makes war on no one but Selvan these days," I said. "And this town is far from those battles."

"It must have something to do with the Shades, then."

I shook my head. "If that were the case, and the town had been attacked, Yue would never have let us in."

"Then guess at the answer yourself, if you are so wise," grumbled Mag. "One thing we told Yue was the truth: I want a bed to sleep in, and quickly."

We had a fair bit of coin on us—with the excellence of Mag's ale, she had never wanted for money—and so we asked after the Sunspear and found it before long. Its sign hung over the door, a spear thrusting up with a red-rayed sun in the background. I glanced at the spear on Mag's saddle and bit my tongue. A girl at the stables took our horses, and we purchased dinner in the common room for a handful of pennies. The food and ale were fine enough, but I found myself longing for Sten's cooking and Mag's brew.

Before we had finished eating, an old man walked into the common room. There were only a handful of people there aside from the two of us, but they all looked up eagerly. The man's eyes were grey and blind with age, and he picked his way through the room with a walking stick. One patron quickly moved a chair from his path to ensure he would not strike it as he walked. Though the top of his head was entirely bald, he had thick, bushy grey brows and a long grey beard down to his waist. He wore deep blue clothes in a common Dorsean style, with a shirt that tied at the side and loose trousers collected at the ankle. Despite his stooped figure and slow walk, his lips curved in a smile that seemed nearly permanent.

The old man sat on a small platform near the unlit hearth, sitting with his legs folded and his walking stick across his knees. A barman appeared beside him with a bowl of broth and a cup that looked to be filled with wine. The old man took a few sips of the broth and a deep swig of the wine, and then settled himself on the platform. I noticed that he had not paid for the meal.

And then he leaned back, lifted his head, and began to sing.

From the very first notes, I knew I was in the presence of a master. Here was a man who had been singing—and, unless I missed my guess, telling tales—for decades before I was even born. Though his frame was diminutive, his voice was thick and powerful, and I could feel it thrumming in the wooden chair upon which I sat.

He sang some songs I knew by heart, and others I had never heard before. He sang some songs I knew, but to strange tunes, and some songs with new words, but set to tunes that were as old as the hills. I had to keep reminding myself to eat, for I kept staring at him, spellbound by the sound of his voice and his effortless command of melody. I was not the only one. All conversation in the common room ceased as everyone listened to the old man. Mag, who had far less appreciation for song and story than I, was yet as entranced as I was. Though the man sang alone and without any instrument, it seemed to me that I could almost hear a troupe behind him: a pipe and a lute and one steady, thudding bodhran.

After mayhap a quarter hour, the man subsided into silence and reached again for his broth and wine. I shook myself as if waking from a dream and turned back to my stew. It had very nearly gone cold.

"That was astounding," I said, surprised at the reverence in my own voice.

Mag smiled at me. "Sky above, you look jealous. I always said you would have made a better bard than a mercenary."

I pointed my spoon at her. "That was not a compliment when you first said it, and it is not a compliment now. Where would you be if I *had* pursued a life in a king's court, and had not been there to look after you?"

Her eyebrows shot for the ceiling. "Oh, I would surely have perished long ago," she said, straining mightily to hide the joke in her voice.

"And do not forget it." I glanced over my shoulder at the old man, who was still resting before he resumed singing. "Besides, it is hard to say that I should have been a great and renowned bard when in the presence of one who deserves the honor so much more."

"If you are so enchanted with the man, go and speak to him," said Mag, chuckling.

"In fact, I think I shall," I told her. "And not just for my own entertainment. We want information, and who better to give it to us than a man who tells tales for his supper?"

So saying, I stood and went across the room to sit beside the old man. He heard me coming, and his head tilted up as he listened to my footsteps approach. His milky eyes looked just over my left shoulder, and I smiled, entirely forgetting he could not see the expression.

"Greetings, friend," I said. "I wished to give you my praise for your songs, and your voice. I have rarely heard a singer so fine."

"Rarely?" said the old man. His grin revealed a few missing teeth in the back. "I am losing my touch, then. I must work harder until it becomes 'never.' But I thank you for your kind words."

I chuckled and pulled up a chair to sit beside him. "That would be a tall order. I have traveled to many lands and been in many fine courts of nobility."

The old man's bushy brows rose. "Courtly bards," he scoffed. "If you ask me, they are limited in skill to the moment when some foolish noble hires them. They think they were hired for the songs and stories they already know, and so they never bother to learn any more."

"That is an interesting thought, and I am somewhat glad to hear it," I said, smiling still wider. "I sometimes think I should have become a bard, but if it would have stunted my skill, I am glad I never did."

He laughed at that, and then he held out his hand. I grasped his wrist and shook firmly.

"They call me Dryleaf here in this town," he said.

"And what do they call you elsewhere?" He smiled and did not answer. "I am Albern of the family Telfer."

"Telfer?" he said, cocking his head. "From Calentin then, are you?"

That made my heart skip a beat. Of the many people I had met across the nine kingdoms, only a handful had ever recognized the name Telfer. Even when they did, it was rare they could place the kingdom it came from.

I tried to speak easily, passing off the moment of hesitation. "I am indeed," I told him. "But you do not look like a man from my homeland."

"Nor am I," he said. "I am from everywhere, as they say. In my day I was a wandering peddler who roamed all over the nine kingdoms. But one day my eyes went"—he pointed to the milky white orbs—"and once they started going bad, it happened fast. I was on my way north, but I was injured crossing the Blackwind just outside this town—I had an uppity horse, and it threw me, and my leg broke. It was not such a bad injury, but old bones are slower to heal. By the time I was ready to ride again, my traveling days were over. Since then, I have waited for anyone traveling to Selvan, hoping I could beg to come along, but the opportunity has never presented itself. It must be . . . three years now? Lan Shui does not lie on any of the great roads that cross Underrealm. We rarely see travelers at all—and even more rarely, lately."

His mention of Selvan dampened my mood. Even now, the Shades would be pursuing Loren through the Birchwood, and I doubted anyone who lived there was safe. I thought to myself that it was a good thing Dryleaf had never reached his destination. Sometimes fate is kind in cruel ways.

But the last thing he had said caught my attention. "I thought something seemed amiss when I came here. Why is everyone so afraid? We were questioned quite closely by the constable when we arrived."

"Yue, you mean?" said Dryleaf. "She is a good sort, if a bit stern. But if she let you in, you will have seen that for yourself."

I noticed that he had deftly avoided answering my question. "A good sort indeed. But why did she suspect us so?"

Dryleaf pursed his lips and nodded a few times, as though bobbing his head in time to some beat I could not hear. His bushy brows had drawn close together. "I am not so sure I should speak of it," he said. "After all, you are a stranger, if an exceedingly polite one. Some strangers are folk of pure intent, but others are less so."

"And have you met any of the latter sort?" I asked. "Anyone in the town who seems not to have the best interest of the people at heart?"

He shook his head, but he did it with a little smile. "I am sorry, but I will not say more. Not yet. If you remain here for a while, we might discuss matters in more detail. But for now I think it is best if you look to yourself, and I do the same." He shifted where he sat and reached for his meal. "And now, if you will forgive me, I must have a few bites before I get back to what earns my meal. I wish you well, and I hope we speak again."

Despite his courtesy, the end of the conversation came so abruptly that I felt myself at a loss for a moment. Yet it seemed clear that I would glean nothing more from him just now, so I politely excused myself and returned to Mag.

TWENTY-THREE

"What a strange old man," said Sun.

Albern laughed. "He was."

"He has died, then?"

"Oh yes," Albern said quietly. "He was old even then, and as I said, this was decades ago."

Sun frowned. "I do not understand. Why was he so polite, and yet unwilling to help? He said strangers could not always be trusted, but if that was the case, why would he speak with you at all?"

Albern's somber mood vanished. "You must learn to allow the elderly our peculiarities," he said. "Oftentimes we do things only to make your life difficult, as revenge for the toll time has wreaked upon us."

"But the town was in danger!"

"And how did he know it was not in danger from me?" said Albern. "That is pulling a little ahead of the story. But you should remember not to be too trusting of strangers, even if you still manage to be courteous to them."

"I should not have trusted you, if I took that advice," muttered Sun.

"True enough," said Albern. "But as Dryleaf himself would discover, I am no one of ill intent."

He remained silent for a good long while, staring down at the reins he held in his hand. He did not look as mournful as when he had recounted Sten's death, but Sun thought she could still sense a deep sadness in him.

"What is wrong?" she asked.

"Nothing exactly," he said. "It is only that I have not recalled Dryleaf in a very long time. The old man and I rode many long miles together. When you get older, you will find that all your stories are laced with grief, for they always concern at least one person who is no longer with you. It is a curse that grows worse the older you get—that fewer and fewer people are left who attended the most important parts of your life. But enough somber talk. In truth, I was only thinking that our expedition tonight is rather like those adventures then, though of course I am much younger now than Dryleaf was, and you are much younger than I was."

Sun blinked. "You mean that Dryleaf is a part of the story?" she said.

Albern smiled. "Oh yes, very much a part of it," he said.

"He did not seem very important when you met him," said Sun. "I thought he would be just another name in a tavern, heard briefly and then never seen again. Like Elsie, who you left in Northwood. I have never heard of him in any other tale of you and the Wanderer."

"But you had never heard of Sten either, and yet you can see how important he was," said Albern. "None of this would have happened without Sten. Indeed, I was just some man in a tavern when first you laid eyes upon me. Yet now here we are, riding off together."

Sun raised her eyebrows. "We are not riding anywhere together. You are riding, and I am walking."

That made Albern laugh aloud, his voice ringing through the night to be swallowed by the trees on either side of the road. "A privilege of age. And you will not have to walk for much longer."

"I am pleased to hear it."

Albern smiled and shook his head. "In any case, you should never discount strangers met by chance—if, indeed, you believe in chance at all. My own thoughts on that matter are far from settled, and my opinions have changed much over the years. But the more I see in my life, the more I begin to believe that there is indeed some great pattern that binds everything together, drawing certain people closer to each other before pulling them away.

"I do not think it was chance, for instance, that brought Mag and Sten together. The moment those two met, it was as though they had been together all their lives. Sten was a simple farmer in northeastern Selvan, and Mag and I were passing through in one of those years when we served no mercenary company in particular. We only intended to stay in the town for a day or two, but then, there was Sten. We had been there almost a week before I even realized we had remained longer than we planned. And that was strange, for I had spent most of those days alone, while Mag and Sten had gone walking together. I usually only shared their company in the evenings, when we would sit and talk and drink in the way that only young people can drink, with no fear of the pain morning will bring. Yet it all seemed . . . right. Natural. I was traveling with Mag, and Mag belonged in that town, at that time, by Sten's side. And so nothing seemed untoward, as far as I was concerned.

"We left the town after three weeks, and we joined another mercenary company soon afterwards. We campaigned for some months, and then we returned to northeastern Selvan—and we went back to Sten's town while we waited for the company to get hired again. We only stayed a week that time—but the next time we returned, we were there for two. Every time the company came home, Mag and I found ourselves in that town, and Mag found herself by Sten's side.

"Now, as I have told you already, Mag was not the sort to seek out bedfellows. She had had one or two whirlwind romances while I had known her, but they never went past a certain point. But in those early days with Sten, it never even went that far. It was as though she and Sten did not even think of each other as lovers. Rather, Mag seemed to have adopted the attitude that time spent away from Sten was simply foolish. If she had to, for our duty to the company, of course she would part from him. But given the option, she would always be with him, and that was simply the way it went.

"Not long afterwards, the company went out on one of the longest campaigns I have ever seen. Almost a year we were on the road, and Mag's mood grew more and more dour. About six months into the campaign, Mag approached the captain and requested a leave of absence. 'To visit family,' she told him, but I knew full well that Mag had no living family. Of course, she told me where she was really going—she was returning to northeastern Selvan for a month, to see Sten, because she was worried how he was getting on.

"The captain was loath to let her leave, but he did it anyways. Mag was gone for three weeks, and then she returned. In some ways, it seemed as though a great weight had lifted from her shoulders, and she joked more often and laughed more readily. But I could tell she was troubled, and when she thought no one was looking, I caught her staring into the distance, her expression one of deep thought.

"At last I approached her. 'Mag,' I said. 'Something happened while you were gone. Would you spit it out and tell me, so that I can stop worrying about you?'

"She looked entirely confused. 'What do you mean?' she asked. 'I am the same as I have always been.'

"'May the dark take me if that is true,' I said. 'You seem relieved ever since you visited Sten, but it also seems as if something else troubles you. Why are you upset?'

"'I am not upset,' she assured me. 'Though I suppose you are right that something has bothered me. But it is not my own sadness—it is Sten's. He was happy to see me, of course. But something weighed on him, and no matter how I asked, he would not tell me what was wrong. There was a great sadness in his eyes when I left him, and I have not been able to stop thinking about it since.'

"Then I laughed at her, laughed long and loud. 'Mag, you are the greatest warrior I have ever known,' I told her. 'And you are also the greatest idiot. Sten is troubled because he loves you with all of his heart. And judging by the fact that you took leave to go visit him—when you have never taken leave in all the years I have known you—I would guess that you love him, too, and are too stupid to realize it.'

"Mag dismissed my words as preposterous, and the conversation ended soon after. But deep down, she knew I was right, and it did not take her long to realize the truth. Over the next year, something changed within her. Battle and warfare, which she had always loved, suddenly became distasteful to her. She no longer loved to throw herself into a fight, nor to spar with me and the other sellswords. Before, she had loved to practice, no matter how easy it was for her to beat us every time. Now she could hardly be mustered to the practice yard even for mandatory drilling.

"A year later, she officially tendered her resignation, and I did the same. Our captain begged and pleaded with us to stay—Mag more than me, of course—but she would not be dissuaded. We left together, and we returned to Sten, and soon they married and moved to Northwood.

"Sten was nothing special—and I say that as one of his dearest friends. He was a farmer's son like many others across the nine lands. But he was exactly what Mag needed, in that place, and in that time. The life of a mercenary had nothing new to offer her, but she could not see that. So she met one who would teach her the lesson, instead. The timing was too perfect to be mere luck.

"The same has always proven true, at least in my experience. Mayhap it was chance that put Dryleaf and me in that tavern together at the same time, all that long while later. But I have had my doubts, and those doubts have not slept in the many years since."

"What else would it be, if not chance?" said Sun.

Albern leaned low in his saddle, and his voice grew somewhat hushed. "Can you look at everything that has happened across Underrealm—everything that is still happening now—and tell me you do not think there is some greater power at work? Some great force we cannot understand, pulling our strings like puppets?"

Sun frowned up at him. "I . . . what power? What force?"

He straightened and shrugged. "If I had the answer, I would surely sell it to a king for a wagon full of gold. But I will advise you not to be too ready to believe in chance. The smallest actions can have the most profound effects, and we can hardly guess at them. For even the most mundane of occurrences, there may be reasons we can but guess at."

That was not an entirely pleasant thought, and it lingered in Sun's mind. If even the ordinary choices in her life could contain some great and hidden purpose, then what of the more consequential ones? She had thought her adventure with Albern tonight was little more than a lark. She did not like to imagine what else it could be.

These thoughts troubled her more and more as they went on, and as Albern resumed his story.

TWENTY-FOUR

I WAS SOMEWHAT DISGRUNTLED AFTER MY CONVERSATION WITH DRYleaf, but there was little I could do about it. Mag and I slept well that night, happy to have a mattress beneath us instead of a bedroll on the hard ground. The next morning, we broke our fast quickly and then returned to our room to discuss what we should do.

"I think it is clear what danger threatens the town," she said. "The people here are frightened of the Shades. They must be terrorizing the countryside."

"But then why would Yue let us in?" I asked.

"Mayhap they know the Shades, or know what they look like," said Mag. "You and I are no friends of theirs, certainly. Mayhap Yue knew it when she permitted us to enter."

I shook my head. "That seems quite a guess."

She spread her hands. "Do you have a better one?"

"No," I admitted.

"Then let us carry on as if I am right until proven otherwise, unless you would rather sit in this inn and wait for the weremage to come to us. Any plan of action, carried out with certainty, is better than no plan at all."

I had to laugh at that. "Do not throw Victon's words at me after all these years."

"You obeyed him easily enough when we fought for him," she said with a grin.

"And that has not been for a very long while."

Despite my protests, I knew she was right. We had no better ideas, and even if a thorough search did not reveal the Shades themselves, it might lead us to another answer. Still, I was nervous we might draw attention to ourselves. Constable Yue had made it clear that we were not to cause trouble in her town, and we were planning to do exactly that.

For caution's sake, we set out into the streets with our cloaks on and our hoods up, despite the heat of the day. Soon we were both drenched with sweat. I did my best to ignore it, but Mag complained mightily. We worked our way through shops, ostensibly to pick up supplies so that we could continue on our journey.

"If the Shades are indeed terrorizing this town, the people will know where they are," said Mag. "Keep an eye out for places that the townsfolk avoid—even if they only avoid looking at them."

We did so, but we soon realized we had a problem. The town was much the same as it had been yesterday; the people were afraid and despondent no matter where we went. It was hard to find a place they were avoiding when they seemed to be avoiding going outside at all. Few townsfolk would look at us, and in every shop we visited, the owner would conduct business as quickly as possible without speaking. When we tried to make conversation, they gave short, clipped answers or simply asked us to leave. And most curiously, when we told them we were looking for supplies to leave Lan Shui and continue our journey, they looked at us with terror in their eyes.

Probably out of frustration, Mag's course became increasingly erratic, crossing back and forth through the town on a dizzying path with no pattern that I could discern. At last, just past midday, she stopped in the middle of the street and balled her hands into fists.

"Let us get ourselves a meal and something to drink."

"That would be a welcome relief," I said. By now my shirt was clinging to me with sweat.

"Mm-hm," said Mag with a nod.

Something in her manner was strange, and I grew alert at once. She seemed distracted.

"Mag?" I said in a low voice. "What is it?"

"Mayhap nothing," she said. "I might say more when we find a place out of the sun."

Though I was intensely curious, I followed her without further questions. She stepped into the first tavern she found and paid for a light meal of bread and cheese and ale. Leading me to a corner table, she sat facing the door with her back against the wall. I sat beside her, facing out into the rest of the room.

"Well?" I said.

"I thought I saw someone following us," she told me. "They were being careful not to be seen, but stealth did not seem to be their strong suit. There! Look at me and pretend we are talking."

We turned our heads towards each other. "We *are* talking," I pointed out.

"Yes, good," said Mag. "Just like that, as though we are really having a conversation."

I laughed at the joke, but also to help the ruse. The laugh gave me an excuse to turn my head back towards the rest of the room, and I saw the person Mag must have been talking about. He was a young man with bulging eyes and short black hair, his light brown cloak thrown back over his shoulders in the heat. As soon as he had entered the room, he had gone straight to the proprietor, and was speaking with him now. Their words were inaudible from where we sat.

"The boy?" I said, turning back to Mag.

"Yes," she said. "I kept seeing him on whichever street we were on, no matter how wildly I turned our path."

"So that is why you took such a strange route through the streets," I said. "I was wondering about that."

"He is leaving," said Mag, glancing out of the corner of her eye.

"We should go after him."

"Do you think so?" said Mag with a smirk. "Be careful, though. Capturing him will be useless, and of course we cannot kill him. He looks young. I think he will be easily frightened. Let us spring an attack that fails. He might lead us straight back to his masters."

"Unless he is the weremage in disguise," I said.

Mag sighed and shook her head. "Albern, you know I love you, like one loves a helpless pet, but you can be intolerably foolish. We know the weremage can take a bird's form. If she knew we were here, and if she were following us, she would watch us from the sky."

She stood and made for the tavern's front door without waiting for my answer. I lifted one finger and opened my mouth to call out a retort, but could think of nothing. Lowering my hand, I stood to follow her, grumbling many ominous things about *pets* and *helpless* and what I would show her about intolerable foolishness. I was careful Mag heard none of my words, of course.

We left the tavern and headed down the street, back the way we had come. As we did, a figure detached itself from a nearby wall and followed us, trying to stick to the sparse shadows cast by buildings. Mag had been right about one thing: the boy was about as stealthy as a troll with an arrow in each eye and a spear in its backside.

"Now," whispered Mag, and ducked suddenly down an alley.

I dashed after her. We ran to the end of the alley and split up on the other side, each of us hiding behind a corner and waiting for the boy to follow. We heard his hurried footsteps drawing nearer. Mag gripped her spear and nodded to me from across the alley mouth.

The boy cried out in terror as we leaped upon him. Mag brought the butt of her spear around and struck him in the ribs with it. It was a light tap, but he squealed like a shot squirrel. I had already drawn back my fist to swing at him, but when he doubled over, my fist sailed over his head and into Mag's jaw. She stumbled back, apparently stunned for a moment, and then attacked again. But she seemed to overestimate the swing of her spear this time, and the butt crashed into my shoulder instead of the boy's face. I fell against the building beside me, grunting in pain.

The boy, who had all the wit of a bit of over-cured leather, stared at us in confusion. I growled at Mag through gritted teeth.

"Stop just standing there, or he will *get away.*"

As though the idea had never occurred to him before, the boy screamed and ran back through the alley the way he had come. Mag seized my shoulder and pulled me after her.

"You swung a bit harder than you needed to," Mag remarked.

"My deepest apologies. I am only a helpless pet, and cannot always control my own strength."

Mag snorted and redoubled her pace, for the boy had vanished around the side of the buildings up ahead. Mag and I followed him just as he had been following us, but with one important difference: we knew what we were doing. We hung back at each corner, only peeking around to make sure we saw which way the boy had gone.

It seemed to me, however, that we hardly needed to take such precautions. The boy did not glance back even once, and he did not seem to complicate his route at all, but led us straight to the heart of Lan Shui. At last he threw open the door of a ramshackle house and then slammed it shut behind him. Mag and I skidded to a halt just outside the door, looking up at the building.

"Is there any reason not to follow him straightaway?" said Mag.

"This is a large building that could contain a dozen enemies or more," I said.

"Any *good* reason, I mean?"

I drew my sword. "None."

Mag grinned as she hefted her spear. Together we launched ourselves forwards, slamming our shoulders into the front door.

It burst open, and I took in the room at a blink. Just before us stood the boy, his eyes bulging more than ever with terror at the sight of us. He stood with two others, a thin Heddish man and a fat Dorsean woman—Shades, I guessed, though they did not wear blue and grey. A fourth Shade stood in a doorway at the other end of the room. She was older, but hale, and wore her grey hair in a braid.

"Well met," I said. "Did we see each other in Northwood? I have such a terrible memory for faces."

"Pantu, you fool," hissed the woman with the grey braid. Then, to the others, she cried, "Kill them!" But she did not heed her own advice, instead turning and fleeing deeper into the house.

The thin man shoved the boy out of the way and rushed us, unsheathing a sword. The woman picked up a warhammer before doing the same. I braced myself to receive the man's first lunge, but that turned out to be unnecessary. Mag gave a savage thrust, and his sword arm was dangling useless at his side, while his blade clattered to the floor. The fat woman swung her warhammer twice, driving us both back one step, but then Mag pounced. Her spearhead pierced the woman's gut, making her gasp, before withdrawing and striking again, this time straight into her heart.

I almost relaxed, before I saw the thin man trying to retrieve his sword with his left hand. My own sword came sweeping down, and the Shade fell to the floor.

The boy cowered in the corner of the room, his hands raised helplessly before him, terrified. Mag advanced on him, but I darted forwards and took her arm. She whirled on me, and I flinched before her dead-eyed gaze.

"Mag," I said. "Look at him."

She hesitated and looked down at the boy. He looked back up at us, terrified. I felt the tension bleed from Mag's arm.

"Run for your life," I told the boy. "And if you know what is good for you, stop working with these Shades. They will come to ruin in the end."

I tossed my head, and the boy bolted through the open front door.

"There will be more of them," said Mag, her voice the emotionless monotone of her battle-trance. "Let us clear the house, and quickly."

She started for the door to the left, but I took her arm and stopped her. When she turned on me, I tried not to flinch at her dead eyes.

"Wait," I said. I pointed to the room's second door on the right. "If we chase the woman, she might be able to circle through the house and come out this way. One of us should stay here to guard the exit."

"There could be a back door, too," she said tonelessly.

"There could be, but we *know* about the front door," I said. "Go after her before we waste too much time."

She nodded and darted through the left-hand door. I felt a twinge of shame at how easily I had let her go off on her own. But both of us knew that, if one of us should go alone into the house, it should be her. I could be overwhelmed if more foes waited within. Mag could not.

I took a stance by the front door, sword ready in my hand. After the first few moments, the house was silent; not even Mag's footfalls could be heard. My pulse thudded loud in my ears, but it was thick and muddy. I shook my head, trying to clear it.

What was wrong with this place? The air was heavy with more than the midday heat. I could feel an evil energy seeping from the very walls. I had heard wizards talk of sensing magic at work. This felt like what they described, but of course I was no wizard. Even if there was magic here, I would never have been able to sense it. Yet I could sense . . . something.

Footsteps came pounding from behind the left-hand door. I tensed, raising my sword—and then I realized that it had to be Mag. No foe could have gotten past her to flee here.

The door opened to reveal the Shade woman with the grey braid.

She skidded to a halt at the sight of me, her well-lined eyes going wide. She, too, held a blade in her hand, but it dipped for a moment as she dragged a hand down her face.

"This was not supposed to happen," she muttered, almost as if talking to herself. "You were never supposed to come here."

I shifted my stance slightly, watching for a trick. "I am sorry to be such a disappointment, though you may be relieved to know I have always been such, according to those who know me best."

She spat on the wooden floor. "Shut your prattling lips. You were not meant to die here, but dark take me if I will let you kill me instead."

"Now, be calm," I said. "There is no reason anyone has to—"

She lunged before I could finish, and I barely blocked her overhead swing. But hardly had her blade rebounded before it came again, swinging from my left this time. I tried to twist out of the way, but I felt the tip of the blade slice a deep cut in my forearm. I grimaced in pain and tried to step away, but she followed.

"You people do not poison your weapons, do you?" I said, trying to keep my tone light.

"Do you think servants of the Lord have no honor?" she said. Then she smiled. "You will have to find out, I suppose."

She attacked again. I warded her blows, but each one forced me another step back. I could not risk a glance behind me, but I could *feel* the closed door at my back. The woman saw it, and she gave a grim smile. She was a better fighter than I was, and we both knew it. I took a wild swing that forced her a half-step back. But even as my sword came around, I could feel myself losing my balance. I stumbled, and she saw her opening.

"Die, wretch," she hissed, swinging for my side.

The only thing I could do was fall to the floor. My sword clattered out of reach. Her blade hissed harmlessly through the air where I had stood a moment before. But I had only prolonged the inevitable. I rolled desperately onto my back, hoping against hope that I could roll out of the way of her next swing.

But the woman was not standing over me with her blade held high. In fact, she was only standing at all because Mag's spear had pierced straight through her head and embedded itself in the wall. Now the woman hung feebly from the middle of the spear, bouncing up and down slightly with its spring. Her eyes were cold and empty.

I looked over. Mag stood in the right-hand doorway, blood spattered all across her clothing. She had arrived just in time to throw her spear across the room and through the head of my foe. Even as I watched, her battle-trance slipped away and warmth came back into her expression.

"Five, Albern," she said. "I took five of them, and still I had to help you against one."

"In a building like this, yes," I said. "Put me on an open field and put a bow in my hand—"

"—and stand your enemies in a line facing you like practice dummies, and do not give them any weapons to fight back, yes, yes," said Mag. She came to me and held out a hand to pull me up, forcing a slight smile. "We cannot always fight in perfect circumstances, you oaf."

"Oh, be silent," I grumbled. "And would you take back your spear? That is unnerving." I pointed at the grey-haired woman, still suspended where she stood by Mag's weapon.

Mag's little smile died, and she went about the messy business of retrieving her spear. Once she had extricated it from the woman and the door, she cleaned it on the woman's cloak. I went to where my sword had fallen and picked it up, keeping a suspicious eye on both doors leading out of the room. I did not want to be taken by surprise again.

Mag noticed my attitude and shook her head. "I got them all. The house feels empty."

"But still evil," I remarked. The air was still thick with the curious power I had felt earlier.

"Yes, still evil," said Mag.

"How did the woman get past you?" I said. "She emerged from the left-hand door—the same one you went through. Did she slip by somehow?"

Mag turned to look at the door, frowning. "She did not. I circled the whole house and came back around the other way, and I did not see her until I killed her. But I passed a staircase leading up. The woman must have run upstairs, and then come back down after I had passed. She, and three others—they found me in the back room, surprising me by attacking from behind."

My eyebrows shot for the ceiling. "However did you survive."

Mag put a hand over her heart. "It was a near thing."

I could not quite find a chuckle for her joke. A mercenary learns to lighten their mood, even in the midst of the grim business of killing, but I was never able to laugh in the presence of an enemy's corpse.

"I wish now that I had not killed all of them," said Mag. "I did not think to let any of the others live, for I thought we could interrogate this one." She pointed at the corpse of the grey-braided woman.

"Interrogate . . ." I closed my eyes and sighed. The weremage. She was not here. In the fighting, I had almost forgotten about her. "Sky. I had not thought of that."

"Clearly not," said Mag. "In any case, we did not find what we sought, and I feel it would be unwise for us to remain here overlong. Let us be on our way."

"A sensible suggestion," I said.

I turned to the front door and threw it open, relieved, at least, that I would be able to escape the oppressive feeling that permeated the house. The open air outside felt like cool springwater on a midsummer day. I stopped just past the threshold and took several deep breaths. Mag was not so dramatic about it, but I could see the relief on her face as well. She planted the butt of her spear on the ground and leaned on it with a sigh.

"You!"

The voice—new, but still familiar—froze my blood. I looked up, the sinking feeling in my stomach growing worse, to see Yue marching towards us, her face red beneath her shock of bristling yellow hair.

"Dark take the both of you—you are under arrest, under the authority of the King's law."

TWENTY-FIVE

"Constable Baolan," I said, raising a hand to wave at her. "Well met, again."

She stalked up to us in a huff, hands balled to fists by her sides. Behind her were the same two constables we had seen at the gate the day before. They looked at each other warily, hands near the handles of their clubs.

"I told you not to make trouble while you were in my town," growled Yue. "And then, a short while ago, someone came and told me they saw you chasing a boy through the streets."

"He was following us," said Mag easily. "We wanted to know why."

"He is from this town," said Yue. "You are not. And before—wait."

She stopped abruptly and pulled her club from its hook on her belt. Her companions did the same, though more slowly. Yue pointed at Mag and me, glaring.

"That is blood."

I winced as I looked down at myself. "It . . . is. We were attacked."

"Where?" snapped Yue.

I pointed into the house behind us. Yue glanced at it and then looked back to me.

"You go in first," she said.

There was nothing for it. I did as she asked, with Mag just behind me and the constables bringing up the rear. We filed into the front room, and Mag and I stepped to the side. The bodies of the first two Shades, along with the grey-haired woman, lay on the floor in clear view. Blood had already begun to pool around them.

Yue hissed and raised her club as if expecting us to attack. But I had already raised my hands in surrender, and Mag had made no threatening move, though she still held her spear.

"Drop your weapon," Yue ordered.

Mag sighed and did so, slowly raising her hands just as I had. "Constable, as my friend has already told you, we were attacked. We only defended ourselves."

"After breaking down the front door, if I am not mistaken," said Yue. My spirits, already low, plummeted further. The front door *had* plainly been smashed open, a detail I had not recalled until Yue mentioned it.

"We did, it is true," I said. "But only in haste."

"Because of the boy, you claim," said Yue.

"Yes," I said. "He fled once his companions attacked us. He is young, between a child and an adult. He has short hair and wide, prominent eyes."

Yue's face went white. "Pantu? Did you—"

"We did not harm him," I said. "And he made no move to harm us—only these ones did so. He fled soon after the fighting started."

"If that is true, we shall soon find out," said Yue. "Sinshi, go and fetch him."

The constable hesitated a moment, looking uneasily between us and his master. But when Yue fixed him with a furious look, he hastened to obey, awkwardly trying (and failing) to close the front door behind him.

My stomach did another turn. We could hardly expect the boy to speak in our defense—though he had not seemed as bloodthirsty as his Shade companions, we had chased him and then murdered his fellows. We had to figure out a way to turn Yue to our side before the boy got here, or else we had to hope he had already hidden himself so well that the constable could not find him.

"May I explain our case further?" I asked Yue.

"I think I have heard your side," spat Yue. "Now I would hear from the boy you chased, for no good reason that I have heard yet."

"Is it so strange?" I said. "You know we are travelers, and you can likely tell that we are no strangers to battle and fighting. We are in a strange place, and then someone starts following us. Would you not be curious, if you were us?"

"Of course I would be," said Yue. "But I imagine that, were I in your shoes, my path would not have ended in murder."

"Not murder," said Mag. "We told you—"

"Yes, that you defended yourselves," said Yue. She looked at me. "You are right, Albern of the family Telfer, in that I can tell that you are no strangers to fighting. And given the chance, I would do much to avoid any sort of fight against your friend Mag, here. Tell me: if she is so great a warrior, could she not have defended you both without taking three lives?"

Beside me, Mag tensed and gave me a quick look. As I met her gaze, my mouth twisted as though I had bitten into a lemon.

"Albern—" began Mag.

"What?" snapped Yue. "What is it?"

Ignoring Mag's urgent look, I spoke softly to Yue. "These are not the only three," I told her. "There are three more in the back room."

Yue's face went as pale as the corpse of the Heddish man on the floor. But to her credit, her voice seemed entirely calm when she spoke again. "I see. And they were killed in self-defense as well, I take it?"

"Albern, you fool," muttered Mag.

"Do you think she would not have found them?" I said. I met Yue's gaze without flinching. "We should not be afraid of telling the truth, for we have nothing to hide."

"That is a noble sentiment, though one I find hard to believe," said Yue. She turned to the constable beside her. "Ashta, collect their weapons." Ashta hastened to obey while Yue fixed us both with another hard look. "Indeed, the only reason I have not clapped you in irons already is that I can hardly believe two murderers as ruthless as you appear to be would behave so foolishly that they would let themselves be caught by constables and then freely admit to their own killings."

"That is one point in our favor, then," I said, taking off my sword belt and handing it to Ashta. Mag grimaced as the constable picked up her spear.

"Do not be flip with me," said Yue.

"Why do the deaths of these people bother you so?" said Mag suddenly.

The rest of us froze—even Ashta, who had been halfway back to Yue with our weapons. Slowly, all three of us turned to stare at Mag.

"Are you . . . are you joking?" said Yue. "You have murdered six people in my—"

"Six people, yes, but not six people from this town," said Mag. "None of these people are from Lan Shui, are they? I think the boy is local—Pantu, you called him?—but none of the others look Dorsean, or even half-Dorsean, like you. And they all seemed to be living here, in a house that looks to have suffered many long years of disrepair. I would guess that no one from Lan Shui has lived here in mayhap half a decade, and that you did not know the house was occupied at all. That means they were living here for some secret purpose, under your nose. And they are fighters, just as we are. What noble purpose could such warriors have for dwelling here, out of sight of the King's law?"

Yue said nothing for a long moment. Ashta frowned as she drew near her sergeant again—but it was a frown of deep thought, not of anger or denial. Mag had struck upon something I had not even considered, and from the looks on the constables' faces, I could tell her guess was at least close to the truth.

"Regardless of any of that," Yue pressed, "the King's law still applies, whether these people were born in Lan Shui or not."

"Yet the King's law provides for defending oneself against unprovoked attack," I said.

"You keep saying that," said Yue. "How far do you think such an excuse will stretch? There are *six* corpses in this house. Why did you not simply flee after the first two attacked you?"

My mouth opened, but no words came for a long moment. "Well . . . it all happened very quickly," I said at last, well aware of how weak the excuse sounded.

I was spared further embarrassment as the front door opened and Sinshi returned with the boy, Pantu, in tow. Pantu did not look to have come entirely of his own free will. I was afraid his bulging eyes would nearly fall from his skull, and he was covered with a sheen of sweat that I guessed was not just from the heat outside. When he saw Yue looming over him, he flinched.

"I found him, Sergeant," said Sinshi.

"Hello, Pantu," growled Yue. "I thought we had moved past the point where I would find you involved in some sort of trouble every other week, and yet here we are."

Pantu looked resentfully at her from under his hooded lids. "I did not do anything wrong," he mumbled.

Yue thrust a finger at Mag and me. "These strangers say you did. Did they attack you and your friends here first, or was it the other way around?"

The boy stared at us for a long moment. The room went utterly quiet, and it felt as if time itself had stood still. The only sensation in my body was the same oppressive weight of power that had pressed upon me since the moment we first entered the house.

"These ones attacked first," said the boy, pointing at the corpses on the floor. "The strangers only defended themselves."

Yue's shoulders sagged. She looked utterly flabbergasted as she thrust a finger at the corpses. "You are saying you were *with* them, boy," she said. "If they committed a crime, you are complicit. And you are telling me they attacked Mag and Albern for no reason?"

"*I* did nothing," whined Pantu. "These ones shoved me out of the way before the fight began. I wanted to escape, but they were blocking the door."

"That is true," said Mag quickly. "He did not join these others in the attack, and only—"

"Enough from you," said Yue, her face flushing. She spoke derisively to Pantu. "Your friends are dead, and you will not even speak in their defense. Why did you even truck with them, boy?"

Rather than cowering further, Pantu straightened and pointed at his own face. An angry bruise shone on his cheek, a few fingers beneath one bulging eye. "They were not my friends. They paid me, and I ran errands for them, but they were never grateful for my work. They were a bad lot, and I thank the sky that these strangers rid the town of them. We did not need them here any more than we need the vampire."

"Hist!" cried Yue, knuckles going white as they gripped her club.

"Vampire?" I said. "What vampire?"

"Nothing," said Yue. "Ignore him. He is a foolish boy." She seized Pantu's shoulder and pulled him to her side, as though protecting him from Mag. "With the only living testimony on your side, I cannot hold you. But I am warning you now: you are no longer welcome here. Fetch what supplies you need, and then ride from Lan Shui with all haste. Trouble follows the two of you like a heavy storm, and I will not tolerate it. Now get out."

"We still want to know why he was following us," I said to Yue.

"I suggest you accustom yourselves to disappointment," she replied.

"What was that talk of a vampire?" said Mag. "If this town is in danger—"

"I said it was none of your concern," said Yue. "Fetch what you need, and go."

"Yesterday you told us you did not want us to leave without speaking with you first," I pointed out.

"Consider those orders changed," said Yue. "If you are gone before the day's end, it will not be too soon."

We collected our weapons from Ashta and left the house. I did not glance back over my shoulder until we were several streets away. Finally I stepped to the side of the street, Mag beside me.

"Well, that was a near thing," I said.

"Near indeed," said Mag. "Not that I was in any great danger. I could have trounced those constables with my eyes closed. Though I can understand why *you* would be frightened."

I glared at her for a long moment, and she met my gaze without flinching. But both of us could only last a few moments before our faces broke into grins, and we chuckled together.

"Sky above, I thought we were doomed when that boy stepped into the room," I said. "I wonder what made him speak in our defense?"

"I would like to ask him," said Mag. "And we should ask after the weremage, too, since he is the last person alive who might know anything about her."

"Yet he is with Yue," I said. "And I think we would be pressing our luck if we tried to seek him out again, after all the trouble we have raised today."

"Agreed," said Mag. "Home, then, or what passes for it."

We turned our steps towards the Sunspear.

TWENTY-SIX

As we ambled away from the Shade hideout, Kaita watched us go, rage and grief burning in her heart.

She wanted to swoop down on us. She wanted to claw our eyes out in her raven form, and then she wanted to take her cat form and rip us limb from limb, feasting on our steaming flesh. No, that would be too quick. She would drag us off into the wilderness and play knives across our skin, and then leave us bleeding in the night to be a vampire's feast.

None of the Shades were supposed to die. Dellek, especially, was not supposed to die. It was only supposed to be Pantu. Instead, he alone had survived. What an evil joke of the darkness below.

She had thought of intervening when she saw us enter the house. But she still feared the cold fury in Mag's eye, and the brilliant flash of her spear. And in the end, she had hesitated too long. She had seen us emerge from the house, bloodstained but still alive, and she knew that all the Shades inside had been murdered.

Now she would have to find another way to lure us along the trail. But first she would kill the boy. With his own blood, he would atone for the far, far more valuable lives that had already been lost.

She watched the constables emerge from the house, Pantu in tow. Sinshi still had him by the scruff of the neck, dragging him like a wayward pup. Yue seized his shirt and pulled him away from her constable, shoving a finger in his face to give him a final admonishment. When she had finished with him, she shoved him away, and Pantu went scuttling down the street.

Kaita took wing, flapping to catch up with Pantu and watch him from above.

He ducked around the first corner he could, then poked an eye around it to watch Yue and the other constables. They stood in conference for a moment before Yue bade them all leave. From so high in the air, Kaita could not hear what she said to them, and she did not care. The constables vanished into the streets of the town.

And then, to her great surprise, Pantu snuck from cover and made his way back towards the Shade hideout.

Kaita swooped lower, watching him, her mind whirling. What was the boy doing? Did he have something stashed away in the hideout? Or did he have no other home in Lan Shui to which he could return? Suddenly she regretted not having learned more about the boy from Dellek. He had seemed so insignificant.

She watched as Pantu opened the hideout's front door. He paused there for a moment, recoiling with a hand over his mouth. If she had had lips, Kaita would have sneered. *Weak. Weak, and a fool.* But after a moment he mastered himself. He slipped inside the door, shutting it behind him.

Kaita felt a thrill race through her. She had him now.

With a flap of her ebony wings, she landed in the alley beside the hideout. Her eyes glowed, and in a moment she had resumed her human form, complete with the form-fitting clothes she was able to bring with her during transformations. After listening and watching to make sure there were no witnesses, she crept to the front door of the hideout and slipped inside.

The house was utterly silent. She felt the pulse of the evil magic within, seeping up through the floor from the chamber below, where the Shades had performed their rituals. It pulsed through her body, far more powerful thanks to her magic. She breathed deeply, relishing the feeling of the power.

For a moment she considered: should she seize the strength of the cauldron? Could she even do so? No one knew what it would do to a wizard.

Best not to risk it. Not yet.

Silent as a cat, she crept from room to room, ready to reach for her magic in an instant. But the house seemed empty. Frowning, Kaita sped to the stairs leading up. She climbed them, impatience making her incautious—her footfalls were now audible. But if the boy was upstairs, he would not be able to escape her anyway, even if he did hear her.

He was not upstairs. She searched every room, even under the beds, as though this were a child's game of catch the imp. After searching under the last bed, Kaita straightened. She looked towards the stairs leading down, her eyes narrowing.

There seemed no possibility the boy knew of the basement. Dellek would never have permitted him to learn of it. Yet it was the only place left.

She returned downstairs and opened the secret door. Ignoring the torch, she leaped down the steps two at a time, soon reaching the underground chamber. There she paused for a long moment, letting her eyes adjust to the thin shafts of light that came through the floorboards above.

The chamber was empty.

Kaita gave a low, outraged cry. He had heard her. She did not know how, but he must have, and he slipped out of the house when she was searching for him. Or mayhap he had climbed out a window. Either way, he was not here.

She had another thought. Avoiding the cauldron, she went to the cabinet at the end of the room. Stooping, she opened it. But it, like the chamber, was bare. There should have been a store of magestones. But it seemed that when the hideout came under attack, Dellek had hidden them somewhere. Or mayhap she had thrown them into the cauldron. They were not where they should have been, in any case, and Kaita could waste no time seeking them out.

She tried to calm herself with long, slow, shaking breaths. The boy did not matter. He was insignificant. Less than nothing. Revenge would have been sweet, but it was nothing compared to her mission. And she wished she had the stones, but mayhap it was better this way. This way, she did not have to break her vow to Rogan.

She would let it go. Mag and I were all that mattered, in the end. Whirling, she climbed the stairs and left the house.

Pantu waited a very, very long time, likely longer than he needed to, until he was sure she was gone.

When her footsteps had long since faded away, and the creak of the house's front door was a near memory, he emerged. He pushed open the door of the cabinet and uncurled himself from the cramped space within.

He stood now in the underground chamber. The massive cauldron sat before him, and sunlight glinted through the floorboards high above.

Still shaking with fear and drenched with sweat, he nevertheless looked behind him at the cabinet with a little smile. He might not be a fast runner, and certainly he was no fighter. And as he had learned just that morning, he was awful at trailing a mark without being spotted. But hiding? Yes, Pantu was very good at hiding. It was, mayhap, the only thing he was good at. Certainly his father would have said it was the only thing he was good *for,* dark take the man.

Pantu still did not know how the day had gone so wrong. But now the Shades were dead, and the only one left—Kaita—seemed to be hunting him.

I wonder, these many years later, if he thought of going into town and finding Mag and me and telling us what had transpired. We would have helped him, of course, the poor fool. But whether he wanted to or not, he did not do it.

Instead, he went to the cabinet—the one Kaita had searched.

Then he moved around the side of it, reaching into the gap between the cabinet and the wall, where he had stuffed a small pile of packets wrapped in brown cloth.

The Shades had not known that Pantu knew about the black stones. Indeed, they did not know he knew about this chamber. The same skill that made Pantu so good at hiding was the same reason he was an expert at being ignored. He had discovered long ago that he could go almost anywhere, so long as he did not try to hide it, and everyone around him would simply ignore his presence. In truth, it was what he had tried that morning with Mag and me. Only Mag's heightened sense of danger had discovered him and led to all the rest of the day's madness.

And so, lurking in the background and keeping to the shadows, Pantu had learned much of the Shades' doings. He had seen the ritual they performed with the cauldron of black liquid. And he thought he knew what they were doing.

He pulled one of the packets open to reveal a small pile of black, almost translucent crystals. Magestones. Simply owning them was one of the highest crimes listed by the King's law. Using them was even worse. Eaten by a wizard, they granted a terrible power—but, too, they ate away at the mind, creating a hunger that overpowered all reason.

Magestones had given Xain the power to save my life in the Greatrocks. Magestones had driven him mad to the point that he almost killed me.

But Pantu knew none of this. He knew only that the Shades burned the magestones in a fire under the cauldron—and he thought he knew why. The Shades had been secretive about their motives, of course, but Pantu had made several guesses, helped by the papers the Shades left strewn about their shelves and desks. Pantu had never learned to read, but the papers also bore many sketches of vampires.

A vampire plagued Lan Shui. The Shades were performing a ritual that had something to do with it. It stood to reason, in his mind, that they were trying to drive it off, using some magic that was beyond the King's law.

Therefore, Pantu now drew five magestones from the packet. He stuffed the rest back in the cabinet they had come from, leaving the door unlocked.

The Shades had only ever used two at a time, added to the fire once every two days. But Pantu was tired of that. He was tired of hearing about attack after attack, townsfolk and those beyond the walls slaughtered in the night. Entire families devoured by a beast that no one had lived to speak of.

Five stones. Five stones would drive it away for certain.

Taking the stones in his hand, he crept beneath the cauldron. The fire still burned there, black as night, its flames somehow draining light from the room, rather than bestowing it. Pantu cast the stones into the fire. It swelled, licking at the bottom of the cauldron.

The evil energy in the house swelled. Pantu clutched at his chest, feeling for a moment that he could not breathe. The feeling passed, and he backed away from the cauldron on hands and knees, shaking.

There. That sensation would spread, now. The vampire, frightening as it was, could not withstand such a ward.

Or so Pantu thought. But then, he had never seen what the Shades had put into the cauldron that they heated with their darkfire.

His work done, Pantu left the underground chamber as fast as he could.

TWENTY-SEVEN

In a dejected frame of mind, Mag and I returned to our inn and went to our room. With Mag's help, I bandaged the cut on my arm. It was not so deep as I had feared, though it still stung when we put a healing poultice on it. Once we were finished, we changed out of our bloody clothes and into fresh ones. Mag threw herself on her back atop her bed, while I sat in our one chair, in the corner of the room.

"A vampire," I said. "Now I understand the fear in the eyes of these people."

"And Yue's words make sense," said Mag. "Do you remember? When we first arrived, she told us to inform her before we left. I imagine no one has been able to leave or reach Lan Shui since the vampire arrived. We only managed it because we came from the Greatrocks, into which the creature will not tread."

"And why would it?" I said. "It has plenty of food here."

"We must help these people," said Mag. "Though I have never fought a vampire before."

I cocked my head as I regarded her. "I am glad to hear you say so. I feared you might wish to pursue the weremage."

Mag scoffed. "The weremage is well beyond our reach, and we have little hope of finding out where until we can get our hands on that boy. But even if I knew she was just over the next horizon, I would not abandon these people to the slaughter. Do you think me heartless?"

"I do not, and I am glad to be proven right," I said. "Very well. Like you, I have never hunted a vampire before. But we may have to pursue it regardless, even without information. Time is not on our side. Yue has made it clear that she wants us gone."

"Have you heard tales of them?"

I snapped my fingers, for her words had given me an idea. "I have not. Yet there is one here who knows far more tales than I do. That old singer, Dryleaf. He said we should poke around the town and tell him what we found. I have a feeling this is what he meant."

Mag's mouth twisted. "I wish he had spoken plainly to us, rather than leading us on with such games. But mayhap he had his reasons. Let us find him, then, and ask."

Together we went down to the common room and found the barman. I feared he might not wish to tell us where Dryleaf's room was, but he offered no resistance whatsoever. It seemed it was not uncommon for the townsfolk to seek the old man's wisdom.

Dryleaf had a room on the first floor, towards the back of the inn and just next to the door leading to the privy. The smell was rather awful, but mayhap he did not mind. Or mayhap he appreciated the ability to relieve himself at a moment's notice—often a requirement for older folk, as I can now tell you from experience.

He appeared soon after our two brief knocks, and when he opened the door he stood there for a moment blinking over our shoulders, pulling his blue robes closer about himself.

"Yes?" he said at last. His voice was bright, but weary, and I wondered if we had woken him. "Who is it, and how can I help you?"

"Good day, Dryleaf," I said. "It is Albern. We spoke yesterday. My friend and I are the visitors from the Greatrocks?"

"Ah, yes, of course," he said, wrinkles deepening in a wide smile. "How can I help you both?"

"That is rather a long conversation," said Mag. "Mayhap we could take you to the common room and buy you a meal?"

"I do not pay for my food here, but of course I will accompany you," said Dryleaf. "A moment."

He turned back to his room, but I held the door open. "Can I help at all?"

"Oh, sky no," he said. "I have it all arranged, you see. Can find everything by touch. But bless your path for offering. No, go sit, and I will see you shortly. Or at least, we will speak shortly." He gave a little chuckle at his own joke.

Mag and I went to the common room and sat. Neither of us was hungry, but we both ordered ale, and Mag even managed not to turn her nose up at it when the barman was looking. Soon Dryleaf emerged from the back of the inn. I called to him, and he used his stick to poke his way over to us. I helped him into a seat.

"How has your morning been?" he said, once he had settled himself.

"I will not say 'good,' but certainly eventful," said Mag. "We found some in this town who were up to evil deeds."

"Ah," said Dryleaf carefully, folding one hand over the other. "I may have heard something of them. And what did you do when you found them?"

"We fought," I said. "They lost. They will do no more harm."

Dryleaf's face went somewhat paler. "I . . . please tell me, friends. There was a boy—"

"Pantu," said Mag, cutting him off gently. "He is fine. Frightened, I am sure, but unharmed."

Dryleaf gave a deep sigh of relief. "Thank the sky. He is not a bad child at heart, but he has often landed himself in trouble. He is a poor judge when it comes to choosing companions."

I leaned in closer. "We learned something else today, Dryleaf. When you and I spoke yesterday, why did you not speak of the vampire? Why has *no one* spoken about the vampire?"

Dryleaf shrugged. "I told you as much yesterday: you two are strangers here, and these are uncertain times. I said nothing, for I thought you might be one of those ruffians, aiming to see how much I knew about your doings here in town. I did not *think* so, for you did not sound the sort—but I could not be sure. As for the rest of the townsfolk, can you blame them? You are strangers from beyond the walls. Seeing a town weak and afraid, some might try to take advantage of the situation. You would not be the first highway robbers to think they could leave Lan Shui with more gold than they brought."

"Well, that is not our aim," I said. "We seek a weremage who attacked our home in Northwood."

Mag cocked her head at me, and I frowned at her. Only after a moment did I notice what she had: I had called Northwood *our* home without thinking of it. A flush crept into my cheeks, and I turned back to Dryleaf.

"She attacked Northwood and killed many who are dear to us," Mag said, covering for my sudden, awkward silence. "We followed her trail here. We have not found her, but we think those we fought today were her companions."

"Hm," said Dryleaf. "That may be. They have not been here long. Indeed, many in Lan Shui did not notice their arrival at all. I always keep a sharp ear out for the town's news, and I only heard vague rumors of their presence—most of those through Pantu. But the town has been very different since they arrived."

"Different?" I said. "Different how?"

"Well, for one thing, the trouble with the vampire only began after they arrived," said Dryleaf, pursing his lips. "I have tried to point this out to some in the town, including Yue, but they ascribed it to coincidence."

I frowned, suddenly doubtful. "I . . . cannot say that I blame them. I have never fought a vampire, and I know little about them. But they cannot be controlled by any human, that much is certain."

"That is as may be," said Dryleaf. "But still it makes me uneasy."

"I am not overly interested in the vampire's arrival in Lan Shui," said Mag. "I am more interested in how we can kill it."

Dryleaf was taken aback. "Kill it?"

"Yes," I said. "We are pursuing the weremage, as we said, but we cannot with clear hearts leave Lan Shui in danger. We will help get rid of the vampire before we leave."

The old man sighed, his shoulders drooping. I was surprised—I thought he would be happy to hear that we were going to help. But he seemed to have been overcome by some old sadness, something he had been able to forget but had suddenly been reminded of again. He overcame it quickly, though, seeming to marshal himself even as we watched.

"Well, I am grateful for your help, as I am sure many in the town are—or would be, if they knew of your aim. As for the vampire, I will tell you what I know. It has struck near the village, but so far it has not come within the walls. They prefer to attack victims who are alone and unaided."

"Well, your words explain the abandoned farms we saw outside the town," I said.

"Just so," said Dryleaf. "The vampire seems to be watching Lan Shui. It was after the second attack—three weeks ago now—that we became certain of what we were facing. When we did, Yue sent a messenger to the Mystics in Bertram to request their help. But that messenger was discovered a few days later in the wilderness. Her body had been torn apart and drained of blood. We sent another, but he met the same fate. No one would go a third time—or rather, Yue would not send them."

"But that seems almost intelligent," said Mag. "I thought that vampires were like animals."

Dryleaf shook his head. "In some ways, yes, but not entirely. They have no society or culture, the way that satyrs do, and they never work together. They are solitary hunters. No one is sure where they come from, since they do not seem to breed, or at least there have been no sightings of vampire young. But in any case, they are possessed of incredible cunning, and they will study the actions of their prey with a single-minded obsession. The vampire could easily have seen the messenger and known they were going to get help."

Mag frowned. "That is ill news. I wonder how it keeps watch. It would be difficult to watch all the roads leading away from Lan Shui to other, larger towns and cities nearby."

"To us, it does seem incredible," said Dryleaf. "But vampires are possessed of astounding speed and agility, and they can see in the dark. Sunlight, on the other hand, is poisonous to them, and they hide from it. But the messengers stood no chance when the vampire stalked them in the night."

"Well, it will not find me such easy prey," said Mag. Then, glancing at me, she smiled. "And I shall ensure it does not eat Albern, either. Now, how do we find it, and how do we kill it?"

"The second question is more easily answered," said Dryleaf. "Wood is poisonous to a vampire. Stab it with a steel blade, and it will only become enraged and kill you faster. But pierce it through with wood, and it will die as if it had drunk pure nightshade oil. A stab in the heart is best, for that will kill it instantly. You can also cut off the head, or burn them, though that is much harder to accomplish."

"Easy enough," said Mag.

"The much harder prospect is how to find them," said Dryleaf. "The best advice I can give is what I have already told you: they avoid civilization, and sunlight burns them. Therefore they are forced to lurk near lairs where they can ensure no sunlight will reach them. That usually means caves, and Lan Shui lies at the very feet of the Greatrocks. Though I think you are more likely to find this beast somewhere in the western spur that lies between us and Bertram."

"That was my thought," I put in. "If this creature has found and stopped two messengers, we will not find it to the east."

"You will find a home northwest of Lan Shui, on the lower slopes of the spur," said Dryleaf. "It was attacked six days ago, and everyone who dwelled there was killed. The barman should be able to point it out to you upon a map."

"Then our path is clear," said Mag. "We head west, search the spur, find the vampire, and kill it." She clapped her hands and stood.

"I only hope it is as easy as you make it sound," said Dryleaf, a cloud of doubt passing across his expression.

"We will set out at once," I said, rising to my feet. "If we hurry, we should be able to get there in plenty of time to stalk it to its lair and set a trap."

"One more ale for the dusty road," said Mag, turning and making for the bar. Dryleaf chuckled as her footsteps retreated.

"She is a fighter, that one," he said.

"Indeed. Sometimes I think she is too much of one." I sighed.

"You sound troubled," said Dryleaf, frowning.

"We were both fighters, once. We served in a few mercenary companies, spending many years with the Ruby Crowns in particular. But we left that life behind a long time ago. Now I have been unable to rid myself of the feeling that I dragged Mag back into a world that she was much happier to have left behind."

"Yet you seem to be more reluctant, at least when it comes to this hunt," said Dryleaf.

"True," I said quietly. "I suppose I have less to avenge."

"Vengeance is a shadowed road with a mournful end, whether you are victor or victim," intoned Dryleaf.

"I have not heard that wisdom. I cannot say that I like it, but it has the ring of truth."

Dryleaf gave a grim smile. Then he cocked his head. "You say you served with the Ruby Crowns. I used to travel, as I told you, and I heard many tales of that company. Would I have heard of your exploits?"

"Mine?" I said. "I doubt it. But Mag is another matter. Did anyone ever tell you of the Uncut Lady?"

The effect was immediate. Dryleaf straightened at once and gave a little gasp. "The Uncut Lady? You cannot mean that she is your friend, just across the room right this very minute."

"I do," I said, grinning.

"To think that I have been speaking with her, and never realized," said Dryleaf. "Her voice is far more beautiful than I had imagined it would be."

"Do not tell her that, I beg you. She thinks highly enough of herself as it is."

Dryleaf giggled. "If half the tales of her are true, she deserves to think so. I must shake her hand."

I shook my head and laughed. "Sky above. The last thing Mag's ego needs is an admirer like you."

Dryleaf smiled in reply. The deep lines around his eyes crinkled when he did it, and his bushy beard jumped. But the smile faded almost as quickly as it had come.

"The two of you will take care of yourselves out there, yes?"

"We will," I told him. "As much as I can 'take care' of her."

"Do not undervalue yourself too much," said Dryleaf. "I am a fair judge of people, and that is just as easy to do when you cannot see them. I would say that the love and the companionship you give to Mag are worth more than a thousand swords at her side. From what I know of her, in any case, she has never needed help when it comes to fighting."

I studied him a long moment. "I will try to remember it. Thank you."

Mag returned with a mug of ale. It was half-empty already. "We should be off. I have told the barman to ready the horses for us. Dryleaf, you have our eternal thanks for your counsel. It is a pleasure to encounter such a wise and helpful mind this far from home."

Dryleaf's mouth opened, and a thin squeak came out. Mag frowned. I seized her arm and hurried her away from the table.

"Sky above, let us get on the road before he musters the strength to speak."

TWENTY-EIGHT

The horses were being led out of the stable when we walked outside, and we rode out at once. The main road led north out of the town and continued that way for some leagues before turning west in the direction of Bertram. But we abandoned that direction quickly, turning upon a smaller side road that led to the farms and homesteads across the land that led up to the western spur.

Just as Dryleaf had said, the barman had been able to tell us where to find what we were looking for. There were many homesteads and farms this way, but they became fewer and farther between as one drew away from Lan Shui. At first we rode through farmlands just like the ones we had seen when we first came to the town, and just as then, many of the farms looked abandoned. But soon the land was all wild, open countryside, with no one around. Trees began to grow thicker about us, until soon we were riding through a small wood, through which we could occasionally still glimpse the rising spur of land ahead.

Finally the ground began to climb, and the trees thinned again. We crested a slope and, as if it had sprung out of the ground to meet us, we came upon the homestead we had been searching for.

At the center of it was a house, and a little farther off, a barn stood at the bottom of a steep slope. Some crops had been grown on the lands surrounding the house, but weeds had begun to spring up among them unchecked.

Mayhap thirty paces from the house were the blackened remains of a funeral pyre.

We burned them, of course, the barman had told us. *It was the only . . . well, the only proper thing to do. But their child was—well, they had two, and we found the elder with his parents. The younger son . . . well, we never found his body.*

We paused at the sight, surveying the cleared land for a moment. Mag studied the pyre with a dour look on her face, and I wondered if she was thinking of Sten. After a time, she nudged her horse again.

"Come," she said. "The day is young, and there is hunting yet to do."

She led me to the house, and we took a brief look inside. If the cold pyre had cast a shadow over our mood, the house plunged our souls into darkness. Though the people of Lan Shui had removed and burned the bodies, they had done nothing further to clean the place. Pieces of smashed furniture lay strewn about, and blood stained the floors and even some of the walls.

"They had a back door," I said, pointing to it. "I wonder why they did not try to escape."

"It must have attacked too quickly," said Mag.

We left the place. It was clear that there was nothing inside to help us in our hunt, and I had no desire to remain there a moment longer than I had to. In the clearing outside, we spent a moment gathering ourselves. Mag's expression had soured still further, and I worried that she might do something rash. Not that I knew what that might be—we had no idea where the vampire had gone, nor, indeed, where to start looking.

"Let us explore the wilderness," I told her. "If I had to guess, I would say it came from the west. That is where the land rises again, and where there are most likely to be caves."

"As you say," said Mag.

She swung into her saddle at once, and I followed her a moment after. We guided our horses towards the wilderness out in back of the house. But as we drew within ten paces of the trees, I heard a sharp rustling in the underbrush.

"Hist!" I whispered.

We leaped down from our saddles again. Quick as blinking, I had my bow up and an arrow nocked, and Mag held her spear ready to strike. We approached the woods one step at a time. Behind us, the horses nickered nervously.

"Remember, they said it was fast," whispered Mag.

"It is not the vampire," I said. "The sun is up."

Mag frowned. "What, then?"

I said nothing, for I had no answer.

And then, from the shadows between the trees, a creature leaped forwards. I almost loosed my arrow but stopped myself just in time. My mind had seen a wolf, but in the space of a heartbeat I saw that it was only a dog. Granted, it was a large beast—a wolfhound of a kind common in Dorsea. Its fur was mottled brown with black spots. The hound growled at us, hackles rising.

"Mayhap it belonged to the family," said Mag.

"That was my thought," I said.

I could not help a small measure of disapproval as I looked at the beast. It must have run off into the woods when the vampire came. I knew it was only a dog, but in my homeland, we trained hounds to be loyal to their masters.

And then I caught another movement in the woods.

"Wait . . ."

A small, pallid figure peeked out from behind a trunk. As soon as it saw me looking, it vanished again.

My eyes widened.

"The child," I breathed.

I loosened my draw and stowed my arrow. Mag quickly put up her spear and knelt, extending a hand. The hound calmed down at once, its growls ceasing. But it did not relax its stance, nor move from its position between us and the boy.

"Hello," called out Mag. "We are here to help. We came from Lan Shui."

The boy poked his head out from behind the tree again. My heart ached to see the stark terror in his wide eyes. His hair was disheveled and matted with days' worth of dirt and grime from the woods, and his clothes, though sturdy-looking, were almost black with filth.

"Hello," Mag said again. "Will you come out? We will not hurt you. I swear it."

Slowly, achingly slowly, the boy took a step out from behind the tree. The hound at last relaxed its stance, straightening and turning to trot by the boy's side. He seemed to draw strength from its presence, for he walked forwards a bit more confidently, though he still kept a good distance away from us.

"You are from town?" he said. His words cracked, the sound of a voice that had not been used for days. "I do not know you."

"We are travelers," said Mag. "When we passed through Lan Shui, they told us what had happened here."

His pale face whitened further. The dog whined.

"But we do not have to speak of it," said Mag quickly. "We only want to help you. Can we take you back to town?"

"I do not know you," the boy repeated.

"As she said, we are not from Lan Shui," I told him. "But Mag speaks the truth. We mean you no harm."

The boy said nothing, but only tightened his grip on the hound's fur. Mag went from kneeling to sitting, and drew back her hand.

"What is your name?" she said.

The boy's nose twitched. "I am Liu," he said softly.

"Liu," said Mag. "Some others came before us. Did you not see them?"

"When?" said Liu.

Mag looked up at me, and I answered. "Mayhap three days ago."

"I was in the woods," said Liu. "Oku and I hid there. We hid as far away as we could. I was afraid to come back until yesterday."

"His name is Oku?" said Mag, pointing to the hound. Its tail wagged once and then stopped. The hound tossed its head, as if it had realized what it had done and was slightly embarrassed.

"Yes," said Liu. "He went with me when I . . . when I ran."

Tears welled up in his eyes, and his lip trembled. I felt my chest grow tight.

"That was very smart and brave of you," said Mag, her voice thick.

"Mama told me to," whispered Liu.

"And you were very wise to listen to her," said Mag.

"She died," said Liu, his tears beginning to leak down his cheeks. "And Papa, and Qinsha. Did they not?"

Qinsha must have been his older brother. I looked at Mag helplessly, but she never took her eyes off Liu.

"Oku went with you," she said. "He seems like a very good dog."

Liu did not notice that she had avoided his question. Oku's tail wagged again, twice this time, and he padded slowly towards Mag. He sniffed tentatively at her feet before submitting to a gentle pat between the ears.

"He likes you," said Liu.

"I am glad," said Mag.

Liu took his first step forwards since emerging from the forest. Another long pause. Another small step.

"Are those your horses?" he said at last.

"Yes," said Mag. "But the brown one is an idiot. He is so stupid, my friend named him Foolhoof."

Liu giggled. It sounded as if the noise had been pulled from him against his will. "What about the grey one?"

"Her name is Mist. She is much smarter, and she loves children. Would you like to meet her?"

Liu gave a tentative nod, and Mag rose at last to her feet. I feared Oku would be startled by her movement, but the hound accepted it easily enough. It trotted behind her as she went to Liu and reached out. The boy took her hand and let her lead him to the horses, who had begun to drift off. I noticed that Oku seemed to be limping a bit as he walked by Mag's side.

"Here, boy," I said, walking over to him. Oku paused and looked up at me, his wide eyes glistening. I knelt by his side and extended a hand, slowly, towards his left rear leg. Oku tensed, but I kept my movements slow, and he let me take the leg. Part of the fur was matted, and probing it gently with my fingers, I felt a light cut.

"He has been hurt," I said, looking up at Liu.

"The monster did that," said the boy. "Oku tried to fight it, but it hurt him."

"I have some things in my saddlebag for that," I said, rising and going to Foolhoof. The gelding looked at me suspiciously, but he stood still as I opened a saddlebag. From it I drew some dried yarrow, crushing it in my fist and mixing it with some water from my skin. I returned to Oku and spread it on the cut. The wolfhound submitted to my ministrations, though he whined about it.

"Do not hurt him," said Liu, frowning.

"It stings a bit, but it will help the wound heal," I said.

"Liu," said Mag. "Did you see anything after you ran into the woods? We want to make sure no one else gets hurt."

The boy went silent for a long moment and avoided our gazes. But finally he nodded. "I saw the monster afterwards. It came from that direction, and it left the same way." He pointed towards the trees in a northwesterly direction.

I went that way, leaving Foolhoof behind me. Sure enough, right where Liu had pointed, there were tracks on the ground. They were not human, that I knew. Each step had torn deep gouges in the dirt, and I thought of the clawed limbs that vampires were said to have. It also seemed to run on all fours.

"I have it," I told Mag. "It will be an easy trail to follow."

"Thank the sky," she said. "Let us get them back to town quickly. We should be able to return with plenty of time to follow it before night comes."

Mag hoisted Liu up into the saddle before her. The boy seemed delighted to be riding atop a horse. I would have wagered that he had never been on one before. Oku ran by our side, and despite the wound in his leg, he kept pace with our horses' trotting easily enough.

We rode away from the homestead, careful to keep Liu on the northern side of the clearing, where he would not see the pyre upon which his parents' and brother's corpses had been burned.

TWENTY-NINE

ALBERN DREW HIS HORSE TO A HALT. SUN WALKED ANOTHER FEW PACES before she realized the old man had stopped, and she hastily returned to him.

"What?" said Sun. "What is wrong?"

"Nothing at all," said Albern. "We have arrived."

Sun, who had become lost in the story again, blinked hard and looked around. They stood in a clearing in the woods, a good distance southwest of the town. She had a vague memory of Albern leading her off the main road and down the side path that took them here, but she had hardly noticed at the time. Above them was a rise in the land, and not far away was a cave with a deep, black mouth. It seemed somehow to loom over them in the night. Moonslight let her see only a few paces within the entrance.

"Would you help me start a fire?" said Albern amiably after dismounting. "I can manage it, but it is somewhat harder."

"Of course," said Sun. "Do you have flint?"

"Naturally," said Albern, pulling it from a pouch at his belt. As Sun collected dry leaves and twigs for kindling, Albern went to the trees and pulled down a few small branches to get the fire going. But when he had returned with those, he went to a small hollow nearby and retrieved some larger logs that looked to have been cut with an axe.

"Those were here already," said Sun. "You have been here before."

"I have," said Albern. "Just today. I told you I planned to come here tonight."

With Sun's help, he laid the logs in a crossing pattern. When it was done, Sun took a knife from her boot and struck flint to it, sending sparks across the leaves. They caught easily, and in no time a merry fire burned before them.

"How did the boy survive?" said Sun as Albern worked.

"It was only a few days."

"A few days without food is long enough to be perilous for one so young," she said. "A few days without water will kill anyone."

"There was a stream in the woods that his family would drink from, and he went there on occasion," said Albern. "I think it is likely he collected some roots and berries, too, for his parents would have told him if any were safe to eat. But more than that, do not underestimate the will to live. Even in a child, it can be strong enough to pull us through times of great peril. You would not enjoy a few days without food or water, but I imagine you would survive them."

Sun found a nearby branch to use as a poker, and then she settled herself on the ground next to Albern, staring into the flames. It was a little while before the old man looked at her, his eyes alight with interest.

"You seem to be deep in thought," he said. "If it is no imposition, may I ask what you are thinking about?"

Sun looked at him like one just waking up. "Hm? Oh, it is no great matter. Only, I do not quite understand what a vampire is. I have heard the name, but never a proper tale of them."

"Ah," said Albern. "A fair question indeed. Vampires were rare in those days, and they are more so now. But there is not much to tell beyond what I have already said. They subsist on blood. Though they will gnaw on corpseflesh, they seem to do so only to drain as much blood as possible. No hair grows upon their bodies. Their ears are pointed like an Elf's—though of course they are in all other ways entirely different from those terrible beings—and they walk sometimes hunched on two legs, sometimes on all four. They can leap several paces from a standstill, and their claws are sharp enough to sink into wood and most stone, meaning that walls are no proof against them."

Sun shuddered. "How horrible."

Albern nodded. "Yes. They are quite terrifying, especially if one does not know how to defeat them—which I did not, before Dryleaf told me."

"A good thing that he was there," said Sun. "You were most fortunate."

"Was I?" said Albern, and his eyes crinkled as he smiled. "I have already told you my views on fortune and luck. But if I may, as an aside—would you hold my bow?"

The question was so unexpected that Sun stared at him for a moment, blinking. "I . . . yes," she said at last. "But why?"

"Because we are in the woods at night, of course," said Albern. "I doubt anything like a wolf will approach our fire, but just in case it should—well, let us say that I am not quite the shot I used to be."

He lifted the stump of his right arm, and Sun could not help but laugh. Albern's smile deepened, and he reached for his bow, which he had placed on the ground at his feet. Sun took it with reverent hands. She had heard enough tales of Albern to know how much he had accomplished with this bow, what deadly foes he had faced armed with nothing else. He handed her the string, and she strung the bow, marveling at the ease of it. Then, seized by a sudden impulse, she drew. It pulled far more easily than she had thought it would, and yet she could feel the power contained in it. She felt that she could shoot farther, and with greater power, than any bow she had ever held in her life.

"It is a masterpiece," she breathed. "You made this yourself, did you not?"

"I did," said Albern. "And if I may be forgiven a moment of pride, I am glad you knew that."

"Whenever you are spoken of in tales, your skill with a bow is always listed first among your traits," said Sun.

Albern laughed at that, shaking his head. "If only those tales were true. I am a talespinner myself, and so I know something of how the truth of my stories must have been twisted through the years, becoming a count of accomplishments that I would scarcely recognize."

"Yet I have heard it said, on good authority," said Sun, "that tales are not meant to be believed."

"Then you have been well advised."

Sun smiled, but it died quickly upon her lips. "I must ask you another question, if I may be so bold."

"You have well earned at least one more honest answer."

"What under the sky are we doing here?" Sun gestured at the empty clearing around them, at the stars above and the black, looming mouth of the cave not far off.

Albern nodded, pursing his lips. "A fair enough question. Let me answer only that I am expecting someone. Do not trouble yourself overmuch; I expect them before long. After they have arrived, and then left again, we can be on our way. You can go back to . . . well, to whatever you were doing before you found me. Does that answer satisfy you?"

"Will you give me a better one?" said Sun, her brows rising.

"Not at present," said Albern with a grin.

"Then I suppose it will have to do."

"I thought it might. And now, would you like me to continue the tale?"

"Please," said Sun, settling herself upon the ground.

We rode into town with Liu and Oku. Guards must have spotted us approaching, for we found a small reception when we arrived. Several of the folk of Lan Shui were there, as well as Constable Baolan.

"What are you doing back here?" said Yue as we pulled to a stop before her. Her glare did not look promising.

"We found this boy near his homestead," said Mag. "We heard that it was attacked only a few days ago."

Yue looked at Liu again, and color rose in her cheeks. "Sky above. The Ton boy."

"Just so," I told her. "Is there anyone here who can care for him?"

"Give him to me," said Yue, rushing forwards. She extended her hands for Liu, but the boy recoiled, pressing back into Mag's body.

"Go with her, Liu," said Mag, urging the boy forwards with a gentle push. Though he still seemed reluctant, Liu let himself be pulled down from the saddle and into Yue's arms. She handed him off to a man from the town, who took off his coat to bundle Liu up in it.

"Now then," said Yue. "What are you doing back here?"

Mag and I both balked at that. "We returned a boy you thought was dead," I told her. "That should earn us at least some leniency."

"I do not deny our gratitude," said Yue. "But I thought you left this morning, for good, and I was not sad to see you go."

"We are staying for a little while at least, to help with the—" I shot a glance at Liu and cut my own words off. "With the creature that has been seen in the lands around here."

Yue scowled, and she, too, looked at Liu. "That is not a matter for you to concern yourself with. We are taking care of it."

"Are you?" I said, my blood rising. "Is that why we found this boy alone, abandoned in the woods? Despite your obvious desire to see us only as troublemakers, we are not here to harm you, or anyone in this town."

Yue turned back to the boy, and then back to us. Her hands were twitching, as though she sought someone she could feel justified in seizing and throttling. "Why did you go looking for the creature?" she said. "What is it to you?"

"A danger to the people of your town," I said. "And we think we can end that danger. As you have said before, we are rather well-armed travelers."

"You turn my words on me like a jest," she said. "Forgive me for thinking this hardly matters to you."

"Because I do not always look like I am chewing on a lemon rind does not mean I am not serious."

Her scowl deepened, and she strode towards my horse. I jumped down from the saddle and planted my feet as she stalked up to me, looking down into my eyes. I did not realize until just that moment that she was almost a full head taller than I was. Mag tensed in her saddle, but she did not yet climb down to help.

"You think you can insult me in front of the people of my town?" growled Yue, too quiet for anyone but me to hear. Her breath washed over my face, and I was surprised to find it unexpectedly sweet.

"That is the first time I have done so," I said in an equally low voice. "Yet your words to us have been a never-ending stream of disrespect. I appreciate your position, constable. For once, try to see ours."

She looked over my shoulder at Mag. I felt some of the tension bleed from her, though she did not back away. "What position is that?"

I waited until she met my gaze again. "We want to help. We have other business that will carry us far away from Lan Shui, but we will not abandon your people while this monster threatens them. What do you have to lose? The worst that may happen is that the beast kills us. The best that may happen is the reverse."

She seemed to want to argue further. But the eyes of the townspeople were upon her, and they were pitiful. At last she stamped her foot in frustration.

"Fine," she said, loud enough for everyone to hear. "If you wish to go riding off after this beast, I suppose I cannot stop you. But do not expect me to go trooping off after you."

"We will not," I said. "Now, if you will excuse us, we mean to do more hunting before the sun wanes."

Yue's face went from dark to pale in an instant. "The sun is lowering. Night will be here soon."

"We mean to lure it out of its cave just after sundown," said Mag. "Better, we think, than following it into its lair, even during the day."

The constable shook her head. "I cannot say that is a wise course of action. But it seems clear you will do whatever you want."

"Take Oku!"

Liu's thin shout came from nowhere, and I looked up at him in surprise. The boy still clung to the man holding him, but he looked at us in earnest appeal.

"Take Oku," he said again. "He is a good hunter."

"Thank you, Liu," said Mag gently. "But we can look after ourselves."

"Oku is a good fighter. You will need him." The boy's eyes welled up, and before we could answer, he burst into tears. "He kept me safe," he gasped between sobs. "He will keep you safe, too."

My eyes stung, and I blinked hard before looking to Mag. She met my gaze and sighed. Oku sat near the villagers, his ears cocked as if he knew what we were saying.

"Oku," I said. "Tiss."

The hound's mouth parted in a smile, his tongue lolling to the side, and he trotted up beside Mag's horse. She gave a sigh and wheeled around, riding away from the wall. I remounted, looking down at Yue again—mayhap for the last time, I suddenly realized.

"We will return when we have killed the beast, or not at all," I said. "I wish you and your people good fortune."

I turned and rode after Mag, hoping I cut a suitably impressive figure as we trotted towards the northern horizon.

THIRTY

Now that we knew where we were going, we pressed the horses harder, and we had returned to the homestead in what felt like no time at all. But looking up, I could no longer see the sun over the western spur ahead. Daylight would remain in the sky for a while yet, but we were running out of time. Oku kept up with us easily, apparently untroubled by the slight wound in his flank. As soon as we stopped in the clearing with the farmhouse, he trotted around the perimeter, sniffing at the ground.

I led Mag to the woods where I had seen the tracks earlier. "We can follow them easily. But I am not sure whether we should bring the horses or not. They will make the journey faster, but I do not want them to panic if the vampire should attack us."

"Let us bring them, and if we sense we are nearing the end of the trail, we can leave them behind, or tether them to a tree," said Mag. "I want to find the creature's lair in time, or we may not catch it as it tries to slip out to hunt."

That seemed a sensible point, and so I did as she suggested. We nudged the horses into the woods, and I kept my eyes fixed on the ground, only lifting my gaze every so often to take stock of the land around us.

It was unsurprising that the vampire followed no trail I could see. Its path plunged straight through the trees and underbrush, paying no heed to any obstacle in the way. It was also unerringly straight—wherever the vampire had been heading, it knew the direction well.

The light was dim in the sky when we came to the end of the trail. It led into the mouth of a large cave, which came looming at us from the side of the slope ahead. We stopped half a span away. Oku began to whine immediately. I glanced down at him.

"I think we have found what we are looking for," I said.

"So it seems," agreed Mag. "But we do not have much time." Daylight was vanishing quickly.

"Let us tether the horses a little farther away and make ready."

We did so in short order, leaving them back down the trail we had followed to get here, their reins tied to the springy branches of a willow tree. Oku stuck close beside us now, and he began to whine the moment we approached the cave again.

"If we take care not to get injured, it should not be too difficult of a fight," I said. "You have your spear, and I have my arrows. If we pierce it through, the wood should do the rest of the work for us."

"Simple," said Mag.

We took up position near two trees that stood close to each other. I pulled some dried meat from a pouch on my belt and ate it, suddenly realizing I had not had a meal since the morning. I hoped I would not regret that in the coming fight. As the light faded further and the blue edge of night bled into the sky, the moons showed themselves in the east.

"I think I should lure it forwards," said Mag. "It will see me with my spear and, I think, approach me first. You can lurk in the trees, and when you have a clear shot, you can take it. Hopefully that will end it quickly."

"A good plan," I said. "As long as you do not let it spring upon you."

"It will be your fault if it does," said Mag with a wry look. "Do not wait too long to shoot."

I snorted. "As you say."

"And take the dog with you," she said. "It might distract the beast if it remains by my side."

"Careful," I said, glancing at Oku, who was watching Mag with his tongue lolling. "He is a clever hound. You would not want to insult him."

"Would I not?" said Mag indifferently.

I chuckled despite myself. "Tiss, Oku."

The dog leaped up and trotted to my side. Mag looked at me and frowned. "You said that earlier. What is it?"

"Tiss," I said. "A common command for trained hounds."

"How do I tell it to go away? I suspect I shall want to."

"Now you are just being cruel," I said, reaching down to scratch Oku behind the ears. His tail wagged with delight. "Do not listen to her, friend. She is nowhere near as fierce as she sounds."

Mag snorted and rose at last to her feet. The sunlight was nearly gone. I took Oku off into the trees, finding a place to stand that gave me a clear view of the cave mouth but did not put Mag in my line of fire. To the left of the cave mouth was a sort of natural wall in the side of the slope. The top of it was almost flat, and it climbed like a jagged stair up the side of the mountain and wound away out of sight in the woods. I guessed it would carry one closer to the peak of the spur, though I would have been hesitant to try the ascent with any speed. But I took position near it, one arrow held loose in my hand near the string.

Night advanced, and the stars twinkled above us. Still we saw nothing, heard nothing. When would the vampire rise? Did they ever have nights where they did not rise at all, but slept through to the next day, like a soldier just returned home from campaign? I wished I knew more about them, or that someone else in Lan Shui had been able to explain more—but then, if they had, they would likely have dealt with the creature themselves.

And then Oku growled.

I grew alert at once. The hound bristled, his nose pointed straight towards the cave, his paws spread. But his growl would not carry to Mag's ears. I hissed, and she glanced over. I pointed to Oku and then at the cave, hoping she could see the gesture in the moonslight. She nodded and hefted her spear and shield, planting her feet wide.

A few moments later, we heard a scraping sound. And then the vampire emerged into the night. It walked on two legs like a man, but it was grotesquely hunched, bent almost double so that its hands nearly scraped the ground. If it had straightened, I know it would have stood at least three heads taller than me. Its skin was mottled, pocked, and pallid. It reminded me of the skin of those who have been badly burned and then healed, covered with a mass of scar tissue. Its hands and feet ended in curved claws each as long as a human hand, and it clicked and clacked them against each other as it moved. Its eyes were black, black as a wizard's who had eaten magestones, and its pointed ears, which jutted backwards, flitted and twitched, straining to hear any sound. But once I saw its mouth, I forgot every other detail. It was round and wide, almost a circle, and the teeth were bared in a constant grimace. Those teeth were long and pointed and sharp, and stained so badly that in the moonslight they looked to be covered with fresh blood.

All this I took in with a moment's glance, and I felt my limbs seize with fear. My right hand, holding the arrow, was slack, and my bow arm lowered towards the ground. Oku gave a tiny whimper and slunk back behind my legs.

But Mag, of course, felt no fear at all—or if she did, she hid it perfectly. Without hesitation she took one step towards the creature, taking no care to soften her footfalls.

The vampire, which had seemed to be snuffling at the ground, snapped its head up towards her. It bared sharp teeth and let out a long, hateful hiss.

"Sky above, you are ugly," said Mag. "Come, let me wipe that hideous grimace from your face."

If the creature understood her, it gave no sign, but it did begin to slink towards her. I wondered for a moment why it moved with such caution—it knew something of humans, clearly, and had already killed many of them. Why would it not think that Mag could be hunted as easily as anyone else? Mayhap it was uncertain because Mag was so brazen in her defiance, because she did not show the slightest hesitation or dread.

And then I recalled that I was not just a spectator, and that I had remained inactive for too long. The vampire was a few scant paces away from Mag now, and soon I would lose my shot.

The arrow was already nocked. I lifted my bow, drew, and fired straight towards the creature's heart.

It moved.

When people of other kingdoms see the archers of Calentin, they are astounded at our skill. Most who met me thought my bowcraft was something of legend, that I must surely be the greatest bowman who ever lived in the nine kingdoms. Indeed, I am a skilled archer even by Calentin standards—or I was, in those days when I had both arms. And yet, for all my ability, I have met many masters who far surpassed me at the height of my skill. I was trained by a woman who could fire arrows faster than heartbeats, faster than blinking, and send them all with enough strength to pierce chainmail. If an enemy shot at *her,* she could shoot their darts from the air with her own. I know because I saw her do it. Her eyes were unerring and sharper than an eagle's, and her limbs were a blur.

And yet the vampire moved faster than her. It saw the arrow from the corner of its eye, turned, darted aside, and snatched the arrow from midair before I realized what was happening. Then it flipped the dart around and threw it *back* at me—not with the strength of a bow, but still fast enough to pierce skin. I was saved more by luck than reflexes—I tried to duck, almost too late, and slipped on a patch of loose leaves. I struck the ground hard, the wind driven out of my lungs.

Sky save me, I thought. *How is it so fast?*

I heard an inhuman screech and looked up just in time to see it charge me. All four limbs ripped and tore at the earth to propel it forwards, sending clods of dirt in all directions.

But as fast as it was, Mag was able to catch it. She ran and leaped in between me and the vampire, and it skidded to a halt before her. But hardly had it paused before it struck with one clawed limb. Mag blocked the swipe, and I heard the deep rending of claws on wood. She stabbed in retaliation, but the vampire spun out of the way. It tried to turn the movement into another attack, but Mag's shield was there again to stop it.

It was not until that moment that I realized something about Mag. I had only ever seen her fight another human or animal. When she did so, it was a slaughter. I had never seen her face another opponent who had stood a chance. But now, facing a foe that was so much stronger than a human could ever hope to be, Mag's skill was displayed in full. My eyes, sharp as they were, could not follow the speed of her swings and thrusts. My mind could not comprehend how she knew where the vampire would strike next, nor how she could twist in *just* such a way to avoid it, place her shield in *just* the right position to block its swiping claws. Once or twice the vampire struck her mail instead of the shield, and I winced. But after the first time, I realized that even that was part of Mag's plan. She only let it strike her when the blow would glance from her armor, and when it gave her the opportunity to attack with her spear. Her armor was part of her, just like her shield and spear, and she fought now with her whole body instead of only her weapons.

Unfortunately for me, the vampire still outmatched her in strength. That meant she had to be more nimble than it was—and after a few heartbeats of frantic battle, that meant she had to leap out of the way of a swipe, landing on the vampire's other side.

It turned on me in an instant and pounced.

I shrieked—and not a noble battle-cry, either—and barely managed to leap to my left as its slashing claws sailed past. But now it had me backed up against the steep slope, with nowhere to run.

From the corner of my eye, I saw the natural wall that climbed up like a stair.

Nowhere to go but up.

I jumped atop the stone surface just as the vampire lunged, and it slammed bodily into the slope. Oku came flying from nowhere, snarling and yapping, and the vampire recoiled from the hound. Then Mag attacked, and the vampire screamed hatred at her as it retreated. But it, too, had nowhere to run other than the top of the wall.

It hopped up, still facing back down towards Mag. Suddenly my perch was far more dangerous than the ground had been. I edged towards the lip of the stone, readying myself to jump down. But the vampire spotted the movement out of the corner of its eye. It must have thought I was attacking, for it swiped at me again, forcing me a step back.

Three more steps up we fought that way, and now I was too high up the slope to jump down to the ground without risking a broken leg. Oku stood in front of Mag, trying to help but only, in fact, blocking her spear. And the vampire turned back and forth as it tried to pin one of us down, unable for the moment to do so.

My bow was useless with the vampire so close, and I drew my sword. But that proved to be even more futile. I swung, and for an instant I thought my strike would be true, for the vampire did not try to duck it. But that was only because it caught the sword in its hand instead. I felt the steel bite into flesh, but I did not lop the hand in half the way I would have a human's. It only hissed at me through its pointed teeth, dragged the sword from my grasp, and tossed it over the ledge.

"Blast!" I cried, my hand outstretched futilely towards the sword as it fell to the ground some ten paces below.

And then I saw something.

The vampire swiped at Oku, who leaped back only to become tangled in Mag's legs. She cursed as she spun, flipping over the dog, her green cloak flying about her.

But the moment's distraction had given the vampire an opening. It stalked towards me, black eyes glinting in the moonslight.

"A fair hunt," I said. "But I do not wish to grant you an easy meal."

I leaped over the ledge.

"Albern!" screamed Mag, her battle-trance breaking for a moment.

The vampire roared and leaped after me. A fall from this height would likely kill me—but the vampire would survive, and it would have a meal waiting for it at the bottom.

But then I grabbed the thick, outthrust branch of the pine tree that I had spied from the ledge.

The vampire's roar grew much louder, and then faded as it fell scrabbling past me.

I swung up and landed kneeling on the branch, slinging my bow off my shoulder and drawing an arrow in the same motion. I lined up the shot at the vampire, which was still falling through the air, and loosed.

The vampire landed. I heard nothing break, but the impact obviously winded it. Still, it looked up at the sound of the flying arrow, catching it in midair. It hissed up at me as it snapped the arrow between its dirty claws.

Then Mag's spear struck it in the neck, flying straight through it and into the ground. The vampire's eyes went wide with shock, even as a black corruption spread from the spear's wooden shaft through its skin. It looked like rotting meat, but it spread as quickly as flame.

Around us, the woods settled to silence except for Oku's throaty growling. I looked across the gap between the tree and the slope, and Mag looked back at me, panting.

"Sky above," she said. "That was a fight."

"It was," I said. "What do you think of your helpless pet now?"

"Much the same," she said. "After all, I still had to kill the thing."

My lips formed a thin line. "Only because I distracted it."

Mag chuckled. "That does seem to be what you are best at. Oh, do not look so offended, Albern. After all, we have a true pet now." She pointed at Oku.

I sighed. "Just get back to the ground. It will take me a little longer to climb down."

It did take me longer to reach the clearing than it took Mag, but not by much. When I joined her, she had already extracted her spear from the vampire's corpse and was cleaning it.

"We should take the head," I said. "Just to put Yue's mind at ease about the truth of our words."

"A good idea," said Mag. "And mayhap now she will not look upon us with such disdain."

"Mayhap," I said. "Where did my sword land?"

Mag pointed. Then, as I went to fetch the blade, she took the vampire's head off with one sweep of her spear.

We found the horses, who shifted nervously at the stench of the vampire's corpse, and rode back through the woods towards the road that would take us to Lan Shui. As we emerged from the woods into the clearing with the farmhouse, I took one last look at the darkness beneath the trees.

Something within me was still uneasy. The forest held no answers, only menace—and now a vampire's corpse. So why did I think I would not rest this night?

"It is irritating when you do that," said Sun. "When you ask a question like that, and then the story turns in another direction. You already know the answer. Why are you asking me? You could tell me if you wanted to. You choose not to."

"Hush," said Albern. "Let me have my fun."

THIRTY-ONE

Pantu paced in one of the upper bedrooms of the Shade hideout. He strained to hear any sound of fighting, of struggle, in the town outside.

That was a ridiculous urge, and he knew it. Even if the vampire *did* strike tonight, it would do so in the fields, the farms, a long ways away from Lan Shui itself. He would never hear it.

If it *did* strike tonight. But mayhap it would not.

Tonight was the night. Tonight was the test. Come morning, he would know whether or not his mad scheme had worked—whether he had finally driven the vampire away from Lan Shui for good. He had been trying to sleep, hoping to wake to a bright and happy morning, but he could barely lie down, much less close his eyes.

A floorboard creaked on the first floor.

Pantu froze. As he stopped pacing, the floorboards beneath his feet gave another, louder creak.

Had he imagined the sound?

But no. Now he heard something else. Someone coming up the stairs.

Someone? Or something? He heard claws scrabbling on the wooden steps.

Claws. No. Not possible. Not here.

He burst out the door of the bedroom onto the second story landing. At the top of the stairs crouched a figure. But it was not the vampire that Pantu so feared. It was a cat, dark of fur with a white tail, like one would find in the mountains. Pantu knew the sight of it well—every child of the foothills knew of mountain lions.

Even as disbelief struggled to work its way through his mind, even as he tried to reason out how the beast got this far into the town, the lion pounced. It gave two great swipes of its claws. Pantu felt them slice into his flesh like daggers. He gasped, his chest laid open, and felt the alien, terrifying sensation of cool air on his insides.

He fell on his back, the mountain lion perched on his chest. Its amber eyes, pupils like gibbous moons but wide as coins, stared into his own.

And then the lion said, "You were the one who was supposed to die."

Pantu blinked through the pain, through the darkness creeping in at the edge of his vision. This had to be a dream. A nightmare. He would wake. But then he realized the truth: the lion's eyes were glowing. It was already partway through a transformation—it had already formed a human mouth with which to speak. As he watched, the transformation finished, and Kaita knelt over him, one hand on his throat.

"Dellek should be alive," she said. "All the others should be. Why are you the only one who survived? You are the weak one. The worthless one."

Despite the terror, despite the knowledge of his own death, Pantu gasped out a laugh. Blood came with it. "Not so worthless. I have saved Lan Shui."

Kaita hissed and narrowed her eyes. "You have saved nothing."

"I completed the ritual," said Pantu, wheezing. "Five magestones. It is finished now. The magic will drive the vampire away forever."

He had expected Kaita to grow enraged, to storm at him, mayhap even to finish him off quickly. Instead, she only stared at him in amazement. And then she began to laugh. The laugh grew louder, ringing on and on, even as Pantu felt himself slipping into darkness.

Mag and I rode back to Lan Shui.

Though it was the middle of the night, we found many people awake and there to greet us. Yue stood among them, watching from the wall atop the north gate. Sinshi, one of the other constables, was there with her. The gate was closed, but as we rode up, Yue ordered it open before descending the stairs to meet us on the street.

"What happened?" she demanded, before we could even pull our horses to a stop.

"We fought the vampire," said Mag simply. "We won."

She cut the leather thong with which she had tied its head to her saddle and threw it into the street. The crowd recoiled and gasped. Yue's hard features were pale. "I . . . how did you—"

Most of the faces in the crowd had turned worshipfully to us, and I quailed under their gazes. "I played but a small part. I merely distracted it so that Mag could strike the killing blow."

"He almost killed it twice," said Mag. "Indeed, he might have had more clear shots if I had not gotten in his way."

I could see that Yue was growing frustrated with our modesty, and in the moment I agreed with her—at least when it came to Mag. I knew without a doubt that Mag could have defeated the creature alone, and that the same could not be said for me.

The small crowd now pushed in close around us, wanting to know more about the battle. Oku was nearly crushed against my legs by the press of people. He slipped through them and stepped away from the crowd, looking somewhat miffed.

As Mag, suddenly uncomfortable, tried to answer their questions, I looked over the heads of the crowd. There, near the back of the group, I saw the boy Pantu. He wore plain, grubby clothing, his face smeared with dirt. It looked as though he had been working all day. I hoped that meant he had at last found a more honest line of labor. Beside him stood Dryleaf, one hand holding his walking stick and the other hand on the boy's shoulder. The old man beamed a pleasant smile, his eyeline a bit to my right. But Pantu's expression seemed strange—eager, but not as joyous as most of the other townsfolk.

I pushed past the crowd, which seemed preoccupied with Mag, and went to speak with the two of them. As he heard my footsteps approach, Dryleaf turned towards me.

"Is that Albern?" he said. "I imagine it could not be Mag, for it seems she has quite a following."

"It is," I said. "Greetings, Dryleaf. And to you, Pantu."

Pantu gave a start, as though he was surprised to have been noticed, and ducked his head. Dryleaf chuckled and patted the boy's shoulder.

"Do not mind him. He is only a bit shy. We heard what you did. This town will never be able to properly express its gratitude."

"As I tried to tell them, Mag did most of the work, and all the hardest part of it," I told him.

"I suspect you are underestimating yourself again, though I am sure the Uncut Lady fought admirably," said Dryleaf. "But no matter. I am here for quite another reason. Pantu came to me. He said he had something urgent to tell you, and so I brought him here so that we could both wait for you to return from your hunt."

I looked at Pantu in surprise. He ducked his head again. "Is that right? What is it, boy?"

His bulging eyes glinted up at me, though he hardly raised his head. "I think you should both hear it at once." He hardly stuttered, as he had last time, and he did not whine.

"A moment, then," I told him, and turned back towards the crowd surrounding Mag. Pushing my way through them, I put a hand on Mag's arm and spoke quietly. "If you are done playing the grand hero, I think we should return to the inn. I could use a meal and a bath. And that boy Pantu wishes to speak with us."

"Sky above, yes," muttered Mag.

We excused ourselves from the crowd. They did not wish to see us go, but Mag got rather insistent, and then at last, Yue commanded them all to be off to their homes before she started making arrests. I gave her a grateful nod before we left, but she stepped close for a final word.

"I will not deny my gratitude for your actions, nor your right to a warm meal and rest," she said. "But I would speak with you again before you leave Lan Shui."

"Why, constable," I said, feigning surprise. "We would be honored. I thought you could not wait to be rid of us."

Her familiar scowl returned. "We shall see if I end up changing my mind on that count."

I laughed, and she stalked off. Mag and I went to Dryleaf and Pantu, who now stood alone on the torchlit street.

"Well?" I said. "Here we are. What do you have to say for yourself, boy?"

"And why have you said nothing before now?" said Mag sternly.

Pantu avoided our eyes again at that. "I . . . I am sorry for what happened before. I was too ashamed to come speak with you right away. But I realized you needed to know something. About the weremage."

I tensed, stepping closer to him. "The one working with the Shades?"

He nodded. "Yes, that one. I know little about her—but I do know where she is going. She told all of us. She said her next destination was the town of Opara, in Calentin. They—the Shades—they are up to something there. She never said what it was, but it sounded important."

The boy's words struck me like a hammer blow between the eyes. Mag, too, suddenly wore a grim expression, though hers was mostly out of concern for me. My heart must have shown on my face, for Pantu looked at me curiously.

"What is wrong?"

"Nothing," I said. "Thank you very much for telling us this, Pantu. You did the right thing."

He nodded and turned, heading off into the town. It was as if he had forgotten Dryleaf was there. But the old man did not seem to notice, much less mind, for he only kept beaming in the general direction of the two of us.

"Do you see what I meant?" he said. "A good boy, if sometimes misguided." He swallowed hard and put out a searching hand to shake. "Now then, ah . . . I understand I have the honor of addressing the Uncut Lady. Is that correct?"

Mag suddenly looked just as confused as she had seemed grim a moment ago. Without thinking, she took Dryleaf's wrist and shook, frowning down at him.

"I . . . have been called that, yes. But please, call me Mag."

"It would be my highest honor," said Dryleaf. "Sky above, to think I should have lived to see you in person. Or, to meet you, I should say." He gave a hearty laugh, and Mag gave a weak one as she tried to join him. "You are even better than in the stories."

"You are very much too kind," I told him. "Truly, I mean that. But come. Let us walk you back to the inn. It is late, and surely you are tired."

Dryleaf frowned at me—not out of anger, but with a sudden, strong interest. "It is late, but I am hardly weary. You are trying to cut our conversation short. Why?"

I opened my mouth, trying to summon a lie. But above us, a raven called, and I looked up at it. The bird perched on the edge of a nearby building, staring at me unblinking. My nerves tingled, a sensation that crept up and down my limbs, leaving me anxious and wishing to move. Whatever lie I had been dreaming up fled my mind.

"Pantu's words trouble me," I told him truthfully. "If the Shades are truly in Calentin, and if they are plotting something there . . . well, I wish to find out what they are doing, and why, and then I wish to stop them as quickly as I can."

"We should search their hideout," said Mag. "We hardly had any time to investigate it, the last time we were there. And I do not think Yue will begrudge us a little look about the place now."

"I would be surprised to find anything there," I told her. "But for lack of any better ideas . . . yes, let us go. In any case, I wish to ride for Opara in the morning."

"Agreed," she said. Together we turned and set off down the street, but we had not gone two steps before Dryleaf, who I had entirely forgotten, piped up behind us.

"Wait!" he said. "Wait for me!"

I clapped a hand to my forehead. "Sky save me, I am sorry. Of course I will walk you back to the inn."

"The inn?" said Dryleaf, stepping briskly up beside me. "Do not be silly. I will come with you. I would not wish to delay you for an instant, and it would be my great pleasure to accompany the Uncut Lady on one of her adventures, even such a small and uneventful part of the tale as this."

I looked over my shoulder at Mag. She shrugged. "What harm could it do?"

"I will try not to take that as an insult," said Dryleaf, his bushy eyebrows shooting skywards.

"Very well," I told him. "It will be our pleasure to have your company."

"Of course it will," he said, beaming. As we set off together, Oku fell into step next to the old man, his tongue lolling to the side.

THIRTY-TWO

DAWN WAS STILL A WAYS OFF, AND THE STREETS WERE MOSTLY EMPTY. We saw only a few people about, early risers pulling carts or hefting sacks in preparation for the day's toil. But despite the hour, they seemed almost cheery compared to when we had first arrived in the town. One of them even gave a happy smile and a nod to Mag, which she returned after a moment's hesitation.

When we reached the building where we had fought the Shades, we saw that the front door had not been closed, but still hung open. I helped guide Dryleaf through it, helping him avoid the jagged edge of the shattered doorjamb. The Shades' corpses were gone, but the bloodstains remained. For an uncomfortable moment, I was reminded of the shattered homestead to the north where we had found Liu.

Dryleaf paused inside the doorway, cocking his head back and forth as though listening. "This place has an evil feeling to it."

"It does," I agreed. In fact, the feeling had grown worse. It was stronger, more penetrating, like a thrumming in the air—a monstrous heartbeat that seized my own pulse and forced it to match time.

"Let us have a look about, then," said Mag.

"You can go with her," said Dryleaf. He released my arm and leaned on his staff. "I have my stick, and you can return to me if you have questions."

"We will be quick," I said. "Come, Mag."

From room to room we went, circling all around the first floor. All we found were some discarded scraps of food and rubbish. No messages or any other signs of what the Shades had been up to. We went to the stairs and climbed to the second floor, but it was just as barren as the first—though, thankfully, it was free of the bloodstains that spattered the first floor. Indeed, the floors of the bedrooms upstairs looked fresh-scrubbed. There were no possessions to be found. Even the clothing had been taken. Mag and I poked at the mattresses in case something had been concealed within, but there seemed to be only feathers.

"Yue has been here already," said Mag, frustrated. "If there was any clue, she has taken it."

"Well, we can ask her tomorrow," I said. "She said she wanted another word with us before we left town."

"If she *has* found anything, I doubt she will tell us," grumbled Mag.

"I think we have earned at least a little trust from her," I said. "Come. Dryleaf will likely be wondering what has happened to us."

Constable Ashta settled into her chair at the constable station. She would get no sleep that night, she knew. But the next day, for the first time in a long while, she thought she would be able to rest, well and truly.

She leaned her chair back against the wall, tilting her head back to rest against the wooden planks, and kicked her boots off. They fell to the floor, dripping a bit of mud. Twisting her feet, she reveled in the cool air washing across them, and released a deep sigh.

And then a thought occurred to her. A small, nagging thought, and yet it gave her no peace—the curse of a constable who held her duty as a sacred trust.

Did she forget to order the gate closed?

With a heavy sigh, she tilted the chair up again and reached for her boots. She was a citizen of Lan Shui. She had been born and raised here. But she still felt entirely fed up with the townsfolk sometimes.

They would not wipe their own rear ends if the constables did not remind them.

Pulling on her boots—hating the warm, sweaty feel of them—she stood and strode out into the night again, turning her steps towards the north end of town. The streets were empty, thankfully, and so she was able to make quick progress. And the north gate was not far from the constables' station. She would ensure the gate was closed, and then she would return to the station, and enjoy her night's duty. Mayhap she could even sneak a nap. The sergeant would be in a lenient mood tonight.

Finally she rounded the last corner and came into sight of the north gate. Sure enough, it stood wide open. Ashta shook her head and looked skyward. She could not recall who was on gate duty that night. Was it Shen? That seemed likely. The woman had a mind like a sieve, and more than once Ashta had caught her sleeping in the guardhouse, or neglecting her duties in favor of a game of Moons.

Well, Ashta would give her a scare. Hopefully Shen would remember it, at least for a time, and not shirk her duties in the future.

She strode straight up to the guardhouse door and threw it open hard. The heavy iron knob slammed into the wooden wall behind the door, sending a loud *crack* reverberating through the night air.

The constable stopped dead in her tracks, her mouth open, a shout ready but already dying on her lips.

The guardhouse was empty.

Mag and I came downstairs to find Dryleaf had left the front room and gone to the sitting room on the building's western side. The chairs had a thin film of dust. Oku sat by the old man's side, huddling against his legs. It was clear the hound was put off by the evil energy that suffused the building.

"And?" said Dryleaf. "Was your hunt fruitful?"

"Sadly, no," I said. "I fear we have only wasted our time, and yours."

Dryleaf shook his head slowly, clucking his tongue. "Do not trouble yourself over me," he said, shuffling towards the back of the room and feeling out the floor with his staff. "I am only sorry I could not be of more—"

He stopped.

Slowly, he turned and walked back the way he had come.

He stopped again.

"Dryleaf?" I said tentatively. "What is—"

"Quiet," he said, so sudden and brusque that I found myself complying at once. It was like the order of a battlefield commander, and I realized rather suddenly that I knew almost nothing about the old man's past. Mag, too, had fallen completely silent.

Back and forth Dryleaf walked, and now it was as if he was sniffing. But I could smell nothing other than whatever terrible, nameless stench seemed to permeate the very air in this place. At last he stopped near the center of the room. Then he turned and strode right towards us.

"Move," he said, again speaking in a voice that brooked no disobedience. Mag and I stepped aside, watching the old man. As he passed us, Mag looked at me, raising her eyebrows. I shrugged.

Dryleaf stopped at a tapestry hanging on a wall. He reached out and felt it with his hands before pulling it aside. He probed the wall behind it with his fingers. Then, suddenly, his fingers sank into the wall—or rather, a piece of the wall moved, taking his fingers with it.

There came a sharp *click,* and a section of wall beside the tapestry swung open to reveal a dank staircase.

The old man turned to us, folding his arms over each other and around his staff. I eyed him for a long moment.

"When I was a child," I said slowly, "I heard stories of blind people whose other senses grew sharper than was natural. Their other senses became so good, in fact, that they almost replaced the missing sight. Some of them could perform incredible feats, like seeing through walls, or catching arrows in midair. But I never believed such stories."

Dryleaf snorted loudly. "You were wise not to," he said, grinning. "Such tales are ridiculous, at least so far as I have experienced. I cannot hear a mouse fart from a span away, or some such nonsense. But without my eyes to distract me, I do pay a bit more attention to my ears. That is why, when I was walking about, I heard *this.*"

He walked to the middle of the room. There, he took his staff and struck the floor at his feet. Then he struck the floor again a pace away.

Thoom.

Thunk.

Mag stared at him, astonished. "They sound different."

"Indeed they do," said Dryleaf. "Because there is a hollow spot here, and a deep one. A chamber under the house."

"Well," I said. "I suppose that makes more sense than my first thought."

Dryleaf grinned. "Sometimes, what appears to be magic is simply a matter of paying attention."

Constable Yue stalked through the street, entirely irritated. Ashta had come and fetched her as soon as she had found the north gatehouse unoccupied. Ashta would have gone to find Shen on her own, but she did not know where the woman lived—and so it fell to Yue, as so many things did.

Yue hardly thought it was worth it. Shen was probably in her home getting drunk, celebrating the vampire's death. That was what Yue had been in the middle of doing, before Ashta came pounding at her door.

Two lefts, and then . . . and then a right? Yue frowned, stopping in the street and looking around. It had been this way. She was almost certain of it. But in the middle of the night, and with two cups of wine in her belly, it was suddenly less clear.

Kaw

Yue looked up. A raven perched on the edge of a building above her, looking down. It seemed to be studying her. For a moment Yue had the nonsensical thought that it was waiting for her to do something.

"Shoo," she growled at it. "I have little patience for anything tonight, least of all you."

The raven did not understand her, of course, and so Yue surely imagined the vague expression of amusement in the way it tilted its head at her.

She had had just enough wine that she did not wonder what a raven was doing out at night.

"Ah, there," she said, recognizing Shen's home and happy for a reason to leave the bird behind her. Shen lived in a small, two-room house wedged between a smith on one side and a tavern on the other—a tavern where she and Yue had shared many drinks in the past. Sky as her witness, Yue was going to make Shen buy her plenty of drinks to make up for this cursed nighttime adventure.

The front door stood slightly open. Curse the woman, she must be well and truly drunk. Yue threw it open unceremoniously.

"Shen!" she cried. "Where in the darkness below have you gotten off to?"

But the front room was empty. Yue gave an exasperated grunt and stalked towards the bedroom in the back. She threw it open, but the bedroom, too, was empty.

That gave her pause, and she looked back into the front room, frowning. Where under the sky had Shen gone?

And then she heard a scraping against one of the walls.

Of course. The alley between Shen's home and the tavern. There was a privy there. Shen was having herself a piss.

"Shen!" roared Yue, stalking towards the alley. She would likely wake up some of the neighbors, but she did not care. Let them take their frustration out on Shen, once morning came.

She rounded the corner. There was the privy.

And there was Shen. On the ground, slumped against the wall, her face deathly white, her tunic covered with blood—but not as much as Yue would have expected, judging from the gaping wound in her neck.

Yue froze.

No, she thought. *No, that is not right.*

The vampire did not come within the walls.

Yet there was Shen.

The vampire was dead.

Yet there was Shen.

Even as she watched, Shen's fingers scrabbled futilely against the cobblestones. She shuddered one last time and died.

Yue turned and sprinted for the constables' station.

Dryleaf took my arm, and together we followed Mag down the stairs into a wide chamber beneath the house. With every step down, the evil feeling in the air increased. Oku whined, trotting just behind me, his steps hesitant. I thought about sending him back to wait outside the house, but I wanted him close to protect Dryleaf, in case of danger.

Below, I felt the air open up into a large space. But everything was pitch black, with no faintest light reaching us from the stairway.

"Is there a torch?" I said. My voice vanished into the empty space.

I heard the sound of Mag fumbling along the wall. "Here is one," she said at last. "Give me a moment to light it."

Sparks glinted in the shadows as she worked. Finally a flame sprang to life, and Mag lifted the torch high.

The chamber was large—larger than the first floor of the house, which meant it extended under the buildings on either side. There were desks and tables around the edges of the room, some of them littered with papers. But in the center of the room was a massive cauldron filled with a liquid I thought was entirely black. It was only when we took a few steps forwards, and the light of Mag's torch fell upon the cauldron, that I saw a glint of red.

"Sky above," I breathed.

Mag walked up to the cauldron and took a closer look. Oku went with her, growling in his throat at the cauldron. Mag sniffed. When she turned back to me, her expression was grim.

"Blood," she said. "Old blood. It smells almost . . . rotten."

I knew instinctively that this must be the source of the evil feeling in the house. But how could that be? It was a great deal of blood, true, but it was not as though we could smell it through the floor.

"Let me get another torch," I said. I removed Dryleaf's hand from my arm and went to the wall, fetching another torch and lighting it with Mag's.

"What is it?" said Dryleaf. "Tell me."

"My apologies," I said. "There is a cauldron here, filled with blood. It is paces across."

"Sky," whispered Dryleaf. "How much? How many . . ."

He did not finish, but I heard the words as plainly as if he had spoken them. *How many people died to fill this cauldron?*

I went to Mag's side and knelt, thrusting my torch close to the ground. A pit had been dug beneath the great iron bowl. The stones within were blackened and twisted. I could see no fuel. Whatever had burned there had burned away . . . but it had melted a great deal of the surrounding stone.

"Darkfire," I whispered. "These stones have been melted by darkfire."

"Darkfire?" said Mag. "What is that?"

"An evil magic," said Dryleaf. "You have heard of magestones?"

Mag frowned. "I know that they are a dangerous substance."

"Forbidden by the King's law," said Dryleaf, nodding. "When a wizard eats them, they gain immeasurable power according to their branch. Firemages gain the power of darkfire. It is a black flame that consumes light instead of giving it, and it will melt almost anything."

"But there is another way to create darkfire," I said. "Setting fire to magestones will do it."

"I have never heard that," said Dryleaf.

"Neither had I," I said. "I learned it only recently." It had been in the Greatrocks, with Loren.

"So these Shades you were hunting," said Dryleaf. "They used darkfire to heat the cauldron. To . . . to boil the blood."

"But for what purpose?" I said.

"The vampire," said Dryleaf. "It must have been. The feeling in this place . . . the *smell.* Mayhap that is what summoned the vampire. I was right all along, though I wish I had not been. The Shades *did* bring the creature. But why? What did they hope to gain?"

"Some sort of weapon," said Mag.

I looked up in surprise. She was across the room, standing by one of the desks that lined the walls, and she had a stack of papers in her hand through which she was riffling. "These mention the vampire. The cauldron appears to be part of some ritual to summon it—to unleash it on the Shades' enemies. Using a magestone fire infuses the blood with the stones' essence. It increases the strength of it, gives it some sort of . . . magical property. I am not certain. There are many things written here I do not understand. But that is what brought the vampire out of the mountains, if indeed that is where it came from."

That was a thought so dark, I was stunned to silence for a moment, and Dryleaf seemed to feel the same way. Only Mag still moved or made a noise, flipping through more and more of the papers.

"I do not understand," I said in a hushed voice. "A vampire cannot be controlled. But even if you could set it loose in a town and unleash it, it is . . . well, it is still just a creature. If we had not arrived to kill it, the people of Lan Shui would have done so in time. They would have gotten word to the Mystics eventually. And if the Shades mean to use this as a weapon of war, it is an even worse idea. In a large city, one worth conquering, there would be many guards and constables, and even Mystics, to hunt it. That is what happens whenever a vampire is desperate enough to attack a city by its own choice. That is why they prey on the weak and the isolated."

"There is more," said Mag, scanning a page. "Something about . . . empowering the vampires. Strengthening them. I cannot entirely understand, but it seems they had some scheme for making the beasts even more fearsome."

"The beast, you mean," I said. "Only one."

Mag stopped short. "I suppose you are right," she said. "Though . . . though they speak of more than one in these pages."

I felt a sensation like ice sliding down my throat and into my gut.

"Mag," I said, my voice coming as a whisper. "How far would this ritual reach? How close would a vampire have to be for the magic to draw it in?"

"Sky above," said Dryleaf. But Mag only stared at me. My words were still working their way through her mind.

"Mag," I said again.

"It says . . . it says many leagues," she told me.

I felt the blood drain from my face. "Lan Shui stands at the feet of the Greatrocks. There is nowhere in Dorsea, and few places in all of Underrealm, where vampires can be found in greater numbers."

"But . . . but vampires never work together," said Mag. "You both said so."

"That is what the stories say," muttered Dryleaf. "But you should know better than to believe every story you hear, child."

And then in the town above us, the screaming began.

THIRTY-THREE

"Leave me here!" said Dryleaf. "Close the chamber door while you go and help the town."

"We cannot," I said. "They are coming for this place. You are in danger while you remain here. Come, we will hide you upstairs."

We hurried him up to the second floor and made him lock himself in a bedroom. Then Mag and I burst out of the house's front door. In the open air, we could finally place the direction of the screams—north. We flew that way, our boots slapping on the cobblestone streets.

A pallid, hissing form leaped out of the night.

I skidded to a halt, but the vampire had not been attacking me. It fell instead upon a man I had not seen, who had been cowering in a doorway. The man's scream was abruptly cut off as claws sank into his neck, and the vampire bit hard into his throat with its needle teeth.

"No!" cried Mag, flinging herself at the creature. But the vampire, having already taken deep gulps of the man's blood, chittered and fled. It leaped straight up an impossible height, landing on a roof above and vanishing from sight.

I fell to my knees beside the man and threw off my coat. I bunched it up and pressed it to the gaping wound in his neck. He sputtered and gasped, but each desperate attempt at breath only sent a new gush of red cascading down his shirt.

"Mag!" I cried.

"Coming." She ran to me.

"No!" I said. "Go find them. Kill them. Drive them off from the town. I will do what I can for the people. You are the only one who can face the creatures."

She stared down at me, face white as a sheet, eyes filled with fear for me. And then, even as I watched, the mask came down. The life died in her eyes, and her expression went slack.

Without a word, she turned and ran off into the night.

In mountain lion form, Kaita lurked on a rooftop above me. From her perch, she could see me and Oku battling against another vampire that had come swooping at us. We were hard pressed without Mag there—I fought with a sword in one hand and an arrow in the other, trying to drive the wooden shaft into the creature. Oku snapped and snarled whenever the vampire pressed me too hard, driving it back for only a moment at a time.

At last the vampire decided it had had enough and fled to search for easier prey. It leaped up on the rooftop where Kaita lurked. She ducked back just in time, her black fur melding with the night sky so that I did not see her.

The vampire landed several paces away on the rooftop. It stopped short and turned to her, sniffing. Kaita met its gaze and growled, the deep, rumbling sound shaking the shingles beneath them both.

The vampire sniffed harder and recoiled. Why feast on a mountain cat when there were so many delicious humans nearby? It knew the taste of lion well enough, and it much preferred two-legged prey. It stalked off into the darkness.

Kaita snorted. Then she turned to the corpse lying at her feet. Pantu. The boy's bulging eyes were pointed up towards the moons.

Kaita seized his leg in her wide muzzle. She threw him over the edge of the roof, listening as he landed on the street beside me with a *thud.*

"Sky above," she heard me say. "Pantu. Pantu, are you . . ."

My voice trailed off as I saw his sightless eyes. Kaita smiled in her mind and slunk away.

Mag flew down the streets, searching for her prey. There were screams in all directions, but they rose and faded too quickly for her to get a good sense of where she should go. Only one thing was certain: the Shades had succeeded in their aims, and there was more than one vampire in the town now. From the sound of it, there were at least half a dozen.

The citizens of Lan Shui scrambled and fled in all directions, like chickens who had just found a fox in their henhouse. But no one seemed to know which way to go. Mag saw one group fleeing east collide headlong with another group running west. After some of them slammed into each other and fell to the ground, those still standing kept running the way they had been going. Away from danger, or towards more of it, Mag could not know.

A moment ago, she would have grown frustrated. But her emotions were gone, pushed to the depths of her soul, and only the killer was left. The killer could not afford the thought necessary to care for these people, to be anguished at their terror and their pain. That would be later, when she was herself again.

Finally she heard a scream close by, from the next street over. She turned on the spot and rushed towards the sound. And there, at last, she found her prey.

A vampire crouched over a figure on the ground. A figure in red leather armor. Sinshi, the constable, whose arms still beat feebly at the vampire's shoulder, even as it sucked its meal from his jugular. On the other side of the creature, a man and woman watched in horror from where they sat on the ground. It looked as though Sinshi had pushed them out of the way as the creature attacked. But their terror left them unable to flee, and it would only be a matter of time before the vampire pounced upon them.

If not for Mag.

She ran up to the beast from behind, lunging the last pace. It heard her at the last instant and spun—but just a bit too slowly. Her spearhead slashed a deep rent in its side, and it fell back, giving a horrible, guttural screech.

The vampire crouched, hissing and showing its teeth. Mag fell back to defense, her shield up. The vampire began to edge left, trying to circle her, and she did the same, so that they maneuvered around each other. She got herself between the vampire and the bystanders.

"You should be going," Mag said over her shoulder. The townspeople stared at her for a moment in terror before turning and scrambling away.

The vampire's eyes shifted away from Mag to watch them go. It tried to leap over her to catch them, but Mag predicted the movement. Her spear stabbed upward, the head sinking into the vampire's shoulder. It screeched and landed hard on its side in the street, rolling and coming up in a crouch. It glared at Mag and hissed again. Over its head, she saw the townspeople vanish behind a building.

"Good," she said. "Let us finish it, now."

She leaped to the attack, and the vampire lunged to meet her. Her shield blocked its first swipe, and her spearhead sank into its gut. The vampire screamed as it fell on its back, trying to escape. But Mag followed, thrusting harder on the spear. It pierced flesh and guts, driving through the vampire's back and into the ground below. The skin around the wooden spear haft turned black and wilted, curling back and away from the wound like paper in a flame. The vampire tried to seize the spear—to pull it out, or mayhap to snap it in half. Mag kicked its claws away.

The vampire shuddered and died.

Mag looked up just as Ashta ran into view. The constable's eyes fell upon Sinshi lying dead in the street.

"No!" she cried, falling to her knees beside him. She tilted his head to look into his eyes, but they only stared blankly through her.

"Are you hurt?" said Mag.

Ashta shook, gripping Sinshi's shoulders hard. At last she mastered herself and looked up.

"No."

"Good. I have to go after the others."

"What others?" said Ashta. "They have gone."

Mag paused. She straightened and cocked her head, listening. Lan Shui had gone utterly silent. No more screams, and no more bestial roars.

The fight was over. And deep inside herself, with the ease of long practice, Mag released her trance. Her emotions, her fears, everything came rushing back. For a moment it was overwhelming, and she took a deep breath to maintain her calm. Her shoulders rose and fell, and she was back.

"The wounded will need help," she told Ashta. Even in her own ears, her voice sounded completely different than it had a moment ago. "Whatever you can do, do it. I have to find Albern."

THIRTY-FOUR

DAWN BROKE.

There were many dead strewn about the streets. The constables—those who remained—began to organize the townsfolk to collect the bodies and to heal the wounded. We gathered Dryleaf from the Shades' hideout, returned him to our inn, and went to help the survivors.

Yue found us shortly after the vampires fled. She stopped dead on the street, staring at us, and we met her gaze. She looked beyond weary, swaying on her feet, her eyes blinking too rapidly. It was a far cry from the proud, stocky warrior we had met when we first arrived at the town.

I wondered what she was thinking, in those long moments. Did she blame us for the attack? We had returned to the town full of pride and boasting of victory, but those boasts had proven hollow. Yet we could not have known, any better than Yue could, that the vampires had gathered in numbers.

At last she spoke. "We are collecting the wounded at our station," she said. "If you are not leaving town, then help us bring them."

We did as she asked. That part was easy, for the dead greatly outnumbered the injured.

It was Northwood all over again. I saw the same despair in the face of everyone we passed, the same confusion. Why? Why had this happened to them? They were simple folk. They farmed, and they worked, and they crafted, and they lived their lives. Horror and death had come upon them without warning, without reason. They did not deserve this, and they could scarcely hope to combat it.

When we had fetched all the wounded who had been found in the town, Mag and I stood silent in the street for a while. The night air was cool, and it helped to chill the heat we had worked up with our grisly task. I looked up into the sky, trying to regain a sense of space after spending several hours looking only at dead and dying townsfolk within arm's reach. Mag stared down at her hands.

"Let us get food and something to drink," I said at last.

Mag only nodded. I led her through the streets to our inn. Dryleaf was in the common room, leaning against a wall in the corner, nodding into his chest. I did not want to wake him—the old man had been up most of the night, and he deserved a good rest.

As I went to the barman and ordered breakfast and tea, Mag slumped at a table near the hearth. She stared at her hands the whole time, even as food was brought to us, even as I began to eat. She did not touch her own food. I kept glancing over at her, but she did not meet my gaze even once. Something was weighing on her, that was clear.

Finally I had had enough. "Come on, Mag," I said. "Eat something. And say whatever it is you must say."

She took a bite of the bread on her plate. Then another. Then she started devouring it ravenously, as though her body had only just realized how hungry she was. Her tea was cold by that time, but she drank it down regardless. When she had finished everything on the table before her, she settled back in her chair with a sigh.

"Better?" I said.

"Somewhat," she muttered. Then, to my surprise, she fished into a pouch on her belt and withdrew a copper sliver. She tossed it at me. It gave a heavy *clink* as it landed on the table, and then it rolled across the wood to bump my arm.

"The meal is paid for already," I told her. "Keep your money."

"Look at it, Albern."

Her voice was as solemn as I had ever heard it. Frowning, I scooped up the copper. I looked at it carefully, but I could not see anything amiss. The face of Andriana the Fearless stared up at me.

Then I flipped it over. And still, I looked upon Andriana.

"Ha!" I said. "You see these every once in a while. It gets stamped with the same sign on both sides. I used to have a silver—"

"Latrine duty," said Mag.

I looked at her, not understanding.

"In Northwood, before we rode out. You wanted to go after Loren. I wanted to ride into the Greatrocks. We played latrine duty."

The full weight of what she was saying crashed down upon me. I went very still.

"A coin flip. I keep that copper around as a keepsake, a curiosity. But in that moment, I used it to cheat you. We would not be here if I had not lied. Latrine duty."

I shook my head. "When you make an agreement . . ."

"I stacked the odds," said Mag. "I wish I had not, Albern. I am sorry. You deserve better than—"

"Oh, be quiet," I said. "Honestly, Mag."

She bowed her head, avoiding my gaze. "Of course. I . . . should I leave you alone for a moment?"

"Of course not, you great ass." I laughed. "Latrine duty."

Mag's eyes widened at my laugh. "Are you not upset with me?"

"Am I? I suppose so, a little. But . . ." I sighed and passed a hand over my eyes. "Mag, I . . . I told you much about the Greatrocks. With Loren, I mean, before I came to you in Northwood. But I did not tell you everything, because . . . well, because I was ashamed.

"Loren met me in Strapa. And when she came into my bowyery, she was with a Mystic named Jordel of the family Adair. A finer man I have never met in Underrealm. I could tell they were in some trouble, that they were going somewhere far and doing something important. And I wanted to go with them. Mag, I wanted to go with them so desperately. Yet when I offered my services as a guide, they refused me.

"That piqued my interest, and so I asked around. In no time at all, I discovered that they were hiding their true identity and trying to avoid notice. The Mystics were after them. And so I told the Mystics where they could be found. Soon they were on the run again, fleeing from those who wished to deliver them to the King's justice—and then, who appeared to rescue them, but me. Again I offered my services, and that time they happily took me as their guide."

Mag was looking hard at me. Guilt was still heavy in her eyes. "That is different, Albern. If you had not taken them into the mountains—"

"Jordel would never have discovered the Shades," I told her. "And now Loren will tell the Mystics of the threat, and a great disaster will be averted. I did an evil thing. I betrayed them. And great good came from it. You did nothing nearly so dishonorable. And if we had not come here, Lan Shui would be facing these monsters alone. Instead, they have us. They have you. That means they have a chance."

I pushed back my chair and stood. "If you have done evil against me, I forgive it. That may not entirely assuage your conscience, but if not, that is on your account." I thrust out a hand.

Slowly, Mag rose to her feet. She took my wrist and shook. "Very well," she said quietly. "Thank you."

"You wish to thank me? Give me a week's sleep, a barrel of your finest ale, and figure out some way to kill these vampires before anyone else in Lan Shui gets hurt."

That forced a laugh from her, as I hoped it would. "I cannot help you with the first two. But . . . I may have thought of something when it comes to the vampires."

That took me utterly by surprise. "You have?"

"The Shades' magic summoned them here," she said. "We know that now."

"We do," I said. "And it is an evil like I have never heard tale of, though I know many tales."

"Yet evil may be turned against itself."

I frowned at her. "How do you mean?"

Mag fixed me with a look. "The vampires hunger for the burning blood. And we mean to hunt the vampires."

My eyes widened. "Mag, no."

"Oh yes."

I leaned heavily on the table. "Dark below."

"No, this darkness is within," said Mag. "Within the heart of Lan Shui itself. Let us invite our foes straight into that heart and let the darkness consume them."

THIRTY-FIVE

We went to find Yue before noon. After hearing of the plan, she looked about as convinced as I had been.

"You want to *let* them into the town," she said, as though certain she must have misheard.

"With all the people hidden," said Mag. "No one will be in danger."

"Except whoever stands between the vampires and their goal," said Yue.

"Which will only be us," I said. In truth, I had to force a great deal of confidence into my words—this was Mag's idea, and I was determined to support her, but my fingers kept twitching when I took my attention off them, as though they were desperately trying to flee the impending doom of the rest of my body.

Yue chewed on the inside of her cheek, seemingly unappeased. "Show me," she said at last.

We took her to the Shades' hideout and down the secret staircase to the underground chamber. She stood awestruck in the doorway, looking at the size of it.

"How under the sky did they build this?" she muttered.

"I think they had an alchemist, or more than one," I said. "The people we killed here . . . they have many powerful friends across Underrealm, powerful and evil. I would wager they had whatever resources they required."

We showed her the cauldron and the pit beneath it where the fires had burned. Her expression darkened considerably when we told her of the magestones.

"If magestones are involved, then we should notify the Mystics," she said.

"You have tried to reach them already," Mag pointed out. "And even if you could, how long would it take them to reach us?"

Yue did not seem to have a counterpoint to that. "So your plan," she said slowly, "is to lure the creatures using this cauldron? Can they even smell it from outside?"

"They smelled it from leagues away," I told her. "It is what brought them to Lan Shui in the first place."

"We fight them first on the streets outside," said Mag. "They will be focused on an objective, and we should be able to kill some of them as they move towards it. There are only five left."

"Only?" said Yue—at the same time as me. It had slipped out of me despite myself.

Recovering quickly, I looked at Yue and gave her a sage nod. "Only."

"But if we need to fall back," Mag pressed on, glaring at me, "we can do so safely. We can fight them in the house above, while they try to figure out a way down into the basement, and if any of them make it to the cauldron, we can attack them while they feed."

"Try and explain, again, how this is better than fighting them at the walls," said Yue, folding her arms.

"What are walls to these beasts?" I said. "They can leap up them in one bound."

"Did you ever serve in a king's army? In a mercenary company?" said Mag.

"No," admitted Yue.

"Then take it from the two of us, who have fought on many battlefields across nine kingdoms," said Mag. "An enemy who dearly wants an objective is easy to manipulate. If you can force them to approach it, you can plan your attack. Our enemies have an advantage in their speed and their strength. But we also have an advantage, for they are little more than animals. We have to out-think them."

There was a long moment of silence while Yue looked slowly between us and the cauldron in the center of the room.

"Very well," she said at last. "But we will take additional precautions."

"Such as what?" I said.

"They must be watched as they enter the town," said Yue. "To make sure they do not deviate from the course you intend them to take. I will not invite them into Lan Shui, only to have them turn aside and rip open the homes of innocent villagers who will be unable to defend themselves."

I glanced at Mag. "Constable, you have seen how quickly the beasts move. Mag and I cannot track them from the walls all the way back to this house quickly enough to try and defend it."

"No, you will remain here," said Yue. "Ashta and I will see to the safety of the town. I am sure some others will want to help, as well."

"Your lives will be in grave danger if you do," said Mag quickly. "You would do better to—"

"No," said Yue, swiping her hand through the air like a knife. "This is my town. You may go through with this plan, but only if you do as I say. We may be at some risk, but we would rather face that danger than let others face it in our stead. And once I tell the townsfolk what you plan to do, I doubt you will be able to keep at least some of them from trying to help. Better to accept the help, if it cannot be turned away, and use it to ensure that as few lives are risked as possible."

Mag could hardly argue with that. "Very well, constable," she said. "I wish you would allow us to face this danger alone. But I thank you nevertheless."

"And I, for one, do not wish to face it alone," I said. "If that matters to anyone, which it does not seem to."

Mag held forth her hand. It took a moment, but Yue grasped her wrist firmly. "Just make sure you kill the things."

"We will," I promised.

The rest of the day was spent in frenzied preparation. Yue and Ashta put word out through the town, and the folk of Lan Shui rushed to secure themselves in their homes. Of those who were physically fit to fight, many volunteered to take up arms against the vampires. Yue took most of these and stationed them throughout the town, to hide with the others and act as guards. If the beasts deviated from the path we had planned for them, these guards would be the first to respond. The rest, mayhap a dozen of the fittest townsfolk, were stationed between the walls and the house—the first line of defense if the vampires should turn aside from their hunt.

We finished our work just in time. The sun lowered in the west, its edge just beginning to slide beneath the top of the land spur. The warm day had begun at last to cool. Someone brought a cold meal to Mag and me at the Shade hideout, and Yue joined us there to eat. We sat on the ground outside the house, scraping the last of the food from our bowls with our fingers. While we ate, I noticed Yue giving us sidelong looks—though she did not seem as suspicious as she might once have been, which encouraged me.

"Is this what you do?" she said, as Mag discarded her bowl on the ground and I gave mine to Oku to lick clean.

"What?" I said, blinking at her.

"The vampires. The ones who used to live here, in this house. Is it your duty to seek out such things and end them? Are you some special sort of . . . of Mystic?"

Mag and I laughed together, though we probably should not have done. "No, constable," I said. "This is not something we do often—that we have ever done before, in fact."

"What brought you here, then?" she said. "And do not give me the same lies you told when you first arrived. I have placed much faith in you today. I want a real answer."

Mag and I exchanged glances. But truth seemed the only option.

"We come from the town of Northwood, as we said," Mag told her. "Some weeks ago, it was attacked."

Yue's brows rose. "Like here?"

"No," I said. "Not vampires. By an army. They call themselves Shades. The ones who dwelled here were their compatriots." I jerked my thumb at the Shade hideout beside us.

"Who are they?" said Yue, eyeing the building.

"In truth, I know little of their aims, or where they came from," I said. "That boy, Pantu—may he rest in the darkness—he told me they came from Calentin. All I know for certain is that they had a stronghold in the Greatrocks, until a wizard came and drove them out of it. Then they attacked Northwood in great strength and nearly razed it in revenge."

"And when they did, they killed my husband," said Mag softly.

Yue let a long moment of silence pass. "That is an ill thing to hear," she said at last.

Mag pressed on. "There was a weremage. She led their forces in Northwood. She took the form of a lion and killed my Sten. And when they withdrew, she fled west into the Greatrocks. We followed her trail here to Lan Shui. We hoped to find her here, though of course now we know she left this place before we even came."

"Yet you remain," said Yue.

"Of course," said Mag, shrugging. "We are not without a conscience."

I smiled, and Yue appeared to hide a smirk. "Well. You should not have kept all this from me when you arrived," she said.

"I suppose the King's law would say so," I said. "Would you have allowed us in if we had been honest?"

"Do you jest?" said Yue. "Of course not. Yet I suppose, after a fashion, that I am glad you came."

"That is how latrine duty often works," I said.

Yue blinked at me. "What?" she asked, while Mag tried hard to suppress her laughter.

"Nothing."

Stars had begun to appear in the sky above. The moons had not yet risen, but I could almost see the glow of them in the east. I pushed myself to my feet.

"Time is nearly upon us," I said.

"In my experience, time is always upon us, depending on what time you mean." Yue got to her feet and held out her hand a final time. She took Mag's wrist first, and then mine. "Do your best not to get killed tonight."

"Of course," said Mag. "You have made it clear to us how much trouble it is to get rid of bodies."

"Not so much trouble," said Yue. "The vampires will only be acting in self-defense, after all. Does that not excuse any amount of killing?"

I laughed at that. "Keep yourself safe as well tonight, constable."

"I will try."

She took off down the street at a trot, making for the gate where she would stand with the vanguard. Mag and I prepared our weapons and made ready for the night's battle to come.

THIRTY-SIX

THE WOODS AROUND THEM HAD GROWN COLD, AND THE FIRE HAD BEgun to burn low. Albern huddled farther under his cloak for warmth.

"Would you mind throwing some more wood on the fire?"

Sun shook herself and rose quickly. "Of course," she said. "Forgive me for not noticing sooner."

"Think nothing of it," said Albern. "I think we both lost ourselves there for a moment."

"I cannot imagine it," said Sun, slowly adding logs to the fire. The flames swelled and crackled, and she relished their sudden warmth. "Sitting there in Lan Shui, knowing the vampires were coming and intending to face them head on. I think I would have died of fright."

"Well, you must remember that we were hale and hearty youths in those days," said Albern. "Much as you yourself are now."

Sun could not help but laugh, though she quickly stifled the sound, which was far too loud in the silent forest. "I do not mean to be rude, but you were already a fair bit older than I am now."

Albern frowned with mock severity. "I was barely past my fortieth year, thank you kindly."

"And I have not quite seen my twentieth," said Sun. "You will forgive me, but that is more than twice as old."

"Ah, but life's summer lasts long, and our leaves had not yet begun to brown—only to grey a little bit around the temples." Albern's eyes twinkled in the firelight.

"In any case," said Sun doggedly, "that only proves my point further. You were grown, and warriors as well. I do not think I could sit and wait for such a creature to come for me. The fear would be too great."

"Oh, I think you have a great deal of courage in you," said Albern. "And I can tell by your walk and the strength in your arms that you are a warrior in your own right, even if you have not yet been tested."

Sun could not help the blush that put in her cheeks, though she shook her head to try and dismiss it. "You cannot win an argument with flattery."

"Oh? I seem to recall having done so before." Albern scratched absentmindedly at his stump. "But I do not mean to flatter you. What you have said is the same thing everyone says, until they are thrown headlong into a fight. Some see it coming. Others never do. Either way, they come out the other side a warrior, or they do not come out at all. After you have seen it happen enough times, you tend to pick up a gift for knowing the outcome in advance. I would not say you were a warrior in the making unless I believed it."

A feeling like a cold weight settled in Sun's chest. "I wish I could believe that were true."

Albern gave her a long, searching stare. "Sun, why did you come into my tavern tonight?"

Sun avoided his gaze. "You have not asked me any questions about myself," she said quietly. "You said it did not matter who I was before I walked through that door."

"You do not have to answer," said Albern.

The little clearing settled to silence. For a long moment, Sun planned to do as he suggested, and remain quiet. But then, almost without meaning to, she began to speak.

"Ever since the War of the Necromancer, my family has been dishonored. You know . . . well, everyone knows how it ended. And most know how we have been viewed for our part in that ending. Now everyone in my family seems obsessed with regaining our honor."

She fell silent for a moment. Albern had not removed his gaze from her. His hood cast shadows over his angular face. "That is not such an evil wish," he said quietly.

"Except that they seem more interested in *having* honor than in *doing* honorable things," said Sun. "They no longer want to be viewed as traitors, as cheats, as faithless scoundrels. Yet none of them seem willing to see *why* we are seen that way. They think they can reclaim their status by building alliances, by strengthening our trade connections, by amassing more power. To me, it seems that such actions are what brought about our dishonor in the first place."

"I would tend to agree with you," said Albern.

"They want me to act like they do," said Sun. "They want me to want what they want. But I . . . I do not. I would rather do good deeds unpraised than receive accolades I know I do not deserve. Does . . . does that make sense?"

"It makes all the sense in the world," said Albern. "And if the opinion of an old man matters to you at all, I think you have the right of it, Sun of the family Valgun." He leaned closer to the climbing flames. "I think I had better carry on. We are nearing the end of the tale."

Sun balked. "We are?"

"Oh yes."

Sun could not help herself; she pouted. "I suppose I have no one to blame but myself," she grumbled. "I had harbored a hope . . . well, you told me you were not giving the tale of your arm, but I thought that might be a ruse. I thought mayhap you were going to surprise me and tell the story I really wanted."

"No, I am afraid I spoke only the truth," said Albern. "And despite what I have told you earlier tonight, it *is* all the truth, though it did not always seem that way."

"What do you mean?" said Sun.

"What I am telling you now is the truth as I know it now," said Albern. "I thought the story was somewhat different when I was living it. And afterwards, I thought it was something else again. Whenever I give you a tale, I try to tell the truest version of it that I know at the time."

"Humph," said Sun, holding her hands out towards the fire. "I still think I would rather read a history book."

"Who are you going to believe?" said Albern, smiling slightly. "Some scholar from your family's court, or the man who lived the tale?"

"If I were to heed a wisdom I have only recently learned, I would not *believe* any of it," said Sun, feeling almost ashamed at how good it felt to say the words.

Albern laughed. "An excellent riposte. But I have only my tale. Shall I finish it?"

Sun nodded.

Just after sundown, Mag and I entered the Shades' hideout and descended to the basement. We broke open a locked cabinet on the back wall and found several small packets of brown cloth. I untied one to find a collection of black crystals about as large as a finger. Magestones. Oku sniffed at them and growled.

"How many should we use?" I said.

"All of them," said Mag.

I looked at her. "That might burn straight through the bottom of the cauldron."

"I do not think we will have that long before the vampires reach us."

"A heartening thought," I said. "As you wish."

We piled the magestones up under the cauldron and lit them. They caught the sparks easily, like dry leaves, but they burned with a black fire that immediately sucked light from the air. I hastily snatched my hands away from the flames.

"That will do it," I said, edging backwards as waves of heat rippled across my body. "Let us return to the street."

Together we ran up the stairs, weapons in hand, and stopped on the street outside. Mag stuck out a hand, and we gripped wrists.

"Let us become heroes," she said.

"You have been one a long time," I countered. "Tonight I might finally join you."

"Fah." Her grip tightened for a moment. "In earnestness—be careful. If you let yourself die, I may have to kill you."

"And you as well," I said. "Though I suppose you would have to let me."

"I will," she said. "But enough words. Climb, little squirrel."

I headed around the side of the building. Oku started coming after me, but when he noticed Mag holding her position, he paused, looking between the two of us and whining.

"Kip, Oku," I said. "Mag will need you more than I will, I think."

"Kip, is it?" said Mag. "I will remember that when I want to get rid of him."

I frowned at her until, with a disgusted expression, she scratched Oku behind the ears in apology. Then I left her.

Around the side of the house, the roof descended close to the street. I jumped, just catching the edge of it with my fingertips, and hauled myself up. From there I climbed until I was near the roof's peak, where I knelt and readied my bow. I took half the arrows from my quiver and jammed them into the soft wooden shingles of the roof. Another I held loose in my right hand, ready to fire.

The sun had been down for nearly an hour when we heard them.

First there were cries of alarm from the north end of town. The guards on the walls had seen them. We had left the gates open. There was no point in closing them when the vampires could leap over them anyway.

The cries of alarm spread, coming from different directions but always moving south towards us. That was good. It meant the vampires were not stopping for anything, and none of the townsfolk had been drawn into fights. The battle would happen here, in the street in front of the hideout, as we had planned.

And then, at last, we saw them.

Two of the pallid, twisted, screeching creatures burst into sight at once, a distance down the street straight ahead. One had a narrow, jutting jaw and teeth that stuck out from between its lips, and the other had massive arms, thicker than my legs. For half a heartbeat they paused, sniffing at the air.

"Biter," I called down to Mag, pointing to one and then the other, "and Shoulders."

She glared up at me. "They are not pets."

"Oh, come now. Would you not love to take one home?"

The beasts focused on the door of the hideout, and on Mag standing before it. She hefted her spear. Oku bristled and growled.

The vampires screamed with fury and hunger as they charged.

My right hand moved in a blur, nocking, drawing, loosing. They did not expect the first arrow, but my aim was imperfect. The arrowhead nicked Biter in the arm, but no wood pierced its flesh, and it hardly seemed to feel it. After that they kept an eye on me, and they dodged every shot.

In no time they had reached Mag, and a deadly dance started on the street. By Mag's side, Oku snapped and snarled as he tried to catch hold of Shoulders, but it moved too quickly. Mag slashed and weaved, looking for an opening. The vampires kept trying to push past her, attempting to reach the building, but she managed to stop them. Twice when they tried it, she scored a hit with her spearhead, but not deep enough for the wood to penetrate the skin.

In the space of a few moments, I realized I would not be able to get a clean shot from my position on the roof. I scanned the streets all around the building instead—when more vampires came, I would be Mag's first warning. And the other townsfolk—not to mention the constables—should be coming soon, once the rest of the vampires arrived.

But in watching the streets, I forgot the rooftops.

I caught a flash of moonslight on Elf-white skin. That was the only warning I had before the vampire launched itself through the air, flying from the next rooftop onto my own. I managed to catch its wrists and keep its claws from sinking into my chest, but the momentum bowled me over. We tumbled back onto the rooftop, sliding down the wooden shingles, which shook me hard enough to jar my very bones.

At last I managed to tumble, kicking the vampire off me and slowing my headlong descent. I had my sword in hand before I got to my feet, and I fell back into a defensive position. My bow was up near the roof's peak, useless, but I had a few arrows left in my belt quiver. Slowly I drew one, trying not to move suddenly and provoke an attack. The vampire hissed, but it hesitated, studying me through its beady black eyes. A mottled pattern of black spread across its face, outwards from the nose like someone had thrown an ink pellet straight between its eyes.

"Inkstain," I told it. "That is what I will call you."

Inkstain snarled and lunged just as I got the arrow into my hand.

Twice I fended it off with my sword, trying desperately to find a chance to sink the arrow into one of its swiping limbs. It was impossible. The creature's speed was beyond comprehension. The only thing that saved me was that it recognized the danger of the wooden arrow, and that made it cautious in its attacks. I could not begin to understand how Mag managed not only to match them, but beat them. It took all my mind's panicked, animal instincts just to keep me out of reach of its claws.

Then a shingle gave out under Inkstain's feet. It went crashing down, and it grabbed wildly for something to hold onto.

"Something" turned out to be my leg.

We slid down the roof again, and this time we could not stop our descent before we pitched over the edge. I went over first. For one moment I knew weightlessness. My heart felt as though it wanted to pound my guts until they were unconscious. Then I came slamming down on top of a market stall that had been set up against the side of the building. The cloth enveloped me, breaking the fall.

I scrambled out of the tattered, brown fabric just in time. Inkstain came down right where I had been. The market stall collapsed, and the vampire vanished amid the cloth. Its screams redoubled as it thrashed. I saw a clawed hand burst out of the fabric.

Abandoning my sword, I took an arrow in each hand and leaped, plunging them into the flailing mass. Both darts bit flesh, and Inkstain's screams turned from rage to pain. One iron-hard limb smashed into my head, and I fell back onto my rear, my ears ringing.

Fire flashed in my eyes as a torch came sailing through the night. It struck the fabric of the market stall, which caught almost at once. The flames licked and spread, and soon the whole stall was ablaze. Inkstain shrieked and shriveled. What skin I could see blackened and twisted, and soon the cloth stopped moving altogether.

I looked up in shock. Yue stood there, huffing in her armor and with a nasty bruise on one cheek. She extended a hand without speaking, and I took her help to stand.

"Mag needs us," she said.

"Take me," I said, and followed her at a dead run towards the front of the building.

THIRTY-SEVEN

With the crystal clarity of her battle-trance, Mag saw it when Inkstain bounded over the street to go after me, but Biter and Shoulders kept her too occupied to spare much attention. She trusted me to handle myself, and she kept fighting, kept trying to impale one of the vampires with the wooden haft of her spear. There were only two. She was unlikely to get a better chance.

Then a fresh roar announced the arrival of a third. It sailed through the air, limbs outstretched and rotten teeth bared. On instinct, the other vampires skittered away from it, hissing in anger as it landed between them. The distraction gave Mag a moment to recover, bringing up her shield and facing off against the trio, eyes darting back and forth between them. Oku edged to her side, growling and panting at the same time. The wolfhound was growing weary from trying to keep out of the vampires' grasp.

This new vampire was larger than the others, its limbs even thicker than Shoulders' were, but all in proportion. As it stalked towards her, Biter and Shoulders drew back from it, glancing at it in subservience. They had encountered it before, clearly, and they had not enjoyed the experience.

King. Mag named it in her mind without even thinking. And then, behind her battle-trance, the part of her mind that could still feel had the thought, *I am going to punch Albern.*

Thoughts danced in her mind, far-off music in the calm of her trance. Three vampires before her, and one on the roof. That left one still unaccounted for. And where on earth were the rest of the townspeople? Some of them should have arrived by now, at least.

And then the vampires attacked again, and even her background thoughts vanished.

Her one saving grace against the beasts was that the vampires were clearly unused to fighting together. They were loners, never hunting in packs, and so they had no idea how to approach in a coordinated fashion. For one moment Mag's mind flashed with an image of Victon, her old sergeant, drilling the vampires and teaching them to operate as a unit. If not for the trance, she would have laughed out loud.

Yet the same thing that made them unable to work together also kept her from surprising any of them. When she fought one of them, the other two did not wait idly, thinking their fellow would surely bring her down. They waited for their own chance to fight, and as soon as Mag turned on them, they reacted quickly enough that they almost seemed to be expecting it. She knew she could push herself harder, further, than any person she had met, but if she never managed to bring them down, even her trance would wear out eventually.

Then there came a great commotion from down the street. Mag withdrew by one pace and glanced over the heads of her opponents at the source of the disturbance. King and the other vampires, too, glanced behind to see what was happening.

The final vampire came skidding into the street, crouched on all fours, hissing and spitting. Behind it, from side streets and alleys, came pouring a flood of townsfolk—nearly two dozen of them, and all armed with weapons and torches. Immediately they formed up facing the vampire, thrusting their steel and their flames towards it. The vampire shrieked and swiped at them, but the townsfolk stood strong together, giving it no chance to reach them.

All this Mag saw in a flash, and then she tried something new. Throwing her arms wide, spear pointing one way and shield another, she gave a battle-roar that shook the walls of the buildings around her.

The attention of Biter, Shoulders, and King snapped back to her at once. Biter jumped forth, matching Mag's pose and scream of defiance. For one heartbeat they faced each other, roaring in hatred, neither willing to back down.

Mag caught just a glimpse of brown fur as Oku saw his chance and lunged. His teeth sank into Biter's throat. It gave a warbling cry and tried to swipe at Oku, but the hound kicked off its chest and swung, avoiding the blow.

Mag's spear pierced Biter's eye and drove all the way through the back of its head.

The vampire's body went slack in an instant. Blackness spread from around the haft of her spear, rippling through the vampire's body until it looked burned.

But with her strike, she had opened herself to an attack. King seized the opportunity, and Mag barely got her shield up in time. The blow was heavy enough to break her arm if she had taken the brunt of it, but Mag managed to turn it. Still, it flung her through the air, and she slammed hard into the side of the Shades' hideout.

Oku darted to her side, snarling and bristling as he turned to face the vampires again. But the vampires could not have cared less about him. Ignoring both Mag and the hound, they rushed the building's front door and vanished inside. The last vampire, brought to bay by the townsfolk, gave up the fight and joined its fellows, running into the hideout and disappearing from view.

Mag seized Oku's fur and used him to help pull herself up. Oku whined and licked her hand, but Mag was already searching for signs of me. Just then, Yue and I came rushing around the corner of the building. Relief must have been obvious on my face as I ran and embraced her, for Mag gave a cold smile.

"Were you worried about me?" she said tonelessly.

"I should have known better," I said, looking at Biter's corpse. "You got one, then."

"And you? I saw it come for you, but I was distracted."

"I killed it," I told her. "Or rather, *we* did." I motioned towards Yue, who came to us, frowning.

"The others?" she said.

"All inside," said Mag. "Only three left now. It will be harder to fight them in an enclosed space, but I think we can do it."

Yue's eyes widened, and she looked up at the house. "Why risk it? Burn them instead."

Mag looked at me, frowning. "That could work. Unless they escape the flames."

"We will surround the house." Without waiting for another word from us, Yue turned to the townsfolk, who had gathered a few paces away. "Torches! Throw them into the building and onto the roof! Burn it down! And guard it against their escape!"

They obeyed her at once, flinging their torches at the building in great, fiery arcs. Some bounced from the walls or rolled off the roof, but many flew in through open windows or rolled to a stop on the shingles, which began to smoke and smolder. Soon, what looked like a dozen small fires burned through the house. Smoke began to leak out from the windows of both floors.

Yue strode to the front door, which still hung open, and turned to face us. "We three should spread out and guard the easiest exits," she said. "We cannot let them escape. Hopefully the cauldron keeps them busy enough that—"

We had no warning. There was a shattering cry, and then, faster than a blink, pallid, clawed limbs shot out of the doorway. They seized the back of Yue's armor and dragged her into the house before she could even scream.

THIRTY-EIGHT

We did not stop to think. We rushed in after her. It took Oku a moment to brave the flames, but after a few furious barks, he charged in behind us.

By the time we got inside, the vampire had already vanished from the front room. The left and right doors were both open, giving no clue as to where it had gone. Smoke made the room hazy, and the flames licking at the outside of the building lit our way.

"I do not hear her," I said. "Which way do we go?"

"Split up," said Mag, her voice still a monotone. "I can trust you to stay alive if you take Oku with you?"

"We shall see. Oku, tiss."

The wolfhound ran by my side as I darted to the right and through the door, sword in one hand and an arrow in the other. I did a quick search, looking behind the furniture, but found nothing. Suddenly Oku eyed the door to the next room and started bristling. I heard a sharp cry.

That was good enough for me. I ran and threw my shoulder into the door, and it burst open.

There on the floor lay Yue. Above her crouched a vampire—the final, unnamed one. She had one of its arms by the wrist, barely keeping it away from her face. The other hand was clamped over her shoulder, and the claws were digging into the armor. The vampire hissed and drooled, gobs of its saliva dripping onto Yue's face, which twisted in pain from the creature's grip.

Oku snarled and attacked. His teeth penetrated the vampire's leg before the creature could react. It shrieked and released Yue's shoulder, but she did not slacken her grip on its other hand.

I shoved my sword through its back. It reared up, screaming in pain, and I jammed my arrow into the back of its neck. Its scream cut off at once, and its free claws scrabbled at its own throat, trying to pluck out the deadly dart. Yue shoved hard, and the vampire fell sideways off her, wide, black eyes spinning in their sockets. As we watched, it curled up on itself, its skin going black.

"Are you all right?" I said, helping Yue to her feet.

"Shoulder, and the smoke," she said, coughing heavily. "But I will survive. Mag?"

"Looking for you as well. We split up."

"That was idiotic."

I raised my eyebrows. "My apologies, constable. We would have consulted you on the rescue plan, were you not the one we planned to rescue." I pulled up my shirt, covering my mouth against the smoke, which was growing ever thicker. Flames were now licking at the edges of the room's window.

Yue ignored my words. "The vampires were going mad," she said. "They were tearing the place apart, trying to get at the chamber beneath the house. But their claws seemed unable to penetrate the floor. I do not know why. It looks like simple wood."

"Enchanted, likely," I said. "Many mysteries, and little time. Come. Let us find Mag."

We ran towards the back of the room, where another door would lead us to the back of the house. I lifted the latch and pulled on the handle.

THOOM

An explosion launched me backwards. I struck Yue, and we both came down hard on the floor. Oku yelped and scuttled away. I pushed up on my elbows, groaning. The back room roared with flames. They had gathered, waiting for a fool to come and open the door, and I had proven to be just such a fool.

"Mag could have been in there," I grunted, struggling to my feet.

"If she was, she is dead," said Yue, taking my arm. "But I think she is smarter than that. Come. To the other side of the house. If she lives, she will need us."

Together we ran back the way I had come, circling around the house the long way.

THIRTY-NINE

When I ran right, Mag went left. She sped through into the second room with the secret entrance to the underground chamber. Half of it was aflame, and the smoke was thick and black.

And there she found the vampires—Shoulders and King, the only two left.

For a heartbeat, the creatures did not seem to notice her. Both were screaming and tearing at the floor, but their claws did not so much as scratch it. That was strange, but Mag had no time to think about it. The creatures noticed her, and they wheeled around to attack.

She fought only two now, not the three she had faced outside. But the room's small size constrained her. As she dodged and turned, her cloak kept striking the walls and furniture. Pushing the vampires back with a wild swipe, Mag reached up with her shield and undid the clasp. The cloak fell to the floor. That was better, but not enough to give her the advantage. Her spear strikes had to be somewhat restrained, or she risked striking the walls and knocking herself off balance.

Mag switched her strategy, pressing in closer and using the spear more as a staff. It brought her within reach of the vampires' claws, and she had to block them both with the spear haft and the shield. But with a clever twist, she managed a solid kick into Shoulders' chest.

Shoulders flew away, tumbling over the back of a chair that had caught on fire. The flames erupted across the vampire's skin almost instantly, and it shrieked and tried to bat at them even as its back slammed into the tapestry on the wall.

The vampire was so busy with the flames, it did not see Mag launch herself through the air. Her spear impaled it through the chest and sank deep into the wall behind. The wood and flames spread through Shoulders together, and it died with black blood dribbling from its jaws.

Too late, Mag realized that she had punched a hole straight through the door that led to the underground chamber. She turned, wrenching her spear from the wall and the corpse. King stood there in the center of the room, its head back, sniffing at the air.

It turned on her, its black eyes narrowing to slits.

Mag tried to spear it as it flew through the air towards her, but it caught the spear in one hand and threw her aside with the other. Its claws sank into the wooden wall, and it ripped the door from its hinges, throwing it into the flames on the other side of the room. With a rending screech, it vanished into the shadows of the stairwell.

Yue and I burst into the room just as Mag was getting to her feet. Yue had one arm over my shoulders, and her other hand held the wound near her neck. Oku whined as he ran to Mag and licked her hand.

"One left," said Mag. "It got in."

She wasted no more words, but ran down the stairwell after the thing. Oku gave a bark and ran after her.

"Leave it, Mag!" I cried. "Let the flames finish it!"

"A little late for that," growled Yue.

"Dark take her," I mumbled. "I will get you to the front and then get her out of the cavern."

"No time," said Yue. "I am coming. You both came in here for me." She pushed off of me and drew her short sword in one hand, hefting her cudgel in the other.

"We have no time to argue, but let us pretend I did," I told her. "Come, if you cannot be stopped."

Just inside the doorway was a torch on the wall. I took it and lit it from the flames at the edge of the room before running down the stairs, Yue just behind me. We reached the bottom to see Mag and Oku locked in combat with King. But its proximity to the magestone-infused blood seemed to have given the creature a new surge of strength. Even as I tried to work out how to enter the fight, it sent Oku flying with a kick and swiped at Mag so savagely that she was forced several steps back.

Before any of us could react, the vampire rushed to the cauldron and stooped over the side, plunging its face into the blood.

We all watched, struck dumb and paralyzed with horror, as King threw its head back and roared. The roar turned deep, guttural, until I could feel it shaking and vibrating within my chest. The vampire's pallid skin began to darken, a deep crimson spreading through it as long-dry veins refilled. The red suffused all of its body from top to bottom, and the skin rippled as bones shifted and rearranged themselves beneath. Then the creature shrieked, and my heart leaped, for it sounded like a cry of pain. But then ridges of bone sprang out through the skin, running down its back and arms, with huge spikes protruding from the elbows. All the while, the vampire's body continued to grow, until it stood now at least three heads taller than me, even hunched over as it was.

Yue and I were frozen in horror, but Mag had kept her wits about her. As the transformation neared completion, Mag brought back her arm and heaved her spear straight into King's now-massive back.

King whirled and held up a hand. It did not catch the spear. It let the weapon pass straight through its flesh. The spear shuddered to a stop halfway through the claw, its wood coming to rest deep in the vampire's flesh.

The vampire scowled down at the wound. Then it dragged the spear the rest of the way through and flung it, contemptuously, at Mag's feet.

For a heartbeat we hesitated, waiting for the wood to poison the vampire, to send it cowering to its knees.

Nothing happened, except that the hole in the vampire's hand began to seal itself shut.

"Dark take it," muttered Mag. She stooped to pick up her spear, ignoring the black blood that coated its length.

"This was the aim of the ritual," I said. "The documents spoke of strengthening the vampires somehow."

"How do we kill it?" said Yue. "I thought wood was poison to these things."

"It used to be," said Mag. "Mayhap fire will still do the trick."

"We could retreat," said Yue. "The building is burning. This thing will burn with it."

I looked at King. It had stooped over the cauldron again to take another deep draught. "This chamber will not burn. The floorboards are enchanted. And even if it begins to, I think the creature will burst out before it perishes."

As if King could understand my words, its head snapped up towards the ceiling for a moment. Slowly it turned its gaze upon us. Black eyes shone with hate.

"I think it heard you," Yue pointed out mildly.

"I have my torch," I muttered. "If I can get an opening, I can throw it at the vampire, and we will hope it catches."

"Yue should get one, too, and quickly," said Mag. King had begun to stalk closer.

Yue pulled a torch from the wall and lit it with the flames of mine. "Spread out," I said.

I edged right, Yue left, and Mag stood in the middle with Oku. King, seeing us split up, stopped moving, crouched low, and swiveled its head back and forth to keep an eye on all of us.

"Do it as soon as you can," said Mag suddenly, and then she threw herself at the vampire. Oku was only a half-pace behind.

They danced around each other in the center of the room. But Mag could no longer hold her own against the thing. Whereas before she had held against the vampires' strength and somewhat outmatched them in speed, now she was like a man fighting a tiger. She and King traded blows twice in the blink of an eye, but then the vampire's claws slammed into Mag's shield, and she fell on her back. Instantly she rolled, coming up on her feet again, but the vampire was just behind her. This time its claws raked her scale shirt, and she was thrown away again.

Yue and I charged, torches high. But the vampire turned on us and swiped. Yue dropped to the ground to avoid it, but I was too slow. I felt its putrid claws bite into the flesh of my arm, and I cried out with pain.

Before it could follow up, Mag was there again, her spear thrusting, but each time the thing dodged or turned aside her blows with claws as long as my hands. That gave me the time I needed to scramble away from the fight, now cradling my shoulder. I backed away from the spinning, screeching creature and caught Yue's eye from across the room.

"I will try to give you another opening," I called out to her.

"Never mind that," she said. "We have to distract it."

And then she ran for the cauldron.

I cried out a warning before I could stop myself. The vampire heard, drove Mag off with a wild swipe, and turned just in time to see Yue seize the edge of the cauldron. She heaved, trying to upend it.

The vampire roared and launched itself at her. Yue spun on the spot, thrusting her torch up straight into its face. The creature recoiled, but only for a moment. Then it seized the end of the torch in one clawed hand. It shrieked, its black eyes going wide. But it tightened its grip, digging its claws into its own flesh as it completely enveloped the flames with its hand. Its whole body shuddered, spiny ridges jumping back and forth like mountains in an earthquake.

The flames guttered out. The vampire hissed straight into Yue's face, pained, but very much alive.

"Ah," said Yue.

The vampire scooped her up, its clawed fingers wrapping all the way around her torso, and flung her bodily across the room.

CRACK

She struck the wall, slid to the floor, and was still.

"Yue!" I cried. I tried to dart around King, to run to her, but it spun at the sound of my voice. One limb lashed out. I avoided the claws, but the palm struck me like a bear's paw. I, too, flew into the wall, and my head struck it so hard I nearly blacked out straight away.

"Albern!" cried Mag. "The blood!"

I tried to look at her, tried to focus in a world that was suddenly swimming and hazy. She had reached the cauldron, just as Yue had. But Yue's distraction, and mine, had given her the time she needed.

She heaved. It did not look as if she should have been able to move the giant iron bowl. But Mag knew leverage—knew how to get more out of the human body than anyone had a right to expect.

The cauldron upended. The blood flooded over the stone floor, splashing all across it, crashing against the vampire's legs like the ocean against rocks, soaking its lower body in black liquid.

The vampire screamed in livid fury. But it was too focused on the blood to try and claim vengeance against Mag. It fell to its knees, trying desperately to lap up the blood on the ground, pressing its nose and tongue into the stones.

"The blood!" cried Mag again. "With your torch, you idiot!"

Her voice dragged my attention back from King. I frowned at her. The blood? Yue had already tried that. She might be dead. My torch?

I looked down. I still held my torch in my hand, where it burned brightly. When the vampire had struck me, I had dropped my sword, but somehow I had held onto my stupid torch.

Stupid torch. Why should I care about it. The vampire had put Yue's flame out. Fire had caused pain, yes, but it had not killed the thing.

Then Mag was there, kneeling over me, snatching the torch out of my hand. "Honestly, I have to do everything," she said mildly.

And then she flung the torch into the blood that soaked the floor.

It caught at once, like lamp oil. Black flames rippled out across the stones, consuming all the blood in a flash. It rushed up King's arms and legs, its torso, all covered in the black liquid. The creature's screams were terrible. It writhed, but that only sent it splashing through more blood, through more flame. The darkfire consumed it, its body bubbling and popping, sick, hot, wet spurts of fat and gristle sizzling across the room, splashing in the flaming blood, sending it flying up in little sparks.

"Come on," said Mag. She hauled me to my feet and helped me across the room, careful to give the flames a wide berth. We found Yue collapsed at the bottom of the opposite wall.

"Is she alive?" I said.

"We have to hope so," said Mag. "But I cannot carry you anymore, for I will need your help with her."

I took my arm from Mag's shoulders, and between the two of us we hauled Yue up. She did not stir or groan, but I did not have the time to check for breath or a heartbeat. We merely held her between us, her arms across our shoulders, the way we had hauled so many wounded fellows from battlefields in our youth.

The stairs were difficult to navigate, carrying Yue as we were. When we reached the top, we saw that we had almost been too late. The whole house was consumed in flames, so thick that we almost could not push through them to reach the street again. But we managed it, bursting out through the flames to the shock of the many frightened onlookers, most of whom had to have assumed we were dead already. Oku gave great leaps as he bounded around us, baying with joy and terror.

"Back!" I said. "Someone get me water!"

We laid Yue down between us, and I fumbled with the straps of her armor. Ashta appeared, helping me. We got Yue's armor off, and I pressed my head to her chest, listening desperately, trying to feel the rise and fall of her breath.

And then at last . . .

Pa-pump. Pa-pump.

"Get. Off me," groaned Yue.

I fell back on my rear, closing my eyes and heaving a deep sigh of relief. "Thank the sky."

"Here, Sergeant," said Ashta, relief nearly causing her to drop the waterskin. "Drink this."

"Lift her head," said Mag wryly, "or she will drown instead of burning alive."

She had fetched her singed cloak from the house on our way out, and now she fashioned it into a pillow for Yue. The constable drank deep of Ashta's water, until finally she pushed it away, sputtering and coughing.

"Are you all right?" I asked her.

"I am alive," she said. "That is more than I think I should expect. The vampire?"

"We killed it," I told her. "Something we could not have done without you."

"I am not proud to have been mere bait, but I suppose I am the only one who had the courage for it," said Yue.

"Certainly, it is something I have never volunteered for," I told her.

Yue snorted. "Of course not." Then her countenance grew stern, and she held my gaze. "In all earnestness, thank you for your help. And, I suppose, for saving my life."

"Oh, constable," I said, grinning at her. "You cannot think we did that for you. I have it on the very best authority that corpses are simply a nightmare to take care of. The paperwork alone."

Her brows drew together. "I could still arrest you. Both of you."

I patted her shoulder gently. "You are welcome to try."

Some of the townsfolk who had skill at healing had been summoned, and they came forwards to care for her now. I stood and went to Mag's side. Oku was with her, but she paid him no attention. She had turned from us, and now she stood surveying the Shades' hideout as it burned. Some of the townsfolk had set up a watering line, passing buckets from hand to hand and dousing the nearby buildings to ensure they did not catch alight. But the flames seemed to be self-contained, and there was no wind. The night's danger looked to be well and truly over.

"The blood," I said. Mag did not look at me, so I pressed on. "How did you know about the blood?"

"We all should have known," she said lightly, free from the battle-trance. "From the moment we read their notes. The process infused the blood with magestone essence, remember? I have never seen a substance that catches fire more easily than magestone."

I shook my head. "It was a guess. You risked all our lives on that strategy."

"It was the only idea we had," said Mag. Then at last she turned to me, and a wide grin was plastered across her face. "And what are you complaining for? It worked."

I laughed at that. "I cannot argue with you there."

Wordlessly we embraced, clutching each other tight in the light and warmth of the flames. And in that moment, for one brief instance, I felt as though Mag—the old Mag, the one I had known since we were both young—held me in her arms, and that she would never leave my side again.

FORTY

THE FIRE WAS PUT OUT EVENTUALLY, BUT LONG AFTER WE HAD ALREADY gone to bed. We tried to stay up and help the townsfolk, but they insisted we return to our inn and rest. Ashta, who Yue had deputized until she had recovered, was particularly insistent. When we finally returned to the inn, Dryleaf was nowhere to be seen. We were too tired to search for him that night, and went straight to bed.

We woke the next morning well past dawn. In fact, when I looked out the tiny window of our room, it looked as if even noon had passed us by. It is possible there were some parts of my body that did not hurt, but I could not have told you what they were. Every motion made me groan like an old man.

Mag, sky bless her, seemed fine. She moved lightly on her feet, and there was no sign of ache or pain within her. I saw no bruises on her skin, and of course, as you can imagine, there were no cuts or scrapes, either. I shook my head at it more than once, as we readied ourselves to emerge from our room. Even vampires, inhumanly strong beasts though they were, had been unable to injure Mag in any lasting way. She had been part of my life for more years now than she had not. Yet not even age, it seemed, had proven able to catch her in its inevitable grasp.

When we made our way at last to the common room, we found Dryleaf sitting by the fire, in the very same place he had been when first we met him. I crossed the room to speak with him while Mag went to settle our account with the innkeeper. Dryleaf seemed to recognize the gait of my footsteps, for he tilted his head up eagerly, his milky eyes staring just over my left shoulder.

"I hear you have become heroes," he said.

"Some seem to think so, yes," I told him. "But we were only two among many who fought bravely last night."

"Yes," said Dryleaf, his bushy brows dancing as he nodded. "Yue suffered some injury, I hear, but it sounds as though she will make a full and speedy recovery."

"That is good," I said. "She stood bravely against the monsters."

Dryleaf's shoulders rose and fell, as though with a sigh, but he made no sound. "And I suppose you have seen to your purpose here in Lan Shui, then. Will you be leaving town?"

"We will," I said. "We have business elsewhere."

"Most people do, when they come to visit Lan Shui," he said. "Yet a place may be a way-stop, and still people make for it when occasion arises."

"I thought I would ask—if you do not mind—would you accompany us this morning?" I said. "We want to visit Yue before we go, and I know you are fond of her. And I would appreciate your company."

Dryleaf got up so fast, I was afraid he would hurt himself. "It would be my great pleasure," he said. "And for my part, I give my word to keep your pace and not impose a moment's delay. Now let us go and meet with Mag, for if my ears do not deceive me, I think she is having some sort of trouble with the innkeeper."

I took Dryleaf's arm and led him towards Mag. The old man had been correct. Mag was engaged in a heated argument with the innkeeper as we came up, though the innkeeper himself only met her angry words with a beatific smile, which he turned on me as I drew up to the bar.

Mag whirled on the two of us. "Ah, good," she said. "Dryleaf. Help me convince this idiot that he does not know how to run a business."

"Before I try, I would rather hear the details of the situation," said Dryleaf diplomatically.

"Mag, what under the sky is going on?" I said.

"This man," said Mag, thrusting a finger at the innkeeper's face—the innkeeper's vacant smile widened—"will not take my money."

"No, I will not," agreed the innkeeper, his massive mustache jumping as he sniffed.

"We stayed here for *days,* you ox!" cried Mag. "Take our money!"

Instead of answering, the innkeeper reached into a purse at his belt, produced two pennies, and laid them on the pile of coins that lay on the bar in front of him. The pile seemed somewhat larger than it should have been, considering the time we had spent in Lan Shui.

"And he *will not* stop doing that!" said Mag, sounding quite ready to throttle the man.

"No, I will not," said the innkeeper, sounding absolutely delighted.

"Listen, friend," I said. "No one appreciates your generosity more than we do. But you cannot survive on good deeds and well wishes alone. Take some of our coin."

The innkeeper answered only with another two pennies laid on the pile.

"Stop telling him to take money," growled Mag, who seemed to wish to ignore the fact that she had just done the same thing. "It only makes him give us more."

"I think you should leave," said Dryleaf. "It seems an untenable situation for the two of you, unless you wish to rob the poor man blind."

The innkeeper nodded gaily, as though he had never heard truer words.

"But we *are* robbing him blind," said Mag. "I used to own an inn myself, you know. And I am—well, in all honesty, I am insulted on his behalf."

To my surprise, Dryleaf put his hands on his hips and scowled in Mag's direction. "If you do not wish for people to give you gifts, to say nothing of praise, then I would cease your frankly ridiculous habit of running around and saving them from danger. Many people in the nine kingdoms see this as the only natural reaction to such a thing."

"I did not come here to save anyone," grumbled Mag, avoiding looking at either Dryleaf or the innkeeper. "And so be it, if they are too foolish to take my money—*put them back.*" She snatched the pile of silver away from the innkeeper, who had been reaching for another pair of pennies from his purse.

We beat a hasty retreat from the inn and out into the street, Mag scowling, Dryleaf chuckling mightily, and me trying to restrain myself from joining him. Mag was still trying to cram the coins into her purse several streets later—the innkeeper had given her quite a lot of them. But we both stopped short as we saw Liu standing there before us.

The boy was not alone. Next to him was the man who had taken him in when we had brought him back to Lan Shui. I had never learned his name. But beside them both sat Oku. The dog grinned up at us, tongue lolling from its mouth as it panted in the heat of the day.

"Liu," said Mag, crouching at once to speak with him at eye-level. "How are you?"

"I am well," he said. "You killed the monsters?"

"We helped," I told him. "Many in the town fought them together."

"I am glad," said Liu. "I am glad they are dead."

Mag looked a little sad at that. But she reached out and ruffled his hair. "We have to be going now, but we know we leave Lan Shui under your protection. You will watch out for all these people for us, will you not? Many of them are not very smart. They will need you."

Liu smiled at that. "Of course. I am going to be a constable one day."

"I think you will be a great one."

"I think Oku should go with you," said Liu.

I took a step forwards. "Liu, that is very kind of you," I said. "But he is your hound. This is his home."

"His home was in the mountains," said Liu. "So was mine. But I think he needs to go and protect other people's homes now. That is what you are going to do."

"Let him stay and protect you," I said.

Liu's eyes began to well with tears, and his cheeks flushed. "I am safe now. You killed the monsters. But there may be other monsters out there. I want to know that you are safe, too."

Mag had moved behind the boy, and she was giving me a scowl he could not see. And in my mind, that settled the matter. I gave Liu a warm smile.

"Then it would be our pleasure to take him along with us."

Mag barely stifled a groan. But she plastered a smile on her face as Liu turned and hugged her legs. Then the boy went to Oku and clutched at his dark brown fur.

"Take care of them," he said. "Mayhap I will see you when we are both older."

"We will make sure to come and visit," I said. "Thank you, Liu."

"Fare well," said Mag. She gave the boy another tight hug and then headed north. I followed her, Dryleaf on my arm. Oku took two tentative steps after us, but then he stopped and looked back at Liu.

"Kip, boy," said Liu. "Go with them."

Oku looked at us, and his mouth snapped shut. He looked back at Liu and whined.

"Oku, tiss," I said.

The hound met my gaze. He ran back to Liu and licked his face twice. Liu laughed and gave the dog another hug. Then Oku ran after me, trotting at my heels. Just before we turned the corner out of sight, he gave one last glance back at Liu. Then the boy was gone.

I had forgotten the way to the constables' station, so we followed Dryleaf's directions to find it. A sharp knock produced Constable Ashta in short order, and she ushered us in to visit Yue. The sergeant had been laid upon a wide, soft bed in the back room of the station, where she was propped up on many pillows. She appeared to have been dozing when we arrived, but her eyes snapped open as we entered. She shifted herself so as to appear more upright. As we came to her bedside, she surveyed us with stern, uncompromising eyes.

"You lot are off, then?" she said brusquely.

"We are," said Mag. "But we wanted to ensure you were well taken care of."

"Of course I am," said Yue. "And entirely unsurprised to see you scuttling off after having made so much trouble."

I chuckled. "Yes, but at least we leave you with our apologies. That must be worth something."

"Hardly," said Yue. "But actually, there is one matter that must be tended to before you sally off. By the King's law, there is a bounty on vampires. Any killed and turned in to the law are worth five gold weights each. You have killed seven while you have been here. I never learned my numbers very well, so let us call it forty weights."

Mag gave a loud, frustrated groan and turned to me. "Darkness take all these people. Do they not realize that coins are worth *money?* Why are they so eager to be rid of them?" But then her eyes lit up with an idea, and she whirled back to Yue. "No! Keep the coins. Use them in our name, to support those who lost homes and loved ones to the vampires' attack. And start with that *absolute* fool of an innkeeper whose custom we took. Will you do that for us?"

"Lan Shui has more than enough helping hands to take care of those who are bereaved," said Yue. "And I am afraid the King's law is quite clear about the terms of the bounty."

"Sky above, you—I will not—this—" Mag ended in a sputter, thrusting a finger at Yue. "I am not taking your gold. So unless you mean to get out of that bed this instant and *pursue* me out of town to hide a coin purse in my saddlebags, I am afraid you must be disappointed. Albern, I am taking my leave. Say your farewells, and then let us ride on from this haven of woodenheads." She stalked out of the room, only pausing for a moment at the door to turn and give Yue a final "I am glad you will recover" before vanishing.

I stepped up beside Yue with a smile. As I did, Ashta passed Mag on the way in. She stared after Mag, who had stormed off in a huff, and shook her head as the door slammed shut behind her.

"You shoved the purse in her saddlebag?" said Yue.

"I did, Sergeant," said Ashta. "And judging by the look on her face, I am glad she did not see it."

"Despite her admonishment," I said to Yue, "Mag herself has never been good at holding on to coin. I hope you will forgive her rash words."

"If she follows the King's law, I will," said Yue, arching an eyebrow.

"Thank you, constable. Though you know, you helped us kill two of the beasts."

"Yet constables are exempt from the bounty," said Yue.

"That seems unjust," I said.

"I do not write the laws," she said. "I only enforce them."

I placed a hand on her shoulder, squeezing her through the thick bandages she had there. "And I think you do excellently at it. Fare well, constable. I am sorry to have disturbed the peace of your people."

"Things are better now than they were when you arrived, I suppose," said Yue, meeting my gaze. "If you ever draw near to Lan Shui again, I would not mind if you visited us. You did not get to see many of the town's more attractive features. This bed, for example, is quite comfortable when it is not holding a convalescent."

I do not mind telling you that my cheeks went absolutely wine-dark with color. From his place by the door, Dryleaf gave a conspicuous cough, and Ashta became suddenly very interested in something out the window.

"I . . . I am sure it is," I said finally. "Mayhap I will take you up on your offer, if ever I return this way."

"You would be fortunate to," said Yue with a snort. Then her eyes slid past me to Dryleaf. "Still your giggling, old man. I have not forgotten the help you gave to these people when they were still strangers. I have my eye on you."

"And it is only that fact that lets me feel safe when I lay my head down at night," said Dryleaf, bowing. "I am glad you are well, Yue."

"Of course you are," said Yue. "Well, enough of both of you. I have been ordered to rest well in order to speed my recovery, and I always listen to my healer."

"That is a lie," whispered Dryleaf, as we beat our hasty retreat. "She is one of the most obstinate patients in the nine lands. The healers have told me so. I think she was as stunned by her words to you as you were, and wanted an excuse to kick us out."

We returned to the inn, where we began to ready our horses for travel. Foolhoof looked at me as suspiciously as ever, while Mist, of course, easily took the blanket, bit, and bridle as Mag put them on. Dryleaf sat on a little wooden stool near the front of the stable, a gentle smile plastered on his face. It looked forced.

"Mag," I said quietly, stepping close to her for a moment. "Do you think the innkeeper has any spare horses for sale?"

"Any innkeeper worth their salt does, and he is too much of a fool to be worth that much," said Mag irritably. But she glanced around the stable. "No, in truth, I think he does. There are too many horses here for the number of guests I have seen in the common room, at least. Why do you ask?"

I glanced over my shoulder at Dryleaf, sitting by the stable's front door, and then met Mag's gaze. I raised my eyebrows. She pursed her lips and looked at the old man, considering. At last she looked back at me and nodded.

I left my horse for a moment and went to the old man, sitting beside him on the bench at the front of the stable. "Dryleaf," I said. "I have been thinking much about what you said."

"Hm?" said Dryleaf, shaking himself as though he had been pulled from deep thought. "I have said many things."

"I mean about how you came to be in Lan Shui."

Dryleaf sighed. "Oh? Have you?"

"I have," I said. "And I thought—though you may have no interest in such a scheme—I thought you *could* come with us, if you so desired. We have no plans to visit the Birchwood Forest. But we might go there one day."

For the second time that day, Dryleaf moved with the shocking speed of a much younger man. He leaped to his feet, hands trembling, and I saw tears well up in his cloudy eyes.

"I . . . if you took me with you, I would—I swear I would be no burden, and I would—"

"Sky above, man, of course I know that," I said. "You have forgotten more leagues of travel than I have ever ridden. And for my part, I would be happy to have your wisdom at our side, and I swear we would keep you safe. And something tells me we may have tasks ahead of us for which we will require your help."

"Anything," said Dryleaf. "If my old bones can do it, consider it done."

"Very well. I have your first task for you." I pulled out my purse. "Go and see the innkeeper, and purchase yourself a horse. I think he would refuse to take any of our coin, but I think he might take yours."

Dryleaf let out a laugh that almost turned into a sob, shaking his head. "Even your first task for me is a gift. I am in your debt, Albern of the family Telfer, and I will not forget it."

"You will not have time to," I assured him. "Before long, the hardness of the road and the open fields upon which we make our beds will have reminded you of why you abandoned them for comfort and safety. But while you are seized with this madness, I will take advantage of it."

"How very shrewd of you," said Dryleaf. "But now excuse me—I must purchase myself a horse."

The business was done before we had finished saddling our mounts, and soon the three of us rode out of the stable, Oku trotting along beside our horses. As we passed through the streets, townsfolk waved and wished us well—especially Mag. She rode high in her saddle, her back straight. Her eyes were fixed on the road ahead, the way they had been when we rode into Lan Shui. But now she turned her sight upon the people who called out to her, and smiled at them, and wished them well.

And I was proud to ride by her side, as we made north for Calentin.

For home.

FORTY-ONE

"A good tale," said Sun, as Albern's voice trailed away to nothing. "A good tale, and well told."

Albern did not answer her for a moment. He stared at the fire between them, the flames dancing in his eyes, his arm across the top of his knee, and his fingers hanging idly before his face. For a moment he resembled nothing so much as a statue, a warding figure placed in the woods to guard them from death and darkness, and to provide comfort to any traveler who came his way—comfort, but no help.

Finally he stirred and looked at Sun across the fire. He stared at her for a moment, as though he were hearing her words again in his mind, and then he smiled. "I recognize the words of praise that were customary in your family's court, and I thank you for them."

"Now tell me about your arm."

Albern laughed. "No. Not yet. That is the *end* of the story—or the only ending most people care about. But endings are useless if you do not know where things began. The journey, the whole of it, is what a story is all about. In this small tale I have just told you, imagine how much drier it would have been if I had just told you about Lan Shui and fighting the vampires, without telling you about Northwood first. Imagine how little you would have cared about Northwood if you had not known about Sten."

It was a fair enough point. But the spell of the old man's tale was wearing off now, and it left her feeling cold and alone in the woods, despite the fire and Albern's presence. "Well then, I suppose we had better—"

"Quiet," rasped Albern, so suddenly that Sun obeyed without question.

The old man rose, and from his belt he drew a sword—old, battered, but well sharpened and polished. Sun got to her feet as well, though she did not know why. Without thinking, she drew an arrow and fitted it to the string of Albern's bow, peering out into the night beside him. She had not heard whatever had alerted him, but now she could feel it. The woods were too quiet, and there was a presence. Something was out there, watching them.

"What is it?" she whispered. "A wolf?"

"Not a wolf," said Albern.

And then a creature of nightmares bounded into the firelight. Man-sized and man-shaped, but horribly twisted and bent. It landed on all fours, and there it crouched, hissing at them. Pallid, white skin. Hands that ended in claws as long as Sun's fingers, and a mouth full of pointed teeth.

Sun might have had difficulty identifying it, if she had not heard it mentioned so often already that night.

Vampire, her mind screamed.

And then it roared as it attacked.

First it leaped for Sun, but Albern gave a great cry and jumped in between them. His wild, swinging sword drove the creature back a pace or two, and Albern sidestepped to draw it farther from the fire.

Sun's whole body had gone rigid, but then she realized what Albern was doing. He was stepping aside so that she would have a clear shot. With that thought, her body seemed to move of its own accord. The bow came up, she drew, and she sighted down the arrow.

Albern gave a cry and swiped at the vampire. It lunged to the side, arms wide. And Sun loosed.

With everything Albern had told her that night, she fully expected the vampire to dodge her shot. But to her surprise, it pierced the vampire straight through the wrist. The creature screamed—a terrible, ear-shattering noise that threatened to deafen her, especially in the deep silence of the woods.

The vampire wrenched the arrow out of its limb. The edges of the wound began to turn black. It whirled on her, hissing, but Albern attacked, sword flashing in the firelight.

With a shriek, the vampire leaped off into the woods and the darkness.

The clearing settled again to silence. And as it did, Sun realized that *now* she was shaking, *now* she was quivering and breathing so hard that she did not think she would be able to stand for more than a few heartbeats. The bow clattered from her hand to the ground, and suddenly she was sitting, though she had made no move to lower herself. Her tailbone hurt, but it was a dull, distant sort of pain.

"What . . . sky above, what was that?" she gasped, though she was not truly speaking to anyone.

"Too bad, is what it was," said Albern. "I had hoped we could kill the thing, but it got away. Ah, well. They tend to do that, as I have told you already tonight. And the wound will fester—if it does not die from the infection, it will at least be easier to finish off."

"That was a vampire!"

"Of course it was."

Sun looked at him, eyes wide. "You *knew?* You *knew* that creature was coming?"

"Why, yes," said Albern. "That is why we came out here. And was I not right? You are a warrior true. I can tell. I can always tell. Even back then, I could tell, and I am better at it now."

"But I—but you met me in a tavern by chance!" said Sun, rising shakily to her feet. "What would you have done if I had not come? You could not have faced that thing alone!"

Albern smiled at her, gently and with a little sadness in his eyes. "We met in the tavern, but not by chance. This is the thirteenth town you have visited on your family's trip, Sun. The sixth one was the first time you slipped away from the caravan. You have done it again in every town since. You have been looking for something."

"You . . . you were following me?"

"Sky, no," said Albern. "But you have been seen, and many remarked on it as something strange. The rumor of you reached my ears, and I determined to find you tonight. The constable? He helped me. When Tunsha signaled to the tavern with his ring, he was also telling the constable that all was well and his job was done."

"Then you tricked me," said Sun. "You led me along on a scheme."

"I did," said Albern. "I think you needed me to. But it is done now. And if I was wrong, then you can go. You can return to your family, whom you despise, and go along with their plots, which you disdain."

Sun was standing again. She had no more memory of rising than she had had of sitting down. "Or?"

Albern cocked an eyebrow. "Or what?"

"You make it sound as though I have another choice. I could go home. Or . . . ?"

"Or you could come with me, and I could tell you another story."

She looked away from him. "Where are you going?"

"Lan Shui."

"The town where—"

Albern nodded. "The town from the tale, yes."

"What are you doing there?"

"I am visiting a friend," said Albern. "And then I am taking care of some business. It is somewhat akin to our business tonight, but until I have your answer, I do not think I will tell you any more."

"How do you mean to fight another monster like that one if I do *not* come with you?" said Sun.

Albern smiled at her again. "You were here, in the right place at the right time, tonight. But if you had not come, someone else would have. And if no one shows up, I can hunt someone down. But tonight it was you, and I am glad. You may believe whatever you wish, Sun, but I told you. I no longer believe in chance as I did when I was your age."

"I . . . I still do not understand," said Sun.

"What?" said Albern, spreading his arm wide. "Ask me anything you wish, and I shall do my best to explain."

A thousand questions whirled in her mind, but none of them seemed like the right one. She tossed them aside one by one, until at last she had the question she truly wanted to ask—the only one, really, she *could* ask.

"Should we go after it?" she said, looking Albern in the eye. "If it escapes, we may regret it."

"Well, we may," said Albern, suddenly cagey. "But we may regret it even more deeply if we pursue it in the woods by moonslight. We do not have a warrior like Mag at our side, and I have my doubts about battling the beast twice in one night."

"Oh, but once was fine," said Sun, shaking her head.

"For a young one like that, yes," said Albern. When she gave him a look, he nodded. "Yes, very young. I would not have brought you out here to fight a creature like the ones Mag and I faced. They were old, very old, nearly as old as the bones of the hills whence they came. I doubt the one we saw tonight is much older than I am."

"That is quite old," said Sun.

Albern's mouth twisted. "Always ready with a barb. I admire that. In any case, you said you wanted to do good things more than you wanted accolades. Well, you have done a very good thing tonight, though I doubt anyone shall ever hear of it. Return to your family if you wish."

So saying, he strode to her and took his bow from the ground. In an instant, he had unstrung it and stowed the string in a pouch at his belt, and then he set off through the trees towards the place where he had left his horse. Sun, for the second time that night, found herself staring after the old bowyer, dumbstruck. Just before he vanished from sight, she ran after him.

"Wait!" she cried. "What if I *do* want to come with you?"

Albern stopped and looked back at her, squinting in the moonslight. "You seemed quite angry, and so I gave the cause up for lost."

"I *am* quite angry."

He shrugged. "Well, then. You can find your way back to town, can you not? You know where the road is—just there. I do not think you will meet any more dangers in the forest tonight, but I could give you my sword, if you wish. Morled should still be there, if you hurry, and I do not doubt that she would be glad to see you."

Sun looked off through the trees. There, far in the distance, she could just make out the lights of the town: a soft, fiery glow over the top of a hill, that poured through the trees in little shafts.

It had been a long time. Half the night. Her retainers would be nearly frantic, and Mother and Father would have been alerted that she was missing by this point.

But she could still go to them. She could go on through the rest of their tour of Dorsea, and then return home to Dulmun. She could carry on with only the memory of this one little adventure.

She looked at Albern instead.

"I want to come with you."

With one hand on his saddle, Albern regarded her. "Are you certain?"

"Yes."

"Why?"

Sun lifted her chin. "Is my company unwelcome?"

"You will have a hard time turning back if you go on with me tonight," said Albern. "So I would like you to be very sure of your choice before you make it."

"I do not hate my family," she said. "Yet for a long time, I have not been able to say that I love them, either, and I think their feelings are the same towards me. In my kingdom, parents adopt children often, and those children are treated just the same as if the parents had bedded to make them. You need not share your family's blood to love them—yet neither must you love them simply because you share blood. I am not desperate to escape them, and I would not die if I remained. Yet I need a better purpose in my life than that. I need something more to pull me through each day than the thought that things could be worse."

She took another step towards Albern, and now they were eye-to-eye. "You are a trickster. I do not like that. I do not like being led along a path I cannot see beneath my feet. But tonight, you and I did a good thing. I want to come with you, if you can promise that we will do more good in the nine kingdoms. I want to come with you, if you promise not to trick me into doing the right thing, but trust me to make the right decision."

Albern gave her a long, careful look before answering. "I can promise both those things," he said quietly. "One last time. Are you sure?"

"I am sure," said Sun, and she realized it was true. She did not want to go home. The whole time she had been in this strange, foreign kingdom, she had been looking for some escape—some way to leave, and never have to return. Now that she had found such a chance, she would not turn her back on it.

"I am sure," she said again. "The beginning of the story has been good. I want to hear the rest of it."

Albern smiled his widest grin yet. "And I would be happy to tell it to you. Come on, then. Let us get moving. The road is long, and it always grows darker before revealing at last the sun."

"As you say," said Sun. "But as we go, please, carry on."

Slowly, Albern nodded. "Until the tale's true end."

EPILOGUE

You did not think I forgot about Kaita, did you?

She was there, in Lan Shui, observing the three of us as we rode forth on horseback, Oku trotting beside us.

Kaita still mourned the deaths of Dellek and the other Shades. And for the sake of petty revenge, she wished the vampires had claimed more lives before Mag and I had destroyed them. But she had realized that we would never ride north for Calentin until the threat to Lan Shui had been ended, and so she had let it happen without interfering. And now, things were mostly going according to her plan again.

All except the old man. "Dryleaf," he called himself. Kaita had not predicted him, and she feared there might be more to him than there appeared. So she had taken the form of a few of the folk of Lan Shui, and she had gone poking about, trying to see if the old man had some hidden agenda that had caused him to take up with us.

She had discovered nothing. It seemed he had joined up with us by sheer luck (if you believe in luck). Ever since he had arrived in Lan Shui, he had taken no interest whatsoever in the great events of Underrealm. He was a fixture of the town, an elder who gave advice when he could and sang songs when he could not.

Indeed, the only thing Kaita had managed to learn was that he had not always been known as Dryleaf. Long ago, when he first came to Lan Shui, he had gone by another name, though the old one sounded just as nonsensical to Kaita.

After all, who ever heard of an old peddler named Bracken?

Stone Heart

BEING BOOK TWO
OF THE FIRST VOLUME

OF THE
TALES OF THE WANDERER

ONE

A warm sun rose, its crisp rays bathing Sun's face, and with it came an unpleasant truth.

It is the day after I left my family.

It was hard to believe that only a scant few hours ago, she had fought a vampire. It was even harder to believe that she had won. Since then, she had had a few hours' sleep before Albern had woken her to take the second watch. But despite having slept and woken already, she could not shake the thought that this had to be a dream. She was sure that soon she would wake again, the way she sometimes did in dreams, rising through layers of illusion before finally emerging into the waking world. Any moment now, she would find herself in the luxurious tent her parents' servants had built for her, and hear Mother commanding her to get ready for another day's ride with the caravan.

Yet here she remained, sitting against a tree just inside the edge of an unknown forest in western Dorsea. The dew beneath her felt real enough, as did the rough bark of the tree against which her head rested. A chill wind blew across her face, the last of the night's cold wisping away with the coming of the day. It was almost *too* vivid to be real.

Had she made a mistake? Never had she entertained the thought of running away from her kin, except as the most passing flight of fancy. When the opportunity had presented itself, it had *felt* like the right thing to do, but now she was filled with doubt.

Albern stirred in his bedroll.

Sun looked over at him, watching his stubbled chin as it waggled, the old man murmuring as sleep began to creep away from him. Albern of the family Telfer, a figure of legend in his own right, and longtime companion of the mightiest warrior Underrealm had ever seen—if you believed the stories. And Sun found she *did* believe them, no matter how outlandish Albern's claims seemed. Not only that, she wanted to hear the tale go on.

In the end, that might be all that matters, she told herself. *You may have your doubts, but ask yourself: do you regret your decision?*

She could not bring herself to say that she did.

Albern's eyes opened. He lifted his head slightly, looking around as if disoriented. When he spotted Sun sitting by the edge of their campsite, he seemed to focus at last, and he gave her a little smile.

"Good morn," he said, his voice a frog's croak. He cleared his throat and tried again. "Good morn. No sign of danger while I slept?"

"There were many," said Sun. "A pack of wolves arrived not an hour ago. I told them how old and bony you were, and they slunk away in search of better game."

"No respect for your elders," said Albern, grinning as he sat up nimbly despite his missing arm. "Then again, I had none myself at your age. We shall have a bite to eat and then head off to Lan Shui."

"And what are we doing there?" said Sun.

"I mean to visit a woman there."

Sun arched an eyebrow. "A woman?"

Albern laughed. "Not a lover, if that is what you are implying. Though I would not have you think I am incapable of such things, despite my age. I can still—"

"Sky above, stop talking," said Sun. She went to his pack to fetch some meat and bread, then thought better of it and found some twigs to stoke their fire. It had dwindled down to coals. The forest turf sank pleasantly beneath each footstep, soaking in the morning moisture.

"Noble children," scoffed Albern, pulling his blanket closer around his shoulders.

With a short while's work, the fire sprang to life again, and Sun laid sturdier branches across it to help it grow. She went for the food, then, handing some of it over to Albern. The old man tore at the meat with teeth that looked surprisingly healthy, if somewhat stained with age.

"I have a question," said Sun.

"You may or may not get an answer," said Albern.

"I thought so, but I have to try. Is this . . . is this what you do now?"

Albern frowned at her, then glanced around as if expecting to see someone else there. "Now, just what do you mean by 'this?'"

"Not *this.* I mean last night. Hunting vampires. Is that your . . . your trade?"

That made him smile. "No. I am not a monster hunter, except when I need to be. And when I am, it is not only vampires I seek. I have fought all sorts of creatures. After all, you do know *something* of how I lost my arm, do you not?"

Sun's jaw clenched. She had begged him for that story already, but the man was maddeningly reticent. "Something, but not as much as I would like."

Albern chuckled. "You shall have to suffer under what I am sure is the crushing weight of your disappointment, at least for a while longer."

It was impossible to be *too* angry at the old man when his attitude was so genial and friendly, but that did not stop Sun from trying—nor from trying to hear the story she had wanted him to tell in the first place. "Now that I have agreed to go with you, will you not, *please,* tell me—"

"I will not," said Albern. "Our arrangement remains the same. I will keep telling you stories, as long as you want to hear them—but I will choose them. Can you accept that?"

"I suppose so," grumbled Sun. "I thought that would be your answer, in any case. But I have my own condition. You are a storyteller, and if you say you must tell your stories in a certain order, I will believe you. But we are also traveling companions, and in that, I do not call you master. I do not want to follow along at your heels, chasing you like the wolfhound from your tales. If we are to ride together, I want to be treated as your equal. A partner, not a lackey."

Albern looked mildly surprised. But then his gentle smile grew into a wide grin, and he clapped his hand on his knee. "Why, I could not agree more—and I apologize for making you feel that you were ever anything less. We *are* traveling companions, and neither lord of the other. I vow I will not forget it. What more can I do?"

"Tell me of this woman in Lan Shui, for one thing," said Sun.

"Ah, gladly," said Albern. "She is a medica, and I am seeking her services."

Sun's heart seemed to pause for a moment. "I—are you ill?" A sudden fear clutched at her heart, that the man she had just befriended might be in peril, about to be ripped away from her just as she had begun to value his company. And another, smaller part of her—a part she was somewhat ashamed of—wondered if she was about to be cast out alone upon the road, just as she was wondering if she had made the right choice in the first place.

"Oh, sky no," said Albern, and his easy smile dispelled her terror in an instant. "Do not worry yourself in the slightest. It is simply that old bodies need a little more care than ones your age. My friend in Lan Shui makes sure I stay healthy."

"Ah, I think I see," said Sun. "Because you are ander?"

"Well, yes and no," said Albern. "That plays a part—but age catches up with all of us, and it causes quite a bit more problems than a wending ever has."

Sun let a little sigh of relief escape her. "Well, I am glad to hear it. At the risk of imitating Mag, I have to say: if you were to die before telling me the tale I wish to hear, I would have to kill you."

Albern laughed loud and long at that, and the sound rang hearty and cheerful among the dark trunks that surrounded them. A bird chirped indignantly as it leaped into the air from a branch above him.

"I shall endeavor not to earn your wrath," he said. "In any case, after I have seen the medica, I have other business. There is something near Lan Shui that needs looking into."

"Another vampire?" said Sun, trying not to quail visibly.

"I should certainly hope not," said Albern. "It seems to be a more mundane sort of evil. Banditry, mayhap, but we shall see. These are the errands I mean to take care of in Lan Shui. After I have seen to them—with your help, if you are willing to give it—we shall plan where to go next. Together. Is that acceptable?"

"Of course it is," said Sun. "You could have simply told me so in the first place."

She had meant no insult by it, and she thought she spoke the words lightly. Yet Albern's smile faltered. When he spoke, it was in a subdued, almost mournful tone.

"I am sorry, child," he said. "You are right, of course. It is only that as I tell you these tales, I cannot help but think of the times I traveled with Mag. And when I rode by her side . . . well, the two of us were so close, you see. We almost knew each other's minds. Many things passed between us, plans and decisions, that never needed to be spoken aloud."

He fixed Sun with a gaze that was suddenly clouded. She shifted where she sat. Her meat was in her lap, untouched and now forgotten.

"I hope this causes you no discomfort," said Albern, his voice scarcely above a murmur. "But you remind me of her in many ways. I suppose I fell into old habits. But that was a different time, and I must always remind myself to see the world around me—as it is, not as I remember it. I should know better by now. Can you forgive me?"

"Of course," said Sun, answering a bit too quickly.

"Thank you." The old man's smile grew. "But I must also ask a boon. I reserve the right to surprise you with *some* things. Any good tale must have a few twists and turns, after all, lest we grow bored of it. But I promise that the next part of this story should be very interesting to you—especially considering what you have told me about your family."

Sun could not help herself—she smiled like a girl whose parents had just promised her a treat. "I cannot wait."

"Then let us get ourselves upon the road, and I will talk as we ride."

"You mean as *you* ride."

Albern chuckled. "Your point is well taken. We must see about getting you a horse of your own."

"I would greatly appreciate that."

They packed up their camp—a quick process, for they had not unpacked all that much, simply their bedrolls and some small dishes for eating. As they had laid it all out the night before, Sun had thought she would have to do much of the work, but in fact Albern was much quicker at it than she. The same was true now; his bedroll was on the saddle long before hers was, and by the time she was ready to gather up their simple dishes, he had already bagged them all and slung the sack, too, atop the horse. As she had last night, Sun chided herself for her assumption. It was plain that Albern had been traveling all across Underrealm for many years since he had lost his arm. He had adjusted himself to taking care of the small business of life long ago, and was likely a much better campaigner than she was.

Albern climbed into the saddle and smiled down at her. Their breath poured out in a heavy mist in the still-chilled morning air, mingling far above their heads as it stretched up in search of the light clouds floating overhead.

"Are you ready?" he asked.

"Of course," said Sun.

He nodded and nudged the horse into a walk. Sun strode by his side, one hand hanging idly from his left stirrup, as the old man continued his tale.

TWO

AUTUMN CLUNG TO THE LAND, SLOW TO RELINQUISH IT TO WINTER. The days were cloudy, casting that gentle semblance of sunlight that illuminates the shadows nearly as much as everything else. It rained often, and sometimes it snowed lightly, but we hid beneath our oiled cloaks and rode on regardless. The trees all around us were a thousand shades of red and orange and gold, casting their leaves into the wind to gently brush against us as we carried on.

Our journey had taken us some weeks. After proceeding to the city of Bertram from Lan Shui, we had eschewed the King's road and struck out west, carrying on all the way to the coast before turning north. There the road is often within sight of the ocean, that endless expanse that stretches forever, a blue blanket strewn with a thousand diamonds. In northwestern Dorsea, just before we turned east for Opara, Dryleaf had fallen ill, and we had halted for a few days to let him recuperate. As we drew at last to the borders of what had once been my homeland, I held on to a hope that our hunt might be at its end.

You will remember, of course, that in Lan Shui we had learned that Kaita was heading for Opara. You will also remember that we thought that message came from Pantu, the young boy who had once been a servant of the Shades, but that it had actually been Kaita in disguise. But of course we did not know that as we approached the city. We thought we would go unseen, and that our quarry had no idea we were even after her.

During our travels, I had engaged in a small project of my own. I told you of Jordel, the Mystic with whom I had journeyed through the Greatrocks, and who had perished before that journey's end. I had promised the boy, Gem, that I would write a song for him, a song of celebration for a life more eventful than most. I had not had the time to begin it in Northwood, and the road to Lan Shui had provided little opportunity, for we were in a dangerous land. But on the long road to Opara, I spent many nights on watch and many days idle in my saddle with little else to do. And so I had begun my ballad. It was grueling work, for I had never tried my hand at songwriting in those days. It is not as easy as some think—not if you want to do it properly. Sometimes I could summon no words at all. Other times, a part of the song would stick in my mind, repeating itself over and over again, demanding to be improved, until I was rocking back and forth in my saddle, muttering and humming to myself under my breath.

"Are you going mad over there?" said Mag, drawing me out of my thoughts. "We can seek a healer in the next town."

I looked at her somewhat ashamedly. Mag sat straight in her saddle, prouder than any Mystic knight, her green cloak fluttering in a light wind. Though the journey had been long, and though we had faced darkness along it—not only the vampires we slew in Lan Shui, but highwaymen and brigands in the wilderness—she looked better than ever, hale and healthy and with a focus honed like a razor's edge. Indeed, if I was honest with myself, she looked far more natural, far more *whole,* somehow, than she had back in Northwood. Mag had been happiest there, in those days she had spent with Sten. But there are the things that make us happy, and then there are the things that come to us naturally, and it is an exceptionally fortunate few who can find both things in the same place or circumstance. I think Mag belonged on the road, on a campaign, such as it was, whether or not it was what she desired.

"Forgive me," I told her. "I had not realized how loud my voice had grown."

"Really?" she said, arching an eyebrow. "I have been unable to pay attention to anything else for some time."

On Mag's other side, Dryleaf chuckled, his sightless eyes drifting aimlessly. I had been most worried for the old man when he had fallen ill, but now he seemed even stronger than when we had met him in Lan Shui. He, too, seemed to be a man who belonged on the road—and in his case, it did seem to be his great love, as well. I knew he had been a wandering peddler for many years, long before he met us.

"Oh, do be gentle with Albern, dear girl," he told Mag. "Any art requires time and patience, and songs most of all. They come to us in dreams, in our mind's wanderings, a piece at a time. Then we must sit there with the parts of them, shoving them about like a child with a tinker's puzzle, often going days or weeks without seeing the way they fit together. And then, all of a sudden, the pieces form into a whole, and then the world is forever blessed with a new and beautiful thing. Nothing can fly through the ages like a song."

"Thank you kindly," I said, nodding before I remembered he could not see it. "Your support is greatly appreciated, though I can defend myself against this one." I pointed past Mag at the old man and gave her an admonishing frown. "Do you see? That is how one true friend supports another. With encouragement, not heckling."

"If I were heckling you, I would have found some rocks to throw," said Mag. "Carry on with your mutterings, then. There are many beekeepers in this part of the kingdom. Mayhap one of them will sell me some wax to plug my ears."

I reached over and tried to shove her. Mag snatched my arm and nearly pulled me from the saddle, before catching my shoulder on her knee and launching me back upright. I snatched wildly at the saddle horn to steady myself. Foolhoof, my gelding, snorted loudly and danced beneath me, as though he had sensed an opportunity to try to escape.

"You hush," I told him, slapping his shoulder—but gently. "You will not rid yourself of me that easily." I glared at Mag. "Even with her help."

Mag laughed aloud, dragging a smile out of me. "If I wanted you out of the saddle—"

"—it would already be done," I finished. "You should be more careful with me, you know. You may be able to best me in a fight, but I am learning to write songs. I could immortalize you in verse as an utter buffoon. That sort of victory lasts forever, but you can only trounce me as long as we are both alive."

A curious expression came across her, one so tragic and . . . and *weary*, that I felt at once that I should apologize, though I did not know what I had done wrong. She smiled at me, but I thought I saw her eyes glisten as she did it.

"You are welcome to your eternal victory," she said, and the spell broke. Her voice was so cheery, her smile suddenly so genuine, that I felt I must have imagined what I had seen. "I prefer to defeat the person right in front of me, rather than the idea of them many years later."

I laughed, for it seemed clear that that was the response she needed. Mag and Dryleaf joined in the merriment, while Oku barked and ran two quick circles around our horses.

We fell silent as we rode on. Yet I thought long upon what I had seen, and the way Mag sounded. My words must have reminded her of Sten, I thought. So much had happened since the battle of Northwood, that sometimes I forgot it was barely two months before that Mag and Sten were still living happily in that town, foreseeing no darkness in their future.

"You know, Albern," said Dryleaf after a time, "I could offer my services in your attempt. I have written a fair few songs in my time, and received praise from kings and princes for them."

"I know it, friend," I told him. "I would have guessed it from the moment I first heard you sing. But this is too close to my heart to share with anyone. At least for now."

Dryleaf pursed his lips and gave a deep nod, pushing his long beard into his chest. "A song of mourning, is it? Very well. You will know when you have healed enough for my advice to be more help than hindrance."

I glanced again at Mag, but from the corner of my eye so that she would not notice. Mayhap I need not have worried. Her gaze was distant as she let it rest on the horizon, and I doubted she had heard a word Dryleaf or I had spoken.

The old man had said I would know when my heart had healed. But some wounds, I wagered, never healed at all.

THREE

The next day, we reached the city of Opara, which stands at the foot of the mountain Tahumaunga.

I do not know how far you have traveled, but I doubt it is as far as me, and I can tell you this: there are few sights as glorious, as awe-inspiring, and as frightening as that fiery peak. Tahumaunga looms over the land all around, its crest often wreathed in smoke, which drifts away south and east. There are higher mountains in the nine kingdoms, but none stand so tall in isolation, dominating the horizon and commanding one's attention.

There are tales from the time before time that say it spouted its flames often, sending great rivers of molten rock cascading down its slopes and flooding the wilderness all around. But those flames had long since subsided when Roth's armies conquered the nine kingdoms. Now it belched forth its fires mayhap once in a lifetime, and they were gentle and slow when compared to the mountain's ancient fury.

Opara had been built at the foot of the mountain long ago. The King's road did not pass through it, but it was still sizable, for it was an important waypost on the kingdom's southern border. The Tongarn river poured from underground caverns within the mountain, and the city had been built around the place where the waters reached the lowlands. The south gate stood open as we approached, but the guards there raised a hand to stop us, and one stepped forwards to take Mag's reins, for she was at our head. He looked at each of us in turn with a studious gaze. He and his companions wore the black and red armor, trimmed in white, that marked them as servants of the Calentin king. A curious feeling, somewhere between longing and discomfort, came over me as I beheld them.

"Good day, friends," said the man, a short and stout fellow. I do not know how many Calentin citizens you have met, but we often decorate ourselves with tattoos scarred deep into the skin of the face. They covered this guard's chin, which jiggled when he spoke. "Whence have you come?" One of his fellow guards edged closer and knelt a pace away, extending a hand towards Oku.

"Southern Dorsea, and before that, Selvan," said Mag. "We hail from the town of Northwood."

"A long way to travel," said the guard. "I am Ari, of the family Parata. What is your business in the kingdom?" Oku had drawn tentatively closer, and finally he allowed the other guard to scratch him behind the ears.

"I am Kanohari," I said, speaking before Mag as a way of reminding her not to give her true name. We had discussed this before. Mag and I would use false names, in case word of us somehow reached the weremage and warned her of our approach. Dryleaf would need no such precautions, we thought, since he meant nothing to the Shades. "I am returning home, and these are my friends, accompanying me on the journey."

As I spoke, I dismounted and threw back my hood. The guards' faces lit with recognition, and Ari gave me a warm smile. My father was a Heddan, but my mother was of old Calentin blood, and the features of my homeland were plain upon my face, even if my skin was a bit pale.

"Welcome home, countryman," said Ari. He pressed his fist to his forehead. "How long away?"

"Too long," I said, giving him a smile that I did not feel. "Many years."

He chuckled and clapped a hand on my shoulder. "Well, you will lose that Selvan accent before long." He shifted his attention back to Mag, giving her a nod. "You are true friends to accompany your fellow on such a long journey." Behind him, Oku had gone belly-up to allow the other guard to scratch him. One hind leg kicked wildly at the air.

"Oh, do not worry," said Mag, smiling at me. "It has all been a long ploy. I mean to get him drunk and then steal all his coin."

"She is joking," I said quickly, scowling at her.

Ari chuckled, but then his countenance grew stern. "You are welcome to Opara, but I am afraid we must inspect your belongings. Orders from the Rangatira, and none but his servants are exempt."

"Of course," I said easily. Yet in my mind, a warning bell began to toll. Inspecting travelers at the border? That was something I might have expected in the eastern regions, the mountain passes where I grew up. But the southern border had never been a place of great watchfulness. It had never needed to be, for Dorsea knew better than to bring their aggression here, and they turned it instead upon Selvan, or Feldemar, or sometimes Hedgemond.

Fortunately, we carried nothing suspicious upon us. We were indeed simple travelers, even if our ultimate goal was not quite so simple. After perusing our rations and travel gear and Mag's considerable stock of coin, the guards waved us on through the gate. Oku leaped up with a yelp and, after giving the guard's face a quick lick, he came pelting after us. Ari raised a hand to wave farewell, and then they were out of sight.

Riding into those streets was a strange sensation for me. The scent of cooking food wafted on the air towards me, bringing the aroma of dishes I had not smelled in years, but recognized at once. Most people around us had tattoos, and more than once I caught myself staring at them, tracing their twisting designs with my eyes.

I was something of a rarity, you see. Most people of Calentin do not travel very far from home, and so I had not seen them often since I left. Yet the smells, the sights, and the few snatches of song I could hear in the streets and alleys, all of it came together to pitch my mind straight back to my youth, as though I had never been gone.

"Those guards were very friendly, even if they did search our belongings," remarked Dryleaf. "That is one thing I have always liked about Calentin. Not only is it a beautiful kingdom—or I considered it so, back when I could see—but the people are simply wonderful. They seem so happy here, tucked in their own corner of Underrealm and untroubled by the affairs of the wider world."

"Calentin has its own troubles, and they are plenty." The words came harsher than I intended. Dryleaf cocked his head in surprise, and Mag gave me a stern glance. "Do not look at me like that," I told her. "I speak only the truth. No kingdom is an idyll."

"We know it, but that is no reason to be such a grouch," said Mag. "We are leagues and leagues away from your family. No one here will recognize you."

I gave her a small and sheepish smile. She had seen to the heart of my poor mood right away. "I know that. But this is the closest I have come to my family's domain since I left them."

"Ah," said Dryleaf, nodding sagely. "Bad blood, is it? Well, this is your home kingdom, and you would know more about it than I do. At least we do not have to go to your family's lands. That is one hopeful thing."

I hid a grimace and turned my attention back to the streets. But Oku seemed to sense something of my dark mood, for he whined and stepped closer, nudging my foot with his head. "Thank you, boy," I told him, and looked up at Mag. "Do you see? Even the hound knows how to be a good friend."

Mag snorted and leaned over from her saddle towards mine, wrapping me in a one-armed hug that almost lifted me into the air. "Here. Is this affection enough for you?"

"Release me before I faint," I wheezed.

She let go and pounded me on the back, which only hurt worse. "That is more than enough support for now. I shall give you another dose tomorrow."

"Please do not. I quite enjoy having ribs."

Dryleaf laughed aloud, and I felt my dark mood dissipate somewhat. Mag sometimes made me feel inadequate, but that was through no fault of her own. It was only that she was impressive in so many ways. Yet she was always a true friend, never letting me wallow in my own misery, and doing anything she could to pull me out of it. In that moment, I appreciated it a great deal.

"Let us return to the matter at hand," said Mag. "We are here for the weremage. We need a place to start looking."

"A difficult proposition," I said. "She could be anyone. We could encounter her at any time. In truth, she could have been one of those guards at the gate, and we would never have known."

We had discussed this, of course, on the long road north. Dryleaf had raised the idea of telling the Mystics about the weremage—hunting down rogue wizards was one of their duties, after all. But Mag and I refused. The Mystics would never allow us to join them in hunting the weremage down. They never partnered with others for such a task, except in very rare cases where they had no other choice—or if they were an exceptional person, like Jordel, who had been far more trusting than most. Indeed, if we had told the Mystics of our aims, not only would they have barred us from the hunt and brought the weight of the King's law against us if we persisted, but it is unlikely they would even have told us if they were successful. We had to do this on our own. The weremage had slain Mag's husband, slain my friend. She would die by our hands. On that we were agreed.

Mag nodded at my words. "Our one advantage is that the weremage does not know we are coming for her. The only way she could have found out is if the satyrs sent word. No other servants of their Lord found out about our hunt and lived to tell the tale. And certainly none of them know Pantu told us we could find her here."

"Yet we cannot hope to simply run into her on the street," I said.

"You should seek out these Shades, I think," said Dryleaf. "We know she meant to join some of them here. A weremage can be nearly impossible to hunt, but unless all the Shades are also wizards, they will be easier to pin down. Find them, and you will find her."

"I think that is our best hope," said Mag. "It will still require a good deal of work, but that can wait for the morning. It is already late, and we still need to find a bed for the night. Albern, do you know where we should seek lodgings?"

"No," I said, shaking my head. "I visited Opara but rarely, and that was decades ago. We shall simply have to choose an inn by the look of it."

"I think you two will be better at that than I," said Dryleaf, chuckling. "Though I think I will be a better judge of the food and the beds."

It took us some time to find a place that looked suitable, and by the time we found it, darkness had begun to creep into the sky overhead.

The sign hanging over the door named it the Ugly Squirrel—a joke, it seemed, for the building was beautiful, with a grid of dark beams framing tight wooden slats that had been painted a deep crimson. But then we met the place's owner, and his face more than made up for the building's beauty. His forehead swooped down low over his eyes, which pointed in different directions, and his jaw was misshapen so that he looked to be constantly grimacing. His name was Nuhea, if I remember correctly, and he was a delight. He chuckled as we introduced ourselves.

"The name is for me, not the inn," he said, lisping slightly. "For even ugly squirrels make their nests in beautiful trees."

He took our orders for food and lodgings, summoning hands to care for our horses and carry our few belongings to our rooms. But I noticed him giving me little glances from the corner of his eye—or at least, I thought he did, for it was hard, sometimes, to tell where he was looking. I was somewhat unnerved, even though I knew there was precious little chance of the man recognizing me. In hindsight, I now think that Nuhea must have seen something of my mother in my features. He must have thought I looked familiar, though he could not place why.

In any case, we paid him for his trouble and retired to our rooms, where food was soon delivered to us. We ate quickly and readied ourselves for sleep—though Mag and I still traded watches through the night, just in case. Weary as we were, we had no wish to be surprised, on the off chance that we had been spotted entering the city.

It was our weariness, however, that kept us from noticing the woman who entered the inn just behind us. Her skin was pale and her hair was fair, though she hid both under a grey cloak. She watched as we dealt with Nuhea, she took note of the rooms to which he brought us, and then she slipped out into the night.

FOUR

KAITA HAD BEEN WAITING FOR US IN THE STRONGHOLD OF MAUNWA not far away.

She had been there for some days. When we had ridden from Lan Shui, she had trailed us for a little while, stalking us in raven form, until she was sure we were heading for Opara as she had intended. Then she had cut straight across the countryside towards Calentin, bypassing the roads and traveling a long, harsh route through the wilderness. It had been taxing, but she was eager to reach the city far ahead of us.

But when she reached the Shades there, she found a nasty surprise. The old captain in the area had been given a new assignment. The new captain was a woman named Riri, and the hatred between the two women was thinly veiled, even in service of their Lord. For some days Kaita had been trying to get Riri to prepare for our arrival, but every council had devolved into an argument before long, and so they had barely gotten anything done.

Now Kaita sat in Riri's council chamber again, bored nearly senseless, listening as two officers delivered reports of troop movements, of information and intelligence gathered about the constables, the Mystics, the Rangatira and his rangers. None of it mattered to Kaita. She had only one aim: to continue to lead Mag and me north, to the lands I had once called home. Just as Rogan had commanded her.

And then the door opened, and the woman with pale skin and fair hair entered the council room, casting back her hood.

Kaita looked up, every nerve in her body suddenly alight. The look on the woman's face told her that her long wait was over.

"They are here," said the woman. She nodded to Kaita. "The travelers matching the description you gave."

"At last," hissed Kaita.

Riri gave her a cool look for a moment before turning to the messenger. "Where are they?"

"The Ugly Squirrel. One room for all three of them. I have a contact there, we could strike—"

"We do not aim to kill them," Kaita snapped. "Our job now is—"

"You are not in command here," said Riri. Kaita scowled. She did not need the reminder; Riri had not let her forget it for so much as a moment since her arrival. Riri looked to the messenger once more. "Thank you. That will be all. The rest of you may go as well."

The messenger nodded and left, and the two Shade officers at the table took their leave. Kaita waited in frustrated silence as they shuffled out of the room—too slowly, she thought, and she wondered if Riri had secretly given them an order to annoy her as much as possible.

When the room was finally empty, Riri studied her for a moment. Kaita said nothing. Riri liked to wait for Kaita to speak, and then interrupt her. It was just the sort of petty, vindictive trick she had always cherished—and she had used it often enough against Kaita in the last few days. And so Kaita remained quiet, refusing to give her the pleasure.

"Well?" said Riri at last. "What do you think they mean to do next?"

"They will look for me," said Kaita. "We will have to watch them."

"It is dangerous for my people to visit Opara too often," said Riri. "The High King knows about us now. The nobility is on alert. We are only here to watch for Calentin troop movements. Our secrecy is more important now than ever."

"You do not have to tell me that," said Kaita. "I know Rogan means for us to remain in the shadows, for now. I was there in the room when he said it—and, too, when he commanded us to begin *striking* from those shadows."

Riri's hands clenched on the arms of her chair. Kaita wanted to smile, but she was smart enough to conceal it. Riri had never understood why Rogan kept Kaita so close. She had never understood that Rogan knew just how useful Kaita was, in a way no one ever had before.

Even those who had claimed to, when Kaita had been young.

"In any case," said Riri, "sending my own people into town to watch these stragglers will endanger our more important work. You brought this problem to Opara. You can watch the strangers."

"I can," said Kaita, fighting not to say it through gritted teeth. "But I cannot stay in raven form all day. And even if I could, night will come, and I have to sleep sometime. You cannot simply bury your head beneath your blankets and hope this blows by. If Mag speaks with the King's law, they will come hunting for you."

"They would not find us," said Riri calmly. "None of their agents have come this far outside the city in a long while. The only danger would be if one of our soldiers were caught—which is why I will not continue to send them to Opara on your errands."

Her foolishness grated on Kaita's nerves. The constables might not have made a habit of visiting the stronghold of Maunwa, but it was far from concealed. It was an entirely foolish place to make one's secret hideout—but then again, it played very well into Riri's idea of her own importance. Why should she lurk in caves or some backwater buildings, when she could set herself up in this place of strong stone and imagine herself a grand lord? Never mind that she had only a dozen soldiers at her command.

But Kaita had pointed this out already, and Riri had ignored her. She must adopt a diplomatic tone now, if she wanted Riri to see wisdom.

"Do not underestimate the redbacks," said Kaita. "You do not want them to be on the alert. That is what is important now. The sooner you help me lead Mag and her party north, the safer your mission will be. Abandon this place, and leave evidence that points a trail north. Albern and Mag will discover it. It is only a matter of time. Speed the process, and you can have them out of your life all the sooner."

Riri frowned. It was a good point, though she clearly would not admit that. She scratched one nail against the wood of the table. For just a moment, Kaita thought she might agree.

"No."

Kaita balked. "No? That is all you have to say?"

"It is all I need to say," said Riri. "I am the captain here. I take my orders from Rogan, not you. And the last thing Rogan told me was to keep entirely out of sight, remaining unknown to anyone. And he said that if we were discovered, that we were to eliminate any witnesses. You have been a fool, and have led our enemies right to our doorstep. But I believe you when you say that Rogan wishes for them to be killed. I will do so, fulfilling my duty to him while also cleaning up your mess."

"Are you . . ." Kaita stopped, aghast. "Are you mad? You will not do anything of the sort. If you try, you will die. Mag will slaughter you and anyone foolish enough to follow your orders. I must lead her to Tokana. No human can defeat her, but our allies in the north can."

"Oh, Kaita," said Riri, giving a scornful smile. "Simply because you have proven too incompetent to deal with her, does not mean that I am."

Kaita shot to her feet. "Incompetent?" she roared, as her eyes began to glow. "Never forget who you are speaking to."

She lunged, sprouting a pace taller. Her clothing sank into her flesh even as her hands turned into a lion's massive paws. The air hissed as her razor claws came slashing forwards.

Riri ducked the grasping talons. A knife appeared in her hand, too fast for Kaita to see where she pulled it from. Twisting, she avoided another swipe.

Her dagger flashed. Kaita felt a stabbing pain in each thigh. A thick, guttural scream erupted from her enlarged throat.

Unable to keep her feet, she crashed to the floor on her front. Riri was atop her in an instant. She snatched Kaita's arms and wrenched them behind her back, squeezing until Kaita screamed again.

And then Riri seized her temples. Her fingers dug into the flesh there, pushing, crushing. Kaita's whole body went rigid. She tried to cry out, but all that came was a choked gasp.

She felt the magic slipping away from inside her. Her body slowly resumed its natural form. Her tight blue and grey clothes sprouted out of her skin again. In a few heartbeats, she was herself, and still pinned under Riri. Tears sprang into her eyes at the agony in her legs.

"I will release you so that you can heal those wounds," said Riri. "But only if you will promise not to be so foolish again. Swear to me."

"Only Rogan and our father receive vows from me," said Kaita, gritting her teeth and trying to pull an arm free.

Riri twisted harder. Kaita had to bite her own tongue to hide another scream. "Then I can hold you here as long as I need to."

"All right," said Kaita, hating the whimper in her own voice.

"Say it."

"I swear."

Riri let her go and rose, backing away quickly. But Kaita could not even think of breaking her word. She could only think of the pain in her legs. She focused upon it, and her eyes glowed once more. Slowly, painfully, the flesh turned fluid and melded together. The skin rejoined last, sealing the wound. Kaita gave a sigh of relief and let her magic slip away once more.

She got to her feet. Her arms still pained her; no weremagic could heal a twisting like that. Leaning heavily against the table in the center of the room, she glared at Riri, who now stood by her chair.

"Darkness take you and your Mystics' tricks," snarled Kaita.

Riri smiled. "You have remained the same girl you were in our youth, but I have not. I have grown stronger. And if I have learned the secrets of the mage hunters, now I use them in service of the Lord—a service you have been unable to render. Go now. If Rogan wishes for you to continue your work in Tokana, then you had better scurry off. I shall finish what you could not."

"When Rogan hears of this—"

"Oh? And will *you* tell him?" Riri gave a derisive bark of laughter. "The once great Kaita, scurrying to the heels of her master when she is defeated. I think you will not. I think you will try to forget that this ever happened, out of shame."

Kaita fumed, her breath coming hot and fast, a haze settling over her vision. Almost she reached for her magic again. Almost she transformed and attacked. Never mind defeating Riri—she wanted to kill her.

She smiled instead.

"Very well. You wish to fight the Uncut Lady? You are welcome to her. I wish you every chance of success."

Riri arched an eyebrow. "What are you playing at?"

Kaita did not answer. She turned and stalked out of the room, throwing the door open so that it slammed against the wall outside. Two guards stood beyond, both of them looking nervously over Kaita's shoulder. They must have had strict orders not to enter unless Riri called for aid, but it was clear they had wanted to. They stared, dumbfounded, as Kaita swept past them.

The low stone hallway ran a short distance before reaching a double door. Kaita flung these open to reveal a large main chamber, the centerpiece of the fortress. It was no grand place—not as finely decorated as the Shades' fortress at The Watcher, and not as venerable as their former stronghold in the Greatrocks. It had been built long ago by kings whose names were long forgotten—forgotten because they never rose to the greatness of Roth's generals in later days. Only recently had the Shades reclaimed this place for their own use.

Many of Riri's soldiers sat in the hall now, eating their evening meal. At the loud crash of the doors, most of them looked up, and the rest followed suit as the hall slowly fell silent.

"Hear me," called Kaita, her voice ringing in the still air. "Hear me, my siblings. Your father loves you, as he loves me and all his children. And if his love has a flaw, it is that it leads him to trust those who are not worthy."

Footsteps came down the hall behind her. Riri was coming.

"Father would want you to survive," Kaita went on, more quickly now. "And I say this: if you wish to live, abandon Riri. She is a fool, and she will throw all of your lives away. But if you remain, and if any of you live, your father's mercy will remain—in me. Go north. Find me in Tokana. I will welcome you with an open heart, ready to return you to our father's embrace."

Riri skidded to a stop behind her. Kaita turned and smiled, pleased to see the look of shock and fury on Riri's face.

"What under the sky are you doing?" growled Riri. "This is worse than insubordination. It is treason!"

"Bold words from one who refused Rogan's orders," said Kaita. "Strike me down, if you think you can. But you had best pray word of it never reaches Rogan or our father."

Riri's hands tensed. For a moment, Kaita thought she would actually try it. But finally Riri thrust a finger towards the chamber door leading out.

"Go. Never let me see your face again, lest I plant a dagger within it."

"No, you never will see me again," said Kaita. "You will die shortly after I leave, after I continue my service to our father. You think you have grown strong since our youth, and that I have remained the same. But I *did* change. I have grown wise, while you have remained foolish. Farewell, *Ririti.* For the last time."

Kaita turned and swept from the stronghold.

FIVE

"Why did Riri hate her so?" said Sun.

"They knew each other when they were girls, as you will have guessed," said Albern. "Their feud began then, and it worsened the older they grew. That is not always how it goes, of course. Many times we make enemies in our youth, only to reunite with them later and laugh at old, petty grievances. But that usually requires our paths to draw apart for a time, only to reunite when years of wisdom allow us to see our early days with a more honest eye. Kaita and Riri never had that chance. They were never apart for long, and their conflict worsened each time they clashed."

"They were not sisters, were they?" said Sun. "I have no siblings, but I have known others who do. They fight more than it seems possible two people *can* fight."

Albern chuckled at that. "I have seen the same. But no, they were not."

They journeyed now through green lowlands, across fields that stretched for leagues to the west and east. In the west they met suddenly a great spur rising up out of the land—Sun recognized it from the story Albern had already told her of Lan Shui. To the east, the land climbed into the foothills of the Greatrock Mountains, which stood imposing above them, reaching for the sun, which was still climbing into the sky. The cool air had warmed now, and Sun had cast off her cloak and opened the ties of her outer skins as she walked, trying to keep from overheating. A raven soared above them. Sun glanced at it and was unpleasantly reminded of Kaita, and the way she had stalked Mag and Albern from the air for so long. She shuddered and returned her attention to the road.

"It is all so different," murmured Albern. When Sun looked up at him curiously, he waved his arm at their surroundings. "The landscape, I mean."

"When was the last time you were here?"

"Longer than a while, less than an age," he said, chuckling. "Some time after the Necromancer's War, but not long after. Leaving for such a length of time makes all the changes seem far more stark. When you remain in a place, or when you see something every day of your life, you can miss the subtler changes as they happen."

Sun peered up at him, for his face was still somewhat shadowed by his hood. He had not thrown it back, despite the sun. "You mean as someone grows older?"

"Certainly, but it is true for more than just people." Albern rolled his shoulders. Sun was beginning to recognize that as a sign that he was about to tell another, smaller story, as part of the whole. "I am of the family Telfer, as you know, and my kin dwell in the northeastern mountains of Calentin, in a land called Tokana. That is near the northern end of the Greatrocks, whereas we are now close to their southern tip.

"Our main stronghold is nestled in the mountains, on a ridge overlooking a small dale. That dale was my favorite place when I was a child. The way the land seemed to spill down into it, tumbling from the heights to level out and grow smooth far below our home. The city surrounding our keep was built into the folds of the land. In the morning, the clouds would surround us like a blanket, and as the day wore on, the sun would cast that blanket away from us, welcoming us to its warmth. The stars . . . I have never seen so many, never seen them so clearly. It was like the sky viewed from the ocean on a clear night, but more so.

"Of course, I know now that I was viewing things through the eyes of childhood, and circumstances are rarely as good *or* as bad as we think they are when we are young. But still, it was a beautiful place. I would often go walking and riding, for I was always a lover of the wilderness. When I was very young, my middle sister, Ditra, would accompany me, along with a few attendants. When I was older, I ventured alone.

"In the center of the dale was a tall kauri tree. Every time, I would stop and spend a little while observing it. I told myself stories about it. I imagined climbing it one day, though I never did. The idea of it was something beautiful, and I feared that if I ever went to it in fact, if I put my hands on it, I would find that it was real, and inevitably disappointing.

"The tree never changed. It was always there, always watching over the valley. Kauris are evergreen, so it did not even lose its leaves in the winter. I imagine it was growing, but that was impossible to notice from so far away. And because of the tree, I thought that the land, too, was unchanging. To my mind, the city of Kahaunga was much the same every time I went out on one of my adventures, and the wilderness beyond was always a joy to ride through. I have told you that Mag's happiest days were in Northwood with Sten. Mine were in those mountains, before I grew older and realized something was wrong in my life.

"That changed when, one day, someone cut down the kauri tree."

Sun frowned at him. "What? Who?"

"Some logger, I imagine," said Albern. "I never found out. But the next time I went riding, something felt wrong. It was like going on a journey and realizing after a week of travel that you have forgotten your cloak, though you would have sworn it was on your shoulders. Or, I suppose"—he raised the stump of his right arm—"it is like suddenly missing a limb. It took me some time to realize that the tree had been cut down, and it shook me. It shook me far more than it ought to have. But then, once I had recovered from *that* shock, I began to look around, and I realized that things were even worse. The dale no longer looked as it once had. The town had spread. It was a city now. A pall of smoke hung in the air, the smoke of many cooking fires and smiths' forges. I realized suddenly that the once-brilliant stars above me had grown dim and red. It had happened over time, so that I hardly noticed. And now that I studied it more closely, I realized that *many* trees had been felled in the dale, not just the tall kauri. Now there were more rooftops than trees in the valley. The tall kauri was only the latest victim; I had missed all the others because it had held all of my focus.

"I ran to my mother, the Rangatira, and demanded to know what had happened to the kauri. She dismissed my concerns with a snort, saying that it had had to come down for the good of the people in the dale. I myself thought that the dale had been better before everyone had torn it down to the turf. Mayhap the kauri had only been a pretty thing for me to look at, as my mother tried to tell me, but I did not think so at the time.

"That was in my fourteenth year. Until then, I had been mostly happy with my life. But seeing the great changes that continued to spread around me . . . it made me realize that I, too, had changed. I was never quite as satisfied again. I left before seeing my twentieth year."

"You did?" said Sun, jerked suddenly out of the spell of the story. "Why, I have only seen nineteen years. You left at the same age as I did!"

Albern smiled down at her. "Correct. Do you not think that is odd? Do you understand a little better why, when I first heard about a daughter of the family Valgun sneaking away from her family, I thought I might understand why?"

Sun grew somber. "Mayhap. But your family does not sound quite so bad as mine."

She expected him to refute her, but he only pursed his lips. "Mayhap. I suppose we shall both have to see. For now, let us return to Opara, where Mag and Dryleaf and I had taken our lodgings."

We woke in the morning after a restful night, more restful than any we had had since we set out from Lan Shui. In truth we slept overlong, waking a good few hours past dawn. The smell of food drifting up from the kitchen filled my nostrils as I stretched upon the bed, which I had taken after Mag had replaced me on watch. She sat with her back against the room's door, dozing, but her eyes snapped open as she heard me groan.

"Good morn," she said. "I think I shall fetch us some breakfast."

"Make sure to bring some to Oku as well," I said. "He is likely angry with us, for spending the night inside and apart from him, after so much time of being able to share our tents."

"Your tent, mayhap," said Mag, sniffing. "I never allowed him into mine."

"That is patently untrue," I said. "But in any case, I would much appreciate it if you got us some food."

She nodded and went to do it. I had Dryleaf up by the time she returned, and we ate in silence, enjoying our sliced sweet potato and sour bread.

"Sky," I breathed, once I had finished eating. "That was good."

"A taste of home for you, I imagine," said Dryleaf.

"Time for business, then," said Mag, before I could answer Dryleaf and tell him that I barely remembered the dish, for I had spent longer outside of Calentin than within it. "We must determine how to hunt down the Shades, and hopefully Kaita."

"I am afraid I do not know where to start," I said. "This place is almost as strange to me as if I had never been here before."

Mag grinned. "There is someone we can call on."

I frowned at her. "Who?"

"Victon."

My eyes shot wide. "Victon? Victon is *here?*"

"He is," said Mag. "We sent each other letters on occasion. After he retired from the life of a sellsword, he moved here to Opara and began a winery."

Dryleaf's brows shot for the ceiling, and he licked his lips. "Did he? It has been some time since I have been able to enjoy a good, rare vintage."

"Victon," I said, shaking my head. "I can scarcely believe it."

"I hope he will be happy to see us," said Mag, "and that he will be able to aid us."

Laughing, I said, "Happy? I have never known Victon to be anything but a happy man. Let us ask the innkeeper if he knows where the vineyard is, and then let us report to our old captain."

SIX

You may remember my mentioning Victon earlier. When I joined the Upangan Blades, he was my first sergeant. We fought together for a good long while, and unlike many of my other superiors, he and Mag and I were always fast friends, partially because of something that had happened when I had only been with the company for a few months.

He and I were scouting through the jungle towards an enemy camp when a bear plunged out of the underbrush and attacked us. I was a few paces ahead of Victon, but my focus was on the tracks we were following, and so Victon noticed the bear first. He leaped forwards to shove me out of the way of its charge. It struck him instead, sending him careening into a tree. He sagged to the ground, groaning.

I gave a shout and drew an arrow from my quiver. The bear turned on me at once. It came roaring towards me with a fury that told me it must have cubs nearby. Nothing else could have provoked it into such unreasoning rage.

As it charged, I managed to loose a single arrow. But panic sent my shot wide, and the arrow only entangled in the fur of the bear's shoulder. It struck out, and I barely threw myself out of the way in time. Its paw snapped my bow in two. I ducked behind a tree as it swiped again. Its claws ripped through the tree, nearly toppling it.

Even as I prepared to run for my life, Victon came charging with a cry. He went for a stab, but the bear rounded and struck him a heavy backhanded blow. He crashed to the ground. The bear reared, ready to fall upon him and crush him with its massive bulk.

I had been about to flee, but seeing Victon helpless gave me just enough courage to rejoin the fight. I drew my short sword and charged. I stabbed the beast in the side, but fear had weakened my sword arm. A few fingers' worth of steel pierced the bear's flank, but that was all.

Still, it turned and thundered in rage at me, forgetting Victon. I barely managed to duck another swing. The creature's speed and ferocity were incredible.

I had only one thought: I had to draw it away from Victon. There was no use in both of us dying out here in this sky-forsaken wilderness. I ran off into the jungle, hoping to lose it. But the bear was never more than a few paces behind me. My breath grew short. I could practically smell the thing, and I thought I was doomed.

But then came Mag.

She had been assigned to the same squadron as I, and she and a few of our fellows had remained behind to wait for Victon and me to return. She heard the sound of the bear's attack from far away through the jungle and came running as fast as she could.

Even as I was searching for some place I could climb, or some hole I could hide where the bear would not be able to follow, I heard the tone of its roaring change behind me. I turned and found Mag had engaged with the beast. This was long before she had acquired her spear in Dulmun, so she had a simple broadsword. But she had not even bothered to draw it before flinging herself at the bear.

It growled and swiped at her, but Mag evaded the blow with such ease that she looked lazy doing it. Then her boot flew up and struck the bear hard in its chin. I heard a *crunch,* and its head snapped back. It gave a confused grunt.

Before it could raise another paw to strike, Mag leaped forwards and jabbed at its eyes with fingers she had pressed together like daggers. I heard a wet *thunk* as she pierced one of the bear's eyes, and it gave a terrified scream of pain and fury.

It struck, but again Mag avoided the blow. When she came back up, her sword was in her hand. It sank into the soft flesh underneath the bear's foreleg, piercing deep into its rib cage. Its cry came out wet and wheezing.

The bear turned and fled. It limped on three legs to favor the fourth that Mag had maimed. She turned to me, the battle-trance like a mask over her expression. It shook me then, as it always did.

"Are you all right?"

"Victon," I gasped. "It is heading for Victon."

She seized my arm and pulled me up, and together we pelted after the beast.

Its trail through the jungle was plain to see—and then, half a span before we reached the place I had left Victon, it turned right and vanished into the underbrush. I stopped at the spot, and Mag ran a few more paces before she stopped and looked back at me.

"What is it?" she said.

"It turned. Headed off that way." I pointed where the trail had gone.

She saw the trail after I pointed it out and nodded. "I am going after it. We have to make sure it does not wander into our enemy's camp and alert them. See to Victon."

Without waiting for my answer, she bolted off between the trees. I carried on towards the clearing where we had been attacked. There I found Victon. He had crawled to a nearby tree and sat with his back against it, panting and grimacing, holding his side. Blood seeped out from between his fingers.

"Victon!" I cried. "Are you all right?"

I ran to him, and he smiled up at me, his white teeth shining against his dark skin. "Fine," he said, chuckling. "Its claws got me, but not very badly."

He lifted his hand, and I could see it was true. There was a gash, but nothing life-threatening unless it became infected.

"It needs cleaning," I said, reaching for a flask of ale at my side. "I wish I had something stronger, but this will sting badly enough to do the job."

"How comforting. Wait." Victon seized the flask and took a deep pull, wincing at its poor taste. He handed it back to me. "All right."

I poured it on the wound. Victon growled out his pain and then laid his hand back on the wound when I was done, putting pressure on it with the edge of his cloak.

"There now," I said. "The healers back at camp can tend to it further."

"Mag?" he said.

"Went after the bear. She did not want it to wander towards our enemies, lest they discover other soldiers are here in the jungle."

"Smart of her," said Victon.

"Yes, it annoys me," I said lightly. "No one should be that good a fighter *and* have a mind for strategy."

Victon chuckled. And just then, Mag returned to the clearing. The battle-trance was gone from her, and there was a deep frown on her face.

"You finished it?" I asked her.

"No," she said. "It vanished."

"You lost the trail? It was not exactly trying to be stealthy, after the trouncing you gave it."

"For which I thank you, by the way," said Victon.

"Yes," I said. "It is not everyone who can defeat a full-grown bear with only her hands."

Victon stared at me incredulously. "Her hands?"

"At first," I said, smiling. "I think she wanted a challenge before she deigned to draw her sword."

"Oh, be silent, both of you," said Mag. "And I did not lose the trail. The bear vanished."

I rolled my eyes and grinned at Victon. "That bolsters my confidence, at least. She may be better with a sword than anyone I have ever seen, but she is as useless in this jungle as you are, sir."

Victon burst out laughing, though it looked like it hurt him. "You two have saved my life, and that is not something easily forgotten. Thank you. Now help me up."

We stooped to lift him, and I walked him off through the jungle with his arm around my shoulder. Mag took his other arm, bloody sword still bare in her hand.

"You are too kind, by the way, sir," I said. "I did not save your life. That honor was Mag's."

Victon grinned again. "You drew it off, and you tried to fight it, at least. We cannot all be the Uncut Lady."

Mag grimaced. I had only recently coined that name for her. Victon and I laughed again. Our true friendship began in that moment, and it would last for the rest of our lives.

And it is rather important to me that you know this story, for reasons that shall become plain.

Our innkeeper did indeed know where the vineyards could be found, and he seemed somewhat jealous when we said we and Victon were old friends. It seemed that Victon was rather well known in the area, and his wine much sought after.

With Dryleaf in tow, we rode for the place with light hearts, for we were eager to see our friend again after so long. We cast our hoods up and moved quickly, doing our best to pass unnoticed, just in case the weremage was in the city and happened upon us by chance. We still thought we had the element of surprise. Of course, you know that all our precautions were in vain, but we did not.

We spotted Victon's place almost from the moment we passed through the city's eastern gate. He had a very large estate, hectares of vines stretching across the feet of Tahumaunga, which loomed high above. There was a west wind that day, and so the air was clear, the mountain's lazy smoke blowing away from us. Once we were a good distance out of town, Mag threw back her hood.

"If the weremage is watching us from the sky, that is because she already knows we are here," she proclaimed. "And it is far too wonderful a day to stay sweating under that hood any longer."

I smiled at her. We let the horses proceed at their own slow pace, with Foolhoof occasionally trying to wander off the road towards a particularly delicious-looking patch of grass. Oku padded happily beside us.

A light wooden fence surrounded Victon's land. It would have been proof against nothing more determined than wandering deer, and the gate at the front stood open. We walked up between the rows of vines, seeing no one nearby. Only when we drew closer to the house at the end of the path did we finally see six figures, bent and plucking the last of the year's grapes. So deep were they in concentration that we drew very close indeed before one of them noticed us. Her plump face, brown skin further darkened by the sun, crinkled as she squinted at us.

"Visitors," she said, loud enough for us to hear.

Two of the figures, the ones closest to the path, raised their heads. One of them was a young man, the other a woman, and from their jet-black skin and features, I knew them for Victon's kin. When they saw us, they stepped away from their vines and came walking up. The rest of the workers gave us only a cursory glance before returning to their jobs.

"Good day," said the woman as she approached. "I regret to inform you that we have no stock available for sale. Last year's wine is not yet ready, and it is all reserved, in any case."

"That is ill news," said Mag. "Or it would be, if we were here looking for wine. We have come to see Victon. He is an old friend, even if he is now of such stature that others must greet us when we visit. Am I to guess that you are his children?"

They looked uncertainly at each other. "We . . . are," said the boy. "How do you know our father?"

"From the days of our youth," I said. "Or hers and mine, at least, for Victon is older than either of us. We were sellswords together, in the days when he fought for the Upangan Blades."

A flash of recognition shot across both their faces. They looked up at the two of us with renewed interest, and the girl's eyes shone. She pointed to Mag.

"You . . . are you the Uncut Lady?" she asked.

Mag scowled. I strangled a bark of laughter before it could break free. "I am Mag, if that is what you mean."

"Sky above," said the boy. He came to me, extending a hand. "Well met, friends. And what is your name?"

I am afraid I looked quite thunderstruck. It was Mag's turn to hide her laughter. "You mean Victon never told you about me?"

They both looked embarrassed, and the boy slowly drew back his hand. "He . . . he might have?" he said, making it sound like a question. "Only not well enough that we would know you by sight."

"I am Albern," I said. They both blinked. "Albern of the family Telfer?" I said, struggling mightily to hide a note of desperation.

At last the girl's face lit, and she smiled. "Oh, of course! The Uncut Lady's follower!" She turned to her brother. "You remember. He was the one who ran away from the bear."

"What?" I rather shrieked.

The boy, who appeared not to have heard me, burst out into laughter at the girl's words. "Oh, *him!* Sky save me, Father always makes me laugh when he tells those sorts of stories." He extended his hand again. "Well met, Albern. I am Nuru of the family Victon, and this is my sister, Zuri."

"Well met," said Mag, recognizing that I was quite incapable of speech for the moment, though I did take Nuru's hand and shake it. "You know the two of us already, and our elderly companion is called Dryleaf."

"And are you an old friend as well?" said Zuri. "I do not recall Father mentioning you in his stories."

"I am sorry to say I am not," said Dryleaf, who was still wiping away tears of strangled laughter at my reaction. "Though from everything I have heard, as well as your excellent manners, I think I will enjoy meeting your father to a rare extent."

"Come with us," said Nuru, gently taking the bridle of Mag's horse, Mist. "Father will be overjoyed to see you."

"It will be our pleasure," I managed to growl. Zuri approached Foolhoof, and the dark-taken gelding actually nuzzled into her outstretched hand. "Oh, have you decided to forsake me, too?" I asked him.

Zuri looked up at me, aghast. "What?"

"The horse," I said, dismounting and letting her take the reins. "Never mind me. Thank you."

SEVEN

The house was large, but not opulently so. The walls were light brown stone, but the roofs were curved red tile, which I had not often seen outside of Dorsea. It made for a wonderfully attractive combination, especially with the great wooden doors through which Victon's children led us inside the house.

Victon was napping, and so we met his wife, Nuri, first. She was positively radiant, with a round waist and eyes that danced, her skin even darker than her children's. She was delighted when they introduced us, and she went to fetch Victon as soon as we had finished our greetings. When he emerged, still blinking bleary eyes from sleep and leaning heavily on his crutch, his face beamed with a smile that burst into laughter as he saw us.

"Sky save me if I expected this today!" he said, coming forwards and seizing us in a hug. "What are the two of you doing here? I thought you were both living in Selvan."

That cast a shadow over our mood, and he saw it. His own smile faded a little as he watched ours die.

"We were," said Mag. "Much has changed."

He looked us both over, taking note of Dryleaf. I suspected he was looking for Sten. They had never met, but of course Mag would have mentioned him in her letters.

"I can see that," said Victon at last. His smile returned now—still happy, but somewhat more weary. "Well, come in. We are about to eat. I shall fill you with food and flood you with wine, and we shall talk of what we must, and what we can, and what we wish."

Rarely have I enjoyed a meal so much. The courses were a mixture of Calentin food and dishes from Victon's homeland of Feldemar. First we ate sour flatbread and sweet potatoes, but dipped in a delicious sauce made from beef grease and filled with spices. Then the beef itself came, smoked with manuka wood and cooked with whitefish, soft and tender and soaking in still more sauce. With it came plates of greenshell oysters, dipped in pepper and garlic.

I remember every bite of that meal to this day. I can see Oku, who waited patiently at the side of the room until I offered him a morsel of food. He trotted forwards to eat it gently from my fingers. Mag fed him as well, but only when she thought I was not looking, which of course I was. Victon called Oku to him at one point, and the hound came obediently.

"A finer wolfhound I have never seen," said Victon, holding Oku's face between his weathered hands. "Who has ever seen such a well-mannered boy? Not I, no, not I." Oku nuzzled his hands and licked his face, and Victon laughed and asked the kitchen to give him whatever bones they might have. Oku lay happily in the corner for the rest of the meal.

I remember, too, the wine, which was not only plentiful, but among the best I have ever tasted. It was just sweet enough for you to drink it in great swallows, and more than heady enough to send us into peals of laughter at even the slightest joke. It was dark and smoky, with the faintest hints of charcoal that mingled perfectly with the well-smoked meats we ate. I had a few glasses, and I am positive Mag had more than a bottle. Wine and ale had never had much effect on her.

The food I remember. The conversation, however, comes to me now in bits and snatches. We told Victon of Northwood, and what had happened to Sten. Then we told him of our journey through the Greatrocks, of the satyrs we found there, and of all that happened in Lan Shui. When we told them of the vampires, Victon's face paled, and his wife reached over to clutch her son's arm.

We finished our stories around the same time that the whole table finished their meal, and we all leaned back in our chairs, groaning pleasantly at the tight feeling in our guts. I looked to Victon.

"I cannot remember the last time I enjoyed myself so thoroughly, old friend. Barely half the day has passed, and yet I wish I could lie down."

"But you can," laughed Victon. "I have a room for just such a purpose. Walk with me a moment, and I will show you my land, and then we can rest."

He walked us out of the back of the house and pointed at the different plots, telling us the different sorts of grapes he had, which I am sure are important to a vintner, but which I cannot remember at all. In the middle of the fields were built a series of houses, each seeming just as grand as Victon's own. When we asked him who lived there, he smiled.

"Why, those who work the fields with us, of course."

"They must be grateful to you, for building them such fine homes," said Mag.

Victon cocked his head at her with a wry look. "Grateful to me? They built those homes on their own. I only helped a little."

Mag seemed somewhat at a loss. "Forgive my mistake. I thought the field hands were your servants."

Victon laughed at that, slapping one hand against his hip and the other against his crutch. "Servants? Giving and taking orders? Sky above, Mag, have we not had enough of that in our lives? We make the wine together. We sell the wine together. We live together. Some even bed together when they think their parents are not looking—is that not right, Nuru?" He took his son's arm and gave it a little shake.

"Father, please," said Nuru, blood rushing into his cheeks.

"The only trouble we have tending our fields," Victon went on, "is when he and one of the Turei boys suddenly go missing. But we always find them before too long, and their cheeks are a little rosier when we do."

"Father!" cried Nuru, aghast.

Victon laughed harder and led us all back into the house. He brought us to a room full of couches, each of which was laid with many tasseled pillows, and we lay down as we continued to talk. I learned that Nuru was an ander man, like me. He had come to realize he was ander much younger than I had—I was a bit of a special case, for it usually happens in childhood. The two of us spent a good deal of time speaking privately of our wendings, and all the other little details that only another ander person can truly understand.

Sometimes Dryleaf would be reminded of one of his stories, and then he would tell it. He was better at it than any of us. We listened attentively whether he spoke or sang, and he made Victon's family weep with the beauty of the songs he gave them, so ancient that I had never heard them before, and rendered in the high speech that had once been common in the courts of the nine kingdoms. We talked until dinner, and then we talked all throughout that meal—even better than lunch had been, and with still more wine—and then we talked for a good long while afterwards.

But sometime in the evening, when the sun had long since set and the moons were making their intrepid way across the sky, we came to business. Victon's children had long since gone to bed—Nuru somewhat sooner than Zuri, for I had spotted another boy lurking outside the room, beckoning to him. It was only the five of us now, and Oku in the corner, of course. Mag sat up on her couch. Victon and Nuri rose as well, sensing the mood in the room shift.

"Victon," said Mag. "This day has been the best of long memory. I have not Dryleaf's gift with words, nor even Albern's, and so I cannot tell you what a balm it has been to all of us after the long road that brought us here. But we did not come here only for a visit, however long overdue that might have been."

He sighed, leaning forwards to scratch at the stump of his leg. "Well, of course not. That would have been a long journey to make to see my ugly old face." Nuri reached over and slapped his arm lightly, and he grinned. "Tell me, my friends. What do you need?"

"We told you of the weremage," I said. "We are hunting her here in Opara. We know she still works with these Shades, and we think she came here to join more of them."

Victon frowned and scratched at his stubble. "I have heard nothing of any rogue weremage. Nor have I heard of these Shades. I did not even know about Northwood; there was some rumor of an attack on Selvan, but I took that for Dorsea's usual malcontence. What could bring them here? Opara may stand on the border, but it is hardly a hub of trade."

"The Shades have long been devising a plan both hidden and evil," said Dryleaf. "We should not presume it will be easy to guess at."

Victon reached over to take Nuri's hand. "I suppose I was a fool to think I was done with war forever."

"You still can be," said Mag. She left her chair to kneel before him, putting her hands on his leg. "We will take care of this matter. You left your fighting days behind you."

"So did you," said Victon. Then he chuckled and pounded on his stump with one hand. "But I suppose there is more than one reason I should not return to the field."

Nuri's brows lifted. "Not to mention the fact that your wife might kill you if you tried."

"Another fair point, and one I had not considered," said Victon. "Yet I may still be of some use. I may not know where to start looking for your renegade wizard—but I know the person who *will* know where to look. It happens that I am acquainted with Conrus of the family Matara."

I squinted, thinking, before I recalled the name. "The Rangatira? It . . . might not be wise for us to speak with him."

"Oh?" said Victon, looking vaguely alarmed. "Are you in some trouble with the King's law?"

"No," I said. "But I do not wish my return to Calentin to be widely known, especially among the nobility." I had known Conrus when I was very young. That was a long time ago, and I had had my wending since, but still I did not like the thought of presenting myself to him.

"Yet we could hardly ask for better assistance than we would get from a border lord," said Mag. "Worry not, Albern. I will do most of the talking."

"And I will visit him with you," said Victon. "He has been expecting a bottle of my special reserve for about a week now. I meant to entice him to visit, but it seems fate has given me a better use for an unpaid favor."

"Fate," I laughed, like a fool. "If you say so, old friend."

"But come," said Nuri. "It is far too late for you to make your way back to the city tonight. You must stay here with us, and the lot of you can go in the morning."

We made all the right sounds of protestation, but she did not have to work very hard to persuade us. Nuri set us up in some of the finest rooms in their very fine house, and we slept even better than we had at the inn the night before.

EIGHT

Nuri woke Mag, Dryleaf, and me just after sunrise. We broke our fast with her and Victon. I had a slight headache after all the wine, and Dryleaf looked to be feeling even more delicate, but none of the others seemed any worse for wear.

Our meals were done, and we were picking through the remains of the tastiest morsels left when Victon clapped his hands. "We shall make for the Rangatira first thing," he proclaimed. "I readied one of my finest bottles last night before I went to sleep."

"Will you be accompanying us?" Dryleaf asked Nuri, who was sitting beside him.

She arched an eyebrow. "Do you wish for me to?"

He lifted her hand to kiss it. "How could I wish for anything but more of your astonishingly beautiful company?"

That made Nuri giggle, even as she shook her head. "I could ask no greater compliment, for the blind see the only sort of beauty I have ever cared about. But no, I have many duties here, and I will be little help to you."

When we were ready, we left the house. In the front courtyard we found that the horses had already been brought from the stable, as well as a horse for Victon. Nuru and Zuri were there, and they grinned at us as we emerged into the strengthening daylight.

"A good morn to you all," said Nuru. "Did you sleep well?"

"Wonderfully," said Dryleaf. "And I thank you for your courtesy."

"Mag," said Victon, "will you do me the honor of helping me to the saddle? I learned how to do it myself after the leg, but it is still easier with help. And I could ask for no greater honor than being squired by the Uncut Lady."

"Squired, is it?" said Mag with a wry smile. "Of course I will."

She took his belt and helped heave him up, while I went to aid Dryleaf. Once the two of them were mounted, Mag went to her mare, and I went to Nuru, who was holding Foolhoof's reins. The gelding eyed me suspiciously.

"Did he give you any trouble?" I asked Nuru.

"Not a bit," said Nuru. "He was most well behaved."

"Oh, you will obey *others,* will you?" I said, glaring at Foolhoof even as I rubbed his nose.

He snorted on me, and a bit of phlegm splattered on my hand.

"Do you see?" I asked Nuru, shaking it away. "This is what I must suffer through."

Nuru laughed. Then he held forth a hand. I took his wrist and shook. "It was an honor to meet you, as well as a pleasure," he said. "I am always pleased to meet another ander person, and more so when they are a companion of the fabled Uncut Lady. And a stalwart warrior in their own right," he added quickly, as I gave him a sour look.

"Well spoken, at least at the end," I told him. "Mag has stayed in touch with your father over the years, but I have not. I will do so from now on. And once I have a place where he can send me letters, I would be most pleased to hear from you as well."

The boy's face split in a brilliant grin. "I promise I shall write until you are sick of me."

I laughed and climbed atop my horse. With Victon leading the way, we rode from his home towards the city. The streets were nearly empty, for it was not yet time to go to market, and all the farmers were already out in the fields. Victon took us to our destination with the unswerving air of one who had made this journey many times before.

In the center of Opara stood the Rangatira's keep. It was surrounded by a strong stone wall, the back side of which pressed close to the river. Guards patrolled the top of the wall, but they had the sluggish look of soldiers who almost wished for trouble, simply so they would have something to do.

The guards opened the gate once Victon explained why he had come. I looked down at Oku.

"Kip, boy," I said.

Oku looked up at me and whined.

"I am sorry. But we will return soon."

He trotted off to the side of the gate and lay there, watching as we vanished through it. Attendants took our horses, and Victon led us to the great doors of the keep, which also stood open. A page there raised her chin and looked upon us expectantly.

"I have come to see the Rangatira, bearing a gift I promised him," said Victon, raising the bottle of wine. "And I speak on behalf of my friends here, who have come to beg a boon."

The page looked us over. "Very well. We will take your weapons."

"Of course," I said, unbuckling my sword. I left my bow, for it was unstrung, hanging on my saddle. Mag looked somewhat disgruntled, but she handed over her spear and shield. The page handed the weapons to a doorman before leading us into the keep's great hall.

There were tapestries on the walls inside, as well as many fine weapons with gold inlay—pieces for ceremony and show, but they looked fit for battle if need be. Lord Matara clearly had not forgotten his primary purpose as an agent of war. The furniture was solid and sturdy even when it was beautiful, and the doors looked well-kept and easy to bar against intrusion. Through the hall we were led and into a small chamber off to the right. There were many cushioned chairs inside, and the page beckoned us in.

"I will deliver your request to Lord Matara," she said. "He is in council at the moment. You will be summoned when he is ready."

Mag looked exasperated, but I spoke quickly before she could express it. "Of course," I said. "Thank you for your assistance."

She gave a thin-lipped nod and vanished, closing the door behind her. I helped Dryleaf over to one of the chairs and eased him down into it.

"Oh, this is a fine seat," he said with a sigh. "Though not as fine as your couches, Victon."

"I despise all this waiting." Mag wore a scowl, and she did not sit, but stood in the center of the room with her arms folded. "You nobles seem to have perfected the art of making people wait on your beck and call."

"I have not been a noble for some time," I said.

She was about to respond when the door to the chamber opened again. It had only been a few moments, and so we all turned to it in surprise. There stood the page again, looking almost as startled as we were.

"The Rangatira is ready to receive you," she said, as though she herself could not quite believe it.

I barely kept myself from asking, *Already?* But Victon gave us a knowing grin. We helped Dryleaf stand again, and followed the page back out into the main hall and up a short flight of stone steps to a large door at the end of the room.

Beyond lay the Rangatira's audience chamber. It was the bottom floor of the keep's central tower, and so it was circular, with a wall towards the back that obscured the staircase leading up. In front of that wall stood a small dais—nowhere near so grand as the king's, as I knew from personal experience, but imposing enough. And upon that dais was a chair, where sat the Rangatira. He was a little older than I was, with a thick and braided beard that reached the middle of his chest. Some grey flecked that beard, as well as his temples, just like mine. He had extensive tattoos on his cheeks and chin. Upon his brow was wisdom, and in his eyes burned the fire of courage. His arms were thick with both muscle and fat, and he was clothed in practical garments that were fine enough for his office, but not ostentatious. I felt myself instinctively straightening my posture, standing like a soldier in formation. This was a leader, and no mistake.

"You address Conrus of the family Matara, Rangatira of Opara and of southeastern Calentin," said the page.

I bowed with a fist to my forehead, and after seeing me, Mag did the same. After I straightened, I went to Dryleaf and carefully guided his hand to his forehead. But before I helped him bow, Lord Matara raised a hand.

"That is not necessary," he said. His eyes shifted to the page. "That will be all, thank you."

The page bowed, fist to her forehead, and left. The chamber settled to silence as Lord Matara studied us. At last he beckoned to Victon.

"Greetings, old friend," he said. "I see you have finally brought that which you owe me."

Victon beamed his most charming smile and approached with the wine. "And it is my pleasure to do so."

The Rangatira smiled in return and came down from the dais to accept the bottle. He turned it over in his hands once before placing it on a table near his chair, and then he came over to us, studying us with keen eyes.

"You are the ones who have come to ask a boon?" he said.

"We are, my lord," said Mag, bowing again.

He turned to her, clearly assuming that she was our leader—which suited me just fine. "My duties keep me rather busy, and so I must be brief," he said. "How may I help you?"

"We were hoping, lord, that we could inquire as to whether there has been any unusual activity in Opara of late?"

Lord Matara frowned. "You shall have to be more specific. Odd goings-on are all I seem to deal with. That is the lot of a Rangatira."

Mag gave me a quick glance. How to inquire without tipping our hand?

"Rangatira," I said. "Has anyone, by chance, reported any sightings of a rogue weremage? A Calentin woman of about my years?"

The effect on him was immediate. His dark face grew darker still, and he glanced quickly back and forth between the two of us. "A weremage? I cannot say that I have heard of one, no. But that is a matter for Mystics. Are the two of you redcloaks in disguise?"

"We are not," said Mag quickly. "But we have a special interest. Have there been any crimes recently, mayhap, something outside of petty theft or a street brawl, where the perpetrator has not yet been caught?"

"Nothing that has come to me," said Lord Matara. "Though I could make some inquiries. But what do the two of you want with a rogue weremage? You would do better to turn this matter over to the Mystics and let them track her down, if you can give them a report as to the crimes she has committed."

I sighed and reached for my right sleeve, drawing it up to the elbow.

There, on the inside of my forearm, was my family's mark. I showed it to Lord Matara.

You will already be familiar with noble marks. The family Telfer's is made of three arrows pointing down, and behind them lies a bow. It is somewhat reminiscent of the Mystics' symbol. There mine sat, etched into the skin with black ink.

"We have come from the family Telfer," I told Lord Matara. "We have pursued this weremage a long way, and Lord Telfer's grudge against her is quite personal. For that reason, we would rather not involve the Mystics. The redcloaks would not allow us to pursue our hunt, but would take it upon themselves. We would prefer to handle things quietly."

I could see Victon's surprise. Of course, he knew I was a Telfer. But he also knew that I had not been home in many years, and this story was rather different from what we had told him. But he was wise enough to play along.

The Rangatira, for his part, suddenly looked rather stony. Instead of answering, he turned and walked back to his dais, climbed the stairs, and sat down upon his chair. The message was clear: this was no longer a personal matter, a favor bestowed by him upon his friend, Victon. This had just become official business.

"Why did you not tell me this before?" he said sternly.

"As he said, we wished to handle this matter quietly," said Mag.

He kept his gaze fixed upon my face. "I do not know that I know you," he said, "though you have the Telfer look."

"I do not know that I know you either, Lord," I replied, "though you look like a Matara."

The words were mayhap brazen, but they drew a small smile from him. "What is your name?"

"Kanohari."

His gaze slid past me. "And she?"

"This is Chao," I said, pointing to Mag. "She is an old friend of the family, and a loyal companion in a fight."

"And the other?"

I frowned, though I tried to hide it. When it came to matters of Rangatira and rangers, I did not know why he should be so interested in my companions. "He is Dryleaf. An advisor, and one with much expertise in the matter that drew us from home."

"The matter of wizards, you mean," said Lord Matara.

"I do," I said. "Forgive me, Rangatira, but why do you ask? By which, I only mean that so many questions tell me something is amiss here in Opara."

Lord Matara considered me for a moment, deep in thought.

"When was the last time you were in Telfer lands?"

Quickly I added the time up in my head—not the true answer, of course, but the time it would have taken us to get here from Tokana if I first rode into Feldemar and then traveled in haste.

"What is the date, my lord?"

"The eighteenth of Yanis."

"Then it was over a month ago," I said.

Lord Matara nodded. "That is as I thought. There have been recent developments that I have only recently been made aware of. The High King has sent word to the nobility across the land, asking us to be especially alert for strangers passing through our domains. But if you are supposed to know why, it would be proper for you to hear it from your own lord, not from me."

That put a tremor in my heart. And despite myself, I could not keep from asking the obvious. "And yet, my lord, if you are supposed to be suspicious, why did you allow us to enter your council chamber?"

"Because you came with Victon," he said. "And I have verified that this *is* Victon. I have my own wizards, and though you did not notice them, they probed your party for magic as you entered, to ensure he was no weremage in disguise."

"A wise measure," said Mag.

Lord Matara glanced up at her, looking annoyed for a moment.

"Forgive her, my lord," I said, glaring over my shoulder at Mag. "She has been a family friend for so long that she has grown somewhat lax in decorum, and she is such a skilled warrior that my lord tends to overlook it."

To my immense relief, he smiled at that. "I suppose there are some in Opara whom I treat the same—Victon among them, though that is for his wine, and not his skill in battle. Though I have heard that that was prodigious in earlier days."

"Nearly an age ago now, Rangatira," said Victon, giving another bow.

Lord Matara smiled before turning back to Mag. "If you are so skilled a warrior, I would enjoy sparring with you sometime, if you remain in Opara long."

Before Mag could say something else idiotic, I replied, "I am afraid that is not our plan. We wish to find and eliminate this rogue weremage, and then to return home as quickly as we may."

He nodded. "Fairly said. Very well. If you have been hunting this weremage for almost a month, there is little chance she has anything to do with the matter the High King warned us about. That is reassuring, but it also means I cannot spare my personal attention for the matter. I will send for my lead ranger to assist you."

He lifted a hand in a clear gesture of dismissal, though a kindly one. I bowed, fist to my head once more, and ushered Victon, Mag, and Dryleaf from the room.

NINE

"Sky above, Mag, would you *please* try to keep at least a modicum of respect?" I said, once the page had escorted us back to the waiting chamber and the door was closed.

"I was plenty respectful," she said. "And I took his measure before I spoke. That was a man who respects bravery and a good laugh."

"She is right," said Victon with a chuckle.

"He seemed an honorable man," said Dryleaf. "I could hear a strength in him."

"Strength, and wit, and many secrets," I said. "I knew him, when I was young, before I had even seen fourteen summers."

"Before your wending, then," said Mag. "No wonder he thought you looked familiar."

"The years have altered my appearance at least as much as the wending," I said. "Not all of us have retained our youth so well as you."

She gave me a brittle smile. Dryleaf sighed as he settled back in his chair cushions. "It is good for you that you were not recognized," he said. "It seems you do not have as much to fear in your homeland as you thought."

But I was not entirely convinced. Certainly, here in Opara, it was far less likely that anyone would recognize me than it would have been in Tokana. But all it would take was one member of my family—even distant kin—and then I knew word would make its way back home. To my mother.

I feared to think what might happen then.

Victon spoke up. "This is where I should let you go your own way, I think," he said. "I know little of these matters."

"Of course," said Mag, clasping his hand and pulling him into an embrace. "Thank you for everything, Victon. We will try to see you again, if we can. Will you be all right, getting back to the farm on your own?"

"I told you I can mount my horse," he chuckled. "Besides, the Rangatira's servants are always willing to help me."

"Then thank you again," I said. "May the sky smile upon you, and the moons light your way through the dark."

"I enjoyed our time together more than any I have had in a good long while," said Dryleaf, reaching out to allow Victon to take his wrist. "May the time before our next meeting be short, and may the reunion be joyous."

"With your presence, of course it will be," said Victon. "I would give much to have you tell more tales and sing more songs for my family."

"Nothing would please me more," said Dryleaf. "Once this business is taken care of."

"Of course," said Victon. Then he took Dryleaf's shoulder and gently placed his forehead to the old man's. "Until next time."

He left. We settled ourselves into chairs to await the arrival of the lead ranger.

"I was interested in that secretive business the Rangatira mentioned, about the news from the High King," Dryleaf said, once the chamber had settled to silence again.

"It must be the Shades," said Mag.

"That was my guess," said Dryleaf. "Yet Conrus thinks our weremage has nothing to do with them. I wonder just what Enalyn told the nobility."

I could not help getting somewhat rankled. "The least you two could do is refer to Lord Matara and the High King by their proper titles."

Mag waved an airy hand. "We leave such niceties to you nobles," she said. "You just told me I have a poor grasp of decorum."

Before I could argue further, a thought struck me like an arrow between the eyes. I grinned, prompting a confused frown from Mag.

"Mag," I said, struggling through a throat that had suddenly gone tight. "If the High King warned the nine kings of the Shades, that means she received the message."

She looked every bit as thunderstruck as I felt, her hands clenching to fists. From his place in the cushioned chair, Dryleaf turned his head back and forth, arching an eyebrow.

"Eh? What message?" he said. "You did not tell me you were on speaking terms with the High King."

"Not us," I said. "Friends of ours, ones who barely escaped the destruction of Northwood. They were trying to deliver news of the Shades to the High King's Seat, but they were pursued. We had feared for their safety."

"I see," said Dryleaf, nodding gravely. "Then I am happy for you both that they survived."

"Mag, we know where they are," I said. "We can find them. We can go to the Seat and find—"

"Of course we can," said Mag, giving me a small smile—but a stern one. "Once the weremage is dead, we are free to go wherever we wish. We will visit the Seat then. I swear it."

I felt crestfallen. In my joy over realizing that Loren had survived and fulfilled her mission, I had almost forgotten about the weremage, about anything but my sudden desire to mount Foolhoof and ride for the Great Bay as fast as his legs could carry me. But of course, we had come this far, and there was still the weremage.

"Naturally," I said. "After we have finished here."

"And speaking of which," Mag continued, "if the nobility knows of the Shades, it could become a problem for us. If the Rangatira seeks information about them, but he is trying to keep their existence a secret, then his servants might withhold information from us. It is understandable, of course, but contrary to our aims. But I know how to solve the problem."

Before I could ask what she meant, the chamber door opened. In stepped a person whose golden badge marked them as the lead ranger. They were twixt, short and thinly built, with sharp eyes and hair cut only a finger away from the scalp. Their clothes were much finer than mine, but had clearly seen just as many miles and just as much wear. The tunic's sleeves ended just past the elbow, and I saw scars and calluses on the fingers that told me at once this was an archer, and a well-practiced one.

"Greetings," they said. "I am Tuhin of the family Matara. I serve the Rangatira."

"His lead ranger," I said, stepping forth and offering my hand. "Greetings, friend. I am Kanohari of the family Telfer."

They took me by the wrist and shook, sizing me up for a moment. They had to look up into my face, for they were a head shorter. "Well met indeed. It is a long while since I met a ranger from Tokana."

I smiled weakly. "And a long while since I met one from Opara."

"I have met the Lord Telfer, you know. She came to visit some years ago. An honorable woman, though a hard one."

This caught me so thoroughly by surprise that I was unable to respond for a long moment. I was terrified of my mother discovering my return, but I had managed to put thoughts of her aside—until Tuhin spoke of her so brazenly. A response seemed far out of reach, but I summoned it.

"She certainly is a hard woman," I said at last, forcing a weak smile.

Tuhin chuckled. "Doubly so to her rangers, I imagine. Still, it seems to get results. When she came, she only brought Maia, her lead ranger, but he was a fine man. Rarely have I met a ranger with such skill."

I began to get a sick feeling. I knew no one named Maia. It had been many years since I had spoken with my family, of course, but I had thought that my middle sister, Ditra, would have been the lead ranger. Had something happened?

But of course, when we were younger, Ditra had been more like me—nearly as "soft," as my mother would have put it. I could well imagine that Mother might have decided not to elevate Ditra to the position.

Especially not after what had happened to Romil, my other, eldest sister.

"Maia is a fine man indeed," I said, feeling as though I had pulled the words from the depths of a bog.

"If they set you to this task, you must be a capable warrior," said Tuhin. "And if by any means I can help, I shall. Out of respect for them both."

Though I felt sick, I nodded and waved to the others. "This is Chao, and my elderly friend is Dryleaf."

"A pleasure," said Dryleaf, holding out his hand for them to take it. "The Rangatira's lead ranger! We stand in mighty company. Why, I would guess you have wandered nearly as far as I have."

"I can only hope, Grandfather," said Tuhin warmly. "Well met. Now, I hear we have a weremage to hunt. A dangerous prospect at the best of times. You should tell me all that you can."

They beckoned us over to the chairs, which we moved to surround a table near the back of the room. Mag and I carefully explained what had drawn us here, though I took the lead in the storytelling, changing the details to match the tale that we had come from Tokana. They listened as I described a road east into Feldemar, which then cut south through that kingdom into Dorsea, and then circled back around to head north into Opara.

Tuhin frowned. "Why would she come back towards Calentin if she fled it in the first place?"

"Because she has friends here, or so we have gathered," I said.

Tuhin nodded slowly, pursing their lips. "Hm. If she is lurking near here, there are only a few places she could be—especially if she has company."

"We hoped you would be able to point us to some of them," I said.

They leaned back in their chair, looking pensively at the table and tapping their chin. After a while they rose and went to a cupboard at the other end of the room. From it they pulled a wide scroll, which they unfurled on the table to reveal a map of Opara and the surrounding area. On the eastern end of it was half of Tahumaunga, the fire mountain, with many notes scratched around the area of its foothills. Some had been rubbed away, leaving only a smudged stain behind. Tuhin leaned over it.

"If the weremage is up to no good, and is trying to avoid the law, there are many places she could be hiding," said Tuhin. "Of course, being a weremage, she could be anywhere, even in plain sight."

Mag nodded. "We think it will be easier to find her by way of the friends we mentioned earlier. Someone in one of the previous towns we passed through heard her talking about coming to Opara to join them."

"And what sort of friends are they?" said Tuhin.

Mag shrugged innocently. "She is a criminal on the run from the law. I imagine they are other criminals." Then she fixed Tuhin with a piercing look. "Though of course, the Rangatira seemed rather suspicious of the whole matter. Tell me: are the two of you worried about the Shades?"

She might as well have pulled the ceiling down on us with mind-magic, so great was the effect upon Tuhin. Dryleaf's brows shot for the sky, and his grip tightened on his walking stick. I tried mightily to keep an expression of calm, but I must admit I wondered for a moment if Mag had quite lost her mind.

"How do you—" began Tuhin.

"When we were following the weremage through Dorsea, the rumor of these 'Shades' was thick across the land," said Mag. "We heard they have already attacked a town in Selvan—some place called North Forest, or some such." She gave a look of surprise so genuine that I almost believed it. "But you look shocked. Are they meant to be a secret?"

Tuhin frowned. "They are. Blast. My lord will not be pleased to find out that rumors of the Shades have spread to the commonfolk—though I am happy to hear that it seems to have started in Dorsea, and not here in Calentin."

Mag cocked her head, her eyes widening slightly in perfectly innocent curiosity. "Who are they?"

Tuhin shook their head slowly. "The Rangatira has told me that you should hear that news from your own lord. But if your weremage has something to do with the Shades, then—"

"Oh, we are certain she does not," said Mag, shaking her head emphatically. "There was not even a rumor of them in Tokana. We only heard about them in Dorsea, and never related to our search for her. And we heard less and less about them the farther we came north."

I understood at last. As long as Tuhin thought we knew nothing about the Shades, they would not speak of the matter with us—but they would harbor a secret suspicion about our weremage, and might even withhold information. But by assuring Tuhin that yes, we did know of the Shades, but that we were certain our weremage was in no way related to them, Mag hoped to put Tuhin's mind to rest on the matter. It made sense, though it still seemed a wild risk, and I wished we had had time to discuss it first.

Tuhin was silent a long time. Their brow furrowed, and they looked between Mag and I. "What did this weremage do, exactly? Why did Lord Telfer command you to hunt her in the first place?"

"She killed someone," I said quietly. "Someone dear to us, and dear to Lord Telfer. It was a spiteful, personal fight that spun out of control." Mag's expression turned grim.

Tuhin sighed. "I am sorry to hear it," they said. "Very well. If the weremage has friends hiding her from the law, and they are not lurking here in the city, that should narrow it down. She is likely somewhere in the foothills of the mountain."

"We came from there just this morning," said Mag.

Tuhin nodded. "So I heard. There are many folds in the land in that area. Opara is an always-changing place. People move here, and people move away. Abandoned homesteads are common near the edge of the wilderness. So, too, are neglected strongholds even farther away. Some are built by bandits and thieves and left empty when we drive them off, but then there are abandoned fortresses, relics of ancient kings, some stretching back to the time before time. They often have an evil air, and criminals usually avoid them, but not always." They thrust their finger at the map. "We should begin with the stronghold of Maunwa. The last time it was occupied was three years ago. After we drove bandits out of the place then, the Rangatira kept a watch on it. But that watch was relaxed a year ago, and now it is visited but rarely."

An evil stronghold in the mountains. I did not much like the sound of that. But Mag had focused on something else Tuhin had said.

"You said 'we' should search the stronghold? Kanohari and I had planned to go on our own."

Tuhin grinned up at her. "Did you? Well, I am the Rangatira's servant, and it is my duty. He assigned me to help you."

I gave them an easy smile. "We are grateful, of course."

"It seems your plans are set," said Dryleaf, who had settled back in his chair. "Though I am afraid I will not be much help in such a venture."

Tuhin nodded and knocked their knuckles once on the table. "It is settled, then. The day has worn on too long for us to go now. I will arrange for you to be quartered here in the keep tonight, and we will set out first thing in the morning."

"You are too kind," said Mag. "But we have lodgings in the city."

"I would rather not have to seek you out," said Tuhin lightly. "And besides, you are servants of a Rangatira. It is only right that we should house you while you visit our domain, as well as spare your coin." But they had a careful look in their eye, and I wondered if they wanted to ensure we did not try to investigate the fortress on our own.

"Then I suppose the matter is settled," I said, just as amiably. "We thank you for your help."

"Of course," said Tuhin. "Let us get you to your rooms. Our servants will rouse you before dawn, and then we shall all see what may be done about your weremage."

We set about retrieving our things from the Ugly Squirrel, and Oku was allowed within the keep walls to bed with the other hounds they kept. But as we set about readying ourselves for another night's rest, I found myself wondering whether Tuhin's presence by our side would be a help, or if they might inadvertently keep us from the end of our long hunt.

TEN

IT TAKES A SPECIAL SORT OF PERSON TO BE A RANGER LIKE TUHIN. ONE must be a fighter as well as a tracker, and able to survive alone in the wilderness for weeks on end. I never wanted to be one. Not because I lacked the skill—I was better in the wilderness than most, and a good archer, as well as a passable swordsman. But I did not want to fight for my mother, to be another soldier serving at her command. As a consequence, my mother thought I was rather useless, and that was the only quality she could not forgive in a person. She doted—as much as she ever doted—upon my eldest sister, Romil. And she tolerated my middle sister, Ditra, because Ditra at least tried to play the part our mother demanded.

When I was young, it was hard for me to tell how much of Ditra's demeanor was an act, and how much was genuine. She could adopt a hard-bitten, stern manner when she wished to please our mother. When she was following orders, she would grow stone-hearted, cold, even ruthless.

But I knew another side of her. She was kind to me, and to others, when not under my mother's eye. She was assigned several retainers close to her own age as she grew older, and she grew to love many of them—or at least to bed most of them. I was not supposed to find out, but I did, though Ditra swore me to secrecy.

It happened when I was fifteen, and Ditra would have been . . . oh, she would have been about nineteen? I had woken after a nightmare. I had such dreams often in my youth, though never after my wending, which tells you something. In any case, when I woke up frightened in the night, I would creep down the hall to Ditra's room. Never to my mother's, certainly never to Romil's.

And so there I found myself, creeping along the hallway in the thin moonslight pouring through the windows—when suddenly, the door to Ditra's room opened.

Out came her retainer, cloaked in shadow and little else. I could scarcely see her in the darkness. But she saw me, and she fled at once as if in terror. I stood staring after her, and only after a moment did I realize that Ditra now stood in the doorway. She was clothed in a thin robe, one hand on the door's edge, red upon her cheeks and a scowl upon her face.

"Do not say a word," she whispered in the dark. "Not one. If Mother finds out, she will put me in the stocks."

"Mother would never do that!" I protested. But Ditra gave me a long look, and I wilted under it. "I mean . . . well, obviously, I would never say anything in the first place."

"Good girl," she said, because none of us knew any better in those days, least of all me. "A bad dream?"

I nodded, though I had almost forgotten why I was there. The nightmare was fading. "A small one. Do not trouble yourself over it."

"Oh, come in," she said, opening the door wider. "But sky above, please pay attention in the future, will you? And if you should come to my room, and my door is closed, knock before you open it."

"I will," I promised her.

"Very well," she said. "Tell me what you dreamed."

I entered her room, which smelled sweet, and told her all about the dream, which I do not remember now. And at last I fell asleep in her arms, and felt just a little safer than I had before.

That is what a ranger should be. It is why I always thought Ditra would be an excellent ranger, if she had *not* had to serve my mother.

But it is why I never thought I would be a good one. Because Ditra could always make me feel safe, but that was not a gift I felt I could give to anyone else.

A ranger's first duty is always to keep their people safe. Or at least to try, even when faced with threats against which they are powerless.

On the same night that Mag and I conferred with Tuhin, there was trouble in my homeland of Tokana.

In a small village north of my family's stronghold in Kahaunga, a woman named Whetu and her husband Paora had just put their children to bed for the night. They were sharing a cup of wine before they, too, went to sleep. They rested in wicker chairs in front of their home, watching the stars make their slow turn through the sky.

Whetu had been a ranger long ago. She was the one who heard the sounds first. A heavy stomping, along with a deep, guttural snuffling.

She shot to her feet. "Paora," she whispered.

Paora rose, though more slowly. "What is it?"

"Something is coming. I think—"

A loud, heavy crash shattered the stillness of the night. Towards the northern end of the village, someone screamed.

Whetu turned. "The girls."

They ran inside the house to the back room. Their daughters were sitting up in bed, listening in terror as more screams rang out in the darkness. Together Whetu and Paora scooped them up, running for the front door.

CRASH

The wall to their left shattered inwards. A piece of wood whizzed through the air to jam straight into Whetu's thigh. She managed to bite down on her scream, turning it into a grunt instead, but her daughter fell from her arms onto the floor.

"Whetu!" cried Paora.

"I am fine," wheezed Whetu. "Get the—"

Her eldest daughter screamed, pointing at the new hole in the wall. A massive face was looking through it. The skin looked stony, with small formations of crystals looking as though they had erupted through the skin, and moss clinging to the cracks. Two tusks were visible in the bottom jaw, and two in the top. Huge ears, like miniature sails, swept back from either side of the head, twisting every which way. Small, beady eyes glinted with the light of a nearby fire.

The troll opened its mouth and roared.

"Run!" screamed Whetu, forcing herself to her feet. She seized her daughter's hand and pulled her along, half-dragging her out the door and into the night, forcing herself to keep up with her husband despite the pain in her leg.

Together the family fled south, beyond the bounds of the village and up a rise. Most of the other villagers had gathered there. Whetu and Paora stopped in their midst, clinging to their daughters as they turned to look back at their home.

Trolls were ripping the village apart. There were at least a dozen that Whetu could see. Wooden timbers cracked in their grip as they ripped roofs and walls off of houses, as though they were peeling away the skin of great beasts to reveal and eat the insides. There were only a few stone buildings, but even those could not stand before the monsters—the trolls simply smashed their fists into the stone, and after a few blows, it crumbled before them. A fire had caught in one of the buildings, and tongues of orange licked up into the night. The trolls gave that building a wide berth.

"Why did they attack us?" said one of the villagers.

Whetu's expression was grim. The village had been her home ever since she had retired from the Rangatira's service. Ten years she had lived here, and they had been the happiest years of her life. Watching the trolls rip it apart was like watching them tear her life into pieces and scatter them to the winds.

"Who knows?" she said. "It does not matter now. We must make for Kahaunga."

"She is right!" cried Paora, turning to the others. "We will be safe there. The Rangatira can protect us."

Whetu held her tongue as she pushed through the crowd, leading them off south in the darkness. She wanted to say that Paora's hope was misplaced. They needed to reach the city because they needed food and shelter. But if the trolls attacked Kahaunga, Lord Telfer would not be able to keep them safe. No one would.

Whetu wanted to say it, but she did not. She was no longer a ranger, but she had been. And a ranger was supposed to make her people feel safe. No matter what.

ELEVEN

We were guests of honor in the Rangatira's keep, and our quarters were more than comfortable. Mag distributed our possessions between the bedrooms we had been given. Dryleaf smiled broadly as I walked him about the place, letting him run his fingers along the bookshelves and push them into the deep, plush cushions of the furniture.

"We have gone from comfort to comfort the last few days," he said. "Why could not the road from Bertram have been this gentle on my old bones?"

I laughed. "If only it had, friend. Let yourself relax. You will remain here while we set forth tomorrow."

"Naturally," said Dryleaf. He gave a sigh. "I never thought I would rest inside noble quarters again. It has been some time since I resigned myself to dying in Lan Shui."

"It was our pleasure to change your fate," said Mag.

Dryleaf chuckled. "Oh, I do not know if anything can do that. It depends upon whether you believe in fate or not, I suppose. But I certainly never suspected that I was destined to embark upon another adventure so late in life. The Birchwood was all I ever wanted, for a good long while."

At that moment, a knock came at the door. Supper had been brought for us, though the sun was still well above the horizon. We would go to bed early that night, so that we were well rested when they came to wake us up before dawn. Servants set the dishes out for us, and we began to tuck in. The fare was nowhere near so fine as the meals at Victon's had been, but it was still better than anything we had had upon the road.

"What was it about the Birchwood you so loved?" I asked Dryleaf as we ate. "Why there, and not any of the other wondrous places you must have visited in Underrealm?"

"A fair question," said Dryleaf. "The Birchwood is a place of small wonder, but great peace—which is a wonder in itself, if a less obvious kind. There was something about the trees. Not the sight of them, mind you—that matters little to me, especially now. But there was a feeling to them, a peace beneath their boughs. Four branches of magic there are, wizards will tell you. Yet I have often found myself wondering whether there are other, older magics in the world. It seemed there was always a spell of tranquility upon the Birchwood—something that relaxed your muscles, that made you wish to dip your feet in the cold, clear water of its rivers. I was happy there."

His expression darkened. "Though others were less fortunate. The other reason I wished to return was to look after some friends."

Mag's face twitched. I noticed it, though I did not understand it.

"Old friends?" said Mag.

"Not old the way I am," said Dryleaf. "They were only children, and I had known them for most of their lives. I was mostly concerned with the girl, though there was also a boy who loved her. It has been . . . well, it has been many long years since I was last able to visit them, and when last I was forced to leave them . . . well. The girl, Loren—"

Mag and I had both frozen, her with a bite of food halfway to her mouth. A dawning realization had been creeping upon me as Dryleaf spoke, and when he spoke Loren's name to confirm it, I nearly choked.

"—she had parents with evil hearts," Dryleaf went on, not noticing our sudden silence. "I always worried for her, and as time went on, I would return to visit her more and more frequently. The boy, Chet, was moonstruck for Loren from a young age, and I worried it might get him into trouble with her parents. Particularly her father. I did not know exactly how to help them, but I thought, if I could be there when she came of age, I could somehow . . . some way . . ."

He fell silent. Still I could not move, could not speak. But now Mag was looking at me from across the table.

"Albern," she said quietly.

I stared at her.

Dryleaf frowned. "What is it? Is everything all right?"

Mag turned to him. "Dryleaf . . . this girl from the Birchwood . . ." She fell silent, seemingly unsure what to say.

He pursed his lips. "Yes?"

"We told you of our friends who rode from Northwood," I said. "The ones who delivered word of the Shades to the High King."

Dryleaf went very still. His sightless eyes brimmed with tears.

"It was Loren," said Mag. "And Chet was with her."

His jaw quivered as the tears spilled down his cheeks. When he spoke, his voice had dropped to a whisper.

"Loren is alive?"

We told him everything. Everything we knew, that is, which was not, in fact, everything there was to know. Loren had told me only bits and pieces of what had happened on the long road between her departure from the Birchwood and our meeting in Strapa. But I told Dryleaf everything that had happened after that, and he asked me many questions, so that no detail was missed. He went very pale when we told him of the attack on Northwood, and gave a great sigh of relief when we told him how Loren had escaped the fighting. That was the end of what we had seen, and as my tale subsided, Dryleaf asked me another question.

"Her parents," he said. "Do you know what became of them?"

"We do not," said Mag. "She was not very willing to speak about her home, or her past."

Dryleaf sighed. "No, I suppose she would not have been. Something evil lurked in their souls, and they took it out on their only daughter. Theirs was always a house of secrets—secrets, and pain. I feared that if she remained in that home, she would not survive it."

"You should be happy, then," said Mag. "She escaped, and if I know anything about her, she will never again fall under their sway."

"No," said Dryleaf. "That seems clear. And my heart sings to know that Chet is with her now. He has loved her for a long time, and though I suspect Loren never felt quite the same way—or at least not to the same degree—it will be good for her to have a reminder that not everything in her past came from suffering."

"And she has the children as well," I said. "She may not have known them as long as Chet, but they are a great source of comfort to her. She thinks she protects them, and I suppose she does. But they are better for her than she realizes."

"Good, good," said Dryleaf. "It sounds as though she went through many hardships on her road—and she may still face hardship even now. But as long as she has Chet, I am confident she will be well cared for."

"How did you first meet Loren, anyway?" said Mag. "Why did you keep returning to the Birchwood to see her?"

Dryleaf tilted his head. "You have met her yourself. You know how remarkable she is. She was always that way, and I knew she could do great things, if she could only escape her horrible home. It was always something that just seemed to happen to me: finding the lonely and the lost, and trying to make their lives somewhat easier, if it was in my power to do so. Loren was not the only one, though she was a particularly urgent case. I knew an orphan girl in Cabrus, who has run away now, and is lost in the nine kingdoms. A merchant boy in Idris, who finally broke his family's shackles and lives on his own now. A child of nobility in Hedgemond, who needed more love than her mother felt she could spare. She is a Mystic now, and a fine officer of that order."

My expression darkened, and I picked at a loose thread on my sleeve. I was not from Hedgemond, of course, but Dryleaf's words would have been most apt for my own mother.

"But these others had already managed to escape, sometimes with my help, sometimes on their own. Loren was the last. She never knew me as Dryleaf, by the by. In the Birchwood, they call me Bracken. But after Loren, I had thought I would be done. My bones were already getting too old for travel, and the Birchwood seemed a good place to live out the end of one's life. I had only just resigned myself to do so in Lan Shui instead, when you arrived."

"But Dryleaf," said Mag. "Or, wait. Should we call you Bracken?"

He waved a hand. "No, no. One name is as good as another after all these years, and I will not say the name my parents gave me, for there is a reason I left it behind so long ago."

"Very well," said Mag. "My question is: what now? You know Loren was making for the Seat, and you are free from Lan Shui. Do you wish to run off and find her?"

"We could make arrangements," I said.

Dryleaf settled deeper into his chair and sighed. "I will not lie to you: I greatly wish to go. But no. For now, at least, it is enough for me to know that she escaped her parents. I am content to remain with you for a while yet." His lips curled in a smile. "You may need my help, after all. And besides, it seems likely that you shall cross paths with Loren again, and mayhap sooner than later."

"That is my wish," I said.

"Then until that day," said Dryleaf, "I will happily ride by your side, if you will continue to have me. But wait!" Suddenly his face lit up, and he gave a broad grin. "We must write her at once."

I blinked. "Write her?"

"Why not?" he said. "We know where she is."

I looked to Mag. Writing to Loren had not even crossed our mind on all the long road since Northwood—but then, we had no idea that she had succeeded in her mission. And with that came a chilling thought. "Mag," I said quietly. "She thinks we are dead. She must."

"Sky above," breathed Mag.

"And I doubt she thinks I am still breathing," said Dryleaf. "Had I thought her parents would let her read a letter, I would have written one long ago. As far as she knows, I simply disappeared."

That settled it. We asked one of the stronghold's servants for paper, quill, and ink. Together we sat down and drafted a letter, which Mag rendered in a firm hand. When we were done, I folded the parchment up and handed it to Dryleaf.

"I will see to the arrangements tomorrow, while the two of you are off on your adventure," he said. "Someone should be willing to walk me to the constables' station to send it off."

"Thank you," I said. "I only wish I could see her face when she reads it."

"As do I," chuckled Dryleaf, "though that chance passed long ago."

"At least she will know we are alive," I said. "And if we should meet her upon the road, and you wish to go with her then, no one will begrudge you that—least of all me."

Mag gave me a careful look as I said it. I thought she must be wondering if I, too, would ride off with Loren, were I given the chance.

But now it was time for bed. We had spoken a good long while into the night, and we had to rise early for tomorrow's hunt. I helped Dryleaf to his bed and retired to my own room, undressing by moonslight.

Sky above, let our hunt end tomorrow, I thought to myself. *Let it be over, so that we can find the children again, and see that they are safe.*

But of course, you know enough about the Necromancer's War to know my hopes were in vain. And even today, part of me wishes I had not waited.

TWELVE

One of Lord Matara's servants awoke us before dawn. Mag and I left Dryleaf asleep as we roused and dressed ourselves and then made our way out of the stronghold. The moment we set foot in the courtyard outside the keep, Oku came dashing up to us, yipping in excitement. I knelt and scratched him behind the ears.

"Did you sleep well, boy?" I said. "I hope so. We have a long journey ahead of us."

Oku licked my fingers and trotted over to Mag, sniffing at her leg. I looked studiously away so that she could pat his head and think I had not noticed.

Tuhin soon joined us, leading a horse by the reins. Two stablehands followed, bringing Foolhoof for me and Mist for Mag. We mounted and rode through the streets of the city. Tuhin was silent as we went, and I thought they might still be ridding themself of the last vestiges of sleep. Yet they seemed alert and watchful, peering down each street as we went, though there was no one around. They even looked up into the sky. It struck me that they were likely looking for any sign that the weremage was stalking us.

Once we had left the city through the eastern gate and were a good distance away from the wall, I finally spoke. "Did you see any sign of pursuit?"

"No," said Tuhin. "But I am always cautious when going on an expedition, especially when pursuing a wizard. They are not to be underestimated, especially weremages."

"I have fallen out of such habits on our long road," I said, "but I will try to resume them. I have grown nearly as lazy as Chao." I looked over at her. "Remind me never to grow so inattentive again."

"But what if I am too lazy to do so?" said Mag.

Tuhin smirked. "You can rest easily, Kanohari," they said. "I saw no one paying us any undue attention."

"That is a relief," said Mag. "Wake me if you see any signs of danger. I will be dozing in my saddle, as it seems is my wont."

"Oh, be silent," I grumbled, "or we will make you ride at the head of the party."

"But I do not want to," said Mag, giving an exaggerated frown. She reached to her belt and pulled out a copper sliver. "We should flip for it and let fate decide. Tuhin, have you ever heard of latrine duty?"

"Do not answer that," I said quickly, even as Tuhin opened their mouth to answer.

Tuhin shook their head, still smiling, and took the lead. They made their way down the same eastern road we had taken to reach Victon's estate, but they soon turned north, on a smaller road that curved east after a time, wrapping around the foot of the mountain.

Dawn broke at last, and we increased our pace now that we did not have to worry about striking a rock or sudden pit in the dark. Though we traveled east, the sun did not immediately fly into our eyes, for we had entered a series of low but steep hills that thrust up around the road on both sides. The road grew faint, but it still had very clear edges. I could tell that it had once been well-tended, and mayhap paved with stone.

And then I noticed the tracks.

"Tuhin," I called out.

"I see them," they said, pulling their horse to a halt. Mag and I stopped as well.

"Would anyone else have a good reason to use this road?"

"Not much of one," said Tuhin. "There is no good hunting this way, and there are no dwellings at all."

Mag frowned at me. "What in the dark are the two of you talking about?"

"Signs of others," I said, pointing at the road.

She shook her head. "I see nothing."

"What did I tell you?" I said, giving Tuhin an exaggerated shrug. "Lazy."

While Tuhin hid a laugh, Mag nudged her horse closer and punched me hard in the arm. I gave her an easy smile.

There were not all that many—around a dozen distinct trails that I could make out. They could easily have been made by the same person going back and forth several times. I saw no hoofprints, though if someone wished to approach Opara on horseback, they would likely have looped around and approached by the north road.

"We carry on," said Tuhin. "But we should abandon the road. I wonder if we should leave the horses."

"Though it is tempting," I said, frowning down at Foolhoof's flattened ears, "I would rather draw closer first. How far away is this stronghold?"

"Another two hours if we press the horses, mayhap three or four on foot," said Tuhin.

"Then let us ride for another hour, off the road, before we leave our mounts."

"A fair plan," said Tuhin, and they turned their horse at once, walking off the road and into the wild.

We wound our way through the dips between the hills, slower now without the bridges that crossed shallow cracks in the land, or the rises that had been leveled to accommodate it. Tuhin led us skillfully, though it was clear they had not been here for some time. After a while, the land dipped into a gentle gorge, through which ran a narrow stream with easy banks. The land began a steep climb after we crested the other side. Soon we came upon a broken hinterland, with steep cliffs that threatened to drop us a span or more to the ground below. All around us were piles of black rock, pitted and pockmarked, signs of the mountain's ancient fury.

"This is where I think we should leave the horses," said Tuhin. "They will be no faster than we will be on foot, especially on the fireglass."

Mag arched an eyebrow. "Fireglass?"

I pointed to the black rock. "Leavings of the mountain. Lava after it cools off."

"Ah," said Mag, arching an eyebrow. "The mountain is not going to drop its leavings on us, is it? I am not fond of dangers against which I have little power."

"Not every danger can be staved off with a spear," I told her, slipping down from the saddle. "Worry not, wanderer. We will not let the mountain's rage consume you."

Tuhin chuckled and waved a dismissive hand towards Tahumaunga. "It is only a grumpy old man these days. You are lucky we do not wander at its feet during the time of its youth, when the tales say it was as wrathful as a dragon."

We found a small cluster of trees well away from the fireglass, with brilliant green turf springing up on the ground all around. Oku danced about as we dismounted and brought the horses together. With a hatchet from my saddle, I quickly cut a few sturdy posts from the branches of the trees, and we gave the horses a loose tether that would allow them to wander. They began to nibble at the grass almost immediately, except Mist, who nuzzled Mag's shoulder first.

"There there, girl," said Mag. "We will return before you know it."

"A fine mare," said Tuhin, patting Mist's flank as she began to graze with the others.

"Far better than that one," said Mag, pointing at Foolhoof.

"Do you expect me to argue?" I said, arching my brows. "He is never more than a bad mood away from being turned into sausage."

"That is simply cruel," said Tuhin. Foolhoof raised his head to nudge them gently with his neck, the dark-taken traitor. "Do you see? He is a gentle soul."

They ignored my sudden grumbles and led us off again. Soon we were breathing somewhat heavily. The land kept climbing, and we had to take many sudden turns and detours to avoid pits and cliffs that seemed to appear out of nowhere. Mag, curse her, did not seem winded at all, despite her shirt of metal scales. But then, that was to be expected. I kept Oku close by as we went, and he was more than capable of matching our pace.

I began to notice that Tuhin was looking around uneasily as we went. "What is wrong?" I asked them.

Tuhin's mouth twisted. "The land is quiet."

I felt a tenseness creep down from my neck into my shoulders. "Do you think we are being watched?"

"I am not certain," said Tuhin. "I have been searching for signs, but I have found none yet. We should be wary, just in case."

"I am always wary," said Mag.

"That is a lie," I said.

It became clear, the farther we went, that the cliffs we kept encountering were in fact one long cliff, the edge of a trench that ran for miles. Tuhin's guidance meant we encountered it rarely, and only when they became turned around for a moment. But I realized after a time that it was far too straight to be natural. It was a man-made trench that must have been dug in ancient days. I remembered Victon's words, that it had been put here to divert lava away from Opara and into the surrounding land. I marveled at the thought of it. Magic must have been used in its making, for I could not imagine that even an army could have dug so deep, and for such a great distance.

"Halt," said Tuhin suddenly.

We stopped short behind them. Just ahead of us, the path delved into a slice through a hill, both sides slick with fireglass. Half a span in, the path curved sharply to the right and out of sight.

"Maunwa is on the other side of that passage."

They unslung their bow from their back, and I did the same. Mag had her spear ready, for she had been using it as a walking stick. Now she hefted her shield off her back and onto her arm. Tuhin pressed close to one side of the path, creeping forwards to the sharp turn. I was just behind them, with Mag bringing up the rear.

Tuhin came to the corner at the end of the path and stopped. I pressed forwards a bit, trying to see around. Tuhin saw me edging towards them and beckoned me closer. I leaned over, my shoulder to theirs, and looked around the bend.

Only a few paces from where we stood, the steep-sided path emerged into the open air. And there, mayhap three spans away, sat the fortress of Maunwa. It perched upon the top of a rise, but behind it the land fell off into the sheer cliff of the trench. A thick iron gate sat in its northern wall, visible from our vantage point, and a road ran out of it—the same road, I knew, that we had been following before we left it for the wilderness.

An uneasy feeling came over me. I had approached a stronghold in the mountains in much the same way not that long ago. Then, as now, I had anticipated foes within, and then I had lost someone dear to me.

I shrugged the feeling away. Yes, there might be Shades here, as there had been when I had led Jordel to his doom. But I had not had Mag by my side, then.

"I see no one on the walls," I murmured to Tuhin.

"Mayhap it is abandoned," they said, frowning. "Yet I am still uneasy. We should check to make sure."

We crept forwards. I whispered hasty instructions to Mag and Oku to stay well behind the two of us. For all her skill at fighting, Mag was no master of stealth.

I followed Tuhin's lead until we were out of the narrow path, and then we split up and cut wide, creeping between rocks and mounds of fireglass. I kept my eyes firmly fixed on the stronghold, wary for any sign of movement inside. But there was nothing. The gate remained open, and it looked as though it might have been that way for years.

Of course, we could not know that the Shades were aware of us. We could not know that Kaita had warned them, and that they were fully aware we had left the city, thanks to an agent of theirs in the Rangatira's keep. Nor could we know that they had sent their best scouts to shadow us, agents so stealthy that even Tuhin did not detect them, except as a vague sense of unease. We did not know they had us surrounded.

Until they struck.

THIRTEEN

I HEARD THE WHISTLE OF AN ARROW A BLINK BEFORE IT STRUCK MAG, too late to do anything about it. Too late for me, at least, but not for her. She whirled on the spot. Her cloak billowed around her with the movement, and the arrow passed harmlessly through it.

"Down!" I cried, flinging myself behind a boulder that jutted out of the ground, its bottom half embedded deep in the earth. Oku yelped and pressed against my legs. But no sooner had I hit the dirt than I spotted a flash above me. Sunlight reflecting on metal. Without thinking, I threw myself down and rolled.

An arrow splintered against the rock. If I had been a moment slower, it would have struck me in the chest.

I came up ready to fire. My shaft sped for where I had seen the archer above me. But they were too wily, and had already hidden themselves. My arrow passed futilely through the air.

"Agh!"

Tuhin cried out as an arrow impaled their right shoulder. I spared them only a glance before looking wildly around.

The archer who had fired at me had been opposite the one who shot at Mag. They were in a half-circle that wrapped around us, and we could find little cover out here, despite the boulders. For a mad moment, I thought of running for the fort, but that would put us in open ground long enough for them to fill us with arrows. I looked around desperately.

There. A small depression, not quite a cave, in the side of the hill nearby. It would block vision from above.

I sprinted for Tuhin and seized them by the back of their shirt. Ignoring their grunt of pain, I dragged them towards cover. Oku came pelting after us, whining.

"Chao!" I cried over my shoulder.

Mag had been peeking out from behind a boulder, looking for a way to approach the archers above. She glanced over, saw what I was doing, and ran to join us.

"Dark below," I grunted, releasing Tuhin once we were in the half-cave.

"Thank you," they gasped, seizing their wound and squeezing to keep it from bleeding.

"Save your gratitude until we survive this, if we do," I told them. "Do you have bandages?"

"Here." They drew them from a sack at their belt.

I snapped off the arrowhead and pulled the shaft out of the wound. Tuhin grunted in pain, but they kept their wits and handed me the bandages. I wrapped them around the shoulder, and Tuhin helped me hold them in place until I was done. When I finished, they sighed in relief and leaned back against the cool earth.

"Again, thank you."

I stepped away from them to take stock of our situation. In the half-cave, the Shades could not see us. But neither could we see them, and we could not step out to shoot at them. I had an arrow nocked, but it felt useless between my fingers. My mind whirled, trying to devise a strategy.

"These friends of your weremage are ready for a fight," said Tuhin with a grim smile.

I snorted. "Fortunately, so are we."

"I should have been more watchful," said Tuhin, wincing against the pain of their wound. "I grew lax after we left Opara."

"You were the only one who thought anything was wrong on the road here," I pointed out. "You and Oku. I should have been less moonstruck by the fireglass and the trench. But this is no time for blame. We must—"

"Stay alive," barked Mag.

Before I could even look at her in surprise or ask what she meant, she ran out into the open. Oku gave a sharp bark and ran after her. I reached for them both with a cry.

But though arrows came streaking for them, they missed. Of the two that would have struck Mag, she caught one on her shield. The other passed through her cloak, and I gasped, certain it had pierced her side. But she ripped it from the cloth and flung it on the ground—it had rebounded from her armor. She darted out of sight, Oku hard on her heels.

"What under the sky is she doing?" gasped Tuhin. "There are at least a dozen of them. We need to flee, not fight!"

"That is not how Chao prefers to go about things," I said, shaking my head. "But as tempting as it is to let her take care of them, I cannot allow her to fight alone. There was a tree not far from the stronghold. I am going to sprint for it. It is close enough to the trench that I will have one direction, at least, from which they cannot fire at me. While I give you cover, you must try to go in the same direction as Chao. You can lose yourself in the hills."

"I will go with you," said Tuhin. "I can still run, and I might draw arrows away from you."

"I can do it alone."

"Of course you can," said Tuhin, and they sprinted into the open air.

"Dark take you!" I cried, sprinting after them.

They kept their lead, and the two of us dodged and weaved, taking sudden turns to try and confound the archers. Arrows hissed all around us. One found Tuhin before we reached the tree, but it merely stuck in their cloak.

We fell to the ground on the tree's other side. It was a thick oak with high branches, and for a moment I simply sat there, panting and pressing the back of my head against the rough bark. At last I risked a glance out. I ducked back at once, as five arrows streaked through the air towards me. Three stuck into the tree, the other two embedding themselves in the ground near our feet.

"Only five arrows," I said. "Chao has been busy. We should help her finish the job."

"That shall fall to you, I am afraid," said Tuhin, pointing to their shoulder with a rueful smile. "Unless you think I should throw arrows at them with my good arm."

"As amusing as that would be, I think not."

Quickly notching an arrow, I darted around the other side of the tree and fired at the last place I had seen one of our foes. Her head popped into sight, but a heartbeat too late, and I missed. She fell back behind cover again, and I did the same—but then I froze as I heard a scream from her location.

I risked another glance out. There she was—Mag, standing just in the spot where I had fired my arrow. She had plunged her spear down where I could not see it, but when it came up again, it was red with the blood of the woman I had tried to shoot. I heard a furious barking from Oku, and then Mag vanished.

"Sky bless and dark take her, both at once," I muttered, as I hid once more.

"Chao?" said Tuhin.

"She killed another one. Mayhap more. I think I am going to try to draw their fire again, to give her as much opportunity as I can."

"There are many rocks close by, and I think they are far enough away from the hills. We should mayhap run for one."

I nodded. "One. Two. Three. Four!"

We pelted out from behind the tree. But only two arrows came streaking down this time. *Sky above,* I thought, *did Mag kill that many already?* I struck the ground hard, groaning as my ribs slammed into the rock I had hidden behind, and I heard Tuhin grunt as they did the same several paces away.

From the edge of my vision, I had taken note of where one of the arrows came from. I drew, leaped up, and fired. This time the arrow flew true. A man in a blue cloak appeared just in time to take the shot in the eye. His head jerked back, fletching protruding from the socket, and he toppled out of sight.

"One!" I called out, hiding again. "At least Chao is not having all the fun."

"You two have very odd ideas about your entertainment," said Tuhin, and I gave a shout of laughter.

Footsteps.

They came pounding across the turf, running from the pathway through which we had emerged. From the sound of them, they were making for the stronghold. Mag? No, the steps sounded too light.

I risked a look out. A young woman in a grey cloak was sprinting for the gate. I looked up at the surrounding hills. No shots came flying towards me.

Dropping my bow, I broke from cover and ran after the woman.

She was panicked, her dark skin flushed with exertion and fear. She did not hear me until I was almost upon her. At the last moment I leaped, and only then did she begin to turn to see me. I struck her hard in the side, and she crashed to the ground with me on top of her.

Her hand darted for a knife at her belt. I seized her wrist with one hand and struck her in the face with the other. It dazed her for a moment, and her head lolled to the side. I drew the knife and threw it away before flipping her over to lie on her face, dragging her arm behind her back and holding her immobile. With my free hand, I patted her waist and boot to make sure she was not hiding another weapon.

"I think it is over, Tuhin," I called out. "Help me secure her."

Tuhin emerged into the open, though they still walked hunched over, darting from rock to rock. When no more arrows were forthcoming, they straightened at last and came over.

"Here," they said, drawing a pair of iron manacles from a pouch at their belt. These they clamped around the woman's wrists, securing them behind her back. Together we hauled her to her feet. The woman's eyes were wild, and they darted about frantically, seeking some means of escape. Her shoulder-length hair swung across her face with her movements, though it could not entirely obscure the sizable birthmark that covered her left cheek.

"None of that," I told her. "I am afraid your time here is over. Please do not make more trouble than you already have. I would hate to have to sling you over the back of my horse as we ride back to the city. I have seen a long journey made that way once, and it was most uncomfortable."

"I have done nothing," the woman said. Her voice was low, but thin, and it shook with terror.

"Nothing lasting, though not for lack of trying," I said. "But you shot my friend here, or one of your companions did. Tuhin, what penalty do you think the Rangatira will mete out for such a thing?"

"Oh, imprisonment and hard labor would normally be enough," said Tuhin, raising their brows. "But then, I am a representative of the King's law. The punishment for *that* shall be much more severe."

"Dark below, you are frightening the poor girl," called Mag.

I turned. She had just emerged from the path. Oku padded at her heels, looking up at her and whining. A great deal of blood had spattered across Mag's clothes, and she had her hands on another one of the Shades. This one had her blue hood cast back, and her hair was wild as she struggled and jerked in Mag's grip.

And I knew her.

FOURTEEN

THE WOMAN MAG HAD CAPTURED WAS A NOBLE—OR AT LEAST, SHE HAD been. Her family lived in Opara. They had served the Rangatira when last we had met, far back in my youth. I struggled to remember her name. Riri, that was it. And yet there was no trace of recognition in her eyes.

Shock and a flood of memories caused me to slacken my grip. The woman I was holding noticed it, and she bolted towards the stronghold, her arm tearing out of my hands. But with her arms bound tightly behind her, she could hardly hope to outpace me. I caught up after only a few paces, catching her and wrestling her to the ground once again. It was only when I looked up that I realized we were hardly a pace from the edge of the trench, and spans of empty air stretched before us to the hard ground far below.

"Careful," I told her. "You almost went over. And if you are not cooperative with my friend, she may pitch you over regardless."

"Are you all right there, Kanohari?" said Mag. She drew nearer, her hand firmly clutching Riri's arms behind her back. "I caught one on my own. I thought you would be able to handle another, with help."

"Cease your boasts," I told her. "Are there any more hiding out there?"

"None," said Mag. "I accounted for all of them. There were twelve. Only these two remain. I left this one alive because she is in charge." She hefted Riri's arms up, bringing her slightly off the ground, like a prize on display. Riri snarled and made a fresh break for freedom, but she could not budge with Mag holding her. "I heard her giving orders. The one you are holding escaped while I was killing one of her fellows, and I trusted you would catch her."

"Assuming your faith is genuine, I appreciate it," I told her.

I noticed something odd. Oku had remained close by Mag's side. He kept nuzzling her leg, as though checking to make sure she was all right, and small whines issued from his throat. Mag ignored him.

"Well, now to get them both back to Opara," said Tuhin. They pulled out another pair of manacles and went to bind Riri.

"There is one problem," said Mag, as Tuhin did their work. "I saw no sign of the weremage."

"There is more than one problem," said Tuhin. When we blinked in surprise, they gave us both a stern look. "These are Shades."

I did my best to look shocked. "These two?"

"And their companions," said Tuhin. "They wear blue and grey, which we have been told are the Shades' colors. And something tells me you are not quite as surprised by this news as you are trying to appear."

Mag shrugged. "How could we know? The weremage dwelled long in Tokana. We had no reason to suspect her involvement with them."

"Hm," said Tuhin. "Or mayhap you thought the Rangatira would not let you join the hunt, if he knew you were in fact hunting Shades."

Mag's expression of innocence was perfect. "Would he not?"

"Hm," said Tuhin again. Then they rolled their eyes. "Since we have, in fact, cleared out a hidden stronghold of Shades, I suppose I have done my duty, and I need not press the matter."

"We thank you," I said. "But we are, in fact, after the weremage, and that mystery remains. Unless she is one of these two."

It was only then that I realized Riri had gone very quiet. She looked no less enraged, but she had stopped trying to pull away from Mag. Her eyes went from Tuhin to Mag, and then to me, calculating, assessing.

"I think that if she was disguised as one of these two, she would have taken a more dangerous form already, trying to kill us," said Mag.

"You cannot be sure," said Tuhin. "And you have forgotten someone else." They gave a small smile.

I frowned at them. "Who is that?"

"Me," said Tuhin. "You lost sight of me for a moment there. It would have been easy for her to replace me, if she was nearby, and watching. If you are going to hunt a weremage, you must always be alert, and never trust anyone—least of all the ones you feel certain about."

An uneasy feeling crept through me. "But if you were her, you would never tell us this."

"Unless it were part of a grander ploy," said Tuhin, raising their brows. "I could be luring you into a false sense of peace. Why, after this, I imagine the two of you would march me straight to the Rangatira, where I might be able to strike him down."

"Except the Rangatira has his own wizards to detect that sort of thing," said Mag.

Tuhin gave an exasperated look. "But the weremage might not know that, and I rather wish you had not mentioned it in front of the prisoners."

Oku pulled his attention away from Mag for a moment and trotted to Tuhin. Tuhin knelt to greet him, and Oku sniffed at their wounded shoulder. He gave it one brief lick and then went back to Mag, whining at her again.

"Oku seems to trust you," I said.

"I could fool him, too, if I were particularly skilled at magic," said Tuhin. "There is only one way to ensure we know who the weremage is."

"Please," interjected the younger Shade woman in my grip. Her eyes had begun to brim with tears. "I only served them for the coin, I do not—"

"Shut your mouth, girl," said Riri harshly.

"This is ridiculous," said Mag, looking annoyed. "The weremage would never tell us everything you have."

"They are masters of deception," said Tuhin.

"They are not the weremage!" said the younger girl, tossing her head at Tuhin. "She left!"

"Hoko!" cried Riri.

"She might have appeared to leave, but remained behind," said Tuhin. "You would never know, girl. There is only one way to tell for certain."

"What is it?" I said. "Though I suppose you will tell us, and then tell us that we cannot trust what you have told us, because you could be the weremage."

"You are getting the idea now," said Tuhin, grinning broadly.

They came towards me and the younger Shade—Hoko, she had been called. She recoiled, but Tuhin ignored it.

"There are two points just behind the temple," they said, pointing to their own head. "Just here, where the skull dips. As I understand it, the magic passes through there, no matter what form the weremage takes. And if you strike them—"

They lunged forwards, striking with their uninjured hand in a chopping motion. Hoko reeled under the impact. But nothing happened—no glow in the eyes, and no shifting of her form. Tuhin strode towards Riri next.

"Do not touch me, kingsworn scum," snarled Riri.

But Mag held her still, and Tuhin struck her just as they had done to Hoko. Riri grunted at the blows, but again, nothing happened.

"That is most interesting," said Mag.

Then she moved almost faster than I could see. First she shoved Riri in my direction, and I caught the woman's arm in surprise. Mag struck Tuhin twice, once in each temple, before I realized what had happened. Tuhin nearly fell over from her strikes, but somehow they kept their feet. Their gaze looked unfocused for a moment.

"Yes," they said weakly. "Just like that."

"Chao!" I said indignantly.

"No, she was quite correct to do so," said Tuhin, raising a hand. "I could have been the weremage, and I could still be, if I have been lying. You should bind my hands for the journey home."

"I will keep you close," said Mag. "You will not escape us unless I want you to. Assuming you are, in fact, Tuhin, where did you learn this skill?"

"I was never a Mystic, but I have served alongside them many times," said Tuhin. "This is a trick I learned from their mage hunters."

Suddenly a memory came to me. I, too, had traveled with a Mystic—Jordel, who had also been a mage hunter, once. I had seen him do something I would have called impossible, if I had not seen it myself. He pressed his fingers to the temples of Xain, the wizard, and forced him to use his firemagic.

I met Mag's gaze. "I think they are telling the truth. I have seen something like this before."

"You should bind me regardless," said Tuhin.

"I have already said you cannot escape from me if I do not wish you to," said Mag.

A thought struck me. "Tuhin," I said. "You are trying to warn us about yourself. But you have said nothing about Chao. We both lost sight of her. She could be the weremage, for all you know."

Tuhin grinned. "I wondered when you would think of that. Oku trusts her. Animals have a sense for these things, and none more so than wolfhounds. For a weremage to be able to fool Oku, they would have to be so powerful that you would not have survived the long road you took to get here."

I glared at them. "But you just said Oku's trust of *you* was no proof."

Tuhin shrugged. "Not if I am a strong enough weremage."

"This is making my head hurt," said Mag. "We should be getting back to Opara, lest we return after dark."

"Then you must take the three of us to the Mystics," said Tuhin. "They will know the same trick I have already told you, and they will tell you I am who I appear to be."

"The Mystics?" cried Hoko in terror.

All of us turned to look at her—including Riri, who suddenly fixed the girl with a razor-sharp glare.

"Why, yes," I said. "We need to know what happened to the weremage who had been working with you. And no one is better at gathering information than the Mystics."

"I will tell you!" shrieked Hoko.

"Hoko!" said Riri sharply, tensing in my grip.

"The weremage went to the Telfer homelands! Tokana!" cried the girl.

I froze.

"Hoko!" snarled Riri. "Dark damn you, you traitorous sow!"

"Save your breath," said Hoko, who sounded close to sobbing. "I have been under the Mystics' knives before. I will not go there again for anything—not for you, and not for the Lord."

The girl's words rang in my ears. Tokana? My homeland? What would draw the weremage there?

"Why?" I demanded. I shoved Riri away and gripped Hoko by the shoulders. "Why Tokana?"

I had meant to shove Riri towards Mag. I failed.

She spun with my shove and charged at my back, bent almost double. I heard her just in time to step aside and turn to see what was the matter.

Riri caught Hoko in the stomach with her shoulder.

She did not stop. Both women pitched headfirst over the edge of the trench.

"No!" I cried, running to the edge. Mag leaped forwards and seized my arm, drawing me back.

Riri remained silent, but Hoko's scream lasted an obscenely long time before being sharply cut off.

"They are gone," said Mag quietly.

I ripped my arm out of her grip, and she let me. "Dark take me," I said savagely.

"You were distracted," said Mag. "And you have reason to be."

I glared at her, but I could not do so for long. I turned away, even as Tuhin stood on the edge of the cliff, looking down to where they had fallen.

"We . . . we should investigate," they said after a moment, sounding like someone coming out of a dream. "The stronghold, I mean. We should ensure no one else lurks within. And one of you must remain with me as a guard. Or mayhap we should stay together—I could heal this injury and overpower only one of you."

"Sky above, Tuhin, *you are not the weremage,*" I growled.

They gave me a grim look, only faintly amused now. "You do not know that."

"Let us all search Maunwa, then, and be quick about it," I said gruffly. "The sooner we can return to Opara, the better."

"Do not look too worried," said Tuhin. "If the weremage is heading for Tokana, that means you can set your steps for home."

They could hardly have said anything *more* worrying, though of course they could not have known that. I struggled to don a smile. “That is good news, at least.”

But it was not. I knew it, somehow. Just as I knew that this had become very, very personal.

I did not know exactly why the weremage had turned her steps towards Tokana. But I knew, down to my core, that my family was in terrible danger.

In raven form, Kaita watched the whole thing from the air. When we captured Hoko and Riri, she spun lower in the sky so that she could hear. Hoko told us that the weremage was headed for Tokana, and Kaita felt an enormous wave of relief.

That relief turned to grim satisfaction as Riri and Hoko pitched over the cliff.

Dark take her, the fool, thought Kaita.

Her anger at Riri faded quickly. Now she was free to journey to Tokana. She would travel by air. It would be exhausting, but she had the strength. The end of the game drew near.

Kaita could not defeat Mag herself. But even the Uncut Lady would be helpless against the trolls.

And if she were not—if even the trolls proved unequal to the challenge—Kaita had Rogan’s word. If the trolls could not finish what she had started, then Father would give her the strength she had long craved.

But that would come later, if it came at all. In the meantime, at long last, she was going home.

FIFTEEN

ALBERN FELL SILENT AND GLANCED DOWN AT SUN. THE CORNERS OF HIS mouth curled up, though he seemed to be trying to fight the smile. Sun frowned. What was the old man smirking for? Then she realized she was fidgeting with her fingers as they walked. A flush crept into her cheeks as she stilled her hands.

"You look fit to choke on whatever unasked question plagues you," chuckled Albern. "Spit it out."

Still she hesitated, and when she did speak, it was slowly. "You said you would only give me certain stories. I do not want to ask for a tale you do not wish to tell."

"I will only tell you what I wish, but you can always ask," said Albern. "I do not promise to answer, but I might."

That was good enough for Sun, and her words came out in a rush. "Whenever you speak of Kaita, you say she thought of Calentin—and now Tokana, I suppose—as 'home.' Was it the Shades' home, or *her* home? Did she live there as a child? Did you know her?"

Albern shook his head. "I did not know her, because she was not a noble."

Sun frowned. "What does that matter? I was a noble as well, but I knew plenty of common folk in—"

"Calentin is not Dulmun, and my family was not like yours," said Albern. "The commonfolk in Tokana obeyed us, but when I was a child, we were not particularly well loved. Nor did we mingle often. My mother, in particular, was very strict about it. You recall the story of Ditra and her retainer? She feared Mother would punish her severely if they were found out, and she was correct."

It still made no sense to Sun. "Still, you must have known *some* commoners in your youth, unless you never left your family's stronghold. But you have already told me that was not the case."

He sighed. "You are not entirely wrong. My mother's attitude is, mayhap, an excuse I use to feel better about the way I acted. We all like to think better of our younger selves than we might deserve. The truth is that I rarely tried to befriend anyone outside my family, or even converse with them. I never paid much attention to anyone but other nobility, and even that was scant compared to the attention I gave to the wilderness. You might not believe it, but I think I have spoken more to you, in the short time we have known each other, than I ever spoke to my eldest sister, Romil."

Sun balked at that. "That cannot be true."

"Stories and truth," said Albern with a smile. "But that is how I remember it. Romil saw me as little more than a family asset, and a poor one at that, and I wholeheartedly returned her lack of affection. The only person I was close to was Ditra, and even we drifted further apart as we grew older.

"It was not until I was free from my home, out from under the sway of my mother, that I began to appreciate the people around me. I had been so starved for friendship and affection that I began to bestow them with great vigor. You think I am friendly now, but I doubt you would have so enjoyed my company if you had met me when I was your age. I was too focused on my family, on how they treated me. In short, I thought only of my own difficulties. Once I had put them mostly behind me, it felt like my attention was suddenly free, and I was able to behold a world I had never noticed before. And only then could I spare enough thought for my own desires to decide what I wanted to do with my life. That is when I realized I was ander. I could never see it in Tokana, when I was too focused on my dissatisfaction with my family to see how I was dissatisfied with myself."

Sun shook her head. "I still want to know why you left your home in the first place. You have told me of the tree in the valley, and your mother's lack of care. But neither sounds dire enough to flee your homeland, especially as a noble."

"You did not ask about this before."

Sun threw her hands in the air. "I did not want some dark-taken answer that 'Every part of the story must be told in its proper turn, or the whole thing will collapse.'"

Her imitation of his Calentin accent was passingly fair, and Albern laughed loud and long at it. "I suppose I can explain a bit more of my decision without ruining the whole tale," he said at last, wiping a mirthful tear from his eye as his laughter finally subsided. "I did not leave because of the tree. As I told you, that was only what first made me aware of my discontent. The urge to leave built steadily after that. My mother's unkindness was another part of it. My father was a bannerman first, a parent second, and he died when I was young. All I had was Ditra, and she was only a few years older than me. She was not a good substitute for a parent. And why should she have been? She had no one to learn from—certainly not our mother."

He cut himself off suddenly, and the smile he forced was sour. "That sounded resentful."

"You *seem* resentful," said Sun. "But not without good reason."

"I should have left this bitterness in the past long ago," said Albern. "I should not still be angry about it, but I am."

It made Sun uncomfortable to hear such familiar sentiment from someone so much older than she was. "I understand," she said. "Truly, I do. My parents act the same way."

"As I suspected," said Albern with a sigh. "It is as though . . . as though people become parents, and suddenly they feel a sense of duty to 'the family.' But they forget, or so it seems, that the family is made of people. A family is not a name. It is not a legacy, not a list of ancestors, not the house you live in. It is the people. Your kin, by blood or by law, or by choice. If the people are not well, the family is not well."

He paused again—but this time with a wince of pain, and his hand moved to his side, clutching near his ribs. Sun's heart skipped.

"Are you all right?" she said.

"Fine," he said. "It is . . . something. I am not sure. Mayhap it is an old injury, or mayhap just a product of age. It is one of the reasons I wish to see the medica."

"Ah," said Sun. "You seem to be traveling quite far to meet her. Have you known her long?"

"Oh yes," said Albern, his smile returning. "She is the one who performed my wending when I was your age. She is hardly any older than I am. That was quite a shock, when first we met. There I was, having only seen nineteen summers, having only just realized that I was not my mother's daughter, as I had always thought, but her son. I had just left home, and I was very anxious about the wending, as most are. And in walked a young woman in a medica's robes, who had seen only twenty-two years, and who *looked* even younger than I was.

"Well, I must have seemed nervous, because Dawan laughed out loud. 'You think I am young, do you?' she said. 'Well, you are right. But I am one of the High King Enalyn's personal medicas. Masada, the one who performed Enalyn's own wending, was my mentor, and when he passed into the darkness, I took up Enalyn's service myself. If I am good enough for the High King, I daresay I am good enough for you.'

"Her manner was so forthright, and yet so friendly, that I was immediately put at ease. We got along famously after that. And though she had to travel often, being a medica, we always stayed in touch—better, in fact, than I would stay in touch with Mag in later years. And whenever I was due for a new visit, to ensure my health had remained good since the wending, I would always seek her out if I possibly could."

Sun was staring at him in fascination now. To have the High King's own medica . . . she would not have been more surprised if Albern had revealed that he and Enalyn were closely related by blood. Albern was looking at her carefully, and he continued studying her while she attempted to gather her thoughts.

When Sun spoke, it was not about Dawan. "What happened in Opara next?"

Albern chuckled. "In Opara? Not a great deal. But on the road north, and in Tokana . . . why, yes. Quite a bit happened."

SIXTEEN

As I have mentioned, my family has long dwelled in our stronghold in the city of Kahaunga. And in Kahaunga, while Mag and I were returning from our fight with Riri and the Shades, the Lord Telfer received dire news.

She was in her council chamber, poring over the map of her lands. Her lead ranger, a man named Maia, was by her side. He stood off to the side, leaning against the wall, one hand idly toying with the hilt of the sword on his hip. He knew better than to interrupt his lord when she was deep in thought. She had been a stern woman as long as he had known her, and she did not take kindly to being interrupted.

There was another woman in the room, waiting somewhat less patiently than Maia. Her name was Callen of the family Incab, and she was a representative of the Calentin king. One such representative is stationed in the home of each Rangatira, to provide counsel and to send independent reports to the king. Callen was a reedy woman, and Lord Telfer had never liked her—a sentiment that Maia fully shared. They particularly resented the woman's presence in the room at that moment, but Lord Telfer could think of no proper way to dismiss her.

A knock came at the chamber door.

Lord Telfer growled as she looked up. "What is it?"

The door swung open, and a messenger made her hasty way inside. She pressed a fist to her forehead and bowed.

"Lord Telfer," she said. Her voice was too loud in the modest chamber, full of the frantic energy of one who is both eager to please, and terrified because they bear ill news. "The trolls have attacked another village."

Callen's brows rose in faint surprise. "Sky save us," she said in mild worry, turning to regard the Rangatira.

Lord Telfer ignored her. She straightened, her hands gliding across the smooth parchment of the map before her. "Another? Which one?"

The messenger shook her head. "No name, my lord. It was little more than a collection of homes. One of the survivors is here."

"Here?" snapped Lord Telfer. "Why would you bring—"

The door swung a bit wider, and another woman entered the room. It was Whetu, the woman who had once been one of the Lord Telfer's rangers, but long ago.

"Whetu!" cried Maia, stepping forwards to embrace her. They pressed their foreheads together for a brief moment. "It is good to see you once more."

"If only the circumstances were otherwise," she replied. Stepping past him, she put a fist to her forehead and bowed to Lord Telfer. "My Rangatira."

"Be at peace," said Lord Telfer. It was a soldier's command, and Whetu had not been a soldier for a long while, but Lord Telfer did not much care at the moment. "Report."

Callen looked at her Rangatira in faint surprise. "But this is a villager."

Maia's eyes flashed with anger. "She was a ranger."

"Was," said Callen, tilting her chin up ever so slightly.

Lord Telfer slammed her hand on the desk, and the room fell silent. "Report," she snapped. "The rest of you, keep your flapping lips shut."

"The trolls destroyed our village," said Whetu. "Every building was torn down. Our crops and any stores of bread were raided. The trolls ate most of them before we managed to escape."

"Was anyone slain?" said Lord Telfer.

Whetu shook her head. "No, Rangatira."

"How many trolls?"

"I did my best to count. I saw at least a dozen, but there might have been more."

A dozen, thought Maia. That was a sizable pack.

"Why did you not get a full count?" said Callen sternly.

Whetu did her best not to glare at the representative. She pointed to a bandage on her leg, red with blood. "I was injured. And my husband and I had our daughters to think of."

Callen snorted dismissively. It was a rich reaction, coming from her. Maia knew full well that the king's representative would have fled at the first sight of a troll, and likely kept running until her heart gave out.

But Maia had a thought, and he grew troubled. "Whetu," he said quietly. "Where was your village?"

"Ten leagues out."

Lord Telfer's eyes shot wide. "Where? In which direction?"

Whetu met her gaze with a grim look. "North, Rangatira." She came forwards and pointed to a spot on the map. "There. It is not marked on the map, but it was there."

Maia gave his lord a swift glance. He could see the sudden tension leap into her muscles, the way her knuckles whitened as they gripped the edge of the table. There was a sense of building energy in the air, as though a firemage had summoned a ball of flame and was threatening to unleash it. He gave his lord a moment to answer, but when she remained silent, he turned to Whetu.

"Thank you," he said, nodding. "That will be all."

Whetu nodded and turned to leave the room. The messenger who had brought her left as well, relief plain in her expression at the chance to escape whatever explosion was about to take place.

"That settlement," growled Lord Telfer. "It was clearly within the bounds of the pact."

Maia restrained a sigh of exasperation. "Rangatira," he said carefully, "the last *two* settlements were within the bounds of the pact." *Not that anyone listened to me when I mentioned that,* he added only in his own mind.

She shook her head. "Those were questionable. They could have been interpreted to be within the trolls' territory. But they were close enough to the border that it could have been viewed as a mistake. This time it is obvious. The trolls are making a statement."

"A statement?" scoffed Callen. "They are trolls."

Lord Telfer's fist tightened again, but this time on the hilt of her dagger. Maia held his tongue. He was the Rangatira's closest advisor for a reason. His disarming smile, his wry wit, his charm—these helped stave off Lord Telfer's darker moods, and she knew enough about herself to know how valuable that could be. But Maia had no quip for this, nothing to say that would diffuse the sense of danger in the air.

He turned to the king's representative. "Callen, may I speak with my lord alone?"

She frowned. "This is an important matter. My counsel may be—"

"It concerns a private affair," said Maia, giving his best smile. "I promise, I shall tell you as soon as we have finished. We consider your advice invaluable."

Callen's eyes narrowed. Maia knew she did not entirely believe him. But she gave a conciliatory nod and left the room.

"If she had remained in here one moment longer . . ." Lord Telfer let the words trail off.

"Yes, I rather thought our situation might be further complicated if you were to throttle her," said Maia. He leaned over the map. "You are right, my lord. The trolls are encroaching upon our lands. That has never happened before. I do not see how it can continue without coming to war."

"War," said Lord Telfer, her expression souring. "War, against those creatures."

"Rangatira, how can we . . . what would that mean? We have never gone to war with the trolls. Not since the days of—"

Her eyes flashed as she looked at him.

"—not since ancient days that no one remembers, and few tales speak of," he finished, quickly catching his mistake. "We know how to fight them, though it has not happened in an age. But we have no great stores of oil, and if they continue to advance at their current pace, we will not have time to gather more. If it comes to battle, many will die."

"And if we continue to allow this invasion?" countered Lord Telfer.

"The trolls have not killed anyone. Not yet. And after a dozen villages, I cannot believe that that is an accident. It has to be their intent—not to slaughter our people, but simply to drive them from lands the trolls see as their own."

"Yet the pact is clear."

"And have we ourselves not violated the pact for almost a century?"

Both her hands came crashing down on the table. Maia straightened at once, snapping his hands to his sides.

"These are my people!" she roared. "We never pushed into lands the trolls occupied! We never raised a hand against the beasts! We only took what space we needed to live on, only felled the trees we required for new dwellings. Go and find the refugees who flood into Kahaunga every day, and tell *them* they have violated the treaty. See if that is sufficient comfort to them after losing their homes."

"I apologize, my lord." Maia stared straight ahead, just over her shoulder. "I spoke without thinking."

"You are my counsellor, yet you offer no counsel," said Lord Telfer. "You invent theories why the trolls are behaving this way, but you provide no solution. What would you do about it?"

"Send me to treat with them," said Maia. His eyebrows rose imperceptibly, as though he was struggling to keep his expression neutral. "Or send Callen if you wish. She is a diplomat, after all."

Despite her anger, that made Lord Telfer snort. "She has other uses here. And I will not throw your life away to the trolls. You are too valuable to me."

She turned away. That meant the matter of his insubordination would be set aside, for now. He *had* spoken out of turn, but he had said many worse things through the years, and received no reprimand. Maia was useful. That meant he could get away with much. Only occasionally did his lord feel the need to remind him that he could not get away with everything.

"We will have to decide what to do about the trolls," said Lord Telfer after another long, uncomfortable silence. "But in the meantime, we will protect our people. Send out our messengers to every mountain settlement—all those beyond the pact's borders. And anyone within a league of our side of the border as well. They must leave their homes and join us here in Kahaunga. Tell the rangers to be vigilant. The trolls are not to be trusted. Muster every soldier that can be gathered, in case this should indeed come to war. And finally . . ." She sighed and played with her ear with two fingers. "I will compose a message to the king. I am not yet willing to ask them for aid, but I must inform them of these events. Have our fastest messenger ready to take my scroll."

"Of course, Lord Telfer," said Maia, nodding. He turned at once and made for the chamber door.

"Maia," said Lord Telfer, just as his hand came down on the doorknob.

"Rangatira?" he said, looking back over his shoulder.

"When you are done—and only when you are done—speak with my daughter. Tell her I cannot confer with her tonight."

Maia hesitated a moment. "My lord . . . if she asks to visit you here in your chamber, instead?"

"Refuse her," snapped Lord Telfer. "This is no situation for one as soft as she. She would be useless, and I must have all my wits about me."

Once again, Maia had to restrain a sigh. "Yes, my lord," he said, and left the chamber.

He knew, of course, that Lord Telfer loved her daughter. He only wished that, for once in her life, she would show it. Even if only to him.

The trolls were still picking through the remains of Whetu's nameless village.

Chok, their leader, stood on a hillock overlooking the village, resting on his haunches with both fists planted on the ground. His back was straight, his shoulders thrown back. His thick tongue, corded and muscular like a stout human's arm, dug crumbs from his back teeth. As the trolls of his pack searched the buildings for plants and grains and the other foodstuffs they so loved, he gave a rumbling *huff* of pleasure. They had eaten well already, and the feast would last into the next day.

His gaze turned upon Apok as she stepped out of one of the human homes. Her shoulders crashed into the doorframe as she passed, but it did not slow her in the least. The wood shattered under the impact, shards and splinters of it raining upon the ground. Apok paid no attention, but merely climbed the hillock towards Chok, a large cloth-wrapped bundle under her arm.

She reached him and bowed her head. Chok rose up to his full height, rolling his shoulders, a sign of calm and peace. Apok lifted her bundle and unwrapped it to reveal several brown loaves of bread.

"More food?" she asked, lifting one of them towards him.

Chok grunted and took it. He broke it in half and handed one back to her before shoving the rest of the loaf into his mouth. An involuntary moan shook him as he tasted the sweetness of the baked bread. Trolls had not, in those days, learned to grow their own crops or cook their own food. The mountains they chose to live in were not well suited to farming, and they had never much wanted to bother with it in any case. But they relished the taste of the good crops we humans grew, and when they were baked or cooked into bread or other foodstuffs, with no spices to hide the natural flavor, trolls would go to great lengths to acquire and devour them.

Apok ate of her own half-loaf, only eating once Chok had already consumed his own. She watched her leader from the corner of her eye, and Chok saw it. It made him somewhat uncomfortable. Apok was a loyal follower. She did not question his plans in front of the others, and she never countermanded him. But Chok knew she did not approve of the pack's recent actions, these attacks upon human settlements, pushing ever farther south and west. Yet even now, she only watched him, speaking no word of whatever doubts she may have held.

"This was a good day," rumbled Chok. "We have done well."

And it was true. It had been a good day. An anger had been growing inside him, building since long before their first attack on the humans. He did not like it, but he could not deny it. Now that they had pushed even farther south, past the border of the pact, just far enough to remind the humans of their power, the anger had finally abated.

But it flared up again as he saw Dotag approaching.

Where Apok was a good follower, Dotag always cast doubt on Chok's plans. Where Apok obeyed Chok's orders, Dotag would only do what he was told if he was harangued, or sometimes beaten into it—even if he had suggested the plan in the first place. Every troll in the pack knew that Dotag longed for Chok's place at the head of the pack. But Chok would die before giving it to him.

An involuntary growl rumbled through Chok's body. Apok heard it and turned quickly. When she saw Dotag approaching, her ears spread wide from her head, and she hunched her shoulders. She did not growl, but it seemed as though she wished to.

"This was a good day," said Dotag.

Though he had said the same thing only a moment ago, Chok felt a surge of irritation. He did not want Dotag's agreement. He did not need Dotag's approval.

"Get ready to leave," said Chok. "Be ready to go when the sun rises."

Dotag frowned. "We have not done what we came for."

"Tell me if you think the humans will challenge us again," said Chok, speaking louder now. "They broke the pact, and we have driven them back beyond its borders. They will obey it now, because they know we will return if they do not."

"There are more villages," said Dotag. "There is the city. We can go farther."

Chok snarled and took one leap forwards, landing almost within arm's reach of Dotag. He slammed his fists into the ground. "Stop asking for more like a greedy whelp. Look at the bounds of the pact. We are past them. We came here to keep the humans out of our land. After this, they will not creep into our mountains again. Get ready to go home."

Dotag showed his teeth. "Gatak told us—"

"Do not speak as if Gatak leads us!" roared Chok. "Tell me where she is. Tell me how many times the moons have changed since we saw her. Be wise, and be silent."

Now he did step within reach of Dotag. He could sense Apok just behind him, ready to help if it should come to blows. But he did not need her help to defeat Dotag. Age made him huge and strong. None of the pack could challenge him—not that any but Dotag would dream of trying.

Dotag took a submissive step back, but despite his fear, he glared up at Chok. "Gatak will return. When she does, you will not be so brave. She brings a new master. One stronger even than you."

All the anger within Chok came surging up. He leaped forwards and seized Dotag's neck, throwing him down on his back. Both stony fists rose and came crashing down on Dotag's chest. The smaller troll gave a rumbling shout of pain. Chok wrapped his massive right hand around Dotag's cringing face and brought their eyes within a hand-breadth of each other.

"How would *you* know what strength is?" he growled at Dotag.

He shoved Dotag's head into the ground and turned, striding away from the village. Just before he crested a hillock and passed out of sight, he gave a great roar and slammed his fists into the ground, creating two craters large enough for a child to sit in. The trolls in the village looked in that direction for a moment, and then they returned to their scrounging.

Dotag fought his way back to his feet, trying not to wince at the pain in his chest. Apok looked disgustedly at him, and other near-by trolls gave him quick sneers. He glared at them, showing his teeth again.

Chok had to die. Dotag had wanted to kill him and take control of the pack for as long as he could remember, for seasons beyond counting. The pack thought Chok was strong, but he had a weak heart. Chok could not see the coming future. Not the way Dotag could.

He had intended to wait for Gatak's return before he challenged Chok. But as he lumbered into the village, searching for more scraps, he began to plan.

SEVENTEEN

We returned to Opara. Tuhin tried to insist that we bring them to the Mystics for inspection, but we refused. If we took the matter to the Mystics, there would be awkward questions about *why* we thought the Rangatira's lead ranger might be a weremage, and that would be bad for everyone involved. We settled for taking Tuhin back to the Rangatira, and his own wizards confirmed that Tuhin was who they appeared to be.

"Well, at least you know something more than you did," said Tuhin amiably. "And you now have a valuable skill indeed, as you continue to hunt your weremage."

After that, we had to report to the Rangatira. Tuhin told him that we had not found the weremage, but that we had stumbled upon a cluster of Shades in the wilderness. Lord Matara looked quietly suspicious, but he did not question us, and he set about making plans to increase his guard so that the Shades would not be able to claim another stronghold in his lands.

We took advantage of his gratitude to solve another problem. Now we meant to ride into Calentin, across the domains of two different

Rangatira on our way to Tokana. Armed travelers needed an official writ to pass through another lord's domain, and that writ had to state the purpose of their journey. We were able to convince Lord Matara that we had not received such a writ when we began our hunt, since we had ridden out of Calentin, not into it. Tuhin spoke on our behalf as well, urging the Rangatira to help. He agreed, giving us a writ in his own hand. It would let us ride unhindered all the way to Tokana.

All our affairs that afternoon took only a few hours, but I chafed at what seemed an unforgivable delay. I could not stop hearing Hoko's words in my mind. The weremage was headed for Tokana. I did not know her aim, but I knew it had to be evil. Despite what I have told you already about bad blood with my family, the thought that they were in danger from the Shades filled me with a sick terror, and I could not pull my thoughts away from it. And we did not know when the weremage had left. At best, the journey home would take us just over two weeks. Who knew what havoc she might wreak in that time?

I was all for riding out that very night, but by the time we were done with Conrus, the sun was close to setting. Mag insisted we spend one more night in Opara before we set out, and once he heard our tale, Dryleaf agreed with her.

"You have been long on the road, my boy," he told me. "The journey here might have been gentler to you than it was to me, but not by much. Sleep in a soft bed while you can, lest you find yourself ill prepared for the end of your road."

Mag and I had heard that wisdom many times in our days as sellswords, but now I chafed at the advice. Still, with both of them set against me, I had to relent. We spent another night in Conrus' keep, sleeping in comfort and with good food in our bellies. But I asked his servants to wake us at least an hour before dawn, and when they did, I roused the others quickly. We were riding north before the sun showed its face.

Thus began our journey north through Calentin. My hope that we could reach Kahaunga in two weeks proved futile. The early days of winter unleashed their full strength upon us. Snow and ice-cold rain plagued our road north. I bought sturdier cloaks—two for Dryleaf—and pressed on as hard as I dared. But still I despaired at our pace.

My sour mood, however, hardly seemed to affect my comrades. Mag and Dryleaf knew the importance of our mission, so they were not exactly jovial. But they did not fall into dark periods of silence, as I did. They complained about the road, but they smiled as they did it. Once, when we were forced to make camp in between towns because I had pushed us to ride into the early evening, we were huddled around a meager fire beneath some trees. The rain made it impossible to see more than half a span in any direction. Suddenly Mag looked over at Dryleaf and laughed.

"Well, old man," she said lightly. "You are on the road again. I daresay it is not as pleasant as you had dreamed, when you were back in Lan Shui."

Dryleaf chuckled. "You are wrong, dear one. I feel almost young again. But remember, I had been sitting in the same spot for so long. Years of holding still. Of course it feels good to be moving again now—I have only been doing it for a few weeks. Let us speak again in a few months, and I will tell you how I feel then. I only hope I do not hold you up again the way I did in Dorsea."

Despite my foul temper, his guilt made me feel guilty in turn. "We have told you not to trouble yourself over that," I said. "No one can help it when sickness finds them in the wilds."

"Yet it happens to young folk like yourself less often than to the old."

"Less often to me, mayhap," I said. "But never to Mag at all. She has never been sick a day in her life, that I have seen. Even when dysentery would sweep through our camp, forcing the captains to patrol the tents and ensure every fool washed their hands and boiled their water before drinking it, Mag never suffered from it. They used to say she was Elf-blessed."

Mag shrugged. "And I always said that I simply took better care of myself than you did, and I say it again now."

"I took perfectly good care of myself," I countered. "Certainly better than you. Some folk have all the luck."

She shrugged again. Oku, who had been lying near my feet, raised his head and licked my hand. I scratched his ears.

"Do you see?" I said. "Even Oku agrees with me."

"Oku was not there," Mag pointed out.

"He is wise beyond the measure of a normal wolfhound," I insisted, lowering both hands to fluff his face. "Nothing escapes him."

The hound licked my face, and I laughed as I wiped it off. Then I sighed. "I know I have not been the cheeriest companion since Opara," I said, only just loud enough for them to hear over the rain. "Thank you for putting up with me."

"We understand, my boy," said Dryleaf. "And I hope we have not seemed indifferent to your plight. No one blames you for worrying about your kin."

"Friends have a duty to friends, and soldiers on campaign to each other," said Mag, speaking so lightly that it almost sounded false. "Do not try too hard to hide your worries behind an insincere smile. The two of us will not let you sink too deep into an evil mood. Have I not already said that you are awful at taking care of yourself?"

I scowled. "It was not I who ran off into the mountains alone after enemy archers, eschewing the hiding place that kept the rest of us safe."

Mag and Dryleaf both chuckled, and the old man shook his head. "You should listen to your friend, my dear. Just wait until age catches up with you. You will not find yourself so impervious to sickness then, nor to injury."

We fell into silence, and Mag stared at the flames for a while longer, deep in thought, while Dryleaf and I ate and went to sleep.

I kept working on Jordel's song as we went north. It would not leave my thoughts, as though Jordel himself were there and anxious for me to write something to commemorate him, before the matter passed from my mind. As if I could forget a man I had loved so well, with whom I had shared a bedroll more than once while we traveled through the Greatrocks—a tryst springing from lack of options as much as anything else, but no less earnest for all of that. Dryleaf heard me singing or writing it in snatches, and though he kept prodding me to share my work with him, I was not yet ready.

"You have spent a great deal of time on it," he said.

"Not that long," I told him. "I started shortly after we left Lan Shui. And I want it to be perfect."

Dryleaf scoffed. "My boy, there is no such thing as perfect, especially when it comes to songs and stories. I think you are letting your own conceit get in the way of your work."

"Conceit?" I said. "I only want to ensure it is a fitting tribute to a friend. A friend who was important to me."

"Your friend," said Dryleaf. "What would he think, if you sang him the song you have? Right now, with no further work upon it?"

I scowled, for I knew the answer. And I gave it, even as I tried to explain it away. "Jordel would praise it. He would tell me it was wonderful, because *he* was wonderful, and always full of praise. But that does not mean he would be right. He would say the same thing if I wrote and sang it with a troll's grace. I have to make it worthy of him."

Dryleaf kept staring sightlessly northwards, but dissatisfaction twisted his lips. "You have told me you are inexperienced when it comes to this sort of thing. I would advise you to trust my judgement. But I know, too, that such advice is hard to hear, especially at the beginning. If you wish to keep it to yourself, I will stop hounding you."

I could hear wisdom in his words, and it made me feel guilty. But still I was not ready. "Thank you. And I promise: when it is ready, you shall hear it."

The old man nodded. I think now, looking back upon it, that he knew his job was done. He had planted a seed of thought in my mind, the idea that my own pride might be standing in the way of my accomplishment. Dryleaf's wisdom had been valued in Lan Shui for a reason. I think he knew that, in time, I would see the truth of his words, and come to him for the help I was not yet ready to admit I needed.

And he was right.

EIGHTEEN

As you might suspect, the Shades had a stronghold in Tokana not far away from my family's dwellings. From there they carried out their plans, organizing their efforts according to the instructions they received from Rogan far away, but dealing with ordinary day-to-day matters on their own.

And then, some time before Kaita rejoined them, they received another visitor—one they did not expect, and far removed from their usual routine. It started with shouts as guards on the wall raised an alarm. Before anyone knew what was happening, the gate burst inwards with an ear-shattering crash.

Chok, leader of the troll pack, thundered into the bailey. Standing in the center of it, he slammed his stony fists into the ground and let out a roar. Everyone in the stronghold heard it, and the Shades on the walls dropped their bows in fear.

A Heddish man named Phelan had been placed in charge of the Shades at the outpost. To his great credit, he emerged from the central stronghold to speak with Chok—though he brought a guard of six Shades to accompany him, all armed.

"Ch-Chok," he stammered, trying and failing to wear a diplomatic smile. "What is it? What is wrong?"

The massive troll stumped up to the man, walking on all fours, his fists leaving broad cracks in the stone. He loomed over Phelan, nearly twice as tall as the man, glaring down at him with eyes that smoldered under heavy brows.

"You are still here," he growled, speaking in the common tongue of Underrealm.

Phelan blinked. "I . . . I do not understand."

"You are still here," repeated Chok, his voice rising in irritation. "You helped us drive humans from our lands. You told us where to strike and when. Now they are gone. But you are still here. These are troll lands."

"But Chok," said Phelan, doing his best to sound placating through a voice that still quaked with terror. "The Telfers are our enemies, just as they are yours. That means we are allies. We work together."

"We worked together," said Chok. "Because they went past the bounds of the pact. Now they are gone. Only you remain. A human in troll land is the enemy."

The last word came out in a growl that Phelan could feel in his chest, and he very nearly soiled his grey breeches. "But you . . . we thought you would keep pushing into the Telfer homelands. Gatak told us—"

Chok roared in his face, and Phelan lost control of his bladder at last. The troll raised his fists, and Phelan knew he was about to die. But even as the guards behind him raised their blades, Chok slammed his fists into the ground on either side of Phelan, splintering the stone.

"Do not pretend Gatak speaks for us!" roared Chok. "She has been gone for months. She is your creature, not ours."

"She is an emissary," whispered Phelan, unable to put any more strength into his voice. He hoped the troll did not notice the piss now running down his legs. "She struck the deal in the first place."

"Tell me where she is now," snarled Chok.

"She will arrive soon!" cried Phelan desperately, with a small surge of courage now that he was in more familiar territory. "And when she does, if you and your pack have pushed the Telfers out of the mountains, you will receive a great reward. More crops than you can handle.

As much bread as you can eat. That promise comes directly from the Lord, who never lies."

Chok seemed about to answer. But then another stone-shattering crash came from the direction of the gate. Chok whirled.

Dotag stood in the entrance to the stronghold. The troll's shoulders were raised in an attempt to seem larger, and his nostrils flared in and out with each breath.

"You come here?" he roared, speaking in the trolls' own language. Most of the Shades in the courtyard looked at each other uncertainly, for the words were unknown to them—but Phelan understood. "You come here and threaten our allies?"

"Allies?" roared Chok. "They are in our mountains. They are no different from the humans we drove from our territory. The only difference is that these ones hold you under thrall."

Dotag snarled and took a leap forwards. "I am no slave to humans."

Chok advanced, more calmly than Dotag, and leered. "You would have us lick their boots in exchange for one loaf of bread. You are nothing."

Dotag struck, fist ripping through the air. But Chok caught the blow. He seized Dotag's arm and threw him. The smaller troll flew through the air, over the heads of the Shades, who scattered out of the way. He crashed into the keep wall, buckling it. A hole the size of a human now gaped in the stone.

"You think to challenge me?" roared Chok.

The Shades fled. But even as he cowered near the edge of the courtyard, Phelan waved frantically at his soldiers stationed atop the wall. He motioned to them, cupping his hands and tilting them over, as if pouring a bowl of liquid onto the ground.

Dotag shook his head, woozy from the impact. This time he was more patient, waiting for Chok to strike first. When the larger troll's fist came flying, Dotag ducked. Chok struck the wall instead, widening the hole he had already made. Dotag struck twice under Chok's arm, and the larger troll grunted as he fell a step back.

"You fight like a coward," he rumbled.

"I fight to win," snarled Dotag.

Chok attacked again. But his blow was a feint, and when Dotag sidestepped it, Chok struck with his other fist. It connected under

Dotag's chin, sending him staggering backwards. He struck the outer wall of the courtyard, and only barely managed to throw himself out of the way as Chok's following blow slammed into the stone. Above them both, a Shade lost her footing and pitched over the other side of the wall with a scream.

"You are weak!" cried Chok, coming after Dotag, who tried to scramble away. Chok caught one of his flailing legs and spun, launching him into the keep again. He struck the double wooden doors headfirst, splintering them both.

Phelan looked to the top of the keep. His soldiers were ready. He clenched his fists, beseeching his Lord for good fortune.

His prayers were answered. When Dotag saw Chok coming for him, he scrambled back, deeper into the building.

"Cowering with your human friends," sneered Chok. "Tell me again how strong you are."

Chok reached the front of the keep. He stooped, reaching inside and trying to seize Dotag.

"Now!" roared Phelan.

The Shades atop the keep lifted their huge wooden levers. A massive vat of oil tipped as they strained against it. As it came spilling out, they plunged torches into it, setting it ablaze.

A waterfall of burning oil crashed down upon Chok, dousing his whole body.

The troll screamed in agony and stumbled back. The burning oil coated him, roasting his softer insides, his iron-hard skin no proof against the blazing heat. Blinded by the inferno, he flailed wildly about, seeking something he could hold to steady himself.

Dotag charged out of the keep. He brought both fists around in a wide arc, smashing them into either side of Chok's head. The troll leader stumbled back, dazed. Dotag punched Chok in the gut, and he bent double, groaning. Dotag clenched his fists together and brought them down on the back of Chok's head, crushing it into the stone courtyard.

He did it again. And again. And again, until Chok stopped moving.

Slowly, Dotag backed away from the corpse, his shoulders heaving mightily with every panting breath. He lost his balance for a moment and fell on his rear, propping himself up with one arm. Then he seemed to realize that he was still in a human stronghold, and they were looking at him. He fought back to his feet, shaking his head to clear it, and turned to look at Phelan, who was now cowering near the keep entrance.

"I lead the pack now," said Dotag. "We will do as the Lord has bid. But I want Gatak."

Phelan, hoping that the danger had passed for the moment, emerged into the open. "She shall soon return. We will send her when she does."

"See that you do," snarled Dotag. "And when we drive the other humans out of the mountains, we will expect your reward."

Phelan could do little more than nod. He watched as Dotag went to Chok's body and lifted it in his great, muscular arms. He struggled under the weight, but he carried it out through the gate and off into the mountains.

Dark take me, thought Phelan. *I need a new pair of breeches.*

Once he was out of sight of the Shade fortress, Dotag dropped Chok's body. Then he began the messy process of scraping off the oil and the burned skin that covered most of Chok's form. The other trolls could not know that the humans had helped Dotag with their fire.

After removing most of the evidence of burning, Dotag found a large rock. He slammed it into Chok's corpse over and over again, mashing it to a pulp almost beyond recognition. The wounds, the exposed flesh, and the black blood all worked together to hide the last signs of flame.

Dotag took up Chok's arm and began to drag him along again.

It was nearly sundown by the time Dotag returned to the rest of the trolls, still carrying Chok's body. As soon as they saw him appear over the rise, the trolls moved forwards. At their head was Apok. She saw what Dotag carried in his arms, but she could not quite believe it. Her heart sank as she finally recognized Chok's face, mashed to a pulp but still bearing his telltale ripped ears.

"What have you done?" she cried.

Dotag answered by throwing Chok's body down before the pack. He snarled and puffed out his chest, slamming his fists into the ground. "I have taken leadership from Chok. He was weak, and he was a fool. I am stronger than he. I lead the pack now."

Apok cried out—but a peal of grief, not an angry roar. She fell on her knees by Chok, gingerly touching his chest. Chok lay unmoving, his eyes staring past her, unseeing.

Dotag ignored her, looking over her head at the rest of the pack as they gathered near. Some of them looked at Chok's body in wonderment, some in shock. But none bore the same anger, the same grief, as Apok. They seemed attentive. Ready to hear what he had to say. Ready, mayhap, to obey.

"The humans are our enemies," declared Dotag. "We have driven them from our lands. But how long did they dwell there? They ignored the pact. Now we will teach them to fear us. These mountains are ours, as our ancestors declared in the beginning!"

He thrust a fist into the air. Some of the trolls joined him, unleashing great, bestial roars.

But Apok looked up at him, still cradling Chok's body. "They are within the bounds of the pact already," she said. "And they were never close to us. They never took any land we had already claimed. If you attack them now, you will be marked as a betrayer."

"They betrayed us first," snarled Dotag, pressing his face close to hers. "They cast aside the pact. They cannot claim its protection now."

"Yes!" cried a troll in the pack. "Let us drive them from our mountains!"

"And let us start with these strangers who still lurk in their stone walls!" roared another. "We will cast them down!"

Dotag's attention was diverted from Apok for the moment. "No," he said at once. "The humans who serve the Lord are still our allies. They have not betrayed us. And they have promised us rewards beyond our reckoning if we drive the others out of the mountains. We will not harm them. They serve the Lord, and so do we."

Apok did not speak again. She did not call him a weakling for allying with the humans. But her eyes said much.

Dotag ground his teeth with a sound like shattering rocks. But she had not challenged him, not openly. He could not kill her, not now in front of the others. They would never accept him as their leader if he did.

Apok would live. For now. Until he could find another way to get rid of her.

“We move south,” he declared, turning his back upon Apok. “We must be ready. Our allies will tell us when it is time to strike, and where to attack. Until then, we wait. We wait for battle.”

And for Gatak, he said, but only in his own mind.

NINETEEN

In the middle of the month of Febris, Mag and Dryleaf and I reached Tokana at last.

I will admit that when we crested that last rise to look upon the city where my family had long dwelled, I feared the worst. We had been almost a month on the road. I was certain the weremage had arrived well ahead of us. Whatever evil the Shades were plotting in my homeland, I knew it would be directed against my family. I half-expected to find our keep razed, and the city burned to the ground, with mayhap an army of Shades still camping on the remains.

Instead, I found that things looked almost exactly the way they had when I left home two decades before. So much so, in fact, that I was struck by a wave of memory so powerful I pulled Foolhoof to a stop. Mag and Dryleaf, too, halted their horses. For a long while I sat there, at that familiar point where the road reached the crest of the plateau, and surveyed the city before me.

The land ran relatively even to the north and south, until after dozens of spans, it finally climbed into new peaks, too sharp and steep for any dwellings. But to the north was a great lake in the mountains, and it spilled into a river that came running south into the dale before us. The wide ridge upon which we stood fell off to form the dale's western slopes, and it was here that Kahaunga had been built. After centuries, the town around it had been spilled into the dale and become a true city. The colors were bleak with winter, except for the kauri trees. I sat there, feeling tiny and inconsequential against the size of the city before me, and the swelling heights of the mountains all around, and I did not notice as tears streaked silently down my cheeks, born of a feeling I could not understand and would not have dared to name.

At last, Mag nudged Mist closer to me and took my arm. "Come, you great fool," she said gently. "I would rather not camp here on the mountainside when there are inns so close by."

I scrubbed hastily at my face with my sleeve. "Of course," I said quickly. "Forgive me."

"There is nothing to forgive, lad," said Dryleaf kindly. "Homecoming is never easy when one has been long away."

I nodded. But his words reminded me, too, that this was my home, and one place above all others where I did not wish to be recognized. If word reached my family that I was in Tokana . . .

Somewhere on our journey I had acquired a scarf, and now I pulled it up and around my face to hide my features, while at the same time I pulled my cowl down low over my eyes. It left me with only a single small slit to observe the land as we approached, but I felt more comfortable at once. There was almost no chance that the guards at the wall would recognize me, but I was unwilling to take even such an infinitesimal risk.

"The Rangatira here is named Thada," I told Dryleaf and Mag. They knew she was my mother already, and I did not wish to say so aloud, even though no one was nearby to hear. "She is the ruling authority, and I imagine her daughter, Ditra, helps her in her duties. Have our writ from Lord Matara ready—it will get us through the gates."

Sure enough, when we reached the wall, the guards asked about our business, paying special attention to Mag's spear, and to my bow and sword. They found Lord Matara's writ to be in order, but they did not let us through immediately, first asking us a few more questions about our business in Tokana. We had prepared a story: we were seeking to deliver a message to a member of Lord Matara's family, who was here on diplomatic business.

The guards looked at each other in surprise at that. I frowned, forgetting my desire for discretion for a moment, and spoke. "My good servants, why so many questions? A writ is normally enough to secure passage across the kingdom."

"Normally, yes," said one of the guards, an elderly man with a thick beard who did not take too kindly to such a challenge from an uppity youngster. "But you have been on the road, and have not heard the news. The High King's Seat was attacked near the end of Yanis, and the High King herself narrowly escaped death in the battle."

The words struck us like a hammer blow. Mag and I shared a glance, and Dryleaf went very still in his saddle.

"Attacked?" said Mag. "By whom?"

"The kingdom of Dulmun," said the guard. "A good distance away from us, you might say, but they have many citizens across the nine kingdoms. If you serve a Rangatira, you should be able to appreciate a little extra caution, given the circumstances."

"Of course," said Mag. "If only the Dulmish king were as loyal as you good people, this would not be such a dark day."

That seemed to pacify them, especially the old one, and they waved us on after only a few more questions. Dryleaf had remained silent all the long while, answering only when one of the guards asked him a question, and then only in brief, clipped words. As we passed from earshot of the guards, he spoke at last, scarcely above a whisper.

"The Seat. Loren."

"I know," I said.

"She may be fine," said Mag. "Loren is a clever girl. She has survived worse."

"Worse than a battle on the Seat?" I said. "They may say it was Dulmun, but I do not think that is the whole truth. The Shades were involved, or I am a fool."

"Both things may be true," said Mag. Before I could respond, she quickly went on. "If Enalyn survived, her forces must have won the battle. And you know Loren is not a fighter. She would not put herself in the middle of a conflict like that."

"Those who do not wield blades can still die upon them," I said.

"And one battle will not be the end of it," said Dryleaf. "Who knows what may have happened since?"

"Not I, and not you," said Mag. "I am as worried about Loren as either of you. But we cannot know what may or may not have happened to her, and even if we set out for the Seat this minute we could not find out for months. Keep your mind on our task here, and once we have completed it, then we can look after her."

I sighed. "Very well. It is true enough that we cannot get answers either quickly or easily. And the weremage will not wait idly if we decide to go find Loren."

Dryleaf shook himself. "You are right, of course. And if she survived, she will receive our letter soon. Mayhap she already has. That is some small comfort, at least."

"It is," I said with a smile. Mag murmured in agreement, though she seemed troubled.

We turned our attention back to the city around us, and I tried to remember what I could, in order to direct us to a good inn for the night. But I felt that with each new corner I turned, I found some way in which the city had changed. I could not be sure if it was only my poor memory, or if things were truly so different as I thought, but I suspected the latter. I thought much of the tall kauri tree that had been felled in my youth, and I knew that that had not been the end of the changing of my world.

Kaita reached the Shades before we reached Tokana, of course, and she received word the day we arrived.

Phelan, the captain of the stronghold in her stead, delivered the message. He knocked twice on her door, hard. After waiting three heartbeats for a response, he opened it and stepped in. In his hand he held a lantern, and he lit a taper from it, which he used to illuminate two more lanterns on either side of the room.

"Commander Kaita," he said, keeping his eyes studiously away from the bed. "There is news."

Kaita was already sitting up, as was the girl who had joined her in her bed that night. The girl looked somewhat embarrassed at the intrusion, but Kaita ignored her and donned a thin robe. The room was cold for such a threadbare garment, but the chill was as nothing to Kaita.

"Considering I gave you permission to wake me in only one instance," said Kaita, "I think I may venture a guess as to what news you have brought."

"She has reached Tokana."

"With the others?" said Kaita.

He nodded. "The old one known as Dryleaf, and the ranger."

"The Telfer man is not a ranger," spat Kaita.

Phelan did not seem to know quite what to say to that, and eventually he settled for, "They brought the dog as well."

Kaita tried to suppress her irritation. Though our journey to Tokana had taken us longer than we wished, we had arrived just a little too soon for her purposes. Matters with the trolls had progressed more slowly than she would have wished.

"What of the Telfer patrols?" she said.

"We still encounter them occasionally," said Phelan. "Or rather, we see them. We are always careful not to be noticed."

"Are they still out at night?"

The man frowned. "They are. And they have increased their guards since the trolls crossed the border."

Kaita's fingers played with her hair, braiding it absentmindedly as she considered her plans. "Very well. The trolls' efforts must be increased. Gatak shall have to go and visit them, especially now that Dotag has taken leadership. And keep someone—or several someones—watching Mag at all times. But sky above, do not let her notice. I shall join our agents monitoring them, when my other duties permit me."

The man bowed. "As you say, Commander."

"That will be all."

He nodded and left. The room settled to silence, and the girl in Kaita's bed looked uncertainly at her.

"Would you like me to go?"

"If you wish," said Kaita. "Or you may stay. It is your choice." She removed her robe and lay back down on the bed, staring at the ceiling with her hands clasped under her head.

The girl looked annoyed. "In that case, I think I will take my leave."

Kaita barely heard her. The first real notice she took was when the room went suddenly dark, as the girl snuffed the lamps before leaving. But she remained deep in her own thoughts.

Mag and I had arrived in Tokana at last. Kaita had lured me all the way home.

Soon, the long hunt—which had lasted much longer than the paltry past few months—would come to an end.

TWENTY

I WAS, AS YOU HAVE GATHERED, RATHER TERRIFIED OF BEING DISCOVered by my family. To help you understand why, I should tell you something of my eldest sister, Romil, and of something that happened soon after I had fled from home.

My mother had no tolerance for what she saw as my "foolishness," by which she meant my desire to be happy. She still thought I could be useful to her, and so she sent Romil to bring me home. Romil was very like my mother, which is to say that she was cold and uncaring. Growing up, we hardly ever spoke to each other more than was absolutely required. My mother did not mind. As long as we obeyed her, she cared little for how we felt about each other.

It took Romil some months to find me. I had already had my wending and joined the Upangan Blades before she came stomping into our camp one day. Sentries challenged her, and Romil almost came to blows with them. But I happened to be passing by, and I saw them arguing.

The sight of her froze me in place. I had managed to convince myself that my family would simply . . . let me vanish. That my mother, who had never seemed to care about me one way or another, would forget about me, and be satisfied with two daughters who seemed willing to serve her. I should have known it was a fool's hope.

I approached them and put a hand on the sentry's shoulder. "She is with me," I said. He gave me a doubtful look, but he went off on his patrol, leaving Romil and me standing there facing each other.

She studied me, and I studied her in turn. Behind her was a retainer of our house, but I barely noticed. I could only see Romil. She wore our family's colors proudly. A bow was on her back, and an axe hung at her belt. She had done her hair in a single long braid that fell to the small of her back. Her expression was a mixed one—appraisal, and faint amusement, but mostly anger.

"You look different," she said.

"A wending sometimes has that effect."

She grunted. "So it does," she said. "I hope it has made you happy, as well as cleared your head. It is time for you to return. Mother commands it."

"I no longer follow Mother's commands," I told her.

Her fingers tightened on the haft of her axe. "Of course you do," she said. "You are a Telfer. Mother has need of you, and wending or no, you can still be of use."

It was, of course, a rather abominable thing to say, and I cannot with any honesty speak in her defense. The time after a wending is a delicate one. Doubtless you know the ritual one's friends and family are supposed to perform, for the sake of the ander person. The kindest thing I can say for Romil is that I do not think she spoke out of malice. Mother had given her a duty, and that duty was the only thing she cared about. My feelings mattered to her not at all.

Her response sent my blood rising, and I answered somewhat more rashly than I should have. "I am so glad to hear it. That I might still be *useful* to her. But I regret to say that I am not going anywhere, least of all with you."

She stepped forwards and seized my arm. A few paces away, the retainer's hands balled to fists, though she bore no weapon. "Of course you are, you idiot," snarled Romil. "You have had your lark as an honorless sellsword. But the game is over now. You can ride behind me on my horse."

"No!" I cried, recoiling. But her grip on my arm was like an iron band. "Let go of me!"

"What is all this about?"

Never before or since have I been so glad to hear Mag's voice. I looked over my shoulder to see her approaching from the midst of the camp. Near her was the sentry who had first spoken to Romil. He gave me a grim look over Mag's shoulder—he must have sensed trouble brewing, and gone to fetch her.

Mag stepped up close, and Romil had at least enough sense to let go my arm. She stared Mag up and down with a haughty expression I was well familiar with.

"Who are you supposed to be?" she said.

"A friend," said Mag. Then, as if afraid Romil might be confused, she added, "Not *your* friend, of course."

Romil looked past her to me. "You keep charming company, Vera."

My stomach did another ugly turn. Again I spoke without thinking. "My name is Albern now."

Romil's eyes shot wide, her expression incredulous. Then she gave a loud, ugly laugh. "Oh, it is, is it? I suppose I should have expected as much. You always had the strange notion that you were somehow better than the rest of us, though you never did a thing to prove it."

"And that is about all I need to hear from you," said Mag. "Leave. Now."

"I do not even take suggestions from sellsword scum, much less orders," growled Romil. "Walk away, if you know what is good for you."

Mag looked over her shoulder at me. "I do not much like her. Should I—"

"Leave it." I looked past her to Romil. "That goes for you as well. I am staying here. You can tell Mother you tried. And that you failed."

Romil's face grew dark with anger. "I have not failed at anything, you witless girl."

Mag struck faster than I could see. Her fists cracked twice against Romil's face, flinging her senseless to the ground. I stared at her fallen form in horror and grief. The retainer tensed as if readying for a fight, but Mag stopped her with a look.

"You would be unwise to push the matter," she said. "Take your master and ride away with her. Go back to your lord. Tell her whatever you wish, but get this wretch out of my sight before I send her back with more than a headache."

The retainer did as Mag commanded. I could not even watch. My head hung between my knees as I sat on the ground, angry tears pouring their tracks down my cheeks. As Romil rode off, slumped over her horse's neck, Mag came to sit beside me, throwing an arm around my shoulder and holding me until my grief subsided.

Albern looked suddenly down at Sun. "Do you understand why I am telling you this?"

Sun blinked up at him. "You said I should know something of Romil."

"That is not the only reason. You know, by now, that our families are not entirely dissimilar. Mine tried to drag me back home. Yours may do the same. But your life is your own, and your future is a choice no one can make for you. And if they try to convince you otherwise . . . well, you have a friend who can help you now, just as I had one to help me then."

Sun blinked at a sudden smarting in her eyes. "Thank you," she said, quietly, for she did not trust herself to speak any louder. "That means a great deal."

Albern nodded. "So long as you know. Now, let us return to the tale."

TWENTY-ONE

After a good night's rest at a fine inn near the western edge of Kahaunga, our party woke and began our search for the Shades. First we spoke to our innkeeper and some others in the common room, trading stories of travel through the kingdom for information about events in Tokana.

We learned very quickly about the trolls' recent incursions into Telfer lands. When I first heard of it, I thought it was an Elf-tale, someone spreading stories meant to give the listener a thrill. But when we heard the same thing from three different people, the truth became clear. The trolls were encroaching upon Tokana, and no one in the city knew why.

But I had some idea.

I led Mag and Dryleaf back to our room to speak in private. Calentin inns are tolerant of hounds, so Oku came as well. He flopped down on a small blanket in the corner, tongue lolling from his mouth in a smile. But he looked at all of us with keen eyes as we talked.

"This situation with the trolls," I said as soon as the door closed. "We must learn everything we can about it."

Mag frowned. "Why? It seems a local trouble."

"The trolls are an exceptionally peaceful people," I said. "My family has never had conflict with them. For them to now show aggression . . ."

"You think it has something to do with the Shades," said Dryleaf, pursing his lips.

Understanding dawned in Mag's eyes. "As with the vampires."

"It must be," I said. "The Shades are provoking them to carry out these attacks. Either they are drawing the trolls in with some lure, or they are driving them out of the mountains towards us. Though I know not how such a thing could be done. The trolls are formidable in battle, and very difficult to harm. Only a well-fortified stronghold would have any hope of defending against them, and even then not for very long."

"Are you certain?" said Mag. "Human lords squabble with each other over borders all the time, with little or no provocation."

I shook my head. "The trolls are not human. Nor are they beasts like vampires, possessing little wit. They are cleverer than satyrs, though much slower to anger—which is why you must fear their wrath all the more, for once stoked it can be impossible to quell. They are the titled lords of the Greatrocks, from Calentin's northern border to the city of Woad far to the south. The Calentin king and their border guards are permitted to have settlements on the only three passes that provide easy passage through the mountains, and the trolls rule the rest of it. For them to attack our domain goes against the pact."

Mag shrugged. "They forged a pact, and now they have broken it. It may be treacherous, but these are uncertain times."

"This is not some petty squabble between human lords," said Dryleaf. He leaned forwards in his chair, both hands wrapped tight around his staff. He looked suddenly very old. "The trolls first came into the mountains not long after Roth's armies had conquered Underrealm. That is more than twelve hundreds of years ago. They came from the rocky deserts to the north. No one knows why. When they first came, Calentin tried to fight them, seeing them as just another invader. But the trolls were implacable, as well as being nearly impossible to kill—and even more so in those days, when no one had ever dealt with them before.

"In the end, a captain of the Calentin army first had the idea for a treaty with the trolls. Roth's forces had forged the nine kingdoms, but conflict between kings did not end with the foundation of Underrealm. Calentin had long struggled to keep the Greatrocks secure against incursions from Feldemar, and their forces were stretched thin with the effort. The trolls could protect the mountains better than Calentin ever could, and they would mostly occupy lands that humankind could not settle anyway."

Dryleaf paused for a moment, and then he turned his head in my direction. "That captain's name was Albern, of the family Telfer. And for forging that ancient pact with the trolls, he and his descendants were named lords of the northern Greatrocks, where they live to this day."

Mag looked at me in wonder, and I gave her an embarrassed smile. "Yes. That is where I took the name after my wending. I had heard tales of Albern of the family Telfer all my life. It was quite the legacy to live up to." My smile dampened a bit. "Some in my family felt so overshadowed by our history, in fact, that it consumed them, and became more important to them than the present."

Mag nodded slowly. "And this pact," she said at last, "between the Telfers and the trolls. It has lasted ever since?"

"Without once bringing us into conflict," I said. "Sometimes our people have settled in lands that, strictly speaking, are beyond the borders. But the trolls also come into our lands on occasion. As far as anyone can remember, the relationship has been amicable, and any problems have been resolved quickly. The trolls are easy to deal with, and they enjoy most human foodstuffs, which makes them easy to bribe if all else fails."

"Yet now they are agitated, and no overtures towards peace seem to have been effective," said Dryleaf. "Assuming the Rangatira has made such overtures."

"She would have," I said. "But it is clear they were unsuccessful."

"Because of the Shades," finished Mag. Her face was solemn, but a light danced in her eyes. "I understand. If we investigate this matter with the trolls, it should lead us to the weremage. And we can hope that slaying her will end the problem with the trolls as well."

"We can hope," I said grudgingly. "Whatever the Shades have done to direct the trolls' wrath at Kahaunga, I only pray we can turn it in another direction before they have torn my family's home down to its foundations."

"I have faith in your abilities," said Dryleaf with a smile. "The name of Albern may save these mountains again."

"Not if we never get started," said Mag. "Where do we begin?"

"If we are right in our guess, the Shades will be found lurking somewhere in the mountains," I said. "They could not interact with the trolls from here in the city."

"They say the trolls have been pushing into human territory," said Mag. "What if we find them when next they attack, and follow them back to their home? If they have been dealing with the Shades, we can find them that way."

"No," I said at once, and more sharply than I intended. "You know little of trolls, and so you cannot understand how dangerous such a plan would be."

Mag shrugged. "We have faced danger before. No one thought we could fight a vampire and win."

"This is nothing like that," I said grimly. "You were fast enough to wound the vampires with your spear, and to avoid their blows. But speed will not help you against a troll. You can strike it as much as you like, but your spear will do nothing against their hide. Nor will my arrows, unless I hit one in the eye. And such a small wound will do little beyond angering them enough to crush us beneath their fists. The only thing that can truly harm them is fire, and only the Rangatira's forces have the oil one needs to fight a troll."

She grinned at me, which only served to make me more annoyed. "We will be careful," she assured me. "We will not let the trolls see us. I may know little of them, yet I know they do not have eyesight or a sense of smell as good as our own. They should be easy to track, and without them ever being the wiser."

I huffed through my nose. "We can try. But if you have any sense at all—a doubtful prospect at the best of times—you will follow my guidance when it comes to these beasts. I would rather not see you meet an undignified if long overdue end, crushed by a troll in mountains far from home."

Mag snatched my shoulder and pulled me into a side-armed hug, bouncing me up and down and ruffling my hair. "There is the cheerful Albern I have so missed. This whole matter will be resolved in no time."

I heaved a great sigh, knowing she was wrong, and knowing, too, that I would never be able to convince her.

TWENTY-TWO

We returned to the common room and asked the innkeeper about the last settlement the trolls had attacked. She told us everything she knew, including where to find it. It was a small town called Ahuroa. Hearing the name sent a chill up my back. I had visited it in my youth, both with and without my mother.

Ahuroa was an overnight journey away from Tokana. We left Dry-leaf at the inn, with a plan for him to continue gathering information in the common room and mayhap elsewhere in the city. Mag and I took Oku, as well as our travel packs, and set out into the countryside. My mother was much on my mind as we made our way through the city streets. I remembered journeys we had made, with me riding beside her just as I rode beside Mag now. I remembered trips to Ahuroa, when she had me wait in our dwellings while she tended to business. And I remembered returning from journeys I had made on my own, and Mother being furious that I had left the city without telling anyone.

Indifference when I did my duty, and wrath at any dereliction. It was a fair encapsulation of what life had been like with her.

The guards at the north gate were less watchful than those we had met the day before—leaving the city, it seemed, was less suspicious than arriving at it. When they asked what business we had in the wilds, I told them I had a cousin who had not come with the other refugees from Ahuroa. The trolls had not killed anyone, so I said he must be lost in the wilds. The guards eyed our weapons, but Lord Matara's writ permitted us to be armed, and they wished us luck as we rode out.

The moment we passed into open country, I felt my whole body ease. It was a relief so sharp that it stunned me. Only the day before, I had ridden these same mountains in the open air. One night in Kahaunga had made me tense as a bowstring, yet I had not realized it until I felt it bleed away. A rueful laugh slipped out of me, and Mag glanced over.

"There is no one else around, so I know I did not miss a joke."

I shook my head. "I was just reminded of riding from the city as a child. I always found my home less comfortable than solitude in the wilderness."

Mag was silent for a little while. "I suppose that was true for me as well," she said at last, her voice low. "I spent many years in the woods on my own, when I was young, and forests are still my favorite place to be by myself. They remind me of the peace I knew before I went out into the wide world—before I met you, if I am being honest. It is why I fell in love with Northwood. The trees were only a stone's throw from my tavern, and I would walk among them often."

I will admit I was shocked. Mag had rarely spoken to me of her youth before we met, and I had never pried. She would tell me if she wanted to, I knew. Hearing her suddenly speak of it now was not unlike when I had heard the satyrs speak of a Lord—the words were not strange on their own, but the source turned them quite shocking. I very badly wanted to ask her to tell me more, but I could hear the nervousness in her voice. She was clearly uncomfortable having said so much. I worried that if I pressed her, she might not speak of it again. And so I said nothing.

We rode on for a while in silence after that. Northwest of Kahaunga, the mountains rise up to sharp peaks, which fall steeply away until they flatten out in the little dale overlooked by the stronghold, with gentler slopes on the eastern side. We rode a narrow path that had been cut into that sharp western face, mostly used by rangers who needed to reach far villages and settlements with speed. It gave us a wonderful view down into the dale—though that was spoiled, for me at least, by the sight of how far the city had spread across the mountains. Many trees had been felled, so that the once tranquil forest had been cleared to beyond the dale's eastern side, and homes and settlements had begun to edge up the slopes there. Though it was early morning, a thin pall already hung in the air below us, the smoke of hearths and cooking fires trapped by the mountains, giving the lower city a blurred, hazy appearance, like something half-glimpsed in a nightmare. It was a darker, dirtier thing than the thick, grey cloud cover above us.

At last our path turned around the edge of a mountain, and we were in the wilderness proper. There the road struck the top of a wide ridge, and we were able to kick our horses to a trot, making better time. Oku padded along happily with us. On occasion he would go ranging far ahead, though never out of sight, and then sit by the side of the road until we had caught up to him, before making two turns around our horses' hooves and then running forwards again. The road grew somewhat narrow again, and began to wind around the side of peak after peak.

Shortly after we lost sight of the city, we came to the first stone bridge spanning the gap between two slopes. We stopped at its western end. By the lip of the cliff into which the bridge had been built, there was a small shelf just visible. I tried to ignore it, tried to avoid looking at it entirely. I did not succeed. A dark and hazy memory swam into my mind—a relic of my youth, and a reminder of something I would much rather have forgotten.

Mag, meanwhile, sat staring at the bridge in wonder. It was a half-span long, with its foundations set into the mountains on either end. But it had no supports in the middle, only open air between the bridge and the ground, which was a span below.

"How did they build it?" said Mag. "With no pillars, and no way to have any while they worked?"

"There are tricks," I said. "Not that I know what they are. I am a guide, not a mason. I will admit the bridges never held much interest for me."

"Keen eyes and a dull mind," said Mag. "I am hardly surprised. But an evil mood, as well. Why are you so grumpy?"

"Bad memories," I said. "Let us ride on."

We crossed the bridge. Soon the chasms before the peaks grew less deep and less sheer, and the ground rose to meet the road. We came to another small dale like the one where Kahaunga had been built, and there was the lake that flowed off into the river that ran through the center of the city. But most of the ground here was hard and rocky, ill suited for farming. This vale could support no more than a single small village; I saw it there, on the other end of the lake, its homes perched at the water's edge. A few boats were out.

Our side of the lake was far less gentle. We had to pick our way between boulders and across craggy breaks in the land, sharp fissures that pinched to nothing a few paces down. Oku moved more slowly now, sticking close to us, unsure of his footing on this new terrain.

I found myself growing tense again, distracted, almost irritable. I had to force my attention back to the path ahead of us. It had turned from a solid road to little more than an animal trail, and almost all my focus was required to pick the right path through the rocks and avoid dead ends.

Almost all my focus, but not quite. Suddenly I realized why I was so distracted. My mind was not wandering—it was drawn to something. Tiny noises, which I had passed off as an echo from the stones, but which carried on when we paused for breath.

We were being followed.

I drew an arrow, nocked, and turned in a flash. I paused for a heartbeat before loosing, not wanting to harm some innocent passerby.

There, high above. A woman in grey clothes and a blue cloak, with hard-bitten features.

I fired. If I had not hesitated, I would have struck her in the thigh. As it was, the fletching nearly grazed her rump as she scrambled out of sight.

"Up there!" I cried.

Mag did not question me. Slinging her shield onto her arm, she sprang off of Mist and up the slope towards the woman who had been hunting us.

TWENTY-THREE

I spared no thought for the horses. I ran after Mag.

"Oku, tiss!" I cried, and Oku came bounding after me.

Mag had outdistanced me, but she was looking for a way to climb up towards her prey. The woman dodged nimbly through the rocky terrain, clearly familiar with it. I only caught sight of her for a blink at a time, never long enough for a clear shot. She was much higher on the slope than we were. Mag ran for a sharp incline that would take her up. But when she tried to climb, the land broke under her feet.

"Too soft!" I cried as I ran past her. "We have to find another way!"

Mag growled and tried again. She planted the butt of her spear in the ground to help her, and it held. She climbed up, but ever so slowly. I lost sight of her a heartbeat later.

We were nearing the southern end of the dale. Not far away was the road we had taken to get here. If I could reach the road before the woman, we would have her trapped. I kept glancing up as I sprinted, catching flashes of her blue cloak between the rocks. It would be a near thing. I pushed myself harder, my legs flying.

I rounded a boulder and saw the road a span away. The woman

was still moving between the rocks, but there was a half-span of open ground before the road. I nocked an arrow and drew, waiting for her to emerge into the open. Oku gave a thunderous bark and leaped ahead of me, trying to intercept her.

"Kaw!"

A streak of black feathers swept down upon me. Pain lanced across my face as I felt talons bite into my flesh. I cried out and lost my balance, crashing down upon a rock that struck me in the ribs. Wheezing with the pain, I fought my way back to my knees.

In the air above me, the raven wheeled and screeched again. Oku, hearing my cry, had stopped, and was now looking back. The woman we had been pursuing was mayhap a dozen paces from the road. But I knew the raven that had attacked me was no ordinary beast.

"Oku, attack!" I called out. The hound hesitated. "Haka!" I cried.

He turned and went after the fleeing Shade.

I turned my attention back to the weremage. An arrow was in my hand faster than blinking. I loosed it at the raven even as it wheeled and dived for me again.

The arrow impaled its wing. The raven screamed and crashed into the ground behind a rock a half-span away. I moved forwards slowly, readying another arrow.

Magelight flashed. The weremage's form swelled as she took her human shape, and I caught sight of her behind the rock.

Emotions torrented through me: anger for what she had done to Sten; triumph at the fact that we had found her at last; and fear, for Mag was not there to assist me, and I had no idea where she had gone.

"Mag!" I screamed, my voice echoing off the hard land. "I have her!"

The weremage cried out in pain as she dragged the arrow through the back of her arm. Her eyes flashed again as she sealed the wound. I drew and fired, but she cowered behind the rock, and I missed.

I stopped in my tracks, drawing another arrow. She could not hide forever. Slowly I backed up, step by step, risking only the briefest glances to see my footing.

Another flash of magelight.

The mountain lion with the white tail sprang into view. It was the form she had used to kill Sten. A fresh surge of anger struck me, throwing off my next shot. The mountain lion snarled and leaped to the side, the arrow missing by almost a pace.

I threw the bow aside and drew my sword from my belt. The weremage stalked closer, hackles up, a low growl rumbling from her throat. Fear now joined anger in my gut, churning it, threatening to make me vomit.

"Do it!" I screamed, forcing the terror away. "Do it, you sow!"

The lion roared. It sank back onto its haunches, ready to pounce.

And then a furious stream of barking made us both pause. Oku had abandoned his pursuit of the Shade to help me. He streaked in from the left, a blur of brown and black fur. Teeth flashed in the dull grey sunlight as he drove the mountain lion back a pace. She swiped at him, and Oku dodged it, barking louder.

Then Mag came dashing into view. She was higher up on the slope down which the other Shade had come. I watched as she took in the scene in a heartbeat.

Her battle-trance came over her, the dead-eyed expression crashing down her face like a portcullis.

She charged from behind, but the weremage heard her coming. She looked back over her shoulder, and I could practically see the fear shoot through her as she saw Mag. With a desperate swipe, she drove Oku back and darted towards the road to Kahaunga.

"After her," called Mag, her voice toneless. I recovered my bow, and we gave chase together.

I managed to get off one more shot before the weremage vanished around the first curve in the road. It streaked just past her white tail. We sprinted after her, the slapping of our boots echoing off the mountains.

"Mountain lions cannot run forever," I gasped as we ran. "Bursts of speed, but little endurance."

"Save your breath for running," said Mag tonelessly.

We had only one advantage. The weremage could not turn into a raven and fly away again. If she tried it, I could shoot her down, and she knew it. And in just a few moments, we would reach the bridge. That was a wide open space, and I would have a clear shot.

The hunt was about to end. The other Shade might have escaped, but that would be something to deal with later.

Then we rounded the path leading to the bridge, and I heard the sound of thundering hooves. Confusion made my steps falter, even as I saw the weremage dashing across the bridge in front of us. Beyond her was a party of rangers in Telfer colors, riding towards us on horseback. They were less than a span from the other end of the bridge.

"Now, Albern!" snapped Mag. "Shoot her!"

I shook off my surprise and fired. The arrow flew true, sinking into the weremage's flank. She roared in pain.

An arrow in her side, and a party of riders ahead. The rangers had drawn up short, some reaching for their bows, others snatching spears from holsters on their saddles. The weremage was finished. She had to be.

And then she turned.

At the other end of the chasm, at the edge of a cliff which the bridge had been built to span, there was a small shelf.

A small shelf I had avoided looking at. The source of a bad memory I wished to forget.

The mountain lion leaped down to the shelf. And then she vanished over the other side of it.

From where we stood—and from where the rangers sat on their horses—it looked like she must have plunged to her death. But I knew she had not. I knew that over that shelf was a slope, steep and rocky, and worn smooth by ages of rainfall and exposure to the open wind.

I knew that. And so had the weremage. She had scouted this area better than I thought she could have. She had only run this way because she knew she had a means of escape.

"Albern," said Mag, her voice still monotonous with her trance.

My attention was dragged reluctantly back to the present situation. Now that the mountain lion had vanished, the party of rangers had turned their focus on us. They were advancing slowly across the bridge, weapons raised. Two had dismounted, and they held their spears ready as they approached.

"Drop your spear!" called one still on horseback—a thicker woman with a shaved head, tattoos all over her lower face. "And you, your bow."

"That mountain lion—" I began.

"Your weapons!" she shouted.

I ground my teeth in frustration—but I dropped my bow. "Do it," I muttered to Mag.

Her battle-trance dropped away, and anger showed plain in her features. "Albern, the weremage—"

"We have no choice," I said. "Unless you wish to slay a whole troop of my family's rangers. I believe you could do it, but I hope you will not."

She growled and dropped her spear into the dirt.

The rangers relaxed a bit and came forwards more quickly. We backed a few paces away from our weapons. Oku looked alert, but he did not growl at them, even as the two on foot scooped up the bow and spear.

"Who are you?" said the woman. Now that she was closer, I could see a badge on her chest—my family's symbol, the bow and three arrows, crafted of silver instead of iron. A captain, directly under command of the lead ranger.

"I am Kanohari," I said. "This is Chao. You must listen to us. That mountain lion you just saw—it was a weremage. She is on the run from the King's law."

That gave all of them pause. The whole party gave confused glances to their captain, who frowned down at us from atop her horse. "A weremage?" she said.

"Yes, and she is—" I bit my own words off, glowering at the ground. "She is getting away."

It was too late. By now, the weremage would have reached the end of the slope. She had already had plenty of time to resume her human form, heal herself with her magic, and then take a raven's form to fly away.

She was gone. She had escaped. Again.

Suddenly one of the rangers leaned forwards, peering at our faces. "Wait. I remember you."

I looked up at him in surprise. And then I recognized him. He had been one of the guards at the gate when we arrived to Kahaunga the day before. My heart sank.

"Who are they?" said the captain.

"New arrivals to Kahaunga," said the guard. "They came through the west gate yesterday, along with an old man."

"On what business?" said the captain.

"They said they were delivering a message to a cousin of the Lord

Matara." The ranger's frown deepened. "Which does not explain why they are out here in the wilderness."

"We have Lord Matara's writ," said Mag.

The captain's brows drew close. "If you serve a Rangatira, you know that visitors are not allowed to hunt in another lord's domain, with or without a writ."

"We were not hunting," growled Mag. "We pursued a weremage. She attacked us. Why else would we *chase* a lion through the wilderness?"

The captain paused again. She gave an uncertain glance to the guard beside her, who had begun to look doubtful.

Mag could contain herself no longer. "She is a *Shade,* you fools!"

"Mag!" I said, but too late.

A shock passed through their party. The captain's face darkened, and all doubt vanished from her expression.

"If you know what that means," she hissed, "then you know better than to be shouting it out loud."

"We have hunted her across two kingdoms," I said, spreading my hands and adopting my most disarming tone. "My friend spoke in haste, but she is not—"

"Enough," snapped the captain. I fell silent. "If you speak the truth, and she is a weremage, then she is well beyond our reach by now. And if you are lying, then you have broken Calentin law. In either case, this matter is out of my hands." She turned to her party. "Bind them. We are taking them to the Rangatira."

A pit formed in my stomach, a bottomless hole that threatened to engulf me. I searched desperately for some excuse, something I could say that would save us.

Nothing came. And so I remained silent, as the two guards on foot approached and took Mag and me by the arms.

TWENTY-FOUR

ALBERN LED SUN AROUND THE EDGE OF THE HILL, AND SUDDENLY, there was Lan Shui. He paused the tale, and they both stood looking upon the town.

Sun found herself speechless. She had never seen Lan Shui, and yet Albern had described it in such detail that she felt as if she had been here before. It was nestled by a river that thundered down out of the Greatrocks, the peaks stretching tall and mighty above it. The western spur, which had seemed so large before, was now dwarfed by mountains that were no longer hidden by nearer hills.

"Lan Shui," said Albern. "It has been a long time since last I beheld it. Come. I am hungry, and I long for something to drink."

He nudged his horse forwards, and Sun followed. Though she kept studying the town as they approached, her mind drifted back to the tale Albern had been telling her.

"She got away," said Sun. "Kaita, I mean. You were both such capable fighters, and yet she escaped you."

"As she did in Northwood," said Albern.

"She had help in Northwood," said Sun.

Albern looked down at her, brows raised. "I am afraid I do not see your point, unless you mean to imply that we let her get away."

"Of course not," said Sun quickly. "It is only that . . . it must be the unluckiest thing I have ever heard of."

Albern chuckled. "Luck. I have told you already—"

"That you do not believe in luck," said Sun. "That you trust fate instead. Yes, I have heard you. Many times. But if that is true—if you were not *meant* to kill Kaita then, and you were *meant* to find me in that tavern, and all the rest of it—then why do anything at all? Why make choices? Why . . . why try? If you are *meant* to do one thing or another, if it is all a path laid before you in advance, then what does it matter what choices you make?"

Albern's smile grew a little sad. "It is tragic to see such cynicism in one so young."

"I speak of *your* beliefs, not my own," grumbled Sun.

"And you apply a fatal viewpoint to them," said Albern. "Think of this. One thing is certain for all of us: death lies at the end of our road. That is a certainty. That is a fate no one can escape. So if we know we are fated to die, would you say we should not live? Of course not. Our choices are everything. They make us who we are. And I believe they do shape events. Sometimes, a greater force—fate, I call it, though others have other words—it stops us from making the choice we want to make. But that does not mean our choice is invalid, or that we were wrong for making it. Think of it as a war of forces, a conflict between the things we can choose and the things we cannot. We may not be able to control everything, but we must never stop trying to help when we can, however we can."

It was another one of Albern's sayings that had the sound of deep wisdom, but which made Sun most uncomfortable for reasons she did not entirely understand. It kept her silent until they entered Lan Shui, waved on by a guard at the gatehouse who gave them only a cursory inspection. Within the walls, she let herself get distracted by the sights around her. A strange cast seem to cover the buildings, as well as the mountains and green fields beyond. She was reminded of Albern's tale of the place, of the desperate battle he and Mag had fought against the vampires within these walls. Could she, in fact, see scratches on the buildings from the vampires' claws? Or did they come from a more mundane source, or did she imagine them entirely?

But, too, she thought of the story he had just been telling her, about his little party riding into Telfer lands. The experiences were very similar, and the sensation she had now was familiar as well, the malaise of riding into a foreign town as a stranger, an interloper in another's domain.

"It is different, being a traveler, is it not?" said Sun. "I have not often had the experience of riding into a town or city, unless I was a distinguished guest of some lord there. It is odd to be just a . . . a person. A person who knows no one, to whom nothing is familiar."

"Yes, it can be strange," said Albern. "But I think your discomfort will fade with time, and with practice. Strangers are usually kind. More often than not, you will find yourself welcomed in the places you visit, as long as you bring no evil with you. The experience Mag and I had when we first arrived here, or when we encountered those Telfer rangers in the mountains, is a rare one. Here in Lan Shui, Yue only distrusted us because the town was in danger. In the mountains, the Telfer guards only suspected us because they were on high alert, for the trolls were threatening their home. The kindness with which we were received at the gates of Opara, and at Kahaunga, is the norm, not the exception. In times of peace, people are given to hospitality, and even charity."

Sun looked nervously around at the town again. "Then what sort of welcome do you expect in these times?"

Albern gave a little frown and did not answer.

He pulled his horse to a stop in front of an inn. Sun read the sign over its door: The Sunspear. But she could not reconcile Albern's stories of the place with the sight before her. This building looked almost brand new. And when Albern saw to his horse's lodgings and led her inside, there was a young woman behind the bar, not the older man from his tale.

"This looks . . . rather different from what you told me," said Sun quietly.

Albern paused in his advance across the room. "Oh, yes, it would. Many buildings in Lan Shui were destroyed in the Necromancer's War. The innkeeper who used to own it—the one we met, and who I told you about—was killed. But the inn was rebuilt, and his daughter owns it now. That is her behind the bar. If you find us a table, I will fetch us a meal and some drinks."

Sun did as he asked, finding a spot in the corner. Albern soon arrived with a savory stew that made her mouth water, as well as a mug of beer for each of them. For a time they said nothing, only tucking into their fare and drinking deep. After a quarter-hour they both leaned back in their chairs at the same time, sighing.

"I asked after Dawan," said Albern. "She is here. I have sent word that we arrived, and she should come to see us shortly."

"That is good," said Sun. Then she frowned. "I think."

Albern chuckled. "It is. I only hope it does not take too long. I wish to see to our other business outside of town before the end of the day."

Sun's stomach did a little turn. "I suppose I wish to do so as well."

"It is all right if you are a little nervous," said Albern. "But come. I will return to the tale to take your mind off it, if that is all right?"

"Of course," said Sun.

"You mentioned earlier how strange it was that Kaita escaped," said Albern. "But you have little inkling, I think, of just how right you are. To understand, you need to know how I left my home in my youth, when at last I had decided to do so. I should not have escaped. You might call it sheer luck that I managed it. But I think I was *meant* to get away that night, and it is a tale worth telling."

TWENTY-FIVE

I HAD JUST REACHED THE AGE OF NINETEEN. THERE WERE TWO STORMS that night—one outside our stronghold of Kahaunga, and one within. It was my mother, you see—Lord Thada of the family Telfer, Rangatira of Tokana. She was furious about something or other.

No. That is not fair to her. Because of how she treated me, I sometimes speak lightly of the very real problems she faced as a Rangatira. In this case, a group of Feldemarian bandits had ventured into our pass. My mother had sent a party of rangers to drive them out, and three of our soldiers had fallen. One had been a captain who she had particularly favored. I think she had been meaning to take him as a husband—you will remember that my father was long dead by this point.

In any case, I was in my room, and I was grieving, though for quite a different reason. I had had a hunting hound for much of my youth, a fine beast I had called Kowi. He had died that day. A few days before, while we were out on a trail, he had slipped and fallen when a shelf of land collapsed underneath him. The fall, and the rocks that landed on him after, broke most of his body. I carried him home, and there he lingered for a few days. Our master of hounds had urged me to put him out of his misery, for he had no chance of surviving. I refused, because I loved him, and because I was still very young, and unwise about some things. So when Kowi had finally died, I was abruptly saddled not only with the grief of his loss, but with the guilt that I had made him suffer longer than he had needed to.

It was in this state that my mother found me, alone in my room, my pillow soaked through with tears. I was drunk as well, for I had stolen two bottles of wine from the kitchen and gone through both of them. My sister Ditra was away on a diplomatic trip to the south, and so she had not been there to comfort me. I longed for her company—and so you can imagine my disappointment and dismay when I looked up at the sound of my door opening, and found my mother looking down on me instead.

"Vera," she said, for this was before any of us knew I was ander, "I have need of you."

For a moment I could only blink up at her. "What?" I said at last.

Her mouth pressed into a thin line. She crossed the room and pulled me up off the bed, giving me a shake. "I said I have need of you. You will need to ride out. Get some more useful clothes."

"I . . . what are you talking about?" My voice still shook with sobs, and there was a slur in it as well.

"You are drunk," she said with deep disapproval. "Soldiers from Feldemar have killed three of our people. We are going to retaliate. I am sending you out with the raiding party. It is about time you learned something of real combat."

I snatched my arm away from her, drawing back. "You are riding to Feldemar?"

"No," she said, her gaze steely. "You are."

"You are not even coming with me?" I said. "I have never fought before. I have never killed before!"

Her mouth shriveled into a scowl. "I am well aware of that. But you have had training, just like any of us. It is about time you got your arrows wet. The journey through the pass will sober you."

"No," I said, my voice coming out as little more than a whisper. I shook my head and spoke louder. "I will not."

I could almost feel the tension rise in her body. "You will."

I tried to push past her. "Leave me alone."

She snatched my arm and shoved me down on the bed. Ignoring

my protests, she dragged up my arm and pulled back my sleeve, exposing the family mark. "Do you see this? Do you know what it means? It means you are pledged to the service of this family."

Her grip was too strong, and I could not break free. "I never wanted that mark!"

"It is your duty," she said. At last she let me go, flinging my arm away as though it were something dirty. "You are a child of the family Telfer. It is an honor, and it comes with a responsibility. Yet here you sit, weeping into your sheets about a mangy hound, drinking yourself into a stupor as though you lost someone important."

Before I knew it, I was on my feet, my nose only a few fingers away from hers. "I had him since my eighth year," I said, my voice dropping to a growl. "He was my friend."

"He was a *dog,* you witless girl," said my mother. "And he was mine. Not yours. I am Rangatira. You are not even fit to be one of my rangers—but I will forge you, like a blade, until you are. Get dressed. Do you think I acted this way when your father died?"

"I am sure you did not," I said. "But then, you never really cared about him, did you?"

She slapped me. I suppose it was not as hard as it could have been. Certainly I had taken harder blows in weapons training. But still I went crashing back atop my bed, cradling my cheek with one hand.

"If you were not my daughter, I would put you to death for disobeying me, and I would be within my rights to do so," said my mother calmly. "But being my child will not protect you if you continue in disobedience. Your Rangatira has given you an order. You will obey it, or you will face the King's law."

She turned on her heel and marched from the room, slamming the door shut as she went. Slowly I realized that she was not angry for my words about my father; she was only upset that I continued to disobey her. That was all that mattered. How *useful* I could be to her.

I lay on the bed, fresh tears staining my face and the sheets. I tried to force my sobs to subside, but it happened slowly.

The King's law. Would she truly brand me as a traitor? I thought she might. What would be the penalty for defying one's lord? I knew a soldier could be exiled for that, or executed. But I did not think, even then, that she would order the death of her own child.

That left exile.

And with that thought, my mind was made up. If I was going to be cast out of my home, then I would not wait for her to pronounce that judgement. All the unease that had been building in me for years, all my discontent and dissatisfaction came welling up in me at once.

Ditra was the only person in Kahaunga whom I loved, and she was growing ever more distant as my mother dragged her further into her duty to the family. There was nothing to hold me here. And if I stayed, I would either be miserable for the rest of my life, or accept my fate, as Ditra had, and become one of my mother's warriors, a sword for her to wield, an arrow for her to loose at her enemies.

I would not let that happen.

Quickly I dressed myself—in "useful" clothing, as my mother would have put it, though the plans I was forming would be little use to her. I fetched a pack from my closet and filled it with more clothes, as well as my box of flint and steel. I paused, thinking that mayhap I should run to the kitchens and get some food for my journey. But I had no time. My mother would soon send guards to find me. I would have to hunt on the road. That was fine; I journeyed often through Tokana, and I was able to keep myself well fed as I did so. I slung the pack over my back, took up my bow from where it rested near the door to my room, and left.

No one saw me as I snuck out of the stronghold, but my heart did not ease as I made it into the city. All the guards knew me, and even if I pulled my cowl down over my face, my clothing was too fine for them to think I was simply some passerby. And it was night, besides—no one wandering the streets in the moonslight would pass without suspicion.

Thus I tried to remain alert, watching in all directions for anyone approaching me. But it was hard. My head was still heavy with the wine I had drunk. I know I stumbled, I know I crashed into at least a few buildings as I lurched through the streets. I barely remember any of that. The next clear memory I have is of approaching the city's north gate. I stood there for a moment, trying to think how I could get through.

Then there came shouts, and the gate swung open. A party of rangers on foot came through from the outside—returning from patrol, I guessed. Whatever the case, I seized my opportunity. As soon as the gateway stood empty, I ran towards it. I tripped at the last moment, but I fell to the ground outside just as the gate slammed shut.

My escape had not gone unnoticed. A cry went up, and they labored to open the gate again. I scrambled to my feet and ran. It was not long before I heard them behind me—many voices, shouting in the darkness, hunting for me by moonslight. But that was dim and fey, for rain was falling, and the thick clouds in the sky obscured everything. Despite my drunken state, I was able to keep my distance from my pursuers because I knew the land so well.

My feet carried me north on the same road Mag and I would travel all those years later, searching for the weremage. And they brought me to the bridge. But as I came to the place, the clouds obscured the moons completely, and everything went almost pitch black.

I crashed into someone, and we both fell to the ground.

At first I panicked, thinking one of my pursuers had caught me. But then I realized the person had been in front of me. They had just crossed the bridge from the other direction. They were making for the city.

The clouds parted for a moment, and in the flash of moonslight I saw a face. But it swam in the darkness and my own drunkenness. All I could focus on was the black cloak, trimmed with red. The colors of my family.

I screamed and backed away on hands and knees.

Because, you see, I knew about the shelf by the end of the bridge.

I fell onto the shelf and crawled to the slope on the other side, pitching myself over. It was slick with rainwater, and I flew down it faster than a hawk diving upon its prey. My stomach lurched, and I vomited over the side, my sick splashing upon the valley floor far, far below. But at last I came to the end of the slide.

For a long while I lay there, panting, heaving, feeling ill in both body and spirit. At last I looked back up the slide. The ranger must have seen me. But whoever they were, they had not followed. They had to have recognized me. Yet they had not followed.

I thought that mayhap they had cracked their head when I knocked them over. That they had been knocked senseless, unable to understand what they had seen, unable to call the other guards and point them in my direction.

I thought about them fairly often over the next few months. I hoped they were all right. I thought they must have been; we had not struck each other all that hard. But then how had I escaped? It made no sense.

Do you understand, Sun?

You will.

TWENTY-SIX

The rangers rounded us up and walked us back to Kahaunga, positioning us in their midst. They did, however, show us the courtesy of fetching our horses, when we told them they were a little farther up the road. For our part, we made no trouble for them on the way back to Kahaunga. Oku followed faithfully at our heels, seemingly unconcerned by the new company we kept.

As we went, the captain questioned us, asking where we had taken lodgings and where she might find the old man we had come to Kahaunga with. I barely heard her, and so Mag answered. They went to the place, and one of the rangers went inside to fetch Dryleaf. He emerged with a bemused expression, his hand on the guard's arm.

"Are you there, Kanohari? Chao?" he said.

"Here, Dryleaf," said Mag.

"Ah, good. Your plan of secrecy and stealth has gone swimmingly, I see."

Mag stuck her tongue out and blew at him. Dryleaf smiled.

"Well, I am told the Rangatira requires an audience. We should be honored."

Mag laughed, and even one or two of our guards gave a brief chuckle before biting it off. Dryleaf flashed them all a smile and went to take Mag's arm for guidance. Before we left, Mag looked down at Oku.

"Oku, kip," she said sternly.

The hound cocked his head at her, and a low whine issued from his throat.

"Do as she says, boy," said Dryleaf.

Oku lay down in front of the inn. But he did not take his eyes off us, even as we set off down the street and out of sight.

Our captors led us through the city towards my family's stronghold. I found myself unable to speak, unable to do much more than stew in terror at what lay before us. We were being brought to see my mother. Would she recognize me? Could she? I had not had my wending when I left, and many years had passed since then. But still, she would have to know my face. I was her child.

Then I realized how little that had ever seemed to mean to her, and I felt even worse.

The stronghold gates swung open as we approached, and the rangers led us inside. The captain ordered most of them away, bringing only three with her as she escorted us into the stronghold. Memories struck me like a fell wind as I stepped through the door, leaving my knees weak. Mag saw it, and she put a hand on my shoulder to steady me.

"Easy," she murmured. "We will all be fine. Let me do the talking."

"Gladly," I said, my voice weak. I pulled up my hood and dragged it down low over my face.

The captain stopped us before the huge doors leading into my mother's audience chamber. There she left us with the other rangers while she ducked inside. Our guards removed our bindings. I stood stock still as they did it, staring at my own hands.

"What happened?" said Dryleaf quietly.

"The weremage was following us," said Mag. "We almost ran her down, but our friends here came upon us and mistook our intent."

The rangers gave her a sidelong look, but they remained silent.

"How unfortunate," said Dryleaf with a sigh. "Well, hopefully the Rangatira will understand."

My limbs had begun to shake. My mother, being understanding? It was more than I could imagine.

Another moment's silence stretched. Then Dryleaf cocked his head. "You said she was following you. The two of you did not track her down?"

"No," said Mag.

"So she knew we were here."

A cold dread came over me. She *had* known we were here. It was too far-fetched to assume that she and the other Shade had simply stumbled upon us in the mountains.

"She . . . must have seen us when we arrived to Kahaunga," said Mag, though her voice was tinged with doubt. "It is not as though she—"

"—led us here," I said. "She led us here."

Dryleaf gave a grim nod. "You *have* been given quite a trail of breadcrumbs."

"What, since Opara?" said Mag. "I find that hard to believe."

"Mayhap even earlier," I said. "Always we have gained one piece of information at a time—never enough to bring her down, but only to lead us to the next step in the road."

"But that was true in Northwood," said Mag. "Are you saying that in the mountains, and in Lan Shui, she . . ."

And then she, too, fell to silence. But where I was now wracked with fear and confusion, I saw a burning rage rise in her eyes. Her fists clenched, knuckles turning white.

"But that begs a question," said Dryleaf. "Why? Why all this? You do not even know her name, Mag. What grudge could she bear you that would be worth all this?"

"Only one answer matters to me," snapped Mag. "The same I have sought since the beginning: her head on the end of my spear."

In front of us, the chamber door creaked open. The ranger captain stepped out.

"Follow me."

I steeled myself, following Mag and Dryleaf into the chamber. I remained behind them, forcing myself to stay as calm as I could. Mag would do the talking. Mother would hardly even glimpse my face. She was never interested in visitors, unless she thought they were of some value to her. She would never notice an attendant in the back.

The door closed behind us. I risked a glance up at the dais from beneath my cowl.

I froze.

The room was just as I remembered it, long and wide with a high ceiling. The walls had a series of short windows near the top, impossible for anyone to climb in, just enough to provide some ventilation for the fires that burned in two hearths. The stone pillars running up both sides of the room were of gleaming white limestone, while grey limestone made up the floor. But that grey was now covered with many rugs, which had not been the case in my youth. I saw the furs of bears and mountain cats, but also of creatures from more distant foreign lands. They were well swept and clean, and they made a soft surface for us to walk upon as we approached my mother's dais.

But the woman in the chair was not my mother.

Oh, she had the same sharp chin, the same piercing eyes, the same wide nose. She even wore her hair in tight braids bound up close to her scalp, as my mother had. But she was much younger than my mother. Only a few years older than me.

I looked into the face of my middle sister, Ditra.

This was such a shock to me that it was a good long while before I noticed anything else about the room. When I did, it was only to see that there were a few guards posted along the walls, and that just behind Ditra's chair was a young man wearing the Telfer family colors, as well as a badge of my family's symbol made of gold. Her lead ranger. I did not recognize him, but I remembered Tuhin's words back in Opara: his name was Maia.

My gaze was pulled back to the center of the dais, back to my sister sitting in my mother's chair, wearing my mother's stern countenance, crowned with the silver circlet my mother had borne as her mark of office. It was like seeing my mother all over again, but younger, the way she had looked when I was but a child.

In the end I realized I had been staring too long, and I ducked my head again. For her part, Ditra had not seemed to recognize me in the slightest. Mag and Dryleaf stood in front of me, and so she paid attention only to them, likely thinking me some sort of retainer or guard, and not an equal member of our little party.

That, too, was very like our mother.

Her lead ranger stepped forwards and raised a hand, causing us to stop a good five paces away from the dais. "You stand before Lord

Ditra of the family Telfer, lord of Kahaunga, Rangatira of the domain of Tokana."

My sister tilted her head up slightly. "Well met, travelers," she said. The words were courteous, even if her voice was steely. And suddenly her likeness to my mother was greatly diminished in my mind. Yes, she spoke in a stern tone, but *that* was my sister's voice, a voice I knew better than any but Mag's, a voice I treasured beyond anything else in my life.

I ducked my head still lower, struggling to contain tears. I did not entirely succeed, and I had to pretend to scratch my cheek to wipe them away.

We all bowed low with our fists to our foreheads. "Well met, Rangatira," said Mag. She had given me a brief, confused glance when we entered the hall, but seeing my state, she had not looked at me again. "I am Chao, and this is Dryleaf. We are honored to stand in your presence."

"Kind words, coming from the mouth of one who has been found breaking the law in my domain," said Ditra.

"I have long had great respect for the family Telfer," said Mag, "though it has been long since I was able to visit your noble dwelling. May I ask, where is the former lord, Thada of the family Telfer?"

The chamber fell silent. The lead ranger frowned down at us, but more in confusion than anger, I thought. Ditra had gone rather still in her chair, and while she did not exactly scowl down at Mag, she looked even more solemn than she had a moment ago.

"She passed into the darkness some time ago," she said. "I find it hard to believe you could have met her, for you look as if you would have been very young when she died."

I felt as if the ground had tilted beneath my feet. I gripped the back of Dryleaf's robes, holding him for support, trying not to come unmoored from the very ground. Dryleaf, for his part, tried to keep still, though I am afraid I may have put a great deal of weight on the poor man.

"I am often told that I look younger than I am," said Mag in a quiet voice. "I am sorry for your family's loss. How did she die?"

The lead ranger shifted again, but plainly in annoyance this time. Ditra, too, seemed angered by the question, and her lips drew tight.

"I hope I do not offend," said Mag quickly. "It is only . . . we had the chance to speak once. And I *was* young, as you said. It was a conversation I have never forgotten."

Ditra seemed to relent slightly at that, though she looked no more pleased. "She was riding in the mountains," she said. "Feldemarians attacked and killed her. It was shortly after the death of my older sister."

I could scarcely withstand the storm of emotions now raging within me. And yet, somehow, I did withstand it. What I was feeling . . . it was happening, but I could not let it affect me. I could not let it show in my face. I could not let it reveal anything about me, or draw Ditra's attention to me.

I had been afraid of being recognized when I thought I would have to face my mother. Now I was terrified. And so I controlled myself, despite the agony it caused me. Emotion would be of no help. It would ruin everything. It would cause me to make a mistake, and that would endanger me and my friends. So I simply . . . did not permit the emotion to affect me. I removed it from myself, to a place where it could hold no sway over my actions.

At that moment, I first began to understand Mag's battle-trance. I could not allow my thoughts to control me, and so I simply . . . left. I put myself in another place, so that I could do what I had to do to survive. A part of myself was destroyed as I did it, like I had ripped myself in two. But it was the only way.

And with that realization, the first seed of a question was planted in my mind. What had happened to Mag, long ago, that had made *her* feel this way for the first time? And how, when it was so agonizing to me, had she continued to use it, over and over again, until it became one of her hallmarks in battle?

But all of this passed through my mind in a flash, the way these moments do, to be considered later. Meanwhile, Mag and Ditra continued their conversation.

"No words can express my sorrow," said Mag. "Though years have passed since your loss, I offer my deepest sympathy."

"I am comforted by your kind words," said Ditra, who did not particularly sound as if she was. "But that is not why you stand before me. What are the three of you doing in my lands?"

"We were sent north," said Mag. "We serve Lord Matara."

Ditra frowned. "And what service are you providing him?"

"He ordered us to hunt down a rogue weremage who had been plaguing his domain," said Mag.

"A rogue weremage," said Ditra flatly. "And he did not give this matter to the Mystics?"

Mag hesitated. Dryleaf cleared his throat, drawing Ditra's attention. "Lord Telfer," he said. "This matter concerns secret words that all the Calentin lords have recently heard from the High King's Seat."

Ditra's face betrayed nothing. But she turned and motioned towards Maia with two fingers. He waved to the guards stationed along the walls, and they slowly filed out of the room, closing the door behind them. Ditra turned back to us.

"This concerns the Shades," she said.

"As we told your rangers in the mountains," said Mag, "though mayhap we spoke in haste. The weremage we are hunting—she is a Shade, and she is operating with others in the area."

"Why would Lord Matara not have sent word of this to me at once?" said Ditra. "And this does not explain why he would not take the matter to the Mystics. A rogue weremage falls under their jurisdiction, and even more so if she is a Shade."

"As for your first question, the Rangatira did not know the weremage would come here," said Dryleaf. "Nor did we. We pursued her away from Opara and followed her trail through the kingdom, only arriving here yesterday. In hindsight, it would have been wise of us to come to you before we continued our chase. But we have been on a long trail, and we thought we saw its end within reach. As for your second question, the Mystics in Opara were notified. But they only recently discovered a cabal of Shades in the wilderness near their city, and they have been much preoccupied with rooting them out. They approved of the Rangatira's request to let us handle this matter."

It was a brilliant stroke, all the more so because I knew Dryleaf had made it up on the spot. If Ditra tried to investigate the truth of his words, she would find that yes, a cadre of Shades had indeed been found outside of Opara. As for the Mystics, they would be reticent to give any information about matters concerning a rogue weremage, whether or not they had already heard of her.

"You told my rangers something different when you entered the city," said Ditra.

"Because Lord Matara told us that we were not to speak of the Shades to anyone but another Rangatira," said Mag. She nodded to Maia. "And those they trust, of course."

Ditra considered that for a long moment. I noticed Maia eyeing her out of the corner of his eye, though the man tried not to be obvious about it.

"Why has this weremage come here?" said Ditra at last. "What are she and the other Shades planning?"

"We are not certain," said Mag. "But news has reached us of your recent trouble with the trolls. We think the Shades may have something to do with it."

"I think you know little of trolls," said Ditra, arching an eyebrow, "if you think they have allowed themselves to be influenced by humans—Shades or otherwise. Trolls will treat with us, but they will only take advice and counsel from among their own."

"Of course it sounds unlikely," said Dryleaf diplomatically. "We would say the same thing, if we had not heard of something like it before. Word reached Opara of the Shades doing something similar in Dorsea. They hatched a plan around a magic ritual, one that summoned vampires and drove them into a frenzy of hunger. A town near the Greatrocks was almost destroyed, and would have been, if not for the actions of a few brave heroes."

Mag's mouth twitched.

"Vampires?" said Maia incredulously. "No one can command those savage beasts."

"Yet they did," said Dryleaf, bowing his head. "I hope, then, that you can understand why we think they may have something to do with the trolls."

"That is evil news, if it is true," said Ditra. "Yet I have never heard of, and cannot imagine, any such ritual that would command a troll."

"Nor have we," said Mag. "Yet we suspect it all the same. It was one thing we hoped to learn on our expedition. If we are correct, it is a clear pattern—a strategy the Shades may be using in other places, in other kingdoms, even now."

Ditra tapped her chin with one finger. "Stirring up creatures from the wilds to sow chaos and disruption . . . these are the tactics of a foe fighting a war of stealth and subterfuge."

"Guerilla tactics," said Mag with a nod.

"They cannot stand toe-to-toe with the High King, and so they instigate battles between her armies and other forces, to supplement their numbers." Ditra slid her hands along the arms of her chair and pushed her shoulders back, stretching. "If this is part of their strategy, it will be very useful information in the coming days. I will send word of this to the king, and advise them to relay it to the High King."

We all bowed deeply. "Thank you, Rangatira," said Dryleaf. "You prove yourself wise beyond your years—or at least, so I guess from the sound of your voice."

Ditra gave a little smile—almost, it seemed, against her will—and said, "Thank you, Grandfather." Then her eyes swept across us again. "So you and the quiet one in the back are rangers?"

Dryleaf and Mag paused for a moment that stretched too long. I realized that they were reluctant to answer, afraid they would miss some intricacy of Calentin politics and make a misstep. Though I badly wished to hold my tongue, I spoke. "No, Lord Telfer. Simple soldiers. We have no marks."

"So he has not fallen asleep back there," said Ditra. I ducked my head lower, hoping it looked like I was embarrassed, and not trying to hide my face. "I can believe the two of you are soldiers, especially since you have Conrus' writ." She turned to Dryleaf. "But I think your fighting days are behind you, if you will forgive my saying so—was it Dryleaf?"

"It was, and it is, Rangatira," said Dryleaf, smiling broadly. "And you are correct. I am one of Conrus' advisors. In my youth I had many dealings with the Mystics, and I learned from them many secrets of dealing with rogue wizards. These two are sellswords working for hire."

I winced, but it was too late. At the word "sellswords," Ditra's small smile vanished, to be replaced with a dour expression.

"Strange that Conrus would trust mercenaries with such an important task," said Ditra. "Stranger still that he would relay to them the information he had received from the High King. Foolish, one might even say."

"We have served him for many long years," I said quickly. "The

Rangatira knows he can trust in our discretion. Indeed, we would have joined his rangers long ago. But we were somewhat involved in a disagreement with him and the Rangatira Hauru of Tonga, and Lord Matara was reluctant to bring us into his service, for fear of causing offense."

Ditra's stern look did not relax any, but she did lean back in her chair with a sigh. "Sky save us all from politicking," she said irritably.

"On which point we could not agree more," said Dryleaf. "And I hope you will believe me when I say that I have rarely encountered two more worthy soldiers in all my years of being a councilor. And with that, I believe we have taken up as much of your doubtless precious time as can be spared. Though if you wish it, I would be honored to sing for your dining hall tonight, or any night that you would have me."

She seemed to be more irritated than ever, though she still maintained a thin veneer of decorum. "I do not wish it. My position leaves me no time to sit idly and listen to songs."

Mag, sensing the tension in the room, spoke again. "In that case, Lord Telfer, we would beg your leave. We should set about our business of tracking down this weremage. With your permission, of course."

"Normally, I would not give it," said Ditra. "This matter has moved into Tokana, which means it falls to me to settle it. But my rangers are already stretched thin to ensure none of my people are harmed by the trolls. Therefore I will permit you to continue your hunt. You may speak with my lead ranger, Maia, if you require anything from us." She waved a hand at him, and he gave us a slow nod. "I will also order the soldiers of my house to be on the alert while they patrol. They know the Shades' colors, but any information you have on the weremage would be useful."

"She has Calentin features," said Mag. "When we have seen her in human form, she has worn her long black hair in a braid down her back."

"That narrows it down not a whit," said Ditra. "What of her animal forms?"

"We have seen two, though there may be others," said Mag. "A raven, and a brown mountain lion with a white tail."

Ditra did not respond to that. Her eyes did not widen, her hands did not clench. I doubt that Mag or Dryleaf noticed anything change in her appearance. But I sensed *something* in her demeanor. Maia, however, did not give her a second glance, and I told myself I must have imagined it.

"That is something to go on, at least," said Ditra. "I will relay it to my rangers. You are dismissed."

"Thank you, Rangatira," said Dryleaf, bowing low once again. Mag and I did the same, and then I took Dryleaf's arm, guiding him along as I followed Mag out of the room.

TWENTY-SEVEN

I MANAGED TO KEEP MY EXPRESSION IMPASSIVE AS WE MADE OUR WAY out of the stronghold and into the city streets. But I could not keep my grip on the emptiness inside of me forever. Once we were out of sight of my family's home, hot tears slid from me, and my arm began to shake under Dryleaf's hand.

"There now," said Dryleaf gently. "We will be back soon."

Mag looked over her shoulder at his words, and when she saw my face, she came to me at once. "Here," she said softly. "I will take him."

She gently lifted Dryleaf's hand from my arm and placed it on her own. I cast my hood down lower and wept, trying to stay silent at first, but in the end I let myself feel the grief that had been building up in me since I first saw Ditra on my mother's chair. When we reached the inn at last, Oku came bounding up, but he seemed to sense my mood and did not bark at us. Once we reached our room, I sat on the edge of the bed and cast my face into my hands. Mag helped Dryleaf to a chair in the corner, shrugged off her shirt of scale mail, and then came to sit by me, wrapping her arm around my shoulders and pulling my head to her chest. Dryleaf bowed his head, and the two of them sat in silence while I poured my woe into Mag's tunic. She did not speak a word, but only held me tighter, occasionally patting my hair. Oku curled up at my feet, his head resting on my boot.

It did not take all that long, considering. I had mourned the loss of my mother long ago—though because she had not been truly gone, there was always at least some hope that we might reconcile our differences. What I mourned in that moment was the loss of that hope. The knowledge was heavy upon me that it was over now, and things would never be right between us.

And, too, I wept for the sight of my sister. My sweet, loving sister, the only one who had comforted me when the world had not cared, now sitting in our mother's chair, and every bit as hard as she had ever been.

But at last my tears subsided. I scrubbed the last of them away on my sleeve, shaking my head and trying to bring myself back to the moment.

"Thank you," I said quietly. "Thank you both."

"You have nothing to thank us for, dear boy," said Dryleaf. "You have had a hard day."

"We do not have to talk now," said Mag. "If you need time—"

"I do not," I said. "I would rather get to work. It will keep my mind from matters of grief."

"As you say," said Dryleaf carefully.

"Do you think my idea unwise?" I said, trying not to sound irritated.

"I think that open wounds need time to close, or they may become aggravated," he said. "And that goes for others as well. The Rangatira still harbors some grief."

"She seemed very comfortable on that chair," I said bitterly.

"She sounded like a lord secure in her position, it is true," said Dryleaf. He paused before continuing, picking at a thread on the knee of his robe. "Are you certain you do not wish to tell her you have returned?"

"No," I said at once. "She would not react well."

Dryleaf subsided. I could almost taste his unspoken questions, but he had enough sense, bless him, to let them be.

"Then if we are resolved, let us speak of what has happened," said Mag. "We know the weremage is in the wilds to the north."

"And we can guess that she was watching us before that," I said. "That means she will know where to find us. We should find new lodgings, quickly, before she has time to put a new watch upon us."

"Will that help?" said Dryleaf. "If we mean to go out into the wilds again, we will encounter her eventually. Then she can take her bird form again, and follow us back to wherever we are."

Mag frowned. "That is a fair point. But we must have some way to ensure you are safe when we are not here."

"You are worried about me?" said Dryleaf, smiling broadly. "You two are the ones riding out into danger."

"And leaving you unguarded," I said.

He waved his hand. "Why would the weremage care about me? Besides, this room is just next to the inn's common room, and the lock on the door is sturdy. She could not hope to strike me here without causing quite a bit more trouble than she has seemed to seek thus far."

"Very well," I said. "But you must be wary. That ranger in Opara had many wise things to say about trust and weremages. We will establish a password, and you must never unlock the door for either of us until we have spoken it."

"If it will make you feel better," said Dryleaf, inclining his head magnanimously.

"Then we should set back out and continue searching the site of the trolls' attacks," I said. "Not today—it has grown too late. But tomorrow, and every day, until we have tracked down the weremage."

"And ended her," said Mag.

"So we all hope." I paused, looking down at my hands as they rested in my lap.

Mag smiled. "Very well. Let us continue with our original plan. Back into the mountains tomorrow. The way will be easy without having to worry about Lord Telfer's patrols rounding us up."

"Easy," I said with a bitter smile. "I only hope we do not encounter any trolls in those mountains. If we do, you will learn just how 'easy' they are to deal with."

While we conferred at the inn, Lord Telfer was having her own discussion with Maia. It turned out that I had not, in fact, imagined her reaction when we told her of the weremage's animal forms. For a long while after we left, she sat in her chair, chin resting on her fist, her eyes seeing nothing. Maia stood silently by, knowing it would be foolish to disturb her until she was ready for him. In the end she sighed and stood from her chair.

"Let us retire to my chamber," she said. "We must discuss these matters."

"Of course, Rangatira," said Maia, giving a half-bow. He followed her to the back of the room, to the door leading to a staircase up to her private chamber. There Maia moved towards the chairs surrounding her table, but Ditra walked past them to her window, and Maia stayed on his feet. Another long silence dominated the room.

"Wine, Rangatira?" said Maia at last.

"Hm," she said.

Deciding to interpret her answer in the affirmative, he poured two cups. She took a sip when he put hers into her hand, but her gaze remained fixed out the window. Maia joined her in looking at the valley. From this vantage point, high in the keep's central tower, they could see almost the whole dale. The day was still cloudy and grey, and the sun was lowering behind them, but it still gave more than enough light to see signs of movement far below. Thousands of people milling together, going about their lives.

But Maia knew, though he could not see it, that there were refugees in the city, servants of his lord who had been forced to flee their homes, and who now choked the streets, the inns, anywhere they could find to sleep. Kahaunga looked much the same as it always did, but there was an unrest in the city now, a fear under the surface, and a tension that threatened to burst, like the snowy clouds in the sky above them.

For her part, Ditra's thoughts were only partially for the city. Mag and I had brought her evil tidings, and she was pondering them. But apart from our news, she was thinking of me. She could not understand why her thoughts should so dwell on a quiet man in a brown cloak standing behind his companions, who were clearly leading our little mission. She had gotten a good enough look at me to know that I was half Calentin and half Heddish, but that was common enough, especially in Tokana.

In the end, her thoughts turned away from me to the weremage. A weremage who took the form of a brown mountain lion with a white tail.

Sky above, thought Ditra. *After all these years.*

At last she nodded, as though in answer to a question. Maia stood straighter. He knew his lord. She had decided something, or she was ready to do so.

"Yes, Rangatira?" he prompted.

"You have been seeing to the patrols and organizing the housing of those who have had to flee from the outer villages," said Ditra. "You must give those duties to another. I require something else of you."

"Of course," said Maia. "What is it?"

"I need you to track down this weremage."

Maia was somewhat surprised, but he hid it well. "As you wish. I shall be working with the newcomers, then?"

"No," snapped Ditra, turning on him with such a furious glare that he swallowed through a suddenly dry throat. "No," she said again, less angrily, taking a deep drink of her wine. "You must do this on your own. Find her, if she can be found in the wilderness. Find out where she is and what she is doing. Take no action against her until you have done this and reported back to me."

"As you command," said Maia. "But Rangatira . . . the newcomers are searching for her as well."

Ditra lifted her chin as she regarded him. "Are you a ranger of the family Telfer, or are you not? I am certain they are capable fighters, if Conrus took them into his service. But they are strangers to this place. They do not know these mountains. You will find Kaita before they do."

Maia frowned. "Kaita?"

Ditra went very, very still.

"The weremage," she said after a moment. "They mentioned her name was Kaita."

For a moment, Maia was unsure how to answer. Of course we had *not* mentioned that her name was Kaita, and Maia knew it. But the look in his lord's eyes told him he would be most unwise to mention it.

"That must have escaped my notice," he said at last.

"See that it escapes any mention as well," said Ditra. "Tell no one what you are doing. And if you discover anything about the weremage or her whereabouts, you are to bring it to me immediately. Do you understand?"

"Of course, Rangatira." Maia gave a low bow. "If I may ask, does this have anything to do with—"

"You may not." Ditra turned from him to look out the window again. "We are done."

Maia bowed once more, though she did not see it, and then he left.

TWENTY-EIGHT

"I have a question," said Sun.

Albern smiled. "I enjoy your questions immensely."

"You hardly ever answer them," said Sun with a frown.

"Sometimes that is what makes them enjoyable."

Sun rolled her eyes and drank more of her beer. They had both finished their meals long ago. "You said you were going to tell me another story about Mag. But this story seems to be about you."

He seemed to consider that for a long moment, pursing his lips and nodding. "Yes. Yes, I suppose it is. This part of the tale took place in my homeland. A great deal more happened to me—at least in my own mind—than happened to Mag. Are you not enjoying the tale?"

So disarming was his smile that Sun felt he would truly not be offended, no matter her answer. But the truth was that she *was* quite enjoying it. And yet hearing of the manner of his return, the way he had been marched into his own home like a prisoner, had caused her own chest to grow tight, her breath catching in her throat.

"The thought of returning as you did terrifies me," she said. "I almost felt ill when you described it."

He nodded. "It may be the freshness of the parting that makes you feel so. You may feel differently in twenty years. In fact, I hope you do. Because whatever else may be said about my return to Calentin, it was good for me, in the end."

Just as Sun was about to ask him what he meant, a voice spoke nearby. "Are you boring some poor girl to death with tales, young man?"

Sun gave a start and looked up. Standing just beside the table, so close it seemed impossible Sun could not have heard her approach, was a woman. She looked to be somewhat younger than Albern. Her dark skin and long locks of hair spoke of Feldemarian descent, but she wore robes of gold, trimmed with white. Her face was round and soft, and she filled out her robes nicely, her form falling to the floor in wide curves like the bouncing of a child's ball.

"Dawan." Albern stood at once and embraced her, and she patted his back gently. He slid around to another chair on the far side of the table, offering his own to her. "My heart sings to see you again."

"It should not be doing that," said Dawan, her brows rising. "I shall have to take a look at it."

Albern chuckled, and Sun did the same, once she realized it was a joke. She had not stopped studying Dawan's face. "Albern told me you were older than he is," she said. "I can hardly believe it."

Dawan laughed, a deep, rich sound that made Sun feel comforted and warm. "I have lived a life of great comfort and safety, even when travel has taken me away from the Seat. Meanwhile, this fool keeps throwing himself into one dark pit after another. Always climbs back out, however, which is good, especially if he is now picking up traveling companions as young as you are."

"As kind as always," said Albern, giving her a smile. Dawan returned it. Then she clasped her hands before her.

"I have much to do here and elsewhere, and less time to do it in. May we retire to my room?"

"Of course," said Albern.

He drained the last of his mug, and Sun hurried to do the same. They rose and followed Dawan out of the common room into a hallway. She stopped at the second door on the left and opened it. As Albern and Sun filed in, Dawan remained by the door. When they were inside, she paused and looked to Albern.

"Would you prefer for us to be alone?"

"That is up to Sun," said Albern. "I do not mind either way."

"I would like to stay, if that is all right," said Sun. The truth was that she was not even sure what she was staying for, but curiosity had a hold on her now.

"It is," said Dawan. She closed the door and locked it. "You will have to go if I ask you to, however."

"I will," said Sun.

Dawan motioned her to a chair on the other side of the room, and Sun sat. Albern rested on the edge of the bed. Dawan went to him and took his face in her hands, tilting it back and forth and looking at him from all angles.

"Your eyes are still sharp, I see."

"They are, thank the sky," said Albern.

Dawan nodded. Then she placed her hands on either side of Albern's throat. From behind her, Sun saw the soft glow of magelight from the woman's eyes. She gave a little gasp before she could stifle it—as a child of nobility, she had often seen wizards performing magic, but it still sent a thrill through her every time.

From what Sun knew of spellcasting, she thought that Dawan was using her alchemy—transmutation, wizards called it—to look into Albern's body, inspecting for any signs of injury or illness. They both remained completely still for a moment, Albern's eyes closed as he let Dawan inspect him. After a short while, the glow in Dawan's eyes faded, and she sighed.

"All seems well here. Your shirt, please."

Albern nodded and began to peel his tunic away from his body. It was stained with sweat and with much travel, but Dawan did not flinch as she helped him lift it off and hung it on a hook by the door like a fine garment.

"Where was it?" she asked, peering at his chest.

"Here," said Albern, pointing. It was awkward, for the spot was under his left arm, but he had no right arm to make the motion with.

"All right," said Dawan. She did not use her magic at first, but poked and prodded at his torso like any healer Sun had seen. Albern took her ministrations without comment, his gaze wandering idly about the room. Once he met Sun's eyes and gave her a gentle smile, which Sun returned with some embarrassment.

"You do not have to remain if you do not wish to," he said.

"I am all right," said Sun.

Albern nodded and said no more. When Dawan had finished looking him over, she again placed her hands on his body, her eyes filling with magelight as she touched him first in one place, and then another. It took considerably longer than Sun would have expected. She thought that alchemists could see straight through something in just a heartbeat, but that seemed not to be the case.

Dawan finished at last and stepped back with a sigh. There was a second chair nearby, and she sat down in it, seemingly fatigued for a moment.

"I can see it," she said. "It does not appear to be from your wending, which is a good thing. And I do not think it is an illness, either. It looks to be the remnant of some old injury, likely from a battle."

Albern pursed his lips. "It has never troubled me before."

"You are old," said Dawan flatly, though she softened the words with a smile. "Medicas can do much with the body, but they can do nothing about such injuries, nor about age itself."

"Well, then," said Albern, nodding. "That is the best news I could have expected, and I am glad to hear it."

"It would not be so agitated if you settled down and led a quiet life," said Dawan.

Albern smiled. "Mayhap one day."

"Days run short, my friend," said Dawan quietly. "For both of us."

He shrugged. "Who knows what the future holds?"

"Only one thing is certain," said Dawan. "But come. These thoughts are too gloomy. Let us finish your inspection." She turned to Sun. "You may remain, as before, but I will ask that you avert your eyes."

"Oh, I . . . of course." Sun felt her cheeks flame as she looked away. She was vaguely aware of some activity between Dawan and Albern on the other side of the room, but she busied herself studying the grain of the wood floor beneath her.

"Have you suffered any pains?" said Dawan after a bit.

"As you have said, I live a hard life."

"Aside from the usual, of course," said Dawan, her voice betraying only a hint of annoyance.

"No," said Albern.

"Good," said Dawan. There was more activity just beyond the edge of Sun's vision. "All right, girl. We are done."

Sun looked back. Albern was fully clothed again and smiling at the medica. Dawan had gone to a table beside her bed, where a small bowl of perfumed water stood. She dipped her hands in it, wiping them gently before drying them on a cloth. When she finished, she fixed her gaze on Sun, and there was a keen interest in her eyes.

"Have you ever seen a medica at work on an ander person before?"

"No," said Sun quietly. "I have known ander people, of course, but this is . . . new. I have always been somewhat curious about it."

"Well, you will rarely have a better chance to ask questions," said Dawan, spreading her hands. "What do you wish to know?"

Sun leaned forwards, flattening her hands against each other before her chin. "I have seen medicas heal wounds, but then I have heard that they do not truly *heal* wounds."

"That is true," said Dawan. "In the case of grievous injury, the best we can do is a sort of . . . a sealing. It holds the wound shut so that our charge does not bleed to death. True healing must come from within. Our seal will wear away after a time, and there can be aftereffects."

"Why?" said Sun. "Why can you not truly heal the wound? And why is a wending different? The changes an ander person goes through do not wear away."

Dawan licked her lips slowly, shaking her head as though frustrated. "And there you have asked the greatest question of our art. The answer is that no one knows. A therianthrope can heal their own wounds, but though a transmuter's power is a mirror of that branch, yet we cannot heal others. And no one knows why."

Sun blinked, confused. Albern saw it, and he smiled. "Therianthropy is what wizards call weremagic, and transmutation is alchemy."

"Ah," said Sun. "Thank you."

Dawan smiled and shook her head at them. "In any case, to understand why it is this way, we would have to know why bodies grow the way they do in the first place, and that is a mystery beyond anyone. All I can tell you is that we consult with our charges for a long time, making sure the patient knows exactly the way they wish their body to be, and that they have put that picture in our mind in as much detail as they possibly can. It is easier the younger they are, but then, most who are ander know it from an early age. But only once this picture is clear can we use our magic to realize it. If our job is done well, the body accepts the changes very naturally."

"With no . . . no changing back to the way it was before," said Sun.

"Correct. It is called reversion, in our craft." Dawan paused, considering. "This is not part of our training, but . . . in my own experience, and from what I have seen, it is . . . it is as though the body was always *supposed* to be that way in the first place. We only use our magic to get it back on track, if you will. It is more like righting a ship so it can resume its course, than truly 'changing' anything. Which is why many ander people do not get a wending at all. They enjoy themselves just the way they are. The body was never off course in the first place."

"I still do not see how that is different from an injury," said Sun. "Is a wound not just a body getting 'off course,' as you put it, in what is clearly an attempt to relate to my Dulmish sensibilities?" She smiled.

Dawan gave a loud guffaw before she could help herself, and then turned it into a more dignified titter. She glanced at Albern. "Oh, I like her. As for your question, girl: that might be the case, but it does not mean medicas can accomplish true healing. We cannot, and the results can be very dangerous if we try. Things can be different with a disease, or some injuries a person may be born with. Sometimes our magic can treat such a disease, other times it cannot. But since the side effects can be so severe, it is rarely attempted unless a life is at stake."

The room settled to silence. As Sun pondered what the medica had said, she realized that Albern and Dawan were both looking very intently at her. It was the same look Albern had given her earlier that day, when she had asked him about the time he left home. Suddenly she felt self-conscious, and she rolled her shoulders as if casting off a cloak.

"What is it? Did I say something wrong? I did not mean to . . ." She trailed off, for she did not know what she had not meant to do.

"Nothing like that," said Dawan. She came over and crouched before Sun, looking at her from eye level. Her warm, soft hands wrapped around Sun's own. "I must ask, and there is no wrong answer—even no answer. Do you think you might be ander?"

Suddenly Sun understood their reaction. She smiled at them both. "Ah. I see. I . . . I have thought about it. I do not think so, though I am not entirely sure."

"And you do not have to be," said Dawan quickly.

"Of course not," said Albern. "I am glad to hear you have given thought to it, though. That was more than I had done, when I left Tokana."

"Now I know why you were giving me all those looks this morning," said Sun. "You could have simply asked me."

"That is a conversation that must be had in the right time and place," said Albern. "As I know better than most."

"He is not entirely a fool," said Dawan. But the look she gave Albern was so fond that Sun could not believe any of the chiding in her tone. "And with that, we are done here."

Sun stood from the chair. She had not realized how much time had passed until her leg muscles suddenly screamed in protest. "Sky above, I need to walk."

"I am sure you will, if I know anything about Albern," said Dawan.

Albern stood from the bed, tugging gently on his tunic to adjust it. "Thank you, Dawan, as always."

"You are most welcome, old friend." Dawan went and gave him a quick peck on the cheek. "And do not try any of your tricks this time. I have already given the innkeeper gold—more than enough to cover my time here. You will not be able to sneak a payment to her for my services."

His face twisted in a scowl. "Dark take you. Old age has made you wily."

Dawan laughed. She went to Sun and took her hand for a moment, squeezing it. "It was an honor to meet you."

"Honor does not begin to describe it," said Sun. Then, seized by an impulse, she stepped forwards and embraced the medica. Dawan seemed shocked for the space of a heartbeat, but before Sun could pull back in embarrassment, she felt the woman's plump arms wrap around her.

"Please," whispered Dawan. "Please, take care of him for me."

Then Sun did draw back, but in surprise. She looked into Dawan's eyes and found them glistening. But her face was turned from Albern, and she had spoken so quietly that Sun knew he had not heard.

"Thank you again," said Sun. She gave Dawan a look, hoping the medica could see the answer in her eyes.

"And you," said Dawan, nodding.

Albern ushered her out. Dawan closed the door behind them. "You see?" said Albern. "What did I tell you? Dawan is one of the nine lands' greatest treasures."

"She is," said Sun fervently. "I wish we could have stayed with her longer. But I will accept, as a poor substitute, a return to your tale."

Albern chuckled. "Very well," he said. "I will tell you a bit more—but as we walk. Remember, I had other business in Lan Shui, and I still mean to take care of it."

"Agreed," said Sun, following him out of the Sunspear.

But as they walked through the streets and out through the north gate, she caught herself looking often back over her shoulder, thinking of all that Dawan had said.

TWENTY-NINE

The day after our meeting with Ditra, Gatak finally returned to the other trolls.

She strode into the pack's midst soon after dawn, the sun just cresting the eastern horizon and shining on her back. The smaller trolls roaming around the edges of the pack saw her first. They went stock still, staring in wonder as she approached. Gatak ignored them. Ambling on all fours, she picked her way between the trolls who were still sleeping. The air buzzed with their snores.

Apok stepped into her path.

Gatak was larger than most of the trolls, but Apok was larger still. Gatak looked up, betraying no concern. They stared at each other for a long, silent moment.

"You have been gone for many turns of the moons," said Apok at last.

"Yes," said Gatak.

"Where have you been?"

"I have traveled far," said Gatak. "I have seen the end of the mountains. I have seen the eastern sky and the western sea."

“I think you have been lurking with your human friends,” said Apok.

“They are friends to all of us,” said Gatak. “Their Lord promises many gifts.”

“Chok did not think so,” said Apok.

Gatak showed her teeth. “And where is he?”

Apok’s nostrils flared. But before she could answer, a barking command came from behind her.

“Apok! Enough!”

Dotag strode up, shoving Apok aside when he reached the two of them. For a moment he stood there, looking Gatak up and down, his ears folding back in contentment. Looking around, he found another troll who still slept, his arm curled around a half-eaten loaf of bread. Dotag snatched it away.

“For you,” he said, proffering the loaf.

Gatak growled in pleasure as she took it from him and ate it in a single bite. But she tossed her head as she swallowed the last of it.

“Good,” she said. “But old.”

Dotag’s face fell. “We last attacked the humans five nights ago. We will get more.”

Gatak peered up into his face. “Have you fought many battles? Have you driven them out of the mountains?”

Instead of answering, Dotag looked around at the rest of the pack. “Let us talk alone.”

That earned a stony silence from Gatak, but she followed him as he strode away. They broke into a run as they left the pack, and Dotag thrilled to be running with her again. Soon they came to a broad cliff that climbed straight up the side of a mountain. Dotag roared and plunged his hands into the stone, grabbing handholds and propelling himself upwards. Gatak followed, but quietly.

Half a span up, they came to a wide ledge that almost looked to have been cut into the mountainside. The ground was soft and overgrown with grass, which formed a soft cushion for them to sit down on. Dotag cast himself down, looking out from the cliff over the mountains as they spun away south. Far away—but not too far—he saw the pall of smoke that marked the humans’ city, the one they called Kahaunga.

“We are close now,” he said.

"Close, but not there," said Gatak. "Tell me what you have done."

"We have attacked many villages. The humans flee from us. They gather in their city." He drew a crude map of the pact's borders in the turf, digging into it with his stubby finger. "This is the pact line. We are here." He dug a great circle where the pack now resided.

Gatak snorted. "I know where we are. Why have you not attacked the human city?"

Dotag's ears spread wide and began to quiver with his sullenness. "We have been moving closer," he said. "The pack was reluctant."

"When Chok led them," said Gatak. "You lead now. They will follow you."

"They do follow me," said Dotag angrily. He stood and slammed his fists into the ground. His crude drawing was flung to dust.

"How many humans have you killed?"

Dotag almost deflated as she watched. "None," he said. "The others still do not wish to kill. They say there is no reason to. The humans flee whenever we come."

"They flee, but then they gather," snarled Gatak. "And they do not leave the mountains. They infest our land like ticks. They will not flee their city and let you take it. You must kill them. You should have killed many already."

"We will," said Dotag. "I will. And then the others will follow me. We will drive the humans out of the mountains. For you."

That seemed to please Gatak. She pawed the ground. "For the Lord."

"For you," Dotag said again. When she let the matter lie, he went to sit beside her again. "You were right. I lead now. The others follow me. And I can mate as I wish."

Gatak's ears went up. "When did that ever stop us before?"

That very morning, we had set out into the Greatrocks, seeking the weremage.

It did not go well.

Yearsend was almost upon us, and it was the harshest time of winter. We rode out into the snow and the cold, and snowy and cold we remained, day after day. Our first expedition told us nothing. Any clues to the trolls' actions or whereabouts was lost to the winds and a fresh snowfall that started the day we rode out.

Rather than return straight to Kahaunga, we traveled east aways, for I remembered another village in that direction, and I guessed that it, too, might have been attacked by the trolls. I was correct, but it did not help us at all. The attack had clearly happened earlier than the first village, and so the clues were even older. The only thing we could tell for sure was that the trolls had stolen every bit of produce and baked goods from both villages, which was in keeping with what we knew of them already.

We returned to Kahaunga in poor spirits—and then our mood was worsened further when we heard the news that Dryleaf had managed to gather in the meantime.

"There have been more attacks," he said. "Three of them, and all in villages closer to Kahaunga."

"Dark take me," I said, clenching my hand to a fist. "We should have come home straightaway."

"We should have," said Mag. "But no use worrying about it now." Though her smile was gentle, it put me ill at ease. She had been treating me gingerly ever since our meeting with Ditra, and I was growing sick of it. I would much rather have had her usual teasing.

"There is more," said Dryleaf, his expression grim even as he continued to scratch Oku behind the ears. "The trolls have started killing."

I stared at him, stunned. Mag leaned forwards in her chair.

"How many?" she said.

"Very few," said Dryleaf. "Still, it marks a change. No matter what, they never killed before. It was too obvious to be anything but deliberate. The word around Kahaunga is that they have given up trying to drive humans away from their lands. The people of the city fear they mean to wipe us out."

"And where did you hear that?" I said. "You were supposed to remain safe here in our room."

Dryleaf waved a hand. "One must eat."

I sighed. "Please do not risk yourself. But as long as you are gathering information, I suppose we should use it. You say not many were killed. How many is not many?"

"Less than a dozen, by all accounts," said Dryleaf. "And that tells us something, considering that the trolls have driven hundreds out of their homes. The people are frightened, and that is understandable, but I think fear is making them foolish. If the trolls wished to wipe them out, many more would have fallen."

"It is still too many," I said.

"Of course," said Dryleaf, bowing his head. "I do not mean to make light of those who are lost."

"The ones who died," said Mag. "Did they try to fight the trolls?"

Dryleaf frowned. "Some, yes. Not others. A few were old and frail, and merely trying to escape. Most were simple farmers or craftsmen, without even a weapon to their name, much less in their hands. But . . . but there were also children."

A cold feeling came over me, starting in my gut and making its way up towards my heart. "The trolls have killed children?"

"That is . . . unclear," said Dryleaf. "No one has said such a thing. Not exactly. But children have gone missing. And there was one man . . . I had to ply him with much wine to get him talking, for he was distraught, weeping and rocking back and forth in his chair. But when I finally got him to talk, he told me—and he said as well, mind you, that he had already told others this, but that they had not believed him—but he said the trolls took his children away. Two of them, a son and a daughter. He said that two trolls scooped them up into their great stony paws and carried them off."

Mag and I looked at each other, and I knew she must be feeling the same terror and disgust that I was. The story was all too familiar to us. Children had also been taken from Northwood when it was attacked.

"As if we needed more proof that the Shades are working with the trolls," muttered Mag.

We rested in Kahaunga for one night, and then we set out into the mountains again. Now a fresh urgency spurred our steps. We pushed the horses as hard as we dared, riding for the village that had been attacked most recently. When we reached it, we found all the same signs as before—destroyed buildings, raided storehouses empty of produce and goods, huge footprints tracked everywhere. But now, too, there were bodies. When we could, we burned them, for it was too dangerous for the families to travel out so far and do so.

We kept at it for days. For over a week we explored the mountains, ranging ever farther north, seeking for the trolls while also trying to avoid being seen by them. There seemed to be no pattern to their attacks. First they would strike to the west, and then to the east, then farther north, and then so close to Kahaunga that the refugees reached the city on the same day of the attack. Anywhere humans had been foolish enough not to retreat from the wilderness, the trolls found them. They could travel almost straight across the land, while we had to navigate the roads and paths around the peaks and over the cliffs and crevasses. Whenever we found their trail, it would always lead into rocky terrain and vanish, or straight up sheer cliffs where we could not follow. Still, we made some progress. I began to see a pattern in the way the trolls moved. Always their attacks came from the north, and always they retreated to the east. That was some clue, at least.

But I began to notice something else. Sometimes I would get a sense of being watched. It put Mag and me on high alert, for we were certain that the weremage was stalking us again. But I could never catch sight of anyone, Shade or otherwise, and I saw no ravens in the sky. Then we began to find campsites—but small ones, just a trampled-down area and the remains of a fire, hastily hidden.

"The weremage?" said Mag, when we found the second one.

"I do not think so," I told her. "Why would she leave a campfire? She does not need one."

"Unless she has been remaining in the wilds for days at a time," said Mag.

I frowned. "Mayhap. We should stay wary."

On one of our return trips to Kahaunga, I found a mapmaker and bought a map of the area. I began to plot out where the trolls had struck, and our best guess of where they had run off to. Slowly I began to narrow down the area where I believed we could find them. But the more we searched, and the more I plotted on our map, the more I began to realize something. The noose was tightening. The trolls were massing for an attack. We were hearing reports of dozens of trolls at a time now, swarming from the mountains like an army. The pattern of their attacks seemed to be random, but they were steadily moving in one direction: straight to the heart of Kahaunga.

They were close, and getting closer. And I did not know if Ditra could stand against them. My only hope of helping her was by finding and killing the Shades. And especially the weremage.

"Where are they?"

Maia frowned. "The two from Opara?"

Ditra scowled at him. They were in her private chamber, and she was slouched in her chair at the head of her table. Maia stood in a position of rest at the other end of it. She had not invited him to sit down. "The Shades," said Ditra. "I care nothing for the strangers."

"I have not found them yet," said Maia. "But I believe I am drawing closer. Then again, so are the strangers."

"How?" demanded Ditra. "You are my lead ranger. You were born to this land. How are they keeping up with you?"

Maia shrugged, projecting a nonchalance he did not feel. "I do not know, Rangatira. They seem to know the area fairly well. Certainly at least one of them has been here before."

Ditra found herself troubled by that, though she did not know why, and she did not greatly wish to speculate upon it. "Well, you must avoid them if you can."

"I have, so far," said Maia. "It has sometimes been a near thing. But I may not be able to avoid them forever. We are on the same trail, after all, and it is leading us both to the same end."

"Then you must beat them to it," said Ditra. "Mayhap you should take others with you."

"No," said Maia. "That would only slow me down."

"You do not seem to be moving particularly fast," snapped Ditra, slamming down her mug. A bit of ale splashed over the side of it onto the table.

Maia said nothing, but only clasped his hands behind his back.

Ditra gave a disgusted snort and stood, making her way over to the window. She stared out into the sky. Another snow was falling, heavier than it had been in the last few days.

"Find the Shades," she said. "Before the strangers can. We have to end this before it begins. We *cannot* engage in an open battle with the trolls."

"Of course, Rangatira." Maia bowed and left the room.

Ditra stayed at her window a long while, looking out into the gusts of white flakes.

I cannot let this come to open war, she thought. But she feared it might already be too late.

THIRTY

I suppose it was foolish of me to hope that we could go on forever without encountering a troll. But I did hold that hope, and it proved to be wrong.

We were investigating yet another destroyed village. This one was only an hour's hard ride from the sight of Kahaunga's walls. The trolls had slain a score of people in the attack, throwing Kahaunga even deeper into panic. It was hard to tell if the trolls were growing more bloodthirsty, or if more people were dying because more people were fighting. Now that the trolls had started to kill, townsfolk were less likely to simply abandon their homes. Many fought to keep them.

Whenever they did, they lost.

We crept up on the village stealthily, though in truth we were not as cautious as we could have been. This was the eleventh village we had investigated, and we had not found trolls in any of them. So although we dismounted a good distance away and approached the village on foot, I did not range very far ahead of Mag to scout the place.

That almost proved disastrous.

Mag and I were picking our way through the buildings when we heard it: the heavy thud of a foot on stone, and a great snorting, snuffling sound. It was close—within half a span, certainly. Terror nearly stopped my heart.

"Oku, kip," I whispered, motioning furiously to the dog as I dragged Mag out of the street and out of sight. We ducked into a half-wrecked home with a massive hole in the wall. Part of the ceiling hung down into the main room.

We waited a long moment. A sharp *crack* sounded not far away—a timber breaking. The troll was digging into another building, likely breaking it apart just like the one we were in now.

"They left one behind?" whispered Mag.

"Or it returned," I whispered back. "From the reports, it sounded as though this raid was quicker than most of the others. This troll might have snuck away from the rest of its pack, hoping to find some foodstuffs the others left behind."

"Mayhap we should ask it."

I stared at her in horror. A smile crept across her face.

"I am joking."

"Do not do that."

Oku growled low in his throat.

"Kip, Oku." He subsided, and I turned back to Mag. "We must get out of here, and as quietly as possible. It sounds as though it is a little distance off. We should be able to get away without it spotting us."

"This could be our chance, Albern," said Mag. "We could follow it back to the others, and from them, to the Shades."

"We cannot risk being discovered," I said harshly, my voice a little too loud. "You do not know these creatures, Mag."

"The entire reason we came out here was to find trolls." Mag pointed through the hole in the wall. "There. I have found one."

"We came to find a trail. Letting a troll see us would be beyond foolish."

"There have been nearly a dozen trails, and they have not led us anywhere. Now we have—"

I covered her mouth with my hand, my eyes wide. She fell silent. I swiveled back and forth, listening, while Oku quivered beside us.

"What is it?" Mag hissed, her voice muffled by my fingers.

"I do not hear the—"

THOOM

The wall on the other side of the building crashed inwards. Shards of wood and plaster showered us. A wooden beam as thick as my leg flew by, missing me by a handbreadth. The troll's stubby fingers reached in, probing for us. It roared in fury.

"Run!" I screamed, dragging Mag out the door. "Oku, kip!"

The hound fled, yelping in panic, and we were just behind him. I heard the troll crash into the building where we had been hiding, but I dared not turn back to look. Mag's arm was still in my clutches. But suddenly, to my horror, she yanked herself free and stopped in the middle of the street.

I skidded to a halt, and Oku did the same. My stomach did somersaults as I looked at Mag.

She had cast her cloak back and off her shoulders. In her right hand was her spear, and upon her left arm was her shield, held up in defense. The troll had stopped thundering after us, coming to a stop several paces away. It seemed more confused than anything as it glowered down at her, showing its teeth. They were mostly grey and blunt, but there were four huge tusks, two on the top and two on the bottom, that jutted from between the lips like latches holding a book closed. It regarded Mag for a long moment, heavy breaths huffing from its nostrils to steam in the frigid air.

"Greetings," said Mag amiably. "I am Mag. We are looking for some friends of yours."

The troll's brows drew close. "You are human," it said.

"And you are obviously a very bright specimen of your kind."

"Mag, you fool!" I cried. "Do not taunt the thing. Run!"

"No, I do not think so," said Mag, before speaking to the troll once again. "You will never have heard of me, I suspect. In many of the nine kingdoms, I am called the Uncut Lady. Though I am not one to flee from battle, I have no wish to fight you. Tell us where we can find the humans who have been working with your pack, and you and I can part as friends."

The troll's scowl deepened. "I am friends with no human," it snarled.

"Except the Shades, I suppose?"

The troll roared and slammed its hands into the earth before storming towards her.

"No chance of peace, then," said Mag. "I suspected as much."

"Mag!"

I was too late. She crouched for a moment and then leaped, spear up and shield forwards.

The troll struck her a backhanded blow. It caught Mag from below and to the left, crashing into her shield. She sailed over the roof of a nearby building like a stone from a catapult, vanishing from sight.

The sight of it froze me in place. I had tried to tell her. I had said she could not treat the trolls like any other foe. And now one of them had dealt with her like she was no more threatening than a gnat. I prayed to the sky that she was still alive, and I could not imagine she was not badly hurt.

I forced my attention back to the troll. Mag would have to wait for a moment, for I could not help her if I was dead. Like Victon with the bear, I had to survive, and draw the danger away.

The troll had stopped in its advance, shoulders hunched, fists planted on the ground. Its wide, angry eyes fixed on Oku and me. The hound had sunk back on his haunches, fur bristling, a low growl in his throat. But he made no move to attack. He wanted to protect me, but I could practically feel the fear radiating from him. I tried to think of what to do.

Fire, I thought. *Dark take me, I need fire.*

I somehow doubted the troll would let me take out my flint and steel to start a blaze. I risked a glance around. None of the buildings showed any signs of smoke—their cooking fires and hearths would have extinguished themselves long ago.

My attention was dragged back to the troll as it took a step forwards. I raised my bow just a touch. But what good was an arrow against its hide?

Mag had tried to speak with it. But she had tried bluster. Mayhap there was another way.

"I do not wish to fight you," I called out.

It gave a sound that was almost a grunt, but closer to a growl. "Get out of our mountains."

"We will leave you in peace. You are welcome to the foodstuffs here."

That was a mistake. My whole body jerked as the troll roared and slammed its fists down again. "You do not give us anything. We have taken it!"

"Of course," I said. "I did not mean to—"

It was too late. The troll charged. I whipped my bow up and fired a shot, aiming for the eye. But it was moving too fast, and the arrow ricocheted from its stony forehead. Oku and I dived out of the way behind the corner of a building just as the troll sped by both of us, slamming its shoulder into another structure. The wooden timbers shattered under the impact, and the roof collapsed.

"Oku, kip!" I said. "Go!"

With a panicked yelp, the hound ran off and out of sight. No use in both of us dying.

I had to decide what my aim was. If Mag was still alive, she had to be hurt. Thus it seemed my best chance of accomplishing anything lay in drawing the troll away from her, and then losing it so I could swing back and find her.

Every part of me screamed in terrified protest as I turned back to the troll, who was only now emerging from the wreckage of the home it had destroyed.

"All right, then, beast," I called out. "You want a fight? Come and get one."

My heart skipped as it gave another wild roar. I drew and fired just before it charged. But fear made my shot go wide again, and the arrow bounced from its hide.

I turned and fled around the corner of the stone building, thinking that might give the troll pause. I was wrong. Two earth-shattering crashes shook the ground as the troll slammed through the opposite wall, and then the near one just behind me. A stone struck my shoulder, and I stumbled.

I tried desperately not to panic as I turned another corner. I could not outrun the thing, and I could not safely hide behind any of the buildings. I had to make it lose sight of me. But I was nearing the village's edge, and soon I would be in open terrain. My mind whirled, searching for some solution.

Another turn. Another. If I could only stay out of sight a moment longer . . .

The wall to my left exploded outwards, flinging me through the air. I struck the wall of the building opposite and slumped to the ground.

Gasping in pain, I looked up. The troll loomed there, framed in the hole it had put in the building. Its eyes narrowed as it looked down at me, ears angled up. The earth trembled as it stalked forwards on stony fists.

The terror in my heart turned to rage. I struggled to my feet, leaving my bow where it had fallen and drawing my short sword. Sheer disbelief stopped the troll in its tracks.

"If I am to die, then I will die," I said. "But on my feet." *In Tokana. Like my mother. Like Romil.* That was a bitter thought.

The troll snorted. It took another lumbering step forwards.

There came a flash of metal to my right. Mag came rushing at the troll's flank. Her spear leaped, the edge skittering along its stony side. It roared, turning to swipe at her. But Mag ducked with inhuman speed, and her spear slashed up again. This time the tip of it flashed dangerously close to the troll's eye, and it reeled back in confusion.

"Your bow," said Mag. Her voice was toneless, her eyes lifeless with her battle-trance. "That sword will do little good."

I barely heard the words. I could only stare at her in wonder. She was covered in dirt and mud, but she was utterly unharmed. She did not limp, or hunch over like a fighter nursing a broken rib. I could not even see a bruise, though I imagined there had to be many beneath her clothes and armor.

"Mag, are you—"

"Your bow," she snapped.

The words pierced my confusion at last. With shaking hands I stowed my sword in its scabbard and stooped for my bow, keeping watch on the troll. It was staring down at Mag, seemingly just as astounded as I was. But even as we watched, confusion turned to wrath.

"Mag—"

"Aim for the eyes," she said, and attacked.

I was glad to see she had learned her lesson after the last time. The troll tried to bat her aside as it had before, but this time Mag ducked the swing. Her spear flashed up, and the troll recoiled as the blade passed across its cheek—not breaking the skin, but again drawing too close to the eye for comfort.

It took two stumbling steps back, but Mag followed. She slashed again and again. The long, bladed edge of the spear could not hope to pierce the troll's hide, but it provided an ample distraction. I reached to my quiver and drew another arrow. With Mag occupying all of the troll's attention, I had enough time to draw, to hold, to sight along the shaft.

A long, slow breath escaped me.

I loosed.

The arrow sank into the troll's eye, deep enough to strike the skull behind.

It screamed and stumbled back, swiping at the air as if trying to swat away a fly. Black blood dribbled down its face, staining its teeth as it bared them. Mag tried to make another strike, but its flailing arms drove her back.

Something flashed in the sun as it flew towards the troll. A glass vial struck the beast in the face, and dark, oily liquid spilled all over its body.

We froze. So did the troll. It swiped at the oil, black as its own blood, and stared at it in confusion.

"Hail, friend."

Mag and I looked up. Standing on the roof of a nearby building was Maia, Ditra's lead ranger. He had thrown the flask. Now he stood in an almost languid position—but he had an arrow nocked, and its tip was wrapped with a flaming rag.

The troll looked up at him, squinting with its one good eye through the oil.

"Well met," said Maia amiably. "You are covered in flammable oil, and I have a flame to light it. I highly suggest you turn and run."

At first the troll seemed too angry to understand, but gradually it made sense of the words. It looked down at itself, smelling the pitch that covered its body.

It looked back up, and even I could see the fear shining in its remaining eye.

The troll fled from the village, climbing over a hill and out of sight.

THIRTY-ONE

MAIA WAITED UNTIL THE TROLL WAS OUT OF SIGHT. THEN HE TURNED as if to leave.

"Wait!" I cried.

He paused. I saw his shoulders heave with a sigh before he turned back and gave Mag and I an easygoing smile.

"Yes?" he said.

"You saved our lives," I said.

"Oh, you seemed to be doing well enough," he said. "I only wanted to make sure."

Mag had let her trance fall away. Now she arched an eyebrow up at him. "I suppose we are grateful. Though I do question what you are doing out here in the first place."

He gave another sigh and climbed down from the roof. I came over to stand beside Mag.

As I neared her, I heard the padding of soft feet. Oku emerged into view, coming to take his place at our side. The poor hound looked almost ashamed, as though he had dishonored himself by fleeing, even though I had told him to.

When Maia reached the ground, he looked us over. "Are the two of you all right?"

"We are fine," said Mag. "Though as I said, I have questions."

"I was simply passing through," said Maia. "I heard the commotion and came to help."

"Are you not in troll territory?" I said. "I am surprised to learn that Ditra—that the Rangatira would send her rangers out this far, when they should be patrolling the lands that you are still trying to protect."

"You yourself are beyond those lands," said Maia.

"And the Rangatira gave us permission to be here," said Mag.

Maia looked slightly uncomfortable. "As she did with me."

"Yet she told us her rangers would be too busy to aid in the fight," said Mag. "What purpose brings you here?"

Maia looked over his shoulder as though searching for aid. "I should be leaving."

A realization struck me. "You are the one I have sensed in the wilderness. I felt as if someone was nearby. We found campfires. That was you."

"I was not actually following you, if that is any comfort," said Maia. "Our paths simply lay in the same direction. Indeed, I did not think I would encounter you at all in the mountains. But you are very skilled. I suspect one or both of you must have spent some time here before, though I do not remember you."

"It has been . . . a long time," I said. "In my youth. I do not remember you either, if that is any comfort."

"No, I suppose you would not," said Maia. "I came to Kahaunga some eighteen years ago as a boy, when my father wed the Rangatira. I became a ranger as soon as I came of age."

I almost did not hear his last words. The realization struck me that Maia was Ditra's son by law, and that made him my nephew. I might have lost members of my family since I left home, but it seemed I had gained others. I wondered what other new relatives there might be within my family's stronghold.

Things had been quiet for too long. Mag was studying Maia as though she were trying to decide if he was a threat. I forced a smile. "That explains why you are so much more skilled here than I am. Though it does not explain what you are doing here, as my friend asked before. I suppose you have been sent to watch us."

"Not at all," said Maia. He gave another heavy sigh, but this time it looked as though he had finally come to a decision. "In fact, I was sent out for the same purpose as you—to track down the Shades. The only problem is that I was supposed to greatly outpace you in the hunt. In fact, I was strictly ordered to."

"We are very sorry to have made your duty so difficult," said Mag, giving him a wry smile.

"I am sure you are," said Maia.

"Mayhap we could work together," I said.

Maia's mouth twisted. "That . . . is not quite possible."

"Because the Rangatira ordered you not to," said Mag. When Maia narrowed his eyes at her, she smiled. "I may not be as familiar with this land as either of you, but I have some understanding of soldiers, and those who order them about."

"Well, you have guessed aright," said Maia. "I am sorry, but I cannot disobey my lord."

"But Ditra—the Rangatira," I said quickly. *Dark take me for a fool, I have to stop doing that.* "She gave us permission to find the Shades. You mean to tell me she did not actually want us to succeed? If we do, we will put a stop to your entire conflict with the trolls."

Maia only shrugged. "I do not pretend to understand everything, nor to be privy to all of the counsel the Rangatira may receive. She is my lord. I do her bidding. Although . . ." His look grew crafty. "Although I suppose there is a way we could both achieve our aims, and better serve the Rangatira at the same time."

"How is that?" said Mag.

Oku had come over to sniff at Maia's boots. He knelt and scratched the hound behind the ears, and Oku stretched up to lick his face. "You mean to hunt down the Shades. I have been ordered to find them, but not to engage with them, and only to relay their location back to the Rangatira. If you can agree to do the same, I would not object to working with you. Our skills would be more effective if we combined them, and I would save myself a great deal of time if I could focus only on the hunt, and not on avoiding you in the wilderness."

"If we find the Shades, you would wish for us to stave off our attack until you have informed your lord?" said Mag. She folded her arms, making their muscular lines more prominent. "That would imperil the success of our attack."

"You would not have to wait long," said Maia placatingly. "My lord wishes to end the threat of the Shades. It is her duty. I am not certain why she wishes to hear from me before she attacks, but she *will* attack. We can join the main Telfer forces in eliminating the Shades. I will have done my duty, and you will have what you want. Everyone's aims will be satisfied."

I thought hard about it, but I could see no reason not to do as he said. It seemed a wise course of action. Ditra was playing some game I did not understand, and it had hampered our search so far. This would solve the problem without harming either party.

"That seems agreeable to me," I said. "Chao?"

Mag was still for a moment before she remembered that I had used her false name. But rather than nodding in agreement, she gave a grimace. "I suppose I might be able to. As long as when it comes to battle, I am the one to kill the weremage."

"The Rangatira might not like that," said Maia with a sigh. "Though I do not know what she could do to prevent you. What is your grudge against Kaita, anyway?"

I froze.

"Kaita?" I whispered.

Maia's eyes went wide, and his face went a shade paler.

Kaita.

THIRTY-TWO

I WAS A CHILD IN MY FAMILY'S STRONGHOLD, CREEPING TOWARDS DITRA's room after having a nightmare. Suddenly, the door opened. Out came Kaita, cloaked in shadow. I could scarcely see her in the darkness. I did not recognize her face.

But Kaita saw me, staring at her wide-eyed in the moonslight. If the Lord Telfer found out that she had been caught in Ditra's bedchamber . . . no matter how useful Kaita was, she would be flung out into the streets to beg for her food.

She fled in terror. I looked after her for a moment, before realizing that Ditra now stood in the doorway, and I forgot all about her retainer.

It was the night I fled from home, drunk with wine and pelted by rain. I had left the city already. I had reached the bridge.

I crashed into Kaita, and we both fell to the ground.

The clouds parted for a moment, and I caught a flash of moonslight. I saw Kaita's face, but it swam in the darkness and my own drunkenness. Yet I screamed at the sight of my family's colors on her cloak, and I backed away on hands and knees.

Kaita watched me scramble over the shelf by the end of the bridge. Then she saw me fall off the other side. She barely stifled a cry as she leaped forwards, expecting to see my broken body far below her.

Instead, she saw me sliding away on a steep, rocky surface slick with rainwater.

She looked on in wonder until I turned a corner out of sight. For a moment she debated going after me.

Then she smiled.

I was gone. The youngest Telfer child, and the most useless.

Kahaunga would be well quit of me.

She turned and carried on her way back to the city.

It was the day Romil found me in the mercenary camp. She stood before me, but behind her, by the horses, was a retainer. Kaita.

Mag struck faster than I could see, flinging my sister to the ground unconscious. I stared at her fallen form in horror and grief. Kaita reached for her weapon, but Mag stopped her with a look.

"That would be unwise," said Mag. "Take your master and ride away with her. Go back to your lord. Tell her whatever you wish, but get this wretch out of my sight before I give her more than a headache."

Kaita did as Mag commanded. I did not even watch them go, for I was sitting on the ground, arms wrapped around my knees, lost in my grief.

I was in the jungle with Victon and Mag. The bear turned and fled, limping on three legs to favor the fourth that Mag had maimed. Mag turned to me, the battle-trance like a mask over her expression. It shook me then, as it always did.

"You are all right?"

"Victon," I gasped. "It is heading for Victon."

She seized my arm and pulled me up, and together we pelted after the beast.

The bear fled from us, bleeding from wounds it had never expected to receive. Suddenly it lurched to the right and lumbered off into the underbrush. It carried on, heedless of the trail it left behind. Even Mag would be able to track it.

But it would not be there when she arrived.

When the bear had lumbered a span away from the main path, it stopped. Without even bothering to look behind to see if it was being followed, it hunched over.

Its eyes began to glow.

In a moment the transformation was done, and Kaita's form emerged from the bear's. She stifled a cry as she felt the wounds in her body seal up, lances of pain shooting through her as flesh and skin joined together.

She took two deep, shaky breaths that wracked her body. But she could not remain still for long.

Again her eyes glowed. She shrank, her tight clothing sinking into her flesh. Black feathers sprouted across her skin. In a few heartbeats, she had taken the raven's form. She flapped desperately, winging up and away. She glanced down only once—to see Mag burst into the clearing where she had just been. Panic seized her, and she flapped harder, flying away from the jungle as fast as she could.

It was the battle of Northwood, and I knelt by Sten's side. Across from me were Mag and the medica, whose eyes were glowing as she gripped the torn flesh of his throat, desperately trying to seal the wound. Mag and I held his hands, pulling them away so the medica could work.

And Kaita lurked nearby, hidden just behind the edge of a building. My back was to her. My attention was all for Sten. I was exposed.

"Try to be silent," said the medica sharply. "It will only be worse."

"Almost, my love," said Mag. "Hold on."

Kaita's eyes glowed. She took the form of the mountain lion. In the long years since the jungle of Feldemar, she had obsessed over her first fight with Mag. She had made a mistake, then. She had sought power, rather than speed. The bear had been mighty, but it was too slow. She should have chosen the lion, long her favorite form. It was fast. Faster than Mag, or so she believed.

The medica finished her work. "It is done," she said. "He is not out of danger, but—"

Kaita bounded out from behind the building and leaped for me. I saw the flash of movement from the corner of my eye.

"Down!" I dived out of the way, seizing Mag and the medica and taking them with me.

Kaita landed on Sten's chest, her claws sinking into his flesh with a biting *shunk.* His fingers grasped for Kaita's throat. And then he died.

"No," said Mag. "No."

She rose to her feet, and her hands curled to fists at her sides. Kaita growled at her. Mag did not even have her sword. This would be a simple kill.

But it was not. Try as she might, she could not lay a claw on Mag. And as Mag screamed *No!* over and over, she took Kaita apart with her bare hands.

Kaita resumed her human form, recoiling and holding her wounds.

I saw her. And memories tugged at the back of my mind. But there was Mag, and there was Sten's corpse, and the battle of Northwood still raged around us.

"Sow! You feckless sow!" screamed Kaita. Shades came running into view. "Kill her!" cried Kaita, thrusting a finger towards Mag.

She turned into a raven and flew away.

"You knew her!" cried Sun, her voice ringing with something between betrayal and triumph.

"I did not," said Albern.

"You did!" insisted Sun. "You saw her in Tokana again and again, and probably another thousand times that you have never told me about. Yet you told me you had never seen her before."

"I said nothing of the kind," said Albern. "You asked if I knew her. I did not."

"That is splitting hairs," said Sun, folding her arms. "You know what I meant."

"I do know what you meant," said Albern. "But you have been thinking about it all wrong. Tell me: did you know every soldier who served your family?"

Sun frowned. "I knew our master of arms. Her name was Hilde, and she—"

"I said everyone."

It felt as though she was being drawn into a trap, but Sun did not know how to get out. She waved her hands in irritation. "There were dozens of people running in and out of our kitchens," she said. "I did not meet every baker and scullery maid, if that is what you are asking."

"And we had dozens of rangers, of which Kaita was not one, not to mention hundreds of guards, not only in Kahaunga, but all across our lands," said Albern. "And I have told you already that my mother strictly forbid us from becoming too friendly with anyone, least of all those who were not even of the nobility."

Sun huffed and shook her head. "You could have told me about Kaita from the beginning."

Albern grinned at her. "What was it you said this morning? Every part of the story must be told in its proper turn, or the whole thing will collapse. You were quite right, though you hardly knew it."

"Dark take me for a fool," growled Sun. "Had I known you would throw my own words back at me, I would never have spoken them. This conversation is not over, old man, but fortunately for you, I want to know what happened next more than I want to trounce you."

He chuckled and gave a nod. "Very well. Let us return to Tokana."

THIRTY-THREE

I STOOD IN THE RUINED VILLAGE, STARING AT MAIA IN HORROR AND fury. But that only lasted a moment before I turned and stormed off towards the horses, Oku at my heels.

"What is it?" Mag's confusion was plain in her voice.

"Where is he going?" said Maia.

Mag did not answer, but I heard her footsteps behind me as she followed. Soon Maia joined her. He ran up beside me and tried to get in front of me.

"Listen, friend, I do not know what—"

He stopped as Mag snatched his arm and pulled him out of my way. "I do not know what is happening either," she said. "But I would advise you not to try to touch Albern while I am present."

Maia frowned. "Albern?"

Mag floundered for a moment. "Kanohari," she said lamely. "I meant . . . oh, dark take it all, just get on your horse."

I ignored them both, swinging up into Foolhoof's saddle and spurring him south. I rode hard, slowing only just enough for Oku to keep the pace. Soon I heard thundering hooves behind, and Mag and Maia drew close.

"Albern!" she called out. "What is wrong?"

I ignored her, and she seemed to give up on getting an answer. The three of us rode in silence all the way to Kahaunga.

Farmers in the outlying fields stopped their work and straightened, staring at us as we galloped past. I do not know what went through their minds. Mayhap they thought we were rushing to deliver news of a fresh attack. But I paid them no more attention than I gave to Mag or to Maia. We hit the streets of the outer city. Thankfully they were clear, and I did not have to slow Foolhoof very much. But at last I had to pull to a stop at the gate of the Telfer keep.

"Open the gate!" I called up.

A guard atop the wall peered down at me in confusion. "Who under the sky are you to issue such an order?"

"I am Albern of the family Telfer, and I have returned to my homeland," I answered her. "Open the gate!"

The woman's eyes went wide with shock. She looked past me to Maia, who was just as surprised.

"The family Telfer?" he said to me.

I pulled down my sleeve and showed him our family's mark. He stared at it in wonder for a moment, sighed, and looked back up at the gate guard.

"For good or for ill, I think you had better do as he says."

That seemed good enough, and the guards hastened to open the gate. I spurred Foolhoof forwards as soon as it was high enough for me to avoid hitting my head. Once I reached the keep, I dismounted and left Foolhoof behind as I stormed up the steps. The doors stood open, and I passed through them to stalk down the wide entrance hall.

"Albern," said Mag. It was one of the few times in her life I had heard her sound nervous. "Are you certain about this?"

"More certain than I have been about anything since we got here," I growled.

Two Telfer guards stood at the door to Ditra's audience chamber. They stepped forwards, hands tightening on their spears as I approached.

"Let him pass," said Maia in resignation. "I am with him."

They did not look pleased about it, but they did as he said. I threw open the double doors as hard as I could, and they slammed against the stone walls on either side. Ditra sat on her chair atop the dais, and her head snapped up in shock as I entered. A small cluster of advisors huddled before her, and they, too, turned to stare at me in amazement.

"Kaita!" I roared.

Ditra's eyes went wide. The guards at the edges of the room stepped forwards, ready to defend their lord. Among the councilors I spotted a woman in robes of Calentin colors—the king's representative. She studied me with great interest.

"Kaita!" I said again. "She is the weremage. And you knew. You knew! And you sent your ranger after her because you were afraid we would kill her."

The king's representative looked up at Ditra with a faint frown. "Rangatira, who under the sky is this man?"

Ditra ignored her. A flush crept up her neck into her cheeks as she stared at me. "How . . . how *dare* you—"

"How dare I?" I cried. I advanced to stand at the foot of the dais, and the king's representative hastily gave way before me. "You have the gall to ask how dare *I?* You are the Rangatira! You serve the king of Calentin and the High King of Underrealm. And you wanted to let a murdering witch escape justice just because you used to share her bed!"

Ditra's face went from crimson to nearly purple. She looked past me to Maia. "You allowed him in here? What were you thinking?"

I lifted my arm and dragged down my sleeve. The Telfer mark shone against my skin. Ditra stared at it for a moment, speechless. And then I saw recognition flash in her eyes as she looked upon my face. Emotions, one after another, played in her expression. Joy, I think, at seeing me again. Despair that I had discovered her secret. And then, slowly dominating the rest, a cold, mounting fury.

"You return here . . ." she said, the words grinding out of her like a blade on a whetstone. "You return after decades. *Decades.* You parade yourself in front of me, in plain sight but still skulking like a coward. And now you have the audacity to accuse *me?* Arrest them."

The guards began to come forwards.

"We are not your enemies," I said. "Kaita is. You know that, and yet you act to protect her. It is beneath you, Ditra."

"I am the *Lord* Telfer," she snapped, shooting to her feet. "Rangatira of Tokana and servant of the king of Calentin. You are nothing. You gave up any right to speak to me thus when you fled our home. And now you may sit in a cell until I figure out what to do with you."

"That would be a poor idea," said Mag, grip tightening on her spear.

I sagged. All my fury had flowed out of me in my outburst, and suddenly I was very tired. I lifted a hand towards Mag. "No. Do not harm her servants. They are only doing their duty." I glowered up at Ditra again. "Which is more than might be said of some."

While Ditra fumed, Mag spoke to me in a low voice. "Albern. I can keep us from going into a cell in the first place. But if she puts us there . . . no one can bend steel bars. Not even me."

"Then do what you must," I told her. "As for me, it seems I am going to be imprisoned." I raised my wrists, ready for the manacles that one of the guards had already pulled from a pouch.

Mag rolled her eyes and did the same. But she smiled at the guards as they bound her. "You should enjoy yourselves. One day you will be able to brag to your children about capturing the Uncut Lady."

Ditra now seemed to be trying to avoid looking at us. The king's representative seemed almost amused. "Is this man your brother, Rangatira?" she said. "The one who—"

"Get out," growled Ditra. "I will send for you when I require you."

The representative looked affronted. "But we were discussing—"

"Get out!" roared Ditra. The representative jumped, and then she scurried out of the room like a chastised dog. The other councilors followed at her heels.

I had not looked away from Ditra, and just before her guards dragged us off, she met my gaze at last.

"We do not have endless time," I said, all anger gone from my voice. "You have . . . we have both made mistakes. Speak with me again, so that we can fix them. Do not wait too long."

Her scowl deepened, and she turned it upon the guards. "Take them away. Then go into the city and find that old man they came here with. He can join them in their cell."

The guards spun us around and marched us from the room. Maia gave me a rueful smile just before they hauled me away.

THIRTY-FOUR

"That was very foolish of you," said Sun. "Walking in there like that."

"It was," said Albern sadly. "I was young, then, and youth comes with many poor ideas."

"You were older than I am now!"

"Well, why do you think I keep such a careful eye on you?" When Sun scowled, he chuckled. "I am only joking. The truth is that it is easy to look back on our past actions—or the actions of others—and see how they were wrong. But we always think we are wise in the moment. No matter how old you get, you will always think you are smarter than you used to be. You will always look back at your younger years and marvel at what an idiot you were—but *now,* of course, you are wise, having learned so much more."

Sun shoved his shoulder. "I am not an idiot."

"And what about when you had seen only fifteen years?"

"Oh, sky above," said Sun, rolling her eyes. "That was different. You would not believe some of the things I got up to."

"And did you think you were a fool, then? Or did you think you were much wiser than you had been when you were ten?"

Sun opened her mouth to reply, but she could think of nothing to say. Her jaw snapped shut, and she glowered at him.

Albern shrugged. "I only tell you the truth as I know it. And I do not excuse myself. I can look back on the events I am telling you about and recognize what a hotheaded young fool I was. If I live another ten years, I am certain I will look back on today and feel the same way."

"Enough idle philosophy," said Sun grumpily. "Where are we going?"

They had passed back out beyond Lan Shui's northern gate, but the town was not yet far behind them. The sun was lowering, nearly kissing the top of the western spur, and just starting to shadow the countryside. She could see the line of its shade advancing towards them as night approached, a great darkness sweeping over the land. It was a chilling sight.

"Well, it seems there are some less-than-gentle folk plaguing Lan Shui again," said Albern. "This time, though, they seem to be operating somewhere outside the town's borders. We are not exactly certain where."

Sun frowned at him. "We?"

"Why, you and I," said Albern, cocking his head at her. "I apologize—I did not mean to dictate your own uncertainty to you."

"Oh no, please feel free," said Sun, arching an eyebrow. "So how do *we* mean to find them?"

"I do not know if you have heard, but I am something of a good tracker," said Albern. "A wagon was ambushed not far from here just the other day, and I think we will be able to find our foes' hideout by following the trail away from it."

"Why did we not see the location of the attack when we approached Lan Shui?"

"There is more than one road leading into town. I wanted to see Dawan before I went to investigate the caravan."

"And who are these people, exactly?"

He sighed. "Hopefully they are bandits."

"You do not sound very hopeful."

"That is because I do not think they are bandits."

Sun gave a small but very frustrated growl. "What *do* you think they are?"

He seemed to be struggling for an answer, pursing his lips and looking around, as though he was searching his own mind for the right words. When he did speak, it almost sounded as if he was ignoring her question. "Do you remember the tree from my youth? The tall kauri?"

"I . . . do," said Sun, confused.

"When I was young, I paid little attention to the lands of my home. I only watched the tree. It was always there. It changed slowly. It was a landmark, in more than one sense. Only when it was torn down was I finally able to look around and see how all the dale had changed around it.

"The people of Lan Shui are the same. In fact, most people are. If one thing remains the same—a tree, a nation, a king—and if that thing is important enough to them, they think the world is hardly changing at all. Until one day their landmark changes at last, and they realize that things have been happening all along that they paid little heed to. It can be helpful to focus on one thing, one place, one person more than the rest. It anchors us. It can help us find ourselves when the world seems too chaotic, too frightening. But we must remain at least brave enough to keep *looking* at the world beyond our landmarks, to ensure that no danger threatens them—and that the landmarks themselves are still as we imagine them to be."

"And what does this have to do with my question?" said Sun.

Albern pointed. "Look for yourself."

By the side of the road lay the remnants of a destroyed wagon. Sun had been so absorbed by Albern's words that she had not noticed it. The planks looked to be scored and gouged by weapons, and Sun saw at least three arrows sticking out of them. Worse, there were several dark streaks in the dirt of the road. Sun was certain they were blood.

Albern knelt to inspect the dark streaks. Then he went to the wagon, pacing all around it. At first he only looked without touching, but then he stepped closer, running his hand along the wood, peering closely at the grain, the gouges, the arrows. Sun did not know what he was looking at, but there was no hint of uncertainty in his movements.

Then he stopped short, eyes narrowing. He knelt and leaned under the wagon. When he emerged and stood, he held a small piece of brown cloth, hardly any bigger than his hand.

"What is that?"

"It *was* the wrapping of a small packet," said Albern, his tone grim. "They took what was inside."

"Or destroyed it."

"No, they took it." Albern pointed. "The attackers fled that way. Do you see their tracks there, leading off into the foothills of the Greatrocks?"

Sun stared at the spot. She could see nothing. She came to stand beside Albern, trying to view the spot from the same place.

"I do not see any such tracks," she said at last.

Albern sighed. "Mag never did, either. Come along."

He set off in the direction he had indicated. Sun trailed along behind him. It was only then that she realized Albern had not brought his horse from the Sunspear. She guessed that he had left it behind so that the noise of its hooves would not betray their position. She began to walk more slowly, trying to make her footfalls as quiet as she could.

Albern glanced back over his shoulder. "What are you doing?"

Sun felt a blush creep into her cheeks. "I am trying to be quiet. I thought that was why you left your horse behind."

Albern smiled. "It is, but such measures are not yet necessary. Our prey is still a fair distance away. We can talk, if you wish."

"I do," said Sun. "You keep hinting at these people and expecting me to assemble the hints into an answer. I would rather just hear it plain. Who are they? What are they after?"

Albern shook his head. "I am not trying to trick you or deceive you, but to teach you. However, if you wish for an answer, here is the best one I have. They do not have a name that I am aware of. But they have some purpose here. I think, but do not know, that it is something evil—more evil than mere banditry. But because they are hiding it, because it is happening in the shadows and the silence, no one in Lan Shui is paying too much attention. They think they face only bandits. Bandits, themselves, are their own sort of landmark in the lives of the people of Lan Shui. That is an evil they can face, and so they would rather believe in bandits than seek the truth. 'Only in watchfulness lies safety,' said a Mystic to me once. But people do not remain watchful forever, and when they lapse, darkness gathers."

"That is not exactly an answer," said Sun.

"I wish I had a better answer to give you," said Albern. "But failing that, I will continue the tale."

Dryleaf did not seem particularly annoyed when they brought him to our cell, which was a courtesy I had no right to expect of him. He settled quite easily down onto the bench against the back wall, resting against the stone with a sigh. I sat opposite him, on the ground, my back against the iron bars. A quick glance around had told me that the rest of the cells were empty. I took that as a good sign. Ditra did not seem overly fond of jailing people for little reason, it seemed. I wondered if my mother had been any different. I had never bothered to spend much time inspecting the dungeons.

"Well, this is all a great deal of foolishness," said Mag lightly. She stood at the other end of the iron bars from me, leaning against them with her arms crossed, as though she were awaiting a delivery of barley to her inn.

"Yes," I said.

"Unabashed, reckless foolishness."

"It is."

"Now, Mag," said Dryleaf kindly. "Do not be too harsh. Tomorrow is the first day of Yearsend, after all. A time for forgiveness."

"I find her words comforting, actually," I said. "It is when she gets quiet, or tries to treat me too delicately, that I grow worried."

"Then I suppose I retract my scolding."

"So your sister and the weremage used to bed each other, did they?" said Mag.

"They did," I said. "They were young. Kaita started as Ditra's retainer when she had seen only eighteen years, freshly returned from the Academy, and she is only a year or two older than Ditra. I cannot believe I did not recognize her in Northwood. There was a twinge at the back of my mind, but I never—"

"None of that," said Mag. "It was long ago. Your sister did not recognize you, her own brother. Why should you recognize someone you barely even knew?"

I shook my head slowly. "Mag, I . . . this means something."

"I know."

"No, I mean . . . in Northwood. We both thought Kaita was after you. We thought she bore some grudge against you, though we did not know what. But she was never after you. She was trying to get to me. When she attacked, I shoved you out of the way, and she killed Sten instead." I looked up at her, tears shining in my eyes. "But she was never aiming for you. It was me all along."

"I know," said Mag. "I worked that out for myself. I am actually rather clever, as well as being mighty."

"And humble," said Dryleaf.

"Sky above, Mag," I whispered. "I am so sorry."

"You should not be," she said brusquely. "Your actions change nothing. It was not your fault. I would have thrown myself in her path to protect you, and Sten would have done the same. And the only reason he died was that you were trying to protect me. None of us did anything wrong. No one but Kaita."

Her words were little comfort. I bowed my head into my hands.

"We had a sense that she was stringing us along," said Dryleaf quietly. "Now we know why. She wanted to draw you here. To your home, and hers. But why? Why not strike at us on the road?"

"Because of Mag," I said quietly, looking up.

Mag frowned. "Me?"

I nodded. "Do you remember that time we saved Victon from the bear in the jungle?"

Her frown deepened. "I do, but I fail to see what it has to do with anything."

"That, too, was Kaita."

Her eyes went wide. "How do you know?"

"You were confused by how it seemed to vanish. I was, too. It stuck in my mind, so that I still remember it all these years later. That was Kaita. I believe she turned into a raven and flew away, which is why the trail ended so. That was the first time she tried to kill me, I think. But you were there to protect me, and we remained by each other's side for years. She must have given up. And then one day she joined the Shades, and that must have occupied her time too much to think of hunting me down. But then, when she learned that we were together again, and in Northwood . . . she had the strength of an army behind her. She thought she could try again. But even then, you defeated her. She must have realized that she could not defeat you, that no human could. No *human.*"

"The trolls," said Dryleaf suddenly. "She hoped the trolls could do it."

"Sky above," breathed Mag. "And it seems she might be right. I was almost as helpless against the troll as you were."

That drew me just enough out of my dark mood to scowl at her. "If you will remember, it was I who wounded the troll."

She gave a dismissive wave of her hand. "I kept its attention so that you could."

"In any case," I said, soldiering on, "she knew she could lure us here, because I would not let her harm my family. And here, she has a chance of defeating you. Once you are out of the way, she can take her revenge on me at last."

"And your sister."

I frowned at her. "My sister?"

"Of course," said Mag. "If she only wanted to draw us into conflict with the trolls, she could have done that in the mountains farther south. But she and the Shades have driven the trolls into a war with the family Telfer. She cannot think your sister will emerge from such a conflict unscathed. Whatever grudge she bears against you, she includes Lord Telfer in it as well."

That detail had escaped me. But just as I was beginning to mull it over, there came the high squeak of a lock turning towards the front of the dungeon. I made my way to my feet as we heard boots approaching. Two of my family's guards appeared outside the cell, their faces grim. Behind them was Ditra.

"You wanted to talk," she said.

"Did you think you needed these guards?" I said, pointing to them.

"They are not for you," said Ditra. Her gaze shifted to Mag. "They are for her. We have heard of the Uncut Lady even this far to the north."

"Then you know your guards are useless," said Mag with a smile.

An angry flush crept up into Ditra's face, and I raised a hand to pacify Mag. "It is fine. Please, sit, and wait for my return." I glanced at Ditra. "Assuming I *will* return?"

"As long as you do not do anything stupid," she growled in irritation. "Stupider, I mean."

Mag shrugged and went to sit beside Dryleaf. The guards unlocked the cell door, and I joined them in the hallway. We waited while they locked it again, and then I followed Ditra and her guards out of the dungeon.

THIRTY-FIVE

Ditra led me up to the entry hall, and then through the large door to her audience chamber. But she did not stop there. She took me to the back, to the doorway hidden behind a stone wall that led to a narrow stairway. I knew that stairway led up to her personal chamber. It had once been my mother's, and I had no fond memories of it. But I followed her up.

The two guards remained downstairs. But when we reached the upper hallway, I found Maia standing at the door to Ditra's chamber, his hands clasped behind his back. As I emerged from the stairwell, he gave me a nearly imperceptible nod. Ditra ignored him, striding through the door into her room. I paused for a moment.

"Will you be joining us?" I asked Maia.

"Do I need to?"

That made me deflate a bit. "Of course not. I would never harm her."

"So I thought," said Maia. "I will remain outside."

"Actually, you will fetch us some food and wine," said Ditra sharply. It appeared she had not entirely gotten over her annoyance at Maia for the earlier spectacle. After a moment she added, "And have some sent to the others in the cell, while you are visiting the kitchens."

"Of course, my lord," said Maia. He gave a little sigh and left.

I steeled myself. Painful memories swam to the forefront of my mind, of so many times I had stepped into this chamber and left it in despair, or in tears. But that had been a long time ago. I shook off my thoughts and stepped into the room, closing the door behind me.

To my surprise, Ditra had not taken her seat at the head of the table. Instead she leaned against the nearest edge of it, her hands probing its corner idly. The posture was so unlike our mother that for a moment I could see only the sister of my youth.

"So," she began. "Tell me about your friends. The truth, please, and not the lie you fed me earlier."

"Mag was my friend in the Upangan Blades," I said. "We have been close ever since. Dryleaf is an old man we found in Dorsea not long ago."

"Very well." She took a long breath and loosed it through her nose. "There is one matter we must tend to before any others. How are you?"

I stood there for a very long moment, and I am certain I had an utterly buffoonish look upon my face. When the words finally registered, I shrugged. "I . . . I am all right. I suppose."

Her jaw clenched, and she shook her head. "I mean after the wending."

Suddenly I realized what she was doing, and for a moment I could not speak. There is a conversation the family of an ander person is supposed to have with them after their wending, a ritual of long custom, stretching back to the time before time. She was having it with me now.

"Ditra, that was twenty years ago." I could barely choke the words out. My throat had grown tight.

Her nostrils flared. "And you were not here. How are you?"

I could not hold her gaze any longer. I stared at my feet and shook my head, feeling tears close to bursting. "I am fine," I whispered.

She came forwards and put her hands on my shoulders. "You look wonderful. Graceful. Like an adult, and not just for the grey in your hair. You were so very awkward as a child."

Still I could barely choke my answers out. "I had good reason to be."

From the corner of my eye I saw a smile on her lips, and I saw how sad it was. "You did. I wish to be certain—it is Albern now, correct?"

"It is."

"Albern," she said. "As your sister, I am overjoyed. Come, brother. For the first time, let me greet you as the man you are."

She took me into her arms, and I could not withhold myself any longer. I did not fall sobbing into her grip, as I had done to Mag when I learned of my mother's death. But still my tears slipped from me, and I held her hard, pressing my face into her shoulder, the way I had done so many times in my youth, when a nightmare had woken me in the middle of sleep. And when at last we drew back, I saw tears shining in her eyes as well.

But then she took another step back, and I saw her emotions fade away, not unlike when Mag's battle-trance slid into place. In that moment she became not my sister, but the Lord Telfer, Rangatira of Tokana. I, too, pushed my emotions to the side.

"Now. I am not only your sister, Albern. I am lord of these lands, and it falls to me to protect them. What is Kaita doing here? And what brought you here to hunt her?"

"I have only guesses for the first question, though I can answer the second easily enough. I am here to kill her. And I know she wishes to kill me as well. But I think she came here because she wants to kill you, too."

Ditra frowned. "Me? What makes you think that?"

"Many things," I said. "Chief among them being the fact that she led me across three kingdoms to get here."

She shook her head. "Kaita is not trying to kill me."

I was flabbergasted. "You cannot be that naive," I said. Her eyes flashed, and I went on quickly. "Ditra, I know you and she used to share a bed on occasion, but that was—"

"It was more than some idle tryst," said Ditra. "She risked her life to be with me."

"She . . . she what?"

A knock sounded at the door. Maia opened it, bearing a tray with food and wine.

"Thank you," said Ditra briskly. "Give it to him, and then leave us be."

"Of course, Rangatira," said Maia. He gave us both a quick, surreptitious glance, but he did as his lord bid him. When the door closed again, Ditra motioned me over to the table. We both sat, the tray between us, but neither of us touched anything upon it.

"When you . . ." Ditra's nostrils flared again, and she took a moment to master herself. "When you left. Mother sent Romil to fetch you back. She sent Kaita along with her, as a retainer and a bodyguard. Of course, we both know that Romil failed. But on her journey back here to Tokana, she was attacked by Feldemarians. They killed Romil. Kaita tried to protect her, but she barely escaped with her own life. And when she finally returned home, Mother tried to have her executed."

"What?" I exclaimed. "Why?"

"For failing to protect Romil." Ditra's expression had gone dark. It was plain that she thought Mother's decision was wrong, even barbaric. "Mother was enraged. Kaita, who had barely survived the Feldemarian attack, was nearly killed again. But she escaped, and then she came to me, and asked me to leave with her, if you can believe it."

"She thought you would go with her?" I said. "What kind of fool did she—"

Ditra waved a hand in dismissal. "We were in love, Albern. Or we thought we were, the way people do at that age. But of course I told her not to be ridiculous. Mother's decision might have been wrong, but I would not betray our family. I promised I would keep her visit a secret, and then I told her to go."

I shook my head. It seemed I understood at last.

"Ditra," I said slowly, wondering how I could make her see it. "Kaita lost her position in our household because of me. And then she lost you, her lover, when she tried to run."

"She should not have had to run," said Ditra. "If I had been Rangatira, it would never have happened. What Mother did was evil. You should understand that better than most. Kaita was her victim, just as you were."

"You cannot fix all of Mother's wrongs," I said. "If you try, you will doom yourself. Mother was cruel to me, and it made my life miserable—but I shed her cruelty as soon as I could, and I purged it from my life. Kaita has taken that cruelty and made it her own. Now she means to tear the family Telfer down, to raze Tokana and leave no one here to contest her. It is part of the Shades' strategy in their war against the High King. But for Kaita, it is more than that. She is going to destroy everything we have, and she is going to use the trolls to do it. You have to stop her. You must let Mag and me help you."

"I did only my duty," said Ditra firmly. "Kaita was distressed. She might have thought, in the moment, that I would abandon my family, but she could not have truly believed it. This matter between the two of you is something else."

"She is a Shade," I said. "I have faced her on the battlefield. She is a high captain in their ranks. They are the ones behind the troll attacks."

Ditra's nostrils flared. "You did not know Kaita as I did. You barely knew her at all."

"Do you honestly think she still—"

"You never knew her, Albern," snapped Ditra. "You only cared about yourself when you lived here."

I felt my own anger rising to meet hers. "Well, someone had to."

"No!" Ditra's bark made me jump. She stood from her chair, planting her hands on the table as she leaned over me. "You do not get to speak to me that way. *Me,* of all people. Not after you abandoned your duty to our family."

I felt like a pouting child again, but I could not help the sullen expression on my face. "What duty is that?"

"You know what. Maia is a fine man, but you should be my lead ranger."

"I grew up thinking you would be lead ranger, and Romil would be the Rangatira after Mother."

"So you left because you would not have a title?" said Ditra, staring at me wide-eyed. "You were unsatisfied with—"

"I left because I had no reason to stay!" I snapped. "I had nothing here!"

"You had me."

"You were my sister," I said slowly, trying to master my temper. "Yes, we had each other. But Mother . . . Romil . . ."

"They are dead, Albern." Her voice caught. "They have been dead a long time. Yet you never came back."

I could scarcely speak above a whisper. "I did not know Mother had died until I stood in your council chamber a few days ago."

She dropped her gaze from mine and stepped away from the table. Scooping up her cup of wine, she went to the window, raising one arm to lean against it, picking with her nails at the diamond-shaped bolts that held the glass in place. "I know. We tried to send word, but we had lost track of you. And there was so much to do, so much expected of me . . ."

Her voice trailed away. I shifted in my seat. "You do not have to explain anything," I said. "You were—"

"Mother?"

I stopped, frowning. "What?"

She turned to me slowly. "You said you did not know about Mother."

My throat had gone dry. I tried to speak, but I could not.

"You said you did not know about *Mother,*" she said again, fury rising in her tone. "What of Romil? Did you know? Did you receive our letter?"

I could not meet her gaze. I took one of the goblets of wine from the tray and sipped it. "I did."

"You knew," said Ditra, her voice toneless, like Mag's trance. "You knew your sister had died. Yet you stayed away."

"Whose sister?" I demanded. "How was she my sister? She did not help me. She did not comfort me. She did not care a whit whether I lived or died."

"She was our sister regardless," said Ditra. "Or do you think that Thada was not our mother?"

"I do not know what she was to you, after I left. She was never a mother to me."

Ditra scoffed. "You are being ridiculous. She raised us, she—"

"Raised us? What does that mean to you? She never even noticed my existence until she needed me. Until I was *useful* to her." I spat the word. "She never cared about anything we did, anything we wanted, unless it was in her service. You have seen this already."

I lifted my arm and dragged down my sleeve again to show the family mark. Ditra's sleeve was tighter than mine, but she ripped it open to show her own mark.

"We both have one," she said. "But I have not forgotten what mine means, as you have."

"You were away when she gave me the mark," I said. "It was during the same trip you were on when I left. Mother decided it was time for me to receive it, whether I wanted it or not. And indeed, I did not want it. So she forced me. She summoned soldiers and had them *hold me down* so she could carve it into my skin herself. When I fought, she slapped me. No, she was never a mother to me. You were the closest thing I ever had to that."

But that only made the dam burst. Ditra seized the tray of food and threw it against the wall.

"And I *needed* you, Albern!" she screamed. "I had *no one.* No one at all. When Romil died, do you think Mother was there to comfort me? Do you think she took care of me? Consoled me? Do you think she even gave me the cold comfort of allowing me to weep in her presence? After we laid Romil to rest, she called me to this chamber. Do you know what she said? 'You will be my new lead ranger, of course. Someone will be along to show you your duties.' Then she dismissed me. That was all. What did you think would happen? Did you think she would see the evil of her ways, and finally love me the way she always should have? You have never been that great of a fool."

I could not answer. I had no answer to give. This was the true burden of guilt that had hung over me all the long years since I left home. This was what I had never been able to tell anyone, not even Mag. I knew Romil had died, and I knew I should have gone home—not for myself, and certainly not for Mother, but for Ditra. So that she would not be alone.

Ditra's fury now was more than I could bear. I cast my gaze to the floor, unable even to look at her.

She straightened. "I am done with you. Tell Maia to return you to your cell."

You might think it was a strange command—ordering someone to have themselves put back in prison. But I did it. I rose, left the room, and said nothing as I let Maia lead me back to my friends.

THIRTY-SIX

Dotag came to speak with Gatak again that night. They were on a ridge towards the north end of the Kahaunga valley. Gatak had found another cliff to sit on, a place to look out over the lowlands, a place with a good view of the city. Dotag strutted up to her, puffing his chest and rolling his shoulders. Gatak did not look at him right away. Her gaze was fixed on the smoke of the humans' city.

Close now. So close.

After a moment of waiting for Gatak to look at him, to no avail, Dotag finally spoke. "It is nearly done," he boasted. "No humans still dwell in the mountains. Only in their valley. I have sent the gifts we stole from them to other packs, and many of them have joined us. We are ready."

Gatak looked over at last. "Are you?"

"We are many. We are strong. Their homes will not stand before us. They will flee. Any who stand and fight will die."

"Then I hope none of them try to flee," said Gatak. "I hope you kill them all."

Dotag showed just a bit of his teeth. Gatak stepped closer and pressed her forehead to his. They both closed their eyes for a moment and shared a breath. When they pulled away, Dotag's ears were back in pleasure, and he viewed her with a hungry look in his eyes.

But she had other things to see to.

"I must go for now," she said.

Dotag's face fell, and his ears came back up. "Go?" he said. "Go where?"

"To speak with the Lord," she said. "And to ensure our victory."

"We will win," insisted Dotag. "The humans cannot stop us."

"I believe you," said Gatak. "Do not worry. I will return soon."

"You said that before," said Dotag. "You did not come back for a long time."

Gatak lowered her ears and pressed her head into his chest. "A few months are nothing. There are many years ahead of us. But I will not be gone that long this time. I promise I will return to you before the attack."

Dotag seemed comforted at that—and at the feeling of her pressing into him. "You vow it?"

"I vow it," she said. "Watch for my return."

She made her long, slow climb down the cliff. She hated coming down. It always took so much longer than climbing. But it was worth it to view the world from those lofty heights—not as high as a bird, but with solid ground underneath you, like a throne from which you could view the world far below your feet.

Gatak reached the bottom and lumbered off into the darkness, to a place she knew was well out of sight of Dotag, where no troll had any hope of seeing her.

Once she was certain she was alone, her eyes began to glow.

Her form shrank. Her limbs grew slim. Tight clothing sprang from where it had been wrapped deep within her form.

Kaita emerged into the night. She took a deep breath of the air, reveling in her returned sense of smell. Trolls could smell almost nothing, and she always felt like she had a wolf's nose after she resumed human form.

But she had little time to enjoy herself. Her eyes glowed again. She took her raven form and flapped up into the air. The mountain winds were with her, and in no time she had reached the Shade encampment. They had set themselves up in rows of tents, buried deep in the mountains where few had any hope of finding them. Even rangers would not have drawn near to the camp, for the trolls were between them and the city.

She landed in their midst and resumed her human form again. A wave of fatigue struck her, but she shrugged it off. There was a moment's shock among the Shades, but it did not last long. Their commander's habits were well known, and they relaxed as soon as they recognized her. Phelan stepped up, bowing low before her.

"Order everyone to be ready," said Kaita. "The trolls will attack soon. When they do, we shall fight beside them."

"Of course, Commander," said Phelan. "We are prepared to strike at a moment's notice."

"And the special team I tasked you with putting together?"

Phelan hesitated. "They, too, are prepared. Eleven of our best soldiers. They will infiltrate the keep and kill every Telfer they can."

Kaita fixed him with a look. "You have doubts?"

"The Telfer keep is well defended, Commander. I worry for the success of their mission. But I have faith in your plan."

"You should," said Kaita. "I myself will be on that mission."

His eyes widened. "That is too dangerous."

"It is necessary," said Kaita. "I know the keep. I know all of its secret ways, the passages in and out. Do not trouble yourself over my safety. The Telfers are the ones who should be worried."

"As you say, Commander." Phelan did an admirable job of trying to hide his doubt. He bowed again and left her.

Kaita spent a little while longer patrolling the camp, ensuring that everything was prepared and that her soldiers were ready for the battle. Finally she accepted that things were as prepared as they were going to be, and she made her way to a tent to sleep. But she lay awake a long time, staring at the top of her tent, fingers playing at her braid in the darkness and listening to the gentle nighttime sounds of the camp.

Close now. So close.

Maia led me back to my cell. But when we reached it, I found a surprise. Mag stood against the bars, her arms passed through them and her wrists manacled. Two guards were moving a mattress into the cell.

I looked at Mag. "What did you do?"

"Nothing," she said, sounding almost disappointed. "Dryleaf said his cot was too hard for his old back. He asked for a softer mattress, and the guards would only provide it if I let them truss me up. I agreed for his sake."

"And I cannot tell you how much I appreciate it," Dryleaf piped up from the back of the cell. He sat on the cot, smiling broadly, as the guards wrestled the new mattress in and placed it on the floor to the right.

Mag studied my face. She must have noticed my red, puffy eyes, for she frowned. "You look a bit worse for wear. Did she hurt you?"

She had, of course, though not in the way that Mag meant. So I forced a chuckle. "We did not have a brawl in her chambers, if that is what you mean."

"Hm," said Mag.

Dryleaf found his way to his feet as he heard the guards retreating from the cell. He probed at the air, and when he found one of them, he patted her on the back. "Thank you again, very kindly. It is good to see that even in dire times, the hospitality of Calentin knows no bounds."

"That is kind of you to say," said the guard. She looked a little ashamed, as if she had not expected her duties to include imprisoning such an old and frail man.

"Not as kind as you have been," said Dryleaf, his smile widening.

Once they had left the cell, I walked myself in. Maia shut the door behind me, and when I turned, I saw that he was eyeing me carefully. But he said nothing as the guards locked the door again, and he turned to go. The woman Dryleaf had spoken to went to unbind Mag's wrists.

"Thank you for not making this difficult," she said.

"Think nothing of it," said Mag. "I told you it was for the old man's sake."

The guard smiled and unlocked the manacles. She glanced up the hallway where Maia and the other guard had retreated. When she spoke again, her voice was soft. "I . . . I wanted to let you know. I have heard many tales of you, and I know you are no evil person. I hope the Lord Telfer does not treat you too harshly. She is a fair woman."

"You would know better than I," said Mag with a smile.

The woman stepped a bit closer. "I heard a story once . . . is it true that you held a breach in a keep wall for four hours, alone?"

Mag's smile dampened. "It is. That was not a good day. I was only alone because all my companions had died."

The woman's face fell at once. "I . . . I am sorry to bring an old grief to mind."

"Do not trouble yourself." Mag smirked. "And, if I may offer a word of advice?"

She had not yet pulled her hands back within the cell. Now she seized the front of the girl's shirt—quickly, but gently.

"You are a little too close. I could seize you, smash your head into the bars, and steal the keys to escape."

The girl's face flamed as Mag let go of her shirt and gave her a little pat on the cheek. "I . . . will keep that in mind. But I do not think you would do such a thing." She reached to put the manacle keys on her belt—and then she frowned. "Dark take me. It would not have helped you, anyway. I must have put the cell key somewhere . . ."

She froze and looked up at Mag suspiciously. Mag smiled broadly and raised her hands.

"You took all my pouches. I could not hide a key on myself if I wanted to."

The guard sighed and rolled her eyes. "Very well. I believe you. I wish I could say this was the first time I had lost it." With a rueful shake of her head she left us, grumbling under her breath.

"They brought you food?" I asked, once she had gone.

Dryleaf nodded. "They did. And fine fare it was, for a prison. It was when they brought our meal that I asked for the mattress. Thank you for seeing to our arrangements."

"I did nothing," I told him. "Ditra thought of it on her own."

He nodded. "It is as the girl said—she sounds like a fair woman."

"She is, I suppose," I said. "Though just now she is trying a bit too hard to be like our mother."

"That displeases you, I gather."

"My mother was a hard woman. So hard, for so long, that she forgot how to be gentle. And that is all I wish to say about her for the moment."

Dryleaf nodded. I went and sat on the floor by the cell door, just where I had rested the last time I was in here. Mag, too, resumed her position, leaning against the other end of the bars. But when I glanced up, I found her studying me. I did not wish to speak with her any more than with Dryleaf, so I avoided her gaze.

"This is a nice jail," said Dryleaf, not seeming to mind our silence. "I have been in far worse."

That drew me somewhat out of my dark thoughts. "You? In jail? What for?"

"I assure you, only for other misunderstandings like this one," he said, chuckling. "I may be old now, but I have gotten myself into a great deal of trouble under many names. Good people end up in prison all the time. Some of my most popular stories are about just that thing."

"Well, let us hope that your luck holds out," said Mag, "and that this trip to a cell is no worse than your previous ones."

"No, indeed," said Dryleaf. "Already it is a good deal more pleasant. Fear not, my lord of Telfer. I have a feeling this will all work itself out in the end."

"I am not the Lord Telfer," I said quietly, turning away from him.

THIRTY-SEVEN

Ditra sat in her chamber for a while after I left. She stared long out the window, at the gentle snows that fell outside it, into the darkness that was gathering to the north. Then she roused herself and went to bed. The tray of food lay where she had cast it on the floor, untended.

She went through her morning the next day in a dark mood. Again and again she tried to put me from her mind, but again and again her thoughts returned to me. She could sense it affecting her decisions, creating long silences before she realized someone had spoken to her, and that she had to answer. It was hard to concentrate, hard to focus.

During her midday meal, she finally threw her knife down onto her plate and abandoned her pathetic attempt to eat.

She rose and went to the door of another chamber down the hall, knocking at it twice.

"Yes?" came a soft voice from inside.

Ditra opened the door. Her daughter sat at a desk across the room, her quill out, a stack of parchment in front of her. She had been copying from a tome of history recently—a pursuit Ditra did not particularly understand, but it took up her daughter's time and kept her from getting underfoot, for which Ditra was grateful.

"Mother," she said, beaming. She rose and ran to her in the doorway, throwing her arms around Ditra's waist.

"I have not been able to visit you of late," said Ditra, trying to maintain a regal tone. "I thought we could speak for a moment, in this brief calm between storms."

"Storms?" Her daughter looked up into her face. "Is something the matter?"

"You have heard about the attacks in the mountains," said Ditra sternly. "It ill behooves you to play at ignorance, V-Vera."

Ditra stumbled over the name, her throat suddenly dry. It had been my name, of course, before my wending. She had meant it as a tribute to me, especially because she had not known I was ander. But it seemed a poor decision now.

Vera, for her part, looked chastised. It hurt Ditra to see it, but she steeled herself. She had not even been particularly harsh. Vera would need to withstand much worse than this, when she one day took Maia's place as lead ranger, after he became Rangatira.

"Come," said Ditra. "Sit."

She guided Vera back to her chair by the desk, and then she sat on the girl's bed. For a moment they waited there in silence, both staring at their hands, which each of them had folded in their lap. The silence drew on, long past awkwardness and into discomfort.

"Do you . . . do you want to be a ranger, Vera?"

Vera looked up at her, eyes wide. "Why, yes, Mother. Of course. You know that."

"You have said so," said Ditra. "But I have often told you that it is what I expect. I mean to ask . . . do you *want* to be a ranger? Would you, if I were not Lord of Tokana?"

It was clear the girl had not considered it before. Now she frowned and looked away, her eyes growing distant. "I think so. All of our rangers are certainly very dashing. And I am always happiest out in the wilderness." She flushed and looked quickly at Ditra. "I do not mean to say I am not happy here—"

Ditra forestalled her with a raised hand. "I understand what you mean." *Better than you can know.* "Go on."

Vera frowned again, and she began to twist her hands. "I have never fought before, of course. I like my training, but I do not enjoy the thought of . . . of killing. But I know we never do it without reason."

Do we not? thought Ditra. *I always thought Mother was too careless of others' lives.*

She closed her eyes and steeled herself. *Enough.* She had become a confused mess, and she would not serve her people well in this state.

"There have been some . . . arrivals, to the keep," she said to Vera.

"Guests?" said Vera, frowning.

"No," said Ditra. "Prisoners. They may be here on dishonorable business." The words tasted bitter in her mouth. Even she barely believed them.

"I cannot remember the last time we had prisoners in the dungeons," said Vera, her voice suddenly small.

Ditra could not help a snort of laughter. "I could not have said that when I was your age."

Vera smiled at Ditra's laughter, brief and grim though it was. She had always loved it when they laughed together, and loved it all the more for how rare it was.

"I . . . I have something I think I should tell you," said Ditra. "But it is a long tale, and a difficult one. Do you remember—"

A horn sounded. Ditra shot to her feet.

"Mother?" said Vera.

"Stay here," said Ditra. She almost left, but at the last moment she stopped. Turning, she embraced Vera, holding her tight. "Be strong. I will return when I can."

She ran from the room. A door at the end of the hall led her into a passageway onto the walls. Soldiers of her house started in surprise as she emerged into the open and marched down the ramparts. She stopped at the first person she saw—and suddenly she realized that she knew the woman. It was Whetu, the former ranger whose family had narrowly escaped their village's destruction a few weeks before.

"Whetu," she said, nodding. "I am somewhat surprised to see you here."

"Rangatira," said Whetu, bowing with a fist to her forehead. "It seemed clear things would come to a fight before long. I took up your service again, for that seemed better than waiting idly for the trolls to come to us."

"Maia assigned you?"

"He did, Rangatira," said Whetu.

Ditra's mouth gave a wry twist. Maia had not mentioned it, but then, he had been rather preoccupied lately. "I am glad you are here. I am assigning you to guard my daughter's chamber. Find two others on your way and bring them with you, on my authority."

"Yes, Rangatira," said Whetu. "No harm will come to her."

Ditra nodded and walked on while Whetu ran to do her bidding. Ditra stalked up to the short tower overlooking the east gatehouse, and there she found Maia.

"Report."

Maia turned at the sound of her voice, and though he kept a passive expression, Ditra could see the relief in his eyes. He was obviously struggling to maintain his customary good humor, but it was overpowered by a worry he could not entirely hide.

"Rangatira," he said. "Trolls have gathered at the north end of the dale."

Ditra suppressed a shudder. They had all known that Kahaunga was the trolls' eventual aim, but her scouts had guessed that any attack would not come for several more days. Ditra had thought they would have more time—time for the king's reinforcements to arrive, time to work out another solution. Time to find and eliminate the Shades, mayhap.

A thought came to her briefly that that might have happened, if she had ordered Maia to work with us, as he had wished to. But she quashed that thought immediately. This was a time for action, not doubt.

"How many?"

"Many," said Maia. "More than two hundreds."

Ditra's eyes shot wide. "Two *hundreds?*" She realized that soldiers all around them were staring at her, and she forced her expression back to one of impassive calm. "What are they doing?"

"They are holding their position for now," said Maia. "But they may only be waiting until they finish gathering their forces." He paused. "I did not even know there were that many in the mountains."

"Of course there are," she snapped. "The Greatrocks stretch for hundreds of leagues."

"I mean the mountains of Tokana," said Maia. "We have never glimpsed a pack even a fraction of this size."

"Why would you? They have always observed the pact. They have kept to themselves for more generations than the years in your life."

"That seems to have changed."

Ditra frowned slightly. "And we will deal with it."

Maia paused, glancing around. Ditra was grateful that at least he, too, was aware that everyone was watching them, and that morale might depend a great deal on the words the others heard them speak. He leaned close and dropped to a whisper.

"I respect that you must keep a strong front, Rangatira," he said. "But are you not worried? Should we not retreat?"

Ditra leaned on the wall and looked into the dale far below. The mountains hid the northern end of it from this position, but she could almost imagine them there, gathering, milling about.

Preparing to sweep down upon her people and kill them all.

"We do not retreat," she said loudly. "Kahaunga is our home."

Maia looked frustrated, but still he kept his voice low. "A corpse is not comforted that it lies in the same place it dwelled when alive. We cannot hope to hold against a pack so large."

Ditra looked to him. "Do you not see?" she said, lowering her voice to match his. "It is too late for that. Kahaunga is not only our home, it is our best hope. We can defend ourselves on these walls. If we retreat, and they attack us on the road, we will be helpless. We will fight here, and we will win here, or we will die here."

He looked away, eyes flicking back and forth as he surveyed the dale. "What if we order an evacuation of the most vulnerable? Tell all those who cannot fight to leave, while the rest of us hold off the trolls to cover their retreat."

Ditra considered it. The Telfer stronghold could contain a third of the city at most, and that would be an exceptionally tight fit. There would be folk on cots in the cells of her dungeon.

The dungeon. Mag and I crossed her mind. She forced the thought away.

"Do it," she said. "Everyone in Kahaunga who can pick up a weapon must join us here in the stronghold, especially those who can shoot. We will hold against the trolls as long as we can. All other citizens must make for the pass west out of the mountains."

He straightened, relief plain on his face. "Yes, Rangatira." He turned to the others. "You heard her. Order the evacuation."

Ditra turned her attention back to the city below. *This is why Mother was so cold,* she thought. *One must be hard to be a Telfer.*

But as she saw Maia looking at her out of the corner of his eye, she felt a flicker of doubt that she did not think our mother ever had.

Dotag stood on a hillock, observing the trolls as they gathered before him.

Two hundreds. No one had ever commanded a pack so large.

He felt nervous. He felt sick. A doubt was in him now, one he could no longer suppress. No one had ever commanded this many trolls—and no trolls had attacked human lands, as they were about to do. Not since the days trolls first came into these mountains.

That should have been a comforting thought—that he was following in the footsteps of his ancient forefathers. But it only made him more nervous, increasing his misgivings until he felt as though he wanted to vomit.

He looked down and saw Apok. She was staring up at him, not moving, not blinking. His doubt increased tenfold, fear creeping in at the edges of it. He thought of Chok's broken body as he dragged it out of the Shade stronghold, and quickly he tried to think of something else.

Then a commotion caught his attention. As the trolls milled about, moving in great swirls and spreading out across the open turf, a path opened between them. Down that path lumbered Gatak. Trolls gave way before her, and the pack closed again behind her. She was headed straight towards Dotag's hillock.

All of Dotag's fears vanished in an instant. Gatak had come. Just as she had said she would.

Mayhap everything else she had promised would come true as well.

Gatak joined him on the hillock. She turned back and looked over the trolls. They covered the ground, a small plateau at the northern end of the Kahaunga valley.

"I thought there would be more," she said, sounding vaguely disappointed.

Dotag felt somewhat crestfallen. "We are enough. We will drive the humans out. And then all the mountains will be ours."

Gatak turned to him, her ears rising in anticipation. "Then do it."

We had spent an uncomfortable night in our cell—or at least, Mag and I had. Dryleaf, of course, had his mattress. But his snoring had kept the two of us awake, which had not been helped by our hard cots. I understood why the old man had complained. I had spent much of the day dozing, trying to gain what extra rest I could.

But I shot awake when the horns sounded.

"What was that?" said Mag, looking towards the ceiling.

"You have never heard horns before?" I said.

"Is it the trolls?"

"It has to be."

We sat in silence. I did not know what to do. Dryleaf bowed his head with a frown, seeming deep in thought. My hands clenched into fists and then relaxed, over and over. Mag's gaze wandered as though she was considering something, replaying events in her head.

A door crashed open at one end of the hallway, and a guard rushed past us. At the last moment I recognized her as the one who had spoken to Mag yesterday.

"Wait!"

She skidded to a halt, looking at us with wide, frightened eyes. "I cannot—"

"What is happening?" I said, gripping the bars.

"Trolls," she said. "They have gathered in the dale to attack the city."

"How many?"

Her face went a shade paler. "Many."

"Let me out," said Mag. "You know who I am. My friend here is just as remarkable."

I thought privately that that was a tremendous lie, but I was not going to countermand her just then. The guard hesitated. But she shook her head. "I cannot. I am sorry."

"But if you—"

She ran on, rushing through the door at the other end of the hall.

Dryleaf sighed and stood. He shuffled towards the two of us, hand outstretched. "It sounds as though things are getting most dire. I suspect the Lord Telfer could use the two of you."

I slammed my hand against the cell bars. "She could, though she will never admit it."

Dryleaf pulled a key from his sleeve. Mag and I froze. He groped the air for a moment before finding the door handle. Reaching through the bars, he inserted the key and turned it.

Click

The door swung open.

Dryleaf held the key up, dangling it before us.

"I took it when the guards brought the mattress. You should return it to them on your way out."

Mag could barely contain herself. "Why under the sky did you not tell us this before," she growled. It was far more of an accusation than a question.

Dryleaf frowned and held up an admonishing finger. "The guards brought me my mattress because I was old and infirm and blind. It is not right to betray the kindness of anyone who would do that, even if they are imprisoning one. Unless, of course, one does so to save their lives. Just as I am doing now."

Mag and I stared at him. "You have a very strange sense of right and wrong, old man," I said.

Dryleaf's frown cracked, becoming a grin. "I suppose some might think so. Take care of yourselves. I believe I will remain here. The mattress is *very* comfortable."

We rushed out of the cell and down the hall where the guard had gone. Mag threw the door open to the small guard room. At the other end, the guard stood by another door leading up into the keep. She stared at us, frozen in shock.

"We are going to help in the fighting," said Mag matter-of-factly. "And if you give us back our weapons, we will be much better at it."

The girl's mouth opened and then closed again. Her hand twitched as if to reach for her weapon, but she looked at Mag and thought better of it. Finally she sighed and pointed to a wooden locker across the room.

"They are in there," she said. From her pocket she fished a small iron key and threw it into my hand. "At least I did not lose *that* key."

THIRTY-EIGHT

We emerged into the stronghold's main bailey to find chaos.

A mass of people had pressed into a great throng before the keep doors. When I first emerged into the open, I thought they were pressing forwards, seeking safety in the keep itself. But after a moment I realized that these did not look like refugees. They were young and hale people, and they were listening attentively to commands shouted at them by Telfer soldiers in armor, standing on whatever platform they could find, desperately barking orders.

Mag seized the arm of a passing guard. "Where is the battle?" she demanded.

The guard stopped looking her up and down for a moment. "In the city, of course," she said.

"The dale?" I said.

"Yes. Lord Telfer led her forces into the streets. They are trying to slow the trolls' advance while the rest of the city escapes."

"If these people are trying to escape, why do they look like they are forming for battle?" I said.

"These ones are," she said. "Everyone who can fight has been commanded to do so. The rest are taking the western pass out of the mountains."

I took Mag's arm. "To the city with us, then."

We ran for the main gate. It stood open, and more people were still pushing in. We had to force our way through the crowd. Mag led the way, for as with so many things, she seemed to have a particular knack for threading through the mass. But once we were in the open again, we stopped to take in the sight before us. A mass of people was making its way up from the dale, clogging the roads. When they reached the Telfer stronghold, they split into three columns, one passing in through the gate, and the two others curling around it to keep traveling west.

"I wish we had our horses," said Mag.

"They would not help us," I said. "We cannot ride through the crowd and trample these people, and besides, they would bolt at the first sign of the trolls. I will take us on the side streets."

A peal of overjoyed barking drew our attention. We turned to see Oku streaking towards us. He leaped around our feet, yapping and licking our hands and then retreating to bark some more.

"We are glad you are here as well, Oku," I said. "Even Mag."

"Hm," said Mag, who had scratched Oku behind the ears just as much as I had, though she tried to look aloof while she did it. "Let us not waste any more time. If our last tumble with the trolls was any indication, your sister is not having an easy time of it."

I nodded and led the way into the city. We avoided the main roads, and I took them down any side streets I could remember. But even those avenues were full of people, Kahaunga natives who knew their way better than I did and who wanted to escape. We pressed through them as quickly as we could.

It was quite clear when we reached the battle at last.

We slid to a halt in the center of a wide square as a roar ripped through the air. Mag lifted her spear, and I raised my bow. A squadron of Telfer soldiers came pelting into view, fear on their faces.

A troll was just behind them.

I fired as Mag leaped to the attack. My arrow bounced from the troll's shoulder. It did not so much as flinch. But it did stop in its pursuit of the soldiers and focused on Mag, who stood firm before it, her feet wide, her weapon ready. Oku joined her, bristling and growling.

"Albern," called Mag. "Do you have any ideas?"

"Try not to die."

The troll snarled and swung for her. Mag dived to the side. Oku snapped at the troll's massive fist, but darted out of the way as it pressed forwards.

I turned to the soldiers. They had stopped in their flight and now stood in a cluster around me, staring in wonder at the sight of Mag facing the troll with only a wolfhound to join her.

"Oil! Who has oil?"

One of the soldiers blinked at me as though she did not understand. But finally she pulled a flask of it from her belt. "This is the last one we have."

"Someone give me a torch!" I barked.

"We lost them," said one of the soldiers. "We would not have retreated if we had fire."

Growling in frustration, I spared a glance for Mag. She had the troll chasing her all around the square, always staying just out of its grasp. Her flight looked desperate, but I could not tell if she was merely leading it on. Oku trailed behind the troll, sometimes snapping at its ankles, but he did not distract it at all.

"We have to get fire," I said. "Now."

"The . . . the buildings," said a soldier. "Some are—"

I looked past him. To the north, where the battle was thickest, smoke rose into the air. I shoved the flask of oil into his hand.

"Land this on that troll," I said. "Do not miss."

Several of them had arrows wrapped with pitch-covered rags. I snatched two up and sprinted for the smoke.

Three houses down, I found one with flames licking at the outer wall. I thrust the arrows into the flames, and they caught at once. Turning, I sprinted back for the square.

The troll no longer pressed Mag so closely, but I soon saw why. The soldiers had fanned back out around the two of them, trying to distract it so the one with the flask could throw it. Two had been killed. Their bodies lay at the edges of the square, limbs twisted at odd angles.

I readied one of the arrows. "Do it!" I roared.

The soldier looked back at me. In his terror, he almost dropped the flask.

"Now! What are you waiting for?"

He looked ready to faint. But he turned and threw.

The flask sailed over the troll's head. It shattered against a distant wall, the oil splattering over a square area three paces wide.

The soldier turned to look back at me in horror. I was just as shocked as he was.

"It is the size of a house!" I cried. "How could you miss?"

His limbs shook, but he gave no reply.

"All right, all of you, get out," I commanded. "If you can, find another unit and join them. If you cannot, retreat to the keep."

They ran to do as I ordered, scooping up their fallen comrades and carrying them off. I still held my arrow ready, but the flame was useless now. It would not pierce the troll's hide, and without oil, I could not hope to catch it in a blaze.

Mag's desperate turns and dodges were bringing her closer to me with every step. I edged backwards. I could not abandon her to fight alone, but I was out of ideas. In the heat of battle, I could not hurt the troll any more than Mag could, and neither could I dodge its wild blows as well as she.

She glanced over and seemed to notice me for the first time. "Where is the oil?" she called out, ducking the troll's huge fist as it whirled through the air where her head had just been.

"All over that building," I said, pointing. "The fool missed."

Mag had to leap backwards as the troll's hands crashed into the street with a punishing blow. "He *missed?*" she cried. "It is as big as a house!"

"I told him."

She looked over at the building again, and then at me. The troll paused for a moment, eyes narrowing, looking for an opening.

"Light it," said Mag.

The troll snorted and stepped forwards.

"What?" I said, incredulous.

"Light it!" she said, running for the building. The troll screamed in rage as it went after her.

I understood almost too late. Raising the bow, I drew. The flames danced in front of my eyes, almost obscuring Mag with waves of heat. She skidded to a stop in front of the building and turned to face the troll head-on. It was in a full charge now, thundering straight for her.

I loosed. Mag dodged aside at the last possible moment.

The troll and the arrow hit the oil at the same time.

Flames erupted across the building, just as it collapsed inwards with a crash that shook the ground. Oil from the timbers spread all over the troll's body, covering it with flames. The troll's furious roaring turned to panicked bleats of fear. It slapped at itself, trying to put out the flames. But the folk of Tokana had had centuries to perfect their craft, and the oil continued to burn.

Shrieking in terror, the troll turned and ran from the square. Mag looked very much as though she wanted to pursue it, but she stayed put. The building continued to burn, the flames gradually climbing higher until the roof caught as well.

"Are you all right?" I said.

"It did not touch me. Some of your sister's soldiers were not so fortunate."

"Speaking of which," I said, "we should get moving. The battle goes on without us."

Mag nodded, and we turned to head north. But suddenly there came the sound of tramping feet down the city street towards us. A company of Telfer soldiers came into view. They were not exactly running, but they were clearly in retreat. At their head was Ditra. Her face was smudged with soot and sweat, and there was an ugly cut on her cheek. Her armor was dented in several places, and I thought I detected a limp in her gait.

Her steps faltered as she caught sight of us, and the company ground to a halt. I could see the fury rising in her, and her hand tightened on her axe.

"What in the dark below—"

"We heard there was a battle," I said. "I thought you might be able to use us."

"You broke out?" she said. "Who did you—"

"We harmed no one, I promise you," I said.

"And we just saved a squadron of your soldiers," added Mag.

Ditra's gaze flashed to her. "What?"

"A troll pursued them into this square," I said. "Mag held it off while I used oil and fire upon it."

Sheer shock seemed to wipe the anger from Ditra's face. "You faced a troll alone?"

I watched as Mag struggled not to look haughty, and she almost succeeded. "You said you have heard of me."

A crash sounded from behind the soldiers—a fair distance away, but not far enough for comfort. Ditra glanced that way for a moment, and when she turned back, there was a resigned look upon her face.

"If you are willing to aid our fight against the trolls, I suppose I cannot turn you away," she said. "But you will do exactly as my officers and I command, when we command it."

"Of course." I bowed low, and then remembered my decorum. "Rangatira."

"Then follow us. We are pulling back to the stronghold."

"But the trolls—" Mag began.

"Mag," I said. She stopped short. "Do as she says."

She cocked her head, and the corner of her lips twisted. She nodded to Ditra. "Very well, Rangatira."

Ditra nodded and started off, and we fell into step beside her. "We cannot stop the trolls in the city," she said. "We have given our people enough time to flee to the keep, if they mean to fight, or to the pass, if they do not. Our duty now is to consolidate our forces and hold the trolls."

"How long do you mean to hold them?" I said.

Her eyes were grim. "As long as we can."

Dotag stood in the middle of the burning city, his chest heaving, his breath coming out in loud snorts that turned to mist in the air. The humans had fled from their city. He had walked such a long road to get here, and now it was almost over. He could hardly have dreamed that he would be here one day, standing triumphant among the wreckage of the humans' homes, leading a pack greater than any troll had ever commanded.

He roared, throwing his head back and slamming his fists into his chest. Several trolls around him recoiled at the sound of his voice, but when they saw him celebrating their victory, they raised their voices in chorus with his.

At last he subsided as one of the trolls brought him a handful of crops pillaged from one of the human's homes. It was only the first of many tributes he would receive tonight. With a pack of two hundreds, Dotag could hardly imagine the mountain of goods that would be brought before him, for him to pick and choose from, sharing the tastiest morsels with—

Dotag stopped. His brows drew together, lowering over beady eyes as he swung back and forth, searching his surroundings.

Where had Gatak gone?

THIRTY-NINE

WE MADE OUR WAY TO THE STRONGHOLD AND FOUND THE GATES OPEN. Ditra's company was the last to return, and the guards on the wall looked relieved when she ordered them to close the gates after we had entered. She had ordered the rest of her troops to divide and make their way back through the city piecemeal, like the squadron we had rescued before meeting her. The rangers had held the trolls off as long as they could to give the rest time to get away.

The moment we had entered the keep, Ditra turned to Maia. "Summon my councilors to the audience chamber immediately."

"At once, Rangatira." Maia gave us a half-smile and a quick nod before darting off to do as she said. It left the three of us standing in the center of the bailey, crowds milling around us, while Ditra studied Mag and me.

"If you would like—" I began.

"What? You could attend my council?" said Ditra. "How very magnanimous of you. But I do not require the advice of prisoners pressed into service for battle."

"We could save lives." I pointed back towards the city. "We already did. Rangatira," I added, after just a moment's too much hesitation.

"Then when it comes to battle again, I will summon you," she said. "But you will pardon me if I do not consider your advice more useful than my advisors who have lived here their whole lives, and know our situation better."

I bit back the argument that sprang to my lips. She was not wrong. I might have been her younger brother, but we were no longer children, and it was not my place to countermand her, no matter how I hated to hear the word *useful* on her lips. "As you wish, Rangatira."

For a moment I thought I saw her expression soften. But she only turned away to stride off towards the keep.

"A shame," said Mag. "I had hoped the prospect of nearly dying in battle might have bridged at least some of the rift between you."

"Believe me, that was a far more civil conversation than our last," I said. "Let us find Dryleaf and wait. Ditra may not want us to attend her council, but I want to know what is going on the second she comes out to tell everyone."

Ditra strode into her audience chamber, pulling her leather gauntlets off. She winced as she flexed her fingers. They had gripped her axe and shield so tightly that she could hardly feel them now. For a moment she bent and uncurled them while she looked around the chamber. It had been empty of guards, but they were filing back in now as their lord prepared for her meeting.

She noticed something odd. The guards were filing in from the back of the room, from the stairway leading up to the nobility's living quarters. They should have been out in the main bailey, directing the influx of citizens being pressed into fighting service. Ditra supposed they must have been drawn up to the walls to coordinate their defense, and taken the shorter route down to the council room. But she shrugged off such thoughts as Maia came hurrying up, nodding briskly to her.

"Everyone—"

"Vera," said Ditra. "Did you check on her?"

He nodded. "She is safe. Her guards have not left their post since you sent them there."

"Good. What else?"

"Everyone is here. All the captains, and the king's representative."

"Is she still here?" said Ditra with faint surprise. "I half thought she might try to sneak out with the refugees."

Maia hid a smile, though it seemed a near thing. "She still has time. Many are still gathering to flee the city."

Ditra nodded and went to her chair. The councilors gathered around the dais, looking up at her with stern, impassive faces. She saw no sign of eagerness in them, but neither did she see any doubt. They were ready to serve their lord.

"The trolls will not give us much time to rest," said Ditra. "They are looting the lower city now, but it is only a matter of time before they push towards the stronghold. We must discuss the strategy of our defense."

Callen, the king's representative, took a hesitant step forwards. Her tongue crept out to moisten cracked lips. "Can we even hope to defend against them?"

"We have no choice but to do so," said Ditra.

"Your forces have never faced so many," said Callen. "Without reinforcements from the king—"

"The king has sent soldiers and oil in support," said Ditra. "But the trolls attacked earlier than we thought they would, and it seems their strategy is to overwhelm us before any help can arrive."

"Strategy?" scoffed Callen. "They are trolls! They barely have—"

Ditra stood from her chair. Every ranger in the room bowed their head. Callen fell silent, eyes wide.

"They have pushed into our territory. They have avoided our rangers at every turn. They even misled our scouts into believing they would attack at least a week later than they have. You do yourself no favors by assuming them to be mindless beasts, and you serve your Rangatira not at all."

"O-of course," stammered Callen. "Forgive me, Rangatira. But if the king's forces may not even be coming, mayhap we should flee with the rest, for I do not see how we can defend Kahaunga forever."

"The king has sent their army. We might be able to hold the walls until it arrives, or we might not. We cannot know for certain. But we do know that we cannot abandon Kahaunga. If the trolls face no opposition here, they will simply chase our people into the pass, where they will find them defenseless, and slaughter them. We who remain here are a rearguard, to ensure that does not happen."

"You mean we remain here to die!" said Callen. "You have no hope or plan of escape!"

Ditra's anger bubbled up, threatening to burst. But before it could, Maia stepped from her side to face Callen from a pace away.

"I have no intention of dying in Kahaunga," said Maia. "But I will happily throw you over the wall to our enemies, if you see nothing but death in your future."

Callen took a step back. Ditra noticed that the guards at the edge of the room had pressed forwards, as if they were ready to intervene if things should come to a fight. *Fools,* she thought irritably. *Callen would never dare to raise a hand against Maia—and if she did, he would have her on the floor faster than blinking.*

"I have no wish to die," said Callen, making an impressive attempt to rally. "That is why I counsel against this foolish course."

"You serve me, and through me, the king of Calentin," said Ditra, letting an edge creep into her voice. "If you think you serve us best by fleeing with the rest of the city's people, then by all means, do so. Return to the king in Tara and tell them what transpired here. But if you do not wish to die, you might find that a foolish course of action. They have no great love for cowards."

Callen took several deep breaths, each time seeming as if she was about to say something. Her eyes flew wildly about, as if searching for any words that she thought might spare her. At last she shook her head and gave a hasty bow with her fist raised.

"I . . . I think I will retire to my chambers. A new missive must be written and sent to the king about our situation, and I should send it along before all the city's residents have passed us by."

Ditra nodded in approval. Callen turned and began to push through the rangers on her way to the door, while Maia looked up and gave Ditra a wry look. She knew they were both thinking the same thing: Callen would doubtless decide at the last minute to deliver the message herself. She would be gone before nightfall.

Callen reached the back of the crowd, but suddenly she pulled up short before two of the room's guards. Ditra frowned as she realized the guards had come even closer than before. Now the twelve of them nearly surrounded Ditra, Maia, and the six ranger captains who served on her council.

"What in the dark below are you doing?" Ditra barked. "Move aside and let her pass."

The air filled with the hiss of drawn steel as the guards unsheathed their weapons.

FORTY

MAG AND I WAITED IN THE ENTRANCE HALL OUTSIDE. I PACED BACK and forth in front of the doors, while Mag stood stoically, watching me walk by her each time. The hall was in chaos around us, with guards trying to give orders to their new army of recruits, while the new arrivals roved back and forth in great groups, trying to obey those orders but mostly just colliding with each other. Two guards were posted at the entrance of Ditra's council chamber, and they eyed us suspiciously as we walked back and forth. Mag gave them a smile.

"Greetings, friends," she said. "How are you on this fine day?"

Neither guard answered her.

"The Rangatira's council should not take long," I told her as I walked by on my next pass. "Once she has decided what she wants to do, we can determine how to help her."

"I hope it is as quick as you say," said Mag. "Or she will come out here to find a trench where she once had an even floor in her hall. Stop pacing."

I stopped, but I glared at her. "I will, but only because I want to."

"Of course," said Mag.

"This is no time for jokes, Mag. People are already dying, and—"

From Ditra's council chamber came shouts and the clashing of steel.

As one, Mag and I and the guards turned towards the doors. But while the guards were still staring in confusion, Mag and I sprinted for the doorway. At the last moment, the guards turned and crossed their spears to bar it.

"No one is permitted to—"

"Oh, be silent," said Mag, snatching one of the spears and slamming the haft into the guard's head. The woman reeled backwards.

"My apologies." I struck the other in the face. He slammed into the door. With two quick jabs, Mag knocked her guard to the ground, senseless, and then took mine to the floor with a swift kick to the side.

We threw open the doors and rushed inside to a scene of chaos. Ditra's ranger captains stood at the foot of her dais, facing outwards, blades in their hands. Only four remained, including Maia—three lay on the floor in swiftly spreading pools of their own blood. There, as well, lay two people in guard uniforms. But ten more guards remained on their feet, and they were pressing in towards the rangers with blades drawn.

"Ditra!" I cried.

Her gaze snapped up over the combat to see me. But she could not spare more than a glance, as the guards pressed forwards and the rangers tried desperately to hold them back.

Mag threw her spear before we reached their line. It impaled one guard straight through his chainmail. His hands scrabbled at his back, trying to grasp the thing. Mag reached him a blink later, planted a foot on his back, and dragged the spear out with both hands. Oku lunged, latching onto the leg of one of the other guards. The woman fell, and Oku's jaws crushed her throat.

I had nocked an arrow. As Mag did her bloody work, I fired as fast as I could. Two of the guards fell to my arrows. Maia joined his lord on her dais and found his own bow, and he sank a shot into the eye of a third.

But the other rangers had fallen now. One of the guards leaped for Maia and swung her sword for his face. He managed to block it with his bow, which snapped in half.

The guard dragged a knife from her belt and plunged it into Maia's shoulder. Then his gut.

His eyes went wide. His hands scrabbled for the guard's face. But he only succeeded in gripping her helmet and pulling it off.

Kaita. It was Kaita.

Ditra and I froze in horror at the same time. And then Kaita plunged the dagger into Ditra's chest.

She fell back, striking the chair and then the ground.

"No!" I screamed.

Kaita stepped forwards. She raised her dagger to strike again, to be sure.

The arrow flew from my bow. It pierced straight through her forearm. She cried out and dropped the dagger.

In shock, she looked up and noticed me for the first time. Then her gaze fell upon Mag closer by. There were only four guards left, and even as Kaita watched, Mag slew one of them.

Oku lunged at Kaita, bowling her over, and I heard her scream as his fangs sank into her already-wounded arm. Somehow she managed to throw him off. It gave her just enough time to rise and flee. One of the Shades saw her go, and he tried to follow. Together they ran for the back of the room, to the staircase that would take them up into the keep. Oku went after them, silently, hunting.

I sprinted forwards, already nocking another arrow. I loosed it at a Shade on the dais from only two paces away. Distracted as he was by Mag, he never even saw the shot that killed him. Mag slew the last one a moment later.

"Ditra!" I cried, falling on my knees beside her. I seized her shoulder and pulled her up.

She gave a deep groan, fingers clutching the front of my jerkin.

"Ditra!" I said again, my voice breaking. Sky above, she was alive. I seized her tabard and pulled it aside, trying to see her wound.

I saw only metal glinting up at me. Chain mail. Several of the links were bent and pressed into her flesh, but she would survive.

Lost for words, I could only take her shoulders and pull her into an embrace. But Ditra pushed me away.

"Maia," she said, wincing as she clutched at her chest.

Panic had driven him from my mind. I looked over. He lay on his back, hands and arms twitching as he held the wound in his belly. I helped Ditra over to him.

"Albern," said Mag, her voice toneless. "The weremage."

"Go," I told her. "Find her if you can."

Mag started off as I joined Ditra by Maia's side. But he looked up at me with wild eyes. "Vera."

I felt a sickening lurch in my gut. "No. It is Albern. We are here."

"No," he said. His voice shook with pain, grunting between gasped words. His eyes found Ditra's. "My—lord. Vera."

All the blood drained from Ditra's face. Her hands twitched, wanting to hold Maia, wanting to pull away. She looked wildly from him to the doorway through which Kaita had fled. Still unsure, she looked back down at him.

"Maia—"

"Go!" growled Maia, glaring up at her in fury. "Get—out—of here."

I wagered it was the first time in his life he had ever dared to give her an order. But Ditra obeyed it, bolting for the back of the room. Mag hesitated, looking down at me.

"Go," I said. "Guard her with your life."

Mag nodded and vanished.

The room settled to silence as I knelt by Maia's side. A cloak close at hand was free from bloodstains. I ripped it from the corpse it had adorned and began to tear strips off it.

"Keep holding that wound," I said. "I will stanch the bleeding from your shoulder."

"Vera," he gasped.

Another sickening lurch in my gut. "My name—"

"Not—you." For a moment the pain increased, and he only winced and sucked in deep, desperate breaths. "Vera. Ditra's—daughter. Forgive—me."

My hands stilled, and I could only stare at him for a moment. But I forced my mind back to the task, trying to find any way I could to stop him from continuing to bleed.

"Never mind that now," I said. "Just keep pressing that wound."

"No—good," said Maia, managing a smile. His teeth were bloodstained, and each breath came in a deep, hissing gasp. "Too—deep."

"Stop talking," I ordered.

"Seen—it," said Maia. "Many—times. Too—many." He gave a rasping breath that might have been an attempt at laughter. Flecks of blood came out.

"Dark take you," I growled. The cloth I pressed to his shoulder soaked through with blood in an instant. I turned my attention to his gut wound. "A Rangatira needs her lead ranger. You are not relieved of your duty."

"No—choice," said Maia. "She—needs—"

"What she needs is for you to stop talking," I said. "Lift your hands when I say. Count of four. One—"

He lifted one hand from the wound and seized my wrist, staining my skin red. I met his gaze. His skin had gone deathly pale. A thin bubble of blood protruded from his lips and then burst. Each gasp was shallower, but he forced the words out regardless.

"She—she needs—you—to save—her."

"Mag and the Rangatira have gone after her," I said. "They will see to—to Vera."

He shook his head—he could only move it a finger in each direction. "No. Ditra." I felt his fingers slacken on my wrist. "Ditra."

Slowly, as though he were relaxing into sleep, his head sank back. But his eyes never left me. Not even as I bowed my head over him, and the hall around us settled to silence.

FORTY-ONE

"She killed him?" said Sun.

Albern nodded slowly. "She did."

"Did Mag catch her?"

He shook his head, never taking his eyes from the trail they were following. Or rather, that *he* was following, for Sun could not see it. "She did not. Not then."

"She escaped again?" said Sun, incredulous, her voice rising. "Mag was just behind her!"

"We hesitated a moment too long, after Maia," said Albern. "Mag caught the other Shade that tried to flee. But Kaita took her mountain lion form as soon as she could. She was on the wall and in her raven form before anyone knew what had happened, and then she took wing."

Sun glared into the grass, picturing it in her mind, running it over and over as though by sheer force of will she could change what had happened. "I cannot believe how she kept getting away from you. Did Mag not wish to catch her?"

"Oh, she did," said Albern. "More than you can believe. More than she wanted to save the lives of the people of Kahaunga, certainly. Every time Kaita escaped us, it was sheer luck. If I had not lived it myself, I would not believe it. And though I do not mean to cast an even darker pall over what is already an unhappy tale thus far, I will say this: many, many times have I seen evil people escape judgement, while good people meet an early end. The world should not be that way, but sometimes it is."

"I am no child. I do not believe that everything is always just and right. But dark below, at least tell me that she did not kill your—"

Albern raised a hand. Sun stopped short, glaring at him. "Are you shushing—"

"Please," whispered Albern. "Do not speak for a moment. I think we are drawing close to the end of the trail."

Somewhat mollified, Sun fell silent. Albern's bow was in her hand, and his quiver on her belt. She drew an arrow, holding it nocked and ready.

"Where?" she whispered.

"Not far," he said. "Come. Off the beaten path for a little while."

Sun's face twisted. She could see no trace whatsoever of their prey, and certainly not a beaten path. But she followed Albern as he cut suddenly right, working his way around the southern side of a great hill that rose to a cluster of reddish boulders at the top. It brought them to another hill, which Albern circumvented again. But when they came to a third hill, this time he began to climb. Sun followed, and when Albern began to walk in a half-crouch, she did the same.

They reached the crest of the hill. Two trees grew towards the north end of it, and they snuck up to one of them. A few paces from the edge of the hill, Albern lowered himself to the ground, creeping forwards like a jungle cat stalking through grass. Sun did the same, though she had to restrain herself from moving too quickly—it was easier for her than for Albern, with his missing arm.

Together they sidled up to the edge of the hill and looked down into a small dip in the land. Sun barely restrained a gasp.

A camp sat in the lowest flat point in the land. A motley assortment of disheveled individuals lounged about in various positions of rest, many of them near a campfire with some meat suspended above it. There looked to be a few guards posted, but they were scant paces away from the others, and they sat on rocks or the flat ground. They hardly seemed to be looking out for a squirrel to shoot, much less intruders.

But the center of the camp drew Sun's attention immediately. There she saw a sizable cauldron made of black iron, and full of an even blacker liquid. The sun's final rays only gave it a few hints of any color, and that was a dark red. Beneath the cauldron burned a flame—a flame like Sun had never seen before, black instead of red, with the barest hints of blue and grey flicking at the top of it. A flame that seemed to draw light from the air rather than bestowing it.

"Dark below!" hissed Sun. "That is—"

"Please do be quieter," said Albern.

"That is a cauldron of blood," whispered Sun. "And is that . . . is that darkfire beneath it?"

"It is," whispered Albern.

"Then those people are Shades?"

"No," said Albern. "Not quite. But they have some idea of what the Shades were, and despite that, they are trying to emulate them."

His gaze flicked back and forth across the scene before them. He was surveying the scene, taking stock of the people and the layout of their camp.

"Do . . . do you mean to fight them?"

"Fight might be a strong word," said Albern. "But I do mean to stop them."

"But there are so many. I have never fought in a battle before. I cannot defeat a dozen foes. And you . . ."

"Yes," said Albern, shrugging his right shoulder to highlight his missing arm. "Not exactly the stalwart battle companion you might hope for."

"Then you do not think we can defeat them?"

"Look there." Albern pointed to a crate, close to both the cauldron and the campfire. "A guard on either side of it. And they are the only ones in the whole party who seem alert. I would wager that is where they keep the rest of their magestones."

"We should tell the constables," said Sun.

"Hm," said Albern. "I have another idea. Let us get out of sight and wait until sundown."

They slid back, away from the edge of the hill. Once they were out of sight, Albern rose and walked down the other side of the hill, Sun just behind him.

"The two of us cannot hope to win against them."

He smiled back over his shoulder at her. "There are many ways to win. In Kahaunga, we were well outmatched by the trolls. Yet we had an advantage. One we did not yet realize."

"An advantage?" said Sun.

"Oh yes. If you know something your foe does not, you always have an advantage. Let us get somewhere more private and have a bite to eat. We will take care of these conspirators at dusk. That should give us just enough time to finish this part of the tale. That is, if you want me to go on?"

Sun rolled her eyes and reached for the pouch of food at her belt. "You already know the answer, old man."

FORTY-TWO

After chasing Kaita out of the stronghold, Ditra and Mag returned to the council chamber. When she saw Maia lying dead at the foot of her chair, Ditra looked ready to collapse.

"He died bravely," I murmured.

"Who cares for that?" said Ditra, her voice cracking.

She sank to sit on the stairs of her dais, and I sat close beside her. I wanted to ask about her daughter, but I could not quite bring myself to name her. Not yet. "Did you . . . did you and Mag . . ."

For a moment she only stared at Maia's body, but at last she looked up. "We went after my daughter. Albern, I . . . I named her Vera. I wanted to tell you when . . . you should not have found out like that."

"It is all right," I said at once.

"I missed you," she said, her voice cracking. "And I thought . . . after Romil, and Mother, and when you still did not return . . . I thought I would never see you again."

"Ditra," I said, reaching over and taking her shoulder. "It is all right. I am honored."

She bowed her head. "Well. She is safe. The guards outside her room never even saw the commotion. Kaita may have had plans for her, but she had to abandon them after you showed up."

"That is a comfort, at least."

Ditra looked at Maia's body. "I will call nothing a comfort today. Not today."

Two of her ranger captains had been slain, and the other four had been wounded—two of them grievously. They had been carried off to be attended by healers. That left two in the chamber. They knelt beside Maia's body like an honor guard, their heads bowed over him. Now they tried to rise, but they swayed as they did it.

"No," snapped Ditra. "Sit. I will not have either of you fainting in my council chamber."

The rangers settled back down at our feet, grateful looks upon their faces.

"Thank you, Rangatira."

Ditra rose and went to her chair, bowing her head and covering her eyes with one hand. I looked to Mag, who stood a few paces off. Her expression was stony, but not emotionless. The battle-trance was gone. The look on her face was one of disappointment, of frustration at losing Kaita yet again.

"This is not over," I told her.

"Well do I know it," said Mag.

I nodded and looked up to Ditra. "If you still mean to hold council, might I fetch our friend, Dryleaf? He bears the wisdom of many years, and might have valuable advice."

Ditra did not look up. "Why not? I seem now to have a dearth of councilors." She looked up suddenly. "Where is the king's representative?"

"The thin woman wearing robes of the king's colors? Dead."

"First to fall to the Shades," growled one of the remaining ranger captains.

"Of course she was," said Ditra. She waved a hand at me. "Go and fetch the old man."

I bowed to her and went to retrieve Dryleaf. By the time I returned, Maia's body had been removed from the council chamber. Servants had removed many skins from the floor that had been ruined with blood, and they were scrubbing at the stone beneath, trying to remove the stains. Dryleaf bowed low to Ditra with a fist on his forehead.

"Rangatira," he said. "My most grievous condolences for your loss."

"I thank you for them," said Ditra. "And if I was less courteous the last time you offered such graceful sentiment, please forgive me. Fetch him a—" She looked around the chamber for a moment, seeming lost. "Dark take me, I have no one left to fetch you a chair."

"A moment," I said, ducking out of the room again. I went to the first guard I saw. "The Rangatira needs new guards in her council chamber. Choose half a dozen of them—but make sure you know them intimately well, and ask them questions only they would have the answer to. We have already been infiltrated today."

Rumor of the Shades must have spread fast, for her face went pale, and she nodded. "As you say." She turned to run off. I pointed to the next guard, just a few paces away, who looked as though he had been trying to overhear us.

"You. The Rangatira requires chairs for her council. Fetch . . ." I counted us off on my fingers. "Five of them. The most comfortable ones you can find, but do not take too long."

He nodded and ran to do my bidding at once. I realized in that instant that I had begun talking to the guards as I had spoken to them in my youth. That was a disconcerting thought.

I returned to the council chamber. No one seemed to have moved or spoken since I had left. We waited in silence a while until guards filtered into the room, bearing chairs for us. They set them in a semicircle facing the dais, and then they retreated to stand at the edges of the room. Ditra studied them, likely inspecting their faces to ensure she knew them.

"Very well," said Ditra, leaning forwards. Her rangers straightened. "I suppose we had better begin. These are my ranger captains, Huia and Ihaia, both of the family Taumata."

They rose from their chairs and bowed to us. I rose and bowed in turn, and then gestured to myself and my companions. "I am Albern of the family Telfer. This is Mag, the Uncut Lady, and Dryleaf, our friend."

"Well met. We are honored to meet the Uncut Lady," said Huia. She was a thin but wirily muscled woman. The sides of her hair were trimmed to stubble, while the top was gathered into a tail that ran back and hung down to her shoulder blades. Her face was more tattoo than unmarked skin. She gestured to Ihaia. "My cousin and I were little more than whelps when last you were home. I am glad to see your return."

That put me off for a moment, but I managed to nod. "You have my thanks."

"With that out of the way," said Ditra. "Let us begin. We must defend Kahaunga as long as we can. To do that, it would be helpful to know when the trolls mean to attack."

"Our scouts have been returning with regular reports," said Huia. "The trolls are still looting the city. We think it will be some time before they finish and start to climb the western side of the dale. Normally, I would say we could expect their attack tomorrow, or the next day. Of course, they attacked the city sooner than we expected, so we cannot be certain."

"I suspect they will be spurred to action when the weremage returns to them," I said. "She will be incensed by her failure to kill the Rangatira, and since she has ordered the trolls' attacks thus far, fury might lead her to order them to attack at once."

"How do you know that she—" Ditra bit her own words off and shook her head. "No. You have been right about the weremage thus far. I will trust your council in this."

"Your soldiers know how to fight trolls?" said Dryleaf.

"Our trained soldiers, yes," said Ihaia. "The new arrivals from the city . . . well, they shall have to learn fast."

"It is not too difficult," I said. "Cover the trolls with oil, and use flame upon them. We should tell every guard to repeat those words until they are blue in the face. I wish we could drill it, but I think we will not have the time."

"And we cannot waste any oil," said Ditra. "Our stores are low. The king's army will bring more, but who knows when they will arrive? Our new recruits shall learn it as they do it."

"A trial by fire," I said. The moment the words were out of my mouth, I regretted them—it was just the sort of flippant joke I would have made to my mother when I was a child, inviting her wrath. But to my surprise, and not inconsiderable joy, Ditra gave me the tiniest smile, just as she had when we were young, and she did not want Mother to notice.

"You should send scouts to the north and south as well," said Dryleaf. "Just in case the trolls try to maneuver around Kahaunga and attack your folk who are fleeing upon the road."

"But not too many," I said. "I doubt it will be necessary, for I hardly think that even the Shades could influence the trolls in so subtle a way. They will almost certainly attack the walls. Send your scouts, but only two in each direction."

"As you say," said Ditra. She glanced over at Mag. "You are very quiet. More so than the last time you stood in this chamber. Have you no counsel to give?"

"I think these two have the better advice," said Mag. "I came to Tokana for the weremage, and nothing else."

Ditra's mouth set in a thin line. "Then that is your task in the battle. Kill her, if you get so much as half a chance."

Mag bowed. "As you command, Rangatira."

Ditra nodded. "Very well. That is all for now. Go and see to the orders I have given." She turned to me. "Albern. I wish to speak with you privately."

I hesitated as the others rose and prepared to leave. Ditra must have seen the apprehension on my face, for she shook her head.

"This is not an order. Please, brother."

I relaxed. As her rangers went to issue her orders, and Mag remained with Dryleaf, I followed Ditra up the stairs to the same chamber where we had met last. There was a new bottle of wine on the table, and two cups. She stopped in the middle of the room, staring at them.

"One of those cups was for Maia," she said. "I suppose it is yours, now."

"Thank you," I said. I poured for both of us and sat back, but I did not touch my wine. Ditra, on the other hand, drank half of hers in one gulp. She put it back down upon the table, staring at her own hand as it gripped the glass.

"You were right about Kaita."

"I wish I had not been."

"The past is barren ground for sowing wishes," she said, "and the future is fertile for nothing else."

My brows rose. "I have never heard that wisdom. I doubt you learned it from Mother."

"I did not. It came from my late husband." At last Ditra looked up at me. But far from the pain I had seen there last time, her eyes were filled with a profound sadness, almost mourning. "You should have come back, Albern. When Romil died. You should have come back."

"And what would Mother have said?" I asked her quietly. "How could I have faced her? She, who I could never quite say hated me, but simply . . . did not seem to care. Yet she would have cared, had I returned. Romil would not have died, if not for me. She was only on that pass because she was returning after seeking me out."

"Yes, she was," said Ditra. "That does not mean it was your fault."

"I know that. But Mother . . . she would not have seen it the same way. She would have hated me, then."

Ditra nodded slightly. "You are right. She would have. She did. And without you there to turn her hatred upon, she turned it on me instead, and on herself. She spent nearly every waking moment in the pass, hunting down any Feldemarian who dared to enter our domain, until in the end, they killed her. But not before she had let me know just how useless I was to her, in her time of loss."

I shook my head. "Ditra . . . no one should have suffered that. Least of all you. I am sorry."

"No. That was not your fault, either." She sighed and pushed her chair back a few fingers. "And we have no time to worry about it now, in any case. Kaita will be back. I doubted you before, but no longer. If we are to die here, as might well be the case, I would sooner do it by your side than alone. Will you stand with me?"

I nodded. "I will help you save your people."

"Thank you." It came out as a whisper, though I do not think she intended it to. She took a deep breath, obviously steeling herself. "Albern, I . . . my daughter. Vera. I never knew that you were ander, I would never have . . ."

She trailed off. The sound of the name caused my chest to grow tight. But this was nothing like when Romil had said it to me, on the edges of that sellsword camp, or when I thought Maia had said it to me. This feeling was strange.

Because never, in all the early years I had spent in Tokana, had I ever dreamed that someone would be proud to name their child after me.

"It is a perfect name," I managed to say. "I am sure it suits her beautifully. Better than it ever suited me."

Ditra gave the first full, genuine smile I had seen since my return to Tokana. "It does, at that. I am going to send her with the rest of the refugees, and I must do it soon. But before she goes, would . . . would you like to meet her?"

I felt dangerously close to shattering, so I remained silent. But I nodded. Ditra rose and left the chamber. When she returned, she brought a little girl who could not be older than twelve. The girl's eyes were wide and wonderstruck as she looked up at me.

It was like looking at a painting of myself at her age.

Ditra kept her hand on Vera's shoulder, looking at me with obvious apprehension. I smiled and held out my hand.

"Hello," I said. "I am Albern."

Vera's eyes went wide. She looked up at her mother, who nodded, and then back to me. "You are my uncle," she said in a quiet voice, putting her hand in mine.

"I am."

"Mother says I look just like you used to."

Ditra's hand clenched on her shoulder. "Vera—"

"It is all right," I told her quietly, before smiling at Vera again. "Your mother could not be more right. I only wish we had more time to talk. But you have somewhere to go."

Vera's smile dampened, and her eyes filled with doubt as she looked up at Ditra. "I told her I did not want to leave."

"Yet you must. Your mother is doing what is best for you." I met Ditra's eyes. "Parents always try to do that. Some of them fail. But not your mother."

Vera frowned. But she took a hesitant step forwards, and then another, and then she hugged me about the waist. It startled me, and a long moment stretched before I thought to embrace her in return.

"I am glad I met you, at least," said Vera quietly. "Might we talk more, when we return?"

"I hope so, child. In fact, I promise that we will."

FORTY-THREE

KAITA FLEW TOWARDS THE NORTHERN EDGE OF THE CITY. GREAT SWELLS of warm air rose before her from the flames of Kahaunga's burning buildings, but she flapped anyway, powering her wing muscles with sheer fury.

Why in the dark below was Mag there? she raged in her mind. *They were in prison. Both of them. Again, always again, she robs me of my victory.*

At last she reached the city's northern borders. The Shades had gathered there, only showing themselves after the trolls pressed deep into the city streets. Now they waited, unwary, for the fighting had moved far away. Kaita landed in their midst and shed her raven form, even as many Shades stepped away from her in alarm.

"Report," she snarled, as soon as she had the mouth to speak the word.

Phelan, her captain, stepped forth, looking only slightly unnerved by her transformation. "We are ready to strike on your order, Comm—"

"Not my order," snapped Kaita. "I will not be here to command you, and so I leave it to you. Take our forces to the western end of the city. The moment you see the trolls attack, join them at once. You know where to strike to put our numbers to best effect."

"Yes, Commander," said Phelan. "Our soldiers are prepared. We have brought ladders and—"

"I *know* what you have brought!" roared Kaita. "I created the plan, and it is almost complete. Tonight we wipe the family of Telfer from the face of the world. Now move!"

His face reddened, but Kaita had ceased paying attention. She stalked south, away from the camp. Before she had even finished passing through their ranks, her eyes glowed, and her form began to shift again. Shades cried out and dived aside as she suddenly grew gigantic. Grey, stone-solid skin swept across her, and her ears turned to giant flaps that swept out from her head.

In a moment the transformation was complete, and she had taken Gatak's shape. She broke into a troll's gallop, thundering out of sight of the Shades on all fours to vanish into the city. She had never taken her troll shape where the other Shades could see. If the trolls ever discovered her secret, the whole plan would come apart. But everything was nearing completion now. Even if there was a traitor among the Shades, they would not have enough time to tell the trolls before the battle would be over.

She began to spot trolls amid the wreckage of Kahaunga's buildings. They were picking through the destruction, searching for food. The first time she spotted one, she stopped and bared her teeth at him.

"Come. We are readying for the attack. Dotag needs all the pack."

The troll scowled at her, its ears rising. "He said we could rest and eat."

"And now he needs us," said Kaita. "You are of his pack. Come."

She gathered every troll she could find as she went, until soon there were at least two dozen trailing along behind her, though none walked with quite her speed or purpose. She searched for the front lines of the gathered pack. There she would find Dotag. A pack leader had to *lead.* Dotag had been in the thick of the fighting when they had attacked the city, and he would be there again when they assaulted the Telfer stronghold.

At last she spotted him, in a large square towards the city's western end. A great pile of produce and bread had been put before him, tributes from trolls in the pack who looked to curry favor. Dotag was picking at the pile, searching for the choicest morsels to eat first. He looked rather ragged—there was a tear in his left ear that had not been there that morning, and there were burn marks on his right flank. Kaita even saw some broken skin on his right shoulder. A very large building must have fallen on him for that to happen. Kaita ignored it and stalked up to him. Dotag noticed her at the last second, and his ears dipped in pleasure—but they flew sideways in alarm as Kaita pressed her face close to his.

"We have rested long enough." She thrust a stubby finger up the long slope rising to the west. "The humans have gathered in their fortress. Now is the time to tear it down and kill them all."

Dotag very nearly looked frightened of her. "We do not need to attack now," he said. "They have run from their city. They know we have won."

"We have to kill them!" roared Kaita. "They have broken the pact!"

"So have we," came Apok's voice.

Kaita snarled and turned. The younger troll stood at the edge of the square, her stony, angry gaze fixed on Dotag.

"I speak to Dotag," snarled Kaita. "Not to you."

"And you tell him that the humans broke the pact," said Apok, stalking forwards. "Yet we have attacked their city. We have killed them. That, too, breaks the pact."

"Only after they did it first."

"What, then?" said Apok. "Do we kill more? They will bring their armies. They will bring oil and fire. Already today they killed many of us. The pack lost more trolls today than it did in all the years Chok led us."

"Because more trolls follow Dotag than ever followed Chok," said Kaita. "Dotag is a great leader."

"He leads more of us, and he leads more of us to die," said Apok. "The humans will drive us out of this city, and then they will drive us farther. Beyond the bounds of the pact. Even out of the mountains. Will you call that victory?"

Dotag looked more uncertain than ever. Kaita whirled on him. "The Telfers," she said. "They are the ones who broke their word. Do whatever you want after they are dead. But you cannot allow them to live after breaking the pact. The Lord wishes them to be dealt with."

"Trolls do not follow your human lord," growled Apok, taking another step forwards. "Trolls fight for ourselves. We follow ourselves. I think you have left for so long that you have forgotten."

Kaita could feel herself close to the breaking point. But if she attacked Apok, even Dotag would not be able to protect her from the other trolls in the pack.

The pack. Inwardly, Kaita grinned. Apok might speak against her, but she could not speak against Dotag without repercussions.

"I follow Dotag," said Kaita. "He leads the pack, not I. Do you challenge him?"

Apok hesitated. It was a long, uncomfortable moment in the square before she spoke, but Kaita knew she had already won.

"No," said Apok.

"Then be silent." Kaita turned back to Dotag and lowered her voice. "We have the Telfers trapped. Apok is right about one thing. The humans will bring their armies. They will bring their fire. But if we kill the Telfers, no human will ever dare to break the bonds of the pact."

Still Dotag did not look entirely convinced. He pawed at the pavement of the town square, eyeing the pile of bread and produce before him. "We have gone far enough for now. Many have died. More are hurt. We need to rest."

"We *need* to kill them," said Kaita, her voice rumbling with fury. "They will never leave these mountains until we throw them out. You lead this pack now. You must be strong. You must protect us from the humans. And you must do it *now*. The Lord will reward you for it."

Dotag looked more reluctant than ever. But he tore his gaze away from the pile of food before him, looking up towards the western rim of the valley. At last he turned to the other trolls in the square.

"We attack." Dotag tried to make his voice loud and commanding, but it rasped, weary from all his roaring during the battle earlier. "Gather the pack. We will destroy the humans' home. We will rest when they are all dead."

The trolls lumbered off to do his bidding. Dotag turned to Kaita, his expression full of doubt. But Kaita only smiled.

FORTY-FOUR

Maia's body was burned in the center of the stronghold's bailey with everyone in attendance. Ditra had Vera off to one side of her, and I stood to the other. When the flames began to subside, Ditra sent Vera away to join the rest of the refugees. With her went a dozen guards for protection. I could not help but think that a dozen more soldiers would be useful in the coming battle, but I said nothing. Ditra had to know it. But if we died, then Vera would be the last remnant of our line.

Not that it seemed to make much difference to Ditra's soldiers. At first she asked for volunteers, but no one stepped forwards. I was shocked, until I realized the soldiers did not see the assignment as an honor—they saw it as fleeing from the fight. It astounded me, and I could not help but wonder if they would have been so eager to stay and die at their lord's side if my mother had still been the Rangatira.

In the end, Ditra had to order a dozen of them to leave with Vera. The first tried to argue. She subsided when Ditra asked her if she thought Vera's life was not worth saving—in which case Ditra would happily strip her of rank and send her out to face the trolls first. After that, she and the others went along quite meekly, if not exactly willingly.

Mag and I faced much the same resistance when we told Dryleaf to leave the city as well. The old man flatly refused until we threatened to tie him up and stick him in the back of a wagon. He could not help in a fight, and though his counsel was valuable, the time for advice was long past. We sent Oku with him. The hound trotted along at the heels of Dryleaf's horse, looking back at Mag and I often. For once, he did not seem to understand what was going on, and it nearly broke my heart.

With Vera seen to, and all the other preparations at the stronghold underway, Ditra's remaining rangers and I convinced her to rest. She retired to her chamber to sleep, but not before assigning a servant to find lodgings for Mag and me. "If I am being forced to sleep until the battle, then I will force you to do the same," she said.

I was more than happy to obey. The battle in the city had not lasted long—certainly not as long for me as it had been for Ditra—but I was exhausted to the point of collapse. When they showed me to my bed, I paused only long enough to stow my bow and sword before I fell upon the mattress, fully clothed. I have some vague sense that Mag came into my room just before sleep claimed me. If she meant to talk, she left disappointed.

The blast of a horn woke me in an instant. I had slept for three hours, but it felt like no time at all. Groggy, I belted my sword on and slung my bow across my back, stumbling from the room to find Mag waiting for me.

"Did you sleep?" I said, my speech slurred with weariness.

"A bit," she said. Her words were clear, and her eyes looked as sharp as ever. "Less than you, though yours looks to have done you less good."

I waved her words away. "Leave off. Let us go to Ditra."

We found her on the eastern wall, looking into the dale below. The night sky was dark above us, but the landscape was fairly well lit by the fires that still burned in the city, which reflected off the pall of black smoke hanging in the air. A chill wind blew hard into our faces, and I pulled my cloak tighter as I shivered. Ditra looked up at our approach and gave us a stiff nod.

"They are coming."

I squinted down into the darkness. The burning city cast a tint across the world, so that everything was only visible in shades between black and crimson. But I saw no signs of movement down below, no indication of the trolls at all.

"Where?" I said.

"My scouts reported it," said Ditra. "Rest assured, they will be here soon."

"That prospect urges neither rest nor assurance."

Mag laughed and clapped my shoulder, probably a bit harder than she had to. "Relax, Albern. I will be here to keep you safe."

Despite herself, I saw a smile tugging at the corner of Ditra's mouth. "Yes, see that you do, will you? I have waited for the fool to return home for quite some time. It would be a tragic shame to lose him now."

"Like an old pet," said Mag, brightening immediately.

"I am *not—*"

"Yes, exactly," said Ditra, and now she could not stop the grin from spreading across her face.

I subsided, glowering into the darkness of the dale. But despite my objections, the smile on Ditra's face was worth any amount of jibes aimed at me.

Her good mood faded as she returned to business. "You will want pitch arrows," she told me. "There are many stored along the wall. Fill your quiver. There are torches and braziers, too, which you can use to light them." She turned to Mag. "I take it from the spear in your hand that you are not much of an archer."

"Not much of one, no," said Mag.

"You will want oil, then," said Ditra. "Your spear will be little help other than as a distraction. Carry a few flasks on your belt. If you can soak a troll with oil, that will let the archers take care of them. The flasks are stowed near the arrows."

"As you say, Rangatira." Mag bowed to her and went to fetch them. I stared at her retreating back, scowling. Finally I caught Ditra giving me an amused look, and I turned the scowl upon her.

"She keeps bowing to you."

Ditra smirked. "She bowed to me when you all first arrived."

"When she was trying to deceive you," I said. "The last few times, it has been genuine."

"I consider it a great honor to receive such courtesy from the Uncut Lady herself."

Together we peered out into the darkness, searching for the first sign of our foes. "They are coming sooner than we thought. I had hoped they would rest."

Ditra shrugged. "We did not think they would attack the city at all for at least another week. It is the Shades' doing." Her expression grew grim. "It is Kaita's."

"We must look for her in the battle," I said. "If she falls . . ."

Ditra shook her head. "I have little hope that that will stop them. She may be spurring the trolls on, but she seems to be doing so from the rear. And even if we fell her, the trolls do not follow humans. They have been persuaded to make up their minds, and that will not change simply because one human dies on the battlefield."

"It might make me feel better, at least," I muttered.

She sighed, frowning down at her feet. "I suppose I agree."

"Her actions were not your doing," I said.

"I kept Maia from working with you, as he wished to do. I wanted to make it right with her somehow . . . after what Mother did, I mean."

"That was a kind and just thing to do."

"But not a wise thing to do," she said.

"I doubt we would have found her even with Maia's help. And I would not have trusted unsworn strangers from another land any more than you did."

Ditra considered that for a moment, and then she shook herself. "Well, we can never repeat the past. There is only the present, and whatever future remains to us."

"If we can hold until the king sends their army . . ."

"That is doubtful. We have never seen more than a dozen or so trolls at a time. We managed to kill a few in the city, but there are still nearly two hundreds of them, and I have scarcely twice that number of soldiers at my command."

"But you have your walls," I told her. "They were built to withstand trolls."

"Nothing can withstand them forever."

Something in her tone worried me. For a moment I forgot that she was the Lord Telfer, that she was, by rights, my Rangatira. For a moment I saw only my sister. I reached out and gently took her shoulder.

"Ditra. You cannot give up."

She did not look at me. "I will not surrender to them, if that is what you mean."

"I mean you cannot give up hope."

"Hope," she snorted. "I have been so ill acquainted with it for so many years that I no longer know what it looks like. And how am I to be reminded now, when the night is dark and an unstoppable foe lurks just beyond the doorstep? I am Lord Ditra of the family Telfer, Rangatira of Tokana. It looks as though we will be the last of Mother's children to fall. If you had remained in Strapa, that might have left me with some small hope—the idea that you could return and take my place. But if one of us falls tonight, we both shall."

"There is always Vera," I said. "And I never thought I would return here at all. No one knows what fortune may bring."

"Nor whether it will be kind or cruel." At last she met my eyes and smiled, but I could see that it was mostly for show. She reached out and gripped my shoulder. "Go and fetch yourself some arrows. Be ready for the call to retreat—if they take the walls, we will fall back to the keep. Above all, look after yourself. I do not know if we can survive this battle. But if we can, I expect you to emerge on the other side of it."

"I can only promise that I will try," I told her. "But then, I have been trying to stay alive for a good long while now, and I have managed it so far."

"Then take this as an order from your Rangatira: stay alive tonight."

"Only if you do the same." I bowed, and then I stepped forwards to place my forehead against hers, the act of greeting and farewell between family.

We parted, me to fetch my arrows, and her to see to the last arrangements of defense. Soldiers gathered atop the eastern gate and all along its wall, with only a token force left to the western defenses. Shades or no, we did not suspect the trolls would suddenly show a gift for strategy. They had not done so in any of the towns they had attacked. They would throw themselves at the first thing they saw—the eastern wall—and break it.

And why not? We cannot stop them. We cannot even hold them back for all that long.

I stamped that thought down at once. One thing I knew, at least, from my many years as a sellsword: things only become hopeless when you decide to abandon hope.

FORTY-FIVE

THE TROLLS APPROACHED THE STRONGHOLD OUT OF THE DARKNESS, silhouetted by the fires in the city. They gathered well within arrow range, but we loosed no shots. Arrows would be pointless against their stony hides—pointless until they approached close enough to strike with oil, and then flaming arrows.

Every soldier on the wall remained stock still, gazing out at our gathering foe. I cannot speak for the rest of them, but my heart was filled with fear. Trolls had been a story of terror for me since I was a child. They had killed many of the people I had once called mine. And before the night was over, I was sure they would kill many more.

Nearly a hundred archers lined the wall. Besides the bows in their hands, they had stores of oil flasks ready to throw. We expected the gatehouse to be the focus of the trolls' assault. There were two gates, both made of wood reinforced with a grid of thick steel bands. We would defend the outer gate as long as we could, but that would not last long. Once the trolls broke through into the gatehouse, there were great cauldrons of oil ready to pour atop them through murder holes. The second gate would be sturdier, for there were three dozens of soldiers in the bailey ready to bolster it. They were each equipped with bracers, long iron poles like spears, but with flat metal plates at the end instead of pointed spearheads. They would hold the plates against the gate and step on the other end, like infantry preparing for a cavalry charge.

As I looked upon the massive limbs of the trolls arranging themselves before us, I wondered how long the second gate would last.

Ditra joined me above the gatehouse as the trolls looked to be finishing their preparations. Her expression was grim as she surveyed them.

"There is the leader." She pointed to a large troll at the head of the pack. He was not quite so large as I had feared, but he was clearly in charge. The other trolls moved around him, keeping an eye on him if they were close, as though ready to move out of his way, or to follow him if he began the advance. As I watched, he slammed his fists into the ground and gave a loud, barking command.

But then my eyes were drawn to the troll just beside him. I did not know trolls very well, but I thought this one was female. And she did not treat the leader like the others did. She barely seemed to notice him. Instead, her gaze was fixed unswervingly upon the wall, and upon the keep behind it. It seemed strange behavior, and it stuck out in my mind.

My thoughts were pulled back to the present as the trolls charged. Roaring with fury, they crossed the open ground with great, bounding leaps. I could feel the thunder of their coming reverberate through the stone wall beneath my feet. My fingers tightened on my bow, and I fingered the oil flask in my right hand.

"Ready!" Ditra's sergeants echoed her cry along the wall. The troops held their flasks aloft.

The trolls drew close. Now we could see the rage in their eyes. They drew within thirty paces of the wall. Then twenty. I wagered I could throw that far, but no command came. I glanced at Ditra from the corner of my eye. She held steady. The trolls drew within ten paces.

"Throw!"

A hundred flasks of oil arced through the air. Their glass glittered in the light of our braziers.

"Loose!"

I had nocked the second I let go of the flask, and now I fired my flaming arrow straight at it. It shattered, flinging its flaming contents into the face of an unlucky troll right next to the leader. The troll stumbled and fell, screaming. His fellows ran straight over him, pressing him deeper and deeper into the snowy mud. It did not seem to harm him, but only to stifle the flames.

Fire had ripped into the troll's front line. Dozens of them reeled away from the wall. They screamed in pain and tried to batter the blazes that roasted them. But more trolls pushed forwards, slamming into the wall. Fists as large as my torso slammed into the stone. The wall shook, but it held.

Some trolls scrambled up the backs and shoulders of their companions, leaping for the ramparts. Soldiers dropped their bows and hacked at the trolls' hands with steel. Ditra gave a great cry and raised her axe as a stubby hand appeared in front of her. The weapon was called Uira, and it was an heirloom of our house. It flashed with runic light as she brought it down, cleaving straight through the troll's forefinger. The creature fell back to the ground with a roar.

They had massed below us at the front gate. Their leader was off to the side, fighting to push through his pack and reach the gate. I threw a flask at him, but he saw it and batted it aside, where it shattered over the face of another troll. Flaming arrows streaked through the darkness, and fresh bursts of fire exploded over the trolls' heads and shoulders. They surged back. For a moment I thought they might turn and run. But their leader gave a great roar and pressed forwards, slamming his fists into the gate. The others gained new heart, and they crashed into it with all their fury.

It shattered with the sound of splintering wood and rending metal. The trolls poured into the gatehouse and straight into the second gate. It rocked on its hinges, but the soldiers in the bailey held. More trolls crowded into the space, though only a dozen could fit. The leader held his ground rather than enter the gatehouse.

Ditra turned to her soldiers atop the barbican. "Oil!" she roared.

The soldiers seized their cauldrons and heaved. The iron turned on great wooden wheels. I ran forwards to lend a hand, seizing the bottom of a vat and lifting with all my might. Soldiers thrust torches into the oil as it came pouring out, and a wave of blistering heat washed across my face.

Flaming oil poured down over the trolls like the spewing of a volcano. I saw one of them look up just as it came pouring down. Oil flooded her face, pouring down her throat. She fell to the ground, clawing at herself. It lasted only a moment before she stilled forever.

The oil coated everyone else who had entered the gatehouse, killing most in seconds. The others fled back into the open air, slamming into the rest of the pack, smearing them with flames. The trolls' lines shuddered and began to draw back. I saw the first few begin to turn and run, and then it was like a bursting dam. As one they pounded away from the wall, separating themselves to avoid spreading the fire any more. Some did not make it back, the oil and flames claiming them before they could make it more than a few paces away from the wall. The trolls ran out to beyond throwing range again, lurking on the edge of darkness, pacing back and forth and licking their wounds.

Ditra was only a few paces away. Both of us were covered in sweat, leaning heavily against the wall. Her helm had come off sometime during the battle. I saw it two paces away and went to fetch it for her.

"Thank you," she gasped as I placed it in her hand.

Mag approached. She strode between the soldiers who had collapsed in exhaustion against the wall, and she looked for all the world as if she were taking a stroll through the woods. She raised two skins in her hands.

"I have brought water."

Ditra and I each took a skin from her and drank greedily. It was not quite cold, but it was a good deal cooler than the heat atop the wall, drifting up from the pools of burning oil and the flaming corpses of trolls below the wall.

"How did the gatehouse fare?" said Mag.

"Better than it could have," I said.

Ditra's mouth gave a grim twist as she pulled the helm on. "We do not have enough oil to refill the cauldrons. We will have only flasks and arrows when they return. How did the fighting go farther along the wall?"

Mag frowned slightly. "We lost some soldiers. The trolls flung rocks at them from below. I feel useless up here. All I could do was stab their fingers when they tried to climb up, like a wasp attacking a bear."

"Enough wasps can ruin a bear's day," I said.

She pointed out into the darkness. “That only works if there are many wasps and just one bear. This is quite the reverse.”

“Yet even one sting can hurt. Mayhap they will give up and flee home.”

Ditra arched an eyebrow. “That is a poor joke, brother.”

I shrugged. “What other kind is there, on a night like tonight?”

Kaita, still in the form of Gatak, stalked up to Dotag. His right arm was curled up to his chest, and he probed gently at a nasty burn he had received in the fight around the gatehouse. As she approached, Dotag looked up, and Kaita was troubled by his resentful look.

“We have rested long enough,” she said. “We must attack again, before they have time to regroup.”

“Many died,” said Dotag. “We are not ready.”

“They cannot stop us,” said Kaita. “Some died, but we have many more.”

“The gate,” said Dotag. “They burned us. None will go back in there again.”

“That was most of the oil they had,” said Kaita. “They will not be able to pour such fire down upon you again.”

“How do you know that?” said Apok, whom Kaita had not noticed standing close by. Burns covered most of her chest, but her eyes were sharp, and she looked upon Kaita with suspicion.

“What?” snarled Kaita.

“How do you know of the humans’ oil, Gatak?”

“The Lord has told me,” said Kaita. “He knows many secrets. He has much power. He knows we will win.”

“I think your Lord is a meddling human,” rumbled Apok. “A human who wishes to control us.”

Kaita took a lunging step forwards and smashed her fists into the dirt. “You dare to speak ill of him?”

“Gatak!”

She froze at Dotag’s voice. He was scowling when she turned back to him. Immediately Kaita dropped her ears and stooped, making sure she stood almost a pace shorter than he.

“You may trust my words, Dotag,” she said soothingly. “The Lord assures our victory.”

Dotag gave a *snuff.* He looked uncertainly up at the stronghold wall, and then looked past Kaita to Apok.

"Why do you look at her?" said Kaita. "She would have us all turn and flee from this place. She would not have us take these mountains for our own. Does she lead the pack, or do you?"

"He does," growled Apok. "Not me. Not you."

But this was too much for Dotag. He pounded a fist on the ground. "I lead. We attack again." He glared past Kaita to Apok. "I will attack the gate myself. And you will come with me."

Apok's nostrils flared, but she ducked her head and turned away. Dotag grunted and turned to Kaita. He spoke in a lower voice, so low that only she could hear.

"You said the other humans would help us. Where were they?"

Kaita ducked her head. "They could not reveal themselves. We had to break the outer gate. Now that that is done, they will lend their strength to ours. You will take the wall, and then kill everyone inside."

Dotag's eyes narrowed. "You did not say that before."

Kaita suppressed a momentary surge of anger, that a troll would think himself worthy of questioning her counsel. But of course she could not say that. "I told you they would help us take the inner gate. That is what they will do."

He stared at her a long moment. Kaita met his gaze, unflinching. At last Dotag snorted and turned away.

"Tell the others. We attack. Now."

FORTY-SIX

It felt as though we had had barely a moment's respite before the trolls charged again. New soldiers had taken the place of those who fell on the wall, but everyone looked weary enough to fall over. I felt the same.

We rained oil and fire down upon the trolls as soon as they came in range. But they were better prepared this time, and they leaped aside or batted at the vials. Still we scored many hits, and their rending screams cut the air.

Once again they swarmed the gatehouse. This time Mag had joined us atop it. She flung a perfectly timed vial of oil, and I lit it, and our unlucky victim's wild flailing stalled the charge of many behind him. Even so, half a dozen trolls burst into the gatehouse. We ran to the murder holes, throwing flasks and firing flame at them as best we could. Their roars of pain shook the wall, but without the overwhelming torrent of oil we had had last time, they only seemed spurred to greater fury. They flung themselves at the second gate like mad beasts. Dents appeared in the solid steel banding.

One of the trolls at the back of the group could not reach the gate.

She looked up through the murder holes with eyes full of hate. Then a soldier leaned too far over. The troll vaulted upwards. Her hand reached through the opening to seize the guard's head and drag him down into the darkness. His body cracked and popped sickeningly as it was forced through the narrow gap, but his screams were swiftly cut off as the troll battered him against the ground below.

"Stay back!" commanded Ditra. She ran to the back of the barbican, looking down upon the soldiers in the bailey who were still bracing the second gate. "Hold! Hold them! They cannot—"

I heard a whistling on the air. The sound of many arrows. On instinct, I shouted, "Down!" and dived to tackle Ditra to the floor.

But the arrows had not been aimed at us. They fell upon the soldiers in the bailey. I looked up in confusion, and then I heard shouting from the west wall. Peering through the gloom, by the light of torches I saw soldiers in blue and grey swarming along the ramparts there. They had swords on their belts and shields on their backs, but in their hands were bows. Even now they were preparing another volley to loose upon the soldiers in the courtyard. Behind them, I could just glimpse bits of shining metal—grappling hooks, and the tops of siege ladders.

"They have flanked us!" I cried. "Shades from the west!"

Ditra looked down. Corpses littered the stone. Barely a dozen soldiers still braced the second gate, and they were wavering.

She cried out to the soldiers around us. "The walls have been taken, and the gate will follow! Back! Back to the keep!"

They took up the cry all up and down the wall, and the soldiers turned in a rout. I stayed by Ditra's side, wishing she would move faster. But she pushed everyone else ahead of her, determined to be the last to leave the wall. We ran down the southeast battlements and turned down the stretch that would lead us to the keep door. Every living soldier in the bailey had fled, and now the second gate was crumpling under the trolls' onslaught. Even as I watched, it shattered. In three pieces it fell, skittering away on stone that was slick with melted snow, now tinged red with blood.

"Albern!"

Mag's toneless cry brought my attention back to the wall. I heard a coarse rasping, like two stones grinding against each other. The hand of a troll had appeared over the top of the ramparts. They had circled around to the south, and one was climbing up now. A huge, stony head appeared before us.

We attacked it at the same time, but Mag got there first. Her spear plunged into its eye socket, and I saw the jolt in Mag's arm as she struck the skull. As the troll screamed, I hacked at its hand with my sword. Still it did not let go—not until Ditra brought her axe down, and its enchantments hewed the troll's hand in half. The creature roared as it fell away into darkness.

"Thank you," I said, gripping Ditra's shoulder.

"You would have done it yourself, if you held the axe," said Ditra. "But you are welcome."

"I had *some* hand in it as well," grumbled Mag. But her words were lost in the din as we passed through the door and into the keep. The door was iron, and inside it had great iron bolts, thick as my arm, which we slid into place. Not even a troll would be able to break them down, and they were unlikely to try, since they could not fit inside.

We made our way quickly to the main entry hall. Some wise soul had gathered as many bracers as they could from the bailey, and now a dozen Telfer guards stood at the great main doors, bracing them against entry. But I heard no sounds of assault from outside.

Ditra caught sight of Captain Huia. "Have they moved towards the keep yet?"

Huia drew up straight, though she looked ready to fall over both from weariness and the nasty cut below her temple, slicing through her close-shaved hair and soaking her short braid with blood. "No, Rangatira. We are mustering every soldier we have left into this room."

"Post two at each wall door," said Ditra. "The trolls cannot break them, but the Shades may have some trickery left. And see to your wound." She turned to Mag and me. "With me."

We followed her to a circular side stairway that led to the keep's upper floors. She passed them one after the other until we finally emerged onto the roof of the keep, more than fifteen paces above the floor of the bailey—too high for the trolls to throw stones at us. We went to the battlements and looked down.

The trolls were again regrouping, nursing their wounds and preparing for another charge. They were close, pressing together in the bailey, while still more tried to force their way in through the gatehouse. Our only way out was through the keep's front door, and they had it blocked. They were close to victory now, and they knew it. They growled and roared, slamming their hands into the ground and cracking cobblestones.

"They will not wait as long this time," I said.

"They did not wait very long last time," said Mag.

"Their leader," said Ditra. "Where is he?"

I pointed. "There." He stood in the midst of the pack, pacing back and forth, a few steps each way, growling and leering at the keep door like it was a rival come to challenge him.

"Out of our reach, from up here," said Mag.

"I could stick him with an arrow," I said. "It might annoy him."

"Yes, it would please me to know he will be irritated when he breaks in the door and kills us all," mused Ditra.

Mag met my gaze. "What would happen if we brought him down? When they break down the door, you and I try to slay him. I can land the oil if you strike him with the arrows."

I looked to Ditra. "Rangatira?"

She mulled it over. "Even if he dies, I do not think they will simply turn and walk away from the city. But if they at least withdraw from the keep, and take the time to establish a new pack leader . . . it could delay them a day or two. That might give the king's army time to arrive, if indeed they are on their way."

"And if they are not?" said Mag.

Ditra looked grim. "It might give us time to withdraw. We have given the refugees enough time. The trolls care only about the mountains. They will not chase us into the lowlands. It would mean giving Kahaunga up for lost, but that is better than letting everyone die."

Only a week ago, I would have agreed without question. But now, the prospect of retreat filled me with a wild, unreasoning rage. If we fled, we would not only give up the city. We might lose our best chance to kill Kaita since Northwood. I strode to the edge of the balcony.

"Albern?" said Ditra, alarmed.

I drew an arrow, nocked, and loosed. It plunged through the air, striking the line between stones in the bailey just at the foot of the troll's leader. He jumped at the sound, looking down at the arrow in confusion. It was a long moment before he put it together, and his gaze snapped up to see me atop the keep.

"I am Albern of the family Telfer!" I called down to him. "Turn away from here. Go back to your homes. Go back to the borders of the pact."

He bared his teeth at me. "I am Dotag!" he roared, standing to his full height. "I lead the pack. I do not listen to humans."

"Your pack did once," I said. "Go back to the border."

"You broke the pact long before we did," said Dotag. "I will not listen to you now."

"Humans did break the pact, but we never harmed your people. And you do not fight us now because of the pact. You say you do not listen to humans, but you are spurred on by the Shades. They are treacherous. They have used you to attack us, but they will betray you, as they have done to others. I have traveled three kingdoms in pursuit of them, and you cannot trust them."

"We serve no humans!" roared Dotag. "We will never listen to you! Your words mean nothing to us!"

I frowned—but not at Dotag. My attention had moved past him, to the female troll who still lurked by his side. She was not paying the slightest attention to her leader, as the other trolls were. Instead she looked straight at me. The expression of hatred upon her face was almost human.

But my thoughts were pulled back to Dotag as he rounded on the rest of the pack. "We will never serve humans!" he bellowed. "Tear their home to the ground! Kill all you find inside!"

They stampeded towards the door, Dotag leading the way. The female troll was swept along in the tide. They pressed up against the sides of the keep.

"Dark take them," said Ditra. "To the hall! We must try to bring him down."

She ran for the trapdoor leading back into the keep, and Mag was just behind her. But I paused at the battlements for a moment, looking down. To this day, I could not tell you what made me stay, but I did.

A hail of oil vials crashed along the troll's ranks, flung from arrow slits. Flaming arrows came just behind, sending a blast of fire across them. The trolls recoiled, stumbling back from the keep for a moment.

I seized the merlon, leaning forwards, my eyes wide.

The flames struck the troll by Dotag's side, and she recoiled with the others. But she bent her head away, out of sight, and I saw a flash. Magelight. And the flesh that had been struck by flames now stitched itself together before my eyes.

I turned and ran from the battlement. The trapdoor still hung open, and I dived into it, running down the stairs and through the rest of the keep. At the front of the main hall, soldiers were leaning on the bracers, holding the door shut as long as they could. There came a great, shattering crash as a troll threw itself against the doors. I reached Mag and Ditra just at the entrance to the main hall, and I seized Mag's shoulder to pull her around.

"Kaita!" I cried. "The female troll lurking near the leader. She is Kaita in disguise."

Mag stared at me in wonder. Ditra turned at my words, astonished.

"How do you—"

"Fire struck her, and she used her magic to heal herself," I said. "It was only a flash, but I saw it. It is her."

There came a great *crack* as timbers began to splinter on the keep door. Through a hole in the iron grid, I saw a troll's eye peeking through.

Mag's face went stony as the battle-trance settled over her. "Then I will kill her."

"We cannot. You have to expose her."

"Killing her *will* expose her, Albern," said Ditra. "If a weremage is killed, they take their true form."

"She hangs back from the fighting," I told Mag. "You might get close enough to strike her, but I cannot. But there is Tuhin's trick. The one they showed us in Opara."

Mag's face remained impassive. "I remember."

"Use it. Force her to resume her human form in front of the trolls. She has been goading them all along. They have followed her advice because they think she is one of their own. When they realize a Shade has been deceiving them the whole time—"

A thunderous crash rocked the keep as the doors shattered inwards. Timbers and bands of iron went flying, flinging soldiers away from the door. Dotag flew into the open space at the front of the hall, roaring his hatred. Trolls tumbled in behind him—and among them was Kaita.

"Push them back!" cried Ditra, raising her axe and running forwards. "Fire! Fire!"

Flasks of oil came flying from all directions. A brazier stood next to me against the wall, and I lit and loosed. Flame erupted among the trolls. But they were too enraged now to let that stop them. They seized any Telfer soldier they could get their hands on, flinging them into walls, smashing them against the floor, or simply squeezing them until their bodies broke.

But they could not touch Mag.

She had sprung towards them as soon as the doors caved in. Now she vaulted and leaped off a woman's shoulders. Dotag froze in shock as she flew straight towards his massive head. But she landed on his shoulder and jumped again.

Kaita saw her at the last instant. Her wide troll's eyes filled with fear, and she scrambled desperately to try and escape the keep. Even in a troll's form, she was too afraid of Mag to face her in battle. But the crowd of trolls was too thick, and she could not flee.

Mag landed in the midst of them. A troll attacked from either side, trying to seize her, to smash her, to fling her away. She rolled under the grasping hands of one, and leaped over the swipe of another.

She cast aside her spear and shield, landed on one of her assailant's oak-thick arms, and jumped straight for Kaita's terrified face.

I could see nothing else in the hall. The world seemed frozen for a moment. I can remember it now as clear as anything—Mag's fluttering cloak, and Kaita trying desperately to evade her.

Then Mag swept her fists forwards and struck. One fist crashed into each temple, just where Tuhin had showed us in Opara.

Kaita screamed, a deep, guttural roar that echoed through the hall. Magelight poured from her eyes, bright as a beacon fire, lighting the ceiling and walls.

The trolls' assault shuddered to a stop. At their head, Dotag turned and looked upon Kaita in confusion. And as trolls and humans alike watched, frozen in place, Kaita shrank, withered, and became human once more, to fall stunned at Mag's feet.

FORTY-SEVEN

Everyone in the hall, human or otherwise, seemed to be waiting for someone to say something—to explain, to denounce Kaita, anything. Instead, the only sound was a slight scrape of metal on stone as Mag fetched her spear, and then stooped to haul Kaita up by the back of her neck. She turned the weremage to face Dotag, holding the haft of the spear across the weremage's throat.

"A weremage," she said loudly, so that every troll could hear. "A human. She has prodded you into this fight. She has led you to go far beyond the pact boundary, to attack the family Telfer. She has been using you."

Ditra saw her chance and stepped forwards. "This was a base, dishonorable trick," she said. "This woman has harmed both our people equally. We have both lost many of our own here today. But we need not fight any longer, now that we see our common foe."

But Dotag ignored both of them. He only stared at Kaita in shock, his shoulders drooping, his mouth hanging agape. He took one slow, hesitant step forwards. And then he spoke, in the troll's language, which I could not understand. But others in the hall knew it, and they told me later what he and the other trolls said in the moments that followed, and so I will render it to you now.

"Gatak," he said. "Gatak, what trickery is this?"

"Not Gatak," said Ditra, for she knew the troll tongue. "Kaita. Her name is Kaita."

Dotag barely seemed to hear her. "You pretended. You pretended to be one of us."

Kaita, for her part, did not seem to be even slightly interested in Dotag's horror. Her eyes darted everywhere, wild, terrified at Mag's grip upon her, desperate to find some way to escape.

"Answer me!" roared Dotag, so loud that I jumped.

That seemed to snap Kaita's attention back to him. She looked up into his enraged, bewildered expression, and she forced a smile upon her face. "You are so close, Dotag," she said eagerly. "You have come so far. The humans cannot hope to stop your pack now. Finish it. Kill them!"

She struggled against Mag's spear, but Mag, expressionless, only squeezed tighter. Kaita began to gag, the wood pressing into her windpipe.

"You . . . you did this," said Dotag. His shoulders heaved. "You . . . you—"

He straightened and threw his fists wide, unleashing a roar that startled everyone in the hall. Then he charged. I saw Mag hesitate for just a heartbeat, and for a mad moment I thought she was going to let Dotag crush her and Kaita together.

Instead, she wrapped an arm around Kaita's neck and leaped to the side, dodging just as Dotag's fist came crashing down where they had just been standing. Both women fell. Mag tried to get back up, but Kaita was fighting her now. She could not free herself from Mag's grip, but her struggles kept either of them from getting to their feet.

Dotag roared and attacked again. Mag had to roll away. Without Kaita to hamper her movements, she was able to shoot to her feet and strike. Dotag screamed and reeled away. Mag had sliced his right ear clean off.

But Kaita had been given the reprieve she needed. Her eyes flashed, and even as Ditra cried out for archers to stop her, she took her mountain lion form. I was the only one who managed a shot—it flew straight through the crowd, piercing her flank. She yowled, but she did not stop. In a blink she had slithered through the press of trolls, out the door and into the bailey beyond. Another flash of magelight, and then I saw a raven wheel away above the heads of the trolls, screaming in frustration as it vanished into the sky.

Mag stood stock still, watching. Had it not been for the battle-trance, I am sure she would have been shaking with rage.

Dotag hardly seemed to know what to do with himself. His thick fingers probed at the wound in the side of his head. I thought it would enrage him further, but instead he only seemed confused. He looked down at Mag, but he did not try to attack her. He looked at the rest of us in the hall, taking in the many flaming arrows raised and flasks of oil ready to throw.

At last he turned back to his pack. "The mountains are still ours! Fight! Kill them!"

He whirled back, ready to plunge into the midst of Ditra's troops. But he only got two steps before he realized that not one troll had moved to follow him. They were looking at him instead, their faces impassive, studying him like a beast in the mountains. He stopped and turned.

"Fight!" he roared, louder than before. Still they held their ground. Dotag snarled and lunged towards them, smashing his fists against the floor. "I lead this pack. I lead! Challenge me, or obey!"

"I challenge you."

One of the trolls—another female—stepped forwards. She was thick and tall, and imposing despite the small burns on her skin. And I did not need to speak the troll's language to hear the hatred thick in her voice.

"I, Apok, challenge you. You let yourself be tricked by the humans. You followed their counsel when Chok told you not to. You killed Chok to serve the humans. You will lead us to ruin. I, Apok, challenge you."

Dotag looked truly terrified now. But he stumped towards her, spreading his shoulders to appear thicker and bigger than before.

"Get back!" called Ditra. Her soldiers needed no second urging; they backed as far from the two trolls as they could, pressing against the far edges of the hall. Only Mag remained where she was, still staring off where Kaita had flown. I pushed through the crowd and seized her, drawing her away from the trolls.

“Come,” I murmured. “We will find her again.”

We barely got out of the way before Dotag snarled and charged Apok. He leaped at her, swinging both fists with all his might. But Apok stepped out of the way and used his own momentum to slam him into the ground. She struck him twice before he managed to roll away—but when he came up, it was with a powerful blow that flung her back into the wall. She slumped down, and I saw cracked stone behind her.

Dotag pressed his advantage. As Apok fought for her feet, he struck her once in the face, sending her head crashing against the wall again. He struck her twice more, both in places on her torso that had been badly burned in the battle. Apok roared with pain. She lashed out, and the nails of her stubby fingers raked the place where Dotag’s ear had been. He recoiled, falling back a few steps and giving her the chance to gain her feet again.

Mag’s arm tensed in my hand. I gripped her tighter, and she turned to look at me. “Leave it,” I said quietly. “This is their affair, and they will brook no interference.”

“If that one wins . . .” she tilted her head towards Dotag.

“I know,” I said. “But we have no choice.”

Apok approached Dotag cautiously. They were both grimacing, showing each other their teeth. But Apok held herself firm, her gaze fixed on Dotag, whereas he was shifting back and forth, looking about. He might have been searching for some advantage, but he looked like he was trying to find an escape.

Finally Apok attacked again. Dotag ducked her first blow, but her second crashed into his jaw. He went sliding back across the stone floor and came to a stop amid the wreckage of the keep door, curled up like a babe in a cradle. The Telfer soldiers in the room gasped, and there was a murmur among the trolls.

But it was a ruse. As Apok approached, Dotag struck. He had snatched up a piece of the broken iron grid that had held the door, a shard of metal almost two paces long. He thrust it into Apok’s chest, and almost two handbreadths of the metal sank into her flesh. She clutched at it with both hands, falling back on her rear, roaring. Dotag stepped closer, trying to jam it deeper, a low growl issuing from his throat. The rest of the trolls shifted. Some of them gave angry, rumbling shouts, and nearly all of them glared at Dotag. It seemed clear they did not approve of his cowardly trick.

Apok's eyes widened, and she bared her teeth again. She let go the iron shard, and Dotag's weight pressed it deeper into her chest. But Apok's hands rose and wrapped around his throat. She squeezed. Dotag's hands slackened on the iron, and he seized her wrists, trying to pull her away. But Apok had him now. She heaved, throwing him off balance and bringing him crashing to the ground. Apok pulled him up just enough to slam his head back into the stone. Dotag's nails dug into her forearms, but she did not relent. Again and again she sent the back of his head crashing into the floor. A black stain of blood appeared on the ground beneath him, and his arms fell away from her wrists.

Apok stopped. She straightened. With one massive hand, she dragged the iron shard from her own chest. Dotag stirred. His eyes spun in their sockets as he tried to sit up.

Apok rammed the iron shard into his mouth. It pierced straight through the back of his head, pinning him to the stone floor.

Dotag jerked once and then lay still.

The hall fell quiet, save for Apok's great, heaving breaths. She tossed her head as though shaking away a dizzy spell. My gaze shifted to Ditra. She stood near the front of her soldiers, her mouth slightly open, waiting.

Apok turned to her, eyes narrowed. I gripped my bow.

"I lead the pack now." Apok's growl echoed around the hall. She spoke in the common tongue of Underrealm. "Our fight is over."

I nearly sagged with relief, as did most of the Telfer soldiers I could see. But Ditra stood straighter, stepping forwards to separate herself from the crowd. She inclined her head.

"Then we shall part," she said. "And you will leave here pursued by no ill will of my family or our warriors."

Apok nodded slowly. Then, "There is still the pact."

"Yes," said Ditra. "I am Lord Ditra of the family Telfer, Rangatira of Tokana, and descendant of the first Albern of the family Telfer. My ancestor forged the pact with your people. But it has been neglected for so long that it has grown rusted and damaged, like a blade unused. It must be reforged. You and I can do so, as our predecessors did long ago."

That produced a long moment of silence. At first I thought Apok might not have understood. But then she snorted in what seemed like amusement.

"Tomorrow, then," she said. "We do not love many words, as humans do. But you and I will use as many words as we have to, in order to return peace to the mountains."

Ditra seemed taken aback. But at last she smiled. "Tomorrow, then."

Apok turned to her pack. "Leave," she said. "Back to the mountains, and away from the city."

The trolls did not make a sound, but turned as one to obey her. We stood there, all of us, and watched their giant, lumbering forms stalk away into the night. No one moved until the last one was gone. When the hall had settled to silence once again, I turned to Mag. She was staring out into the darkness—out the shattered door through which Kaita had escaped.

I let go her arm and gripped her shoulder. "We will find her."

Mag smiled—but it was a smile of such sadness, and such bone-deep weariness, that I felt my eyes sting.

"I know," she whispered. "I know we will."

FORTY-EIGHT

There was still much to be done that night. Ditra sent the fastest messengers she had left to find the refugees on the road and order their return. She then sent a small contingent of soldiers to meet them on the road and provide protection from ambush. The Shades had vanished after the small part they played in the battle, and Ditra feared further mischief from them.

After that she retired at last, ordering us to do the same. Mag and I collapsed in our beds the moment we saw them. We slept well past midday and rose to find Kahaunga had begun the long process of re-building itself. We helped where we could, and spent our time in rest when we could not.

True to her word, Apok returned the next day, and she met with Ditra on the slopes north of Kahaunga. They discussed the pact again, redrew the boundaries, and pledged that their descendants, and those they commanded, would swear by the new pact from that day forth. Then the humans and the trolls joined each other in rebuilding their lives, with the trolls helping Telfer subjects reclaim and rebuild their homes in the mountains, and the Telfers providing the trolls with great stores of bread and crops, which were gratefully (if messily) devoured.

Early on the third day, Dryleaf and Oku returned to us, along with the rest of the refugees. Oku barked madly as he leaped around us, and Dryleaf beamed.

"I knew somehow that you two would come out all right," he said, "yet I am glad to see myself proven correct."

"I think you had an almost foolish confidence in our success, then," I told him.

"Someone had to."

"Albern may speak for himself, but not for me," said Mag, in a light mood that I doubted was genuine. "If our foes wish to rid themselves of me, they shall have to do better than trolls."

"And speaking of your foes," said Dryleaf, "what of Kaita?"

Mag's false cheer vanished.

"She escaped," I said. "She was last seen fleeing southwest, as fast as her raven wings would carry her."

Dryleaf gave a tired sigh. "I suppose you wish to strike out upon the road as soon as may be, without even giving an old man a night to rest?"

Mag paused for a long moment. Her mouth worked, her lips twisting around each other, as though words were fighting to escape.

At last she simply said, "No."

I gaped at her. "No?"

"No." Mag shook her head. "Kaita led us here step by step. Always she left us a clue, pulling us along until we reached Tokana, where she hoped to have done with us. That game has finished, and she has lost. Now we have no more clues, no signs by which to pursue her. So why should we hurry back to the road? Besides"—and she gave me a gentle smile—"you have returned home after far too long. You have reunited with your family. You should take the time to enjoy that."

"I will," I said. "But my aims have not changed. In Northwood, you and I said we would make Kaita pay. I said I was with you. That promise still stands."

"I am glad to hear it," said Mag, and I could hear how deeply she meant it. "Then enjoy your return to your homeland. Kaita will still be out there when you are done, and we will find her together."

"I, too, am still with you," muttered Dryleaf from his chair. "Though I suppose it sounds less heroically inspiring coming from me."

The rest of our Yearsend was rather pleasant. Ditra's rangers were kept very busy hunting down the Shades in the mountains. When Kaita abandoned them, they melted into the wilderness, trying to hide from all sight and retribution. Most did not succeed. Ditra's forces hunted the Shades down in every hole where they tried to hide. And those who passed farther into the mountains, and were discovered by trolls . . . well, I did not like to imagine their fate then, and I still do not.

We stayed in Kahaunga for more than a week. When Ditra was not too busy rebuilding her city, I spent most of my days with her, and when she was, I would visit Vera instead. Sometimes I would take her riding beyond the walls of the stronghold, and I discovered to my great delight that she seemed to love the mountain wilderness almost as much as I had when I was her age.

My time spent with Ditra was mostly pleasant. In the very first days, we were so thrilled at Kahaunga's salvation that we thought of little else. After that, our conversations turned back to our past and our family. We still had some angry words to say to each other then, things we had not had time to say before the trolls attacked. But I will not repeat it all here, for it worked itself out in the end—the way it usually does, with family. One's true family, at any rate. We found peace with each other, and I took every meal with her and Vera, with Mag and Dryleaf joining us more often than not. Ditra had, you remember, been rather cool towards Mag when she thought she was a sellsword. That was no longer the case, and they grew to like each other greatly in a very short time. Ditra found great amusement in Mag's frequent jokes at my expense, and sometimes the two of them would join forces against me, doing their utmost to make me blush, and falling into peals of laughter when I retreated, muttering, into my wine. On one such occasion, Dryleaf gave a sudden, barking laugh.

"Sky above, I have just realized it." He reached over and patted Mag's arm. "Mag has become your new Ditra."

That sobered both women up rather sharply, and they glared at him. "I certainly have not," said Mag.

"She certainly has not," said Ditra, at the exact same time.

This, of course, sent both Dryleaf and me into hysterics, and Vera giggled at her mother's side. When I had recovered enough to talk, I patted Mag's hand.

"I think he is wiser than either of us, my friend."

It was Mag's turn to retreat to her cup of wine.

Ditra and Vera got to hear Dryleaf sing often during that time. We would sit in her chamber, Vera on my lap or her mother's, Mag by the window with Oku curled at her feet, and listen as Dryleaf shared songs we had never heard before. I never failed to marvel at how many he seemed to know. I thought I could learn a new one every week for the rest of my life and still not match him. The years seemed to fall away from him when he performed; his face shone in the firelight, his stance was firm, his shoulders straight. And as I watched him, and listened, I reflected on a conversation that he and I had had more than once in the last few months.

One day, nearly a week after the battle with the trolls, I saw him alone in his chamber after the others had gone to bed. I had just helped Ditra put Vera to bed; she had fallen asleep on her mother's lap, and I carried her to her room while Ditra tucked the blankets in around her.

"What is it, my boy?" said Dryleaf, brows raised in curiosity.

"I . . . I wanted to share something with you, if you do not mind staying up a while longer."

Dryleaf frowned. "Of course. Is everything all right?"

I took a deep breath. "It is. I have . . . this is still dear to me, and I am reluctant . . . it is the song. Jordel's song."

Dryleaf understood at once, and he nodded solemnly. "Ah."

"I told you of my journey with Loren in the Greatrocks. I spoke more of her than of Jordel, but Jordel was dearer to me, and I promised that I would make a song for him. I . . . I would be honored if you were the first to hear it."

I did not look up at him, even though he could not see me, for I suddenly felt like a very foolish child. But Dryleaf reached over and took up my hand and squeezed it between his leathery fingers. I looked up to find him smiling gently, his gaze seemingly just over my left shoulder.

"The honor would be mine," he said.

And so, in hesitant, stumbling tones, I sang him the song I had spent the last few months writing.

What sorrow feel we
Who mourning raise our hands
To farewell bid to he
Who watchfully guarded the nine lands

Stranger, will not you weep
Do you know he who fell from high
In a bed of stones and there to sleep
And ages will pass him by

Do you know Jordel of Adair
Who walked miles long
His mighty arm, his silver hair
His shining blade, his armor strong

For none could meet one so bold
Or kindness in such measure great
Without weeping when he lay there cold
The master of his own fate

He saw along his own trail
And knew the fate that loomed
With his head high, in shining mail
Jordel rode forth to meet his doom

Our tears we must bring to close
And bitter our grief we must allay
Jordel his own resting place chose
To bring us all through night to day

My voice faded in the chamber, and Dryleaf sat nodding in the firelight, his head bobbing in time with the pace at which I had sung. I could not even look at him, such was my embarrassment.

"You can tell me," I said. "It is not very good."

"I can hear the heart of it. You have done a rare thing. A fine thing."

"How very diplomatic of you," I said, with an embarrassed snort. My face was beet-red. "But those are fair words holding little substance. You are trying to try to make me feel better."

"Stop it, boy," said Dryleaf. It was one of the only times he ever spoke sharply to me. "You think it will make you feel better to hear it, so let me make it plain that you are wrong: No, your song is not very good. Of course it is not. You said you have never written one before, and you have been trying to do it all on your own. And it is not even finished."

"No, just a great deal of time wasted, it seems." I already knew the song was poor, but hearing it from the old man, who was always so kind, was like a knife in the gut.

"Wasted?" said Dryleaf incredulously. "No. You could have brought it to me sooner, and then things might have gone a bit faster. But no work upon a song is wasted. You have done the important work, my boy, you have the most important piece. You have the *heart* of it. Your language is off, the poetry lacks, and your rhythm . . . well. But these are dressings. These are the niceties you drape atop the soul of the song itself. If the soul is weak, all the dressings in the world will yield you nothing. You have spent your time wrestling with the hardest task, the part that too many bards eschew. But your work has borne fruit. Now it is ready to be honed, like a blade on a whetstone."

"I will work on it more, then," I said. "Thank you for your advice." I made to rise, but Dryleaf reached out suddenly and seized my hand.

"Sit down, boy, sit down," he said. "You have struggled too long at this alone."

"It is mine." I could hardly understand the sense of jealousy and selfishness rising up in me, and I did not enjoy it, but neither could I rid myself of it. "I have to do this on my own. It is important to me."

He released my hand and leaned back in his chair with a sigh. "I am sure it is. It is clear you loved him."

My anger abated somewhat, and I spoke softly. "I did."

"Then do him justice, and let the song become something great. You feel you must do this yourself, because you think it would be weak to beg help from another. Forgive me, but it is very like Mag."

I scoffed. "Mag? Mag has no interest in songs."

Dryleaf shook his head. "Not in songs. But in other things. She is the greatest warrior of her age. Everyone knows it. She feels the weight of it. It makes her feel that she must always take on more, and do it alone."

"She fought beside us against the trolls."

"I have no doubt," he said, "that if she thought you would have stayed behind and let her face them alone, she would have. And she took it upon herself to slay the pack leader, and to subdue Kaita."

I looked down at my hands in my lap. "She asked me to come with her, when she left Northwood."

"Did she?" said Dryleaf. "That, then, was a rare moment of wisdom. I think that, if you do not want both your roads to end in tragedy, you must teach her to show such wisdom more often. You should not learn her way of doing things, but persuade her to a wiser course instead. She needs your help if she is to accomplish her aims. If she tries to do it alone, she will fail, Uncut Lady or not." He took a deep breath. "It is a lesson many never learn. Your sister thought she could succeed on her own. But look how she fared here, before you came. In the end, only you and Mag brought even the faintest hope of success."

We fell silent. I thought upon what Dryleaf had said, and I saw, swimming before me, the face of Maia. *She needs you to save her,* he had said to me.

After a little while, I stood and made for the door. But I stopped by Dryleaf's chair and reached down for his hand. He squeezed my fingers again, gently.

"Thank you," I said quietly. "It is late now. But we will speak of the song again soon."

"I cannot wait," he murmured.

FORTY-NINE

After a week and a half of rest, we left Kahaunga at last.

When Mag and I told Ditra of our intention to leave, she went very quiet. We were in her chamber eating our evening meal, along with Dryleaf, but I had made sure that Vera was not in the room. As the silence stretched on after I had finished speaking, I looked uncertainly at Mag, but she never took her gaze from Ditra.

"I had meant to discuss matters with you before now," said Ditra softly. "I thought to ask you to be my new lead ranger. I can think of no one else more suited to take Maia's place at my side."

"And I expected you to say so," I said. "But I have been away from Calentin a long time, and I am happier wandering the nine lands than I ever was here." She began to object, but I raised a hand to forestall her. "It was not only Mother who made me unhappy here. It is the life I was expected to lead. The one you want me to lead now. I am not suited to a noble's life, Ditra. I never was."

She sighed and shook her head. "No. I suppose you are not. I will not pretend I am happy with your answer, but neither can I say truthfully that you are wrong. Mayhap that is why I waited so long to raise the subject."

To my surprise, she turned to Dryleaf. "And what of you, Grandfather? You have ridden a long road to reach us, and a longer one stretches before you still, unless I miss my guess. Would you rather remain? I would treasure your presence as an advisor, not to mention your singing voice."

Dryleaf bowed in his seat. "You are very kind, Rangatira. But my road does stretch on a long way, as you said, and there is an old friend at the end of it, unless I miss *my* guess." He grinned and turned, so that his blind eyes seemed to gaze somewhere between Mag and me. "And besides, what hope do you truly think these young ones have without me at their side?"

That made us all laugh, and our talk turned to other things. With the matter settled, over the next few days Ditra commanded her servants to help us ready for travel. They provisioned us well, and groomed and re-shod our horses. And in those two days, we spent more time with Ditra and Vera than ever, and our meals were all the sweeter for our knowledge that our time together would soon end. Kaita had been seen flying away southwest, and there were some vague reports of strange things happening in that direction. Mag, Dryleaf, and I spent many days holed up in council with Ditra, poring over maps and determining our best course south. She sent word to the Calentin king, to be sent to all their Rangatira, that a rogue weremage allied with the Shades was passing through the kingdom, and that they should be on watch for her. At last we settled on a road that would bring us back to Opara by much the same route we had taken to get to Kahaunga, but with frequent stops along the way to search for any rumors of Kaita's passing. Ditra gave us a new writ, of course, granting us broad, sweeping powers to aid us in our search.

At last, our time came to depart. We rose before dawn on the thirteenth of Martis to find our horses ready by the stables. Ditra was there to bid us farewell, and she had brought Vera with her. The poor girl was still blinking sleep from her eyes. But she came alert and ran forwards as soon as she saw me.

"Tell me you are not really leaving," she pleaded.

"I am," I said, ruffling her hair. "But not forever. We will meet again. And in the meantime, I have taught you much of the wilderness. I will expect you to know much more when I return. I think your mother needs another ranger, if you are willing to be one."

Her eyes shone, and she smiled. "Of course I am!" she cried.

I smiled and patted her cheek. So like me in some ways, and so different in others. She stepped away to bid Mag and Dryleaf farewell, and especially to scratch Oku's belly, while I went to Ditra. She had put on a stern look, very reminiscent of our mother. But her eyes gleamed with love, and with mischief.

"You will write me, of course," she said sternly. "You have no excuses this time. If I do not receive any word from you, I will send all my rangers out to hunt you down, leaving Kahaunga defenseless."

"I promise I will not make you take such drastic measures," I said. "I will write as often as I can. To Vera, at least."

Her mouth twitched, and she slapped my arm. Then she pulled me in for an embrace. "Fare well, brother. Take care of yourself, and your friends. I owe you everything. If ever I can be of service, I will."

I clutched her tight, closing my eyes, trying to freeze the memory in my mind forever—and I succeeded. Even now, I can smell the scent of her hair, feel the smooth weave of her cloak against my cheek, shiver at the cold winter air that blew against my back.

"Thank you," I said. "For your offer, and for all else you have done. I will not stay away so long this time."

"You damned well had better not," she said gruffly, pushing me back to hold at arm's length. "You may think I am joking, but you *will* find rangers on your doorstep if you defy me."

"I will remember it. Fare well, dearest sister. Protect our home."

Tears came to her eyes at that, and the sight of it finally sent my own spilling down my cheeks. It was the kind of weeping that you do not mind, that stems from joy rather than pain, and is sweeter even than laughter in the sunlight.

We mounted soon after, and rode through the rebuilt gate. I looked back often, until the road turned and we lost sight of them at last. I faced forwards then, and heaved a deep breath as I gazed upon the road that would take us west and out of the mountains.

"Are you all right?" said Mag. "You could have stayed, you know."

"I could have," I said. "But then what hope would you have?"

She rolled her eyes. "I am going to trounce you."

I chuckled, but after a moment I looked her steadily in the eye. "I am with you, Mag, until the end of this road. You may be the Uncut

Lady, and I may be only a simple bowyer, but you may count on my help, whether it be through my counsel, or my presence at your side in a fight. To whatever end."

She smiled. "Of course I know it. Do you really think I would let you leave, even if you wanted to?"

"I am serious."

"Do you think I am not?"

I shook my head. "Have your jests, then. But let us speak of Kaita. How do we plan to find her?"

Mag shrugged and nudged Mist to trot a little faster. "I do not know. But we *will* find her. After all, I have nothing better to do."

I nudged Foolhoof to catch up. "Nor do I."

FIFTY

Albern's timing was impeccable. The first edges of dusk were just creeping into the sky as he quietly finished his tale. Sun took a deep breath and released it in a sigh, just as she had the first night, before the vampire had attacked.

"I am glad you fixed things with your sister," she said. "Is she still alive?"

"She is," said Albern, grinning hugely. "She survived the War of the Necromancer, and everything that has come since. Old age has left her slightly less healthy than I am, if you can believe it, and Vera rules Tokana in her stead. She is an excellent Rangatira, well respected by her king, as well as the other lords, and beloved by her people. She has two sons of her own now. I still go to visit them every once in a while. Mayhap you will come with me next time."

"I would love to," said Sun.

Albern nodded. Then his smile died. "Another day, then. For now, we have work to do."

"Yes," said Sun. "Though I am still unclear about just what exactly it is that you *want* to do."

"Our friends over the hill are trying to perform the same ritual the Shades performed in Lan Shui years ago," said Albern. "But they are disorganized. They have neither the reach nor the resources of the Shades of old. If we brought this information to the King's law, they would certainly stop the ritual. But, too, they might claim the magestones for themselves. And in any case, some officers of the law might be killed in the fighting, and likely all of the criminals. I think we can put a stop to their plans without anyone dying tonight."

"A noble goal," said Sun. "But you did not answer my question: *what* exactly do you mean to do?"

"First, you will sneak into position on the other side of their camp," said Albern. "I will distract them and draw them away from the cauldron, and their store of magestones. You will take the stones and fling them into the fire, and then steal one of their torches to throw into the cauldron itself. We will burn away their contraband, and their plans, all at once."

Sun's throat had gone quite dry. "You mean for me to sneak in among them?"

"Only if you are willing," said Albern. "I pitted you against the vampire all unawares. I did it to teach you your worth in a fight, but I will never do that again. If you help me with this now, I want you to do it with both eyes open, and with both of us agreeing to what we do before we do it." He smiled and held forth his left hand. "As partners."

Sun returned his smile, though in truth she felt far less confident than he sounded. She gripped his wrist and shook. "Partners, then."

He pulled his sword off his belt and handed it to her. "Here. I do not mean to let them draw close enough for this to be of use to me."

Sun could not help a moment's trepidation as she accepted the blade. "Do you think I will need it?"

"Not if all goes well, but there is no guarantee of that."

"How comforting."

At Albern's direction, she slipped away down the other side of the hill, circling wide around the camp, out of sight. The day's fading light was just enough for her to see by. She kept a careful eye on the glow of the campfire that shone above the tops of the hills she passed. As she went, she tried her best to silence her steps, though she did not have Albern's gift for it. Hopefully the activity of the camp would be enough to keep them from noticing.

Finally she spotted the gap between the hills that would let her draw as close as possible to the chest where the magestones were being kept. Crouching so low she was almost crawling, Sun edged forwards. Soon she could see the tents. She stopped as soon as the first person came into view. It was a woman, facing away towards the campfire. That was a good thing—it would ruin her night vision. Sun peered through the darkness, searching for the shape of Albern atop the hill on the other side of the camp. At last she caught sight of him—a small black form moving against the stars. She hoped he could see her as well. Then, even as she watched, she saw him raise his arm, and then bring it down swiftly.

Thwack

The sound of a stone striking flesh echoed in the night.

"What in the dark—"

A guard shot to her feet. She was looking at something Sun could not see.

"What happened?" called a voice.

"Something hit Wen."

"What do you mean 'some—'"

Thwack

The voice died abruptly.

"Attack!" cried the woman in Sun's view. "We are under attack!"

She ran off out of sight. Someone came and threw open the flap of the tent closest to Sun, and a figure stumbled out of it into the night. Sun ducked back until the figure was out of sight.

Trotting, but still trying to remain silent, Sun crept up behind the tent. She stuck one eye out around the edge of it, but it seemed she need not have bothered. Ten or so people were gathered at the other end of the camp, but they were staring in Albern's direction, away from Sun.

Thwack

One of the figures fell poleaxed to the ground and did not move. A stone bounced away from his limp form.

"There!" A man thrust his finger up towards the hill where Albern was hiding. "I saw something!"

"Find them!" barked another. "We cannot let them bring word of us to Lan Shui!"

Most of them attempted to climb the hill, while two circled around the base of it, likely hoping to cut off Albern's escape.

Sun moved. Her heart thundered in her ears as she reached the chest holding the magestones and threw herself to the ground behind it. Only then did she see the heavy iron lock that held it shut.

"Dark below," muttered Sun.

She risked a glance at the hill. The Shades—or whatever they were—were not paying any attention to their own camp. After a quick search, she found a large rock, half as big as her head. She hefted it high and slammed it against the lock. The iron held for two strikes, but on the third, it fell open.

With shaking fingers, she pulled the lock out and opened the chest. It was packed to the lid with packets wrapped in brown cloth. Sun pulled one open to find black, semi-translucent crystals. Magestones.

She scooped all the packets up into her arms and dashed towards the cauldron. She threw them into the flame beneath it, but it was an awkward throw, and half of them fell upon the ground next to the fire. She fell to her knees and tried to scoop them up, wincing at the heat of the darkfire that leaped up, licking at the sides of the cauldron.

A hand seized her hair and threw her backwards.

Sun's head struck the ground hard, and she rolled away, stunned. A heavy boot struck her in the ribs. She had just enough presence of mind to roll away from it.

"Glad I came back to make sure the camp was safe," snarled a woman's voice.

Sun heard her foe's footsteps approaching. She threw herself to the side as the woman aimed another kick. Fighting to her feet, Sun backed away, trying to take stock of the situation.

One woman had returned to the camp—the one Sun had seen as she approached. Her face was gaunt, with high, sharp cheekbones, and her head was shaved to stubble. Her clothes were all of thick leather and fur, far too hot for the weather recently. It looked as though she had dressed to be more impressive than practical. But the others were all gone, vanished over the top of the hill. Sun hoped that Albern was all right.

Sun shook her head to clear it. She needed time to figure out what to do. "What are you doing out here?"

"You are not that ignorant, or you would not have thrown the stones into the flames," snarled the woman. She took a step forwards.

Sun drew Albern's sword and held it before her, the tip a pace away from the woman's chest.

"Stop."

The woman paused, but only for a moment. A cruel smile played across her lips. "Do you even know how to use that, girl?"

"Trust me, I do. I am older than I look, if not nearly as old as you."

That earned Sun a snarl. The woman drew two long daggers from her belt and lunged forwards, trying to batter Sun's weapon aside. But Sun had spent many hours training in her family's yard, and she retreated, using her own weapon to block the woman's slashes and thrusts.

Knives, knives, she thought. *What do you do against a foe with knives?* She knew she had learned it, but all thought had fled her mind, and she was moving on instinct. It was harder to remember her lessons when she knew her foe wanted to kill her.

She stepped forwards with a wild swing. The woman took two steps away, breathing heavily. Sweat beaded her brow, made all the worse by the heat of the darkfire behind her. Sun hoped she regretted her choice of clothing.

"You do not look like a killer," growled the woman.

"There is a first time for everything, I am beginning to learn."

"Walk away. What we are doing here does not concern you. And it will make Underrealm a better place in the end."

Sun loosened her grip on her sword for a moment, flexing her fingers. "I am told that your sort always thinks that. But I have learned another lesson. It does no good to ignore evil done in the shadows, no matter how often people would rather do so."

The woman lunged. Again she tried to slap Sun's blade aside—but this time Sun let her. She spun with the blow, sidestepping as the woman's other dagger plunged through the space she had been standing.

Sun brought the sword arcing back around, and with the flat of the blade she slapped the woman's hand. The dagger slipped from her sweat-soaked fingers to the ground. When she stooped to retrieve it,

Sun sliced a thin cut on the back of her thigh. The woman's back arched as she cried out. Sun stepped in close and struck her in the neck with a fist, making her cough and fall back, dropping her other dagger.

She stumbled on the rock Sun had used to break the lock, falling on her back. Before she could rise, Sun stepped up, blade pointed straight at the woman's face, now only a finger's breadth away.

"Please," the woman whispered. "Please do not kill me."

"As I said, there is a first time for everything," said Sun. "But not for this. Not tonight."

She flipped the sword and fell on the woman's chest in one smooth motion, bringing the pommel crashing into her head. The woman's head snapped back and her eyes rolled up, showing their whites for just a moment before they closed.

Breathing heavily, Sun stood again and sheathed the sword. She looked at the hill. The rest of the would-be Shades were nowhere in sight.

Quickly she ran back to the cauldron, scooped up the rest of the magestones and flung them into the darkfire beneath. The flames sprang still higher. They had caught on the sides of the cauldron, though they had not burned through it yet. It was only a matter of time, but Sun found a torch and plunged it into the cauldron anyway. Albern had said to do it, and she guessed he had a reason.

Darkfire sprang up from the top of the cauldron, mingling with the black flames that crept up from the bottom. It began to consume the metal at last, creating holes that sent black blood pouring out into the flames. But Sun did not stay to watch. She sprinted off in the direction she had approached the camp—when she ran head-on into a figure in the darkness. They both grunted and fell to the ground beside each other.

Sun scrambled away from the figure, grasping for the sword at her belt—but then she heard Albern's deep voice in the darkness. "Sky above, that hurt."

"Albern!" Sun whispered. "I am sorry. Are you all right?"

"Well enough, I suppose." He accepted Sun's hand, and she pulled him to his feet. "Is your task done?"

"It is," she said. "What of the other Shades? Or whatever they are."

"They are gone," he said. "I led them on a merry chase south and then lost them as soon as I could. One slipped away from the others, and I feared she might return here."

"She did," said Sun, pointing to the woman's unconscious form. "I dealt with her."

His eyes shot wide. "Did you, now? Well done."

"I will tell you honestly: after fighting a vampire, I found myself rather unimpressed with her."

That made him laugh, though he quickly stifled it. "Well, we should be going. We have done a good thing here tonight—another good deed no one will ever hear about."

"Just as I want it," said Sun.

She followed him as he crept away from the camp and began a long westward loop that would bring them back to the road. Soon they had come out of the hills and begun to walk on open, grassy ground under the light of the stars. The moons had risen as well, and they cast all the world in a silvery pale glow. Sun looked up at them, her heart full, her mind replaying her brief scuffle with the woman in the camp.

"What of the rest of them?" she said. "They got away."

"They did, but it is of little consequence," said Albern. "It took them a very long time to gather the information they needed to steal those magestones. It will take them longer to do it again, if they even have the nerve for it. And if they should do so, well, then, someone will stop them. Mayhap it will be us."

"How do you know how long it took them?"

He grinned at her in the moonslight. "You are welcome to join my adventures, Sun, but you cannot expect to learn everything all at once. I have many friends in many lands who send me much information. And I told you I reserve the right to keep *some* things a surprise."

Sun shook her head. "Then what is our aim now?"

Albern stopped and turned, surveying her in the moonslight. "That is up to us. We are partners now, or so you said you desired."

"I . . . I did," said Sun. "I do. Yet I . . . I do not know what to do next."

"I have often felt the same," said Albern. "Well, we have a long walk back to Lan Shui. We can discuss it on the way."

Sun nodded. "That sounds agreeable."

They walked on in silence for a while, Sun mulling things over in her mind. She thought of the maps she had studied of this part of the kingdom. There were some things she had always wanted to see in Dorsea. She thought of its history, and of the ancient and great figures of Underrealm's beginnings, many of them her long-distant kin.

"What if we went to Bertram?" she said.

Albern looked at her, his brows raised. "Bertram?"

"I have often wanted to see it," said Sun. "My family was going to travel there, though not for some time yet. It was one of the few places along our route that I looked forward to. Renna the Sunmane made her home there, before she built Dorsea's capital of Danfon."

"So she did," said Albern. "Bertram would be a fine place to visit. In fact, there is a man there who owes me some money, and I would be happy to give you a fair share of it, if you will have it."

Sun frowned. "A fair share?"

He tilted his head. "As a partner."

"But what is the money for?"

"Ah." He smiled. "For services I rendered to him, which I shall tell you about once we reach Bertram. But I promise it is a benign surprise, far more innocent than our business tonight. I would split it with you, with your portion being in recognition of your accompaniment, and of your skill with a blade. I am afraid you are a bit of a sellsword now, Sun—at least as long as you stick the road."

Sun smiled. "A sellsword. I think I might like that."

He swept his arm out as if in invitation, and then he continued on west. Sun followed him into the moonslight, full of wonder at what her future might yet hold. Wonder, but no longer any fear.

EPILOGUE

Oh, by the by—you should know something of what Rogan was doing during this time.

Not long after Kaita fled from Kahaunga, he was sitting in a chamber in Dorsea's northeastern reaches. A cup of mulled wine was in his hand, but he drank from it slowly, twirling it in his hands and staring into its depths.

A voice spoke from the shadows. "My son."

Rogan shot to his feet, his eyes shining.

"Father?"

"Kaita has failed."

Rogan's hands clenched to fists at his sides. "She . . . how do you—"

"It is enough that I know."

"Father, tell me that she is not—"

"She lives."

Rogan sank back into his chair in relief, casting a hand over his eyes. "Thank the sky." But then he lifted his head, and there was fear in his eyes. "Do not blame her for this, Father. It was with my counsel that she set upon her road. If she could not succeed in Tokana, no one could have. Do not punish her."

"She did her best. She could not have done any more than she did. But now she is searching for you. You made her a vow."

"As you commanded." Rogan shook his head, staring at his own boots. "I was reluctant."

"Kaita cannot be allowed to find you. Not right away. Not until the time is right. But when you reunite with her at last, you must give her what was promised."

Slowly, Rogan stood from his chair. He went to the table in the center of the chamber. Upon it had been laid a map of the nine kingdoms. Small figures in blue stood upon the map, marking every place where the Shades had an agent or a fighting force. There were many. Far more than we would have guessed, in those days.

"You said you would not punish her," he said quietly.

"It is not punishment."

"I have seen it, Father," whispered Rogan. "If Kaita gets her wish, it will only lead to her death."

"You can see farther than any other, my son. Any other except me. Trust me when I say that this is no punishment." Rogan felt a hand on his shoulder, comforting him. "But yes. I am afraid that if we are to achieve our aims, you are right. Kaita will have to die."

Hell Skin

BEING BOOK THREE
OF THE FIRST VOLUME

OF THE
TALES OF THE WANDERER

ONE

Sun might have been forgiven for wishing the conversation would end. After all, no one had invited her to take part in it, and few things are worse than waiting on the edges of others' discussion, hearing what they have to say and yet having little to offer.

Her meal had gone some time ago, whisked away by a barman who gave her a wink and received a curled lip in return. Albern, however, still made deliberate and slow progress through his food, and the discussion he had begun with the woman at the next table did not aid his speed. Sun could not quite say why Albern had started speaking to her, except that it seemed to be a knack of his. He had a friendly and approachable manner, for all his appearance of a rough old man. Strangers found him easy to talk to, and he always seemed eager to speak to them as well. That was how Sun had met him, after all.

"And I say," Albern responded to the woman, "that the day we are all pleased with our kings is the day the world breaks. I have never known a time in which the commoner had only love for the noble, and I have lived a good deal longer than you have, if you will forgive my saying so."

"Why should I need to forgive a plain truth?" said the woman, chuckling. "And I do not wish for a *perfect* king. I only wish for a better one. This business on the Feldemarian border . . ."

Albern waved the stump of his right arm as if he had forgotten it was missing its hand. "Many lips have passed the news of those troubles to our ears. Who knows what is going on up there? But mayhap I will look into it before long, and then I will bring the truth back to you."

The woman reached out to clasp his left wrist. "A wanderer, are you? Then I accept your offer, and with gratitude. Only take care of yourself on the journey. The roads are not as safe as they were."

"When do you mean?" said Albern, grinning as he shook her hand. "The dream of eternally safe roads is another I have never seen come true. But we will be careful. Good day to you."

The woman gave a rueful laugh and, with a quick nod to Sun, rose to leave. The moment she had disappeared into the crowd of the common room, Sun leaned close.

"About time, old man. I thought you two would talk until sundown."

Albern shrugged. "I would not have minded it. Charming conversation is often in short supply."

Sun's brows rose. "I hope you do not mean to insult me."

"No, indeed. I have enjoyed our conversations more than any in a good long while. I imagine your impatience is what has had you bouncing in your seat for the last half hour? I wondered if you had to relieve yourself."

"In fact, I do. It is only that you kept seeming to be on the verge of finishing your talk."

Sun rose from her chair, though Albern was not quite done with his food. Sighing, he scooped the last few spoonfuls of stew into his mouth. "That is your trouble, Sun, or one of them. Always too eager for the end."

He led her through the common room and out the front door. With a kind word and a few copper slivers, Albern sent the stable girl to fetch their horse—their *horses,* Sun reminded herself. Albern had bought one for her. She could hardly believe that she owned a steed. All the horses she had called "hers" were, in fact, her parents' property.

Besides the horse, Albern had given her a new brown cloak—or new to Sun, at any rate, for Albern had clearly owned it for a while. But it was warmer than the blue one she had worn when they met, and it was also less conspicuous.

"If you need to relieve yourself, do it now," said Albern. "I mean to push our pace today."

"But you said we were an easy day's ride from Bertram," said Sun.

"Easy if we want to make the city by sundown," said Albern. "But I would rather get there ahead of the dark if we can. One of my friends in the city does not appreciate being woken at night—or being summoned, I should say, for he is usually already awake, and accompanied."

Sun scowled at him. "I suppose you mean to tell me that we will not have time for the story."

Albern chuckled. "Oh, were you anxious about that? Then be assured that I do not mean to gallop the whole way."

"That is all I needed to hear. I will return quickly."

She darted around to the outhouse in back of the inn. As with many places they had visited lately, it was only a wooden platform with a hole in it, but her nose did not curl quite so bitterly as it used to. She was growing somewhat used to conditions on the road, which of course were far less glamorous than the luxury in which she had been raised.

It made her wonder what her parents would think if they could see her now. But that thought carried worry in its wake, and she shied away from it. Thoughts of her parents had pressed themselves more and more into her mind of late. Had they halted their procession, sending their guards to seek her across the land? Or would they have carried on, eager to begin the long process of raising their station to its former heights? Sun could not be sure, and it was useless to think too long upon it. Yet in the back of her mind was being scratched, as though by a scribe marking events in a tome of history, a map of where her parents would be each day.

They would reach Bertram before long. Not today, as Sun would. But not too far in the future, either.

Sun did not plan to be there when they came, however. And so she found it easier than expected to banish the last thoughts of her family as she rejoined Albern where he waited with their mounts. Sun patted her horse fondly on the neck as Albern handed her the reins.

"Have you thought of a name yet?" said Albern. "You know it is bad luck to ride a horse with no name."

"That was Mag's superstition," said Sun.

Albern smiled sadly. "I called it so at the time. Yet you already know my thoughts on many subjects have changed since then."

"My opinions have not been tempered by so many years as yours." Sun studied the horse in deep thought. She was a fine steed, though not fit for battle. She was too slight, and just a bit too skittish—trusting of Sun's judgement, but nervous at a sudden noise.

"I will name her Undvikar if it will reassure you. Though I will call her 'Vika' more often, for it comes more easily to the tongue."

Albern smiled, and she wondered if he knew the old tongue of Dulmun from which she had drawn the name. But he said only, "I hope you name her for yourself, and not for my assurance. But I think it is a fine name. Hello, Vika." He reached over and scratched the mare behind the ears, which she hesitantly permitted. "Now, let us be off."

They remained on foot and walked the horses at first, pressing into the busy traffic of the town's main street. Many wagons and carts were plodding their way through the shallow mud, heading east and west in roughly equal numbers. Those heading west were laden with goods, mostly foodstuffs to trade in Bertram. Those rolling east were mostly empty, or else held items from the city to sell in town. But though the crowd was thick, still there was room enough to weave through it, which Albern did with expert swiftness.

Navigating the press kept them silent until they left the town's western end. There the way opened before them, the carts having room to spread out. But before Sun and Albern mounted, she caught his gaze and spoke.

"I want to hear how Mag died."

Albern went still for a moment. Then, without answering, he climbed into his saddle. Sun did the same, but she kept her eye on him all the while. She half expected him to spur his mount, still without answering her. But at last he returned her gaze, peering at her from under his hood, which he had raised against the last chill of morning.

"This is the third time you have asked me to tell you that, and the first time you have said it so plainly."

Sun had expected him to deny her outright. His answer was not what she had asked for, but it was not a refusal, either. "You told me I may ask whatever I wish, though you are not obligated to tell me the story that I want."

Albern sighed and turned his eyes forwards again. When he spoke, his voice was sad and solemn, but strong. It was the tone of one speaking at the funeral of a dear friend: an acknowledgment of grief, but also a resolution to face the future without fear.

"They say the best tales never end, but that is a lie. All tales end. Yours, mine. Mag's. Yet while they still spin, in chorus they weave the tale of the world. And that tale shall never die, even if one day none of us remain to hear it."

He glanced at her again, but only for a moment. "It is as I said in the tavern, Sun. You are too eager to reach the end of the story. You would be wiser to enjoy yourself. Take your time. All things end, yes, but that does not mean we should charge recklessly towards that end, eager to meet it. And neither should we cower from it, afraid for it to find us.

"I have met many people who needed to learn that second lesson. Mag needed to learn the first."

TWO

WINTER HAD YET REFUSED TO RELEASE ITS FORBIDDING GRIP ON THE land of Dorsea when Mag, Dryleaf, Oku, and I rode down out of the Sunmane Pass. Of course, we had clothes to protect us against the weather, but there is a sort of cold that no cloak can entirely dispel, and it shrouded us. The peaks of the mountains at our backs remained snow-capped all year round. But now the snow covered everything from those peaks to the valleys and the wide-open land before us, shrouding it all in white. Even forests made little impression on the snowy blanket. Only the marks of towns and other settlements were plain to see, patches of brown that spouted the grey smoke of hearths into the sky.

You will remember that we had remained in Calentin for some time before continuing our pursuit of Kaita. The best information we had was that she had been heading southwest, and so that was where we went. We took the long road south through Calentin's eastern reaches, bearing my sister's writ, which let us pass unmolested through the lands of the other Rangatira.

In the city of Opara we rested for a few days, visiting our friend

Victon and seeking what information we could. But there was precious little of it. All along our journey north, Kaita had been enticing us with a trail of clues, hidden just well enough to make us think we were terribly clever for discovering them. Now that she no longer wished to be followed, we were faced with tracking down a weremage in a wide-open world. That can be a nearly impossible task. We knew only of her connection to the Shades, and so it was information about them that we sought. All we had found so far was some vague rumor, gleaned from the Rangatira in Opara, of a plot that concerned northeastern Dorsea. And so that was where we had turned our steps.

The search was long and fruitless, and it weighed heavy on us. There is only so much time one can spend seeking one's quarry before one tires of the hunt. Sometimes we were desperate for any sign of Kaita. Other times we were apathetically numb and merely going through the motions of our journey.

No one had heard anything in any of the places we visited. There were no rumors of a rogue weremage. We could find no reliable information about the Shades.

It was now a week since we had come down out of the mountains, and we were drawing near to a small town by the name of Taitou. As we rode, Dryleaf often turned to face the south. He was blind, of course, but he had traveled these lands when he was younger. He knew the Birchwood was close, and he must have been thinking of Loren.

Loren would have been much on my mind as well, but I was preoccupied with Mag. She was my best friend, and we often jested and poked fun at each other. But ever since the Sunmane Pass, a dark mood had come over her. There had been an avalanche in those mountains, and though it posed no danger to us, Mag had been somber since.

I thought she might harbor worry for Dryleaf and me, imagining that she was dragging us along a more dangerous journey than she had at first foreseen. Or mayhap she only hoped, as I did, that the end of the road was near, and all her thought was bent upon it. But as we approached the walls of Taitou, I sought to cheer her up.

"What troubling thoughts leave you so grumpy?" I called out to her. "If you are not careful, your face will freeze in that frown—though I suppose that could only be an improvement."

She did not laugh. In fact, she barely glanced at me. "No troubling thoughts," she said. "Only a hope that the journey will soon be over. But mayhap that is a fool's hope."

"You should enjoy what you can of your wanderings," I told her. "Look at the land we ride in. Is it not beautiful? Drink it in and let your cares go, while they are not pressing."

"It has always been beautiful." Mag tossed her head to the north. "I used to live two days' ride from here, in the northern reaches of the Carrweld Forest. You can see its southern reaches there. Taitou was the closest settlement of any notable size—I once thought it was a great city."

There are few things she could have said that would have been more surprising. In all our years together, Mag had seldom spoken about her past.

"I did not know that," I answered after a moment.

"It was a small village." Her words came slow, her voice careful. "A tiny village called Shuiniu. There I dwelled until . . . well, until I outgrew it, I suppose. One day I had to go out into the wider world, of which I knew nothing, and when I did, I had to pick a direction. South was straight into the forest. I knew of nothing interesting to the west or east. But I had heard tales of Feldemar, and it seemed a grand kingdom, and so that is where I went. And that led me to the Upangan Blades, and you. We met about a week after I left home."

In a few moments, Mag had told me more of her early life than in all the years of our youth. It was just like in Tokana, when she had told me of her love of the forests. And in that moment, as before, I did not know quite what to do. I suppose I was like you, desperate for her to give me more details and continue the story. But, if you will forgive me for saying so, I had the sense to rein in my questions—all but one.

"Do you want to visit?" I said.

Mag gave me a sharp look.

"We do not have to," I said hastily. "But we do not know where to go, and I think we can spare a day, or a few of them. Is there anyone there you wish to see?"

"No." Her answer came without hesitation. Her tone was not harsh, but neither did it leave any room for argument or doubt. And she did not explain further.

"Fair enough," I said, attempting nonchalance. But in truth, I was afraid I had sent her guard crashing back down, and I wished I had said nothing at all.

Two days after we rode out of the Sunmane Pass, a rider came out of the mountains behind us. She stopped at the last crest before the road descended into Dorsea's lowlands. The height was lofty enough to see a great distance, until it was easy to imagine one could view Danfon far to the southeast, though of course that was impossible.

She pulled her cloak a bit tighter around herself. She had been searching for us, and her search had gone on for a long time. Disappointment in Calentin was close behind her, but now the trail was fresh again, and it led her into Dorsea.

With a grumble and a set in her shoulders, she nudged her horse forwards, down into the lands we had entered only days ago.

Dusk was still hours away when we reached the town of Taitou. At the western gate, guards inspected us with suspicion. This, of course, was routine to us now—from Constable Yue at the gates of Lan Shui to the Rangatira's soldiers who guarded Opara, we had practice dealing with servants of the King's law. We had a story already prepared and well rehearsed from long repetition.

But this time was different. In addition to four constables, two Mystics guarded the gate as well.

I knew many Mystics in my day. Some were good, like Jordel of the family Adair, about whom I have told you. A few were cruel. Most were somewhere in the middle. But for the most part, I rarely wished to get involved with Mystics if I could help it. If they were present in any situation, it was because things had gotten much worse than they should have. And with some exceptions, I knew them for a suspicious lot, willing to go to any length to solve a crime they were investigating. They were only too ready to eliminate anything—or anyone—they perceived as a threat to the High King's order.

So you can understand it was with some trepidation that we submitted ourselves to inspection by the redcloaks. More than their scrutiny, I feared that word of our coming might reach unwanted ears.

The Shades had agents in many places, and I did not doubt that at least some of them had infiltrated the redcloaks. Yet there was nothing we could do, other than turn and ride from Taitou with all possible speed—and that would have been suspicious, to say the least. Then the Mystics would have sent out word to their order that three riders of our description had refused to submit to inspection, and that news would have reached Kaita in time.

So I fixed a smile on my face as I stood a few paces off from Foolhoof, my gelding. "Is there anything I can help you with, friend? If you tell me what you are looking for, mayhap I can tell you where to find it."

The Mystic, a stout man with dark hair and a heavy scar on his left cheek, frowned at me. It was his second time going through my things.

"If you were carrying what I am looking for, you would not tell me."

"Contraband, is it?" said Mag. "Or mayhap you seek a blue cloak?"

I winced. Dark take Mag. She almost seemed to enjoy taunting the King's law and those who served it.

Both Mystics gave her sharp looks. "An odd thing to say," growled the second one, a strong-armed twixt with impressive scars on their bare arms. I wondered how they were not shivering with cold. "What makes you think of blue cloaks?"

"Come, my friends." Dryleaf was as polite as ever. "Do you imagine we are ignorant of the rumors about these Shades? Sky above, they attacked the Seat. It does no one any good to pretend at secrecy—not us, and not you, with your mission from the High King."

"Our mission is our own, and we will see to it," said the man. "But as for you three, what exactly do you know of the Shades?"

"Only what everyone knows," I said, shrugging. "They attacked the Seat, and then they vanished. All else is rumors."

The twixt glared hard. "What rumors, exactly?"

"Zhen! Lo!" said a new voice. "I hope you are not being rude to Taitou's newest guests."

Both Mystics yanked their hands from our saddles, smoothed their cloaks, and stood at attention, as another approached through the gate. As he came to a stop before us, the others saluted with fists over their hearts.

The first thing I noticed about the new arrival was his smile, for it seemed ever-present, and it flashed with well-kept white teeth. After that, I noticed that he was short—or a bit shorter than me, anyway—with several layers of fat beneath his clothing. He wore a red cloak, like most of those in his order, and the Mystic badge—three rods bound by a circle, with three-sectioned wings behind. But he also bore an arrow insignia on his tunic that told me he was a captain, the same as Jordel had been. My fingers played with a small bag at my belt holding one of Jordel's clasps, which I had taken from his body in token of memory. I was glad the Mystics had not wanted to search our every pocket and pouch.

As the captain came to a clipped halt, I found myself straightening as the Mystics had. It was the long-honed habit of drawing up before an officer about to inspect you. (Mag, if anything, slouched a bit more).

Dryleaf bowed his head as he heard the captain come to a halt. "Your fine warriors were doing only their duty, I am sure." He stepped forwards and offered his hand.

The Mystic captain stepped forwards and took his wrist gently to shake it. "They are dutiful, no doubt," he said. "Though they often inconvenience new arrivals more than turns out to be necessary. But what can one do? These are dangerous times. I am certain ones such as yourselves understand."

Mag cocked her head. "Ones such as ourselves?"

"Well, you understand me," said the captain. "Warriors."

Mag paused, appraising him for a moment. To cover the sudden silence, I stepped towards the captain and extended my hand as Dryleaf had done. "Of course we understand, Captain . . . ?"

His eyes flashed as he took my wrist and shook. "You recognize the symbol. Few do. I am Captain Kun, of the family Zhou."

I managed to keep my expression neutral, but inside I winced. Recognizing a captain's arrow was nothing a simple traveler would be able to do. He suspected we were fighters, and I had just confirmed it.

But I said only, "I am Kanohari. And my friend here is Chao. Our elderly friend is Dryleaf." Mag and I were using false names, you will remember.

"I may be blind, but I say again that I think you overstate things," said Dryleaf, cheerfully snippy. "If I could see, I do not doubt I would find you almost of an age with me."

The joke was well rehearsed, and I chuckled. Dryleaf smiled. But Captain Zhou's eyes were on Mag. She was staring around as if in boredom, waiting for us to sort out the pleasantries. Kun saw it, and he pointed to her as he laughed.

"Do you see that? Her manner reassures me more than any words the three of you could speak." Still holding my right hand in his, he clapped his left hand over them both and turned to the Mystic behind him. "Look at her—Chao, they say. Not a care in the world. Not afraid of you two searching through her things. You would expect a little nervousness from an enemy warrior—pardon me; you *did* say you were warriors, did you not?"

"We did not," I said. "But I can answer you now and tell you that we *were*. Both of us served as mercenaries in our youth."

Interest sparked in Kun's eyes. "Sellswords? How utterly fascinating. The High King needs soldiers now, with Underrealm threatened by war. Who knows when the armies of Dulmun will strike next? Or indeed, these Shades you were speaking about with such authority. I am certain Her Majesty would rather have you on her side than let the enemy snap you up."

This line of conversation seemed to be drawing into perilous territory. Mag's attention was fully back on the exchange, but I spoke before she could. "Our fighting days are long past us," I told him. "We are merely looking for a friend—another former mercenary who had gone to the coast to visit family. When we heard the Seat had been attacked, we grew concerned. We have journeyed long to seek her, for as you said, these are uncertain times. Fear not on our account. We are true citizens of Underrealm, and we would never lend our blades to vile traitors and rebels." I gave an easy smile. "But we are old citizens as well, and too weary of fighting to pledge ourselves to the High King's armies, even for coin."

Kun did not look disappointed, but only smiled broader and shook his head. "That is a pity. You seem as though you would be good to have in a fight. But I might have guessed that you had left your fighting days behind you, what with your companion. Meaning no offense, of course, Grandfather." He chuckled.

"Oh, that is quite all right, young man," said Dryleaf, matching the man's laugh. "Who could look at me and see a great champion?"

Oku padded forwards to sniff at Kun's boot, and the captain stooped to scratch his shoulder. "Well then," said Kun. "You are free to go on about your business, of course. But be careful. The Shades emerged from the Birchwood in strength, and seemingly from thin air. One wonders where they could be lurking now."

"One wonders indeed." I shook his hand once more and then helped Dryleaf into his saddle before gaining my own. "Thank you for your kindness. It is good to see that even in suspicious times, some have not forgotten the value of courtesy. Sky bless you."

"And may the moons shine upon your path," said Kun. He smiled as we left, and even gave a little wave just before we passed through the gate.

"That could have gone worse," remarked Mag as we passed into the streets of Taitou. "But I think that captain paid more attention to us than he appeared to."

"You are being paranoid," I said. "My only worry about him is that he might be too friendly for his own good. A trusting manner is welcome to travelers, but it might let more sinister folk slip through a net that should be tight."

"I hear your concern," said Dryleaf with a smile. "Yet it is better to find out one was too kind than to find that one has been too cruel and made others miserable for foolish reasons. I, for one, liked Captain Zhou immensely."

As we rode off, Kun watched us go. The constables at the gate, who had watched our exchange nervously, settled back into positions of rest. Zhen and Lo, the two Mystics posted there, remained standing at rigid attention.

"Well, Captain," said Zhen at last, "we shall continue our vigilance."

"Of course you will," said Kun, still smiling. "Nephew, follow these new arrivals."

Lo looked at Zhen in confusion. But Zhen's expression bent towards a frown. His face darkened, making the heavy scar on his left cheek stand out all the more.

"I prefer not to be referred to that way, *Captain.*"

Kun's smile widened. *My little sister-son,* he thought. *So eager to be seen as a man, when it seems only yesterday I had to help his mother dress him in the morning.*

"I am truly sorry," he said. "I keep forgetting. *Lieutenant* Zhen of the family Zhou—take another from your unit and follow them. Keep track of everything they do."

"But Captain," said Lo, "with the way you acted towards them . . . that is, do you think they are suspicious?"

"You think them above question because I was friendly?" said Kun, chuckling. "Of course I was polite. What possible benefit could result from rudeness? Even the darkest circumstances do not demand ill manners. But they are liars, all three of them. Retired warriors? Both of them have bloodstains on their boots and clothes—old stains, but not old enough. They are fighters, and they have fought recently. Within weeks. Follow them, and send any information directly to me."

"Are they Shades, Captain?" ventured Zhen.

"That is precisely what I mean to find out. The enemy surprised us once. I vow beneath the sky that they will not do so again if I can prevent it."

THREE

Now, you will recall that Mag said she used to live near Taitou. She did not explain further at that time. But later, I learned something of the place that she had called home before we met, and I shall tell you something of it now.

Shuiniu was a small village, as she had said. The people there mostly lived on their own merits. They farmed or hunted for sustenance, and they had a smith, a cobbler, and other crafters to see to the people's needs. They had some small trade with what they saw as "outsiders"; Taitou lay not far to the south, and the Dorsean city of Bianje stood on the border a few days to the northwest. Due west was the River Marsden, with many towns along its length. But Shuiniu was too small a place to receive great caravans from any larger settlement. Only small, modest traders came to visit the village, so that it was rare to meet more than a dozen outsiders in a year.

Mag apprenticed under a brewer in the town. The brewer's name was Duana, and she was as good a master to Mag as could have been hoped. Mag took to the craft with great zeal and exceptional skill. Under Duana, she learned the little tricks that would one day make her so renowned as a brewer. But she told me more than once that Duana's ale was much better, and I have often lamented that I never had the chance to taste it.

Now, at that time, there was a man in town named Ciaran. He was a Heddan, but he had moved to Dorsea in his youth. Being from so far away made him feel like an outsider, and deep in his heart was a desire for others to feel the same. He had a caustic manner and a cruel streak, and he was wont to create division between people where none had been before.

Naturally, he did not get on well with Mag, who tried to avoid him where she could. But her master owned the town's tavern as well as the brewery, and so it was impossible to avoid Ciaran entirely. Whenever she was around, he would barb and jab at her in subtle, veiled ways. I am sure you know what I mean—jibes which hide insults, but which he could always claim had been meant to be innocent.

I only heard of two times that Mag rose to the bait. The first was in the tavern, while Ciaran was downing a mug of her latest brew. He slurped at it and gave deep gasping breaths between each swig, a habit he knew she hated.

(That was a bugbear of Mag's, by the way. If I ever wished to annoy her, all I had to do was eat with my mouth open or smack my lips and tongue as I drank. Before long, she would pitch me into the nearest body of water she could find. I usually considered it worth it. I had to take my victories where I could, you understand.)

"This is fair stuff," said Ciaran, slamming his mug on the table a little too hard. "One day, someone might call you skilled at your craft, child."

Mag kept her gaze on the bar as she scrubbed it with a washcloth. "I thank you, of course."

"Then again," said Ciaran, "mayhap you have reached the pinnacle of your skill already. It can be that way. You reach a peak early on, and then you grow worse with time. If you find that to be the case, you must not be too disappointed."

Mag had very nearly scrubbed through the bar's varnish by this point. Her washcloth stopped, and a close observer would have seen her jaw muscles were like iron. She spoke before she could moderate either her words or her tone.

"Well, if I have already reached my peak, at least I can say I have one skill. Mayhap in the future, you will be able to say the same, though I doubt it."

Ciaran's face grew as ugly as his heart. He was a large man, with arms thick and hairy, and a great barrel chest packed with muscle from his work at the anvil. He pushed back his chair with a jerk, the tavern filling with the screech of wood on wood. Most conversations around them hushed, unless the speakers were too drunk to notice the sudden tension in the air.

"I do not take kindly to insults," said Ciaran.

Mag looked quizzically at him. "No one does. That is why they are insults, you steer."

His face went beet red. "Enough. I would have accepted an apology if you had groveled. But not now. Come outside, and I will beat remorse out of you."

Mag's blood was up. Duana was nowhere to be seen. So she gave him a fierce smile. "I am no bard, and so I cannot describe how amusing such a threat is, coming from you."

Now the people around them were getting nervous, that curious tension that always surrounds a bar fight. They did not wish to see anyone get hurt—at least, not too badly—but there is still something thrilling about seeing two foes knock the stuffing out of each other. And never is that more true than when a grudge has long been fomenting.

"Outside," growled Ciaran. "Now." And he strode out the front door.

Mag lifted the hinged panel that locked off the bar and began to follow him. But just then, Duana came out from the tavern's back room. She saw Mag heading off, and then she noticed that Ciaran was no longer in his chair.

"Where are you going?" she asked Mag sharply.

Mag glanced back at her. "One of our customers asked for my services."

"Mag!" said Duana. "Let it go. You have better ways to spend your time."

But customers were hurrying out after Ciaran, eager to see the fray. Mag gestured at them, and then at the emptying tables in the room. "Do I? There are no customers to serve. I will not be a moment."

She stepped through the front door. Ciaran waited in the street for her, hands clenched to fists at his side. He had rolled up his sleeves, revealing hairy forearms. His face was an ugly squint. Mag stepped up to him, and the contrast was striking: this smallish young woman before a hulking brute of a man. Some of the crowd's enthusiasm died.

"I shall give you one last chance to apologize," said Ciaran.

"And I will let you swing first," said Mag.

Then her face went dead. The light faded from her eyes. It was her battle-trance, and it chilled the villagers of Shuiniu to see it. Even Ciaran seemed stricken for a moment, and he hesitated.

But then he glanced around, seeing the villagers, knowing they were witnessing his doubt.

He swung for her face.

Mag grabbed his wrist and twisted. Her hand drove into his armpit like a knife. Ciaran cried out in pain as he doubled over.

Mag's fist pummeled his cheeks, his nose, his chin. She did not strike his barrel chest. Why bother, when thick muscle guarded him like armor? Only when he bent and twisted, trying to escape, did she hit his kidneys with punishing savagery. She knew where to strike to hurt him the most, all the places that can break someone no matter their size.

Ciaran cried out again and again, more plaintive each time. It was not long before he sounded more like a child than a hale and hearty smith.

She did not draw out his suffering. After beating him nearly into submission, she caught his wrist once more. Pinching the nerves, she sent him reeling off balance. With a sweep of her leg she tripped him. Even as he fell, she levered him over her shoulder. Screaming, he flew three paces to land in a heap among the crowd. He struck a few of the onlookers, but they did not seem to mind.

The crowd had murmured before the fight. When Ciaran had thrown his first punch, a few had cried out in excitement. But during the beating, everything had fallen to deathly silence. Now that silence reigned for a moment longer.

And then, all at once, the crowd burst into shouts and cheers. Some gathered around Ciaran's fallen form, trying to help him back to his feet. Others clustered around Mag, talking all at once.

Such was their excitement that not one of them noticed as her battle-trance fell away. For a moment, her eyes flickered with something like fear: the deep uncertainty of one who finds themself in a strange place, disoriented and alone.

None of the crowd saw it, but Duana, watching from the tavern's front porch, did. Her eyes filled with concern, even as Mag moved through the press to the door. Duana took hold of her arm.

"Mag," she said quietly. "Are you all right?"

A moment passed before Mag could force an uncaring smile. "Am *I* all right? Look at *him.*" She tossed her head at Ciaran, and then she gently pulled her arm from Duana's grasp to go inside.

It was the first time Mag ever fought another person. But of course, it was not the last.

"Wait," said Sun. "That cannot have been her first fight."

Albern raised an eyebrow. "Oh? Can it not?"

"Of *course* not!" cried Sun. "Where did she learn how to do that? And . . . and her battle-trance. You told me you experienced something like it in Tokana. But you wondered what horrible fate could have befallen Mag that led her to discover it. You are telling me it happened by chance during some barroom brawl in a town no one has ever heard of?"

Albern shrugged, annoying her further. Not only did it seem he had no answer, but he seemed not to think an answer was terribly important. "She had no idea where it came from—the trance, or her skill at fighting."

Sun took a deep breath, and then another. "I am not asking about her, at that time," she said. "I am asking you, now. Do you know where her ability came from?"

That only earned her a grin. "You have sharp ears, and a sharper wit."

"That is no answer!"

Albern raised his arms as though pleading for mercy, but he kept smiling. "I have some ideas and some rather wild guesses. But they will sound outlandish if you do not know the story behind them. And that is the story I am telling you now."

Sun turned away from him and looked at the road ahead. The town was far behind them, and Bertram was nowhere in sight. They were in open country, with only the Bluewater off to the south to break up the landscape. There were no answers anywhere, and no relief.

"I hate waiting," she growled.

Albern laughed hard. "That is an understatement if ever there was one."

FOUR

It occurs to me that I have said little of Kaita.

She was in northeastern Dorsea at the time, as was our hope. In bird form, she could fly straight over landscapes through which we had to find roads to traverse. But such travel is exhausting to a weremage. A rider passes most of a journey's weariness to their mount, where Kaita felt the full burden of it in her own body. It wore her down more and more, as the days added up to weeks and weeks grew close to months.

But where we were wandering aimlessly, she knew where she wished to go. Thus she was far away from us when she reached an outpost of Shades southeast of the Dunfen lake. There they hid from prying eyes in the thick woods, which no one has ever cleared.

In raven form, Kaita ducked below the canopy of the trees. Flitting from branch to branch, she searched for signs leading to her kindred. Weariness and anxiety made her movements sharp and jerky, and she thrashed in her flight, moving like one enthralled by mindwyrd.

But at last she spotted a path, marked by trees carved with subtle signs that one could only see if they knew what to seek. After following the signs for a league, she at last spotted the fresh-hewn timbers of the

Shades' buildings. The sight made her want to collapse from relief. Instead, she forced herself into one last desperate flight, covering the last few spans with a frenzied beating of her wings.

She landed in the center of the camp. Some Shades looked up curiously—and then all of them turned to her as her eyes began to glow, and her human form emerged from the raven's wings and black feathers.

Her close-fitting clothes were in the Shades' colors of blue and grey. But they were filthy with the grime of the road and threadbare from nights spent in dark dells and caves. Kaita knew it, and so she threw her hands up as the Shades drew their weapons and nocked arrows.

"I serve the master of death!" Her voice was half a croak, traces of the raven's call still lingering in her throat. "I am Kaita. There must be at least one here who knows that name."

For a moment, no one answered. Kaita feared they would shoot her down where she stood. Or they might take her prisoner, wasting priceless time in a cell until someone decided what to do with her.

But then, from the corner of her eye, she saw a wisp of a man straighten, sheathe his sword, and step forwards.

"Kaita?" His voice was as wonderstruck as the look in his eyes. "What in the dark below are you doing here?"

"Horata," she gasped, and her voice nearly broke on the word. She took a step towards him, doing it slowly so that her knees did not give out. "I might ask you the same. I thought you were in Feldemar."

"Reassigned," he said absentmindedly. He turned to the other Shades. "I know her! Lower your weapons. Someone go and get the commander."

The commander. Kaita's heart leaped. "Horata, who is in charge here?"

"Tagata," he said. Kaita's hopes fell. "She is a—"

"I know her well," said Kaita with a sigh. It would be a joy to see Tagata, but . . . She put a hand on Horata's shoulder, more for support than out of affection. "I thought . . . I hoped Rogan might be here."

Horata looked upon her with pity. "I am sorry," he said. "We have not seen Rogan in weeks. Not since the assault on the Seat. I thought he was at the Watcher."

Kaita shook her head, stifling her anger to keep from snapping at him. It was hardly Horata's fault that he was wrong. "He is not. I went there first. They had not seen him since he *marched* to the Seat."

Horata frowned. "Where do you suppose he could be?"

"I do not *know.*" Now Kaita could not entirely keep the exasperation from her voice. "That is what I am here to find out."

Some of her exhaustion must have shown in her bearing, for Horata stepped closer. Putting an arm around her, he led her towards the central building of the compound. "Well, let us get you some food. Not to mention a place to sit down. You look as though you have taken a long road to get here."

"Longer than you know," said Kaita. And though she tried hard to keep an upright, regal bearing, she leaned heavily on him. It felt strange to be walking again after so many hours of powering along on wings. "Thank you, Horata."

Color came to his cheeks. "We are all children of the Lord. We owe each other at least so much."

Inside was a corridor that turned immediately right and left. Horata took her to the right, where soon they came into a mess hall. Some scattered Shades were sitting about the tables, but not many, for it was between the midday meal and supper. Once he had her seated, Horata ran to the kitchen and fetched her some bread and the remains of that day's soup.

Kaita had not realized how hungry she was until the food was before her. She tore into it like a woman starving, and when Horata fetched her some ale, she finished the first mug in but a moment. As she ate more and more, crumbs and ale sticking to her face, Horata's eyes grew wide.

"Dark below, Kaita," he murmured. "What has happened to you?"

"Nothing," said Kaita. "And much. I have been long pursued, many times cornered, and twice has defeat come crashing down at the moment of my victory. And now I seek Rogan, but for *dark's* sake"—she sent a fist crashing down on the table, tipping her mug—"I cannot find him anywhere."

Horata snatched up her fallen mug and replaced it with his full one. "Well, we can help, at least in one respect. Tagata will know exactly where Rogan is."

"Yes," said Kaita, her hands beginning to shake as she took up her bread and splashed it into her soup. "Almost at the end. Finally."

But how many times during this journey had she thought the same thing?

She shied away from the thought. Despair helped no one, least of all the one suffering from it.

Being so preoccupied with her food, Kaita did not notice when another Shade entered the dining hall and approached the table. Only when Horata looked up at the woman did Kaita realize she was there.

"What is it?" said Horata. "Where is the commander?"

The woman—a girl, honestly, barely older than the children—glanced fearfully at Kaita before she answered. "She has gone. Some errand of the Lord called her away, and no one knows exactly why. She took no one with her."

Kaita paused, her mouth partly open, still full of soup-soaked bread. "What do you—" She paused and swallowed so that her speech no longer slurred. "What do you mean, 'some errand'?"

"I do not know," said the girl, her face going pale. "No one seems to. She did not say when she would be back."

Kaita's hands stopped shaking. She went stone-still as she looked upon the girl, whose eyes filled with fear.

Tagata. The one person here who could tell her where Rogan was. And she had vanished just as Kaita had arrived.

"Dark below," muttered Horata. "That is ill fortune beyond belief. I am sorry, Kaita. But still, you are here now. You can rest. We can get you new clothes, and—you will forgive me," he chuckled. "But a bath might do you some good."

"Yes," said Kaita slowly. "Yes, it would. And I will enjoy sleeping in a bed rather than on the ground."

Horata rose and drew her up after him, leading her to the bath and fetching new clothes while she scrubbed the dirt from her skin. But all the while, one thought remained with her, persistent, tapping at the door of her mind and trying to persuade its way in.

Was it possible that Rogan did not *wish* for her to find him?

Was it possible . . . the thought did not bear dwelling on . . . but could it be that the Lord himself did not wish for her to have what she sought? That despite his promises, he did not intend to give her the strength she needed to defeat Mag?

In a rigid mind, the seed of doubt can take long to find purchase. But once it has taken root, it can never be entirely eradicated.

"It is time, my son."

Rogan's hand clenched to a fist, crumpling the missive he had been reading. It told him something he already knew: Kaita was searching for him, and she was running herself to death in the hunt.

But this was the first time his father had spoken of the matter since Kaita had failed in Tokana, weeks ago. When Father had told Rogan that Kaita would have to die if the Shades were to win the war.

He stood from the table in his small room.

"Why now, Father?" he said.

"Do you not trust in me?"

"Always," he said immediately. "Forgive my impertinence."

The Lord's laugh was gentle. "You are too quick to beg my forgiveness. Those who serve us feel the same way towards you that you do towards me—afraid of making the smallest misstep, even when they are only curious. You are always gentle with them. Remember to reserve that same kindness for yourself. To answer your question: it is time because I have seen that it is time. I have no greater understanding than you. I have only a better grasp of the sight."

Rogan shook his head. "Then I trust in you. Only . . ."

"Only you wish to delay the moment as long as possible." Rogan could feel the Lord's deep sigh in his bones, and he felt, too, the sadness that came with it. "I desire the same thing. Yet if we are to achieve our aims . . ."

"I know." Rogan's voice had faded to a whisper. "Very well. I will send word to Kaita and tell her where to find me."

"Thank you, my son."

His father left him, and Rogan felt empty, as he always did.

Soon he left his room. A short hallway brought him to the chamber where his advisors were in council. As he strode in, they were leaning over a map of Underrealm, discussing a new wave of raids into Feldemar. But the moment they noticed Rogan, the chamber fell silent. Everyone present looked at him, eyes shining with love, awaiting his command. Only Ikaia dared to smile, stepping forwards and gripping his wrist.

"Things are proceeding well, brother," she said. "Our brave warriors have done much to foment discord between Dorsea and Feldemar. And by all accounts, no one in either kingdom knows they are ours."

"Good," said Rogan. "And the affair in Danfon?"

"It only awaits your order." Ikaia answered without thinking. But as she caught the reason he asked, she straightened, and her eyes went wide. The air in the room seemed to thicken, and now they were all frozen, looking at him, hanging on his next words.

"The order is given," said Rogan. "Tell Wojin it is time to act."

He paused. Unspoken words hung on the air, and everyone could hear them. No one moved. Almost he stopped there. Almost he left his father's command unfulfilled.

But Rogan was a dutiful son.

"And send word to Kaita," he said. "Tell her where to find me. A long-overdue conversation must finally take place."

FIVE

The rider who followed us through the Sunmane Pass had lost our trail some time ago. Now she wandered from town to town, chasing every lead from barkeeps and constables. The growing spring had given fresh rainfall, and she could not keep it entirely out of her boots. She shook her feet every so often to keep the water from growing too cold with stillness.

Something had changed. When the rider passed others on the road, she met untrusting looks that soon darted away. Some suspicion might be understandable—she wore a hood and a mask, after all. But this was something more. Something must have happened in the area, but she had not had time to stop off and find out what.

Suddenly she spied a troop on foot, making its way west along the road. The rider sighed and set her shoulders as she recognized Dorsean uniforms.

Stay calm, she thought. *And say nothing if you can help it.*

But it did not seem that the sky had blessed her with fortune that day. As soon as the soldiers spotted the horse coming, they fanned out across the road to block its path. The rider pulled up in front of the troop, glaring at them from beneath a dark brown hood.

"Hail," said a soldier, wiping melted snow from her hair. "What is your business in these parts?"

"What business of yours is business of mine?" said the rider.

That seemed to stump the woman for a moment, and she glared at the rider while trying to work out an answer. "I serve the king," she said at last. "The true king. I keep his peace. Who do *you* serve?"

True king? An odd word for a soldier to use. But the rider put that thought from her mind. She could not answer it now, and it was thus only a distraction.

"I serve no one any longer," she said, voice muffled by the mask. "I am only looking for two friends in a strange land."

"A strange land?" said the soldier, eyes sharpening at once. "And what land is that?"

The rider cursed inwardly. "I only mean that I come from western Dorsea. I have never crossed the Greatrocks before."

The soldiers edged forwards, some of them reaching for their weapons. The woman who led them drew her sword halfway out.

"A quick reply, if not an honest one," she said. "I think we have a spy on our hands."

"I am no spy," growled the rider.

"Oh?" said the soldier in mock surprise. "I am sure a spy would never lie about such a thing. Search her belongings."

The rider gave a great sigh, her shoulders drooping as if in defeat. Two guards saw the movement and relaxed, straightening as they came forwards. Their hands neared the horse's reins.

With a great shout, the rider kicked at the horse's flanks. It sprang forwards as though stung, and the rider drove one booted foot into the face of each soldier. They fell back with cries and broken noses. The other soldiers scattered as the horse threatened to trample them. They shouted for her to halt, but their cries were impotent, for they had no steeds of their own. Quickly they faded into the distance.

Dark take it, thought the rider. *A fugitive, now. Another thing to blame the wanderers for, when I find them again.*

But what under the sky had happened in Dorsea, when the king's soldiers were accosting lone travelers on the road?

"The answer, of course," said Albern, "is that there had been a coup in the Dorsean capital of Danfon."

Sun stared at him in wonder. They had stopped for the midday meal, and a bite of dried meat hung in her almost-limp fingers, her mouth half-open.

"You were here in Dorsea when the war broke out?" she said.

Albern smiled at her. "You might have guessed that. I do not doubt you learned the dates of it in your tutoring."

"I did not count the days of your story in my mind."

"I will not dwell overlong on that tale," said Albern with a sigh. "Others have told it elsewhere, and better than I could. I do not doubt that you have already learned something of it from your instructors in history. Suffice it to say that Wojin of the family Fei, uncle and chief councilor of the king, overthrew his liege and took the throne. His efforts went to waste in the end, thanks to the Nightblade—but of course, we did not know that at the time."

Sun shook her head. "What was it like in the kingdom? They taught me it was a horrid, bloody affair, and I cannot imagine that you escaped the fighting."

"No, we did not," said Albern. "The war threw the whole kingdom into chaos. Indeed, it rocked the foundations of Underrealm itself. And word was not long in reaching us—nor was it long before we found ourselves drawn into the conflict."

After Taitou, we spent two eternal weeks in northeastern Dorsea, riding from town to village to hamlet and back again. But nowhere could we find anything to tell us where to go next. Our mood darkened. Winter, at last, began to give way to spring, which should have helped. But instead of good and gentle weather, the sky started to rain almost constantly. It drove into our faces and down the backs of our necks, no matter how we bundled up against it. And yet it was still too cold for the snow to melt away. It turned into a thick and horrible slush upon the ground, mixing into the dirt to turn it into a dark and sucking mud. Mag and I began to grow snappish with each other, and even with Dryleaf, though in his case we at least tried to restrain ourselves.

It was in the town of Huzen, not too far from the coast of the Great Bay, that we began to rethink our plan. We were in a tavern called the Spiced Fiddle, and Dryleaf had his boots off with his stockinged feet up near the fire. Any chance to rest near a hearth, safe from the freezing rain, now felt like a luxury.

The old man had sung earlier, and then he had given me a turn. I had performed my song about Jordel. Dryleaf and I had worked on it ever since I first shared it with him in Tokana, and I had been performing it in taverns for some weeks. Mag, bless her, did not poke fun at me over it, for she could sense how dear to my heart it was. Indeed, the first few times I had sung it in a tavern's common room, I had been unable to finish, and I soon fell weeping back into my chair. But enough repetition had allowed me to keep my tears from falling, though my heart was still heavy as I sat with my friends and discussed our options.

"Mayhap we have been taking the wrong approach," said Dryleaf. "We have avoided large cities thus far, for there are too many prying eyes. Yet at the same time, there are a great many listening ears, and also discerning minds to sift the truth from lies. Mayhap we would find better information in Danfon, or one of the cities on the coast. We might even take a small detour to the High King's Seat. I know some folk there who are able to gather news from all across the nine kingdoms."

Slowly Mag shook her head. "I am not sure that is wise," she said. "If Kaita, or the Shades, are indeed here in northeastern Dorsea, we would waste a great deal of time going all the way to the Seat. Do we not know anyone else who could help us? Someone closer?"

"I do not," said Dryleaf. "The only place I can think of would be Danfon, and that is farther away than the Seat."

"That would be no help, then," I said. "Mayhap we should not go seeking out cities after all. Three of the Shade encampments we found were quite removed from civilization. Mayhap we need to turn away from towns and hamlets and seek them in the wild."

"Oh?" said Mag, arching an eyebrow. "And where in the wild would you have us look? I am no ranger like you, of course, but I have heard the wilderness is rather large."

I glowered at her. "I am no ranger. What would you have us do, then? Dryleaf suggests the cities, and you say they are too far. I suggest unclaimed lands, and you say they are too large. Let us hear your proposal, then."

"Why not simply carry on?" said Mag. "We do not know but that our current course will bring us to our enemies."

"Yet we have no reason to think it will," I snapped. "It is only a vague hope that great fortune will befall us."

Mag frowned at me. "Just as it did in Lan Shui."

I threw my hands in the air. "Oh, certainly. One out of four times."

"Now, now," said Dryleaf. "She may have a point, boy. The wide world is too large for us to search completely. And cities—or smaller towns," he said hastily, nodding in Mag's direction, "have one great advantage: they are peopled. If the Shades cause trouble in the wilderness, and we come to the place a week later, the trees and beasts will offer us precious little information. But if the Shades' actions affect a settlement of any size, the news will linger long enough for us to find it. It will even spread."

I gritted my teeth. That was a good point, though I was not quite ready to admit it. But I was saved from having to answer by a blast of horns outside the tavern.

I shot to my feet. Dryleaf sat up straight, clutching his walking stick. All around us, the tavern's patrons froze and looked anxiously towards the door. Then they began to move, some towards the outside, and some upstairs to their rooms. My mind gave a sickening wrench as I remembered the day Northwood fell.

"An attack?" I said, my voice gruff to hide my fear.

"It could be the Shades," said Dryleaf. "You two should go. I will be safe here."

"Get yourself to our room, at least," I said. He hastened to obey.

My bow rested against the wall, and I strung it quickly. As I did, Mag's battle-trance came over her. When I finished, she hefted her spear and shield.

"Outside," she intoned.

I followed her, slinging my belt quiver on and pulling an arrow from it. We burst through the door into the street, where we found Oku trotting nervously around. He gave a happy bark when he saw us and padded over to stand between us.

"Good boy," I said, patting his head. "Now, what in the sky is going on?"

A scene of chaos greeted us. Armed soldiers were killing each other in the streets. Thankfully, most of the fighting was a good distance away from the inn itself. I half-drew my arrow, but I stopped. There were no cloaks of blue in sight, nor any grey-clad fighters.

"I see no Shades," I said.

"Nor do I," said Mag in the toneless voice of her battle-trance. "It could be Dulmun."

"No, wait," I said. "Look at them, Mag. Every fighter wears the livery of Dorsea. The town's guards are fighting each other."

It was true. To a one, the soldiers before us wore the red and yellow of Dorsea. How did any of them know who to attack?

"Mayhap they are Shades in disguise?" said Mag in confusion. With no target for her spear, she had let the trance slip away.

"Mayhap," I said. A sick feeling was growing in my stomach. Something was wrong here, worse than it had been in Lan Shui or Tokana. "No way for us to tell. We should retrieve Dryleaf and flee."

Mag spun to me. "Flee?"

I pointed at the fighting. "How can we join the battle when we do not know who is on which side, much less which side is the right one? And what if the wrong side wins? Do you think we will be safe here in Huzen?"

"Very well," said Mag. "But where do we go?"

"We need not worry about the direction yet," I said. "This foe approaches from within, and so we must get ourselves without."

We ran back inside and fetched Dryleaf from the room. He took my arm and followed us down the stairs.

"What is it?" he said as we went. "Who is attacking?"

"We do not know," I said. "Dorsean soldiers are fighting each other in the streets. We have to leave the town."

His bushy brows drew together. "Dorsean soldiers . . . ?" he said slowly.

"We have no more answers than that," I said. Mag threw open the inn's door, and we stepped out into the street. "And I would rather discover them from a place of safety, than in the midst of—"

"You! Halt!"

Two soldiers stood before us. The fighting had moved closer to the inn now. The guards who challenged us stood over a man's gutted body. He was wearing the same uniform as them. Now they raised their swords, approaching step by step.

"Go back inside. Now!"

Mag's spear came up, her voice toneless again. "That is not going to happen."

One of them, a bulky man with a scraggly beard, snarled at her. "We are servants of the true king, and you will obey our commands." He rolled his shoulder, the tip of his blade moving in a lazy circle. "Unless you are traitors, in league with the pretender?"

True king? Pretender? What was going on here?

The second guard had stepped to the side, and I was very aware of how close her sword was to Dryleaf. I nudged the old man behind me. Oku bristled and growled at the woman. But while I hesitated, trying to determine the right course of action, Mag had no such hesitation. She pounced on the bearded man. For a terrible moment, I feared she would kill him, but she only struck him down with the butt of her spear. He fell, stunned but not quite senseless, and Mag kicked his sword far out of reach.

The woman put up a better fight, managing to trade two blows with Mag. But then the spontoon's tip came around, and Mag slammed the flat of it into the woman's temple with a crushing blow. She fell to the mud of the street, poleaxed. Her limp body now lay in the pool of blood from the guard they had killed right before we arrived.

"What in the dark below is this?" I said.

"No time to find out," said Mag. "The horses."

All the stablehands had fled, so we fetched our mounts and rode hard for the west gate. Though we avoided the fighting where we could, sometimes we had to gallop straight through the battle. It was a horrible reminder of Northwood. I kept a tight hand on the reins of Dryleaf's horse. He clung to the saddle, bent over his mount's neck to make himself as small a target as possible. I wondered how terrifying this must be for him, hearing only clashing blades and death screams.

The western gate was closed. Four Dorsean guards stood before it, with halberds held forwards in warning. I thought I recognized them from when we had come into the town hours ago.

"Halt!" cried one who seemed braver than the rest. At least her hands were not shaking. "No one is leaving the town!"

"We only wish to escape the fighting!" I called back as we reined in our horses before them. "We are simple travelers. This battle has nothing to do with us."

"No one is leaving," she repeated, and her voice was grim. "By order of the mayor."

I sighed and looked at Mag. "Do you wish to . . ."

"I do not wish to, but I will," she said, and she dismounted.

The soldiers, bless them, stepped towards us, for they saw a clear threat in Mag's stance. But when they thrust their halberds at her, the space where she had stood was suddenly empty. She darted between their stabs and ducked beneath their slashes. Though they were well trained, Mag's grace made them look clumsy and foolish. Oku edged forwards, though he seemed reluctant to join her in the fight.

"Kip, Oku," I said. "She does not need us."

Oku sat.

Mag's spear lashed out three times, and one by one, the guards fell. She did not slash or pierce them but knocked them senseless with the butt or the flat of the blade.

Soon only the guard who had challenged us remained, and now her hands *did* shake. She took two steps back, and now she was up against the town wall.

"No one is permitted to leave!" she cried, voice trembling and eyes wide.

Mag's brow furrowed, as it might have at a growling puppy. Then she knocked the woman's halberd out of her grip and caught both her wrists in one hand. Pushing her up against the gate, she held the haft of the spontoon across her throat.

"Now then," said Mag. "Suppose you tell us what under the sky is going on."

The girl gritted her teeth and tried to free her hands, but she could no more move than she could have taken flight. I saw the moment the spark went out of her. Her shoulders sagged, and a held breath escaped her in a sigh.

"No one knows," said the woman. "Not for certain."

"Suppose you tell us what you suspect, or what you have heard," said Dryleaf. "That might be just as useful."

"And if I do not?" she said, glaring at Mag.

"I will not kill you," said Mag easily. "But I will have to give you the same headache I gave your companions, and we will leave the town regardless. I would rather not do that. We are no evil folk, but merely confused, and likely more so than you are."

"That hardly seems possible," snorted the woman.

She had stopped struggling against Mag's grip, and so Mag released her wrists and took a step back. But I saw that her foot stayed close to the halberd, ready to kick it away if the woman should reach for it.

The guard rolled her head and felt gingerly at her throat, where Mag's spear had pressed against it. "Thank you. In answer to your question . . . word has reached Huzen that King Jun is dead. May he be safe in the darkness. Wojin has taken the throne."

"Dead?" said Dryleaf. "How?"

The woman's face turned sour like old milk. "Wojin says the High King sent an assassin."

I could only stare at her. That was patently ridiculous. What possible reason could the High King have had for such an act?

"Who is this Wojin you speak of?" I asked the woman. "I do not know that name."

But it was Dryleaf who answered. "He is—or was—Jun's uncle." He cocked his head. "But he is not next in the line of succession. That would be His Excellency, Prince Senlin. What happened to him?"

"Wojin says that the High King's assassins killed him as well," said the guard, her eyes flashing. "But I do not believe it, and neither did my companions, and neither does the mayor. We are servants of the king, not Wojin and his hired thugs. It is Wojin's men who have attacked the town, for the mayor refuses to swear fealty to him. He thinks—and I agree—that Wojin staged a coup."

"With help from the Shades," said Mag, her eyes widening.

The guard turned to her, incredulous. "How do you know that?"

"We do not know it," I said. "Not for certain. But we are roughly as certain of it as you are that the High King did not have King Jun killed."

Mag grimaced at me. "It would seem, then," she said slowly, "that these are loyalists to Jun, the true king." She bowed her head to the woman. "I would never have attacked you if I had known. I beg your forgiveness—and theirs."

I held up a hand. "To be fair to ourselves, we *did* ask politely to leave, at first. And in that spirit, please apologize to your friends on our behalf, when they wake up with bruises."

"I shall consider doing so," said the guard. She eyed her halberd, but if she thought to seize it, it was only for a wistful moment. She motioned us forwards. "Go on, then, since I clearly cannot stop you."

In a moment, I had the gate up, while Mag kept a wary eye on the woman, just in case. Then we were through and out into the open countryside, while Huzen burned in battle behind us.

But as the guard went to rouse her comrades and rally them to the fight, two more figures slipped out the gate. They faded into the wilderness at once, following the tracks of our horses. One of them had a heavy scar on his left cheek.

SIX

We rode west until Huzen was out of sight, and then we rode a while longer, for safety. On a bank overlooking a small stream, we pitched our tents to camp overnight. Mag watered the horses while I took a hatchet and began cutting wood for a fire. I ended up cutting more than we needed. It felt good to slam my hatchet into the wood over and over again, taking out my frustration at our formless foe and rapidly worsening circumstance.

All the while, Dryleaf sat on a rock, his sightless eyes staring into nothing. "A civil war," he said after a time. "A civil war in Dorsea. Something I never thought to see."

"Nor did any of us, I am certain," said Mag. "Yet war threatens all of Underrealm."

"Conflict between two kingdoms is one thing," said Dryleaf. "Even the rebellion of a king against the High King—well, while it is hardly common, neither is it unheard of. But a king's soldiers killing each other in the streets . . . that is something else. In the turmoil of these times, I fear conflicts like these will cause the greatest harm: a nation turned on itself, kin against kin. Such a thing has hardly been seen since the days of Roth himself."

"I have no doubt the Shades are behind it," I said.

"Of course," said Mag with a shrug. "They have been behind every crisis we have seen on our long road."

Dryleaf sighed. "I am sure you are both right. It fairly stinks of their work. They have perfected the art of sending others to do their fighting for them."

"If only they would show their faces," said Mag. "I would give much to capture even one of them, to trace our way to Kaita."

"But now she will be heavily protected," said Dryleaf. "She must have rejoined her allies. Thus our way seems unclear. What are we to do?"

"Find Kaita," said Mag at once.

"Without getting ourselves killed," I added.

She smiled. "In a perfect world, yes."

"Mag."

"Dearest Albern."

"Mag."

"I am mostly joking."

"Mag."

Dryleaf wore a frown, and he began to stroke his beard. "Mayhap Kaita should not be our focus—our primary focus, I mean, for the time being."

I arched a brow. "Oh? What do you have in mind?"

"We could seek Loren," said Dryleaf. "Kaita has allies now—and even more than we thought if Dorsea now works with the Shades. Mayhap we should acquire some friends of our own."

Mag's levity vanished in an instant. A very curious expression came over her—uncertainty, anxiety, and . . . and something else I could not quite identify. I frowned as she shook her head.

"Loren and the others could be anywhere," she said at last. "Who knows how long it would take to find them? What strength might Kaita gather to herself in that time?"

I hesitated. That reasoning made sense. Yet I could not shake an uneasy feeling that there was more to it. Mag almost seemed to feel . . . guilty.

Dryleaf's expression had fallen, and he shook his head. "My dear, I think we must be honest with ourselves. We have lost too much time already. It has been two months since we saw Kaita last. If she wished to vanish forever, hiding in some far kingdom where we will never find her, she could have done that by now. If she wished to surround herself with allies, she could have done that as well. We can hardly worsen our situation by spending more time, especially if we spend it strengthening ourselves for the fight to come."

Mag had been resting her spear across her knees. Now she seized it, shot to her feet, and threw it into a tree five paces away. The spearhead stuck in the trunk, quivering, as Mag's hands balled to fists at her sides.

"Mag!" I said, frowning.

"What?" she growled.

"You may not like it, but you have to admit he is—"

"I *know* he is right, Albern." Suddenly her shoulders sagged. "Of course I know it. I have been thinking of little else for the last month. Sometimes I hardly know why we are even here in northeastern Dorsea. Chasing some half-baked notion from a Rangatira? We have nothing. Nothing at all. And even now, with civil war breaking out, there is no sign of the Shades. I am . . . I am tired."

Slowly, she paced over to her spear and pulled it out. Just as slowly, she returned and resumed her seat by the fire. I had sat up, tense for a moment, but now I began to relax again.

"I understand, Mag," I said quietly. "I am tired, too. And you, Dryleaf, may try to hide it, but I can see the weariness in your shoulders as well. So let us rest. Let us slow down, at least a little. We can stop our wandering, and see what we can learn about this civil war, if there is anything to learn."

"I cannot stop," said Mag. "I cannot. I have to find her. I would hate myself if I stopped trying. And you said you would stay with me."

"Of course I did," I said. "And I will. Always."

She looked away from me. "Then trust me. Searching for Loren now would be unwise. Sky above, she will not even kill in a fight. She would be little help in our hunt, and we would only endanger her if she joined it. It would be a waste of time, and we have wasted enough as it is."

I sighed. "All right, then, Mag. We will keep looking for Kaita. We . . . we can continue asking around about the Shades. They may have something to do with this civil war. If they do, they may be easier to find now."

Dryleaf had been listening to us silently, but now his head snapped up. Though his eyes were sightless, I could almost see a light in them.

"There may be another way," he said. "Loren is not the only ally we could seek. We could find others."

Mag arched an eyebrow. "And where do you mean to find them? I know few enough people in Dorsea. And if I do not want to spend a month searching fruitlessly for Loren, I certainly do not want to take the time for a tour of recruitment."

Dryleaf cracked a grin. "You will not recruit anyone. You will be recruited. That Mystic captain in Taitou. Kun, of the family Zhou. If anyone in the kingdom wishes to find and fight the Shades, it will be him. If we can ingratiate ourselves with him, we may learn something of our enemy's whereabouts."

I had to admit that this idea appealed to me. We had been listless and wandering in Dorsea for far too long. And Victon always used to say that even a bad plan, carried out swiftly and with certainty, is better than no plan at all. I could think of worse things than allying ourselves with servants of the High King, Mystics though they might be.

Mag, too, had a spark of excitement in her eyes. "It would certainly be better than our aimless wandering. But I do not know if that Kun fellow was as trusting as he appeared. I heard the smile in his voice, but I also heard a false tone in it, and something steely lying beneath."

"Yet he did offer to recruit us," I said. "And we can prove our worth to him. Only a fool would refuse to have the Uncut Lady on their side of a battle."

Mag scowled. "They will not know about that ridiculous title, because you will not tell them."

I widened my eyes. "Of course not. I would never."

"Albern."

"Dearest Mag."

Dryleaf shook his head, wearing a little smile. "I can hear the eagerness in your voices so plainly, I can almost picture your faces. And I think Kun will be more than grateful to have you."

A reluctant smile pulled at the corner of Mag's mouth. "Well, then. Let us try it. It *has* been a long time since we were sellswords."

"A long time indeed," I said. "Let us get some good rest tonight, then. Tomorrow, we ride to join the war for Underrealm's future."

SEVEN

"I can relate to your situation," said Sun.

"Oh?" said Albern, cocking his head. "How is that?"

"Since meeting you, I have also found myself joining battles I did not expect," she explained. "Though of course, you and I fight no great battles of nations. We are monster hunters, I suppose . . . and whatever one would call it when we stopped those brigands near Lan Shui."

"Do not so quickly discount your actions—or, for that matter, my own," said Albern. "It is easier to see battles on a grand scale when looking through the lens of history. But a king's army is nothing but a collection of people. In ones and twos they join the fight, and in ones and twos they die—or they fight until they cannot anymore. You hear of them as part of a greater whole. But it takes wisdom to see that one is *always* part of a greater whole, whether you fight to save your loved ones, or you are hunting vampires in the woods."

That was a disturbing thought to Sun. After a moment's consideration, she thought she knew why. "But then, to what end? You say that you and I are rooting out evil, the way you and Mag did when you were younger. But if there is still evil today, is that not discouraging?"

Albern only smiled. "Good folk always seek a permanent end to evil. That is . . . well, I will not say it *cannot* be done, but it never *has* been done. But, after fighting for a time, of course someone is entitled to some well-earned peace. This, too, comes to us in ones and twos. A woman like Duana leaves the army in her autumn years, starting the trade she has long desired to practice. A couple like Mag and Sten meet, and fall in love, and build a life together."

Sun's voice grew hushed. "Yet evil found them in the end."

His expression dampened. "It did, at that. Because peace, like war, comes in ones and twos, and rarely to a whole nation, or the world. The world will never know peace. Not forever. But some people can. Doing good in your youth should, if fate is kind—which it sometimes is, despite appearances—let you enjoy a better world towards the end of your days. And that is no small thing to achieve."

Sun sighed, not entirely comforted. After all, Albern was close to the end of his days, and he did not live a peaceful life. But it seemed cruel to say so.

They had neared Bertram's southeast gate. Above them, the sky was now grey and hazy, the combined smoke from thousands of fires drifting up into the clean air. Here, the Bluewater and Blackwind rivers joined as they came leaping down out of the Greatrock Mountains to the east. Their mingled waters were called the Fangrong, and that great river ran to Dorsea's western coast.

Bertram had once been the capital of the kingdom, and it was easy to see the marks of that heritage in its bearing. The walls were among the tallest Sun had ever seen. Long, weighted banners by the gate bore a Dorsean longsword surrounded by a circle of stars, all yellow, on a red field. Over the walls, she could glimpse tall towers with the red tile roofs that were common across Dorsea, and balconies that surely gave a breathtaking view of the surrounding land.

Where the twin rivers met the eastern wall, they churned through two river gates. As the day cooled, the waters threw a slight mist into the air that gave everything a pleasantly dreamy quality. All of it made the approach to Bertram feel like riding up to a place from an Elf-tale, something half-hidden in clouds of vapor and magic, all of which might vanish if Sun turned her back on it.

But thoughts of her family would not leave her, and they spoiled the moment's enchantment.

Albern glanced at her from the corners of his eyes. "You seem nervous."

"Of course I am," said Sun. "Soon, we will be in Bertram. If my parents will discover me anywhere, it is likely to be here."

Albern seemed to think about that for a moment. He was silent so long that Sun finally looked over at him. His brow had furrowed, and his lips pursed, like a man trying to find words for a strange feeling.

"Out with it," she said. "What are you thinking?"

"I am trying to find a way to say what I mean without cruelty," he said slowly. "I understand your fear, Sun. And yet, I think you place too much stock in it."

Her brows rose. "Oh? Do you see my caution as foolishness?" She tried to keep her words light, but they held a bitter undertone.

"Not at all," said Albern. "But it is unhealthy to let fear rule our lives."

Sun wanted to tell him that she was not frightened, that she was only trying to be prudent. But as she thought on it, she realized that he was right. She was afraid. The thought of being dragged back into her old life—and the consequences she might face from her parents—was worse than she wished to contemplate.

She gritted her teeth. "I do not think the two of us can withstand my family's guards if they try to recover me."

"Yet we do not know if they will even find us," said Albern. "And we might ask others for assistance, if it should come to that. I have many friends in the city. And aside from that . . . well." His face broke into a broad grin, so pure that Sun felt her fear diminish. "I think you will greatly enjoy yourself here. Indeed, Sun, I think you will be reluctant to leave Bertram once we are done."

Sun snorted. "Of all you have said, I find that hardest to believe."

"Stories and belief."

They stopped talking as they reached the gate. It was open wide enough for several people to pass through abreast. But two guards with spears flanked the entrance, and they held up their hands in challenge.

"You there," said one. He was a squint-eyed man with bristling black hair and a beard to match. "Business in the city?"

"I have some friends to see," said Albern. "Nothing terribly exciting. I am afraid we are only simple travelers."

"Oh, we know you well enough, old man," spat the other guard, a thin woman with a jutting chin. "Rarely could your travels be called simple, and I suspect the same could be said for your aims in Bertram."

Albern leaned forwards in his saddle, eyes narrowing. "Ah, of course. Beilin, is it not? It is a long time since I saw you last."

Beilin spat. The gob of it hit the ground a few hands away from Albern's horse. "Some might say not long enough."

Sun stared flabbergasted at the guards. All her own concerns with Bertram fled her, and she could not hold her tongue. "I am a new traveler to Dorsea, but I am shocked to see such dearth of hospitality," she said hotly. "You claim to know this man, but I call that a lie. If you were aware of half the deeds he has done in his life—deeds that directly served this land and your laws, I might add–you would throw your gates wide before him and summon an honor guard to escort him through your streets."

Now it was the guards' turn to look shocked. But before they could reply, Albern lifted his hand. A sudden fit of giggling had taken him, and he could barely restrain it. His face had gone red, and his eyes watered as his chest jerked with silent laughter.

"Friends, please," he choked out. "There is no need for such posturing on my account. Beilin, you and your companion are welcome to search our things. We have nothing to hide from two upstanding servants of Dorsea's laws."

Sun stared at him. "But they—"

"They are only doing their best to protect their home," said Albern, still chuckling. "That is their duty. You and I know our intentions in Bertram, and they are not dishonorable. Why, then, should we fear for anyone to question us?"

Sun, in fact, knew nothing of Albern's intentions here, but she was wise enough not to say so. The guards had subsided after their indignation towards Sun. Beilin turned and spat again.

"Get your dark-damned selves in," she said in a disgruntled tone. "But you had best not set one foot out of line, either of you. Rest assured that we will watch you while you are here."

"You always do," said Albern. "We thank you for your service. And send my regards to Captain Stockton, if he still serves the city. It has been long since he and I have spoken over cups, and I might take the opportunity while I am here."

The guards pointedly ignored him, having already moved on to the next in line who wished to enter the gate. Albern and Sun walked their horses through, and then they were in Bertram.

Sun found a smile leaping to her face at the noise of it, the smell, the bustle and the chaos all around. She had always been enamored of a city's frenzy. The press of people went about their lives, each of them caring only for their own affairs and not a whit for those around them. Yet there was an identity to a city. A shopkeeper might not know the tanner she passed in the street, but if an outsider insulted their home, they would unite in an instant against the offender. And as soon as the fight had finished, each would likely forget the other's existence again.

It should have been alienating, but Sun had always found it comforting. Back home, cities gave her a rare chance to feel normal, and in them, no one gave her undue attention because of her birth.

She forced her mind back to the present. "It was clever of you to mention the guard captain," she told Albern. "But I still think you should have boxed their ears for the way they spoke to you."

"I spoke the truth," said Albern. "They were only doing their jobs. I have no doubt the King's law will be keeping a close eye on me while I am in Bertram, but I have grown accustomed to it, and it no longer bothers me."

Sun frowned. "Would that I had your calm."

Her mind drifted back to her parents, and the street seemed to narrow around her. She hunched her shoulders and pulled up the hood of her cloak, wary of being recognized. Albern saw it, and his smile weakened.

"Ah, yes," he said. "I did not mean to call your mind back to troubling matters. But come. Your hood is up, and I doubt they are looking for me. I will continue the tale to keep you distracted while I tend to my business. I mean to introduce you to an old friend—one who owes me quite a bit of coin."

EIGHT

The next day, we left the lands around Huzen and made for Taitou, where we had met Kun and his Mystics. We pressed the horses hard and reached the east gate the next day.

We were not surprised to find it even more heavily guarded than last time. Four Mystics stood watch, instead of the two we had encountered before. As we stopped before the gate, one of the Mystics hailed us with a shout. He was an imposing, older man with a frankly magnificent mustache.

"Who are you, and what business have you in Taitou?" he asked in a gruff bark.

"We are friends to the King's law!" I said. "When last we were here, we spoke to your captain, an honorable man named Kun of the family Zhou. We would speak with him again."

The Mystics looked at each other, and then the older one spoke again. "You would, would you? And why would he speak with you?"

Dryleaf spoke then, in the clarion voice of a bard. He was so often soft-spoken that it was easy to forget the power of his oratory. I would not have been surprised to hear him project his voice through a stone wall two paces thick.

"We can only imagine the burden upon Captain Zhou, now that Dorsea is in open war," he called up. "But we have come to lessen that burden. We are all servants of the High King, and her peace is threatened across Underrealm. Kun knows my stalwart companions are fighters. Tell him they have returned and wish to join him, and I promise that you will have done your captain a great boon."

That gave them pause. After a moment, the older Mystic turned to one of the constables and said something we could not hear. The constable darted off out of sight behind the wall, and the Mystic turned back to us.

"Very well," he called down. "I have sent word, and on your head be it if you waste the captain's time. In the meanwhile, come into the guardhouse. It is too damnably cold and wet out here, and you look as though you have ridden a hard road."

"Sky bless your courtesy," I replied.

They raised the gate for us to lead the horses through, and we hitched them to a post before stepping into the guardhouse. The gruff old Mystic joined us there by the fire while Mag led Dryleaf to a chair. Oku padded around the room, sniffing at everyone's boots. The constables tried to look stern, but I saw them scratch him behind the ears when they thought no one else would notice. The gruff old Mystic even crouched down and pulled a bit of dried meat from a belt pouch to feed him.

"Whence have you come?" he asked us as he stroked Oku's fur. "Have you any news of the civil war?"

"We rode straight from Huzen," I told him. "Fighting broke out in the town. The mayor there is loyal to King Jun. Loyalists battle Wojin's forces in the streets."

He gave a heavy sigh and stood. "The tale is the same in many places. Here, though, it is the reverse. I have heard our mayor is in Wojin's pocket, but he has a garrison of Mystics within his walls. He cannot declare for the false king while we have a sword to his throat, as it were."

Dryleaf clucked his tongue. "But that seems precarious for you, if he were to receive reinforcements. Is it safe to remain here?"

The man shrugged. "No one dons the red cloak for safety. Service to Her Majesty is all I desire."

"And a grand service you provide, I am sure," said Dryleaf. He grasped at empty air until the man took his hand. "I am called Dryleaf."

The man shook his hand firmly. "I am Gang of the family Hua, and you are too kind." His gaze turned to Mag and me. "Who might the two of you be?"

"This is Chao, and I am Kanohari."

"And you are here to join the militia?" he asked.

Mag and I gave each other a glance. It seemed Kun had already begun assembling a force here in Taitou. That would make it easier to join him, or so I hoped.

Before we could answer Gang, the door to the guardhouse opened. In stepped Kun, followed by two Mystics in cloaks with their hoods drawn up. Kun wore the same unquenchable smile as when we had seen him last.

"Sky above and dark below," he chirped. "I had not thought to see the three of you again so soon."

I matched his smile with one of my own. "But you did expect to see us. I suppose you understood things better than we did when you asked us to join the High King's fight."

"I have a gift for understanding things," he said. "And yet, I am eager to gain greater knowledge of the three of you, who have returned from your search for your friend. I confess that I am most curious as to why."

"We have reconsidered your offer," said Mag. "We wish to join your fight against the Shades."

Kun's sunny demeanor dampened somewhat at that. "Oh? And what of the friend you sought?"

I shrugged. "She was safe and sound on the coast. We found her in Brekkur, but she had long been reunited with her family. It was on our way back that the war broke out, and we reconsidered the position we took in our last chat with you."

"Hm," said Kun, tapping his chin. "The strange part is, most folk in Dorsea do not see our battle as being against the Shades. At present, folk either side with Wojin, or they remain loyal to King Jun and his son, who may still be alive."

This put me ill at ease. We had indeed spoken as if we had some inside knowledge of the war that most would not possess. Fortunately, Dryleaf rallied to save us.

"My friends are no masters of statecraft or politics," he put in. "But I have wandered these nine kingdoms a great deal longer than they. From all we have heard, it seems clear to me that the Shades are the true threat and the power behind Wojin's treachery. If the Shades fell, I doubt this civil war would last much longer. And since the Mystics are servants of the High King above all, it seemed to me that you would be most interested in such a course. That is why I suggested to them that we return here and that they enlist in your service."

Kun's smile remained strong as he considered these words for a long moment. His gaze moved slowly between the three of us as if he was trying to read our intentions in our expressions.

"So you are against Wojin, are you?" he said at last.

"Certainly, if he pits his strength against the High King," I said.

"If that is the case," said Kun, "then do you mind telling me why you attacked loyalist soldiers?"

Mag and I were too astonished to speak. And at that moment, one of Kun's Mystics stepped forwards and drew back his hood. The heavy scar on his left cheek was familiar, as was his stout frame, and soon I placed him. He was the young Mystic we had met at the Taitou gates the first time we came here. As I studied him more closely now, I could see that his face shared Kun's features. It seemed they were relatives.

"Lieutenant Zhen," said Kun. "Are these the ones you told me of?"

"They are, Captain," said the Mystic. "I came to the gate in Huzen just in time to see these two—not the old man—attack the guards. They forced the gate open and fled, even while fighting raged in the streets behind them."

Kun fixed a steely gaze upon us. "You followed them to Huzen. Did they ever visit a friend on the coast? In Brekkur?"

Zhen shook his head. "They did not, Captain. That was a lie."

I cursed under my breath. Zhen must have followed us from Taitou to Huzen, looking for us to betray the King's law. He must have had exceptional woodcraft for me to have never noticed him tailing us. It seemed Mag had been right—Kun suspected us from the first.

Kun's brow furrowed, even while his smile remained. "To be clear: did the guards at the gate attack these people, nephew?"

Zhen's expression darkened. "They did not, *Captain.* These two struck first after the guards tried to enforce their orders from the mayor, who is loyal to King Jun."

"Now, hold on," I said quickly. "We were in the middle of a strange town, trapped in a battle about which we knew nothing. We had no idea the guards and mayor were loyal to King Jun. We did not even know about the civil war. We only sought to escape the fighting."

"By harming servants of the King's law," said Kun, nodding as if I was making perfect sense. "Of course, I wish to believe you. But there is, of course, no reason to do so, since you have lied about so much else. There is every possibility you knew exactly what you were doing. And that, I am afraid, is a risk I cannot take. *Guards!*"

The last word was a battlefield bark, so sharp and sudden that I jumped. The door flew open, and four Mystics entered with blades drawn. The constables in the room drew their weapons with grim looks on their faces.

Beside me, Mag had tensed to fight. Dryleaf's head swung back and forth, trying to read the room from the sounds around us. Oku backed up against my legs, whining. But before things could go any further, I threw up my hands towards Kun and the Mystics at the door.

"Wait!" I said, as sharp as Kun had. It stopped everyone for an instant, but that was enough for me to continue. "Listen. When last we were here, we told you we used to be mercenaries. That was true, but not the whole of it. This is Mag, known to many as the Uncut Lady. I know at least some of you must have heard of her."

They froze on the spot, though Kun had given them no order to halt. His eyes went wide as he looked upon Mag with fresh wonder.

"That is right," I went on, more slowly now. "If you have heard of her, you know she did not have to leave a single guard alive at that gate in Huzen. Yet she did them no lasting harm, but only left them with a few lumps. She could kill everyone in this room right now if she wanted to. Or she could do the same to you as she did to those guards, getting us out of here without spilling a drop of blood."

The air in the room felt thick as butter, and still, no one moved—except Kun, who licked his lips.

"I believe she could," he said, "if tales of her exploits have not been exaggerated. Yet neither of you moves. What are we to make of this?"

"We have no wish to hurt anyone," I said. "We told you we came to help, and that is the truth. Take us into your service. With the Uncut Lady on your side, you are that much closer to victory, whatever your aims."

Again the room went silent. Mag, for her part, had not moved since I started speaking. The mask was down, her battle-trance rendering her emotionless, cold, calculating. I hoped she would restrain herself until we were sure there was no other way out of the room.

Still, Kun stared at us. But now his focus was mainly on Mag, and his perpetual smile had faded. I saw calculation in his eyes: factors weighed, measured, and tossed aside one by one.

At last, he managed to summon his smile again.

"I believe that you do not wish to harm us," he said, "or it would have happened already. But neither can I trust you, what with you having attacked soldiers under the king's command. Even your offer now veils a threat of violence, like the peacetime treaty of a warlike king. And I cannot discount the possibility that you might be spies. I am afraid I must ask you to leave. And if you are on the side of the King's law, you will do so without a fuss. If not . . . well. I suppose I shall learn firsthand whether the Uncut Lady deserves her reputation."

I was at a loss. It was heartbreaking to think of leaving Taitou empty-handed. We would be no better off than we were when we fled Huzen, and we would have wasted even more time into the bargain. Worse yet, Kun would doubtless send word of this to the Mystics across the land. We had to persuade him, but I was at a loss.

But Dryleaf was not. Again he spoke as a bard, his voice filling the room and invigorating the heart.

"You are making a mistake, and you are shirking your duty," he said.

The air in the room, already chilled with the outside air, seemed to grow colder still. Kun's eyes flashed.

"You are turning away two fighters who could turn the tide of a battle," Dryleaf went on. "And former military officers who could train this militia you are recruiting."

Kun's smile widened. "Oh?" he said. "You think you can train my fighters into worthy soldiers?"

Mag dropped her mask. I saw the tension bleed out of her, and at the same time, I felt some of it dissipate in the air, making me sigh with relief.

"I can," she said earnestly. "I can turn your farm boys and smiths' daughters into a force of warriors you can *use.*"

Kun deliberated on that for a moment. But then he shook his head. "It is too great a risk."

"Watch us as close as you like," I said. "What harm could we do if you are vigilant around us?"

Kun's smile showed teeth. "You two should know better than most that a soldier you cannot trust is worse than useless."

I gave an exasperated sigh, but mostly because he was right. "Then give us a chance to prove you can trust us! A week, Captain. Just give us a week."

His brows rose. "A week? And just what do you think you could do in that time?"

That gave me pause, and I shared a look with Mag. To be honest, the words had slipped out of me in desperation. I did not know that I *could* do anything with just a week. But Mag answered to cover my sudden silence.

"In a week, I can train a fighter who can beat one of your Mystics."

Kun's smile broke into a full laugh. "I assume you are joking."

"I am not," said Mag. "Let me prove it."

Inwardly, I groaned. Ten days to turn farmers into fighters who could beat hardened Mystics? I would have balked at the challenge when I was in my prime, and I had not trained soldiers in well over a decade. It seemed impossible. But we had little choice.

"Hm," said Kun, stroking his chin. "I must admit, such a feat would impress me. And yet, there remains the matter of your dishonesty. Why should I believe your intentions or your boasts, when you have lied about your purpose in Dorsea since the first moment I met you?"

Mag fixed him with a look. "You strike me as one who knows the value of truth sparsely given. When first we met, you suspected us. You sent one of your agents to follow us and see if we got up to any mischief. Yet when you spoke to us, you were all smiles and courtesy."

Kun tilted his head. "No circumstance demands ill manners."

"Just so," said Mag. "But we had no reason to trust you. If you know anything about the Shades, you know that they have slithered into many corners across the nine kingdoms. We thought it better to keep our intentions far from our lips, lest word of it reach them. I regret it now, but I would do it again."

All was silent for a long moment. Then, finally, Kun shook his head ever so slightly.

"A bit of the truth is better than none, I suppose. Very well. You shall be provisional officers in my force. In one week, there shall be a trial by combat. You choose one of your soldiers, and I will choose a Mystic against whom to pit them. If your champion wins, you can consider yourselves enlisted. If my champion wins, you will be on your way and trouble me no more."

There it was. A week did not seem anywhere near enough time. But it was what we had.

And Mag, of course, smiled and said, "We have a deal."

NINE

We had arrived in Taitou late in the day, and so we rested overnight before Kun brought us to his forces. He made us pay for a room at the inn, but it seemed unwise to complain. In the morning, Kun fetched us and led us towards his encampment on the northwestern end of town. Dryleaf and Oku came along with us. I was afraid Kun might order them to stay behind, but he said nothing.

We had not spent a great deal of time in Taitou before, but even so, I could tell things were different. There was a tension in the air that had not been there before. People in the streets had a new sense of purpose, an excitement above the day-to-day lives of common folk. Wagons and carts moved weapons from smiths and town stores to Kun's encampment. Smithies rang with the music of hammers, and there was an extra note of urgency in every haggling merchant trying to extract more coin from each deal.

As we followed Kun out the western gate, we saw the land that had become his army's training grounds. His troops were housed and fed in the city, but Kun had commandeered a few farms outside the walls to give them a space to train in weapons fighting, as well as to practice marching and moving in formation.

There looked to be at least four hundreds of soldiers formed into ragtag groups. Some were in lines, while some were paired off and battering each other with blunt swords. As we drew closer, I spotted red cloaks moving among the crowds. There were dishearteningly few of them.

"How many Mystics do you have?" I asked Kun.

He looked over at me, his immortal smile never faltering. "Forty, all told. Only ten of them are of the rank of knight. Those, I have assigned as lieutenants or sergeants in this little force. The remaining Mystic warriors are my unit, to form a strong center on any battlefield we may find ourselves upon."

Mag nodded. "That is wise. And how many soldiers have answered your call?"

"Four hundreds and three scores," said Kun. "Not so many, but more than my officers can manage easily. I am quite thrilled to have your help, even if you only remain for a few days."

"We are sure you are," I said, letting a hint of sarcasm shine through. "But if you fear we are spies, why would you tell us the composition of your forces so exactly?"

That made Kun laugh. "Oh, really. Any farmer in his fields could get a good count of my soldiers with hardly any effort. If you worry about the security of information, be assured that I do not intend to tell you anything about my aims, intentions, or plans."

Mag's brows rose. "How heartening."

As we came to the training grounds, Kun gave a tremendous barking shout. "*Tou!*"

Everyone within a span of him jerked, all the soldiers turning to look in his direction. Most of the regular militia simply stared, but every Mystic placed their hand over their heart in salute. The closest redcloak came straight to us, and when he reached Kun, he bowed. He was not as old as we were, but he was not exactly young, either. His frame was impressive, and he wore a short goatee, neatly trimmed, with long hair bundled into a tail that fell just past his shoulders.

"Captain," he said. "How may I serve?"

Kun turned to the two of us. "This is Tou, one of my lieutenants," he said cheerfully. "Tou, please meet Albern of the family Telfer, and Mag, and their friend Dryleaf. I have a wager with them, of sorts. They are to be assigned as sergeants, and each is to train a squadron of militia for the coming campaign. If in one week, they can train a fighter who can defeat one of our order in combat, they are allowed to stay on as part of our force. Otherwise, they will have to leave us."

Tou arched an eyebrow at that. "As you say, ser. I will see to it that they drill hard."

"Oh, do not trouble yourself overmuch," said Kun, smiling wider. "They are the ones being put to the test here, not you. After all, I have no cause to doubt *your* loyalty. But do see to it that they stay out of trouble, will you?"

With that, he turned on his heel and walked briskly away. Tou watched him go for only a moment before turning to us.

"I am Tou of the family Shi," he said, extending his hand. "Well met, even if in strange circumstance."

I took his wrist. "Well met indeed," I said.

"You look to be an archer," he said, and then turned to Mag. "And I would guess that you prefer to fight up close?"

"Right you are, on both counts," I said.

"A Calentin archer is always welcome," he said. "Come. A few of my squadrons lack Mystics to lead them, and I have been trying to manage all of them on my own. Let me introduce them to you."

He led us through the training grounds at a slow pace, in consideration of Dryleaf. Nearby, rows of stuffed targets had been lined up for archers. Too, several large practice rings had been outlined for sword and spear training.

Many people were hard at practice now, and I saw redcloaks moving among them—Mystics giving instructions and barking orders. Some paused in their duties and hailed Tou, waving, and he always waved back. He looked to be a popular man and a respected one, and I hoped that would bode well for us.

"Our forces number five companies," Tou went on. "Each company is led by a lieutenant—me, in your case. Lieutenants wield five squadrons of around fifteen, and each squadron is led by a sergeant. Only a handful of the sergeants are Mystics. The rest are veterans of King Jun's army or former mercenaries." He grimaced. "Or I suppose I should say returned mercenaries, for they are all taking coin to fight once again."

"Not the greatest force we have served in, but not the smallest, either," said Mag. "If Kun can find a worthy target to point us at, we may be able to do quite some damage to the enemy."

"That is the hope," said Tou. He cocked his head. "Though as a matter of etiquette, I must ask that you refer to him as Captain Zhou in the future."

Mag nodded quickly. "Of course. Our soldiering habits are rusty, but I will endeavor to polish them."

At last, we came to a stop in front of two groups of people. A gaggle of archers stood to our right, awkwardly firing shafts at the row of targets before them. To the left, some fighters with practice swords and shields were drilling, though their swings were clumsy and slow.

It was our first chance to get a good look at what Kun had to work with, and it was not entirely heartening. Most of these "fighters" looked to be anything but. They were farmers, craftsmen, and shopkeepers. Every so often, I would glimpse the brawny arms and solid frames of blacksmiths or woodsfolk. But they were few and far between, and they were as helpless with their swords as anyone else. Smiths are usually skilled at crafting steel, but not wielding it.

"Green Squadron! Black Squadron!" Tou's voice ripped through the morning air. "Form up!"

The people around us stopped what they were doing and looked at Tou curiously. One by one, they approached and formed into two ragged lines. They were slow about it, seeming more confused than interested.

"Green Squadron," said Tou, addressing the swordfighters and waving his hand at Mag. "You have a new sergeant. Her name is Mag, and she will see to your training from now on. Black Squadron, you will now be reporting to Albern of the family Telfer."

Dryleaf raised a hand. "And where are my soldiers, if I may be so bold?"

That got a chuckle from Tou, as well as from many of the assembled militia. "An oversight on my part, grandfather," said Tou. "I will find a squadron for you as soon as I am able." He turned back to Mag and me. "You will report to me at the end of each day. Muster is at dawn every morning, and while we train, your soldiers are expected on duty ten days a week. Any questions?"

"No, ser," said Mag and I.

"Excellent." Tou gave a small sigh and looked our squadrons over. "Get to work, then. You have much to do."

"Ser!" Mag and I snapped off salutes, which I thought were passingly suitable for how out of practice we were. Tou waved and left us, heading towards his other units.

Each of us went to our squadrons. I eyed the archers before me critically, and Mag did the same with her swordfighters. My mind began to fall into old habits, and I noticed myself picking out those who stood poised and ready, those who seemed lost, and those who seemed lazy.

"All right, recruits," said Mag at last. "We have watched you dance. Now you will learn how to fight."

As we began our training, Dryleaf headed off into Taitou with Oku, seeking information. I led my squadron over to a row of targets, while Mag took hers to the practice rings. Some of the archers began to line up and prepare to fire, but I called them back.

"Hold a moment. You know my name, but I have not learned any of yours. I can hardly instruct you if I must resort to calling out 'You there!' every time." I pointed to the closest of them, a large man whose black skin and great height spoke of Feldemarian descent. His thick locs were bound into a tail that swayed when he moved. "What is your name?"

He looked uncomfortably to either side of him as if making sure I was talking to him and not someone else. "Chausiku, ser."

"Well met, Chausiku," I said. "If you do not mind my asking, why are you here?"

Chausiku blinked. "Ser? I answered the call to defend Dorsea from—"

"Forgive me, that is not what I meant," I said. "I mean that you look to be at least ten hands tall, and your shoulders are almost as broad as my bow is long. Why are you here, in this squadron, rather than with the swordfighters?"

His dark face darkened still further in a flush. "I am a hunter by trade, ser. I am skilled with a bow already, and I have never wielded a sword, and do not want to."

"Well, you shall have to learn, regardless," I told him. "Bowcraft is all well and good, but if the enemy gets close, you shall be glad of a blade with which to defend yourself. Still, I am glad you are already familiar with your weapon. Who else here already knows something of archery?"

Seven of them threw their hands up, but one woman did so faster than the rest. She was short and slight, with black hair cut to sweep forwards rakishly. Her skin looked only recently sun-browned, as though she were more used to spending her days indoors. Her eyes were sharp and focused on me like a hawk's. I pointed to her. "You. What is your name?"

"Jian, ser," she said, lifting her chin slightly.

"And where did you learn to shoot?"

"My father was a hunter and a bowyer," she said. "I studied bowcraft under him, and I still work with him in his shop."

"A bowyer!" I said, delighted. "I am one myself—or was, until almost a year ago. We shall have to trade techniques sometime."

"I would be glad to, ser," she said. Then her smile twisted. "And I am not afraid to learn how to kill up close, as some others are."

That gave me pause, and I noticed another flush creeping into Chausiku's cheeks—but this time from anger rather than embarrassment.

"Well, I am afraid I must disappoint you, as well," I said, and raised my voice to address the entire squadron. "The most important thing you will learn from me is not how to kill. That is something you will learn as an unfortunate matter of course. But I hope you will focus on another skill that is much more important. First and foremost, I will teach all of you how to stay alive."

Jian frowned and pushed her hair back off her forehead. "It seems to me that the best way to stay alive is to kill one's enemy so that they are no threat."

"And do you imagine your enemy will stand there and let you plant an arrow in their eye?" I countered. "I would say rather that the best way to kill your foe is to stay alive long enough to do it. And besides, there are many more dangers in a campaign than the soldiers you will face on the battlefield. Hunger and cold, and especially disease, have killed far more soldiers than any battle in the long pages of history. Yet the bards will never sing songs of dysentery. Being a good soldier mostly means keeping yourself healthy until battle finally comes. If you do not learn how to survive a forced march, no tricks of archery I could teach you will be of the least use. Do you understand?"

They gave me a scattered chorus of "Yes, ser." Jian mumbled it along with the rest of them, but I wondered if she genuinely grasped my meaning, or if she even wished to. I decided to let it go for the moment. I was new to these people, and it is an inferior officer whose first action is to throw their weight around.

"Very good," I said. "Now, has anyone here fought before? Any veterans at all?"

To my dismay, only one man raised his hand: a man slightly older than me, whose pale skin and flaming red hair and beard marked him as a Heddan. He looked around at the rest of the squadron, and he seemed surprised to be the only one with his hand up. That told me the unit had only recently formed, and most of them had not had time to meet or learn much about each other.

"Well, that is one, at least," I said, trying to hide my disappointment. "What is your name?"

"Hallan, ser," he said crisply, drawing up straight. He spoke with the rolling, lilting quality and strange affects of Hedgemond, and his great beard jumped when he talked. "I'm a veteran of King Kashonnel's army in my youth, though thass nearly a score of years ago now. But I saw action, ser."

"I am glad to hear it," I said. "Do you remember your training drills, Hallan?"

He flashed a grin to reveal bright teeth, but also two gaps in them. "I'm sure they'll come back quick, ser."

His smile was infectious, and I found myself returning it. "Very good. Then let us finish our instructions and get to work. We have much to do and not enough time for it."

TEN

I QUICKLY LEARNED THE NAMES OF THE REST OF MY SQUADRON. BUT NOW, these many years later, I cannot remember all of them. That is the way of things, I fear, and the same is true for all the mercenary companies with which I ever fought. Memory is fickle. Unless a particular story stitched one of my companions tightly in my mind, I forgot them eventually.

Mag and I launched into training our soldiers with great vigor. We set them to the drills we had done in the Upangan Blades. Victon had been an excellent officer, quickly able to turn even the greenest warriors into passable fighters.

And the greenest warriors seemed to be what Kun had given us. Both Mag and I struggled to maintain hope through our dismay. Hallan was the only person in either of our units with any experience in a proper fighting force. I could not tell if Kun had stacked the deck against our success or if our soldiers were representative of the entire army. Something told me it was a combination of the two.

From the start, I began to get a feel for the personalities of those in my squadron. Jian, for example, had a bit of a nasty streak and a frightful temperament.

"You shoot for the head too often," I told her once. "Of course, you will kill a foe if you strike them between the eyes, but it is a much smaller target. The chest is a more reliable hit, and it will remove your enemy from the fight just as quickly."

A savage twist came to her mouth, and I could not quite have called it a smile. "That seems sensible. But what about gut shots, then? I have heard those are likely to kill, and painfully. I would not mind letting these dark-damned traitors suffer before ending them."

I frowned. "They are painful, that is true. But still not as good as the chest. If you shoot for the gut, and your aim is low, you are likely to strike the belt or buckle. That may keep your shot from bringing them down. And if you are off by a wider margin, your arrow might pass between the legs and miss. We aim for the chest because it is the largest target, with the widest margin for error."

Again she nodded, and she did not seem to notice my unease. "That is sensible, as well. The chest it is, then." She showed her teeth for a moment and pushed back her rakish hair. "And then if I miss, I may be fortunate and hit the gut after all."

Chausiku was next to her in the line, and his locs swayed as he turned to glower down at her—far down, for she was less than eight hands tall. "Our purpose is not savagery," he said. "We are here to save the kingdom, not become torturers."

Jian turned to face him. "I am here to punish traitors, not to coddle them."

"Enough, from both of you!" I snapped. "Turn your ire into action. Any more arguing, and you shall be running laps around the training grounds."

"Yes, ser," grated Chausiku.

"I am not afraid of running," muttered Jian. But she turned her attention back to the practice targets, and Chausiku did the same.

Hallan had a more challenging time with his drills at first. I stepped up behind him on that first day and watched as two of his shots whizzed by the dummy.

"Rubbish," he muttered, his beard twitching. Then he noticed me standing there and lowered his bow, straightening up. "Ser. What can I do for ye?"

"I am only observing," I told him. "You have good form. How long has it been since you practiced?"

"Long enough that when last I did, my eyes still worked," he groused. "Form's easy enough, iss getting the target sighted thass tripping me up."

"Why do you not have spectacles?" I said. "Taitou may not be a great city, but surely there is a glass-weaver in town."

"Sure enough there is," he said with a nod. "Juss never needed them much, I suppose. I've been a woodsman for years now, and I can see plenty well enough to bring down a tree. And iss simple living, so I never had much in the way of extra coin to pay for glass."

"Well, you shall need them if you are to fulfill your duty now," I said. "And the coin for it can come from the Mystics. I will speak with Tou this evening and arrange it."

Hallan looked pleasantly surprised, and he bowed, his beard pushing into his chest. "Well, my thanks to you then, ser." He grunted. "Spectacles, on my ugly old face. Who'd've guessed it."

It was not long before I came to treat Hallan as my unofficial second-in-command. He had a good head on his shoulders, and he could make peace if tensions rose among the squadron—particularly with Chausiku and Jian. When I relayed an order through him, my soldiers obeyed as if it had come straight from my mouth. I tried not to favor him too heavily, of course, for I feared the others might grow jealous. But in fact, I think it rather endeared me to them. They seemed to believe that if I relied on Hallan, I must be someone of sound judgement.

But while I did my duty in training my archers, I was much more concerned with Mag's swordfighters. Kun's test would be combat in the ring, not a test of archery, and we had to pass.

On the third day of our training, Tou came by for inspection. I saw him heading for Mag's squadron, and I turned to Hallan.

"Hallan, I am going to speak with the lieutenant," I told him. "If you need me, send someone to fetch me."

"Yesser," he said with a nod, and nocked another arrow.

I went running after Tou and reached him just before he reached Mag's unit. He saw me coming and gave a nod without asking why I was there; I suspect he could guess.

Mag was standing at the edge of a ring, and two men were training in the middle of it. She looked up as Tou and I approached, and she snapped off a salute to him.

"Ser."

"Sergeant," said Tou. "How goes the training? Are you in need of anything?"

"I would enjoy more time to work with them and at least one fighter who had seen action before," said Mag. "But since I do not think those are things you can provide, I will not request them of you."

Tou nodded. "Fair enough. Sad to say, we are all somewhat green here. I myself have never seen combat on the field. The two of you may be the most experienced fighters in the whole force." He pointed at the two men in the ring behind Mag. "Who are these?"

Mag pointed to the younger combatant. He was a strong man, wearing a sleeveless shirt that left his bronzed arms glistening. His black hair was cropped close and dripping with sweat. As I watched, he swiped the sweat away, never taking his eyes from his foe.

"That is Dibu," said Mag. "His opponent is Jie. They are among the better specimens in my squadron. I have tried to pair each fighter up with someone close to them in skill so that all of them get the most benefit from each training session."

Dibu lunged, swinging a horizontal strike. Jie got his shield up, but Dibu managed to catch the edge of it. Jie's shield arm flew wide. As he stumbled back, Dibu pressed forwards. His blade circled around and up towards Jie's face.

I tensed, but Dibu controlled the swipe. It stopped just short of Jie's eye. Jie recoiled, and his foot came down in a puddle of slushy snow. While he was off balance, Dibu kicked his gut. Jie fell, his sword and shield clattering from his hands. Dibu stepped up and pointed his blade at the larger man's face.

"Good!" called Mag. "Reset, and do it again. Jie, you must study your battlefield always. Know where your footing is safe, and where it is precarious. Mud can win a fight faster than skill."

"Yesser," said Jie.

He reached out a hand, and Dibu helped pull him to his feet. But when Dibu looked over to see the three of us there watching him, including Tou, he suddenly seemed embarrassed. His bronzed face flushed, and he quickly turned away.

Tou cleared his throat. "That one does not like performing," he said, stroking his goatee. "Yet he focused well enough during the fight. Who else do you count among your best?"

Mag arched an eyebrow and motioned for Tou and me to follow her. "I have one of particular note. Her name is Li. She has never fought in a real battle before, but her mother was a soldier in King Jun's army, and she taught Li many forms. Between that and the girl's natural talent, Li certainly has the greatest skill of anyone in my squadron. I expect to rely on her to help me teach the rest of them."

I could see at once that Mag spoke true. Li was paired up with another woman, and both of them were light of build but wiry. Yet Li was far more quick and nimble on her feet than her opponent, darting back and forth like a serpent. First her blade was above, then below, and then sweeping in from the side. It was all her opponent could do to keep the sword away from her padded armor, and she could not do so forever.

With the speed of liquid thunder, Li spun around her foe's clumsy strike. The flat of her blade crashed into the small of the other woman's back. She fell facedown in the dirt. Immediately Li straightened, heaved a deep breath, and sheathed her sword.

"A good strike," called Tou. Both women snapped around to look at him. "But you relented the moment you had an advantage. You cannot do the same thing in a real fight."

Li's eyes widened, and she bowed. "Of course, ser. It is just . . . well, I already felled her."

"And an enemy felled can rise once more if you do not finish them," said Mag. "Again. And this time, do not pull back until the fight is over." She waved at the two of them to begin and then turned to confer with Tou and me.

"She moves like you, Mag," I told her.

Mag looked somewhat miffed. "She is quick enough on her feet, I suppose."

"Well, everything seems to be in order," said Tou. "Better than in order, in fact. I still do not entirely understand why the captain made this wager with you, but I find myself hoping you will win."

"As do we, ser," I said. "Do you have any advice for us? Any tips that might secure a victory?"

Tou shrugged. "I have no hidden information, if that is what you mean. The terms are rather clear, and the captain seems confident you shall not beat him. I can do little more than encourage you to do your best, and hope."

I sighed. "Well, if that is the best we can do, then we shall do it. Thank you, Lieutenant."

Tou nodded and left us. I looked to Mag.

"What do you think? Do we have a chance?"

Mag looked at Li, who was again trading blows with her opponent in the ring.

"A chance? Mayhap. Ask me again in a few more days."

ELEVEN

But of course, Mag and I were not the only ones joining together with allies.

To the north of us, close to the Feldemarian border, Rogan had encamped with many of his soldiers. As I have mentioned, they were the ones raiding into Feldemar. They crossed the border in Dorsean uniforms, attacking farms and the caravans of lesser merchant families. In this way, they had been fomenting discord between the two kingdoms and drawing King Jun's attention to the area. This distracted Jun from the coup that Wojin had been planning under his very nose.

Now that open war had broken out in the kingdom, however, Rogan's strategy would change radically. And it was while he was concocting these plans that Kaita found him at last.

Rogan stepped out of his broad tent and into the open air, walking through the center of the camp. All around him, Shades stopped in their tracks and saluted, hands over their fists. He nodded to each, giving them a stern smile that warmed their hearts.

But as he neared the center of the camp, it seemed as if a thought struck him. His steps faltered, slowed, and then stopped. Though no one else had heard anything, Rogan tilted his head back to look into the sky, and the faint smile on his lips fell away.

A raven swooped out of the grey clouds to land on the dirt before him. Some Shades looked on curiously, and then their eyes bugged with surprise as Kaita emerged from the bird's form. But Rogan looked as if he had expected her.

"Kaita," he said. Warm. Welcoming. Grief-stricken.

"Brother," said Kaita through a raspy throat.

She had been ragged five days ago when she received Rogan's summons. She looked worse now. Her clothes were new, but she was dirty and wasted, and gaunt beyond what Rogan had ever seen of her. Still she tried to stand tall, her head up and her shoulders back. But it was a poor showing, and her limbs shook with the effort of attempting it.

Rogan saw it in her eyes, and he motioned her back towards his tent. Kaita followed him without a word. They passed through the camp quickly, and it was all Kaita could do to ignore the stares of the other Shades. Rogan pulled back the flap of his tent, letting Kaita step through first.

He had barely followed her in before Kaita broke. Her face twisted with pain as tears etched burning lines down her face. She paced to the back of the tent and whirled, walking back up to Rogan and glaring up into his face.

"Weeks," she said, managing to keep her voice down so that those outside could not hear her fury. "Weeks I have been searching for you. I went to every encampment I knew of, every stronghold where our siblings have gathered in strength. No one knew where you were, and that is not like you. No one knew how to send you a message, and that is not like you. You left me alone. Alone in the wilderness, with two people hungry for my death, and after you *promised—*"

Her voice broke, and she turned from him. Rogan laid a hand on her shoulder from behind, but she jerked away.

"Do not *touch* me."

"You were never alone," said Rogan softly. "I have heard many reports of your long journey. In Lan Shui, and then Opara, and then Kahuanga, you were with our siblings always."

"But I had no one I *cared* about," snapped Kaita. "Not after Dellek died in Lan Shui. I did not have Tagata, or you, or Father."

Rogan's face grew stony. Kaita knew he wished to admonish her, to tell her that she should care about all the Shades as if they were family. But he held the words back. Mayhap he knew that was not what she needed to hear.

"We made a plan together, Kaita," he said. "And we agreed upon it in Northwood, before you set out on your long road."

"That plan never satisfied me, and you know it."

"And do you think I was happy with it? Do you think I enjoyed making the promises I did? I would rather have had you by my side all this long while. But Mag and Albern were more important to you, and I knew that, and so I let you go your own way. That is the nature of compromise, Kaita, of being part of a family. You and I both thought you had a hope in Northwood, and then in Kahuanga."

Kaita's chin trembled as she looked up at him. Yes, she had thought she had a hope. Better than a hope. How could she have foreseen that Mag would be able to defeat her lion form? How could she have predicted that Mag would find a way to survive even the trolls? They were monsters of campfire legend.

But her plans had failed her, just as her strength had failed her every time she and Mag came to blows. She could not win, no matter what she did. Dark below, she could not even find a way to kill *me,* and I was no warrior of legend. Even my sister Ditra had survived Kaita's attempts to kill her.

The seed of doubt had already rooted in Kaita's mind. Now, for the first time, it ensnared her own idea of herself, becoming a corruption that threatened to destroy the last shreds of her conviction.

Yet Kaita was not the sort of person to accept responsibility when she could instead cast blame. And so her expression went from lost to furious once more, and again she stepped towards Rogan.

"You never gave me the chance I wanted," she hissed. "I told you from the beginning what I need, what I knew I would require in the end. Now I have spent months in useless flight, and you have lost scores of your precious siblings. They have exposed our plans in two kingdoms, all because you would not listen to me until it was too late. *That* is why I demanded your promise. Because I knew all along what it would come to in the end, even if you were too foolish to see it."

She stopped suddenly, fearing she had gone too far. But no anger came into Rogan's eyes, only a more profound sadness. And Kaita wondered if he knew all the unspoken thoughts that had flitted through her head before she finally lashed out.

"I wanted to give you a chance to change—to learn *why* you must change," he said quietly. "Since before we met, you have tried to do everything alone. You wish to rely only on yourself, to have so much power that no one can challenge you. Once, you were loyal to a family, and they betrayed you. You have feared to rely on others ever since. But those you hunt—Mag, and especially Albern—they know the value of friendship, of companions on whom they can depend. They know what it is to fight as part of something greater than themselves, to serve without the desire of personal advantage."

"I have served the Shades loyally," said Kaita, a note of desperation in her voice.

"And you know I love you for it," said Rogan. "And I know you love me, and some other few of our number. But I am no fool, Kaita. Your own goals have always come first. The moment you saw your opportunity, you abandoned everything to pursue what you had long desired. You would break the world to achieve your ends, and you would cast all of us aside to do it. That is why your foes defeat you, Kaita, over and over again. And you will never win until you come to your senses. You must tear down your walls—I cannot do it for you. But I can tell you that leaving yourself open to betrayal is better than living your life alone."

Silent sobs began to wrack her body long before he finished. In one corner of his large tent was a small desk and chair, and she stumbled over to sit. Rogan knelt beside her, wrapping her shoulders in his massive, powerful hands, and he let her cry. In time she turned and buried her face in his tunic, and he held her like the sister she was to him.

But when at last her tears subsided, and her fists loosened their desperate grip on his clothes, she looked up at him. Her eyes were clear once more, and there was a hunger in them.

"I hear you, brother," said Kaita. "I am ready to join the cause with my whole heart, and I am ready to accept the help I know I can find nowhere else. The help that our father promised."

Rogan's heart broke, for he knew that she had not truly understood him. And for a moment, he felt the temptation to refuse her. But he could not. He had made a promise—not only to Kaita, but to the Lord. And though he could not see as far as his father, he knew that he must keep faith with both of them if the Shades were to achieve their ends.

Even if it came at the cost of Kaita's life.

Gently he pulled her hands from his tunic, and then he went to the foot of his bedroll. He had a small chest there, which he opened now using the silver key from his belt.

Out of the chest, he pulled a small packet wrapped in brown cloth.

Kaita's eyes lit at once. "You have them with you now?"

"I always do," he said. "And recently, in particular, I have ensured I had an extra store on hand, for I knew you would come to claim them. I have never forgotten you. Even when I could not see you, you must believe me: you were never out of my mind, and I never abandoned you."

Kaita nodded, but it was an absentminded gesture, for her eyes were fixed on the stones. Again Rogan sighed, and he came over to place the packet in her hand.

"They are yours," he said. "As I promised. But now I must demand a promise from you in turn."

Her eyes flashed as she looked up at him. "And what is that?"

"You must use them at the right time," said Rogan. "Do not plunge after Mag or Albern into the middle of a host of foes. You may kill them if you do, but even with the stones, you will not escape alive. Draw them out first. Use the magestones when they are alone, isolated—even from each other, if you can manage it. Strike only when you are certain of survival. Do not throw your life away trying to end theirs."

For a moment, she hesitated, and Rogan feared she would refuse. He had no right to demand this of her, not really. Already he had sworn to give her the stones, without this condition. But as she looked up at him, Rogan saw understanding in her eyes, as well as compassion.

She stood from the chair and stepped forwards, laying her head against his chest. His thick arms wrapped around her shoulders.

"I promise," she said, "for I know you ask out of kindness and concern. And I will make another promise: I vow to live up to the faith you have shown in me, and that I know Father still has for me."

"And he will until the end," Rogan murmured. His voice was thick with grief, but he knew she would mistake it for reverence. "Now go.

Tagata leads the greater part of our forces west. Join her there, and you will soon have the opportunity you seek."

Kaita looked up at him in wonder. "Albern and Mag will be there? But I thought they were to the south, closer to the Birchwood."

Despite the pain in his heart, he smiled down at her. "They will meet Tagata, and soon."

She lifted a hand and placed it against his cheek. "Thank you, brother," she whispered. "I will not fail you. And I will see you soon."

Quickly she left the tent. In a moment, Rogan heard the flapping of wings as a raven took to the air.

At last, he let his tears come, slow and silent as they worked their way through the lines of his face. Kaita had given him her promise, for she thought it came from his love for her.

But even that promise had been mandated by the Lord.

TWELVE

After the first five days of training, Mag and I took stock of our situation. We were sitting apart from our squadrons, sharing a meal around a campfire. Dryleaf was with us, and Oku had curled up at my feet. The day's rain had faded to a mere drizzle. Our breath misted in the air, dissipating quickly, and our feet squished upon the slushy ground.

"I think you should present Li for Kun's test," I said. "I have seen her against the others. No one can match her speed, and few even come close."

Mag pursed her lips, but after a moment she shook her head. "I do not think so. She has the skill, but something is missing inside her. Her attention wanders as often as her gaze. Nimble feet and quick hands are all well and good, but a true warrior needs something more."

I frowned and paused in feeding Oku a scrap. "What more do you think she needs?"

"A killer instinct," said Mag. "She never presses the fight hard enough, even when she has an advantage. And when she is on her back foot, she all but gives up. She knows her foe is not really trying to harm her, and it makes her complacent. No matter how many times I tell her to take things more seriously, she does not muster the fire she needs to truly crush her foe."

Oku had been waiting patiently for me to finish handing him the bit of gristle I had pulled out of my bowl. I fed it to him and scratched him behind the ears. "That is mayhap a good thing while that foe is another trainee," I said, "but I see your point. Let us hope she can summon that instinct upon the battlefield and survive such a test. But who, then, gives us the best chance?"

Mag was silent for a moment, and then she gave a slow nod as if answering a question in her mind. "Dibu," she said. "If anyone can secure our position with the Mystics, I think it will be him."

Dryleaf's bushy eyebrows shot up. "Dibu? He seems a good man, from the brief conversations we have had. Yet I thought he had not touched a blade until just under a month ago."

"That is true," said Mag. "Yet now he nearly matches Li's skill. I noticed on the second day that Tou seemed to favor him, and soon I saw one reason why. I think if I focus most of my efforts on him, he will surpass Li. He certainly has better instincts. Though he is only training, he never lets up until his opponent is defeated." A small smile crossed her lips. "Or until *he* is defeated. After all, I sometimes train with him personally."

I chuckled. "There is the modesty I have missed in you."

She scoffed. "As if such a malady has ever plagued me."

"How have things been with you, Dryleaf?" I said. "You have been often in Taitou, and also wandering around the army's encampment. Have you learned anything interesting?"

"Nothing I think would be especially helpful," said Dryleaf. "I am making more progress in the town than in the camp, but there is less information there than here. My best sources are at a house of the Guild of Lovers. They are always glad to welcome a skillfully told story or a good singing voice. And of course, many within Kun's army visit them often, including some of the Mystics. But you know lovers."

"Not particularly," said Mag, smirking.

I chuckled. "They are reticent with their clients' information, is what he means," I said. "And well they should be."

"Indeed," said Dryleaf. "They will tell me only harmless little items—interesting, but not especially useful, and with no names attached. Everyone knows Kun is training this army to go and fight, but no one knows where, or when, or for what purpose. He could mean to march on the capital, but I do not think so. He does not have enough troops."

"I agree," I said. "I still think our first guess is the best one. He means to pursue the Shades."

"And that means he is our best chance to find Kaita," said Mag. Her bowl was empty, and she placed it on the ground beside her as she leaned back on her hands. Oku immediately began to lick it clean. "We *must* win Kun's trial. Let us hope that he does not deliberate overmuch on his choice of a fighter. If he thinks the trial will be easy, and that any of his Mystics can defeat our champion, he may carelessly choose someone Dibu can overcome."

I worried about Kun more and more as the days went on, however. He had begun to come around our part of the camp often, looking in on us as we trained our squadrons. He never failed to be exceedingly polite, and I never saw his broad smile falter. "How goes the training?" he would ask, and I would grit my teeth and reply, "Excellent, Captain. You can see for yourself how they are improving." And Kun would inspect the practice dummies and nod in approval.

He would even go to one or another member of my squadron and give them pointers. "Notice how Albern raises his elbow higher than you? That gives his draw more strength, and it shifts the string less when he looses the arrow. Try to match him." Even if he did not wish us to remain in his company, he seemed determined to gain as much benefit as possible from our instruction.

Of course, he took even greater interest in Mag's swordfighters. He would pace around the edges of her practice rings and call out advice or encouragement as the bouts went on. It made some of the soldiers quite nervous. Li, in particular, did not at all enjoy his presence, and her attention wandered even more than usual. Once, she almost dropped her sword when Kun barked at her to press her attack. I began to understand why Mag did not think Li was the best choice.

Yet Kun seemed to have the same opinion that I had held at first. As the days wore on, he focused most of his attention on Li. He observed her evident skill with the blade and the way she toyed with her opponents rather than finish them off. I hoped he thought she would be our champion and that Dibu would be a surprise.

Mag began to guide his thoughts further in that direction. Whenever Kun would come by for inspection, Mag would drill Li personally. She would push the girl to her limits, but not beyond them, making her look as though she could nearly hold her own in the fight. But the moment Kun left, Mag would return to Dibu and resume working with him instead.

Tou was a constant presence during our drilling, wandering around the rings while he brushed his fingers through his goatee. He oversaw three other squadrons, but he spent an increasing amount of time with us. He would even help our troops practice, and I came to learn that he was a powerful fighter. Though he lacked a substantial build, he was surprisingly strong—impregnable in defense and ferocious when on the attack. Mag requested him to pair up with Dibu whenever he came by, and I could see the boy's skill begin to grow by leaps and bounds. Tou knocked him into the slushy ground every time, but Dibu lasted longer and longer against him as days went by. Each time they finished, Tou would confer with Mag and me, giving advice on how to prepare Dibu for the test. Mag was always grateful for his insight.

Though it may sound boastful, I think Tou was quite intrigued by us. I know, certainly, that we became friendly in short order. Tou tried to maintain an appropriate level of separation and distance, but no more than one would expect from one's superior officer.

He was a good sort, but I could tell he placed great faith in military discipline. Though he wanted us to join Kun's army, he had no wish to undermine his superior officer. This put him in a difficult position, but he managed it as best he could. For my part, at least, I wanted to help him, and the best way to do that was to succeed in Kun's challenge on our own merits.

Day by day, we drove ourselves and our troops as hard as we could. But the week seemed to wear away incredibly fast.

THIRTEEN

THE DAY OF KUN'S TEST FINALLY CAME.

Usually our squadrons were mustered for drilling before dawn. That day, Tou let us sleep until an hour after sunup. My eyes snapped open the moment I heard the calls outside my tent. I lay there for a moment, reluctant to move. So much rested on today. Dibu might win, and then we would have taken a significant step towards achieving our aims. Or we might fail, and then we would have wasted another week. We would be no better off than we were at the start: alone in Dorsea, with no idea how to find Kaita. In fact, we would be worse off, for she would have had ten extra days to flee, or hide herself, or gather more allies to her side.

I did not know what we would do if that happened. I feared to think what Mag might do. But there was nothing for it now. I sighed and roused myself, dressing quickly and stepping out of the tent.

Our squadrons were already mustering themselves, as they did every day. As I joined Mag and stood before them, I could not deny a small flush of pride at seeing them form up with precision and speed. Tou seemed pleased with our squadrons' discipline, as well.

I heard footsteps behind us and turned. Kun came marching up, two Mystics to either side of him. I recognized one as Zhen, Kun's nephew, the one with a heavy scar on his left cheek. It had been he who reported on our doings in Huzen.

It occurred to me that Zhen might be the one pitted against Mag's champion. That might be good for us. Zhen seemed a capable man, certainly, but it appeared he specialized in espionage. Mayhap Dibu would have the edge against him when it came to a straight fight.

Kun stopped before us, wearing his usual broad smile. "Well! Good morning to all of you. I must commend you on the presentation of your troops. Few squadrons among our forces show such discipline."

"Thank you, Captain," said Tou and Mag at the same time. Mag stopped short, her mouth twisting, and gave Tou a deferential nod. He smiled slightly and went on. "Your recognition honors us. We await your order."

"Well, I have only one order for you today, in truth," said Kun with a chuckle. "It is the day of the test! I doubt you have forgotten."

"No indeed, Captain," said Tou quickly. "We are ready."

"As ready as you will ever be, I suppose," said Kun. "I am sure we all hope that it is enough. Well." His eyes darted to Li. Out of the corner of my eye, I saw her wandering gaze focus on the captain, her nimble body growing tense. "Who will be your champion?"

Tou looked at Mag, who took a step forwards. "Captain, I have chosen Dibu to represent the best result of our training."

I was gratified to see a look of surprise—on Captain Kun's face, and Dibu's. Li's cheeks flushed red. Meanwhile, Kun's smile faltered for a moment. He looked past Mag to Dibu.

"Well, soldier? Your sergeant has spoken. Step forwards."

Still, Dibu hesitated, looking at Li as if certain he had misheard. Then, at last, he walked towards us, presenting himself as if for inspection. I noticed his bronzed knuckles were white where they gripped his shield and blade.

"Ser," he said. "I am ready."

"I certainly hope so," said Kun. He smiled at the Mystics to either side of him. "And so I suppose it falls to me to select my champion. I have given much thought to the matter." Again his smile widened. "Let us hope I can surprise you at least as much as you have surprised me.

For my champion in today's bout, I select Tou. I expect you to do quite well, Lieutenant."

Beside me, Tou went rigid. My heart sank into my boots. The lieutenant had been sparring against Dibu nearly every day, sometimes for hours on end. He knew Dibu's strengths and weaknesses. Dibu, meanwhile, had been too busy learning how to fight at all to study Tou specifically.

But as I looked to my right, my gaze fell upon Mag. To my surprise, she was fighting to suppress a smile. I wondered what under the sky could be going through her mind.

"And so we begin!" said Kun brightly. "Have you a favorite fighting ring, Dibu? I will let you choose, since I think most would agree you are the underdog."

"I . . . do not, Captain," said Dibu slowly. He nodded at Tou. "The bout may take place wherever you wish, Lieutenant."

I expected to hear defeat in his voice, the apathy of knowing an unfavorable outcome before it arrives. But to my surprise, he sounded thoughtful, as though he was already trying to think his way through it. That lit a new spark of hope in me. It seemed Mag had been right about Dibu's instincts, at least. I did not doubt that if Li had been chosen as our champion, she would merely be going through the motions now, convinced she could never win.

We proceeded to the nearest ring. Tou and Dibu traded their swords for practice blades. They spent a few moments at either end of the space, swinging the blades to get the balance. Dibu kept his eyes on his weapon and his shield, inspecting them closely, as though he might find the secret to victory in the grain of the wood or the dull shine of the steel. But Tou's gaze was locked on Dibu, and his jaw kept working.

"Now, I expect you both to give your best effort," said Kun loudly. "But of course, you are ordered not to cause each other any serious harm. You are both assets of the Mystics, after all, and therefore of the High King. Do not deprive her of a loyal sword arm, nor the soldier to wield it."

"Of course, Captain," said Dibu. Tou echoed him as if it were an afterthought.

"Well then," said Kun. "Begin!"

Tou and Dibu stalked close, both turning slightly to the right so that they ended up circling each other. Slowly the circle shrank until they were a pace apart.

Dibu struck first, his sword arcing around in a powerful side swing. Tou deflected it with his shield. But Dibu seemed to expect it, bringing the blade back around and trying to hit his side. Tou's blade was there to block it, and then he launched a counterattack.

Dibu blocked three strokes in a row, and he did not give ground, but held Tou off where he stood. My heart leaped as he went on the offensive again. Tou was the first to fall back one step. Then he pressed Dibu, who took two steps back.

Each blow clanged harder against shield or sword. Every swipe came faster. Gradually Tou stepped up his speed. But Dibu matched him blow for blow. His mouth was a grim, determined line.

Then Dibu did something I had never seen from him before, something Mag had not taught him. He launched forwards with his shield, which crashed against Tou's. Tou held, but then Dibu's leg swept out, kicking Tou's feet from under him.

The Mystic fell to the ground. Our squadrons gave a great cheer.

But Tou did not lose his head. He rolled away quickly, and Dibu brought his sword down on the ground where he had been. It put Dibu ever so slightly off balance, giving Tou just enough time to regain his feet. Now his brilliant red cloak and black hair were soaked with mud, and he was breathing heavily.

I glanced at Kun, and I saw his smile turn icy.

"Enough, Tou!" he barked. "This is a test, not training. End it!"

Tou's jaw clenched, and I felt my hopes plummet. He had treated this like a practice bout, gradually fighting harder to teach Dibu as much as possible. But he was a military man first and foremost. He would obey his captain's order, and his captain had ordered him to win.

Tou lunged to attack. I heard a gasp ripple along our squadrons. Few among them had seen him unleash all his skill, but they could see it now. Every swing of his sword was as fast as blinking. He struck his shield against Dibu's with every other stroke, knocking it aside, trying to find an opening.

Dibu was on the defensive now. Almost every blow forced him back. But whenever I feared he would step out of the ring, he sidestepped to keep himself inside. Every time, it gave him a new lane of retreat, more room to work.

I realized what he was doing. He was trying to tire Tou out. He knew he could not win an even match. But if he could hold off Tou's attacks long enough, he might conserve enough energy to balance the odds.

Mag had been right. Not only was Dibu a natural fighter, but he was smarter than I had expected.

Yet his wits did not seem to be enough. Twice he almost went down as Tou battered his shield. The third time, Tou brought the edge of his shield against Dibu's, cracking it down the middle. The next swing knocked the shield clean off Dibu's arm, and he winced with pain.

Tou's foot lashed out, catching Dibu in the gut. He stumbled back, dropping his sword a pace away. Even as he tripped, Tou caught him in the shoulder with the flat of his blade. Dibu's padded armor held, but he cried out with pain as he spun and slammed face-first into the ground.

Without thinking, I clutched Mag's arm (which was like seizing an iron bar). But when I looked at her, she still wore the smile she had had before.

"Wait," she whispered.

I looked back just in time to see Tou glance at us. There was an apology in his eyes, but there was also a resolution.

He lifted a foot to step towards Dibu and demand the yield.

Dibu's hand flashed out, seizing his broken shield where it had fallen. He flung it across the mud, and it cracked into Tou's shin. The Mystic slipped on the slush and went crashing into the ground. Dibu sprang, and when he came up, his sword was in his hand.

In an instant, he was standing with one foot on Tou's sword wrist, the tip of the blade at his throat.

Everything went completely silent. I believe I was even holding my breath. Dibu, on the other hand, was panting heavily, and his close-cropped hair was soaking with sweat and mud.

"Do you yield?" said Dibu, between gasps.

Tou looked up at him, brows raised in surprise, clearly impressed. "I yield."

Our squadrons erupted in cheers and yells. They flooded into the ring, surrounding Dibu and pounding him on the back, ignoring the winces they drew through his embarrassed smile. I half thought they were going to lift him and carry him out of the ring on their shoulders.

"Troops!" barked Mag suddenly. "Attention!"

Everything fell silent again as our squadrons turned, hands slapping to their sides.

All eyes went to Kun, who still stood on the side of the ring. His eternal smile had returned. But I saw ice in his eyes as he looked down at Tou, who still lay on the ground. A long moment passed.

"Clearly, I should have chosen another champion," he said at last. "But, well. What can one do in the face of such disappointment?" Then he turned to Mag and me. "Congratulations. The terms of our agreement have been satisfied, and you are now militia serving under the Mystic order. And what good fortune for all of us, for we march to war tomorrow."

He gave Tou one last look. "There will be a council in my tent at sundown. I expect to see you there, and not covered in mud."

Kun turned on his heel and strode off, his two Mystic guards at his side.

We waited a respectful length of time—mayhap not until he was out of earshot, but certainly until he was out of sight. Then I turned to Mag and arched an eyebrow. She smiled, and together we turned back to our squadrons.

"As you were," I said.

The cheers resumed. Now they did lift Dibu by the legs, hauling him into the air and carrying him off. Dibu let out halfhearted cries of protest. He turned back as they bore him away, looking at Tou, who had not yet risen. It seemed Dibu wanted to help his opponent to his feet, for honor's sake, but the rest of the squadron would not have it.

Well. Dibu deserved his celebration. And so I walked to Tou and reached down. Tou sighed, took my wrist, and let me haul him to his feet. He did his best to dust himself off, but with the heavy mud and slushy snow clinging to him, I am afraid it did not do much good.

"It shall be a while before I recover from that," he said.

"He barely touched you," said Mag.

"It was not my body that suffered injury, but my pride." He stopped wiping the mud off and gave us both a stern look. "It is important to me that you both know: I did not let him win. That was a clever ploy on his part."

"Trust me, I am aware," I said. "I saw the look on your face when you went for him. And neither of us holds your effort against you. You were following your captain's orders."

"We are only happy Dibu prevailed," said Mag. But she could not entirely hide another smile. "And if we are being honest with each other, I think you might be somewhat happy about it, too."

Tou's cheeks flamed, and he cleared his throat as he turned away. "It will certainly be good to have the two of you around for the coming fight," he said, absently running a hand through his goatee, which streaked it with mud.

"Hm," said Mag.

"In any case, thank you," I said, and held out my hand. Tou took my wrist, and we shook firmly. "You have been of immense help during the training, and our squadrons have reaped the benefits. Though you lost the match, you also shared in the victory."

Tou shook his head slowly. "I do not know what madness is upon you that makes you want to be part of this war so badly," he said. "But the High King's forces need all the help we can get, and yours more than most. I only ask that you do not make me regret it."

"I promise," said Mag. "You will be glad we are here when it comes time to fight."

FOURTEEN

After Dibu's trial, we had little time to celebrate. Kun had ordered a march for the next morning, and that meant the rest of our day would be spent in furious preparation. Before setting our squadrons to their tasks, Mag and I conferred with Dryleaf.

"Where do you think we are going?" I asked.

"Who knows?" said Mag. "I am sure Kun would not tell us even if we asked."

"Yet he may have told others," said Dryleaf. "You two must see to your preparations, but I will be of little use in that. Let me instead see what I may learn. I should tell the Guild of Lovers, in any case—I am certain they will want to know, and doing them a small favor may repay us all in the end."

"An excellent idea," said Mag, nodding. "Let us know if you learn anything."

Dryleaf gave her a smile and set off towards Taitou, Oku trotting at his heels. Mag and I went to our squadrons and began prodding them into action to pack their things.

Now, even as we had been preparing for Kun's test, the rider had been making her way across the land in search of us.

Her road had grown much more difficult since the civil war broke out, but she was smart enough to keep from being seen. She avoided cities and the major roads, as we had done. Some time ago, she had visited Taitou and learned that we had been there, but she left before we returned. Now she guessed we were lurking somewhere in the nearby wilderness. That was where she had been searching for the past week. But she did not have my skill at finding paths through the wild, and so the going had been slower. She slept in ditches and under trees, muttering complaints about the fact that Mag and I would not sit still and let her catch us.

But because she was being so careful, and quite by accident, she discovered the Shades.

She was leagues north of Taitou, creeping through a wood called the Brackenbough (which, I am sure, would have amused Dryleaf greatly). Day was fading to night. Sheer luck kept the Shades from seeing her. She was only a few spans from the edge of their encampment deep in the woods, but she did not know it.

Suddenly a thought struck her. We might have set up a camp and built a fire, and mayhap she could see the smoke from far off if she climbed a tree. She tied off her horse and found the tallest tree she could. Grunting and cursing, she hauled herself up hand over hand until she had cleared the tree line surrounding her perch. And just as she had hoped, she saw the smoke of a campfire.

But then she saw many more columns of smoke. Not just one campfire. Nearly a dozen.

The rider frowned. She knew the fires were not from Mag and me. But now she was curious why so many people should be camped deep in the Brackenbough.

She made her way back down to the ground, but she did not mount her horse again. Instead, she set off into the woods on foot. From her belt she drew her short sword and her club, one in each hand. Then she moved forwards with every bit of stealth she could summon.

But she never reached the camp. Two figures appeared in the forest ahead, forcing her to stop.

The rider drew up behind a tree. She stuck out one eye, taking a few moments to study the figures before her. They stood a span apart so that they could just see each other through the woods.

Sentries. But what were they guarding?

Then the rider noticed their outfits of grey, with blue cloaks pulled tight about them.

She knew what that meant. She had seen Shades before. From the campfires, it seemed to be a decently sized force. Mayhap two hundreds. That was more than the rider had ever seen in one place.

"Dark below," she grumbled.

She slid behind the tree again and then snuck away south, quiet as a rather large mouse. Soon she had rejoined her horse and untied it from the tree branch.

Now she had a choice to make. This discovery troubled her, and she could not simply ignore it. Such a force of Shades moving through the kingdom could threaten all of Dorsea, and that was more important than Mag and me.

Taitou was to the south, and she knew that town held a small garrison of Mystics. If anyone could deal with this situation, the redcloaks could.

The rider blew out a loud, exasperated sigh, sending it misting up into the wintry air. Then she climbed into the saddle.

"Come on, boy," she said, patting her horse's neck. "We make for Taitou. One more delay I will take out on the wanderers' hides, whenever we find them."

Dryleaf went about his business in Taitou, while Mag and I set to ours in the encampment. We had drilled our squadrons on packing their kit, but they still needed our attention and an occasional sharp word. By the time the sun was lowering towards the horizon, I was nearly worn out. Dryleaf found Mag and me just as we had reunited and started supper.

"I hope your day was fruitful," he said.

"The only fruit borne today was a thistle," I said, "and I feel its needles all up and down my back. Why is it I can travel hundreds of leagues with the two of you and feel fine, but after spending one day helping others prepare for a journey, I feel ready to quit?"

Dryleaf chuckled. "Ask any parent if they were ever as tired before children as they were after."

Mag smirked. "We are their officers, not their parents, and they will have a rude awakening if they forget it. But what of you? What were you able to learn?"

The old man shook his head with a smile. "I should have predicted this, but the Guild of Lovers already knew about the march. They have a wagon ready to follow the army with some half-dozen lovers. Two of my friends, Orla and Nikau, will be coming along. In any case, the lovers must have heard of it from some of the Mystics who are closest in Kun's council—who I would have difficulty befriending, of course. It appears the march was a complete surprise to most of the redcloaks. Even Tou had not known of it."

I met Mag's gaze. "That means Kun was afraid of word getting out," I said.

"And that likely means he is going after the Shades," said Mag, tapping her fingers on her thigh. "This is something, at least. You could learn nothing else?"

"Only that we are marching north," said Dryleaf. "No one knows exactly where."

"North," I mused. "I know of nothing important that way. Other than the town where you grew up, Mag."

Her mouth twisted towards a frown, as though she had almost said something but then thought better of it. "That place is anything but important."

Just then, Tou approached us. He gave us all a quick nod and touched Dryleaf gently on the shoulder to let him know he was there. "I have returned from Captain Zhou's war council."

I glanced at the sun, which had only barely begun to sink below the horizon. "It seems to have gone rather quickly."

Tou nodded, but he looked troubled. "It did. My company will be marching in the vanguard with the captain's Mystics. He instructed that your squadrons be at the forefront, behind him."

That was a surprise, though I quickly realized it should not have been. "He wishes to keep an eye on us," I said.

His mouth twisted. "I am only passing down the order." But I could see in his eyes that he thought I was correct. "When we muster in the morning, you know where to be."

"Yes, ser," I said, snapping a salute where I sat. Tou nodded and left.

Mag's eyes were alight with excitement. "Good for us, I say. I would rather be at the front—anything to get to the Shades faster. We can help root out the Shades and end this war, Albern. I feel it."

I chuckled. "End the war? Why, Mag. You sound almost as though you are truly committed to the fight now. I thought it was only a cover for us to find Kaita."

She did not answer, or even change her expression. But her fist jabbed out and struck me hard in the shoulder. My whole arm went dead, and I cursed and fumed as Mag went to help Dryleaf fetch his supper.

That evening, a wagon trundled up to the camp as we were almost ready to end our night. It was covered entirely in a brilliant blue cloth of a beautiful weave. Mag and I stopped and watched it approach. Hallan and Dibu were with us, each of them discussing some final matters before the morning's march. As the wagon drew near to us, I spied the driver—a tall, brown-skinned man with lustrous black hair down to his shoulders, supple, muscled arms, and large, strong hands. He looked like a man of Calentin, which held my attention. As the wagon slowed, he nodded to us.

"Good eve, friends," he said. His voice was like warm, smooth liquid pouring down the nape of your neck. "We seek a friend of yours. An older gentleman named Dryleaf. Do you know him?"

"Is that Nikau?" Dryleaf thrust his head out of his tent. "Nikau, darling boy! You found me."

Like a mirror of Dryleaf, a woman poked her head out of the blue front flaps of the wagon. She was a slim, delicate young thing, with pale Heddish skin and hair that flamed red like Hallan's, but curly and more lustrous. She leaned her elbows on the front edge of the wagon and beamed down at Dryleaf.

"There he is!" she called sweetly. "We have arrived, dear friend, and we thought to seek a song from you before we slumber. Any journey should be blessed by merriment before it begins, or else who knows what darkness might befall it?"

"Who, indeed? Thank you, my boy," said Dryleaf as Dibu helped him climb out of the tent and stand up. "It would be my utter joy to share songs and stories with you tonight, and on the road as well."

"Am I to guess that you are from the Guild of Lovers?" I said.

“We are,” said the man with a knowing smile. “I am Nikau, as Dryleaf said.”

“And I am Orla,” said the woman, holding a hand towards me. I took it and kissed it. Her fingers were as soft as cream, and almost the same color. “Entirely enchanted.”

I cleared my throat. “As are we. I am Albern of the family Telfer, and this is Mag. These are Hallan and Dibu, two soldiers in our squadrons. Dryleaf has sung your praises ever since we arrived in the town.”

Orla climbed down from the wagon and wrapped her arm through Dryleaf’s, laying her head on his shoulder. “If that is true, I feel simply cheated. How could he sing without me there to hear it?”

“We shall have plenty of chances to hear him on the road, love,” said Nikau with a smile. He kept studying me. I wondered if he was as curious about me as I was about him and if he could see my Calentin features through my lighter complexion. “A pleasure to meet you both. Do not hesitate to seek us out, should you wish our services. It would be our honor to comfort the friends of Dryleaf, who we have come to love so well.”

“I shall, ah. Certainly consider it,” I said, scratching the back of my neck. “My friend Mag, however—”

Mag smirked at my obvious discomfort. “I am not a bedder. But your offer is generous and well-spoken.”

“That is well enough,” said Nikau, giving her a nod, and then me a wink.

“You are coming with us?” said Dibu. “On the march?”

Nikau gave him an easy smile. “We are. And if it means I get to see those arms of yours each day, I, for one, will do so with pleasure.”

Dibu thrust a tongue into his cheek hard to fight a smile, and he shook his head. “I thank you for the compliment. But . . . we are marching to war, or so we all believe. Is it not safer to ply your trade here?”

“Ye need not worry for that, boy,” said Hallan, folding his arms. He gave Nikau a nod, and Orla a wink. “Lovers are much as safe in war as they are in any town or city. Their laws forbid them from taking sides, and so why should anyone seek to harm them? Their trade’s neutral, and a help to either side. And I can say from some experience that a lover can hardly find better clientele than when traveling along with an army.”

"All very true," said Orla, smiling at him from Dryleaf's side. "And I do love a soldier with experience."

Hallan bowed low, his beard pressing into his chest. "I'll recommend some to you, then." His eyes flitted to Nikau. "And mayhap you'll make some recommendations as well."

"I am sure they will hardly be necessary," said Nikau, placing a hand on Hallan's arm. "But for now, we had better see to our arrangements. Come, Orla. I will not build your tent for you."

Orla laughed, and it was like music. "Of course you will, if I ask it," she said. "But I am coming." She leaned in to give Dryleaf a quick peck on the cheek. "Await my return, dear one. We will come to hound you for a song as soon as we may."

She danced away towards the back of the wagon. Behind her, some other lovers descended to the ground, and they began to see to the horses' needs and set up tents near the army's. I noticed Mag's and my squadrons looking at them with interest, and I strongly suspected they would be glad for Dryleaf's presence during the long march before us.

Mag was shaking her head with a slightly amused expression. "At least our march shall not be dreary—wherever we end up marching to."

"No, it certainly will not," said Dryleaf, beaming.

We all sang and spoke and laughed and drank that night, and the next morning we set out from Taitou before dawn. Tou's company marched just behind Kun's Mystics, as ordered. Dryleaf found a place in the army's train near the lovers, among the wagons and carts of the camp followers that accompany any force on a campaign.

Mag and I were marching to war for the first time in many years. Though we walked in grim company, for the first time in a while, I found myself excited to take the next step in our journey.

The rider was headed south towards Taitou on a narrow, little-used hunting trail. The day was cold, and the warmth of her mount was little comfort against it. Sharp hills cracked the land around her, like broken fingers arching towards the sky in pain. Dark mutterings poured in a steady trickle from her lips, promising baneful revenge against Mag and me when at last she caught up to us.

To the south, a flight of birds launched itself into the air, screaming.

The rider stopped. Her eyes narrowed. She moved off the trail into the hills, hiding her horse behind some boulders. Retracing her steps, she found a place where she could watch the path while keeping herself hidden.

It was not long before a column of soldiers came into view. The rider leaned forwards, narrowing her eyes.

At the head of the column, she saw Mystics. Some were on horseback, but most were on foot. Behind the redcloaks were other folk. They looked like artisans and farmers, and almost none of them were mounted. But they carried weapons and shields, and sometimes one or two pieces of armor, though it was ragtag and scattered among them.

Militia, thought the rider.

And then she saw Mag and me. We were close to the head of the column, riding our horses in plain sight.

The rider froze. But only for an instant before she was cursing under her breath and racing back towards her horse.

"Dark-damned, steer-loving, slipshod nuisances," she said, and carried on in like manner as she mounted. The moment she was in the saddle, she dug in her heels with a great cry, riding towards the hunting trail at a gallop.

Kun and his Mystics spotted her while she was still spans off. Immediately the Mystics formed up, drawing weapons and hefting their shields to form a wall in front of Kun. Knights barked orders, directing more of the column to advance and join them.

The rider slowed her horse to a walk, throwing empty hands into the air.

"Hail!" she cried. "My weapons are stowed, and I bear no ill intent. Kindly do not shoot me."

Mag and I came marching forwards with our units. The rider studied us, eyes narrowing in a glare, but she could see that we did not recognize her. And why should we have? She was wrapped head to toe in clothing against the cold. Not even a shock of hair stuck out from her hood and mask.

"That is far enough," Kun called out amiably. "Who are you, and what do you want?"

"Two things," said the rider. "The first is more important. I have come looking for you, for I guess that you are the Mystic garrison from Taitou. I have news for you about the Shades."

The effect on all of us was immediate. Mag and I glanced at each other, and most of the gathered soldiers gripped their weapons tighter.

The woman's voice instantly struck me as familiar. But it was far away and muffled, both by her mask and by the heavy snows all around us. My mind raced, trying to place it, but I could not.

Kun's smile only widened.

"I am curious about your news, as well as why you think I should trust it," he called out. "But you said you wanted two things. What is the second?"

The rider's voice went sour. "I am looking for three people in your company."

Kun's smile vanished. "Are you now." It was not a question, but more of a statement of annoyed anticipation.

"I am," said the rider. "I seek Dryleaf, an older man. And two whom I see before me: Mag, called by some the Uncut Lady, and especially Albern of the family Telfer."

Mag frowned, and a flush crept up into my cheeks. Yet still I could not place her voice.

The rider smiled to herself, drawing a dark enjoyment from our reactions.

Kun, meanwhile, had turned a baleful glare on us. "I see," he said. "Why does it not surprise me that the two of you are connected to this stranger, who rides out of the wilderness with knowledge of the Shades?"

Mag never took her eyes off the rider. "I do not recognize her, Captain."

"Nor I," I added. It did not seem wise to mention the familiarity of her voice, for I did not think Kun would be much pleased. "Who are you, stranger? Show your face."

"Stranger?" The rider snorted. "How would a stranger know your names, or recognize you? You know me, wanderers, even if you do not know that you know me."

She dismounted before removing her mask and pulling back the hood of her cloak.

I had nocked an arrow. Now it dipped immediately. Mag put her spear up at once. Both of us took a tentative step forwards, unable to believe our own eyes.

"Yue?" I gasped.

FIFTEEN

SUN STOPPED DEAD IN THE STREET, HER MOUTH AGAPE.

"Not Yue from Lan Shui?" she said.

Albern's smile was broad and smug, and Sun knew he was immensely enjoying the look on her face. "The very same. Come, keep walking. We have a ways to go."

"But . . . but she . . ." Sun struggled for words, trotting at Albern's side. "What on earth was she doing there? What about Lan Shui? She was a *constable!*"

"She was, but she—"

"Now hold on," said Sun. "I learned much about Yue from you. And if there is one thing I know, it is that she would *never* have abandoned her duty to Lan Shui. She took it so seriously that she was ready to arrest you and Mag just for looking suspicious!"

"Oh, her duty to her king was her highest priority," said Albern. "And that had not changed."

"But she abandoned Lan Shui!" cried Sun. "Why would she do that?"

Albern stuck a tongue in his cheek, biting down on it as if he was trying desperately to quell the grin plastered on his features. "You see," he said slowly, "I was telling you a story, in which I was just about to relay my conversation with Yue, and during which time I asked her these questions, and Yue—"

"All right," growled Sun. "Get on with it."

Mag and I stood there staring at Yue, our mouths hanging open. Or at least, mine was. It is difficult for me to imagine Mag being so flabbergasted, though I know it must have happened at least once.

"Careful," Yue told me after a moment. She could not entirely banish a sardonic smirk. "Winter it might be, but there are still enough flies to be caught in that gaping hole in your face."

"Yue," I breathed. "What under the *sky* are you doing here?"

Mag arched an eyebrow. "And what in the dark below, while you are answering questions."

"Ha," said Yue.

"Pardon me," said Kun. His smile had returned, but it was sharp as a razor's edge. "You are carrying on a conversation as though you are the only ones invested in its outcome. Let me kindly remind you that you are not."

"Of course, Captain," I said at once. "Forgive me. This woman is a friend."

"Though how in blazes she found us is another matter," said Mag. Suddenly she frowned. "Albern . . ."

Her voice trailed off, and I realized what she was thinking. Kaita would have known Yue from Lan Shui, and she might know—or have guessed—that we were friendly. As a weremage, Kaita could hardly ask for a better opportunity to get within striking distance of us.

"Yue," I said slowly. "You remember what we were seeking when we left Lan Shui."

"Of course," she said, irritated. "You left to find the werema—ah." Her brows lifted. "The weremage. And now, here I am."

"A weremage?" said Kun. "What is this about?"

Yue turned to him and bowed. "Captain. I was formerly a constable in the town of Lan Shui. It is a modest place, some leagues southeast of—"

"I know it," said Kun. "Go on."

Yue nodded towards us. "These two traveled through the town some months ago. There was a weremage who caused some local trouble, and they helped me resolve the issue. But the weremage was never found." She scowled at the two of us. "They are afraid I might be her, which is an uncommon display of good sense."

Kun's brows shot for the sky. "You certainly seem familiar with their antics."

"And I guess that you are as well," said Yue, bowing again. "But they are right, ser. I could be the weremage in disguise."

Mag opened her mouth to speak, but I gripped her arm to stop her. She could offer to test Yue—she had learned how in Calentin. But I did not think it wise to reveal that knowledge to Kun, for it might lead to awkward questions.

Fortunately, Kun solved the problem for us. "Prudence is always a wise course. Zhen—forgive me, *Lieutenant* Zhou? Test her, if you would."

Zhen, Kun's nephew, stepped forwards. He sheathed his sword as he approached Yue and stood before her, a pace away. Yue held her ground, but her jaw clenched as she looked at him.

"A test?" she said. "I have never heard of this."

"Most have not," said Zhen. "It is taught to some within the order, and it is quite foolproof."

Yue lifted her chin. "Very well. What do you need me to do?"

"Nothing," said Zhen. "But I must strike you. Nothing too damaging, I promise, but it will daze you for a moment."

She fought a scowl. "You are certain this works?"

"I am," said Zhen.

Yue sighed. "Very well. Do what you must."

Zhen nodded. Then he stepped forwards and slammed his hands into Yue's temples with two powerful chops. Her head reeled back, and she blinked hard against the pain. But her eyes did not glow, and soon her vision seemed to clear. She glared at Zhen.

"That hurt."

I laughed out loud. "Yet it was worth it—at least to me."

I went running forwards to embrace her, Mag only a pace behind me. I struck Yue hard and wrapped her in a hug.

"But why *are* you here, Yue?" I said quietly.

"To find and aid you two, of course, you great idiot," she growled.

"Excuse me," said Kun. "You keep forgetting the rest of us are here, and it begins to border on offense."

"Apologies, Captain," said Yue, stepping towards him. "I have sought these two across Dorsea. If they have joined your efforts in this civil war, then I would pledge my service as well."

"Would you now?" said Kun. "Sky save me. I am nearly drowning in recruits, seemingly whether I wish them or not."

"You could hardly ask for a better sword arm than hers," I told him. "Mag and I will vouch for her."

"That is no surprise," said Kun. "I imagine you have friends scattered all across the nine kingdoms, turning up when one least expects it."

I did not miss the subtle dig. That could also have been a description of the Shades. I thought hard, wondering how I could convince him to let Yue stay on.

Yet I need not have worried, for Yue stepped forwards. The Mystics beside Kun tensed, but Yue stopped while still two paces away. In a tone I had never heard her use before—proud yet deferential, strong but respectful—she spoke.

"Captain Kun," she said. "I am Yue of the family Baolan, former constable of the town of Lan Shui. I am kin to Constable Aroha in Opara, to Constable Pinti in Yota, to Constable Zho in Danfon, and to Constabular Captain Stubhart on the High King's Seat. If letters can be sent to them, they will all vouch for me, as will Constable Ashta in Lan Shui itself. Also, my uncle Joshin serves the Mystics with honor in the city of Bertram, and my grandmother Brinna was a chancellor in Pinkeng in the south until her retirement five years ago. Long has the family Baolan served the King's law, and I have no greater aspirations in this life or any other. I am the servant of Jun of the family Fei, the true king of Dorsea, and his kin, and through them the High King.

"I have fourteen months of training with sword, shield, and club, and nine years' experience using them in service of the people of Dorsea. With these companions, Albern and Mag, I have fought and defeated vampires, and I would throw myself into the maw of a thousand worse horrors to protect the nine kingdoms."

She fell to her knee right there in the slushy mud, and she bowed her head to Kun. "I decry the false pretender, Wojin, who now sits the throne, and all who swear fealty to him. I know of the Shades who threaten the nine kingdoms, and I pledge myself to their defeat. I have fought them already, and I will fight them again if given the opportunity, and I will not stop until their evil is driven from the land.

"If I may aid in your enemies' defeat by the strength of my arm, it is yours. If I may bring you to victory by what courage I have, I pledge it. And if I can uphold the order of the nine kingdoms by either my life or my death, I give them both into your service, as I did when first I donned the red armor of my station."

We all stood frozen. The air fell to silence. Some nearby militia had drifted closer as she spoke, and now everyone present stood in silent astonishment. Kun studied her. His perpetual smile had fallen away, and yet that did not worry me. I could tell he was impressed.

He dismounted, stepped forwards, and took Yue's shoulder. Firmly, but not roughly, he pulled her to her feet.

"I accept your service, Yue of the family Baolan, and I count myself honored to do so," he said. "If every soldier who marched for the High King were of your caliber, I do not doubt the war would be over within a month."

His smile returned, and he looked at Mag and me over Yue's shoulders.

"If all the two of you end up doing is bringing me her aid, I will consider myself well served, and more than compensated for losing our wager."

I bowed. "Thank you, Captain."

His gaze returned to Yue, and he arched an eyebrow. "Vampires? I shall need to hear that tale. But not now. I will summon you for counsel after supper, to hear this information you have on the Shades. Be ready."

Yue saluted with a fist over her heart. "Yesser."

He gave her a sharp nod and then turned to Zhen, who still stood close by. "That is enough of a march for today. Order the column to make camp for the night."

So saying, he set off back to his Mystics. Yue turned to Mag and me, and she folded her arms under her chest.

"Well," she said. "Now that I have saved you from trouble *again,* we should talk."

"We should, but I would be remiss not to send for Dryleaf." I turned to Chausiku, who stood close by. He and the rest of my squadron had observed all these proceedings with wide eyes, and more than a few of them with mouths hanging half-open. "Chausiku. Fetch Dryleaf from the train, if you would. He will want to be here."

"Ser," he said with a nod. For a moment longer, he stared at Yue, Mag, and me, but at last he set off, his tail of locs swinging behind him.

"Hallan," I said. He snapped sharply to attention, beard bristling. "See that everyone gets themselves well situated. Keep the tent lines straight this time, and call for me if you need me."

"Ser," said Hallan with a nod. He turned to the rest of the unit. "You heard the sergeant! Line'em up nice, little ones, or I'll have you digging latrines tonight."

Mag turned to her squadron. "Dibu, Li, can you see to arrangements?"

"Of course, ser," said Dibu with a nod. Li echoed him after a moment, and then slung her pack off her back, her wandering gaze momentarily fixed on Yue.

Yue was now looking at us with one brow cocked. "Sergeants, are you? A mark against my estimation of the captain, if he elevated you so."

I laughed. "I am sure it will reassure you to know that we forced him into it. But dark below, Yue. What brought you here?"

"That is a bit of a tale," said Yue. "As I recovered from my injuries in Lan Shui, I had time to think. When I became a constable, I did it to protect the kingdom. Now it seemed you were doing more for the safety of Dorsea than I was. That was an untenable thought. And by the time I had finished healing, Lan Shui had been quiet and peaceful for many weeks. Ashta, it turns out, is more than capable of dealing with day-to-day affairs. She had even hired a new constable to help her, and I felt . . . unnecessary. So I turned my command over to her and tried to follow you to Opara. But when I reached it, I learned that you had come, and then left, and then come and then left again."

"Wait," said Mag, holding up a hand. "Who told you all that?"

Yue shrugged again. "The Rangatira's constables. A cousin of mine named Aroha serves there."

I raised my brows. "Do all of your kin take the red leather?"

"Those who do not take the red cloak," she said, glowering. "May I tell my story, or will you continue to interrupt me at every opportunity?"

"We make no promises," said Mag.

Just at that moment, Dryleaf came hurrying up, his arm in Chausiku's. At his heels came Oku, and as soon as the hound spotted Yue, he came bounding forwards with great leaps and barks. Yue looked down at him with a frown she could not quite maintain.

"You still have the mutt," she said.

"Yue," I said reproachfully.

"Oh, all right," she said. She scratched him behind the ears as Dryleaf came hobbling forwards, his arms outstretched.

"Yue!" he cried. The moment Yue took his hands, he seized her around the neck and pulled her down for a hug. I saw tears shining in his eyes as he embraced her. "Dear, dear, *dear* girl. When young Chausiku here told me it was you, I hardly dared to believe him."

"Hello, old man," said Yue. She returned his hug, squeezing him mayhap a bit harder than she should have, what with his age. "I am glad to see you safe, but dismayed to find you still following these fools as they traipse across all the nine lands."

"They have taken excellent care of me," chuckled Dryleaf, wheezing slightly in her grip.

"Of course they have," said Yue. "They know that if they let anything happen to you, I would flay the skin from their bodies."

Dryleaf laughed aloud before pulling back and reaching up to cradle her face in his leathery hands. "But sky above and dark below, what brought you all this way?"

"I was just telling them," said Yue. "But I do not mind repeating myself. It has been a long road, and conversation rare. Mayhap after a meal and a, er . . . a rest." She glanced back at Mag and me.

"Of course," I said. "I imagine you have a tent? If not, I am certain one can be provided. I think Kun rather likes you, after that speech."

"Yes, that *was* impressive," said Mag, smirking.

"I am sure it was," put in Dryleaf. "You do not know Yue as I do. Her talents lie far beyond simple skill with a blade."

"They do indeed," said Yue. But she licked her lips nervously. "And speaking of which, there is something I would take care of, now that most of the important business has been seen to, and before we talk further, or before Kun summons me to his council. Before I lose my nerve, at any rate."

That confused me, and I saw my expression mirrored in Mag and Dryleaf. "What is that?" I asked her.

Yue's gaze flicked to me, and then away. "I made you an offer in Lan Shui, and you said you would take me up on it when next we met. Well, now we have met. So, shall you set up your tent, or shall I set up mine? It has been . . . a very long road."

I do not mind telling you that I was struck utterly speechless for a moment. In wild desperation, I looked to Mag and Dryleaf. Though I am no prudish child of merchants, I doubted my cheeks had ever been so dark.

Mag raised an eyebrow. "Well? Go on, then. You know what to do, yes?"

Dryleaf patted me on the shoulder. "Be careful, my boy. Her injuries were severe, and she may still be recovering."

I could only splutter and look up at Yue. *Me* be careful with *her?* She was a head taller and had to outweigh me by two stones, at least.

But then she reached out her hand towards me. And I saw her grow suddenly hesitant, timid—almost shy. There was a question in her eyes, and a fear of what my answer might be.

Well. I was not such an old man yet, and blood ran in my veins. And Yue was, as I have told you . . . a powerful woman.

I took her hand and led her to where Hallan was building my tent for me.

SIXTEEN

Of the rest of that evening I wish to say little, so let us resume the tale after some time had passed. After a while, Yue went to Kun's council. When she returned, Mag and I learned that Kun had assigned her as sergeant to another squadron of soldiers in Tou's company. But to our dismay, Yue would not tell us much of what else they had discussed, for Kun had commanded her to secrecy. All she would say to us was that the army would march west in the morning.

"West?" said Mag. "Why west?"

"Because that is where the Shades were going, as best I could tell," said Yue.

"But there is nothing to the west," said Mag. "Dorsea's large cities are all to the south, and Feldemar's to the north. These are wildlands."

"I only know where they are heading," said Yue, shrugging. "I know nothing more of their aims than you do."

The next day, Kun turned his march away from the rising sun. And now that he had some definite idea of our enemy's movements, he pushed his troops hard. We found ourselves on a forced march, and suddenly Mag's and my experience with campaigning became invaluable.

A fighting force lives a very different life on the march than at home. Wise officers give their soldiers a routine, and wise soldiers follow it. Though it may sound silly, lives may be lost because of the smallest of forgotten details. A battle may turn because you did not build a tent line straight, which led to an injury in the night, which held up the march for an hour, which allowed your enemy to surprise you. Or you may arrive to battle exhausted because many in the camp were woken by the commotion of the night before.

There are also smaller tricks to make the journey easier for each soldier. On the first night of our westward march, I came upon Jian unloading her whole pack and laying out all its items.

"You would do better to save your effort," I told her. "I doubt you will use half those things tonight, and then you will only have to pack them again in the morning."

She paused, frowning down at her pack and pushing back her rakish hair. "But I did not bring much. It only takes a few moments."

"A few moments now may seem trivial," I told her. "But in the morning, you will be even more tired and sore than you are now. Then you will throw your things haphazardly into your pack, which will bounce on its straps all day, tiring you further."

"Trust him, girl," said Hallan, whose own tent was nearby. His fiery beard jumped as he pointed up at me. "He's legged more leagues and fought more fights than even me, though he be younger."

Jian shrugged. "Very well. I suppose I will listen to so *very* many years of experience."

"Fair enough," I said with a smirk. I went on down the line to inspect the rest of them, giving Hallan a nod of gratitude as I went. He waved it off with a smile and began to clean his new spectacles.

Mag and I impressed these little details upon our squadrons as best we could. I noticed that when we did, Tou listened attentively as he stroked his goatee. Before long, I caught him passing our words on to the other sergeants in our company. I suspect he even conferred with the other lieutenants and passed them the same information, for I soon noticed most of the army doing as we had instructed our squadrons.

A hard march through the day under Kun's watchful eye and a tent shared with Yue at night. Life had taken on the routines of the mercenary days of my youth, and I found myself not displeased.

At the end of the day after Yue joined us, we made camp at the northern edge of the Carrweld Forest. Mag had been quiet throughout the day. I wondered if she was thinking of Shuiniu, the village where she had grown up. It was just there, just a little ways into the forest. As we had ridden throughout the day, I had kept an eye to the south. Whenever I saw a road or a hunting trail, I wondered if we could have followed it south until it reached Mag's old home. We could not take the time to visit now, of course. Kun would never allow it, and we were on contract now—we were bound to remain with the army until our next stop in a town or city, on pain of punishment. Yet I was filled with a sudden desire to go to Shuiniu, to see the streets that Mag walked as a child, to visit the people who had known her when she was young.

"You are very quiet," said Yue, driving such thoughts away. "What troubles you?"

We were sitting side by side as we ate our supper. Everyone had left us to eat alone, which I appreciated—I had been surrounded by bodies and shouting voices all day during the march. Now it was quite pleasant to take in a quiet moment with Yue's comforting presence by my side. The evening was milder than they had been of late. Though the sky was dark with clouds, there was no rain, and we had found a log to give us a dry place to sit, free of the slushy snow that covered the ground.

"Oh, nothing very important," I answered, glancing around to make sure Mag was not near. "That forest there is called the Carrweld. Mag grew up in a town there, and I wondered if she was homesick."

Yue snorted. "Strange. It is hard to imagine her growing up anywhere. Something about that woman feels eternal, as though she sprang out of the ground full grown."

I shook my head. "You exaggerate. But then, you are not the first to do so. Many people see her remarkable skill at fighting and ascribe all sorts of other wild notions to her. I suppose I have been guilty of it myself. Mayhap that was why I was so surprised, though I should not have been, to learn she had had a whole life before we ever met."

"Of course she did," said Yue. "We all do. You scarcely know anything about me in the time before we met, and I know precious little of you, aside from what happened to you in Northwood. Though I imagine you were a troublemaker even before then."

That cast a dark pall over my mood, and Yue saw it. She frowned, leaning forwards to get a better look at me.

"What?" she said. "What is it?"

I had a sudden urge to avoid her gaze. "The battle of Northwood was a dark day," I said. "But the time before it was hardly better. I had not thought of it in some time."

Her brows rose. "It must have been bad for you to compare it to Northwood."

"It was," I said. "I lost—" I cut myself short. "It was," I said finally.

Yue waited through a long moment of silence. Then she nudged me with her elbow. "You lost what? Your favorite dog?"

Oku's head came up, but I ignored him. "No, nothing. I should not have said anything, least of all now."

Despite my reticence, Yue seemed to hear much in my words. "Ah," she said carefully, leaning back, her hands on the log. "You lost some-*one.* Someone . . . special?"

I placed a hand on her knee and finally looked her in the eye. "Forget it," I said. "I am enjoying myself now. There is no need to dwell on the past."

"Albern, you are allowed to have had lovers before me," she said. "I had many before you."

"Of course you did. Of course we both did. But it hardly seems the thing to talk about now, does it?"

She shrugged. "And why not? If their memory lingers, I do not mind you speaking of them to me, if it helps."

I sighed, reaching up to scratch at my stubble. I had not had a chance for a proper shave since we left Taitou. "Nothing lingers. It is fine. I have spent enough time thinking about him. I am ready to look ahead. Sky above, how can I complain? It is nothing like Mag in Northwood, losing the love of her—"

My words choked off. I tossed my head back and forth, failing to convince even myself that my mood was light. Yue, who did not seem fooled in the slightest, leaned closer and fixed me with her gaze. Again, I could not meet her eyes.

"Albern, whoever he was, you do yourself no favors by trying to convince me he was unimportant. I think you are trying to pretend for my benefit, but if so, you are a fool. Ours is not some moons-flying romance, you astonishingly foolish man. I am not looking for such a thing anyway. At least not now. Certainly not with someone who still holds a torch for their last lover."

"Of course not," I said. "I know that. You and I are simply . . . it is . . ."

"Enjoyable," said Yue, with the slightest smirk. "So enjoy it. Let yourself feel what you must, and when that feeling is sorrow, take comfort in me." She stuck her tongue in her cheek. "I plan to take comfort in you."

I had just started to take a pull from my wineskin, and now I almost choked on it. "Sky above, Yue," I gasped.

"There we are," said Yue. "Now, come. I am tired after another long day's march, and I want to get to sleep early." She stood and reached down to pull me up. "But not too early."

I sighed and let her lift me to my feet. "Fine," I said. "But only for your sake. I will take no joy in this."

"I am about to make you a liar," she said, heading for the tent.

But before I followed her, something caught my eye. I looked to my left and saw Mag standing there. She was a little apart from Dryleaf and our squadrons, who were all clustered around a fire, listening to the old man tell a story. Nikau and Orla were there, the lovers distracted from business by whatever tale Dryleaf was spinning.

But Mag did not seem to be listening to him. Her back was straight, her arms at her sides, and her gaze was fixed unerringly on the Carrweld. I knew from long experience that she could hold her body still as a statue when she wanted to. But now I saw a twitch in her hands. They hung loose and open, and her fingers would jerk forwards and then back. Forwards, and then back.

She did not see me. I doubted she saw anything but the darkness beneath those branches.

Almost I went to speak with her. But Yue called out to me, and I turned to follow her into the tent at last.

SEVENTEEN

Our march now took us into open wilderness, with no real roads to speed our journey. Still, we made a good pace west, clearing almost four leagues each day. On the third day, we turned from our somewhat northwesterly course to aim southwest, passing from a land of broken hills to one of rivers and marshes. Kun seemed to know the region well, for he led us unerringly around the worst delays in the land.

On the fifth day, we reached a town called Kuan Shu on the banks of the River Marsden. There we found a bridge, and after crossing, we camped beyond the western borders of the town that night.

Captain Kun did not let us spend any time within the walls speaking to Kuan Shu's inhabitants. I believe he did not wish us to spread any word of who we were or what our mission was. But he sent his nephew, Zhen, and some other Mystics into the town, probably to seek information about the Shades.

On the sixth day, Kun stopped the march about an hour earlier than expected. While we halted on the road, waiting, Kun and his advisors deliberated ahead of us. I was about to ask Tou if he wanted to see what was the matter, when Kun sent out the order to make camp for the night.

The sun was still a good hour or two above the horizon. I could think of only one reason why we would halt early. If Kun thought we were to meet our enemy in battle soon, he would want to keep his army as fresh as possible.

But I kept these thoughts to myself as I directed my squadron in building their tents. Then my attention caught on a messenger approaching from the head of the camp, where Kun's tent was being built. The woman went to Tou and spoke quietly with him before leaving at a brisk pace, heading farther back down the column. Tou stood looking after her for a moment, fingers on his chin, before he sought me out and motioned me over to him.

"Trouble?" I asked.

"No," said Tou. "Only a summons to speak with the captain. I may not be gone long, but just in case, would you have one of your soldiers build my tent for me?"

"I will see to it myself," I said. "And your stakes will not be as shaky as they have been in recent days."

His expression lightened, and he rolled his eyes. "Not everyone is as . . . seasoned a campaigner as you are."

I placed a hand to my chest, raising my eyebrows in mock affront. "A jibe at my advancing years? I thought you a better man."

Tou chuckled, seemingly against his will, and flapped a hand towards his pack. "Just build the tent."

"Of course," I said, smiling. The smile lasted until he was gone, and then a worried crease came to my brow. My thoughts were troubled as I built Tou's tent and then my own, and then I knelt to light a fire after Chausiku brought some wood.

Tou finally returned as the last light was fading in the sky. His face was grim as he approached me by my fire.

"Get Mag and Yue and come speak with me," he said.

"Yes, ser," I said, and went to do as he had bid.

When I found Mag, she and Yue were sitting with their squadron and eating. Dryleaf was there with them, as were Nikau and Orla. The lovers spent time with us every night, at least for our evening meal, before they went and plied their services among the army. Yue, it seemed, was in the middle of a tale about our fight with the vampires.

". . . and then they split up," Yue was saying as I approached. *"Split up,* the fools. Unfortunately, Albern was the one to find me, which meant I had to save my own hide. The vampire got a good chunk of my shoulder with its claws, but I managed to shove it into the flames and burn it to death."

"*After* I had already pierced it with an arrow," I put in.

Yue looked up, the surprise on her face too exaggerated to be genuine. "Albern! I did not see you coming."

"Mm," I said. "I am afraid you must finish your tale later. The lieutenant needs us."

The mood of those around the fire darkened in an instant. Without a word, Mag and Yue got to their feet. But as Yue was stepping away, Dryleaf reached up and took her hand.

"Should I come with you?" he asked.

"Tou is in a hurry," I said. "But I promise we will speak with you after."

Dryleaf nodded. "Very well. I eagerly await it." Then he turned to the rest of those sitting by the fire. "And in the meantime, mayhap I should tell you *my* part in this tale of the vampires. It was quite amusing—Albern was so impressed with my wisdom that he thought I could see without my eyes."

Orla wore a joyful expression. "I would not be surprised, dear one," she said, gently rubbing the back of his hand. "The sky bestows many blessings on those who command the magic of talespinning."

A few chuckles rang out behind us as we walked away. I smiled ruefully in the growing darkness. "Why do all your stories seem to make me the butt of the joke?"

Yue slapped my rear end. "Because you are so excellent for the role."

My face flamed, and I hoped they could not see it in the sparse light of the campfires we passed. Mag, however, ignored our flirting.

"Do you know what this business is with Tou?" she asked.

"I do not," I said. "But the moment the march stopped, the captain summoned all the lieutenants. And I noticed that we did not march as long as we could have today."

"I noticed that, too," said Mag.

Yue glanced back and forth between us. "What does that mean?"

"Captain Zhou may be trying to save our strength," said Mag. "And there is only one reason he might do that, which is to have us ready for a battle he believes is imminent."

Yue sighed. "I see."

"Let us see what Tou has to say before we consign ourselves to gloom," I said. "There may be another explanation."

There was not.

"The captain believes we will meet the enemy soon," said Tou, skipping any preamble. "We have stumbled upon signs of the Shades' march."

We stood there in dour silence—Mag, Yue, me, and the other two sergeants in Tou's company. They were both Mystic knights, but for the life of me, I can no longer remember their names.

"They are marching in the open?" I said at last. "That is unusual, from what we have heard."

"So it is," said Tou. "But they are both in the open and not, you might say. These are wildlands. It is unlikely anyone would see them, and less likely that anyone who saw them would know what they were seeing."

"Where are they coming from?" said Yue.

"The captain has a theory," said Tou. "Recently there have been rumors of Dorsean raids into Feldemar. King Alim of Feldemar has sought reparations. But King Jun knew nothing about the raids, and he refused responsibility for them. Diplomats on both sides were trying to sort the situation out. Now the captain thinks he knows the truth: these attacks were carried out by the Shades. They posed as Dorsean soldiers to foment discord between us and Feldemar."

Mag and I glanced at each other again. "That seems a sensible guess," said Mag. "We have had several encounters with the Shades so far, and they are fond of getting others to do their fighting for them."

"And so now we expect to meet these Shades on the field?" I said.

"The captain thinks so," said Tou. "And in very little time. We do not know their destination, but we mean to keep them from reaching it."

"Good," said Mag. "What does he need from us?"

"Only to be ready," said Tou, scratching his goatee. "And to make sure your squadrons are ready as well. You all have good heads on your shoulders and at least some experience in a fight. The same cannot be said for everyone you command. See to their readiness. Prepare them for what is to come."

“Easy enough,” I said. But immediately, I winced. “Or rather, easy enough to understand. Of course, it is no simple thing to prepare someone for their first battle.”

Yue arched an eyebrow at me. “Hm. I wonder what was wrong with me, that when we first met, I thought you had such a silver tongue.”

I rolled my eyes at her before addressing Tou again. “We will see it done, ser. Let us know if there is any other way we can be of service.” Then I turned and looked Yue dead in the eye. “And my tongue may not be silvered, but it has received no complaints of late.”

I turned on my heel and left, while Mag nearly collapsed, trying to hold back her laughter. Yue went beet red and failed to muster any retort.

EIGHTEEN

I woke the next morning with a mission—one not given to me by Tou.

Quickly I broke my fast by the campfire nearest my squadron's tents. Then I headed towards the west end of the camp, where Kun and his Mystics slept. A few curious eyes followed me as I walked past, but I ignored them. Most of the time, if you act as though you are supposed to be wherever you are, few will question you. Such was the case then, for no Mystics came to ask me what I was doing.

At the westernmost end of the camp, I saw the signs Kun had found. A wide trail had been tramped into the ground. It intersected with our path from the north, and there it turned west and headed in the same direction as our march. I gathered all the information that I could. Their number seemed to be around two hundreds, which was less than half of our force. That was close to Yue's best guess at their numbers. I saw no hoofprints at all, which was a heartening sign. If they had been a mounted party, we could not have hoped to catch them. It seemed to me that they had been here only a day ago. But I could not be entirely sure, nor could I tell anything else; Kun and his Mystics had already wandered about the place, disturbing many of the signs.

I turned and headed back towards my part of the camp with the same air of indifference as when I had come. Once again, no one hailed or challenged me. When I reached our row of tents, I saw that Mag was already up and breaking her fast by the fire. She greeted me with a lazy wave. I sat by her and pulled out a packet of dried meat. I had already eaten, but no seasoned soldier refuses a second helping.

"Good morn," I told her. "I have been busy already."

"So I gather," she said. "Looking into the signs of the Shades?"

"Just so. We are only a day behind them, I think. And they are marching west, on the same path as us."

Mag frowned. "West. I still do not understand it. This is not the quickest way to reach any city of import. If they mean to make trouble in Feldemar, they would do better to go north, and if in Dorsea, then to the south."

I shrugged. "Mayhap they mean to practice some smaller mischief, as in Lan Shui."

"What is that about Lan Shui?" came a sleepy, grumbly voice. Yue hauled herself out of my tent. Her short yellow hair stuck out in all directions, black in the roots after so long without dye. "Do not tell me we are heading back home after I spent so long riding away from it. I might just throw a fit."

"I do not think so," I said, chuckling. She came to sit beside me. I brushed a hand lightly up her back, and she stole some food from my pouch.

Mag, meanwhile, did not look convinced by my idea. "I doubt they are doing anything like the ritual that summoned the vampires. Why would they need so many soldiers? The Shades in Lan Shui numbered less than a dozen."

"A fair point," I said. Then I arched my brows. "Though mayhap Yue struck closer to the truth. What if their destination is not on this side of the Greatrocks? They may be making for the Sunmane Pass, there to cross the Greatrocks and pursue some mischief in western Dorsea."

Mag's eyes widened. "No. They do not mean to cross the pass. They mean to occupy it."

Yue frowned. "Occupy it?"

But I understood Mag at once. "Of course. There are only two passes through the Greatrocks. If the Shades could occupy one of them, they would cut the kingdom's trade and travel in half."

"Why only in half?" said Mag, her expression going dark. "I would wager that another force makes for the Moonslight Pass in the south. They will cut Dorsea in two."

Yue and I looked at each other, and then at Mag. "We have to tell Kun," I said.

Mag snorted. "Would he even listen to us?"

"He could hardly ignore you," said Yue.

"You might be surprised," said Mag. "He has suspected us from the start. We only march in the vanguard so he can keep an eye on us."

"But this could devastate the kingdom," said Yue. "What do you mean to do about it, if not tell the captain?"

"She is right," I told Mag. "We have to try, at least. Mayhap if we present a plan of action, along with our guess, we may be able to convince him."

Mag's eyes flashed. "Do you think we could get our hands on a map?"

"I have one," said Yue, to our surprise. "It is nothing fit for kings, but I brought it for my journey, when I was trying to determine where you fools might have gone."

"Yue, you are a gift," said Mag. "Please, fetch it at once."

Soon we had it laid on the ground near the fire. Mag took a piece of charcoal to draw on it, and her brow furrowed as she studied it. She circled a spot. Twenty-five leagues west of our position, there was a narrow pass between a wood to the south and a cluster of hills to the north.

"This place," she said. "It is the northern edge of the Greenfrost. We march right for it, and so do the Shades. It would be a perfect place to attack them. But Kun's army has no hope of catching them before they reach it. Not unless we send a smaller force to ambush them, to delay their march until the rest of the army can catch up."

"It will be a hard trek even so," I said. "But with us guiding Tou's company, we could get there in time."

"Then let us bring this to the lieutenant at once," said Yue, "before Kun begins the day's march."

We found Tou with little trouble. He was finishing his morning meal, and he arched an eyebrow at us as we approached.

"Good day," he said. "What is it? You look as though something important has happened."

"Not yet," said Mag.

As quickly as we could, we outlined our plan. Tou listened attentively, curling his fingers through his goatee and frowning.

"The Sunmane Pass," he said. "I admit, it makes more sense than anything else we have guessed at. But they would have a hard time holding it with no place of strength to defend."

A chill went through me. "They may have a stronghold in the peaks," I said.

Tou met my gaze, nonplussed. "Oh? I know of no such places in those mountains. How could they keep it hidden?"

My throat went dry. "I . . . I have seen something similar before. In the mountains west of Northwood. It is where I first saw Shades, though I did not know who they were at the time."

I was afraid Tou might have heard something of that stronghold and know that there was more to my tale. But to my immense relief, he only nodded. "Well, then. I think you are right. This must be brought before the captain." His expression soured. "Though I wonder if I should bring it to him myself. He is . . . not overly fond of the two of you."

"An understatement if ever there was one," said Mag lightly. "But you will need Albern and me to guide the company if we have any hope of catching the Shades in time."

Tou tilted his head. "You know the area well?"

"She is Dorsean," I told him, "and grew up not far from here. And I was trained as a ranger in Calentin. Though I do not know this land well, I can guide a force through any wilderness if I know where I am going."

Mag's mouth opened and then clamped tight again. I hoped I had not overstepped, saying more than she had wished. But she did not look angry, only conflicted.

"All right," said Tou. "The troops have risen, and most will soon be ready to march. We must speak to the captain at once. Come."

"Ser," said Mag, Yue, and I together.

We followed him through the camp to Kun's tent. A small table had been set up, and Kun was enjoying a meal upon it. Upon another, smaller table beside him, he read reports and letters. As he noticed our approach, he looked up, gave us a beaming smile, and wiped a bit of grease from the corner of his mouth.

"Lieutenant Shi," he said. His eyes roved across the rest of us. "And your sergeants. To what do I owe such a pleasure?"

Tou drew up smartly and gave a salute. "Captain. Mag and Albern have shared some thoughts with me this morning, and I thought it best to bring them to your attention."

"Indeed?" said Kun. "I am sure I cannot wait to hear what is going on in their inimitable minds." He stood and motioned to one of his attendants, who began to clean the remainder of his meal. "Let us speak in my tent."

We followed him inside. Like those of most military commanders, his tent was a grander thing than the one- and two-person tents of the rest of the camp. He had a space in the middle for a desk, upon which had been laid a map of Dorsea, larger and more detailed than Yue's.

"Now then," said Kun. "I imagine this has something to do with whatever Sergeant Telfer was poking his nose into this morning?"

So, someone had reported my investigation to the captain after all. I tried not to look like a guilty child who had been caught stealing an extra slice of apple tart. "Yes, Captain," I said. "I was curious about the Shades and what their aims might be. And I am somewhat skilled at woodcraft, so I thought I might be able to glean some information."

"Lieutenant Zhou is also quite capable in such matters," said Kun. "Tell me: do you think you discovered anything he did not?"

"I am certain he saw everything I did, Captain," I said. "Yet Mag and I might have been able to guess more from the information."

Mag stepped in. "Ser, we believe the Shades are making for the Sunmane Pass. If they can prevent travel through it, and if an equal force can do the same in the Moonslight Pass to the south, they will deal a devastating blow to Dorsea. It will help Wojin hold the throne, and even if he were usurped, Dorsea will be utterly unable to aid the High King against Dulmun."

Kun's brows shot for the tent's ceiling. "That is quite an assumption. Do you know something of the Shades' intentions?"

The meaning behind the question was obvious. Kun rarely missed an opportunity to needle us with the possibility that we were on the side of the enemy. I ignored it, and as Tou rolled out Yue's smaller map atop the larger one, I pointed to the marks we had made with charcoal.

"It may be an assumption, Captain, but I believe it is a good one," I said. "Mag was the first to think something was wrong. She was born and raised in Dorsea, and it bothered her when she saw the direction of the Shades' march. They are headed due west, yet there is nothing valuable between here and the Greatrocks—nothing except the pass itself."

"And two hundreds is more than enough to hold the pass and keep anyone from using it," said Tou. "At least we think so, if the Shades have a stronghold in the Greatrocks."

I blanched as Kun gave him a sharp look. "A stronghold? And what makes you think they have one?"

Tou paused, turning to look at me. "Well . . ."

I took a deep breath. "Captain Zhou. What do you know of Jordel of the family Adair?"

A long moment of silence stretched as he studied me. Tou now seemed uncomfortable, as though he regretted bringing us here. Mag's gaze remained locked on me, studying my face. I suspected she worried for me—after all, she was one of the few who knew all the details of my time with Jordel. More details than I would share now, certainly.

But I was also keenly aware of Yue's gaze upon me. It was only a few days since we had spoken of Jordel, though I had not named him then. Her expression was a mix of curiosity and pity.

At last, Kun spoke slowly. "I did not know Jordel. But I have heard much of him."

"Especially since Northwood fell, if I am not mistaken," I said.

Kun's smile sharpened, and he lifted his chin. "What makes you say that?"

"Because I was with him in the Greatrocks," I said. "I fought by his side when we discovered the Shades there. And I laid his cairn when he fell, and I wept at his grave."

The air in the tent was thick enough to cut with a knife. Kun did not so much as blink, and I could read nothing in his smile.

"Hm," he said. Another moment passed, and then his smile softened. "Well. This is all interesting information that I certainly wish I had had earlier. I wonder if I can believe it. Though if you were trying to trick me, I hardly think you would admit involvement in the death of the last Mystic captain you knew."

For weeks now, I had kept my temper through such remarks. Kun never stopped prodding us, trying to get a reaction. And I understood why, and I forgave him for it. But now I felt my blood rush in my ears, creating a whine at the very edge of my hearing, and a terrible rage thundered in my chest.

"Captain," I said, my voice louder than it should have been, "I will not stand idle while you speak that way. You have your jibes at Mag's and my expense. We hear them beneath your courtesy, and we know you know it. But you will keep your needling words far from the subject of Jordel."

Tou's eyes were wide, and he looked as though he wanted to do something but did not know what. Meanwhile, Kun's smile had again grown sharp and icy. "Oh, I will? Or what? What will you do if I do not comply?"

"There is no 'or,'" I said.

"Albern," said Mag, gently but firmly.

"No!" I barked, cutting her off. Her brows lifted, but I ignored her and turned back to Kun. "There is no 'or.' You will stop because you are a man of honor, and respecting Jordel's memory is the honorable thing to do. If I were a Shade in disguise, intent on your ruin, it would still be right. If I were an assassin with designs on the High King herself, it would still be right. You will not speak ill of the dead or of—" My voice caught, but I forced myself to go on. "—Or of one who loved him. You *will* hold your tongue, not for fear of anything I might do, but because it is right, and because you are worthy of such restraint."

Everything lapsed into silence again. Tou still looked ready to spring into action the instant he felt sure of what action to take. My limbs shook as anger and anxiety coursed through me together. I was prepared to fight, to flee, or to break and weep on the ground, and I could not have told you which I wanted to do most.

But Kun did not look angry. His smile had not gone, but it had eased.

"At last, some honesty," he said quietly.

I frowned. "Ser?"

He dropped his gaze to the map and leaned over the table on clenched fists. "The two of you wrap yourselves in lies. You have since the moment I laid eyes on you. Nothing you have said to me has come without some cloak of falsehood, or a shawl of deceit at the very least. And that is fine. I do not need unshrouded honesty from everyone who serves me. But it makes me suspicious, as is my right." He looked back up at me again, studying me close from beneath his thick black brows. "Yet now I hear you speak with truth ringing from every part of you—your tongue, your eyes, and your heart. It is refreshing."

There was a long pause while I took this in. "Thank you, Captain," I said at last. "So you believe me?"

"I do," said Kun, smiling. "And your sharing of truth deserves the same in turn. I had not meant to tell you this yet, but now I wish to inform you of something Lieutenant Zhen learned in Kuan Shu."

Lieutenant Zhen straightened suddenly, his eyes widening. "Ser—"

Kun waved him to silence with one hand. "Zhen, please. They deserve as much, now that they have laid their hearts bare, as it were." He turned his gaze to us. "Wojin has been deposed."

"What?" said Mag, Yue, and I at the same time.

"Yes," said Kun, nodding. "Reports are murky as to how. But agents in the capital city of Danfon, led by other Mystics, overthrew the pretender king. Even now, he is being held captive there."

"Then who sits the throne?" said Yue.

Kun glanced at her. "His Majesty—formerly His Excellency—Senlin of the family Fei. King Jun was, it seems, killed. That much was true in what Wojin said, if nothing else was."

"But this is wonderful news, ser!" said Tou. "Should we not proceed to Danfon at once to help the new king stabilize his claim?"

"You forget yourself, Lieutenant," said Kun, though his smile remained plastered on his face. "We are Mystics. Our duty is not only to Dorsea, but to the High King, and through her, to Underrealm itself."

Tou bowed his head at once. "Of course, ser. Please accept my apology."

"It is accepted," said Kun. "And to answer your question: no. I do not think that Danfon is where we are most needed. King Senlin remains a loyal servant of the High King, and I have faith that he will consolidate his power in the capital and across the kingdom. But he will not be able to do so if the Shades succeed in cutting Dorsea in two by claiming the mountain passes."

Mag's eyes were alight. "So you believe us, then?"

Kun's smile widened. "Yes. I believe you. Your guess as to the Shades' intentions is better than any of mine. And knowing the lieutenant, you came up with a plan of action before you brought this to me. What is it?"

Tou glanced back and forth between Mag and me, as though he could hardly believe it. But he recovered quickly, clearing his throat. "Well, Captain. Sergeant Mag pointed out this area here." He indicated the spot Mag had marked earlier. "A smaller, faster force could be sent ahead to circle the Shades, ambushing them in the Greenfrost. That could hamper their march long enough for our main host to catch up with them, wiping them out before they reach the Greatrocks."

"Hm," said Kun, thinking. "It would be a hard march."

"Albern and I can serve as guides, ser," said Mag quickly. "I know the area, and Albern's woodcraft is unmatched—or, that is, I am sure it is comparable to Lieutenant Zhou's."

Kun chuckled. "You need not look after my nephew's honor so closely, Sergeant. Very well. I will let the two of you guide this force. Lieutenant Shi, your company will march on the route they have indicated."

"Yes, Captain," said Tou, giving him a bow.

"And I will be coming with you," finished Kun.

That gave all of us pause. Tou looked surprised, but Mag looked suspicious.

"Your . . . presence would be most welcome, of course, Captain," said Tou slowly.

"Oh, not just mine," said Kun. "My entire unit. All of the Mystics in our force, save those who are sergeants and lieutenants in the other companies. After all, if you intend to slow the Shades' march, you will need the strongest fighters you can get." He turned to Mag. "With Lieutenant Shi's company and my unit, we shall have just over a hundred of troops. Will that let you stage an ambush that can halt our foes' advance?"

Mag grinned. "I could do it with half that, ser."

Kun's eternal smile turned just as wolfish as her own.

NINETEEN

DAYS LATER, UNAWARE THAT THE SHADES' POSITION HAD BEEN DISCOVERED, Kaita wrestled with weighty thoughts.

Mag had guessed correctly. The Shades, having fulfilled their purpose on the border between Dorsea and Feldemar, now made for the Sunmane Pass. Most of the western senators had not been loyal to Wojin, and they would wish now to support the new king, as soon as they could muster the armies to do it. The Shades might not be able to prevent that from happening, but they would want to delay it as long as they could.

These matters were much on Kaita's mind. But something else also troubled her thoughts. She wore no furs against the cold—it was nothing compared to Tokana—but she still had on her cloak. She never took it off these days. And as she considered the road ahead, her hand stole into the cloak, probing an inside pocket. There sat the package of brown cloth Rogan had given her.

She could feel the magestones calling to her. Sometimes she even peeled back the edges of the cloth to look at them, as though to reassure herself of their presence. They glinted back at her, dark as the pupil of a giant's eye.

Wild thoughts flitted through her mind whenever she looked at the stones. Rogan had never wanted to give them to her. What if he had lied? What if he had given her fakes? She should eat one, test it, just to be sure, just so that she could know—

Footsteps approached her tent. Kaita snatched her hand away from the stones as the front flap opened. Tagata entered, bent double to fit.

Tagata was a shadeborn, like Rogan. Ten and a half hands tall she stood, and her shoulders were as broad as two ordinary folk abreast. On her back she carried a massive greatsword, which was as tall as Kaita herself. But her most frightening ability was neither her strength nor the surprising speed with which she could move. It was the tattoo inked on the back of her neck, the mark of her lord's favor. That mark could banish death itself, letting her recover from even the most grievous wound in a matter of moments.

She was a killer, born and bred and given a dark blessing. Yet, like Rogan, she was not always cruel or violent. As she entered Kaita's tent, her eyes held nothing but fondness and concern. And as she saw Kaita resting only in her cloak, she gave a little smile.

"Are you not cold, little one?" she said. "But then, I suppose you would not be, after your days in Calentin."

Kaita felt a flash of anger at the mention of Calentin, but it quickly subsided. She knew Tagata meant nothing by the jest, and she did not know as much of Kaita's story as Rogan did. So she smiled in response and beckoned Tagata to sit beside her.

"I find the cold bracing," she said. "But I am not opposed to piling on a few extra furs when I have someone with whom to share them. There are few things as pleasant as sharing warmth and comfort when the world is cold and dead."

"I agree with you there," said Tagata, taking the seat Kaita had offered. Their shoulders pressed together, and even through her thick cloak, Kaita could feel the warmth of Tagata's shoulder. She was like a furnace. It was something she had noticed in all the shadeborn she had ever met, as if they burned with some inner fire that no winter could hope to douse. Kaita leaned into her, resting her head on her shoulder.

Rogan had always told her to love all the Shades like her own family. But in truth, Kaita held most of them in disdain. They were like sheep, like the very people who had made her suffer early in life. She gave her trust and love only to those who deserved it—ones like Tagata, and Rogan himself. Ones who were useful, because they were strong.

But they were also very, very clever. And even as Tagata wrapped an arm around Kaita's shoulders, sharing more of her heat through the cloak, she glanced down at Kaita to give her a quick look-over.

"Are you well?" she said. "Is there anything you wish to speak with me about? Anything that worries you?"

Kaita sighed through her nose. "You should say what you mean. I have not taken the magestones. I gave my word to Rogan. And yet in return, he has sent me to march with you, directly away from where I wish to go."

Tagata frowned. "We must make for the pass. If the western senators can muster—"

"I know the reasons," snapped Kaita. She paused, took a breath, and forced herself back to calm. "Of course, this host can hardly turn around and head east. But I could. I could go on the hunt for Albern and Mag again. I have the power to end them at last."

"You must have faith," said Tagata. "If Rogan told you this was the right thing to do, you must trust him. He would not deceive you."

"I trust in him, just as I trust in our father," said Kaita irritably. "Yet what else am I supposed to think? The last I heard, Albern and Mag were to the east. Yet he sends me to march west. Does he know where they are better than I do? If so, why does he not tell me? Why not tell me *where* and *when* I shall meet them, rather than a vague promise?"

"He would never say it unless he believed it to be true," said Tagata.

"And I wish to trust in that," growled Kaita. "But how can I? How can he know?"

Tagata hesitated. At first, Kaita thought she had no answer. But when Tagata spoke, it was almost as if the words were being forced out of her. "He has . . . methods."

Kaita drew back, feeling her arm and shoulder cool as she looked up into Tagata's face. Tagata, meanwhile, did not meet her eyes, but looked studiously at the tent flap.

"Tagata?" said Kaita. "What do you mean?"

Tagata licked her lips, considering. "He . . . that is, I mean Rogan, but Father as well . . . they have . . . a sight."

She paused. Kaita remained silent, waiting. She felt a curious certainty that Tagata should not be telling her this, and that she should not press the matter, for that might drive Tagata back to silence.

"I do not know quite how it works," said Tagata. Now she spoke more quickly, as though cracks in a dam were widening. "But they can see things. Threads of time and fate, like the future in a tapestry."

"No one has that power," whispered Kaita.

"They do," said Tagata. "I do not know how it works. I do not know where they gained it. Rogan often says that we are all equal to each other—but I cannot be his equal, for this gift is beyond me. I barely know of its existence, and I know nothing of its origin. It seems to me that it is . . . unclear, some of the time. Yet from what I know, it is infallible."

"And what do you know?" said Kaita.

But Tagata shook her head. "I should not have said as much as I have. I will not speak more of this. I only tell you so that you know your faith is not misplaced. If Rogan said you would achieve your aims this way, but did not explain why, then I am sure it is because he has seen it."

Kaita wanted to ask one of the thousand questions whirling in her mind. But before she could prod Tagata to speak on, they heard shouting outside the tent.

Instantly they were on their feet, Kaita casting her cloaks and blankets aside. They threw themselves out of the tent just as a Shade came running up to them, her eyes wide, and pointed east.

"Commander!" she said to Tagata. "One of the eastern outriders has delivered a report. There is a force following us."

"What?" snapped Tagata. "How many? How close?"

"That is unclear, commander," said the messenger. "He saw the smoke of many campfires, but could not see the foe."

Tagata paused for a moment, considering. But a furious excitement sparked in Kaita's heart.

"It is them," she said in a whisper. "It must be."

Tagata frowned at her. "If there are many campfires, it cannot only be Mag and Albern."

"No," said Kaita. "Not just them. They have allied with others, other servants of the High King, to pursue me. Or to pursue us, for I doubt they know I am here. You were right. *Rogan* was right. I should never have doubted."

"You can be forgiven, I think," said Tagata. She turned back to the messenger. "Send word all through the camp. Muster for the march, and be ready to press hard. We must reach the Greatrocks before they catch us."

"Yes, commander," said the messenger, and she ran off to carry Tagata's words through the camp.

"I should go east," said Kaita.

Tagata's eyes went wide. *"No,* Kaita," she began. "You cannot—"

Kaita stopped her with a raised hand. "Be at peace. I do not mean to fight them. But I am your only weremage. Let me scout their position and estimate their number. When I am done, I will come straight back."

Tagata did not seem entirely convinced. The giant frowned down at her. "Will you promise me?"

Kaita gave her a small smile. Not all the Shades had earned her love, but Tagata had done so long ago. "I will do better than that," she said quietly.

She reached into her cloak and pulled out the small packet wrapped in brown cloth. As Tagata stared in shock, Kaita placed it in her hand and folded her thick fingers around it.

"Keep them until I return," said Kaita. "They would slow me down in my flight. And without them, you know I have no chance of striking at Mag and Albern in the heart of their allies."

"Kaita . . ." murmured Tagata.

Wordlessly, Kaita stood on tiptoe and pulled Tagata's face down to kiss her on the cheek. Then she turned, and her eyes filled with magelight. An instant later, a raven took wing into the grey, cloudy sky.

Kaita had to flap hard, for there were no updrafts to cast her sailing through the air. But she relished the burning in her wings, the feeling of blood coursing its feverish way through the tiny veins of her bird form. Her months of fleeing from Mag and me had left her exhausted, but she had had a week of easy travel with the Shades to recover. Now flying felt like a return to honest work after being too long idle.

At last, she spotted Kun's force. She studied it from high up in the air. Her best guess was that around three and a half hundreds of troops lay below her, not counting the camp followers behind. That was almost double the size of the Shade force. Worse yet, she spotted some dozen or so red cloaks wandering among the press—Mystic officers directing the militia.

So. The Mystics were aware of the Shades' march and were hunting them across Dorsea. And they were only half a day's march behind the Shades. At least they had no horses, other than some few officers' mounts and pack animals. Tagata and her troops should still be able to reach the Greatrocks before they were caught, though it would be a near thing.

Kaita was about to swoop lower. She wanted to see if she could identify the leader of this little army. She especially wanted to catch sight of Mag and me, to confirm what she already suspected. But just before she bent her wings to dive, an arrow flew up from the host. It pierced a raven, a real raven, through the breast. The bird plummeted to the ground.

Dark take them, thought Kaita. They were shooting birds in case they were weremages. Even as she watched, a falcon drew too close and was shot down.

Well. In truth, that was all she needed to know. If this host was taking precaution against weremages, that must mean that Mag and I were there. We would have told them about her. She could not get closer to confirm it, but she had all the proof she required.

She turned and powered her wings back towards Tagata and the rest of the Shades.

Of course, Tou's company had left the rest of the host days ago, and Mag and I had gone with him. Under our guidance, the company had marched south for half a day before swinging west. Then, we had raced along a small valley that ran south of the Greenfrost. Kun had directed the rest of his forces, under Zhen's command, to pursue the Shades with all possible speed and distract them.

That was why Kaita only counted three and a half hundreds of soldiers, and she reported that number to Tagata.

That was why she only saw a dozen or so redcloaks—the rest were with Kun, who marched with Mag and me.

That was why the next day, Kaita only kept an eye on the force behind, and never flew ahead to scout the Greenfrost for danger.

And that was why the Shades were utterly unprepared when we found them in the forest the next day.

TWENTY

WE MARCHED AT A BREAKNECK PACE, SLEEPING SIX HOURS EACH NIGHT and pressing ourselves hard during the daylight. Each time we stopped, Mag and I consulted Kun's map again. We evaluated each day's progress and made plans for the next. I put every ounce of my woodcraft to its utmost use, and Mag wracked her mind for every detail she could remember of the countryside.

If Kun's soldiers had not been so green, I doubt we could have carried off the march in time. When soldiers have never seen combat, their first outing seems like a thrilling adventure. They will march and train harder, and they find it easy to call upon inner reserves of strength and energy.

These things fade once they learn the reality of war. But since ours had not yet absorbed that lesson, we were able to push them hard enough to catch up to our foes.

Our force reached the woods a day before the Shades. The Greenfrost is so named because it is filled with trees called pycnandra, which secrete a greenish sap. When winter comes, the trees freeze over, and the sap turns the ice green. Then it is like wandering through a forest of emerald and jade statues. They were still frozen when we passed through the wood. It was a breathtaking sight, though we had little time to appreciate its beauty.

The path where the Shades entered the Greenfrost to the east was winding and sinuous. But halfway through the wood, the road straightened, and then it ran straight as an arrow's path until it reached the western end of the forest. It was on this straightaway that Kun planned our attack.

Tou's company had five squadrons: three of archers, including mine, and Mag's and Yue's with swords. And then, of course, there were Kun's Mystics, all carrying swords and shields, and each wearing chain.

We deployed two squadrons of archers on the south of the road and my unit to the north. Kun would signal the attack by firing a flaming brand into the air, and the archers would loose. Our bowfire would sow confusion in the Shades' ranks, miring them down. Then would come the second strike. Kun's Mystics would attack straight down the center, with Mag's squadron supporting him on the left and Yue's spears on the right.

Kun knew we would not be able to stop the Shades entirely, not with only a hundred of fighters. His idea was to make them retreat instead. We wanted them to run north, where the Greenfrost gave way to a vast, broad land with many hills and dells.

"Captain," said Yue, when Kun told us the plan. "Will they not vanish into the hills? How will we keep track of them?"

"Indeed, we hope they try it, because it will not work," said Kun. He nodded to Mag. "Mag here knows this region. The land there is too gentle to block sight very well. Nor will it let them funnel us into a trap, nor will the gentle slopes give them much of a high ground to defend. The hills only look impressive from a distance. Once inside, they will never leave again."

It was a cunning ploy, and Mag and I were impressed. I think Kun could tell we approved, which seemed to please him, despite himself. Something had changed in his attitude towards us. I did not get the sense that he trusted us, but no longer was he always suspicious of us. He spoke frankly with us as he laid out his plan.

"I wish to impress upon you both," he said to Mag and me, "that your squadrons will be in the path of the Shades' retreat. You must withdraw the moment they move in your direction. I hope you understand that I am not placing you in this position out of any wish of harm to you. With your experience, I know—or hope—that you will be able to lead your squadrons in a disciplined retreat."

Mag cracked a smile. "You can say what you mean, Captain, if you mean to imply we are cowards."

Kun's small council erupted in laughter, which we all quickly cut off. The humor was a good thing—all our faces had been grim, and there are few things more harmful to a fighting force than for its commanders to be too moody.

"Hardly," said Kun, smiling as usual. "Discipline and speed are all I ask of you. Maneuver west, swing around, and join the rest of us in pursuing them north."

"As you wish, Captain," I said.

"Good," said Kun. His smile lost some of its luster. "All that is left, then, is the waiting."

As any soldier with experience will tell you, the waiting is the worst part.

I gathered my squadron and moved with them to the north, positioning them in the forest where Kun had directed us. Mag and her unit came with us. Our troops kept their eyes cast down at the ground, and their fingers were pale where they gripped their weapons. Only Hallan seemed to be in better spirits, and that was only compared to the rest. His mouth was set in a firm line; he told no jokes, but kept his now-spectacled gaze on the beautiful jade forest ahead.

We stopped at Mag's position, and I turned to her to clasp wrists.

"Take care of yourself," she said. "If you are killed, I shall be very cross with you."

"And the same to you," I said.

I glanced over her shoulder at her squadron. Li stood there. Her gaze wandered like always, but her hands were shaking. Beside her was Dibu, who was as still as a rock.

I stepped past Mag.

"Listen to me," I said, loud enough to cut through their stupor. "I know your minds. I was there once. We all were. Even Mag, hard as it is to believe it."

Gently I punched her in the shoulder. She responded with a chop under my bicep, and my whole arm lanced with pain. I shook it hard to get the needles out.

"That is my drawing arm, you sow," I growled. Despite themselves, her squadron chuckled. "Yes," I told them. "That is how you should be feeling. Not thrilled, for you are not fools. But neither should you worry overmuch, for you have one great advantage in the battle you are about to fight. You have her. You have all heard stories of the Uncut Lady. Sky above, Dryleaf has told you plenty of them in the last weeks."

I hooked my thumbs in my belt and threw my shoulders back. "Well, tonight Dryleaf is going to need you. He will need you to tell *him* tales about your sergeant so that he can add them to his trove. I have fought with Mag on more battlefields than most of you have years in your life. She will not let you down. She will do everything in her power—and that is considerable—to lead you home safe from the field. Do the same for her, and each other, and you will be fine."

As I spoke, I watched them straighten. They turned to look at Mag, and then back to me. And in that brief moment, fear turned to resolution.

Once more I took Mag's wrist, and then I pulled her in for an embrace. There was nothing left to say, and so I led my squadron off.

We were half a span away from Mag's squadron when Jian cleared her throat. "Well, Sergeant. Have you any inspiring speech for us? I half thought Mag would speak on your behalf the way you spoke on hers."

"And what did you think she would say?" I retorted. "You have little to hang your hope upon. You are, after all, stuck with *me.*"

That got a halfhearted laugh from all of them. I stopped and turned, for we had reached our position.

"No, but in all earnestness, the most comforting thing I can say to you is that you do not need any comforting today. For most of you, this is your first battle. And it may be the safest one you will ever see. You have an easy job today: shoot an enemy when they do not know you are there and flee before they can retaliate." I raised one finger. "But there *is* something you must remember. You must listen for the moment when I sound the retreat. And you must stay close to me, and to your squadmates, when we pull back. Pay attention to your surroundings, and always keep an ear out for my call. What is far more important than killing the enemy?"

"Staying alive," they all said in chorus. I had drilled it into them hard enough.

"According to you," added Jian, after a moment.

Chausiku's nostrils flared, and his locs shook as he turned on her. "Dark below, Jian—"

"Be calm, you tree trunk," she told him, pushing her rakish hair off her forehead. "It was a jest."

I rolled my eyes. "All right. Find a tree to hide behind. And get ready."

TWENTY-ONE

It was I who loosed the first shot.

That makes me sound like the quickest archer on the field. But if I am being honest with you, it is because I forgot that Kun was supposed to give us a signal to attack.

The Shades came marching down the forest road from the east. Their dark forms slid in and out of view between the emerald trunks of the trees, like imps half-glimpsed in the wild. I watched them come, wrapped thick in their cloaks of blue. None were on horses, and they all bent wearily under their packs and bedrolls. They looked to be far more tired than our company, for we had been able to leave most of our equipment and supplies back with the main force.

Near the head of the column was a giant of a woman who gave me pause. It was Tagata, as you might be able to guess, but of course, I had never seen her before. She was massive, towering over the Shades all around her, with muscles thick as anything. She wore no extra clothing against the rainy chill, and her skin glistened with a sheen of sweat in the afternoon air. I swallowed hard.

The first shadeborn I had met was Trisken, who slew Jordel. When

I first saw Rogan, I recognized in him the same strength, the same viciousness. I saw it again in this woman now. That meant shooting her would be useless, even if I were to plant an arrow in her eye.

Therefore I chose the closest Shade to me as a target instead. He was a young man, mayhap in his twentieth year. His pale cheeks were rosy with heavy breaths that misted in the cold. He was not wary, nor was he looking about for any sign of attack. He would not even know he was in danger before he was dead.

I sighed and waited for the right moment. But as I said, I forgot about Kun's signal. Fortunately for me, Kun and I had the same idea of when the right moment was. I must have loosed my arrow at the same instant that Kun fired his flaming brand into the sky. At the same time that my shaft sank into the young man's neck, and he fell to the ground, gurgling, a searing hiss sounded in the air.

Shouts erupted from the woods all around us as our soldiers saw the signal. Flights of arrows ripped through the air to land among our foes. The Shades recoiled into each other and drew their weapons. But their movements were slow, sluggish, burdened with the weight of leagues behind them.

All but the brute woman. In an instant, her greatsword was in her hand, shining in the thin sunlight through the clouds. She gave a battle cry that shook the trees, and the Shades jumped in response. Suddenly there was vigor in their steps, and they tried to form into ranks.

We loosed another volley—the third, for me. Our hail of arrows struck the blue cloaks, and I watched them fall. We were silent—what use a battle cry when you are almost a span away and drawing no closer? Our only sound was the hissing song of death flying on wings of fletching.

Then Kun led his charge, and the air filled with their roar. A score and a half of Mystics came charging from the trees, and at their flanks were Mag's squadron and Yue's spears.

Snow turned red as blood splashed across it. The Shades reeled back. Their allies behind them tried to shove them forwards again. But they only pushed them onto our blades.

I saw Li there. She stood side by side with her fellows, but she was hesitant, the tip of her sword shaking. A Shade lunged at her with a savage roar. Li blocked his strikes, but she did not retaliate. And as she stepped back, her foot slipped in the blood-red snow.

Before the Shade could finish her off, Dibu was there. His sword hacked into the Shades' raised sword arm. The man screamed, but only for a moment before Dibu stabbed him through the gut.

Another Shade ran up. Dibu traded two blows and then slammed the edge of his shield into her face. She reeled back, nose broken. Dibu's sword hacked at her neck, nearly severing her head. She flopped to the ground.

With a moment of space to breathe, Dibu turned and hauled Li to her feet. She was still shaking, but she nodded at him. Together they plunged again into the fray, driving the Shades back.

But alone among the Shades, the brute held. Kun's Mystics broke like a wave around her. And she, like a boulder in the surf, held them off until they had to withdraw. Her greatsword came around in a grand sweep. A handful of redcloaks struck the bloody slush, never to rise again.

A curse slipped out of me. I had lost sight of Mag in the press. Hopefully, she would recognize the woman's power from my descriptions of Trisken. If she could strike at the tattoo I guessed was on the back of her neck, we might bring her down, which would be a grievous blow to the Shades.

And then a raven swooped out of the sky, and I forgot all about Mag and the brute.

The raven plunged straight into the Shades' midst. No natural bird would have landed there during a battle. And if I needed any more confirmation, it came in a flash of magelight. Soon Kaita was visible among the press, shouting orders to her fellows.

I could not take my eyes from her. My drawing hand had stilled, and no shafts flew from my string. Hallan paused in his firing, looking at me strangely. He reached over and seized my shoulder, shaking it.

"Sergeant!" he cried.

I roused myself from my thoughts. Kaita could wait.

Where was Mag? Still, I could not see her. But there was the brute woman, holding the Shade line firm.

"Everyone!" I cried. "If you are a good enough shot not to hit our allies, loose your arrows at the giant!"

I pointed her out—as if they needed help to spot her—and then drew and fired my arrow. Six more shafts joined mine. Two missed, but that still sent five arrows slamming into her chest, her neck, her arms.

The brute reeled back. The Shades around her buckled in dismay.

Now the Mystics pressed forwards. Three sank blades deep into the brute's torso. I watched her cough up blood.

My gaze darted back to Kaita. She looked at the brute woman, and she screamed. In anger? In grief? I did not know, for I could not hear.

One ambitious Mystic swung his blade for the brute's neck. But she was not as grievously wounded as he thought. With a roar, she caught his sword in her hand. It sank into the flesh, but she gritted her teeth and bore it. Then she seized the Mystic around the neck and crushed his face with her forehead. His whole body went limp, and he fell to the ground.

The other redcloaks drew back, nervous. That gave the brute the moment she needed to stand. Even as I watched, her skin began to stitch over the gaping wounds in her body. She drew in ragged breaths and hefted her greatsword again.

But another volley of arrows fell upon the Shades, and more of them dropped to the ground. The brute looked back at her allies, and I saw her hesitate. She did not know if there were more soldiers in these woods, waiting to pounce.

As the muscles in her jaw spasmed and then clenched as hard as iron, she raised her greatsword and pointed it north.

"Retreat!" she cried, and the word shook the very air, though her voice was thick with the blood in her lungs. "North! Retreat!"

I looked to Kaita again. She had taken up the call as well, shoving the Shades around her towards the trees—towards us.

And then I saw Mag.

She and her squadron had begun to fall back, retreating before the Shades as Kun had ordered. But Mag had stopped. She was looking at Kaita, who stood amid the Shades a span away.

Their eyes met across the battlefield.

Both of them stood motionless, gazes locked. Around Kaita, the Shades fled straight towards us, towards the trees that promised safety. Around Mag, her squadron wavered, unsure, not wishing to abandon their sergeant.

"Mag!"

My voice cut through the battle. Mag swiveled to look at me.

But there was Kaita. Mag turned back.

“Mag!” I barked again. Her gaze drew inexorably back to me. “Not yet.”

She heaved a great sigh. And she nodded, turning to her squad. I saw her order the retreat, though I could not hear the words.

“Retreat!” I called out. “West, into the woods!”

My unit looked ready to melt with relief, for the Shades were now only half a span away. They began to head west, but I hesitated a moment more, looking back towards Kaita.

She had not moved. She was looking at Mag, even as Mag’s unit withdrew. And in that moment, it was as if I could hear the silent words in her mind.

Not yet, I had said. And now I heard Kaita promise, *But soon.*

I turned and followed my squadron. The Shades fled north towards the hills, just as Kun had planned, and we gathered to wait for the rest of our forces to catch up.

TWENTY-TWO

"And was she correct?" said Sun.

"Hm?" Albern was studying the streets and barely seemed to have heard Sun's question.

"Kaita. Was she correct? Was it soon that she and Mag faced each other at last?"

Albern sighed. "Still eager for the end. Well, be assured, it is coming. It was not long at all before it happened."

"Thank the sky," said Sun. "Let us hear it, then."

"Ah-ah," said Albern. "You shall have to wait a little while. We have arrived."

He stopped, and Sun groaned as she skidded to a halt beside him. They stood in front of a building that looked like a simple shop but for the thick wooden beam barring the front door.

"This place?" said Sun. "It looks to be closed. You should keep telling the story while we wait for it to open."

"It is meant to look abandoned," said Albern, chuckling. "Yet it is very much occupied. Come."

He led her around the back of the building. In the rear was another, smaller door. Sun had seen this sort of shop before. Behind the door would be a stair leading up to an apartment. Albern knocked in a strange pattern: three times, then a pause, then once, then another pause, and then twice more.

Moments passed as Sun looked nervously around. They were in a narrow intersection in the alleys between buildings. Though it led to open air in all four directions, Sun could not help a slight feeling of being trapped.

"Keep talking while we wait," she whispered. "At least tell me what Kaita—"

Snap. A latch turned inside the door, and it cracked open. But Sun could see that a thick chain was affixed to the inside of it, which kept the door from opening too far.

Through the crack, she saw a man. His face was of a medium brown and wrinkled—though not as heavily as Albern's. He wore a thin mustache and a scrub of beard that only held to the edge of his chin, but which was neatly trimmed. His clothing had a sort of look Sun was well familiar with from up-jumped courtiers back home: fine quality, but too ostentatious. His hair fell to his shoulders, black but heavily streaked with grey. His eyes were sharp as he took in Albern, and then his glance flitted to Sun. When he spoke, it was with a heavy south Heddish accent and cadence.

"Albern," said the man. He undid the chain and opened the door wider. "You're late."

"Only by a few days, old friend," said Albern. "I had some important business to attend in Lan Shui."

The man sniffed. "Iss always important business with you. I s'pose you should come in."

"We would not want to trouble you."

"Did I say you're troubling me? Come, iss bloody warm in this sun."

He closed the door and undid the chain before opening it again. He waved a hand to indicate they should climb the stairs. It was less the gesture of a well-mannered doorman and more the furtive command of an irritated parent summoning their children in for dinner.

At the top of the stairs was an apartment, as Sun had expected. A large central room took up much of the space. Cabinets and shelves of crockery lined the walls, and a hearth dominated the back right corner, though it was now empty and cold. A large wooden table stood in the center. On this was a map of Dorsea and Selvan, with some of the other kingdoms poking in at the edges. Sun spied some markings on the map in various colors. But before she could get a good look at them, the man threw a thin blanket over the map to cover it.

"Something to drink?" said the man.

"Mayhap a bit of wine," said Albern. "Not too much, though. We need to keep our wits about us today."

The man's eyes sharpened at that. "Some trouble in the city?"

"Not if we avoid it," said Albern. He sounded unconcerned, but his words reminded Sun of her family. A worried knot formed in her stomach.

The man snorted. "Fairly said." His gaze turned upon Sun, and she felt as though she was being inspected like a murky ledger. "You as well?"

She felt her cheeks flame. "I . . . I will have some wine, yes. Thank you."

"Welcome."

The man went to one of the cupboards and pulled out a bottle, tugging the rag from its neck. He produced two glasses and filled them, handing them over. Sun thought it strange that he was not having any himself, and her hackles rose—but then he went to the table in the center of the room. A half-full glass already stood there, and he filled it the rest of the way. Still, she waited for him to drink before she took her first sip.

"How goes business?" said Albern. "Have you had any more trouble along the western coast?"

"Fah," spat the man. "The western coast is nothing *but* trouble these days. Well, trouble and money, which is the only reason I still deal there. But most of the northern pirates have scuttled into dark holes with the hunt on, and so it isn't as bad as it might be."

"That is good to hear," said Albern. He drank deep of his wine. "And how about closer to home?"

For the first time, the man gave a smile. It was crafty and seemed to hide many secrets, but it was still a smile. "Much better, especially with your help. And speaking of . . ."

He went to another cupboard on the opposite side of the room from the wine. Inside, Sun could glimpse several iron cases that she recognized as lockboxes for coin, as well as piles of bags made from black velvet. He danced his fingers along the bags as if the tips could tell the contents merely by touch. At last, he selected one and hefted it, tossing it in the air twice. Satisfied, he returned to the table and upended the pouch.

Gold scattered across the thin blanket covering the map. Sun guessed there had to be more than a hundred weights. She could not stop her eyes from widening. The man spread a hand expansively over the coins.

"Payment rendered for services well performed," he said. "I threw in a little bit extra. Loyalty may be iss own reward, but I find something a bit heavier provides even more motivation."

"And we thank you kindly," said Albern. He began to scoop the gold up, dropping it back into the pouch without counting it, and then he glanced over his shoulder at Sun. "Would you like a separate pouch?"

Her throat went dry. "I . . . A separate one?"

"Why, yes," said Albern. "Half of this is yours, you know."

"I . . . What am I supposed to do with it?"

Albern blinked. "Money can be exchanged for goods and services."

Over his shoulder, the strange man turned away, but not quite quick enough to hide a smirk. "Glad to see yer keeping witty company these days."

Sun's cheeks, already dark, flushed darker still. "I *know* that," she snapped. "I mean, what am I supposed to do with it *now?*"

Albern shrugged. "Tie it to your belt and keep it under your cloak, I suppose. You would not want to lose it to a cutpurse. And try not to spend it all today—I have one more place to visit, and you may find a profitable use for it there."

"But I . . ." Again Sun looked at the size of the purse in Albern's hand. "That is too much to carry around. It will pull my belt straight off!"

Albern turned to give the stranger a look. The man sighed before turning and stepping behind a half-wall that obscured the rear left of the apartment. In a moment, he reappeared, carrying an odd sort of wallet. It was made of well-worn leather, and it had thick, long straps. The man tossed it to Albern, who caught it deftly and turned to Sun.

"You may buckle this around your chest," he said. "It will keep the purse slung against your right shoulder. You will appear to have a slight hunch under your cloak, but it is more comfortable than having the pouch hang from your belt. Or you can fit it into your saddlebag."

"Thank you," said Sun, taking it from him. Then she turned to the stranger. "I can pay you for this."

He gave her a thin smile. "Pray don't worry about it. Call it another bonus—for him, not for you. Mayhap in time, you'll provide enough services to earn such rewards."

Sun did not know quite what to say to that, particularly since she did not know what services had been performed for all this coin in the first place. She scooped her gold into the purse and strapped it over her shoulder. It did indeed hang comfortably on her, and she decided to keep it there rather than put it in her saddlebag. She had never held this much money before in her life. Of course, she had *seen* this much, but it had all belonged to her family, and they never let her touch it or choose how to spend it.

"I believe thass all the dealings we have for today," said the strange man. "Do let me know if you see to that business along the south Selvan border, old man."

Albern snorted. "Scarcely older than you."

"But you *are* older than me."

Albern chuckled and reached out his left hand. The man took his wrist, and they shook. Then Albern motioned Sun to the back stairs before descending them himself. Before she followed him, Sun turned to their host.

"Thank you," she said. "For the coin, and the wine. I am Sun, of the . . . that is, just Sun."

His eyes flashed, but he did not ask about the words she had abandoned. "Iss been my pleasure, Sun. If I can ask: have you met any of Albern's other friends?"

Sun blinked. The question seemed to hold hidden meaning, but she had no idea what it might be. "We . . . met a woman named Dawan in Lan Shui," she ventured.

"No, no," said the man, shaking his head. "Here in Bertram. Never you mind. Juss look after yourself—and him. That man's worth a fair spot of coin to me."

The words were quite mercenary, but Sun thought she caught concern in the man's eyes. It reminded her of Dawan's parting words, a quiet plea the medica had whispered in her ear when Albern was not listening. Nodding, she turned to follow Albern out of the apartment.

Only when they were back outside did she realize that the stranger had never given his name. Sun's mouth twisted, but she decided to leave it.

"Well," she said instead. "I suppose you have no intention of telling me what that was all about?"

"You suppose quite correctly," said Albern. "But you may learn in time."

"If we *have* enough time," said Sun. "I fear that there are not enough years left in your life to tell me of all the years that came before."

"Oh, come now," said Albern, nudging her shoulder. "In only a few days, I have told you the story of many months. You will catch up eventually, and should not feel too badly about being so slow."

Sun whirled on him. "*Me* slow? You are the one—"

But Albern laughed and stepped for the mouth of the alley, back towards the street. Sun followed him, fuming, but mostly for show. She enjoyed the easy rapport she and Albern had built together, and which had seemed to come to them quite quickly. It reminded her of the old man's conversations with Mag.

And as she thought of that, it occurred to Sun that such familiarity might be a double-edged sword to Albern. Surely he enjoyed the return to a time where he had a traveling companion he could jest with, and who would return jokes as easily as she took them. But at the same time, she must be a poor replacement for Mag and a constant reminder of what he had lost years ago.

Her mood dampened. Pulling her cloak tighter about her, she started to follow Albern into the street.

But then she leaped back, dragging Albern with her. Two riders on horseback thundered through the place he had been standing. Sun took an angry step after them, opening her mouth to call out.

She froze as she saw cloaks of black and gold—the colors of her family.

"Albern!" she whispered, her voice full of fear.

"I see them," he muttered.

Together they moved into the alley's shadows, watching as the riders hit a bend in the street and passed out of sight.

"A good thing you are wearing that borrowed cloak," said Albern softly. "They did not recognize you."

"Yet they must know I am in the city!" said Sun. "Why else would they be in Bertram? We have to leave."

"There are a thousand reasons they might be in Bertram." Albern's voice was calm, as though he was trying to talk down a rearing horse. "We knew they might have sent out scouts in many directions, hoping to catch you in a wide net. This might be no more than that. They were not keeping too careful an eye out, or they would have looked more closely at your face."

"I . . . I should get new clothes," said Sun. "And mayhap some sort of mask. The hood may not be enough."

"As soon as we may." A sudden smile crossed Albern's lips. "After all, we have the coin for it."

Despite herself, Sun gave a little smile in return, and her fingers rose to slide along the straps of her new purse. "I . . . I suppose we do."

"They have no way of knowing you are here," said Albern. "Not for certain. We are not in danger yet."

Sun blew a heavy sigh out through her nose. "Mayhap not. But let us keep it that way. We should leave Bertram now. We have enough coin for the next leg of the journey. Whatever your other business here, you can return for it later."

Albern hesitated, and his gentle smile faded away. "I cannot. Someone is expecting to meet me here today, and if I do not appear, it will cause trouble. I am sorry, Sun, but I have to see this through. I hope you will come with me."

A rising tide of panic threatened to make her vomit. "How urgent can these errands be? When we were in Lan Shui, you made it seem like Bertram was one of many choices. Was that true? Or did you always mean to come here, no matter what I said?"

Albern did not hesitate in the slightest. "Both," he said. "We could have gone another way if you wanted. My errands here could have waited a few days, or even as much as a week or two. But I always intended to come to Bertram eventually. And now that I am here, I must finish my business in the city. If you wish to leave Bertram at once, there are places I can arrange for you to go. You can return when you and I are both assured it is safe. But if you stay, I do not think you will regret it."

The offer to send her away was tempting. She feared to stumble into another of her family's guards out here on the bustling streets. And she thought of herself far away, spending her days in an inn, with plenty of coin to pay for food and ale while she waited for Albern to fetch her.

But then she thought of being alone. Of Albern's absence. And what if her family found her regardless of her caution? Then Albern would not be there to help her escape them.

That was not such a tempting thought, after all.

Albern seemed to spy the indecision in her eyes, for he spoke again. "Remember what I told you not long ago. My family tried to pull me back into their clutches, but they failed. You will not be taken anywhere while I draw breath. Something you should do, by the way."

She sucked in a deep gasp of air and then let it out in a rush. For a moment, she felt lightheaded. But then her head seemed to clear, and she came to a decision.

"Very well," she said. "I will stay with you. But for the sky's sake, please do your business in the city quickly."

"As quickly as I may," said Albern. "And if you wish, I will not continue the story until we know we are safe again."

"Do you jest?" grumbled Sun. "I need something to distract me. Say on."

TWENTY-THREE

Well. You remember that we had driven the Shades into the hills north of the Greenfrost. While our company set up camp in the wood, Kun gathered Tou and the sergeants for a small council after the battle. His customary smile was absent. Soldiers had died that day. He found a large rock to use as a makeshift table and laid a map of the area upon it. With one hand wrapped around his chin, he studied it as he spoke to us.

"Our foes will not go far tonight," he said. "They are already weary, for they have pressed their march hard, and now they have wounded to tend to. We can wait for the rest of our force to arrive in the night, and then we can wipe them out at our leisure. Let the company rest and recover themselves. What were our losses?"

"None from Black Squadron," I said. The other archer sergeants gave the same reply.

"None from Green," said Mag. "A few cuts and bruises, but nothing to slow anyone down."

"I lost three, ser," said Yue, in a voice sharp as flint. "And four wounded."

My gaze snapped to her. Her face was stony, and her eyes were not quite on Kun, but staring over his shoulder into the far distance.

Kun sighed. "The bodies?"

"The rest of Blue Squadron is seeing to them now," said Yue. It sounded as though she was about to say more, but she did not.

"Very well," said Kun. "As for my unit, six Mystics fell. Eight more were wounded, but only two very badly. That leaves just over a score at fighting strength. I will have to share the burden of the center line in future battles."

"Understood, ser," I said. Mag looked troubled, and she remained silent.

"At least their lives were not given in vain," Kun went on. "A score and a half of our foes lie dead. My best guess is at least that many more are grievously wounded, which will slow down the rest of them. It is never easy to lose a comrade. But our fellows who ventured into the darkness today made the enemy pay dearly in blood. We who survive must honor them."

"Yes, ser." This time the whole council spoke in unison.

"Good," said Kun. "Lieutenant Shi, see that sufficient sentries are posted to prevent any surprises. The rest of you see to the arrangements of your units. If any soldier has snuck wine or ale into their packs, let them enjoy it moderately—and have them share with their fellows as well. Everyone deserves a drink tonight, if they wish it. Dismissed."

"Captain," I said, throwing up a hand. "One more thing, if I may."

Everyone had been turning to head away, but now they all stopped. Captain Kun looked at me, surprised.

"Sergeant?"

"Ser," I said. "A woman led the enemy today. A tall brute of a fighter."

Kun's expression darkened. Most of the Mystics who had died had fallen at her hands. "I noticed her."

"Then I am certain you noticed her healing from the wounds we dealt her. I have faced one like her before, ser. They are favored soldiers among the Shades, imbued with some dark magic given to them by their lord. As long as the enchantment holds, they can heal from any injury, even fatal ones."

I watched as Kun's jaw clenched twice. "Formidable indeed," he said.

"But not invincible," I said. "I spoke to you before of Jordel of the family Adair. It was he who discovered how to defeat them. The one we faced in the Greatrocks had a tattoo on the back of his neck. That was what contained the enchantment. Jordel destroyed the man's tattoo, and that made it possible for him to die. If we should engage the brute again, we should seek to destroy the tattoo first. It will not be easy, but if we can manage it, we can bring her down."

Kun's gaze roved across the little council. "You all heard him. Relay the instructions to your troops, as I will relay them to my Mystics. Sleep well."

With a chorus of "Ser," we set about our tasks. As Mag, Yue, and I headed for our squadrons, I glanced back over my shoulder. Kun was bent over his map. Still he wore no smile, and his brow was furrowed as he studied the parchment.

I tried to put him from my mind as I turned to the others. "Yue. Are you all right?"

"I am fine," she said.

"We know what it is to lose people in your command," Mag said gently.

"Then you know nothing you can say will ease my mood," said Yue. "Let us see to our duties. I want something to do."

We reached the middle of the camp, which was still being built around us. Before parting from Yue, I stepped up to her and placed a hand on her arm to keep her from running off. It took a moment, but she met my gaze.

"I am here," I said quietly. "Do not forget it."

Yue scoffed. "As if you have ever let me, since the day we met," she grumbled. But her words were not as fiery as she tried to make them sound.

I pulled her into an embrace, and then I went to see to my squadron. They had already put up their tents and were building fires, around which they had gathered with Mag's unit. Hallan noticed me as I walked up, and his beard jumped as he nodded.

"Sergeant." He and some of the others started to rise from where they were sitting.

"At ease," I said, motioning them all to stay down. "Let us get those fires going and have a meal. The captain also gave explicit orders: if anyone has anything finer than water to drink, they are commanded to enjoy it and share it with their fellows. But do not get too drunk."

That got a few laughs from them, as well as halfhearted cheers. Jian dug into her pack and pulled out a large, full skin. She waved it in the air with a grin.

"Wine, Sergeant?"

"Sky above, yes," I said, taking the skin from her.

It was far from the best I had ever had. But as I am sure you have realized since we met, anything you drink after a fight tastes ten times better than it should. I took a deep pull and handed it back to her.

"Thank you, Jian. You handled yourself well today."

"Thank you, Sergeant," she said, taking a swig. Then she turned and offered it to Chausiku, who sat close by. "Some for you?"

Chausiku looked somewhat surprised. "Yes. Thank you."

"Captain's orders," said Jian with a shrug, pushing her hair back. "So, what do you think, now that you have seen a real fight?"

As he lowered the wineskin, Chausiku's expression darkened. "We survived. I call that a good result."

"As do I," said Jian amiably. "I even killed one of the bastards. And with a gut shot as well. I aimed for the chest as you said, Sergeant, but I am glad I was off."

Chausiku did not answer, but rose with a glower and walked away. I frowned at Jian. "What pleasure do you gain from goading him?'

She grinned. "I suppose I enjoy the reaction. It is so easy to get from him."

I sighed. "Jian, you still seem to think this is some kind of game. You want to punish those you see as evil, but you see your fellows as competitors, not allies. When a battle does not go so well, you will wish you were with friends instead of people you have only mocked since the day you met."

Her expression soured, and she took another pull from her wine. "It will be a dark day indeed before I need someone to coddle me."

I shook my head and left her, walking to where Hallan was getting his campfire going. A cloud of thick, acrid smoke poured from the logs he had stacked together. Hallan cursed and coughed into his thick beard, pulling off his spectacles and swiping at his eyes. My nose began to sting as I approached him.

"Hallan?" I said. "Are you all right?"

"Fine, ser," he wheezed. "Iss this damn wood. Burns like darkfire."

"It is the pycnandra," said Dibu. He was there with Li, who was staring at the burgeoning flame. She did not appear to notice anyone around her, but was lost in her own wandering mind. "Their sap is what turns the trees green when they freeze. But it burns like poison."

Mag approached, coming from the line of her squadron's tents. "I knew someone was trying to burn the greenwood. You can smell it from a span off. Find something else for fuel, or we will all be hacking and coughing through the night."

"Oh, they tell me now," grumbled Hallan. He yanked the logs out of the fire and doused them in a puddle of rainwater on the ground before rising to find other fuel. But before he could leave, I saw Tou approaching.

"Squadrons!" I called out. "Officer present."

Mag's and my units stood and snapped to attention. Tou came to a stop, folding his hands behind his back and giving us all a nod.

"Good eve, all of you," he said, his voice carrying through the evening air. "I have come to relay the captain's compliments. You all carried yourselves well today, and the plan was as successful as could be expected. You have his thanks, as well as mine."

"Ser," we replied in chorus.

"As you were," he said. "Enjoy your rest tonight, for you all deserve it."

As most of them returned to their seats, he came to me and Mag. Mag raised a hand in greeting.

"Lieutenant," she said.

"Sergeant," said Tou. "In particular, I wanted to relay my appreciation to you. You were on the front lines, but you did not lose even one sword. That is worthy of high praise."

Before Mag could answer, Dibu stood from his seat and stepped up to join the rest of us. "It is worth more than praise, Lieutenant," he said, folding his bronzed arms behind his back. "Watching her was like witnessing an Elf-tale. She was everywhere in the fight. Her spear was like lightning from the sky."

Mag's jaw clenched. Tou seemed to notice it, for a small smile crossed his lips as he stroked his goatee and cleared his throat. "No doubt she was impressive, and yet she was not the only one who gave a good showing. You fought well today, soldier. Even better than you did against me in the trial."

Dibu's mouth worked. "Thank you, Lieutenant. Your training has been invaluable."

"Good training still requires a good student," said Tou. "It is a rare pleasure to find one who so easily takes lessons to heart. And that goes for all of you."

He placed a hand briefly on Dibu's muscular arm before stepping past him to Li. She still sat on the ground, and she was staring at the fire Hallan had been trying to build. Its embers were dead now, but she did not seem to have noticed.

"How are you, Li?" said Tou, more quietly now.

The sound of her name seemed to break her reverie. Li looked up at him, eyes lost for a moment. "I . . . am fine, ser."

"You survived your first battle," he said. "You should be proud."

She gave a brief, humorless laugh. "How can I be proud of something I had little hand in? Were it not for Dibu, I would be a corpse burning with the others. He saved my life and killed two of the enemy to do it."

"Yet you rose again," said Dibu, stepping up beside Tou. "And you claimed one foe for yourself before the end of the fight. The lieutenant is right, Li. You should be proud."

Li nodded, but from her expression, you would have thought she did not even hear them. Tou gave a little sigh and stood, turning to Dibu once more.

"Well, I do not wish to take up too much of your time. I only wanted to pass on the captain's praise. Dorsea is indebted to you all for your service today. And so am I."

Dibu swallowed hard and bowed his head. "Ser."

Tou gave Mag and me a quick nod, and then he set off to do his rounds with the rest of the squadrons. When I turned to look at Mag, she was fighting hard to contain a smile.

"What are you grinning about?" I asked her.

"Hm? Oh, nothing," said Mag. "Only it seems we are in the captain's good graces at last."

"And about time," I said. "One step closer to Kaita."

That caused her smile to evaporate at once. "Yet not quite close enough."

"Not yet," I told her. "But soon. Come now. Let us get our people situated, and then get ourselves to bed. I will sleep like a rock tonight."

"As if you ever sleep any other way," said Mag.

I snorted and shoved her shoulder, and she shoved me back (which sent me stumbling three paces). I went and checked on my squadron's tent lines, made sure they knew their watch schedule, and then started making my way to my tent. I still had not seen Yue, but I knew it would be best to leave her alone until she was ready. But on my way to bed, I spotted Chausiku. He stood a little apart from the rest of the camp, away from the fires, staring out into the Greenfrost with his hood drawn up. I approached, and as he heard my footsteps coming, he looked over at me.

"Ser," he said, nodding.

"Good eve," I said. "You should be getting yourself to sleep."

"I will, ser," he said. "But my mind is racing now, and I am trying to let it wear itself out."

"I confess I sometimes need the same." I stood beside him, folding my arms over my chest for warmth. "Today was your first taste of battle, and you did well. But how are you, really? I know you did not enjoy it, as Jian did."

Chausiku snorted. "That I did not. I cannot understand that woman, and I doubt I ever shall."

"Give it time," I said. "You are united in purpose, even if you view the purpose differently."

"I know that to be true, yet I find it hard to believe," said Chausiku with a sigh. "Her bloodlust is unnerving. I answered Captain Zhou's call because I care about Dorsea, and I would not see my nation betray the High King. But I could have gone my whole life without killing another person, and I would have been happier for it."

"Would not we all," I said, "if only the world were gentle enough to allow it. Yet still, you and Jian may find common ground in the end. I hesitate to hope for it, for it may require the war to go on for a long while. But if it does, do not be surprised if you find yourselves becoming fast friends."

"Like you and Mag?" said Chausiku with a smirk. "I confess I cannot see it."

"Well, mayhap not like us," I admitted. "Mag is easier than most to be friends with."

"And yet she is so terrifying in a fight," said Chausiku with a shudder. "I could hardly believe it. She deserves every legend I have ever heard of her. How *did* you become such good friends, anyway, when she is so much younger than you?"

That made me laugh. "It will surprise you to learn that she is, in fact, a little older than I am. We met when I had not quite seen my twentieth year, and she was already as good a fighter as she is today."

Chausiku's eyes were wide in his dark face. "Really? I would have thought she was a decade younger than you, at least. I would believe you if you said you were twice as old as her." Then, suddenly, he looked uncomfortable. "Meaning no insult about your appearance, of course, Sergeant."

My easy smile widened, and I shook my head. "I am sorry to disappoint you, soldier. Some people hardly seem to age, and some . . . well." I waved my hand up and down the length of my body.

Chausiku snorted, trying not to laugh. "Well, in any case, you are lucky to have her for a friend. And now I think my mind has indeed tired itself out. I will see you in the morning, Sergeant."

He turned and left me. It always amused me how shocked people were when they learned the truth about Mag's age compared to her looks.

But Mag *had* aged, I knew. I remembered her when she was younger, and I knew her now. She *was* different, if not as different as I was.

Sometimes being close to a tale keeps us from seeing it clearly. A soldier on the battlefield might slay two foes and think the battle is close to won—but the general on the hilltop can see foes sweeping around the flanks and taste the coming defeat.

But sometimes, being close to the tale is what shows us the truth of it. We can see clearly the sunlight on a fish's rainbow scales, while someone on the shore sees only an ugly trout through muddy, churning waters.

That is how it was with Mag and me. Certainly, she was someone you had to see up close to believe—if you *believe* in stories, that is.

Ah, well. I turned my steps towards my tent, and soon I was abed. I was alone for a long while, as Yue spent time with her squadron, mourning their losses with them. But even before she returned, I slept poorly. Roots kept digging into my head, and I could not seem to get rid of them, no matter how I tried to shift on the forest floor.

TWENTY-FOUR

Now, I have commented on Mag's appearance before this. But it is worth noting that she always looked younger than she was, even when she lived in that village called Shuiniu.

Ten years before Mag and I met, she had just begun her apprenticeship under Duana. Of course, she did not have a hand in the brewing straight away. As is the case with many apprentices, she spent her first several months taking care of odd jobs around the brewery. She would sweep up shavings, fix small things that had broken, and haul water and grain from one place to another as required. All the while, Duana would explain the craft to her, indoctrinating her into the finer aspects of the art.

And Duana would tell stories. It seemed she was a talespinner, of sorts, though none so fine as Dryleaf. But mayhap that is one reason Mag and I became such good friends. She always loved stories, and she would listen with rapt attention as Duana told tales of long ago. She heard stories of the time before time and the founding of Underrealm, the dark days of the Wizard Kings, and many great heroes and terrible villains scattered throughout the countless years of history.

And then, one day, Duana said something that made Mag frown and stop in the middle of her work.

"What is that?" said Mag. Her eyes were wide, and her hand stilled where it had been wiping a brewing vat with a rag.

Duana looked at her in mild surprise. With a giant wooden spoon, she had been stirring a large cauldron as it came to a boil. Now she glanced at the spoon, the cauldron, and the beginnings of her next brew. "What is what?" she asked.

"The word you just said," said Mag.

"Meldin? That is the name of the Dragon in the tale."

"Not the name, that other word. The D . . . Dr—"

"Dragon?" said Duana. "What about it?"

A shadow seemed to come over Mag's face, her expression a cloud of confusion. "What is that? Is it an animal?"

Duana studied Mag, who seemed held as if frozen in ice. And the old brewer felt a powerful, mournful sadness enclose her heart. She often forgot how many little things like this Mag did not know, things that most children learned from bedtime stories.

But then, most children heard those tales from their parents, and Mag had had no such opportunity.

"They were not animals," said Duana quietly. "They were . . . something more. Do you know of satyrs or centaurs?"

Finally, Mag moved, but only to give a tiny nod. "You told me of centaurs."

"Then you know they have bodies like animals, but they are clever of mind like we are," said Duana. "Dragons are something like that, but far greater and more terrible. They are more akin to Elves."

Mag nodded quickly, eager to please. "I know of Elves."

Duana smiled again. "Good. If you have heard of them, you can get an idea of Dragons."

"Are they the same size as us, like Elves?" said Mag. "Or are they smaller, like imps?"

"Neither," said Duana, and despite herself, she felt a tremor of fear. "They were vast in size. The span of their wings was like the length of the ships that sail the deep ocean, and they could swallow a horse in a single bite. From their mouths, they could spew a noxious fume that choked the lungs and dissolved the flesh. But they could also command firemagic and set their breath ablaze, and then the fume became darkfire. They could burn whole towns in blasts of flame."

She saw suddenly that Mag was trembling where she stood. Her eyes had filled with tears, and she had dropped her washcloth to the ground.

"Here now," said Duana, rushing to her. She wrapped her arms around Mag's shoulders and held her close, while Mag clutched the front of her shirt and buried her face in her chest.

"Will they come for me?" said Mag, her voice incredibly small.

"Never," said Duana. "They all vanished from Underrealm long ago."

Mag stopped shaking, and she looked up at Duana with a frown. "Where did all of them go?" she said quietly, fearfully.

"We do not know," said Duana. "But we need not concern ourselves with it now. No one has seen them in hundreds of years—not since the very earliest days of Underrealm."

Mag nodded, scrubbing tears from her eyes with the back of a dirty hand. "All right," she said.

Soon Duana had her back to her chores, and Mag's mood rose as she got to work. But it was a long, long time before Duana ever ventured to tell her another tale of Dragons.

TWENTY-FIVE

But let us return to the Greenfrost.

In the hours before dawn, the rest of Kun's army arrived at our camp. Zhen, Kun's nephew, had marched his troops through the night. I was asleep when they arrived, but I woke when I heard the commotion at the east end of camp. There was a tense, silent moment in my tent while I tried to hear whether it was sounds of battle or not. When I heard no shouting or clashing steel, I guessed that Zhen must have arrived. Beside me, Yue was peaceful in sleep, breathing gently through her mouth. I shook her.

"Yue," I said. "Wake up. The reinforcements have arrived."

"Whuz," she mumbled, sitting up in the darkness and rubbing at her eyes. I could barely see her in the dim firelight leaking through the tent.

"The rest of the troops," I said. "Kun may need us. We should get up."

"All right, all right," grumbled Yue. She began to pull on her clothes. I had slept in mine, so I donned my boots and slipped out of the tent into the open air.

The earliest signs of grey had begun to edge into the sky above me as I studied the road to the east. It was filled with people now, marching troops all looking weary but resolute, with wagons and pack animals behind them. As I studied them, a woman ran up. I recognized her as one of the captain's messengers.

"I have a message for Lieutenant Shi," she said, "but he is not in his tent."

"He is not?" I said, frowning. "I will look for him. May I relay the captain's message?"

"I suppose," said the woman. "It is nothing secret. Captain Zhou wishes to send scouts to locate the Shades. They are to be selected from Lieutenant Shi's company since they have had several hours of sleep now. The captain needs to discuss the plan with the lieutenant."

"Understood," I said. "I will send the lieutenant along as soon as I find him."

She nodded and ran off. Just then, Mag emerged from her tent.

"Mag!" I said. "Good morn, or close enough to it. The captain sent word—"

"I heard," said Mag. "Where do you think Tou has gone?"

I shrugged. "I hardly think anything sinister can have happened. The sentries gave no alarm, and everything else seems to be in order."

Mag's mouth twisted. "Let us check his tent to be sure."

We jogged there as the murmur of voices grew towards the east end of camp. Some troops were throwing themselves straight onto the ground, as though they meant to sleep before even building tents. I thought they might change their minds once the slushy snow soaked their clothes.

Tou's tent was empty, as the messenger had said. I turned to Mag with a shrug.

"Mayhap he is at the latrines," I said. "Foreign water can ruin any soldier's rest. At the very least, we know our squadrons are likely to be the ones sent to scout for the Shades. I think we should rouse them to get ready for the captain's order."

"Let us do it, then," said Mag, who still looked worried. "But we need to find Tou as quickly as possible."

"We can search for him while our troops are readying themselves," I said.

Our squadrons' tents were lined up next to each other, with the flaps facing an open lane between them. Mag took her squadron's tents on the left, and I took mine on the right. We went down the line, throwing open the tents and ordering our soldiers to wake and ready for the day. Hallan and Chausiku snapped awake at once, while Jian complained at me until I cut off her words with the tent flap. Mag went down her line, until about halfway down when she reached the tent that belonged to Dibu.

She threw open the flap and froze. I saw it, and I paused. Slowly I approached from behind Mag, my brow furrowing.

"Mag? What is—"

"Lieutenant," said Mag, trying desperately and failing to keep laughter out of her voice.

"Sergeant," came Tou's bleary voice from inside Dibu's tent.

My eyes adjusted to the dim campfire light, and I could see him staring out at us, alongside Tou, both of them shirtless and wrapped together in a bedroll. They looked to have just woken up.

"Orders from the captain, ser," I called out, my expression deadpan. "He requests your presence to discuss the assignment of a scouting party to hunt down the Shades. We are mustering our squadrons in anticipation that it might be us."

"Very good," said Tou in a resigned voice. "I shall be along presently."

"As you say, ser," said Mag. Her gaze swiveled to Dibu. "You have a quarter-hour, soldier."

She let the tent flap fall, and we collapsed in on ourselves. Seizing each other's shoulders, we shook with laughter that we tried frantically to silence. We were reduced to stumbling through the rest of the tents, throwing up the flaps and gasping out *"Muster"* before choking back another peal of hysterics. Yue came to us when we had almost finished, and she scowled down at me.

"What under the sky has gotten into you?" she said. "You look fit to erupt, and I do not like the way that vein is throbbing in your forehead."

I said nothing, but only pointed back down the line as I kept giggling. Tou was just emerging from Dibu's tent. His cloak was in his hand, and he whirled it on against the cold before marching off towards his tent.

Yue stared at him for a moment, frowning. "Oh," she said slowly. Then her face lit with understanding. *"Oh."*

"I knew it," said Mag. "I knew it from the first."

"Knew what?" I said. "The two of them? Wait." A realization struck me. "Is *this* why you put Dibu against him for the test?"

"I did not know the captain would choose Tou, so of course not," said Mag. "I picked Dibu because he was the best I had. But I was *elated* when the captain chose Tou."

I buried my face in my hand. "You are the most conniving—"

"I already told you I had no idea who the captain would choose," said Mag, folding her arms with a smug grin.

"Are the two of you done with petty gossip?" said Yue with a scowl. "Our squadrons are supposed to be assembling for muster."

"You are right," I said. "Let us get them in line."

It was not very long before it was done. Tou appeared, and Kun walked beside him. Kun's smile was back, and it looked no less bright for the early hour. He nodded to the sergeants, and the whole company gave him a salute. Tou studiously avoided looking at Mag and me, and I am confident our foolish grins never left us.

"Good morning," said Kun. "Today, I hope to bring this expedition to a close. We are going to advance into the hills, and we are going to bring our enemies to bay. To ensure our success, I mean to send a scouting party ahead to hamper the Shades' march in any way possible. Lieutenant Shi?"

Tou gave him a nod and then addressed us, fixing Mag and me with a steely gaze. "Black Squadron. Green Squadron. You will form the scouting party. Head north into the hills, track the Shades down, and follow them. Each of you fetch one horse from the train. Use them to rotate messengers back to camp, informing the captain of the Shades' movement."

"Ser," said Mag and I together. I believe we kept our tone somewhat professional.

"The main force will advance behind you," said Kun. "I am giving the reinforcements two hours to rest from their march, and then we will follow you into the hills. We will catch the Shades and wipe them out. A swift and fitting end for those who have betrayed the High King and all the nine kingdoms." Suddenly he paused, and though his smile remained, his brows furrowed. "Sergeant Baolan?"

Mag and I looked at Yue in surprise. She had her hand raised, and she kept her eyes fixed on the captain. "Blue Squadron is available for the scouting party as well, ser."

Kun's smile softened. "Thank you, Sergeant Baolan. Green Squadron and Black Squadron will serve for the purpose, though your willingness is appreciated."

"We owe them a debt of blood, ser," said Yue fiercely.

"And you will pay it," said Kun. He stepped closer to her and lowered his voice so that only Tou and we sergeants could hear. "I am not holding you back to slight you. You lost people yesterday. That is a tragic honor, but an honor nonetheless. Let the fresher squadrons take the fore now."

"Ser—" began Yue.

"No, Sergeant," said Kun, but gently. "This is an order. And if you need any further assurance, think of the fact that I am keeping my Mystics with the main force as well. Do you think that an insult to them?"

Yue's nostrils flared. "Of course not, ser."

"Then be at peace." Kun stepped back and once again spoke to the whole company. "You have your orders. Dismissed!"

"Yes, ser!" we cried in chorus.

Mag turned to me. "Ready for another day on the field?"

I glanced sidelong at Yue, who was fuming and not looking at either one of us. "I suppose so," I said. "But quickly—before we go, we should speak with Dryleaf. I would guess he has been worried about us while he followed along in the train with Zhen."

With Yue, we hurried to the east end of the camp, where Zhen's troops were getting themselves arranged. In the rear of the column, with the other followers, we soon found Dryleaf by the sound of Oku's excited barks. As soon as the hound scented us, he came bounding forwards with a loud baying of joy, and Dryleaf followed behind. Orla and Nikau were with him, each of the lovers holding one of his arms, but for comfort rather than to help him along.

"Are those my friends?" he called out, feeling his way forwards with his walking stick. "How have you fared without me here to protect you?"

"Well enough, old man," said Mag with a laugh, taking his shoulder and guiding him to us. "We appreciate your service in guarding the reinforcements."

"One does what one can, I suppose," said Dryleaf. His head swung back and forth. "Albern? Yue?"

"We are here," I said, placing a hand on his shoulder.

Yue still looked dour, but she said, "And safe enough. Do not worry yourself."

"Not for a moment," said Dryleaf. But the relief on his face gave lie to the words.

I looked to Nikau. "Were things well on the march?"

"Well enough. We did not press ourselves as hard as you did. But we missed you." He put a hand on Yue's arm. "Nothing is as fun when all the most interesting folk have left."

Yue could not restrain a grin, and she scratched the back of her head. Dryleaf's smile widened as he spoke. "Well, here we are, reunited. What fresh dangers do we expect to face now?"

I gave a glance at Yue. "Kun is sending Mag and me to scout for the Shades," I said. "Once we have pinpointed them, he will bring the rest of the force north to wipe them out."

"Into the hills, you mean?" said Dryleaf. "I spoke with Lieutenant Zhou while we have been marching west to catch up with you, and he told me the lay of the land."

"They should be easy to find," I said. "Especially with the wounded we left them with after our last scrap."

Dryleaf's face grew worried. "That is good. But take care that you do not grow overconfident. I know one reason we brought them to bay here was so that the landscape would give them no advantage. But our enemies are wily and may yet have tricks up their sleeves."

"We will be careful," said Mag.

"Too careful, in some cases," muttered Yue.

Dryleaf's head turned towards her quizzically, but when she said nothing more, he let it be. "Good, good. You should take Oku with you when you go. The poor boy has been frantic with boredom during our march."

"Gladly will we do so, now that you have a chance to rest," I said. "Oku, tiss." The hound darted to my side and sat, looking up at me expectantly.

"Rest, yes," said Dryleaf, sighing. "I will treasure the next few hours in my tent. But give them a happy ending, and come back to me safe."

"Safe and victorious," said Mag. "That is a promise—or as close to a promise as one can give in war."

A shadow passed over Dryleaf's face, but if doubt was in his heart, he did not speak of it before we left him.

TWENTY-SIX

From the moment we started our trek north, I could see the truth of what Kun had told us about these hills. They were gentle and easy, mere ripples in the land, like a slightly rumpled blanket. I chose to climb them as we went, rather than sticking close to the trail the Shades had left in the wet ground. It slowed us, but it gave us a better vantage point to see the land around us, and hopefully to spot the Shades from afar.

Their course wound through the dips, and the furrow they had cut in the land was easy to see: a black slash of mud through the shoots of new grass. We advanced as quickly as we could. Three soldiers in each squadron held torches aloft—one in the front, one in the back, and one in the middle, lighting the way for their fellows. Hallan held the front torch in my squadron, so I stayed a good several paces away from him to keep my eyes sharp in the darkness. We climbed over one hill and down the other side to an open space through which our enemies had passed. As we crossed the Shades' trail, Oku ran back and forth across the black swath in the land, sniffing at their steps. A drizzle began to drift down upon us out of the sky.

"Hold," I said. Our squadrons stopped at once. "Jian, Chausiku. With me. Hallan, you are in charge of Black Squadron until I return, but listen to Mag."

"Albern," said Mag, frowning. "Where are you going?"

"To the top of the next hill." I pointed to the marks. "They stopped here for a while before pressing on. I would guess they sent out scouts looking for a better place to camp. Once they found it, they did not go too much farther before stopping overnight."

"I should come with you," said Mag immediately.

"No," I said. "Jian and I are quieter. And if we encounter the enemy, we will not be fighting, but running back to you."

"Then I can help cover your retreat."

"Mag, no. I am going ahead, and that is that. We will signal you to follow if we find them."

Her mouth worked. But I could see she did not wish to have an argument while the Shades could be getting farther away, especially not in front of our squadrons. I turned to Jian and Chausiku again.

"Come on." Oku padded up to my side, but I held out a hand to stop him. "Kip, boy. Stay with Mag." He whined and sat back on his haunches.

We crept up the hill, the mud helping to keep our footsteps muffled. When we neared the top, I held out a hand to tell them to slow down. We approached the summit at a crawl.

Nearly an hour had passed, and the sky kept lightening in the east. I was trying to use that to our advantage. We crept to the top of the hill on our bellies, and I followed the track of the Shades' progress.

There. I pointed so that Chausiku and Jian could see it, too. Outlined against the grey sky far away, I could see a figure. It was only a black silhouette from this distance and with so little light to illuminate it. But as we watched, a cloak fluttered, the motion making it stand out clearer against the sky.

"A sentry," I said. "A posted one, not a rear scout. That means they are camped just over that hill."

"Should we eliminate them?" said Jian at once.

"It might raise the alarm," I said. "Better to bring the others forwards and form a plan together. Jian, go to fetch them."

She rolled her eyes and growled, but she did it. Soon both squadrons came to the bottom of the hill, where I conferred with Mag.

"They are over that crest," I said, pointing. "Across another open space, and then over one more hill. I would guess the distance at four spans."

"Excellent," said Mag. "If they are encamped, mayhap we should leave them be for now."

"I would agree, but dawn is imminent," I said. "I cannot imagine they will stay there past sunup. Therefore I think we should either hold them in place or drive them in the direction we wish them to go."

"How do you mean to do that?" said Mag.

"If we circle to the east and attack them from there, they may think the whole host is coming from that direction," I said. "Then we can tell Kun to attack from the west, and drive the Shades straight into his arms."

"A good plan, save for one detail," said Mag, raising her brows. "Kaita's raven form."

"Dark take me," I said. "I forgot about that."

"There is nowhere to hide from her in these hills," said Mag. "Once they are alerted to our presence, we will not be able to conceal ourselves from her sight."

"Well, first things first," I said. "Jian. Go back to the captain. Inform him of where the Shades are, and tell him we are devising a plan to hold them in place for his advance."

"Send Chausiku!" said Jian at once. "He is faster than I am by far."

I gritted my teeth. "You will be riding a horse. Chausiku's legs give him no advantage in that."

Jian's cheeks flamed, though she tried to hide it. "I mean that he is a better rider," she said. "I have scarcely even touched a horse in my life."

"Fine," I said. "Chausiku?"

"Yes, *ser,*" he said, glaring at Jian. He set off, loping towards the horses we had brought, and soon was galloping away south.

"That leaves us where we started," said Mag. "How do we hold them in place?"

An idea struck me. "Kaita is a problem, but she may also be the solution. We should not try to hide at all. Let her see how few of us there are—and let her see that you and I are here."

Mag's eyes lit. "She will attack, hoping to kill us. Clever. But what if the other Shades convince her to flee?"

I shook my head. "I doubt it. After all she has been through in search of us, I cannot believe she would resist such a tasty morsel now. We will appear alone and isolated, with only a paltry two squadrons to defend us." I turned my gaze across our units. "Little does she know we have the two best squadrons in the army."

Their chests puffed with pride at that. Jian wore a savage grin.

"Very well," said Mag. "You should advance with one or two archers and bring down a sentry from afar. Make a stink about it so they raise the alarm. Then retreat to the rest of us as quickly as you can."

"Agreed," I said. I turned to Hallan once more. "Hallan—"

"I've got them, ser," said Hallan. Then he turned an exasperated eye on Jian. "And you should take this one with you. She's eager enough, thass sure."

"I suppose she is," I said. "Jian, with me. Stay quiet, and do as I say, or I will throw you to the Shades myself."

Her face went pale. I suspect that when she asked to stay, she had not thought she would be going to antagonize the enemy with only me by her side. I will confess I took some grim satisfaction from her expression, but I only let myself enjoy it for a moment.

Together we set off into the drizzle and the mud. Instead of northeast, where the sentry was, I guided her due north to a hill west of the Shades' camp. By creeping around the southern edge of the hill, I hoped to keep out of the sentry's sight for as long as possible. And we would be in the hill's shadow, weak as it was, so that hopefully he would not notice us until it was too late.

Despite her evident anxiety, Jian followed closely in my footsteps. Soon we were at the bottom of the hill where we had seen the guard last time. I could glimpse a bump I thought was their head, far above us. I turned to Jian.

"Here we are," I whispered. "I am taking the kill, and then we are getting out of here. Do you understand?"

"S-Ser," she stammered.

"Good," I said. "Stay here."

I crept up the hill pace by pace. Slowly the sentry came more fully into view. They must have been tired, for they faced only south, never turning to look left or right.

Poor fool, I thought.

I nocked, drew, sighed, and loosed.

The arrow pierced straight through their head with a soft *thunk.* I saw a splash of blood erupt, only barely visible as red against the lightening sky.

I turned and ran back to Jian as fast as I could.

HROOON

A horn sounded behind us. Soon it was joined by others, and then they sang in chorus, screaming the alert, warning of danger.

"That worked perfectly!" I cried as I reached Jian. "Now run for your life!"

TWENTY-SEVEN

After the ambush in the woods the day before, Kaita and Tagata had led their forces into the hills to the north. Their troops were in disarray and greatly hampered by the wounded they had to drag with them in their retreat.

But Kaita cared for only one of them.

"Tagata!" she cried, pressing through the Shades to go to her. Tagata's wounds were healing themselves, the Lord's magic melding flesh and skin together. But Tagata had suffered so many grievous injuries that it was a slow process, and she winced and growled through her teeth with every step.

As Kaita came running up, Tagata raised a hand to forestall her worry. "I am fine," she said. "The Lord's blessing will not fail me."

"This is my fault," said Kaita. "I should have scouted ahead."

"You kept your eyes on the force following us, as we both agreed," said Tagata. "Our enemies were clever, and we underestimated them. If you wish to take the blame for that, you must share it with—"

Her right leg buckled beneath her, and she fell to the ground. Kaita tried to support her, but it was like catching a falling boulder.

"Tagata!" cried Kaita. "Are you all right? Does it hurt?"

"Not the healing, no," said Tagata through gritted teeth. She tried and failed to regain her feet. "But until the wounds have gone, I can still feel every one."

Kaita looked desperately around. They were in the hills now and could not see very far in any direction. But though the rolling land blocked sight, it was hardly defensible. The slopes were gentle, and they could be scaled or descended with little effort. She growled in frustration.

"I am going to take a look around," she told Tagata. Then she raised her voice to bark at the Shades surrounding them. "Halt the march! Stay here until I return."

Gently she removed Tagata's arm from her shoulder and stepped away. Magelight flashed in her eyes, and a moment later, she powered into the air on raven's wings.

At once, she could see things were even worse than she had feared. They were only a few spans into the hills, but nowhere was there any position better than their current one. The only glimmer of hope came from the fact that, looking south, she could see flashes of firelight in the woods. Her enemies had made camp in the Greenfrost and were not yet giving chase.

She dove back to the ground and resumed her human form. Tagata looked up with blood on her lips.

"Are they close?" she said.

"They have set up camp in the wood," said Kaita. "And we should do the same. There is no better place to march tonight, and we must get as much rest as we can. You need to heal, and the rest of us need to be fresh tomorrow. They will not simply let us sit here unmolested."

"Mayhap we should march a little—" Tagata grunted at a stab of pain. She fell back to one knee, clutching the hilt of her greatsword as its tip sank into the ground.

"And that is enough of that," said Kaita. "Everyone! Set up camp. Sentries on every hill surrounding this dell. Someone raise Tagata's tent for her, *now.*"

Her voice cracked like a whip, and the Shades leaped to obey. Kaita went to Tagata and took her hand. Tagata tried to smile at her through the pain wracking her body.

"You need to rest," said Kaita. "Promise me you will."

"It seems I have little choice," said Tagata. "I will be fine in the morning."

"Should I stay with you?"

Tagata shook her head, sending her heavy auburn hair cascading over her face. "I will be fine. And you will get no rest if you are with me. The healing process is not always pleasant, and less so, the worse my wounds."

Kaita browbeat the others until they had Tagata's tent up, and then she helped her inside. But she found little rest for herself that night. Sleep would not come, and after two hours, she gave up. She settled for taking flight once more, swooping low over the camp of Kun's army in the Greenfrost. The glow of our fires refracted through the emerald trunks, like a crystal that breaks sunlight into many colors.

She could not tell which tents were mine or Mag's. Yet she could almost feel us below her. More than anything, she wanted to descend upon the camp in a fury, to find us and destroy us. The magestones were back at the camp, and Tagata was wounded. Kaita could eat them, and she would never be discovered . . .

But Mag and I were among allies, and Kaita had made promises to Rogan. She was worthy of trust, and she had to prove it. And so, many long hours later, she finally returned to her tent and passed the rest of the night in sleep almost as restless as my own.

When she woke, just before dawn, she emerged into the open air to find Tagata standing there.

The shadeborn's eyes were closed and her shoulders back. Her face tilted slightly up, as though the scent of some treasured dish wafted to her on the breeze. Firelight played across her features, deepening the crags and scars splayed across them. All signs of her injuries were gone—the Lord's blessing had done its work through the night. And now, as Kaita approached, Tagata's eyes opened, and her expression turned grim.

"I received a message," she said. "From the Lord."

"When?" snapped Kaita, eyes wide. "In the night?"

"Yes," said Tagata. "He had dark tidings—yet the darkness holds a glimmer of hope. But come. We should speak of this privately."

She threw back the flap of her tent, and Kaita led the way inside.

Sitting so close, she could again feel the heat radiating from Tagata. It almost made her want to cast off her cloak.

"What are these tidings?" said Kaita.

"We will face our foes in battle again soon," said Tagata. "And we will lose."

For a moment, Kaita could not speak, but only stared at Tagata in shock. "What do you mean, we will lose?" she said.

"They will heavily outnumber us," said Tagata. "No strategy we could concoct will work in these hills, and we cannot outrun them. However, this will not be our end. Some of us, at least, will be able to escape."

"Then let us escape *now,*" said Kaita. "They have not come to attack us yet. There is still time."

"We will not find a way out until the time is right," said Tagata. "The Lord did not know how we would get away, but he said we would see a sign. It shall be a fiery wyrm."

Kaita could only stare in shock for a moment. "Is he—" She stopped herself, for she had come dangerously close to insulting the Lord. "I do not understand. I would think you were joking if I did not know better."

"I assure you I am not," said Tagata. She looked at the tent flap mournfully. "We will lose many of our kindred today."

Kaita shook her head. "I do not understand this sign. Does the Lord mean we will see a *Dragon?* That is impossible."

"I doubt it means that," said Tagata. "He tells us what he sees, but it is as I told you before. Things are not always . . . entirely clear."

Her frustration mounting, Kaita took several deep breaths in an attempt to find calm. But it only seemed to further stoke the fires of her anger, like bellows to a forge.

"This message . . . I know it is related to the sight you told me of," she said slowly. "But this seems worse than useless. It seems to promise a hope that I cannot envision."

"Rarely do I understand the Lord's signs when he relays them to me," said Tagata. "But you must keep faith. Every victory we have seen so far, every stride we have taken in our mission across Underrealm, has come because of the Lord—from his cunning, and from his sight that pierces the veil of time."

Again Kaita shook her head. "You say you have followed his wisdom before, and it has not led you astray. Because I believe in you, I will choose to believe in this. But if our enemies should come upon us, and I see no other choice, I *will* devour the magestones, Tagata. Whether Mag and Albern are alone or not. I will not let them kill me—or you—without using every tool at my disposal to kill them first."

She half expected Tagata to be angry with her. After all, she was threatening to break the promise she had made to Rogan, and through him, to the Lord. But Tagata only looked upon her with profound sadness.

"Your choices are your own, dear one," she said quietly. She placed a hand on Kaita's shoulder. "But I hope you will rethink this. Woe betide you if you take the stones outside of the ordained time. His love will be no protection to you, then."

Kaita quailed for a moment at the strength of certainty in her voice. But then she shook herself, steeling her resolve. "I have said what I have said. Let us muster the troops and march from this cursed land."

HROOON

Horns blew outside the tent. Kaita and Tagata both whipped their heads towards the sound. It came from the south, where their sentries were posted on hills overlooking the land all around.

"And let us do it as soon as we possibly can," muttered Kaita.

The horns were still sounding as Kaita took her raven form and launched into the air. Tagata stood beneath her, head tilted upwards, watching her take flight. The sky was still mostly dark, and Kaita blinked hard, trying to make out shapes on the ground below. The campfires had made her night-blind.

There. Two figures running west across the hills. Kaita's heart leaped. Two figures? That could be . . .

She dove closer and recognized me. The person beside me was not Mag, but some other soldier who was unknown to her.

Fierce bloodlust thundered in Kaita's veins. I was practically alone. She would not even need magestones to—

Then she spotted Mag and our squadrons not far off. A quick count told her our number, and she wheeled out of her dive.

Her heart burned with conflict. Only two squadrons. That was barely anything, compared to the force that had attacked them yesterday. Mag and I, with just over two dozen friends. That was isolated, was it not? It was close enough. She could attack us with the strength of magestones, and her promise to Rogan would be—

She growled in her mind. It was close enough to the terms for Kaita, mayhap. But not for Tagata. And Tagata had the stones. Kaita did not think she could lie straight to the shadeborn's face even if she wished to, and she did not wish to.

But mayhap there was another way. She circled back and landed in the Shade camp, resuming her human form and running to Tagata.

"They are here!" she cried. "Mag and Albern. They are just over that hill, Tagata, and they have only two squadrons with them. We could crush them with little more than a thought."

Tagata looked around the camp. "We have wounded kindred, Kaita. They will not be able to join us in a chase."

"Leave them here," said Kaita. Tagata's nostrils flared, but Kaita raised her hands. "They will be safer here, anyway. We can draw the threat away from them. They will be able to escape when we—that is, if they need to." She swallowed hard, for she had almost announced aloud that they were expecting to lose this battle.

But she could see that she had convinced Tagata. The shadeborn turned to the camp, and her great, bellowing voice rang out.

"Kindred!" she cried. "Our enemies await the kiss of our blades over those hills. We will destroy them in the Lord's name! To arms! *Death!"*

"Death!" cried the Shades.

The camp became a scramble. All who could walk fought to be the first to don their sword belts, to heft their shields and ready their armor.

"I will keep watch over our enemies," said Kaita. "Look for me in the skies. I will guide you."

"Be safe," said Tagata. "And Kaita."

Kaita froze as Tagata reached into her pocket. When her hand came out, it held the brown cloth packet. She placed it in Kaita's much smaller hand.

"Take them," said Tagata softly. "If you see your chance, you take it."

"They . . . they will slow me down," said Kaita, hardly daring to breathe.

"You do not require speed," said Tagata. "They are on foot, and you fly with the winds. But you should have them with you if the chance presents itself. I trust you as Rogan does. As our father does."

Kaita could not contain herself. She threw herself up, her arms wrapping around Tagata's neck, and kissed her deep. One massive arm wrapped around her, crushing her into Tagata's chest. When they parted, Kaita's eyes were shining.

"Thank you," she whispered.

"No one is more deserving," murmured Tagata. "We are doomed to lose today's battle, but you may have your chance for revenge. Do not let it slip away."

Kaita nodded and turned. Her eyes flashed with light again. She shrank, her clothes sinking beneath the flesh along with the brown cloth packet. It was an awkward lump in her chest, but she managed it. Feathers sprouted, a beak sprang from her jaw, and the raven form was complete. She launched into the sky again, pursuing Mag and me across the land.

TWENTY-EIGHT

Mag and I led our squadrons in a run to the west. It was tempting to draw the Shades back along their own trail, but I was wary of them seeing through our trap. So we stayed near the trail but swung slightly to the north. If Kun followed the Shades' course, he would see their army chasing us, and then he would be able to strike.

I kept an eye on the grey sky above us, and so I was not surprised to see a raven swooping after us. Kaita would keep us in her sights, I knew, and guide the Shades to hunt us down. I grinned.

The grin faded from my face as a hail of arrows flew towards us from the south.

"Down!" I cried.

Our soldiers dropped into the mud, but not quickly enough for three of them. One of my archers and two of Mag's swordfighters pitched over, arrows embedded deep in their bodies. A shaft struck the ground next to Oku, and he leaped aside with a yelp. One of my archers who fell was the middle torchbearer. His torch tumbled down the hill we were on, rolling awkwardly side to side as it descended. The flaming pitch burned the sparse dew off the new grass, and some of it caught as the torch kept rolling.

I looked up to where the arrows had come from. A party of Shade archers had run ahead of the rest of their force. They had stuck to the lowlands and moved faster than we had, and now they had a clear shot at us atop the hill.

Mag saw it at the same time. "North!" she cried. "Move north!"

We ran up and over the lip of the hill, coming down the other side. But a murmur was on the air, coming towards us from the east. More Shades, advancing quickly.

"Dark take them," I said.

"Retreat to the west!" said Mag.

"Hold that order!"

Mag's gaze snapped to me, and I pointed to the hilltop east of us.

"We should deliver one volley as they come over the top. It should pin them for a moment, at least, and give us more time to flee."

"Very well," said Mag. "Green Squadron, line up behind the archers. Watch for a flank."

"Ser!" barked her squadron.

"Black Squadron, draw!" I cried.

Arrows flew to strings and drew back. We held for a long, tense moment as the murmur of voices grew louder on the air. Oku was beside me, bristling and growling.

I saw a helmeted head appear over the eastern hill.

"Loose!"

A dozen arrows darted through the air, slamming into the first line of Shades. Nearly every one found its mark.

"Again!" I roared, drawing and firing my arrow.

My squadron joined me, and another hail of death fell among our foes. The Shades fell back with cries of dismay. In a moment, they were out of sight behind the crest of the hill.

Mag and I motioned our soldiers west with sharp hand movements. We did not want to cry a retreat and let the Shades know we were fleeing. Silent as shadows, we fled across the mud, looping around the hill on its western side.

"We have to draw them back closer to the trail," I said to Mag in a low voice. "Otherwise Chausiku will never be able to lead the captain to us."

She only shrugged and raised her brows. “You are the ranger. Lead on.”

“I am *not* a ranger,” I growled. “Squadrons, follow me!”

“Certainly acts like a ranger, though, doesn’t he?” said Hallan to Jian, who barely restrained a smile.

The sun broke the eastern horizon at last, peeking its shining face above the tops of the hills. And its light came just in time to illuminate a party of Shades ahead of us. It was the archers who had fired upon us only moments ago. They pulled up short, shock on their faces. They had not expected us to loop around the hills and meet them so soon. I counted no more than a dozen, and they were scant paces away.

Mag leaped forwards, silent in her battle-trance. Her squadron drew their blades and roared with anger as they rushed the archers. Oku charged beside them, baying with all his might. The Shades loosed a ragged volley before trying to turn and flee, but my archers riddled them with arrows. Only three managed to get away by splitting up and vanishing into the hills. The rest fell dead, pierced with arrows or hacked apart with swords or Mag’s spear. Oku brought one down, jaws clamped around her ankle and then her throat. But Mag lost another soldier in the skirmish, and the Shades’ desperate bowfire took two of my archers and wounded another. We each had a dozen fighters left, including ourselves.

“South,” I gasped, as I hauled my wounded archer to her feet. She gritted her teeth as she leaned on me and tried to run as best she could.

The murmur grew louder to the north. And as we drew near to the Shades’ trail once more, the murmur became a roar. I risked a look back and saw the Shades emerge over the hills behind us. There were at least a hundred and a half of them, and they came charging across the mud at us with bared steel. At their head was the brute woman, and above them swooped Kaita in her raven form. She was drawing closer, and I knew it could not be long before she would take the field in one of her animal forms.

Mayhap we can at least kill her before the end, I thought.

“Keep going!” I cried. “Run! As long as you can! We have to give the captain time to—”

Another roar filled the air, hundreds of voices screaming in blood-lust and fury.

The Shades ground to a confused halt, even as I turned my gaze to the east. The rising sun fell into my eyes, and I had to shield them with a hand. When I could see again, the sight nearly made me weep.

Three hundreds of soldiers swept down from the eastern hills. At the head of the charge were the redcloaks, with Kun himself holding a sword high in the air. Their fury shook the ground as they swept down upon the Shades.

"Retreat!" roared Tagata. "Get back to the hills! Retreat to our siblings!"

Kaita watched from the sky as the Shades turned and fled. Tagata waited until the last, holding the rear of the formation as they ran into the hills. The Mystics' militia were coming right towards her forces, and they outnumbered the Shades two to one.

Kaita cursed in her mind. She had been too focused on Mag and me and had forgotten to watch out for the rest of our allies. Now the Shades were going to fall—mayhap even *Tagata* would fall—and it would all be Kaita's fault.

But no. She had to cast such thoughts aside, for they would not help her fix anything. Kaita swooped low, looking for any way the Shades could escape. They made their way north through a narrow gap between two hills. It was the closest thing to a defensible position that Kaita could see. Tagata formed up squadrons of spears before the opening, to hold it against the Mystics as they attempted an offense. But it would not last long—soon, the Mystics would simply move up the hills and around the sides of the Shade formation.

Kaita swung wider, looping in the air and looking for anything to help. There seemed no hope of escape in these cursed hills, and a last stand would serve little purpose. But there had to be a way. Her hunt could not end like this. Tagata's tale could not end like this.

She tilted her wings to bank left, and she felt the odd bulge in her chest.

Kaita's heart nearly stopped.

The magestones. They would give her the strength of hellskin. Kaita had never seen it, of course, but it was supposed to be terrible. What use would the Mystics' weapons be against her hide? How could their shields withstand her claws?

Even if they managed to bring her down, she should at least be able to kill Mag and me before the end.

It was not the promise she had made to Rogan, but darkness take that vow. Rogan was the one who had sent her on this pointless march, promising she would have her chance. That was clearly false, whether or not Rogan had meant to lie to her. If she would never have a better opportunity, then she would take what she could. Who cared if she died in the end if she fulfilled the purpose that had sustained her all these years?

But then her eyes fell upon the fiery wyrm.

She recognized it in a flash, though she had not been searching for it. It was a blazing trail of fire down a hill to the northeast of the Shades' position. My fallen archer had dropped a torch, and it had tumbled back and forth as it rolled down the hill. The grass had caught fire, and tongues of flame had licked the turf as though an artist had painted it with a great brush. It looked for all the world like the shape of a flaming wyrm stretched out upon the hillside.

The Lord had told Tagata that they would see this sign. And that the sign would lead to escape. Was it possible?

Kaita swooped lower, feeling lightheaded. The blazing trail ended behind a cluster of grey boulders pressed up against the side of the hill. But there was nothing there, not that Kaita could see.

Wait. *There.*

Kaita could not see it until she landed on the boulder. It was a cave entrance, though it could only be seen from among the rocks. Anyone walking by the hill, or even on it, would not see the tunnel until they were nearly inside it.

In an instant, she was winging her way back to Tagata.

"Charge!" cried Kun. He wore his smile still, but it was fierce, alive with the thrill of battle. He and his Mystics pressed towards the gap between the hills. It was their third charge against the Shades, and I knew it would be the last one.

"Loose!" I cried. Our arrows flew over the Mystics' heads, landing among the enemy and casting many of them to the ground. The rest of the Shades wavered, and they broke almost the instant Kun's Mystics slammed into them. As one, they turned and scattered, blue cloaks fluttering in the air behind them as they ran north in the mud.

Mag and I guided our squadrons close behind Kun's as he ran in pursuit. But almost from the moment I pressed through the hills, I felt that something was wrong. There were a paltry few dozen of the Shades in front of us.

Then I forgot such thoughts as another roar filled the air.

Zhen, Kun's nephew, cried aloud as he led his company from the east. Kun had sent him east to loop around behind our foe. Now they were flanked and cut off. Four hundreds of our soldiers met in the center of the battlefield.

The Shades turned back and forth, wavering. They did not know whether to face the charge from the south or the one from the east. In the end, it did not matter. They died to a one, their blood staining the muddy ground beneath them as it pooled.

The battlefield fell to silence—that sudden, shocking stillness that comes after the worst violence, the most brutal carnage. It was broken only by a ragged cheer from our forces before everything fell to quiet again. I fell on my back in the mud, panting heavily. I felt like I had run many leagues in our flight from the Shades, and every step had felt even worse with the sucking mud clutching at our feet.

"Oh no, you great idiot," came Yue's voice. "Come here."

I heard her heavy footsteps approaching. I groaned, but I smiled and raised a hand. Yue seized it and hauled me to my feet. Her arms wrapped around me and mine around her. We shared a kiss, which was both poisoned by and sweeter for the death all around us.

"Why, Sergeant Baolan," I said in mock surprise. "Were you worried about me?"

"Dark take you for a fool," she said. "You are not running off and risking your life like that again, and the captain's orders be damned."

"Careful," I said. "That is dangerously close to mutiny."

"Then I am a mutineer," she said, and kissed me again.

But as the thrill of the fight left me, and our little army began to collect itself and take our toll of the dead, my thoughts grew dour. I remembered what I had noticed when we had first run into this killing field.

And it seemed I was not the only one.

"Where did they go?"

The battle-trance was gone. Mag's voice was quiet. Almost fearful.

Yue looked over at her. "What was that?" she said.

"The Shades," said Mag. "We had them surrounded, yet there cannot be more than two scores of them here. I see neither the brute nor Kaita. Where did all of them go?"

I studied the ground. Tracks led into the field from the south, where Kun had attacked. There were tracks from the north, where the Shades had come in the first place. And tracks came in from the east, where Zhen had led his company in the final charge. But there were no tracks leading out of the little dell at all.

A darkness came over my heart, but I tried to shake it off. This was a victory. I was determined to treat it as such.

"We do not know," I said. "But we have time. Time to figure it out, and to finish the rest of them. I have not forgotten Kaita."

Mag did not look convinced. She shuddered as though a sudden fear had seized her. But at last, she nodded and turned to attend to her squadron.

My grip on Yue tightened.

TWENTY-NINE

Kaita collapsed against the rock wall of the cavern, her whole body heaving in deep, shaking breaths. All around her, Shades seized their chance to rest after their desperate flight.

When Tagata learned of the tunnel, she had asked for volunteers to serve as a rear guard while the rest escaped. So many had volunteered that Tagata had been forced to choose thirty of them. The heartbreak it caused her was still plain on her face.

Kaita had guided them all to the tunnel entrance, and they had pushed their way in as quickly as they could. They had vanished beneath the ground mere moments before Zhen's flanking company would have seen them. Filled with battle fury, Zhen missed spotting the Shades' tracks leading to the tunnel. Then his troops had trampled over the signs, obscuring any hint of how the Shades had seemed to vanish into thin air.

The tunnel had turned west and continued beneath the hills for a long way, plunging deep into the earth before leading to a massive cavern. The Shades had torches, but the ceiling was so high their light did not reach it. Stalagmites thrust up from the ground everywhere, like a vampire's twisted, pitted fangs. But the space was drier than the soaking outside, and hidden, and surprisingly warm compared to early spring's chill.

Just over a hundred Shades remained—less than half of those who had started the march. And there were nearly four hundreds of their foes outside, searching for them and ready to cut them down.

Kaita looked over to where Tagata stood. The shadeborn seemed indefatigable. She had not fallen to the floor gasping, like her siblings. She stood solid in their midst, head bowed in mourning. Kaita knew her well. Tagata would blame herself for every soldier who had fallen on this long trek. The Lord had foretold the outcome, and he held her blameless for it, but that did not matter to her.

Slowly Kaita forced herself to her feet and went to the shadeborn's side, placing a hand on her arm, which burned like an oven.

"Tagata," said Kaita quietly. "You saved everyone you could."

"Not enough of them," said Tagata. She lifted her head at last, still avoiding Kaita's gaze, and took a deep breath. "But now we must look forwards. Help me see to everyone's arrangements. I want fires if we can find the fuel. None of us should have to sit in the dark, alone with our thoughts."

"I think I should scout the caves," said Kaita. "We do not have endless supplies. We have to find a way out of here, and I doubt we will be able to leave the same way we came in. The redcloaks will likely make camp in the same dell where they—" She bit off her words.

Tagata's expression darkened. "Where they slaughtered our kindred," she rumbled.

"Yes," said Kaita. "But we will avenge them. I swear it. Let me take my mountain lion form and search for a way out of this place, and then we can plan our retaliation. The Lord told you this place was an escape. There must be a way."

Tagata gave her a small smile. "Who ever thought you would be the one coaxing me to have faith in our father? But you are right, of course. Go then, dear one. I will care for our kindred."

They shared a brief embrace, and then a glow filled Kaita's eyes as she took her mountain lion form. The caves seemed to fill with light in her vision, the sparse torches letting her see almost as well as if it were day. She remained standing there by Tagata for a moment, drinking in the warm air. Her nose filled with the scents of the Shades behind her, and a thousand other smells as well: long-stale dung from animals who had passed through, and fresher deposits from bats. There was no sign of any larger animals having been here recently, which was a relief.

Soon there was nothing more to be learned without setting off to explore. She rubbed her lion head against Tagata's waist and received a gentle caress along the throat. Then she loped off into the darkness.

There were three tunnels other than the one they had used to enter. Picking the first one to her right, she ran down it, eyes and nose open. The passage twisted this way and that. Sometimes it dropped sharply down, and sometimes it rose so steeply that she had to climb, her claws digging into the limestone of the walls.

For a half hour she crept along the passage, her hopes high. The tunnel did not dive deeper into the earth, which was a good sign. If it did not finish in a dead end, then there was a good chance Kaita would find an exit.

And then, slowly, several strong scents began to creep into her nose. The first was fresh air, thick with snow, and her heart leaped. But then she smelled other things. Wood, but with an acrid and bitter undertone. That would be the pycnandra trees.

And she smelled people: a great many of them, and their horses, and wagons, and goods of all sorts.

It was Kun's force. Kaita had little sense of direction beneath the earth, but this tunnel must have looped around to the southwest. It emerged into another hidden place in the hills, right beside where Kun and his army had made camp.

Kaita's heart sank to her paws. But she pressed forwards anyway, just to be sure. The tunnel ended just as the other one had, behind a pile of boulders that blocked sight. Scrambling and scrabbling with her claws, Kaita climbed up, poking her head over the top of the boulders.

There. The Mystics and their allies were barely more than a span away, off to the east. She could see the redcloaks massed towards the north end of the camp, while the army's train was to the south, closer to the caves where Kaita now stood.

Once again, she could almost *feel* Mag and me close by. We were there, right *there*. If she only took one of the magestones, she could plunge into the heart of the camp, find us, and . . .

But no. There was still her promise to Rogan. Kaita growled, and the sound rumbled thick in her chest.

This tunnel was useless for escape unless the Mystics eventually left—in which case, the Shades could more easily leave through the same passage they had first found.

Discouraged, she trotted the long path back to the large central cavern. By the time she reached them, they had set up their camp, tents all in neat rows as they had done above ground. Kaita came trotting up to Tagata and resumed her human form.

"That tunnel is no use," she said, pointing south. "It leads straight to our enemies, like the first. At least they have not discovered its entrance, or not that I could smell."

"In dark circumstances, we must cherish small blessings all the more," said Tagata. "Thank you, Kaita."

"I will go explore the other passages."

She turned to go, but Tagata held up a hand. "Wait," she said. "You should rest. The others tell me you were wakeful through much of the night, and you have run far and overused your magic since before dawn."

"I am fine," said Kaita, shaking her head. "I will rest once I find us a way out of this mess."

"Eat some food, at least," said Tagata. "You cannot tell me you are not hungry." She smiled as Kaita's stomach rumbled aloud.

"Mayhap a bite would be good," said Kaita reluctantly.

Tagata chuckled and ushered her over to one of the noisome campfires the Shades had built. There were only two, for they had had to make them out of dried dung, and there was precious little of that to be found. Kaita sat, her body nearly screaming in relief after its exertions, and they began to tuck into a little meal together with their fellows in the darkness.

THIRTY

Back on the surface, Mag and I had reconvened with Dryleaf and Yue in the wake of the fighting. Kun ordered our camp moved from the Greenfrost into the hills. The move took somewhat longer than it should have since we were all weary with the day's battle. But Kun felt it necessary to consolidate our presence in the hills, at least until we determined where the Shades had disappeared to. Now, close to midday, we ate a meal by our campfire, the same as Kaita below the earth, though of course, we did not know that.

I could see the deep dissatisfaction in Mag's expression. Her mind lingered on the Shades. It was a beautiful day around us, sunlight filtering through the grey clouds to shine from the snowy hills. But her mood was ugly, and she spoke little, only giving brief answers when we tried to broach conversation.

"Where did they all go?" she muttered after a time, placing her bowl on the ground. It was not even half-eaten. Oku's ears perked up.

"They cannot be far, Mag," I said gently. "There is nowhere around here to hide for long. We will find them."

"And in the meantime, there is plenty to do," said Yue. "We have wounded to see to, and troops who need our guidance." But she sounded disgruntled, and she poked savagely at the logs of our fire with a long stick.

"All of that is well and good if it helps us find Kaita and end her," said Mag. "Yet now it is only a delay. She has evaded us before, and it seems she has done it again. But this time she brought a whole army into the shadows with her."

Dryleaf's hand rested on Oku's head, scratching him behind the ears. Oku sat patiently, enjoying it, but his gaze was riveted on Mag's abandoned food bowl. "You fear losing her forever," said the old man. "But I do not think that is how your hunt will end. One day you will have the confrontation you desire, even if it is not here in these hills."

Mag's fist clenched. "No," she said. "It *will* be here. It *must* be."

"Mag, come now," I said. "Why is it so important that—"

"Because I am *tired,* Albern," said Mag. Her voice cracked, and hearing it froze me. "I am tired of having her dangled in front of my face, luring me along like a carrot does a mule. I am tired of wandering endlessly across the nine lands. I want this to be over. Now. I am tired of—"

She turned away, looking towards the center of camp.

"Mag . . ." I said slowly. "I did not—"

"I do not know what comes next," she said, almost whispering. "I have no plan for it. But I want one. I have been trying to think of it, trying to picture it. I cannot. It is as though my road ends with Kaita, vanishing at her feet. It makes my life feel so small, and I am tired of that, too. I want an after."

She stood.

"And I am going to have one."

"Mag?" I said sharply. Yue and I scrambled to our feet as she stalked off. I helped Dryleaf up and brought him along. "Where are you going?"

"To speak to the captain," she replied.

"Mag, wait," said Yue. "Why?"

"I am going to find her."

"What, alone?" I said. "Mag, you are not going anywhere without us. Or me, at least." I gave Yue a furtive glance.

"Us," she said, frowning at me. "She has the right of it. It would be better than sitting here on our rears."

"That is the spirit," said Mag, still walking at a breakneck pace.

"Mag," said Dryleaf. His voice was almost too quiet to hear. But Mag's gait hitched for a moment, as though she had nearly paused but forced herself on. "My dear girl. Do not risk too much with rash action."

"I risk nothing," said Mag. "Every time I have faced her, I have defeated her without taking a scratch."

"Of course she cannot harm *you,*" said Dryleaf, who was breathing heavily now with the pace of our walk. "But what about everyone else?"

At last, Mag stopped. She wheeled on him. "And why do you think I am doing this?" she snapped. "What do you think this whole journey has been for? I started chasing Kaita because of what she did to my home, to my . . . to my Sten. In Lan Shui, she killed many. In Kahuanga, she started a war that killed even more. Even now, though we win each battle, dozens fall every time. It seems clear that I can protect no one by moving slow, by ensuring each step is safe. So I am done with it. I am ready for the end, and I am sick of people telling me to wait!"

"Mag," I said reproachfully. The look on her face was so fierce, I had an urge to put myself between her and Dryleaf.

"It is all right, my boy," said Dryleaf. He patted my arm. "Strong words are of no concern to me. But I beg of you, Mag: if you want to know what comes after Kaita, then turn aside from her. I have suggested it before, though I knew you might not be ready to hear it. You *need* to hear it now. You have allies, friends. You have the good Captain Zhou and this little family that has taken you into the fold. It will not replace what you lost in Northwood—but you are wise enough to know that nothing will ever replace that. Build something new instead. It will be no less dear simply because it is different."

"Mayhap I will," said Mag. "But after. Northwood is not over. Not until she lies dead at my feet."

"And will that help Sten?" said Dryleaf quietly.

"It has never been about Sten," said Mag. "I know that. I am not a fool. It was always for me."

And she turned and set off towards the captain's tent again.

Yue followed her, and I started to do the same with Dryleaf. But he patted my hand and shook his head. "Leave me, boy. I will be of no help, and I may only anger her until she says something foolish to Kun. I will find my way back to our fire with Oku's help."

"All right," I said. "We will return as soon as we may."

I ran after Mag and caught her as she reached Kun. He was in conference with Tou and the other lieutenants, including his nephew, Zhen. The group of them all looked up at us in confusion.

"Sergeants," said Tou, looking confused. It was a breach of protocol to approach him while he was in conference with the captain.

"Lieutenant Shi," said Mag. Then she turned from him to Kun. "Captain Zhou. I request permission to investigate the Shades' disappearance, along with Sergeants Telfer and Baolan."

"Sergeant," said Tou, speaking sharply now. "That is something to discuss with me first, and with the captain only if I approve."

"Apologies, ser," she said, nodding to him. "But time is of the essence. Hours have passed since we saw them. Wherever they are now, we can be certain they are moving farther away. If we do not find the trail, we may lose them."

Kun had looked at her all the while with a surprised smile on his face. Now he cocked his head. "We are well aware of the situation, Sergeant," he said. "Your offer is appreciated, but unnecessary. Lieutenant Zhou will lead the search for the Shades' trail."

"You should use Albern's talents as well, ser," said Mag.

"Sergeant!" said Tou. "Return to your unit and—"

"That is all right, Lieutenant," said Kun, raising a hand. As Tou subsided, Kun looked upon Mag again. "You have some personal stake in this, Sergeant. And you know how I value honesty. Tell me why this means so much to you."

"A weremage marches with the Shades," said Mag at once. "She killed my husband."

"Mag!" I said, more in shock than dismay. It was no business of mine what she did with the truth, but she had withheld it on our road so far.

"She and her fellows invaded Northwood," Mag went on. "She murdered him in front of my eyes. I have been hunting her ever since. Truth be told, Captain, I joined you in hopes that you would come into conflict with her, and now you have. She is almost within my grasp, yet I can feel her slipping away."

Kun never took his eyes from her. His lips twitched, and I could see heavy thoughts behind his eyes. Then, at last, he spoke.

"Killing the weremage will accomplish little in the war for Underrealm," he said. "She is an asset of the enemy, yes, and a powerful one. But only one. Meanwhile, you, Sergeant Telfer, and Sergeant Baolan are three highly trained and invaluable officers in our war effort. Risking the three of you to locate the enemy is unacceptable. If you have any skilled trackers in your squadron, I might consider sending them, if you propose it to your lieutenant first."

"Captain—" said Mag.

"*No,* Sergeant," barked Tou, stepping in front of the captain. "You have pushed things quite far enough already. Your captain has given you a command. He has even deigned to explain his reasoning behind it, which you are not owed. Turn and march back to your unit *now,* or you will face discipline."

I had never seen the lieutenant so angry. Mag looked as if she wanted to argue more, but she subsided. Kun's expression was firm, but I saw pity in his eyes. If I am being honest, I agreed with his decision. An army is nothing if it lacks unity, and soldiers cannot be running off to settle personal vendettas.

Gently I put a hand on Mag's arm. "Come."

She turned without looking at me and stalked back to the tents. I waited a moment more, bowing my head to Tou.

"Apologies, Lieutenant. She . . . It happened very quickly."

His nostrils flared, but he did give me a brief, sharp nod. I took that as the best sign I was going to get, and together with Yue, I followed Mag back to our tents at the heads of our squadrons.

"How did it go?" said Dryleaf.

"Not well," I answered him. "The captain was not amenable to Mag's decision."

"And is that the end of it?" said Dryleaf.

"Not on your life," said Mag firmly.

Yue frowned. "What do you mean? The captain gave his order."

"I am going out anyway," said Mag.

"You cannot be serious," said Yue. "After he told you no?"

Mag looked at me. "Albern? What do you say?"

I hesitated. "I . . . I am not sure, Mag. We asked the captain. Why do that, if you meant to disobey?"

"Because I thought he would say yes, of course," said Mag. "And he should have, because I am right. Your skills are wasted sitting here in camp. He says we three are too 'valuable' to lose. Well, what good is value if he does not use it?"

"Yet if he sends us out alone, and we do not return," countered Yue, "then we are worth nothing in the next fight. I understand your frustration, Mag. But I understand the captain as well, and you must do the same. He is our superior officer. We are soldiers."

"I left the mercenary life for a reason," said Mag. She turned from Yue to me. "I want to go after her, Albern, and I need you to come with me."

Slowly I shook my head. Rarely have I felt more torn. "Mag. Kun said . . ."

"And since when do we care what others tell us?" said Mag. She nodded at Yue. "Yue tried to tell us what to do in Lan Shui. We disobeyed, and we saved the town."

"This is not Lan Shui," said Yue.

Mag shrugged. "Yue, you are an honorable woman and a dark-damned good fighter. But if you had had your way, Lan Shui would now be empty of everything but vampires and corpses. I do not mean that as an insult. You did what you thought was right. But we had knowledge you did not. That is exactly what we face now. We know better than the captain, not through any fault of his own, other than mayhap not enough trust in us."

"He does not trust you enough, and so you mean to betray his trust even further?" said Yue. "How do you think that will help anything?"

Mag, however, kept her gaze on me. "If you worry about us shirking our duty, we do not have to. We are mercenaries. Let us resign."

"We agreed to see this campaign through," I said. "Kun would brand us as deserters and outlaws. He would have no choice—imagine if everyone in this force thought they could simply turn tail for home after a bad day. If we wish to leave when we return to Taitou or reach another city for resupply, that is one thing. But we cannot abandon our contract out here in the wilderness when another battle could be just around the corner."

I do not mind admitting that Mag was frightening me. I knew she was angry—I could feel the fury emanating from her—but she did not yell, nor did she even scowl. It was as though she restrained her rage just beneath the surface. It gave me the uncomfortable feeling of facing her battle-trance, but from the sharp end of her spear.

"Very well," said Mag. "If we cannot break contract, I am afraid we must disobey orders. I mean to seek the Shades' trail the moment the sun is down, which should be early."

"We cannot, Mag," said Yue. "Albern, tell her we cannot."

I struggled for words, searching for some way to make Mag see the foolishness of her actions. Still, she held me in her gaze, and the look in her eyes was so intense that I felt incapable of gainsaying her.

Yue stepped between us, breaking my eye contact. "Albern, you are a great fool, but not this great of a fool," she said softly. "Do the smart thing. Stay here with me tonight. Let us go and invite Nikau to stay with us—he has been trying hard enough to get inside our tent. Forget this madness."

"If that is more important to you than finding Sten's killer," said Mag, "then I suppose I cannot stop you."

Floundering, I turned to Dryleaf, who still sat motionless by the fire. "Dryleaf?" I said weakly.

But he only shook his head. "I am sorry, my boy. I have said all that could be useful. You know I think this is madness. If that does not sway you or Mag, nothing else I could say would do so."

Mag stepped around Yue and put a hand on my shoulder, gripping it firmly. "Albern. In Northwood, we promised each other. Together until the end, until Sten was avenged. In Lan Shui, we said it again. Are you still with me?'

"Are you with *me?*" I said. "Why must your way be the only one?"

"Because my way leads to Kaita," said Mag. "You would have us sit here and wait, and that is nothing either of us promised the other."

I have lost battles in which many of my friends died. I have borne the bitter sting of watching my commander surrender to the enemy in the middle of a corpse-littered battlefield. But rarely have I ever felt so defeated as I did in that moment.

"All right, Mag," I said quietly. "I made my pledge. If you are going, and if I cannot say anything to sway you, then yes. I am by your side. Until the end of the road."

A beautiful smile splashed over her face as if it had been thrown there. She released a sigh, and I realized how afraid she had been that

I would refuse her. But that was never a possibility, really. She turned to Yue.

"Well?" she said. "We are going. Will you turn us in to the captain? Or will you come with us? I want your sword by my side, Yue."

Yue barely seemed to hear her. She was only looking at me. "Albern?" she said. "You agree with her?"

"I do not," I said. "But I promised, Yue. I cannot abandon her now."

"Hm," snorted Yue. "I thought that promise went two ways." She turned back to Mag. "Very well. If I am outvoted, I suppose I will come, too. I am no faithless friend. But we had best be quick about it, and quiet."

"We will," said Mag. "Then our course is set. Tonight, the moment the sun has gone down. The moons are full, and their light should be good for wandering."

"All right," I said. "But we should leave Oku. If we want to be as quiet as possible, it would be best to have just the three of us."

"A good idea." Mag knelt and took Oku behind the ears, scratching him fondly. It was an uncommon display of affection from her, as though she was in high spirits. But I could not shake some persistent feeling that it was an ill omen.

"Kip, boy," she said. "Stay here with Dryleaf until we come back."

His wide, watery eyes looked into hers, and he cocked his head. When she stood, he went to the bard and lay down by his feet. But he kept his head raised, and he did not stop looking at her. A low whine issued from his throat, and it grew louder when we started to walk away.

As we went to ready ourselves for the night, I glanced back once. Dryleaf's blind eyes had closed, and his head bent low, pushing his long beard into his chest.

That evening, Kun sat inside his tent at one of his small desks. A letter was in his hand—a report to the Mystic chancellor of northeastern Dorsea, relating the army's activities in the region so far. But his hand had long ago stilled at the quill, and his eyes stared at nothing. He wore his usual smile, but it was absentminded. He was thinking of Mag and me, of course, and Mag's earnest plea to go and find the weremage.

So she lost her husband, he thought. That made sense to him. It brought many other strange things about her, and me, into a new clarity.

He thought of his sister. Dear, sweet Min. He had cared about her more than anything else in the world. He still saw her beautiful dark eyes whenever he looked at his nephew Zhen.

What would he have done, had she died from a blade instead of the wasting sickness that took her? Would he have lived his life the same way? Would he still wear the red cloak now?

He turned to the door of his tent and called out, "Bring me Lieutenant Shi."

The decision made, his quill sped across the letter again. By the time Tou arrived to speak with him, Kun had finished. He sealed the letter and handed it to the same messenger who stepped into the tent to present Tou.

"Lieutenant Shi," said Kun brightly. "Please, sit."

"Captain," said Tou, taking the seat opposite. "Thank you."

"Of course. We all spent enough time on our feet today." Kun's smile widened. "I have been thinking of your sergeant's little . . . outburst today."

Tou's face darkened. "Ser. I spoke with them immediately after our council. I assigned Mag's squadron to latrine duty for the next three days, and I gave Albern and Yue strict warnings about—"

Kun cut him off with a raised hand. "All appropriate reactions. But I find myself thinking of Mag and her purpose for being here. Purpose drives us, Lieutenant. None take the red and rods but those who have a desire to protect the nine kingdoms—or none should, at any rate. Some soldiers in this force have joined for the coin, but most are here for some other reason. I am sure there are as many reasons as there are soldiers in our force. But those purposes align in one factor: a love of Dorsea. That is what makes them invaluable to us, and through us, to the High King. And we should not disparage the varied reasons that brought them under our command, if those reasons may be aligned towards our common goal."

Tou ducked his head. "Of course, ser. But . . . forgive me, but why do you tell me all this?"

A long moment passed in silence. Then Kun sighed. "I mean to let your sergeants go hunting for the Shades."

Of all the things Tou expected to hear, that was not among them. "Ser?"

"I mean it," said Kun. "Sergeant Telfer is an excellent tracker. Lieutenant Zhou is better, but not by much, as he told me himself. And if Albern should manage to locate the Shades, he may need Mag's help. She was right. Zhen is already out there seeking the enemy. Better to double our chances."

Tou's jaw kept clenching and releasing. But if he harbored any doubts, he kept them to himself. After all, it would hardly be becoming to argue with his captain after he had just disciplined the rest of us for insubordination.

"Very good, ser," he said. "Shall I give them their orders in the morning?"

"You had better do it now," said Kun, glancing at the tent flap. "Night has fallen. They will want to leave first thing in the morning, I imagine, and so they will want to turn in as early as possible."

"I believe the three of them have already gone to bed," said Tou. "I will tell them now in any case, even if I have to wake them, so they can prepare whatever they will need. Thank you, ser."

He stood from the table, saluted, and left. Kun watched him go, still smiling. He pinched the bridge of his nose and pushed back, rubbing at his eyes, the smile never fading.

But it vanished when Tou came running back to his tent only a few moments later.

THIRTY-ONE

"UGH," SAID SUN. "YOU MEAN HE CAUGHT YOU?"

"I am afraid so," said Albern. "Well, *caught* is not quite the right word . . . but you will see what I mean a bit later in the story."

"Before you tell it, though, I have another question," said Sun.

Albern's brows shot for the sky. "Do you indeed? Mark this moment—the first time you asked me to stop telling the story so that we could talk about something else."

"You are most amusing," said Sun, no hint of a smile on her face. "But the question is, in fact, about the tale. When you spoke of Mag hearing about Dragons for the first time . . ." A shadow seemed to cloud the day, and they both shuddered until it passed. "You mentioned she had no parents. Why not?"

"Well, she must have *had* parents," said Albern. "Everyone does, after all. But if they ever did tell her tales of Dragons, she had long since lost those tales by the time she met Duana and came to Shuiniu."

Now, I told you that Duana was a veteran of the Dorsean king's wars. This was not, of course, King Jun, whose death had sparked the civil war in which we found ourselves. Duana was older. She had fought under Jun's father, Wolin of the family Fei, and had served him with honor.

But when Duana came back from the war, she had many scars, and not all of them were of the skin. I am sure you know of veterans who suffer from maladies of the mind. Sometimes Duana would find herself growing anxious when there was no reason to be, breaking out in cold sweats and jerking at the smallest sound. It would come and go in waves, like a fever that resurges after starting to break.

This might have been why Duana knew the signs of Mag's distress when she first told her of Dragons. She knew how unreasoning such terror can be, and how small and weak Mag must have felt before the images in her mind. Thoughts are but wisps and gossamer to most people, but to some, they hold a terrifying power—and sadly, that power is usually wielded most harshly against those who should be in control of it.

The townsfolk in Shuiniu understood this, as do most in the nine kingdoms. They would leave Duana alone if that was what she required, or stay with her and hold her hand through her tremors if she asked them to. But most of the time, when Duana's attacks would grow too much to bear, she would take a long stick and go walking through the woods. That forest was called the Carrweld, as I have mentioned before, and it was peaceful. Beneath the trees, with birds singing and only the sound of her footsteps to accompany her, Duana would find peace again. Her body would gradually calm, her shakes ceasing, her breath coming free and easy.

But one day, the woods were not so peaceful. One day, just as Duana had overcome her fear, she heard something moving in the underbrush nearby.

Duana's pulse raced again—but this time, it was under control. She gripped her walking stick in both hands, holding it before her in readiness.

The sound came once more. The creature was coming closer. Grimacing at the walking stick in her hands, Duana hoped she was not about to face a bear. But it sounded too small for that. Then a worse thought crossed her mind—it might be a cub, and the mother could be close.

Duana was about to turn tail and run for town, hoping she could outdistance the thing, when she spotted the face.

It was a girl. She was in a low bush, barely two paces away, and she was staring at Duana. Her face was so streaked with dirt and grime that Duana had missed her at first. She had wild, ratty hair filled with mud and sticks and who knew what else.

Duana knelt at once. She held out a hand, moving it ever so slowly and speaking in a gentle, coaxing tone.

"Well, hello there," she said. "I am sorry if I startled you. Can you come out?"

Huge eyes blinked at her from that dirt-covered face. Ever so slowly, the girl pushed out from the bushes on either side of her.

She was naked, and the rest of her body was as filthy as her face. All sorts of detritus and dirt was worked into her hair, and all up and down her skin. But that skin was remarkably well-kept otherwise. Duana saw no signs of injury upon her, not even a scratch. But in her hand, she held a sharpened stick like a spear. Fresh blood stained the tip, and it looked as if there were many more coats beneath it.

"Hello," said Duana again. "I am Duana."

Those great brown eyes blinked. "Duana." The girl's voice was halting, but loud, strong.

"Yes," said Duana. She settled back on her haunches while placing a hand to her chest. "I am Duana. And you?"

The girl pointed to Duana's hand on her chest. "You."

"Me," said Duana. Then she pointed at the girl. "And you." Again the hand on her chest and then pointing to the girl. "I am Duana. And you?"

The girl blinked twice more. Then she pointed at Duana. "You. Duana. I." She placed a hand on her chest.

Sudden, clear certainty came into her eyes.

"Mag. I am Mag."

"Dark take you to its depths, and dark take me for a fool for believing in you!" bellowed Sun.

Albern looked entirely alarmed, and he glanced at the crowd surrounding them on the street. Fortunately, no one seemed to have paid much attention to Sun's outburst, for the bustle of a thousand conversations did much to drown her out.

"I am sorry?" said Albern.

"You should be!" said Sun. "All this time, I thought you were leading me somewhere with all this talk about Mag's peerless fighting."

"You did?"

"I thought you were going to *explain* it. You made it seem as if one day, you were going to tell me how Mag learned to fight!"

"I did?"

"You did, and you know it," growled Sun. "You gave me hope, and now I find that you are not going to tell me anything about it at all."

"Am I not?"

Sun reached over and pinched his nose, much to Albern's very evident shock. "Stop answering my questions with more questions."

"Am I? Or, that is, I will try." Albern's voice came out thin and nasal through her fingers.

Sun released him. In truth, she was not all that angry, and she was enjoying his reaction to her sudden outburst.

"You lied to me as well," she said. "You told me that Mag's fight against Ciaran was her first fight. Yet she came out of the woods with blood on her spear. Clearly, she had fought before."

Albern could not help a little smirk. "I am usually quite careful in my wording. And what I said, precisely, was that her scrap with Ciaran was her first fight against another *person.*"

"Albern," said Sun, letting a whine come into her tone, "you cannot be serious about this. Are you trying to tell me that Mag walked out of the woods as a mysterious little child, already knowing perfectly how to fight, and without a scratch on her under all that dirt? Is this your idea of the brilliant tale of the murky past of one of Underrealm's greatest figures? Because I must tell you that it is *horrible.* I have not felt so cheated since my tutor first taught me how to gamble and then stole my allowance for three months straight. My parents banished him from our home when they found out, but they let him keep the gold for his cleverness."

That made Albern laugh. "Now, *that* is a good tale. A premise, a development, and a resolution that is unexpected yet inevitable. Pithy, too. Certainly more economical than this overlong yarn I have been spinning you." He fixed her with an appraising look. "But as for your other question—Sun, what would you like me to say? I am relaying a tale. Would you like me to tell the story of what happened, as best I know it? Or should I make something up? Mayhap you would prefer a tale in which Mag set out to sail the Eldest Deep, battling all of the dark creatures of those terrifying waters, until she found a sea-hag who imparted upon her the secrets that allowed her to become an invincible fighter. That would be a fantastic story. I am certain they would pay me a great heap of coin in any tavern where I chose to spin it. However, it does not happen to be the truth. So. Which story would you rather hear?"

Sun folded her arms as they walked, staring at her feet in a pout. "That is an entirely unsatisfactory explanation."

Albern smirked. "Well, I shall endeavor to do better in the future."

"Get back to your ill-fated scouting expedition in the night," said Sun, waving a hand at him. "I do not want to hear anything more about impossibly perfect children coming from nowhere."

Albern's mouth twisted. "You may not feel the same way, by the end of the tale."

THIRTY-TWO

As night drew on and the moons rose higher in the sky, Mag, Yue, and I slipped out of Kun's encampment, searching for any clue as to how the Shades had escaped. It was a fine night. Both moons shone full above me, and the clouds had parted, letting the land flood with silvery light. In those days, my eyes were sharper, and I could pick out the details in the land as we went.

I went to the dell where we had wiped out the Shades, or at least the rear guard who let the rest of their fellows escape. The tracks looked much the same—the only things different were the signs of Kun's force moving south after the battle, and one set of new tracks from Zhen, whom Kun had assigned to search for the Shades.

"There is nothing new, Mag," I said. "I might have a chance at spotting something in the daylight, but—"

"Albern," said Mag. "Come now. You have to try, at least. Give me that much."

I sighed. "I do not know what more I can do. I can think of no way they could have vanished like this. It is like Elf-magic."

"Let us retrace our steps during the battle, then," said Mag. "We came from that way." She pointed to the west.

“No, we came from there,” I said, pointing to the hilltop where the Shade archers had fired at us. “Honestly, Mag, sometimes you are like an infant lost in the woods.”

A shadow passed over her expression, but I did not notice. I had frozen in place, staring up at the hill.

“Albern?” said Yue. “What is it?”

“That hill . . . that is where the Shades fired at us,” I said. “They killed one of mine. He bore a torch.”

“I remember,” said Mag. “They got two of mine as well.”

“I see where the torch rolled down the hill,” I said. “But I do not see the torch itself.”

We all looked up at the spot together. There was the mark that looked like a wyrm. It was less clear now, for the flames had long since burned out. But there was a black trough burned in the green shoots of new grass, and it looked for all the world like a dragon twisting as it dove to the ground, wings folded back against its body.

“Someone could have found it and picked it up,” said Yue.

“Look at the boulders,” I said. “It should have rolled down them, but it did not. There are no burn marks, no traces of pitch on the rocks.”

I walked forwards, Yue and Mag trailing behind me. And as I climbed up, I discovered the same thing Kaita had seen earlier that day: the hole behind the boulders, invisible unless you were almost inside it. The trail of the rolling torch vanished into the shadows.

“Dark below,” I said.

“In the strictest sense,” said Yue.

“We have them,” said Mag.

“Yes, we do,” I said. “All right. Let us return to Kun and—”

“What? No,” said Mag, looking at me as though I had gone mad. “They cannot be far inside. We have to go in. Kaita could be just a span away from us at this very moment.”

“Mag, you cannot be serious,” I said. “You told Kun you wanted to find the Shades so he could point his troops at them. Was that a lie?”

“It was not,” said Mag. “But Kun refused me. Now we have found them on our own. Let us slip in, kill Kaita, and then return. No one has to be any the wiser.”

“Mag,” I said, shaking my head. “Even if we can get in and find

Kaita, and even if we can kill her—and neither of those is likely—what makes you think we could get back out again?"

"Albern is right, Mag," said Yue. "I agreed to come out here, but I did not agree to throw myself blindly into the midst of our enemies."

"Then let me do it," growled Mag. "I can deal with Kaita easily enough if I can only get my hands on her. Albern, listen to me. How many times have we faced Kaita on the battlefield? When she knows we are coming, or when she sees we are within striking distance, she always flees. She did it in Northwood. She did it twice in Tokana. And neither of us can catch a bird, or even a mountain lion, for that matter. We *have* to take her by surprise. If we do not, she will only escape again. Please."

I sighed. Mag did have a point. It is perilously tricky to hold a weremage in place when they wish to escape you. And if anyone could slip into the midst of our enemies, kill one of them, and get out again, it would have been Mag. But I was not confident that anyone *could* do it, not even the legendary Uncut Lady.

"When *will* you turn back, Mag?" I said. "What if it grows more dangerous? What if they raise the alarm? What if they kill you, or one of us?"

"That will not happen," said Mag at once. "I will not let anything happen to the two of you. And yes, I promise you: if they raise the alarm, I will turn tail and flee with the both of you." A sudden smile twisted her lips. "I will probably run faster than you, Albern, for age has made you slow."

I laughed despite myself, choking it back and trying to maintain a stern expression. "All right. If I have your vow, I will come with you."

"Then it is settled," said Mag, clapping her hands. "Do not worry, friends. I will lead the way."

So saying, she lowered herself into the darkness behind the boulders. I heard her land lightly on the tunnel floor, and then she hissed up from the shadows for us to follow her.

Yue moved to go down, but I stopped her with a hand on her shoulder. She met my eyes, squinting to see me in the moonslight.

"Are you sure about this?" I said. "Mag and I could go on alone. You could return to camp."

"I would feel faithless if I turned from the two of you now," said Yue, though her usual fire was missing. "I only . . . Albern, you do not have to go along with her in everything."

“I know that,” I said. “And deep down, she knows it, too. But while I am joining in her foolishness, I am glad you are with me.” I leaned in and kissed her.

Smiling despite herself, she shook her head. “You are soft, Telfer. But fear not. I will harden you. Come on.”

She dove into the darkness while I flushed and tried to concentrate on finding a way to slide down that would not break something vital. When eventually I landed catlike beside Yue, Mag had already taken a few steps down the tunnel. The moonslight vanished almost immediately, leaving us in total darkness beneath the earth.

“I have torches,” I said, reaching for my pack.

“No,” said Mag quietly. “If they see us coming, they will raise the alarm for certain. We shall have to feel our way along.”

Yue groaned. “Mag, one of us could trip, and the sound of the falling might alert them anyway. Do you honestly expect us to push forwards into the darkness without a light to see by?”

Mag paused for a moment, thinking. “I suppose if they have posted sentries, they will have torches of their own. But still, I do not want them to see us coming. If you must light a torch, stay far behind me. I will push forwards in the dark, and if I see anything, I will run back to you and alert you.”

“Fine,” I said. “But if you wish to sneak up on them, you have to take off your armor. Leave it here at the entrance, and we can recover it when we come back.”

“I can move quietly with it on,” she groused.

“Not quietly enough,” I said. “Come, Mag.”

“Fine.” She undid the straps that held her scales tight to her body and shucked them off, dumping them by the tunnel entrance with a heavy clank. Then she turned and stalked off into the darkness, one hand on the wall to her right. Soon she had vanished.

“All right,” I said. “Get your flint, and let us have some light.”

In no time, Yue and I had the torch going. Once it was lit, I used it to light a second, which I gave to Yue. Together, side by side, we headed down the tunnel after Mag. She was gone in the darkness ahead of us, and we kept our pace slow, to let her have plenty of space from the glow.

But it was not long at all before Mag came running up to us out of the tunnel ahead, emerging into the torchlight so suddenly that my heart jumped. We stopped short, and my hand strayed to my sword.

"What is it?" I said, my voice hushed. "What is wrong?"

"Nothing," she whispered. "I spotted a Shade guard ahead. He has a lit torch, which made him easy to see from afar."

Yue and I shared a glance. "Well, if there was any doubt that they went this way, that ends it," said Yue. "Now what?"

"He looks to be standing at the entrance to a larger cavern," said Mag. "If we can remove him, I believe we will reach the Shades' main encampment. Then we can find and slay Kaita."

I sighed. "It might be easiest with an arrow. But if there are other guards within sight of the first, it may raise the alarm."

"That is a risk we shall have to take," said Mag. "I cannot approach him undetected, for he trains his eyes on the tunnel. And if he raises the alarm, you get your wish: we retreat to Kun and the others."

"Hooray," I said, my expression deadpan.

Mag smirked. "Spoilsport. Now go and end this fool."

"And there is no chance I can persuade you to go tell Kun, now that we know for certain the Shades are here?" I said, knowing the answer already.

"None at all," said Mag cheerfully.

"All right," I said. "Take my torch and give me some space."

She did as I asked, and I advanced into the darkness of the tunnel. Soon I saw what Mag had seen: a faint glow of torchlight reflecting from the rocky walls around me. It made my going easier, and I was able to take more care with my steps, reducing the sound of my passing to no more than a mouse's scurry.

Soon I had the Shade in sight. He did indeed seem to be standing at the entrance to a much more massive cavern. That had to be where the rest of the Shades were. This guard was staring down the tunnel, and it felt as if he was looking right at me. But he held his torch in his hand, rather than finding some way to prop it against the wall behind him. It made his vision in the dark almost worse than useless.

I sighed and nocked an arrow. The angle would be hard. I could not fire too high, or I would strike the tunnel ceiling. But if I fired too low, the curve of the flight would carry the arrow into the floor instead of my foe.

I drew. I sighed. And I loosed.

The arrow sank perfectly into the Shade's throat. Jian would likely have scolded me if she saw me aim for anything but the chest, but I was trying to keep things quiet.

The torch fell from his hands, and he clutched at his neck, seizing the dart and trying in vain to stanch the sudden gout of blood. Slowly he collapsed to his knees, and then to the floor.

I held still for the longest moment I have ever experienced in my life.

No alarm sounded.

Sighing in relief, I turned and stalked back down the tunnel. Mag and Yue's faces were tense as they watched me emerge from the shadows.

"The door is clear, and no alarm raised," I said. "But we had best be quick. They have to change the guard sometime, and then we will be discovered."

Mag and Yue set their torches down. We could retrieve them on the way back out. We continued down the tunnel until we reached the place where the guard had stood. I could see now that his head had been shaved close to the scalp, but he had a long, stringy beard. He stared up at me as I passed, his mouth slightly open. I ignored him.

THIRTY-THREE

Now we could see the vast cavern beyond the tunnel. It stretched for spans in both length and width. Laid out near its center was the Shades' camp. There were several lines of tents, with two low campfires that I could see. Some figures walked around, but they seemed to be either fetching food or heading off to relieve themselves in some distant corner. I saw no posted guards. Kaita must have been convinced that hiding beneath the earth would keep them safe.

I tapped both Mag and Yue on the shoulder and drew them behind a large, jutting rock formation. I began speaking to them in sign, afraid of letting out even a whisper in this place. The Shade camp was a span off, but sound carried far on the harsh, rocky surfaces all around us.

"What now?" I signed.

"We need the officers' tents," signed Mag. "Kaita will be there."

"What in the dark below are you two doing?" whispered Yue.

"Shhh!" I hissed. "We are signing. Do you not know sign?"

Yue grimaced. "I . . . do," she said aloud. "But I have not practiced in—"

I put a hand over her mouth. *"Please* be silent. Follow along as best you can." I turned back to Mag and resumed in sign. "The camp is like most camps. The officers will be in the group of tents near the other end. Past the soldier tents."

Yue signed haltingly. "Past the sword tents?"

I blew an exasperated breath out my nose. "*Soldier* tents," I signed again, emphasizing the motions.

Recognition dawned in her eyes. "I am hungry," she signed confidently, though I believe she meant "I understand."

"Let us circle their camp," signed Mag. "I will go in. You will keep watch. If you see an enemy, fire an arrow at the ground near me. I will hear it and know to run. But they may hear it, too, so only shoot if there is great danger."

I did not like it, but I had no better ideas. "All right," I signed. Then I reached out and gripped her shoulder. "Be careful," I whispered. "Remember, you promised you would run if we had to."

"I remember," she whispered with a smile. And then she signed, "And you should not be talking out loud."

"All right," I signed back. "Let us go."

Sneaking around the camp was the easy part. The Shades were in the center of the cavern, and we never drew closer than a span away from them. I worried about our every footfall and the scuff of our limbs against protruding rocks, but I likely need not have. Even from this distance, I could hear the noises of the Shades, and they were much louder than any noise we were making.

We did not have to go too far before reaching a good position. Mag gave us one last nod before setting off towards the camp. She left her spear with us, exchanging it for a long knife Yue wore on her belt, which Mag now affixed to her own. Silent as an Elf, she crept forwards. I kept my eyes on her, holding my breath whenever she ducked out of sight and releasing it when she emerged into view again.

The first tent was the easiest. It was near the edge of the camp, and the flap side pointed outwards. I was afraid Mag might move straight into it, but she was wise. She stopped two paces away and waited, watching and listening. No Shades wandered near the tent, and Mag must not have heard any sounds from inside, for she soon crept forwards once more.

Like a shadow, she vanished inside. I could not hear it, but I could almost imagine the soft *shunk* of her blade sliding through the Shade's eye, the brief sounds of struggling as she held them down while their body jerked, lapsed, and then lay still forever.

Mag emerged into view again. I could see blood on her hands. I held a brief hope that Kaita had been in the tent, but it did not seem so, for Mag did not return. But at least she had killed a Shade officer. That was something.

Mag did not wait as long before the next tent, and her impatience was almost our ruin. As she began to approach it, there was a commotion close by. Mag threw herself to the ground. Yue and I tensed, and I nocked an arrow.

From a tent five paces down the row, a Shade emerged. She stood tall and stretched, scratched herself, and blinked hard in the light of the campfire. Then she turned and walked towards the camp's edge. Her path brought her perilously close to Mag, but she passed by, and Mag remained unnoticed. Soon the Shade had vanished into the darkness on the other side of the camp, and I lost sight of her.

Yue and I released a long breath at the same time. Mag stirred, rose from the floor where she had flung herself, and crept forwards on all fours. The flap of the second tent rose and then fell again, and Mag was inside.

This time the kill must not have been as clean, for I saw the tent jerk briefly. But it lasted only a moment, and then Mag came out again.

I leaned forwards, hoping she would come creeping back towards us. There were only a handful of officer tents in the cluster—there were fair odds, at least, that Mag should have found Kaita in one of the first two. But it did not seem so, as she turned and crept towards a third tent.

"Dark take it," growled Yue. "This cannot last forever."

But things seemed to be going well so far. Who knew but that Mag might wipe out the Shades' leadership in one fell swoop, and Kaita along with them. The only foe she would not be able to dispatch so quietly would be the brute woman. But Mag was smart enough to know that. She would not even try.

She *was* smart enough to know that, was she not? I certainly hoped so.

As Mag neared the third tent, I settled back on my haunches to wait. It was growing uncomfortable sitting on the cold, hard stone of the cave. But my whole body jerked with fright as a cry went up from the opposite end of the Shade camp.

"Awake! Awake! Foes! Awake!"

My gaze flew to the source of the noise. I could not see who was shouting. Mag, sky bless her, did not hesitate. She turned and began fleeing back towards Yue and I, keeping low.

The Shade camp erupted into frenzied activity, like an anthill kicked by a restless child. Blue-cloaked warriors poured from the lines of tents, drawing their weapons and looking wildly around.

There. Finally, I could see who was shouting. At the other end of the camp, the brute woman came into view. She towered over those around her, and her shaggy mane of hair swung back and forth as she scanned the darkness.

"Enemies!" she roared. "Enemies in our midst! They are murdering your officers. Find them!"

"What in the dark below?" hissed Yue. "How did she see Mag from the other side of the cave?"

"I do not know," I growled. "But we have to get out of here."

Mag reached us just at that moment. "I do not know how they saw me," she said. I could hear the frustration in her voice.

"And I gather you did not find Kaita," I said.

"No." She almost spat the word.

"Well, we will have another chance. But not now. Run!"

We fled through the shadows, sprinting for the cave entrance. I was terrified we might find it guarded. Mayhap the Shades had discovered the slain guard, and that was how they knew we were here. But there was no one there. The corpse lay right where we had left it. And with all the Shades rushing to the officers' tents, no one was looking in our direction. I scooped up the fallen guard's torch as we ran by.

"I do not understand," said Mag.

"Mayhap it was the weremage," said Yue. "She could have been . . . oh, sky, I do not know, a bat or something. Mayhap she saw you and told the large one."

"She would have come after us," I said. "Or raised the alarm herself."

"Well then, you know more about it than I do," snapped Yue.

"We have to get back to camp," said Mag. "If we tell Kun, and he summons his troops quickly enough, we can still wipe them out before they have a chance to run."

"Oh, *now* she wants to tell the captain," I said.

All three of us could not help a bark of laughter as we sprinted through the blackness.

Kaita heard screams. Her head snapped up. She whirled in the darkness and sprinted back down the tunnel towards the Shade camp.

All day she had been exploring the passages tirelessly, but she had nothing to show for it. One of them had gone on for what felt like a league before abruptly reaching a dead end. She had not gone far down the third, the one she was still in now, but it had not seemed promising. She could not smell any fresh air, and it had seemed to plunge ever deeper and deeper into the earth.

But all these thoughts fled her as she pelted down the tunnel towards her allies. Soon enough, she came leaping into the grand cavern, where she found the Shades in chaos. Tagata was there, standing near the officers' tents near one end of the camp. In her arms, she cradled the corpse of one of her captains, one whose name Kaita could never remember.

Magelight flared, and Kaita resumed her human form. "What happened?" she cried. "Tagata, are you hurt?"

"I am not," growled Tagata. "But they killed Harnel and Selnir."

Harnel, that was it, thought Kaita. "Who killed them?"

But even as she asked the question, the answer came to her in a flash. She knew she was right when she saw the mounting fury in Tagata's gaze.

"Mag and Albern," growled Tagata. "As I was resting, I received a message from the Lord. He told me they were here, *now,* slaying our kindred. Thank goodness I received word from him before they took more."

A chill ran up Kaita's spine. If she had stayed and rested, as Tagata had urged . . . they might have found *her*. It could be *her* corpse in Tagata's arms right now. She wondered bitterly whether the Lord would have foreseen that, and whether he would have warned Tagata in time.

But then again . . . if Mag and Albern had come, then they were alone. They were isolated from their allies. Kaita had the magestones, and she could—

"Tagata," she said quickly. "When did they leave? I could still catch them while they are alone."

"No, dear one," said Tagata softly. "Too much time has passed. They will have returned to their allies now. I am sorry."

"Dark take them," growled Kaita. "Will I never get my chance?"

"You will. Have faith. But for now, there are more pressing matters." Tagata's expression grew grim. "They are going to bring the Mystics down upon us. Everyone is preparing to march, but we do not know where. We cannot leave the way we came. That is where the Mystics will come. Have you found another exit?"

"No," snarled Kaita. "Only paths farther down into the earth, and the southern passage that leads right to—"

She stopped short as an idea struck her. And she could see the same thought reflected in Tagata's savage smile.

"Ready the march," said Kaita. "We make for the south passage."

Mag led the way back to Kun's camp, with Yue and me close behind. On the northeastern end of the camp, Chausiku still stood his sentry post.

"Hail!" called Mag in the darkness. "Three rods."

"And two wings," called Chausiku. He had raised his bow at the sound of her voice, but now he lowered it again. Relief was plain in his expression as we crept up out of the darkness. "I am glad to see you safe, Sergeants."

"As are we," I said. "No trouble here while we were gone?"

"None," said Chausiku. "No one seems to have noticed a thing."

My mouth twisted. "That is well. But remember—do not lie on our account. If anyone asks you what happened tonight, you tell the truth, do you hear?"

Chausiku lifted his chin slightly. "I hear you, Sergeant."

It was not an agreement, but I decided to let it be. With any luck, he would not need to face such a choice at all.

A campfire still burned at our end of the camp, where our tents were set up at the end of our squadrons' lines. Mag made to walk straight past them, heading for Kun's tent. But a sudden shout stopped us all in our tracks.

"Hail, Sergeants!"

We froze. Then, slowly, we turned. From the shadows between our tents stepped Kun. Behind him was Tou, a furious expression on his face.

The captain's smile was as thin as new-frozen ice.

"And where, pray tell, have the three of you been?" he asked sweetly.

THIRTY-FOUR

"Captain," said Mag.

"Am I?" said Kun.

Mag, Yue, and I exchanged a glance. "Ser?" said Mag.

"Am I your captain?" said Kun. "Because one obeys one's captain. And yet the three of you have gone to scout for the enemy alone after I explicitly ordered you not to."

That, of course, is the sort of statement for which there is no safe response, and so we said nothing. At Kun's side, Tou looked furious enough to burst into flames. Only deference to his captain seemed to be keeping him silent. I did not doubt he wished to say many loud, angry things to us, and would when Kun had gone.

"Well?" said Kun. "You are all uncustomarily silent. Sergeant Telfer, at least, has a clever tongue that hardly ever stills. What am I to make of you? This is the sort of thing that carries heavy penalties. Limited rations certainly, mayhap stocks, if we had them. Lashes would not be out of the question if anything disastrous should occur as a result of your transgression. Even execution, were the consequences dire enough. I say this not to hound you with empty threats, but to convey the severity with which I must now consider your case."

Mag rallied, speaking in a calm voice. "Ser, we apologize for going against your orders. But our venture bore fruit. We found the Shades. They are trapped, and we can wipe them out if we act quickly enough."

Kun studied her for a moment, his eyes sometimes flitting to Yue and me on either side of her. When he spoke, it was not in response to her.

"Do you know that, when you first arrived, I was positive you were Shades?" he said. "I was convinced of it. The first thing that shook my conviction was Sergeant Baolan's arrival. And then we fought together against the enemy, and I watched you kill them with my own eyes. My last vestiges of doubt vanished, and I thought that was the end of it. Yet now I see things clearly for the first time after a long while spent in the darkness."

"Ser," I said, "we are *not* Shades."

"Oh no," said Kun. "I am even more certain of that now. You are something less evil than Shades, but no less dangerous. You are vigilantes. Folk who think yourselves above the rest of us, who see yourselves as being removed from the petty concerns of the nine lands."

"Respectfully, ser," said Yue, "I love Underrealm with my whole heart, and I will defend my honor on—"

"Be silent, Sergeant!" roared Tou. He bit off the words almost as sharply as they had erupted, and I gained a new appreciation for just how hard he must be clamping down on his temper. "Do not try to defend your honor when we have caught you violating the captain's trust."

Yue's jaw spasmed once, but she fell silent. Mag spoke again, still calm.

"Yet it is true, sers. We do love Underrealm."

"Not as much as you loved your husband," said Kun, and he too was calm. "I do not say this to hurt you. It is no evil thing that you loved him more than a nation. Underrealm is not even a real thing, nothing you can touch, or see, or hold in the darkness when fear and grief press themselves upon you. It is more useful than true. Yet within the false idea that is a kingdom, there are real people. Many of them are as worthy as your husband, though you do not know them. And by your actions, you endanger them. This war that poisons Underrealm is of little concern to you as long as you satisfy your pursuit of revenge—and yet in that pursuit, you are willing to leave others in grief, countless folk who now must seek their own reparations for the loss of loved ones."

He paused for a moment and sighed, and his smile faded a bit. "I changed my mind, you know. I sent for Lieutenant Shi tonight. I told him to assign you to hunt for the Shades tomorrow, as you requested. If you had been less foolish, you would now be free to pursue your aims. And if I had not come around to your way of thinking, I would never have noticed your betrayal."

The captain's words struck me hard, and I could see I was not the only one. Mag's eyes had widened, and her stance had become tense. I could feel the conflict inside her, self-doubt worming its way into her mind.

Again she mustered herself. "Yet we found the enemy. If we act quickly, we can destroy them. But we have to rouse the troops now."

Kun's gaze grew knife-sharp, and his smile grew just as thin as before. "Why?"

Mag blinked. "To . . . to root them out of—"

"Why *now*, Sergeant? Why not in the morning?"

There was a long, deathly silence. Then, at last:

"Because they discovered us," grated Mag.

"Oh?" said Kun, eyes wide with mock surprise. "Did they?"

Again, a silence stretched wide enough to drown in. Finally, I growled out, "Dark take it, Mag, now is not the time to go dancing around half-truths. Captain, we infiltrated the camp and slew two Shade officers and a guard. But they spotted us."

"With each revelation, the situation grows more dire," said Kun, "and your offense more severe. Not for the first time, I find myself confident that you tell the truth. If you were lying, surely you would not keep digging yourself deeper into the grave."

"We are sorry, ser," I said. "But this can be turned to our advantage. If we move now, we can root them out of their hole and end this expedition. Please, ser. We know we were wrong"—I stared hard at Mag to quell any disagreement, though to my surprise, she looked docile—"but give us the chance to make it right."

His smile widened. "Well. At least you express some remorse. And I suppose I cannot deny someone a chance at redemption, whether they deserve it or not. Of course we must march on them, and at once. I have half a mind to leave your company here to guard the camp as punishment. But Lieutenant Shi is quite angry enough already, and I have never believed in punishing an officer for his subordinates' mistakes. Not to mention that if we must fight, I would rather have the Uncut Lady to the fore."

This, at last, seemed to be what Mag needed to hear. She straightened, her grip tightening on her spear. "Thank you, Captain. You will not regret this."

"I hope not," said Kun. "If I do, be assured that you will regret it far more. Lieutenant Zhou will remain behind with one company to guard the supply train. The rest of you get ready to march. I want us to leave within a quarter-hour. Dismissed."

We turned and strode away. But we had barely gone half a span before I heard a growl behind us.

"Sergeants."

I swallowed hard, and we all turned to face Tou. He was still livid, his eyes boring into each of us in turn. His hands were clasped behind his back as if he was restraining himself.

"Lieutenant Shi," said Mag.

"I do not know what changed between Taitou and here, but you had better change it back," said Tou sharply. "I trusted you, and I thought you trusted me."

"Ser," I said, "it is not that we did not trust—"

"Be silent," snapped Tou. I fell quiet. "You went off against orders because you thought you knew better, and your concerns were more important. Everyone knows you two are the most experienced fighters in the army. They have known it since you arrived. But I respected you because you did not *act* superior. You never lorded your skills or your history over the rest of us. Now it seems that was all a ruse, and you held yourselves above us all along."

He stepped up to Mag. "You are not above us," he said. "Just because you could take anyone here in a fight, that does not mean you are better than we are. We know the strength of trusting the people we fight beside, and that is a greater strength than any one person can match. Even the Uncut Lady. I thought you understood that already, but you had better learn the lesson now."

Mag did not look at him but stared over his shoulder into the distance. Tou remained standing there for a moment before he turned and marched away.

"Get your squadrons ready," he called back over his shoulder. "You will not be even an instant late for muster."

An uncomfortable moment passed before Mag looked at us and shrugged. "They will feel differently once we wipe out the Shades," she said.

"Let us hope that is how tonight ends," said Yue.

"We had better go tell Dryleaf we are safe," I said.

Mag shook her head. "Only to tell him we are going back out into danger again? He is probably asleep. Let him rest. We will complete our mission, and then we can come back with tidings of victory. Besides, you have heard the lieutenant—if we are late, he may flog us."

I gave an uneasy look towards the supply train at the south end of camp. "I suppose you are right," I said. "Very well. We will not wake him until we have happier news to report."

Yue snorted. "He may sleep long, then."

THIRTY-FIVE

It was a cold night, and the wind whistled low. Yue growled at it in response, thumping her hands against her arms to stave off the cold. She had joined her squadron of spears, helping them get ready for the fight. She found herself irritable, and she did not know exactly why. Mayhap it was partly because her unit badgered her with question after question about the coming battle.

"Will we face them underground or above?" said one.

"I think underground, but I cannot know for certain," said Yue.

"Will we be on the front line again?" asked another, eyes wide. Her wound from the battle in the Greenfrost was still healing.

"I do not know," growled Yue.

"Sergeant, should we bring—"

"I do not *know!*" barked Yue.

They all fell silent around her. She closed her eyes and put a hand to her forehead.

"I am sorry. That was . . . I spoke to you like Ashta and Sinshi back home. I should not have then, and I should not have now."

"It is all right, Sergeant," said one of them slowly.

"No, it is not," growled Yue.

The wind picked up, needling them all with frozen rain scouring their skin. Again Yue pounded her arms to warm the blood.

"In Lan Shui, I was in charge," she said. "And I knew most everything about my job. Nothing went on in my town that I was not aware of. But here, everything is different. I am not them." She tossed her head in the direction of Mag and me, who were busy with our squadrons. "I am a fighter, and I have been one for most of my life, but I am new to *this* kind of fighting. Before I met you all, the closest I came to war was when the vampires attacked my town. And waiting for them to come . . . I suppose that the threat seemed great, but at least we had a plan to fight them." A spark seemed to light in her eyes, and her squadron saw it. "But that was not why I felt confident. I felt confident *because* of them." Again she nodded to Mag and me.

One of her soldiers snorted. "Mostly because of her, I suppose."

"No," growled Yue. "Both of them. Albern may not be . . . well, he may not be Mag. But he is no slouch, either. I would lay ten gold weights on him against anyone in this little army, except Mag herself. I thought he was a dark-damned steer when first I met him. And do you know what? He *is* a steer. But he is a *good* steer. He is *my* steer. Not just kind of heart, but skilled and wise as well. If there is anything wrong with him, it is that—"

She cut herself off. Her squadron stared at her curiously.

"What, Sergeant?" said one.

"It is that he cannot keep his fool mouth shut when he should," snapped Yue. "Much like others I could name. Now heft those spears. We have a battle to fight."

But before she went to fetch her weapon, she looked at me again, and then at Mag. The wind blew a curtain of rain before her, blocking us both from view.

It was a cold night, and the wind whistled low. I shivered against it, pulling my hood tighter around my face.

My squadron stood in the darkness around me, rubbing or slapping their arms as we waited for the order to march. I walked among them, seeing that they and their equipment were in shape. Here and there I caught a loose buckle or strap and helped to tighten it, and I ensured no one carried anything they did not need.

Chausiku had been called back from sentry duty, replaced by an archer from Zhen's company. From what the other archer had said, Zhen was not pleased to remain behind while we marched off to glory. I was not sure whether the captain was leaving him because he wished to protect him, or because he felt Zhen was a lieutenant he could trust absolutely. Either way, if I could have chosen to remain behind, I would have. Fighting a desperate, deadly battle in narrow tunnels beneath the earth was far from my idea of a good time.

"Remember," I said. "We will be going in first, but only until we make contact with the enemy. As soon as we see them, we are to loose a volley and then run like Elves are after us. Green Squadron will take it from there."

"Yes, ser," said Jian fiercely. She was projecting all eagerness for the coming battle, but I could sense the nervousness beneath. "And mayhap we will have the chance to loose one or two extra shots into the traitors."

"Hopefully, it will be over too quickly for that," I replied.

"Will they not see our torches coming in the darkness?" said Chausiku. His anxiety was much plainer to see than Jian's.

"They might, but there is little we can do about that," I said. "They could do one of two things. They might attempt to hold the tunnel against us, for it is narrow and will render our numbers no great advantage. Or, they might seek a pitched battle in the large cave where they have made camp.

"If they try to hold the tunnel, Jian may well get her wish. The captain will not send our fighters to die against that brute woman who leads them. Instead, we will pepper them with bowfire until we whittle them down enough that they have to retreat. Either way, it will likely end with a pitched battle in the large cave. There, we should be as safe as we were in the battle in the Greenfrost."

Hallan's great red beard jumped as he chewed on a piece of meat, pulled from a pouch as a midnight snack before our foray. His eyes would rest upon me for a moment before darting away. He seemed less than pleased. I had not told him about my plan with Mag before we left. It was strange to feel such disapproval from the man, who was usually the friendliest archer in my squadron.

"Easy enough, ser," he said gruffly. "Anything else?"

"No, that is all," I said. I turned to speak to the rest of them. "Tonight has held more than its share of bad decisions, and for my part in them, I am sorry. But we are all making the best of a bad situation."

Hallan spat. "S'pose you did what you thought was best."

"We did," I said. "And with luck, we will be proven right in the end."

"Hm," said Hallan.

The wind whistled colder, and I shivered again.

It was a cold night, and the wind whistled low. Mag's squadron buckled on their swords and hefted their shields. Dibu and Li swung their arms nervously, trying to stave off the cold just like the rest of us. But Mag seemed unaffected by the weather. The sharp wind's only effect on her was to send her cloak and hair swirling. Frozen rain tried to slice at her face, but it could not find purchase, and soon it melted and ran down her cheeks. Her gaze was fixed to the northeast, where the cave and the Shades waited.

"Is everyone ready?" said Mag.

"Yesser," said Dibu.

"Good," she said. "We will be right behind Black Squadron. That means we will be the first to meet the enemy, when it comes to blades instead of arrows. Let me take the fore then. Focus on staying alive."

"They say this is it," said Li. Her voice shook. "They say this should be the end."

"It will be," said Mag, fervent but quiet.

She thought of her words with Dryleaf, about our plans to leave Kun's army at the next large city we reached. She motioned Li and Dibu closer and spoke quietly enough that only they could hear.

"I have a question. Do both of you mean to see this war through?"

Li's wandering eyes focused, and her brow furrowed. "What do you mean?"

"This war for Dorsea," said Mag. "For all of Underrealm, I suppose. Will the two of you stick with Kun as long as it takes?"

"I plan to," said Dibu, folding his strong arms. A moment later, Li nodded in agreement.

"That is good," said Mag flatly. "You are both good at this. One should not be overly proud to be a good soldier, but one should not be ashamed of it, either. And you could both be great one day if that is what you want. But not me."

Li snorted. "Ser, you must be joking. You are the greatest among—"

"I mean that it is not for me anymore," said Mag. "I used to enjoy it when I was . . . well, not young. But younger. And when I looked back on those memories, I thought I would enjoy myself again now. But I do not. I am not meant for this sort of life anymore. One day, you might not be, either. When that day comes, I want you to try to recognize it. Because I will not be there to tell you. You are going to have to look out for each other." She gave a sad smirk. "And for the lieutenant, I suppose."

Dibu's cheeks flushed.

"Well, not like that," said Mag. "Although, I suppose like that, too. Come. It is time to march."

The cold wind picked up, blasting them all. Nothing about Mag shivered but her cloak.

THIRTY-SIX

AND SO WE MARCHED. FOUR OF KUN'S COMPANIES SET OUT, LEAVING BEHIND the fifth under Zhen's command. Zhen himself stood at the northeast end of camp and watched us march away, his eyes never leaving the column.

I do not know how long he waited, as we all faded into the darkness before him. But I know it could not have been too long.

We reached the entrance to the tunnel in short order. I approached it with some trepidation, afraid that we might find the Shades had come out and formed up for a defense.

Yet the snowy field beside the boulders was empty. No soldiers waited for us with drawn blades, nor were there tracks to show they had come out at all. They were still inside.

We halted, and the column drew up. Kun summoned Mag, Yue, and me to him. Tou was also there, arms folded, glare fixed upon us.

"Well, Sergeants," said Kun. "Where do we go next?"

I pointed. "Behind those boulders is the entrance to a tunnel leading to the enemy."

"We should take care, Captain," said Mag. "They may be guarding the entrance, hoping to hold it against us."

"Indeed they might," said Kun, smiling. "What I would not give for a wizard of any stripe. But very well. It might be best to drop a torch down first and see if we can spook them. If they fire arrows at it, we will at least know if they are waiting, and we can plan from there."

"Yesser," said Mag. "Let me do it."

"Certainly," said Kun, waving her forwards.

Mag took a torch from Dibu and crept up the hillside until she was above the boulders. She waited for the space of a heartbeat, and then she dropped the torch inside.

We all waited in dead silence. But nothing happened. I could see the light glinting around the edges of the boulders at the entrance.

"Nothing, Captain," said Mag, her voice floating towards us in the night.

"Very well," said Kun. "Two should drop down with shields and hide behind them at once. Two others should drop ropes at the same time, in case we need to pull them out quickly."

"Bring a rope," said Mag. "I can go in first alone."

Before we could answer, Mag dropped into the darkness. I heard her boots land on the tunnel floor, and then another long silence.

"Nothing, Captain," repeated Mag. This time her voice was heavy with the echoes of the tunnel. "They are not here. We can proceed."

Kun turned his gaze on me in the darkness, and though he still smiled, his eyes were steely in the moonslight.

"Very well, Sergeant," called Kun. "But while I can sympathize with the impulse to put yourself on the front line, you do yourself no favors by disobeying my orders."

"My apologies, ser," called Mag. "I will not do so again."

"I wonder if I can believe that," muttered Kun

We began to filter into the tunnel. My squadron went first, as Kun had planned. I dropped into the tunnel beside Mag before my archers, and in the brief private moment we had, I fixed her with a look.

"Mag, you have to stop," I told her. "I know you feel guilty, and I understand. But you *will not* get yourself killed trying to make things right. Do you understand me? I will not have it. If you cannot think of your own safety, at least think of me, and of Dryleaf."

"I *am* thinking of you," said Mag. "Do not worry about me."

I shook my head. "Do not give me a reason to."

Then Jian dropped into the tunnel next to us, and I had to bite my tongue. I waited until all my archers were inside, and then we waited a moment longer until Mag's swordfighters had followed. Our squadrons would press down the tunnel, but not too quickly, while the rest of the army trickled in behind us.

Hallan walked near the front, torch in hand. No one else in my squadron held a torch, and Mag's unit hung well back with their torch-bearer, so we had only scant light to go by. But that seemed better than giving the enemy many targets to fire at in the darkness.

That long, slow advance down the tunnel was one of the most nerve-wracking experiences I have ever had. It was not like the anticipation of any everyday battle. We *knew* they were ahead of us, lurking in that darkness. They could not help but see us—we had a torch. Yet we had no choice but to advance straight towards them, helpless in the dark.

We had no grand strategy, not like Kun had devised before. There was no room for it. This would be brutal, messy, and violent. We would fight and die in darkness, in the flash of torchlight glinting off blood-soaked blades. It would be a hard task to clear the Shades from this place, especially if the brute woman took the fore. If that happened, we would have little choice but to pit Mag against her and pray to a sky we could no longer see.

Yet there was no sign of our enemy. We were close now to the great cavern. But no arrows came hissing out of the darkness to fall among us.

When I guessed we were a span away from the large cavern, I stopped. Something about this felt wrong. The Shades would gain no benefit from fighting us in the vast space ahead. It would have made far more sense for them to fight us here in the tunnel, funneling us into a small space. As I sat there in the dark, pondering the mystery, Mag crept up, and not far behind her came Lieutenant Tou and Captain Kun.

"What is it?" said Mag.

"The cavern is up ahead," I said. "Yet there is no sign of them. I cannot read the tale of it."

"Mayhap they are trying to hide," said Tou. His anger at Mag and me was forgotten for the coming battle—or at least he had put the anger away on a shelf in his mind, to be retrieved later. "Mayhap they have holed up deeper in the cave, hoping that we will think they have left."

"I do not think so," I said slowly. "I would call that foolish, and nothing they have done so far has shown foolishness on their part."

"What do you think, then?" said Kun.

"Mayhap they have set an ambush inside the entrance," said Mag. "They left the tunnel open so that we would think the danger was gone, or at least so that we might grow lax in our caution. They hope we will press into the cavern with speed, and they can strike us from the sides when we are in an open space."

"That could be," said Kun. "Very well. Sergeant, take your squadron forwards. Proceed into the cavern cautiously, and keep a shield wall up around you. If they hope to catch us unawares, we must endeavor to disappoint them."

"Why not let me go in alone?" said Mag. "I will provoke as much of a reaction as my whole squadron, and there is no reason to risk more lives unnecessarily."

"Do not be a fool," I snapped. "Mag, even you cannot guard all sides of you at the same time."

"You know how fast I am," said Mag. "If they start to fire upon me, I will retreat into the—"

"Enough," said Kun. "Albern is correct. Take your squadron, Mag. Be careful, and if they fire upon you, retreat."

A moment passed, with Mag's jaw working furiously. "Yes, Captain."

She set off, leading her squadron down the tunnel towards the entrance to the cavern. My archers and I followed behind, all of us with arrows nocked.

Dibu held the torch in Mag's squadron. The others surrounded him with their shields turned outwards, so that the group of them edged into the cavern like an exceptionally watchful turtle. I tensed, expecting a hail of arrows to fall among them. But no attack came.

A long moment passed as Mag kept leading them farther out into the space. But it was, indeed, empty.

Chills began to creep paths down my spine. I shook them off and pushed into the cavern to join Mag.

"Where in the dark below did they go?" she growled.

"An apt choice of words," I said. "Hallan, give me that torch. I need to have a look around."

I took it and went to inspect the place where the Shades had built their camp. There was a great deal of detritus around, small pieces of cloth that must once have held food, as well as some bones and other scraps from finished meals. But there were no tents, no bedrolls, nothing but a few smoldering remnants of the campfires they had managed to build from dung.

"They left," I said quietly. "But where could . . . ?"

Quickly now, I moved to the wall and began circling the perimeter of the cave. Very soon, I found what Kaita had already seen—three other tunnels leading out of the main cavern. I paused at the southern one. There I saw the smooth stone floor streaked with many muddy boot prints. The Shades had left this way.

I ran back to the center of the cavern. Kun was there now with Mag, and more than a hundred of our soldiers had filtered into the cavern behind him. The captain's smile had grown very, very dangerous.

"Ser," I said. He turned his gaze upon me. "The Shades left through another tunnel, this one leading to the south. Either they found an exit that way, or they took it and hoped they would find one. Either way . . ."

The captain nodded. "Yes, Sergeant," he said. "It seems we have little choice but to chase them even farther into the darkness. Your archers will take point again. Forwards!"

We advanced into the tunnel. But this time, I moved with more speed. I was not as afraid they would turn and try to fight us in the tunnel—if that had been their plan, they would simply have done so at the entrance. No, I suspected they were making for an exit with all speed. But they would still be hampered by their wounded. We could come upon them in the open and cut them down as they fled. We only had to press a little farther, a little faster, a little deeper into the darkness.

The passage twisted, it turned, it climbed. Once, we had to put our weapons away and haul ourselves hand over hand up a short rock wall. The cold of the outside world was long forgotten, and I bemoaned my heavy winter cloak that was now soaked with sweat instead of rainwater.

I could see the footsteps plainly in the torchlight. They began to look more hurried, as though the Shades had started to run through the darkness. And then I felt it—a cool breeze wafting towards us. The icy air of the outside world once again kissed my skin, giving relief against the heat.

"Captain!" I called out down the tunnel behind me. "An exit!"

And then the breeze came again, carrying other things this time.

To my nose, the scent of burning. And to my ears, the sound of screams.

My heart nearly stopped.

No, I thought. *Sky above, no. Please.*

THIRTY-SEVEN

THE MOMENT HE REALIZED WHERE WE WERE, CAPTAIN ZHOU PUSHED past me. He abandoned his Mystics, Mag and me, our squadrons, everyone. He ran out of the cave entrance, scrambled over the boulders that hid it from view, and went sprinting into the destroyed remains of our camp.

"Zhen!" he cried out. "Report! Lieutenant Zhou! *Nephew! Report!*"

He did not hear the voice he sought. Instead, a Mystic knight appeared. Her left hand clutched her right shoulder, which was bleeding heavily. The arrow stuck out of both sides of the wound, and the woman gritted her teeth through the pain.

"Captain," she gasped. "Thank the sky you—"

"Lieutenant Zhou," snapped Kun. "Where is he?"

The knight went very still. "Captain. He . . ."

Kun pushed past her, ignoring her grunt of pain as he jostled her shoulder. He ran to the north end of camp, where Zhen's company of soldiers had been.

Had been.

Nearly the entire force lay dead. Arrows had pierced them; axes had hewn them. The Shades had come out of the hills from the west, and they had found most of Zhen's company still asleep. Our enemies had cut them down even as they struggled to emerge from their tents. Some were alive, moaning and crying out in the snow. Few of them would survive the night.

And there was Zhen.

He was near the front line, where the fighting had started. He had not slept after we left. He had meant to stand vigil through the night, waiting for his uncle and the rest of us to return. But then he had heard the sounds of fighting to the west, and he had raced towards them. Two new, much larger wounds now joined the angry scar on his cheek. A blade had pierced his throat, and an arrow stood straight up from his chest like a flagpole. His face was a battle-grimace, determined, resolute.

Doomed.

Kun fell to his knees. His hands shook as he held them out. His nephew, his sister-son, stared past him into the empty black sky, seeing nothing through those familiar eyes. Slowly Kun scooped him up, gripping the boy by the shoulders and pulling him into his lap. There he held him tight, taking off his own cloak to wrap around the boy, as if hoping to bring some warmth back to the rapidly-freezing skin.

Mag, Yue, and I had gone running through the camp like Kun. But we ran for the train, where we had last seen Dryleaf.

Everything was chaos. The Shades had slaughtered drivers, they had broken wagon wheels, they had spilled every store of food and drink into the snow.

The army's very guts lay spread upon the ground. Losing Zhen's company was a devastating blow, but the loss of the supply train was mayhap even more damaging. Kun would have none of the supplies he needed to carry on. The Shades had taken or destroyed nearly everything, everything but—

My heart melted with relief as I saw the blue silk coverings of the wagon from the Guild of Lovers. It was untouched. The Guild was protected, both by edicts of the High King and by laws older than Underrealm itself. After all, what use to kill lovers in war, when their rules keep them from taking sides in a conflict? I had not been sure the Shades would respect such boundaries. But they had, and the lovers favored Dryleaf. Mayhap . . .

We ran to the wagon. "Dryleaf!" I cried. I seized the flap and threw it open.

At once, I fell back, landing hard on my rear. Knives flashed at me out of the darkness, the light of campfires glinting off their steely edges. I scrambled up, holding my hands high, while Mag and Yue did the same. From inside the wagon came a great peal of barking.

"Hold!" cried Yue. "We mean no harm."

Orla and Nikau saw us, and they lowered their knives. The other lovers took the cue and did the same, though they still watched us warily. Oku came bounding out of the wagon, whining and sniffing at my boots.

"Orla," I said. "Dryleaf. Did he—"

"He is here," she said, scooting aside. Nikau pulled back a blanket, and there was Dryleaf, cradled among the lovers.

I gasped, and Yue put a hand to her mouth. Dryleaf had taken a nasty blow to the head. They had wrapped bandages around it, but it was bleeding heavily, and the cloth was almost soaked through. The old man's eyes were closed, and his breath came slow and labored.

Mag looked upon him, her whole body solid and unmoving as a rock.

"They took the camp by surprise," said Nikau in his smooth, liquid voice. "The first we knew of the attack was when an arrow struck someone running by. As they died, they fell upon Dryleaf and knocked him to the ground. He hit his head on a log. As soon as Orla and I realized what was going on, we carried him into the wagon, and we have been here ever since. The attackers left us alone."

"Thank the sky," I said. "How long has he been asleep?"

"Not long," said Orla quietly. She brushed her slim, pale fingers against his cheek. "He stayed awake a long while. We had some dreamwine, and we gave him as much as he could stomach to help with the pain of his wound. He . . ." She fell to silence.

"He what?" snapped Mag. Orla recoiled, and Mag sighed and bent her head. "Forgive me. What were you going to say?"

"He kept asking for the three of you," said Nikau. "He was afraid, and he kept asking us what was happening, but we did not know what to tell him."

Orla began to weep.

Just then, Dryleaf stirred and started to come awake. His hands reached out, grasping. Nikau took one of his hands, and Orla clasped the other where it came to rest on her dress, stroking the back of his gnarled old fingers.

"Mag," moaned Dryleaf. "Albern. Yue. Where are they?"

"We are here, Dryleaf," I said. "We came back."

Dryleaf burst into tears. "Oh, thank the sky," he said, almost whispering. "Where are you? I cannot tell, your voices, they . . ." Tears took the rest of his words, and he shook in Nikau's smoothly muscled arms.

I looked around at the lovers in the wagon. "May I—?"

"Of course," said Nikau. He motioned for the rest of them to clear some space, and I clambered into the wagon at once. Yue followed more slowly, but then we were there, and Dryleaf clutched our hands, gripping us as if he wished never to let us go again. There was not enough room for her in the wagon, but Mag stood at the back, reaching in and holding Dryleaf's leg so that he would know she was there as well.

"We came as soon as we realized what had happened," I said softly. "I am so sorry we left."

"I was afraid you had fallen," said Dryleaf, holding tightly to my hand. "I thought they had killed you all before they came and attacked us. I could not tell where they had come from, not after I fell."

"We are fine," said Yue. "They fled from us and circled around to come after you, the cowards."

Dryleaf said nothing, but only kept weeping, holding on to both of us. Yue looked up at the lovers.

"We can take him now," she said. "Thank you."

"Yes, thank you from the bottom of all our hearts," I said. "Nothing we could do would ever repay you."

"We would never let harm befall him," said Nikau. "He is a treasure."

"He is that," I said.

Yue bent and scooped him up in her mighty arms. Careful as a mother holding her babe, she carried him out of the wagon, while Dryleaf clung to her. Mag moved woodenly out of the way. As Yue walked with Dryleaf to his tent, Mag stared at both of them, unmoving. With a final murmur of thanks, I left the lovers and went to her.

"Mag, this was not your fault," I said.

"Oh?" said Mag. "You told me that in Northwood, and I knew it was true then. I do not think it is true now."

"We could not know that Kaita had found a way to—"

"Of course we could have known," said Mag. "Or we could have guessed, or prepared for the worst. We thought—no, I will stop hiding behind that coward's lie—*I* thought she was mine for the taking. Like an animal I merely had to put down. I was so focused, so foolish, that I forgot she has a cunning mind and a will to match ours. I was the one who alerted the Shades to the fact that we knew where they were hiding. I led Kun's force away from the camp. Dark below, Albern, I was the one who brought Dryleaf on this fool's errand, when he clearly has no place amid a war."

A shiver passed through me. She had reminded me of something—a truth that now pressed itself upon me with an urgent, frantic need.

"Mag. We have to go."

Yue had set Dryleaf down while she tried to recover what she could of his possessions. Now she looked up at me. "Go? What do you mean, go?"

"I mean leave," I said. "We have to. We have no choice. Kun will blame us for this. And he will . . . he will be right to do so. But Mystic justice . . . I will not submit myself to that. Yue, I am so sorry."

Yue shook her head—not in defiance, but slowly, like a bear trying to clear the cobwebs of winter after waking in the spring. "But I . . . but the law. The King's law."

"Please, Yue," I begged. "Nothing you did tonight was evil enough to deserve what Kun will do to you. Please do not submit yourself to it."

"Let me stay," said Mag. "It was me. I pulled both of you along with me. I practically forced you to go. Let me stay. The three of you leave, and let me take the punishment."

"No, Mag," I snarled. "If you will use guilt to connive me into coming along on your schemes, then I will use guilt to force you to flee with me when they go awry. We promised, *until the end of the road.* You forced me into those caves on that promise. Now I will force you to flee because of it. If you stay, I stay. We run together, or not at all."

Mag's jaw set. But she would not consign Yue and me to death along with her, and I knew it. "Then get up," she said sharply to Yue. "And bring Dryleaf. The longer we wait, the more time we give Kun to recover and come looking for us."

Our horses, as well as Dryleaf's, were with the Guild wagon. Yue changed Dryleaf's bandage—I was relieved to see the bleeding had slowed—and then helped him to the wagon, where he said his good-byes. All the lovers gave him gentle words and soft touches of farewell, especially Nikau and Orla.

"Again, we thank you," said Mag. "You are eternally in the favor of the Uncut Lady, and if you ever require my help in any matter, it is yours."

"And there is something more mundane I must ask of you now," I told them. "Do you have any spare tents or bedrolls? We cannot fetch ours before we leave. We can pay you."

"We have no tents," said Nikau. "But there are plenty of bedrolls, and they are of good quality."

"Here is something for them, and for any other more immediate needs you might have," said Mag.

From her saddlebag, she pulled a fat purse, practically bursting with gold, and handed it over. I knew it was nearly everything she had left, but I held my tongue. This was a lighter penance than she wished to pay, I knew.

Nikau took it from her solemnly. "I feel you overestimate our deed. But thank you." He nodded to her and then to me. "I hope we have the good fortune to meet you again." Orla embraced us one by one, unable to summon words of her own.

Our good-byes said, we headed towards the south end of camp, walking and leading our horses by the reins. Only Dryleaf was mounted, hunched over his saddle horn, his shoulders drooping, and his head bowed.

"I feared I might find you here, but I hoped I would not."

My head snapped up. Mag, Yue, and I ground to a halt.

Tou stood there. Beside him were Dibu, Li, Chausiku, and Jian. The four of them looked shocked, as though they could not believe their own eyes. But Tou's face was one of snarling wrath, his eyes ready to kindle into a blaze.

"Lieutenant Shi," said Mag. Her voice was almost too steady, as if she was trying to summon her battle-trance but could not quite manage it.

"Turn yourselves around," said Tou. "Make for the north end of camp, where the captain's tent stands. When he has finished mourning his nephew, I know he will want to pass judgement on the three of you."

I closed my eyes. So Zhen had died. *Dark take everything,* I thought. *He deserved better.*

But Mag kept her gaze fixed on Tou. "You know we cannot do that, ser."

"You told me," said Tou, spitting the words. "You told me when you joined us that I would not regret your presence. And now you are *deserting?"*

His rage cut me to my heart. But that was not the worst of it. Far worse than Tou's anger were the expressions of Chausiku, of Li, of Dibu. They were like children watching negligent parents walk out the door, not able to understand that they intended never to return. I searched for something to say, any words I could summon that would make them see, make them understand why we had to go.

I could find none.

"Please, ser," said Mag. "Believe me when I say that I will regret my time here more than you can know, and not for my own sake. But I will not let you stop us from leaving."

Now Tou *did* spit. "Then do it. Make your move, you dark-damned traitor."

Mag stepped forwards. Tou unsheathed his blade. Dibu and Jian drew their swords a moment later, half-heartedly, torn. Li and Chausiku simply stood and stared.

As Tou advanced, Mag flipped her spear around and jammed the point into the ground. When Tou swung his blade at her, she ducked beneath it, darted up, and struck him under the chin with her fist.

A *crack* broke the air. Tou fell to the ground, senseless.

Everything was silent. Mag stared down at his fallen form. Dibu, Li, Jian, and Chausiku all watched her for a long, quiet moment. Finally, she looked up at them.

"Just step aside," she pleaded.

One by one, they looked at each other. It was Jian who spoke first, stepping forwards to stand over Tou.

"No," she said simply. "We cannot stop you from leaving, but I do not think we will give you the easy way out."

One by one, Mag knocked them out cold. They fell to land in the mud, some of it still red with the blood of those slain by the Shades.

I stepped forwards. I knelt and lifted each of them, sliding their cloaks beneath them so they would not wake up lying soaked and freezing in the mud. After a moment, Yue bent to help me.

Then we mounted our horses and rode south from the camp as fast as we could.

THIRTY-EIGHT

You can imagine what was going through my mind as we fled into the night, cold, miserable, and alone. After all, I told you of how I was exiled from Tokana when I was close to your age.

But it may interest you to know that this was not Mag's first time, either. She, too, had had to run from her friends after a fight she would rather have avoided. It is how she left Shuiniu, the town where she used to live before we met.

Several years had passed since her first scuffle with Ciaran. In that time, Mag had kept her head down and her fists still, happy to be a brewer under Duana. In truth, the fight with Ciaran meant little to her. It had been a petty dispute, and to her mind, it had been settled.

But Ciaran never forgot it. Nor did he ever forgive Mag for it. He was one of those petty, small-minded folk who hold tight to grudges, letting them fester and rot. He did not care if he had to wait years to get back at her if it meant he could be confident of victory in the end.

As part of his revenge, and because people like him always desire power, he sought to become mayor. He was good at manipulating those around him, and so he achieved it before too very long. It would be overstating things to say that anyone in Shuiniu really *wanted* to give him the position. But many folk, if they are somewhat simple or easily frightened, can lend their support to an utter scoundrel because he promises to solve the problems they think they have. Never mind that he always makes things worse instead—all that matters to him is that he gets there. And once planted, such villains can be very difficult to root out.

At first, his appointment seemed to have little effect on the town or Mag. Business was good for Duana, in both the brewery and the tavern, and it did not change much from year to year. But Duana had begun to get old. No longer could her aging body keep up with the pace of the work. She entertained the idea of letting Mag run the tavern, and even broached the subject once or twice, but Mag had little interest. She loved brewing more, as did Duana, and they both wanted to spend their time at their craft.

So when someone in the town offered to buy the tavern for a good price, Duana gratefully accepted. It seemed the perfect arrangement. She and Mag could brew in peace. And the security of their livelihood seemed assured. There was no one else in Shuiniu foolish enough to try competing with Duana's skill, and the tavern would always need ale. They would have more than enough custom to live on.

But almost as soon as the tavern had changed hands, the new owner stopped purchasing Duana's ale. Instead, they began to ship it in from more distant towns, and even some cities.

At first, Duana and Mag could not understand it. It cost far more to transport the ale such a long way. And yet the tavern's new master did not charge any more for his drinks than he had done in the past. It did not seem possible to continue the practice. Not even the cost of rooms and board would make up the difference. And when they tried to find out why the tavern master had stopped buying Duana's ale, they were met with sullen silence, if he would see them at all. Nor could they sell their ale to the townsfolk. Most people cannot afford to purchase kegs at a time, nor do they have the means to store them.

There were, of course, any number of things they could have done. If nothing else, Mag could have built a small bar beside the brewery, and I am sure the folk of Shuiniu would have come to drink at the new bar as they had from the old one.

But while they were trying to determine their course, the truth came out. The tavern's new master was in Ciaran's pocket. Ciaran had arranged the purchase, paying the greater part of the price. That gave him power over the tavern, and so he ordered it to stop purchasing Duana's ale. He also paid a subsidy to the tavern's owner to keep prices the same despite the cost of shipping ale in. Ciaran had spent his whole life hoarding whatever wealth he could, and he was good at it. This new scheme was no more trouble to him than remembering to get dressed in the morning.

Mag was furious when she heard the news, and she immediately went to confront Ciaran, without telling Duana. She accused him of undermining Duana for petty revenge.

Ciaran gave her an ugly grin. "This is simply good business," he insisted. "After all, the town elected me, in part, for my skill at earning coin. Certainly, I have acquired more of it than you and your master, and so the people trust me more in these matters than you. Can you not see that trade with the broader world is the only way to prosperity? If some in Shuiniu, such as yourselves, must fall by the wayside, well . . . that is the price that must be paid, for the good of the many."

"You give them piss and insist they be grateful," said Mag. "And if anyone gave your ledger half a glance, they would see that you are not even earning more coin for the town."

Her hands clenched to fists, which made Ciaran somewhat nervous. But his grin widened, and he spread his hands.

"Any cunning merchant knows that sometimes you must lose coin today to gain more tomorrow. After all, those who travel here to bring their ale bring coin with them, and they spend it in the town."

"At your smithy and the tavern you own, mostly," said Mag.

Ciaran licked his lips. "And why not? I pay the subsidy for the ale. I am risking the coin, and I should reap the benefit. I have to look after Shuiniu's best interests, even if it is harder on my coin in the short term."

Mag barely kept herself from striking him. "How does *this* serve the town's best interests?"

His eyes flashed, and his mouth twisted in an ugly sneer. "It seems unwise," he said slowly, "to continue purchasing anything from someone like Duana, who would employ a girl as violent as you."

Now, there are countless ways that Mag could have responded. She could have withdrawn, and together with Duana, made some other arrangement. If she had been thinking clearly, she would have seen that Ciaran was trying to goad her.

But Mag was not thinking clearly at all, not at that moment. In fact, as she described it to me, the world had turned a peculiar shade of red.

"Violent?" she snarled. "I will show you violence."

And she did. Her eyes went blank, and her expression dead. It was the battle-trance, and Ciaran recognized it, and his whole body quaked in fear.

She trounced Ciaran, right there in his home. She slammed his head on his desk, scattering parchments and missives he was in the middle of, and then she threw him into a bookshelf that fell over onto him. She dragged him out from under the mess, and then she drove her knee into his gut and struck him across the face, splitting his lip. Then she let him fall helpless at her feet.

Ciaran was stunned for a moment. But as he regained his senses, he gave her a savage grin from the ground, blood staining his teeth.

"How dismayed I am to learn I was right about you," he said. "Assaulting the mayor is a grave crime. I could have our constables take you away to jail you in a city. But I think I shall be merciful. I shall merely levy a fine upon you—and your master. It will be substantial, of course, commensurate with your wrongdoing. How I hope you and Duana will have the coin to pay it."

Mag's eyes went wide, and her hands went slack. What could she do now? She could hardly kill Ciaran. His actions might be base and treacherous, but they were hardly worthy of murder. He was not truly evil, like Kaita, but only an up-jumped snake who enjoyed power and dominance over others.

And in this moment, he had won.

Ciaran watched all these thoughts play across her expression, and his face grew crafty.

"Of course, such a fine could be hard to lay upon you," he said. "If you were to flee from Shuiniu forever, for example. I wager you could get away with it. It might take me time to summon a constable. And it would hardly serve the town to fine Duana if you were no longer here to share in the punishment. The tavern master might even see fit to purchase from her again if you were no longer in her employ."

The message could not have been more clear if he had written it into a contract. Mag was to leave and never return. All Ciaran wanted was for her to be gone. He had no grudge against Duana except through Mag. If Mag left, forever, then Shuiniu would return to business as usual.

At least for a time. For peace never lasts, with men like him. They are always hungry for another victim. Anyone weaker than they are, to give them a false feeling of strength.

But Mag did not know that, and she had little choice. So she took a step back from Ciaran, who was still on the floor, propped up on his elbows. He knew he had won, and slowly he levered himself to his feet. He wiped his bloody mouth on the back of his sleeve.

"You will never see me again," said Mag, her voice shaking. "At least not here. I do hope that we meet each other somewhere far away from Shuiniu. It will be my pleasure to teach you another lesson then, though you will be too stupid to learn it."

Ciaran spat. "Get out. Before I rescind my mercy."

Mag left, never giving a backward glance to Ciaran or his house. She took her time wandering through the streets of the town, for she knew this would be the last time she would see them. In too short a time, she found herself back in Duana's brewery. Duana was drinking a mug of her own brew, drawn from the last batch she had made before the purchase of the tavern.

She looked up, and she must have seen the dismay on Mag's face. Quickly she tried to stand from her stool, but she slowed halfway up, wincing at a pain in her leg.

"Mag?" she said. "What is wrong?"

"I . . . I have to go," said Mag.

Duana's face fell, even as her eyes filled with understanding. "You went to see Ciaran, you dark-damned—"

"Too late for chastisement," said Mag. She swiped at a sudden mist in her eyes, though she tried to make it look like she was only wiping sweat from her brow. "And too late to warn me not to do it. Ciaran has banished me. If I try to stay, he will levy a fine against us that we cannot hope to pay."

Duana slammed her mug on the table, sloshing some of the ale over the side. "Dark take it, Mag! You should have known better—"

"I know," said Mag. She said it quietly, but still, it cut Duana off as if she had shouted. And as she looked upon her master, Mag could no longer hold back the tears, and they poured steadily down her cheeks. But she managed to hold her voice steady. "I am sorry. I could have . . . I do not know, but we could have thought of . . . of something."

That was as much as she could safely say without breaking down, and so she stopped. And seeing her distress, Duana sighed. She went behind the table and poured another mug of ale, which she placed in Mag's hand. Mag drained it before Duana could sit back down, but she went to fill it on her own, and Duana settled into her chair.

"Well, never mind any of that," said Duana. "As you said, it is too late to chastise you or to urge another course. What is done is done. And . . . and in the end, this is likely for the best."

Mag's head whipped towards her, a hurt look on her face. "You . . . want me to go?"

"I do not want it," said Duana. "But what we want, and what is best, are not always the same thing. You know you are unusual, Mag. Everyone in town knows it. It is one reason Ciaran has always hated you—for he is petty and trivial, and so utterly unremarkable, and he sees the chasm of difference between the two of you."

"You are more skilled than I am," said Mag. "You cannot say I am remarkable when you can do this." She hefted her mug, which was already half gone.

"That is not what I mean, and you know it," said Duana. She turned her gaze east, and suddenly it was as if she saw across a great distance, through the walls of the brewery and into a far land beyond. "You and I both know you are not like most people. I saw it when first I found you in those woods, and I have seen it ever since you came to live with me. I saw it again when you trounced Ciaran the first time. Selfishness made me keep you here as long as I have. But I think you are meant for other things, Mag. Things far beyond the meaningless bounds of this unimportant town."

Again Mag's throat had grown thick, and words were hard to come by. "It was important to me."

"I know it," said Duana softly. She swiped at her eyes, as Mag had done before, and stood. "But we have both already said how looking back is worthless. Come. I will give you what I can spare. I only wish I still had the tavern, so that I could give you a horse."

They gathered Mag's things, such as they were, and soon she was ready. They shared one last mug—so far as Mag knew, she would never have another cup of Duana's ale again—and then they said their farewells. Mag never told me exactly what they said to each other then, but some things it is better not to know.

And when it was done, Mag set off into the wilderness of the Dorsean forest, alone and penniless. She did not know it was the start of a road that would lead her to me, and one day to Sten. But it would also take her to Northwood, and to that night in the Greenfrost when all hope seemed lost.

THIRTY-NINE

"I HATE THIS STORY," DECLARED SUN.

Albern arched an eyebrow at her. "Do you now?"

"I do," said Sun. "Most every story I ever heard of Mag was a happy tale, an adventure from which she emerged victorious. Yet now you are only telling me of what seem to be her very worst sorrows. And you are hammering me with them, as if they were nails and I were a stubborn plank, again and again. It is as though you want to be absolutely sure I understand how abjectly miserable she was."

"Well," said Albern, "what did you expect when you asked to hear how she died?"

Sun's eyes went wide. "Wait. Are you telling me that story now? When I asked you to tell me, you did not say you were going to do it!"

Albern snorted. "I did not say I would not, either."

Sun snatched handfuls of her hair, for she had a sudden urge to rip it all out. "But Albern, this is all wrong. This is not *anything* like how I heard Mag died. I thought it had to do with . . ." She swallowed through a dry throat. "With that other matter."

Maddeningly, Albern only shrugged. "And not for the first time, I must ask you, Sun: who do you believe? Skalds from your home, or the man who was there?"

Sun folded her arms in a huff. "And yet you will not even say it. Tell me the truth: is this the story of how Mag died?"

Albern stopped beside her in the street. He turned and looked her straight in the eye. Sun felt transfixed by him, by the sorrow she saw in his dark expression.

"Yes," he said. "This is how she died."

They stood there for a long, silent moment in the middle of the street. Passersby moved around them with muttered complaints. The lowering sun cast heavy lines of black shadow across Albern's eyes and cheeks, and his unmoving face bore down into Sun. She felt dumbstruck.

"But . . . so this is the end of the tale?"

"Were you not eager to hear it?" said Albern. "You wanted to get here. Why do you object now?"

"Because . . . because I . . . I do not know why!" said Sun. "But what kind of storyteller lets his listener know how the tale will end?"

"Sun," said Albern slowly, "you *know* Mag dies. You have always known that. One of the first things you ever asked me was how she died. So how can it ruin the tale for you, if you have always known that would be the ending? Any tale would end with the hero's death if talespinners did not cut themselves off at a happier moment of victory. And how many stories have you asked your family's skalds to tell you again and again, no matter how many times you had already heard them? Why did you want to hear those stories after the first time, if you already knew what would happen?"

"That is different," said Sun. But she said it quietly, and she was not sure she believed it. "I felt like . . . those stories had a point, or they seemed to. Whether they ended well or poorly, there was a reason for it all. But I can see no reason for Mag's suffering in the Greenfrost, no greater purpose served at all."

"Well, neither did we at the time," said Albern. "But you have struck on something there. Even in a tale's darkest moments, it is the storyteller's job to make the audience feel as though their time is not being wasted—that there might be some hope at the end of a weary road, or at least some semblance of satisfaction. I am sorry you feel otherwise now. But stay with me a little longer, and when I am done, then you can tell me if you are still disappointed."

Sun sighed. "That prospect holds little hope for me, either. This tale is why we started traveling together. If you finish the story, does that mean we are done?"

Albern's expression, which had been stern and craggy, softened at once. He clucked his tongue for his horse, and together they started walking down the street again. "No," he said. "No, of course not. I will not abandon you, Sun, not if you do not wish me to—and mayhap not even if you do, depending on the circumstance. And if it is any consolation, after this tale is done, I may have others, and you may wish to hear them. But because you have asked me so many times for the end of the story, I wanted you to find out—the way Mag needed to find out—that the end is not something we should rush. We should let it come in its own time. If we rush it, we may regret it."

He fell silent then, and they walked together for a short while without speaking. But even as Sun was pondering his words, a hand clapped down on her shoulder from behind.

"Mistress," came a rumbling, familiar voice. "The Lord and Lady Valgun command you to attend them at once."

Sun felt as though the whole world had fallen in on her in an instant, as if all the buildings along the street had collapsed on her head. She looked up into the face of Niall, one of her mother's bodyguards. He stood a good head taller than she was, and his dark eyes squinted heavily down at her from his nut-brown face.

Dimly, her mind took in other details. There was Ursa, Niall's right hand, and Frida, diminutive and quiet, but lightning fast in a fight. The women stood on the other side of Albern, one of them with a hand on his horse's reins. Albern himself stood stock-still, his gaze darting everywhere. Sun's mind raced in circles until she felt ready to faint.

"Mistress," repeated Niall.

Ursa had fixed a steely glare on Sun, while Frida's look was almost pleading. She was one of the kinder warriors in her parents' employ, but Sun knew she would not hesitate to bring Sun back home by force if that was what was required.

"I am fairly certain she does not wish to come with you," said Albern.

"You are not involved in this, old man," snapped Niall.

"I am feeling rather involved," said Albern.

And then he drove one heavy boot straight into Niall's groin.

Niall collapsed as though struck with a sledgehammer. Even as Frida reached for her weapon, Albern brought his hand into a vicious chop at her throat. She fell back, gasping and hacking, while Albern slammed the top of his head straight into Ursa's nose. Sun heard a *crunch,* and then Albern seized her, and she was following him down the nearest alley, both of them dragging their horses along.

"Sky above!" cried Sun. "Sky above, what have we done?"

"Strictly speaking, *you* have done nothing," said Albern. He was breathing heavily—his burst of motion seemed to have taken a toll. "Those three are used to getting their way. None of them expected resistance. But they will not be stunned long. Well, not the women, anyway." His hand fumbled in a pouch at his belt.

Risking a glance back, Sun could see he was right. Ursa and Frida had nearly struggled back to standing. Niall, on the other hand, still lay whimpering on the cobblestones, clutching between his legs. But then Sun and Albern darted around a corner, and the guards were out of view.

"We are leaving the horses," said Albern. "They should lure your family's guards away. I will send word to a friend to have them rounded up."

"But what are we—"

"Now, Sun."

She slapped Vika's flank. The horse whinnied loudly and ran down the alley to the street. Cries erupted from the crowd there. But Albern had stopped at a door leading into the back of a building. His left hand came out of the pouch at his belt, fingers gripping an iron key. In a flash, he unlocked the door and threw it open. He pulled Sun in after him and shut the door again.

They both waited in the darkness for a tense moment of silence.

The heavy pounding of boots came to the door. Sun's blood froze.

The boots continued down the alley, where the horses had fled. Soon all had faded to silence.

"Dark below," wheezed Albern. "That was a good run. Lucky we were already close to this place when they found us."

"Lucky indeed," said Sun. Her body seemed to be responding properly to her impulses again, but all she wanted to do was collapse. Instead, she looked around at the space they were in. It was a small room, with shelves running along the walls. Only a little bit of light leaked in under the door through which they had entered. Another door to their right led deeper into the building. "But what *is* this place?"

"The back room of an inn that has been unoccupied for some time," said Albern. "Come, let me show you the common room."

Sun frowned in confusion, but she followed him nevertheless. The door to the right opened into a space behind the tavern's bar. The bar was a large, impressive construction, all of black walnut with a fine grind and polish, but rough edges from the tree's natural growth. High rafters converged in the center of the room above them. A large brass chandelier hung from where the beams met, currently empty, but ready to hold dozens of candles. High windows let shafts of sunlight pierce the room and kept it well ventilated. It seemed a grand place for parties, but Albern had spoken the truth—no one looked to have been here in weeks, mayhap months.

"How did you know this place was here?" said Sun. "And how did you have the key?"

"Well, you will already have gathered that I have many friends in Bertram," said Albern. "This place belongs to one of them. They are planning to reopen it soon, and one of my errands in the city is to help them do so. Why, look at that—there is even a cask of ale here. Would you like a drink?"

"Sky above, *yes,*" said Sun.

She went to the bar, dusted off one of the stools, and sat, while Albern moved around to the back and went to the cask. It was a quarter cask, but that was more than enough to enjoy themselves, depending on how long they stayed here.

Albern tapped it and fetched two glasses from beneath the counter—they were free of dust, which told Sun someone had brought them recently. Soon the drinks were ready, and Albern handed Sun's to her.

"I hope that encounter proved to you one thing," he said. "Your worst fear has come true, but you have survived it. Your family found you. And yet you remain free. Let us drink to that."

Sun could not help a small smile. "Very well. To freedom."

They raised their glasses and drank. Sun took one swallow and lowered the cup, pulling a face. It was not the worst swill she had ever had, but it was undoubtedly the worst she had tasted since meeting Albern. The old man had a gift for finding the best cup of beer around, but this seemed to be an exception.

"Dark below," spat Sun. "With ale like this, it is no wonder this place closed down."

Albern barked a laugh. "A good point. This cask is a gift to celebrate the tavern's purchase, but mayhap it should not have been given. The best thing I can say about this ale is that it can get us drunk. And that is good, because the story is about to take a dark turn."

Sun stared at him. "*About* to take a dark turn?"

She had meant it as a joke, but Albern's expression grew mournful. "Darker, I suppose."

After Mag led Yue, Dryleaf, and me out of the hills, we went due south to lose ourselves in the Greenfrost. I took up the rear of our sad little procession, doing my best to hide our tracks from any pursuit. But privately, I doubted they would come after us. Kun would be enraged at the death of his nephew and dismayed at the gutting of his army. But he was a captain first and foremost. His highest priority now was getting the rest of his troops to safety before they starved to death. He might send a squadron after us at most, but I doubted we would earn even that mean of an honor.

And, I reflected sadly, he no longer had Zhen to send after us. I did not know anyone else who would be able to track me, if I did not want to be found.

The night was already half gone when we left. I pushed us to walk until dawn had begun to lighten the sky to the east. Then, at last, I stopped and had us set up camp, building a little fire. With daylight coming, we would not need to fear anyone spotting the glow through the trees.

We were now mayhap a league south of the road where we had first ambushed the Shades. The Greenfrost glimmered in the swelling daylight around us. But where I had once thought the trees looked like eminent sculptures all in emerald, now they were like stern tombstones in jade, bending over us and fixing us with silent stone eyes of judgement. I tried not to look at them.

We cleared snow from a spot on the ground near the fire, and there we set Dryleaf down to rest. We gave him every cushion we could summon, our softest saddlebags, and every extra cloak or blanket we had. He now looked like a prince lounging in a large bed of cushioned pillows. But his body and clothes were still grimy with travel, and fresh blood stained the bandages wrapped around his head.

Mag sat close beside him, never taking her eyes from him. Yue was off to the side, staring unblinking into the fire. I could imagine the torment in Mag's mind, but I could not begin to guess what Yue must be thinking.

Dryleaf stirred. His hand sought Mag, and when he found her, he squeezed her arm gently. "I am afraid I am rather slowing you down at this point."

"Never," said Mag. "If anyone harms our little troupe by being here, it is me."

"Enough, Mag," I snapped. "In a contest of guilt, there is no winner. We all . . . we all need to sleep. We have been on our feet for nearly two days straight. Let us rest. Then we can figure out what to do."

I thought she would argue with me. I expected her to. But she only looked even more defeated, and that frightened me more.

"Very well," she said softly. "I will take the first watch."

"Let me do it," I said. "It will let me inspect our surroundings and get the lay of the land, as well as make sure we have left no trail leading to us."

"Please, Albern," she said, still not looking at me. "I would not sleep, anyway. At this moment, I feel as though I will never be able to sleep again. Let me have a few hours alone to . . . to try to master my thoughts."

I blew a long breath out through my nose. It turned to mist at once, flying up around my head like a Dragon's breath. "Fine. But if you fail to wake me for my turn, I will not let you stand another watch for a week. Do you hear me?"

Mag nodded. "I hear you."

"Promise me, Mag."

She looked up at me. The firelight danced across her face, but I could see no reflection of it in her eyes.

"Do you not believe me, Albern?"

I tilted my head. "Of course I do, Mag. But I know how you—I know *something* of how you are feeling right now. I will not allow you to give up. Nor will I allow you to try and find more ways to punish yourself. Now, I am weary, and I want to sleep. Promise me, so that I can lay my head down without fear."

"I promise," said Mag. Small. Defeated.

Lying, as it turned out.

Another misty breath wreathed around my temples. "All right. Good night."

I pulled my bedroll off my pack. But before I laid it out, I went to Yue and put a hand on her shoulder. "Yue, I—"

She shoved my hand away. "Leave me alone."

I shook my head. "Yue . . ."

"Dark take you, Albern, you were wise enough to leave me be when I lost soldiers in battle. Be wise enough to get away from me now. I am not going to do anything stupid, if that is what you are afraid of. I just want to be alone."

I ground my teeth and turned from her to look at Dryleaf. He no longer held Mag's arm but had his hands tucked under his armpits for warmth beneath the blankets. Silent tears left slow tracks down his cheeks.

"Of course," I said softly.

I went to the other end of our little campsite and laid out my bedroll. Soon I was tucked inside it, huddling for warmth, my back to the fire and to my friends. Eventually, I heard Yue do the same, laying out a space to sleep and soon filling the clearing with little snores.

I fell asleep not long after that.

I woke up close to sundown.

And Mag was gone.

FORTY

MAG WAITED BY THE CAMPFIRE UNTIL THE REST OF US HAD FALLEN asleep. That was not long. Dryleaf's injury sent him back and forth between senselessness and an agitated dozing. Yue and I were bone-tired and soul-weary. Before long, Mag rose from her place by the fire.

A moment's trepidation held her. What if someone came upon our camp while she was gone? But I had told her Kun would not pursue us. And she believed me. She always believed in me.

Even if I could no longer believe in her.

Oku got to his feet and trotted to her, a low whine issuing from his throat.

"Kip, boy," said Mag.

Oku paused, one front paw hanging in the air.

Mag knelt, scratching him behind the ears. Then she pulled him into her arms, sinking her fingers into his fur, holding him close and relishing his warmth. Oku pushed his nose between her elbow and body, nuzzling into her.

"I am going," she said quietly. "You have to stay here, and you have to stay quiet. Do you understand?"

Oku drew back and looked up into her eyes.

"Of course you do," she said. "You are a good boy, are you not?"

He took two slow steps back, and then he sat. He did not move or make a sound as she strode away from our camp.

Before long, she had emerged from the northern end of the Greenfrost. As I have told you before, she was never good at tracking. But even she could see the signs of an army marching across the landscape. There was the trail, the deep furrow that Kun's force had left as it marched out of the woods and into the hills. She could even see, faintly in the distance, the smoke of campfires rising into the sky above the tops of the hills.

She sighed, set her course, and started walking towards them.

Far away, and yet not so far as all that, Rogan sat at a table in a tent, looking at a map of Dorsea. He was alone—or as alone as he ever was. His thoughts lingered on Kaita, and they left him despondent.

Suddenly he felt a presence. The flap of his tent flew back, and a figure strode into the tent.

Rogan looked up, and his heart nearly stopped as he recognized the Lord.

"Father?" he said, frowning. Something was . . . wrong, but his mind was slow to identify it.

Then the Lord came and placed a hand on his shoulder.

Rogan shot to his feet. *"Father!"* he cried, his voice shaking the tent canvas. "You . . . how are you here? You cannot be here! You—"

"Be at peace, my son," said the Lord. "I am here because I must be. Have faith."

"Of course, Father," said Rogan, bowing his head. "Forgive me, I . . . oh, Father."

He leaped forwards and wrapped his arms around the Lord, crushing the smaller man into his chest. And though Rogan, like all the shadeborn, was always as warm as if a furnace burned in his chest, he felt an even greater warmth seeping from the Lord, suffusing him, granting him a peace of mind and a comfort that he had long missed.

"It has been too long, my favored son," said the Lord quietly.

"It feels like forever and an age," said Rogan, withdrawing slightly. "Are you absolutely certain that this is safe?"

"As certain as I can be, and as safe as anything is," said the Lord. "Besides, it could not wait. Much has become clear to me. I finally know the reason, Rogan. I know why we had to send Kaita to her doom, though it was agony to us both."

Rogan's eyes shot wide. "Why, Father?"

"You will soon see. Fetch horses, but only for the two of us. We must move quickly."

As I woke from the day's sleep, I leaped up with a shout. "Where is Mag?"

My cries startled Yue awake. "What?" she grumbled, blinking against the fading sunlight.

"Mag!" I shouted. I should not have been yelling so loud, but I did not care. I ran around the edges of the camp, screaming into the Greenfrost. "Mag!"

Dryleaf had come awake. He tried to push himself up from the ground, but he could not do it until Yue came running to help him. His head swung back and forth, blind eyes blinking anxiously.

"Albern!" he called out. "What is it? What is happening?"

"Mag is gone," I growled, stomping back towards the camp. "Dark take her, I knew it, I *knew—*"

My attention caught on Oku. The hound was trotting back and forth towards the north end of the camp, sniffing the ground and whining.

"What is it?" I ran to him, and he pointed with his nose. The ground there had been swept clean—I had done it myself when we found the campsite, to ensure no one would follow us here. But now there was a fresh set of tracks. It set out from our camp, walking away north between the trunks of the trees.

"Dark-taken sow!" I roared. "How dare she? She . . . she—" I bit my own words off, unable to find words for my rage.

Yue had come to stand beside me, and though she was no better a tracker than Mag, even she could not miss the set of bootprints leading north through the mud.

"We have to go after her," she said.

I bit my tongue nearly hard enough to sever it. "We cannot," I growled at last. "Not both of us. Yue, I am so sorry. I do not deserve to ask anything of you. But please, someone must stay here with Dryleaf. I need you to keep him safe while I rescue Mag."

"Rescue her?" said Yue. "How do you mean to do that?"

"I think she has gone to Kun's camp," I said. "To turn herself in and face punishment for everything that has happened. I can . . . I should be able to . . ."

Yue's face had gone stony. "Be able to what, Albern?"

I shook my head slowly. "I do not know," I said. "Mayhap I can sneak in and . . . help her escape somehow."

"And what if she is guarded?" said Yue. "What will you do to any soldiers watching over her?"

I looked at her, aghast. "Yue. I would never harm them. If there is no way to get her out . . ." I swallowed hard. "Well. If I cannot get her out, then I will get caught trying. I promised her, Yue, that I would stay by her side until the end of the road. I cannot break my word. Not to Mag."

Yue studied me for a long moment. At last she said, quietly, "All right, then. If you promise you will not harm a servant of the King's law, then I will stay and watch Dryleaf."

"I promise."

Dryleaf was trying to rise to his feet. "Albern," he said, groaning the word. "You have to . . ."

The effort was too much for him, and he subsided, sinking back into the bed we had made for him. I ran to his side. "I am here, Dryleaf."

"You have to save her," said Dryleaf. "I have told you before. She needs you, far more than either of you think."

"I do not know if I believe that," I said. "But I will—"

"You *must* believe it," insisted Dryleaf. "You are not her lackey, Albern. Stop acting as if you are—for both your sakes."

I studied him. His expression was so focused that I felt he was staring right back at me. At last, I nodded.

"All right," I said quietly. "I will remember it. And I *will* save her."

One should never make a promise like that. I felt as if I were lying to his face. But I refused to leave him without hope.

I stood and turned to Yue. "Stay safe until I return."

"Just see to it that you *do* return," she growled.

For a moment, I hesitated. Then I nodded, turning to go.

"Oh, come here, you fool."

She seized me and pulled me in. It was not the most affectionate kiss we had shared, and certainly not the most passionate. But it was something, at least. I had feared that whatever had grown between us had died, after what had happened with Kun, and I would have understood.

"I will see you again," I said.

"You had better," she said.

I turned and ran north, following Mag's trail. Oku padded beside me, silent and true.

Tagata and Kaita were curled around each other in a bedroll, in a tent, a league to the west. Their boots, cloaks, and other clothes were scattered all around, as were three skins that had once contained wine. Parts of the bedroll were torn and ripped, letting in the cold air. But Kaita only had to press herself closer to Tagata's massive, bare form to banish the chill from her skin, and so she slept content.

Until Tagata stirred, pushed herself up on one elbow, and gently shook her shoulder.

"Hmm?" said Kaita. She looked up, blinking hard at Tagata's face. The shadeborn's hair stuck wildly out in all directions, much like Kaita's own. "Oh, again?"

She pulled Tagata down for a kiss. Tagata smiled and gave in for a moment, but then she pressed a hand to Kaita's cheek to stop her.

"No, dear one. I have received word from the Lord. Come. We must leave."

Kaita groaned. The wine had not quite worn off, but it was starting to, and it threatened a noticeable headache. "Now?" she complained. "Well, tell the troops to get ready and then come back to me. We can take a short while to ourselves, while they prepare to march."

"Not our kindred," said Tagata, chuckling. "Just us. You and me."

"Why?" murmured Kaita, pressing against Tagata's chest again. "What do the two of us—"

Her eyes shot wide. She jerked up, gawking at Tagata in the darkness.

"You cannot mean . . ."

Tagata smiled. "Get ready," she said, reaching for her vest. "And make sure you bring the magestones."

Soon they were dressed, and they emerged into the frigid cold together. Kaita followed Tagata to the east. And every few steps, her fingers stole into her cloak to probe the brown cloth packet.

I came sprinting out of the Greenfrost, Oku beside me. I could still see Mag's trail. It stood out fresh on top of the many other tracks from recent days. She was not making even the barest attempt to hide her passing. She had to know I would be able to follow her. Did she think I would not go into Kun's encampment? Did she believe me faithless, that I would abandon her to her fate, and not try to stop her, or to save her?

A chill struck me.

Did she think Kun would be so quick to execute her that I would not even have the chance? That when I failed to save her from her fate, I would be forced to turn tail and head back to Yue?

That was a darker thought than I wished to contemplate, and certainly a darker one than I wanted to imagine in Mag's mind.

I put on a fresh burst of speed, hardly even glancing at her trail anymore. It went straight north. That required no skill to follow. I knew where she was going, and I would go with her until the end, even if it were only to find her already—

I stopped.

Mag's tracks turned. They were no longer heading for Kun's camp, but had swung west.

My gaze followed, and I frowned, wondering what Mag could be looking for in that direction.

And then I saw another massive furrow in the muddy ground. One like the trail of Kun's army, but smaller, and heading west through the hills.

The tracks of the Shades. They had left it when they retreated, after destroying the supply train.

My eyes shot wide.

No.

Mag marched west.

She had known what she was looking for when she left the Greenfrost. She had known the Shades were to the west. And so she skirted the edge of Kun's encampment until she saw the signs of their retreat. She was no tracker, and she never had been. But she could read the signs of an army marching across the land.

She was following those signs still. There was determination in her step, but no speed. She was resolute, but she was not eager. This path was inevitable. It was always going to come to this, in the end. She had once deluded herself into thinking there was another way, but she knew now that that had been an impossible dream.

Like her life with Sten.

She swallowed past a sudden lump in her throat and rolled her shoulders. And she trudged on. She would not stop, not now. Not until she reached the end of the long road.

Alone.

She wondered, briefly, if I would ever forgive her.

Above her, a raven called in the darkening sky. Mag ignored it at first. If the bird sought carrion, it would soon have its fill.

Then she stopped.

It was late for ravens to be out.

The bird landed in the mud in front of her a span away. Magelight flashed in its eyes, and Kaita resumed her human form.

And then behind her, over the low hill west of their battleground, came another figure, this one lumbering. More than two heads taller than Kaita, and with a massive greatsword slung across her back. The brute woman.

Mag heaved a mighty breath, letting it out through her mouth to wreathe into mist around her.

She hefted her spear and swung her shield onto her arm.

FORTY-ONE

Kaita could not believe it. Here was Mag, at last. Alone, isolated from her friends. Kaita had kept her promise to Rogan, who received his instructions directly from the Lord himself.

The Lord had known. He had always known, all this time, how it would end. His foresight was perfect. And what was more, he really did love Kaita. Despite all her doubts, all her questioning, he saw her value, and he had granted her the boon she most desired. She would never doubt him again.

A savage grin spread across her face.

"The end of our road," she called out to Mag across the muddy field.

"And not soon enough," said Mag, her tone casual. "Are you going to turn into the cat, or the bear? Or have you grown tired of tricks? I will kill you like this if you want."

Behind Kaita, Tagata snarled at Mag's threats. But Kaita laughed and turned to her. "Dear one, there is no need to worry. Look at her. Alone, without anyone to rescue her."

"I am not the one who will need rescuing," called Mag.

Kaita ignored her, keeping her gaze on Tagata. "Stay here. You know I have our father's strength now."

"But I came here for you," said Tagata, scowling past her at Mag.

"And you *are* here for me," said Kaita. "That is what is important. You can be my witness. But let me do this on my own and help me celebrate when it is over."

Tagata's nostrils flared as she heaved a sigh. But then she nodded and took a step back. "Very well."

Kaita bowed her head towards Tagata. Then she turned back to Mag. Her hand stole beneath her cloak again, as it had done often on the journey here. But this time when it came out, a single magestone was clutched between her fingers.

Mag went very still. And Kaita saw it. This was not the indifference of the battle-trance, the certainty and neutrality that came with her fearless war mask. This was hesitation. Uncertainty. Kaita had never seen it in Mag's demeanor before, and it thrilled her beyond reckoning. For once, for the *first* time, she was the one in control, and Mag was not confident of the outcome of the fight.

A small, quiet pitter-patter of rain began to fall on them, strengthening by the moment.

Kaita stood straighter, spreading her hand at her side to catch as much of the setting sun's light as possible, even as clouds moved across the sky to obscure its dying glow. It warmed her skin, reminding her of Tagata as they pressed against each other in the tent.

Kaita smiled. And she slid the magestone between her lips.

It crunched between her teeth so sweetly, so gently. There was the slightest resistance, like a carrot that had been steamed to perfection. And then the black crystal melted on her tongue, sliding down her throat like sweet honey. It vanished there, in her center, her core, only to come surging back a moment later. Kaita could feel it coursing through her veins, filling her flesh and her skin and every part of her with pure, raw power.

Power. She thought she had known it before. She thought she knew strength in the burly frame of the bear. She thought she knew killing swiftness in the lightning paws of the mountain lion. But she had known nothing. She could feel it within her—every form she knew, every animal she had taken into her canon, now stronger, faster, more nimble.

But beneath it all, in her very essence, she could sense something new. A form she had never seen before, had never even imagined. Now it presented itself to her, offering up every detail, letting her see it in its entirety, the way a weremage must see a creature when they learn its form. Every part of it was now as familiar to her as the raven in which she had journeyed endless leagues.

This was power. This was safety—the strength to destroy any enemy who ever crossed her. No one could ever banish her again. No one could ever cast her aside for being useless, not with this form inside her.

It was everything she had ever wanted.

She let the form flow into her. And she began to change.

Her eyes turned black, and then they began to glow. A sickening darkness seeped out of them and consumed the fading sunlight. Her skin swelled. It flowed out like water and then hardened, turning rigid as glacial ice, and like ice, it was white and translucent. She fell forwards on all fours. Her shoulders and arms swelled like those of an ape of the northern jungles, but half again as tall and three times as heavy. Her face jutted forth, and huge fangs erupted from both top and bottom jaws. Where the skin formed into solid white armored plates, it also grew jagged spikes that erupted out all across her form. Between the blades, the surfaces were rough like tree bark made of razors, so that nothing could touch her without coming away bleeding.

Kaita gave herself one moment—only one. She closed her eyes, inhaled, and then exhaled again, tensing and flexing every muscle in her new body.

She could not believe it. To know that *this* was the strength of magestones. *This* was the power of the Wizard Kings of old. How had they ever lost it? How could anyone have taken this away from them?

No one could stop her now. She should have taken the stones weeks ago. She *could* have plunged straight into the center of the Mystic army. Who could have stopped her? No blade could pierce her hide. No one could live once she had set her sights on them and pronounced their death.

Her eyes snapped open, and they focused on Mag.

A moment ago, Mag had looked uncertain. That was gone. Her face was a deadpan mask again, the battle-trance with which Kaita was all too familiar. Kaita hated it, hated Mag for it.

The rainstorm above them had worsened, and now lightning

cracked in the sky. Thunder rocked the ground, sending waves through puddles of rainwater. And Kaita roared to meet it, and the sound was like every demon in the darkness below. She charged, and it was more terrible than the worst storms of winter.

Kaita's first swipe came faster than the lion, too fast for Mag to dodge. She raised her shield instead, hoping to roll with the blow as she would have with the bear. But it was too strong, and with a crash, she was flung back, sliding five paces through the mud.

For a moment, Kaita stood there, flexing her great clawed fingers, marveling at them. She had never been so fast, never so strong. Why would the Lord not grant this gift to all his wizard children? Underrealm would not stand for a month, not against even a handful of them.

Mag got to her feet. The mud clung too thick for the rain to wash it off. Still, her face was the impassive mask, not a muscle in it twitching.

But that was fine. Kaita did not need to see Mag's fear. She did not need her to scream or to weep.

It was enough to watch her die.

Kaita launched herself across the snow. Mag tried to dodge aside, but Kaita turned, quick as lightning. Her left rear limb struck out, a crushing blow that slammed into Mag's back and flung her facedown into the ground.

When she came up, her lip was split open. Rainwater mixed with the blood, sending it racing down her chin to splash into the mud.

Kaita's heart sang.

Again she lunged, and then again, each time swiping, snarling. Mag tried to avoid her blows, and sometimes she managed it. But Kaita was simply too fast now. She struck Mag once in the ribs, and something cracked. Her claws raked down Mag's spear arm, sending more bright blood to stain the churning ground.

Though it was Kaita's own claws doing the cutting, she almost could not believe it was working. Never in the past had she so much as nicked Mag's skin. From what she knew, no one ever had.

Mag backed off two paces. She was breathing hard now, though her mangled spear arm did not shake. Her lip still bled down her chin and onto her shirt, but her expression had not changed.

As Kaita stood there marveling at her success, Mag leaped. Her spear came up, and she jammed it straight into Kaita's neck.

It struck the chitinous armor. And there it stuck. Kaita could barely feel it—like a playful pinch from a lover.

She bared her dagger-long fangs, a snarl and a smile all at once.

Her claws raked Mag's body. The spear went spinning away. Mag's shirt of scales kept her from being gutted. But the claws punctured it in places. Blood soaked into her undershirt. And now her spear was behind Kaita, far out of reach.

Kaita stepped forwards, planting her claws in the ground on either side of Mag's head. Mag looked up into her ink-black eyes.

I was running through the snow in the fading afternoon light, Oku by my side. Ahead of us, I could hear the inhuman screams of some unknown creature. A new form of Kaita's, I guessed, though I could not imagine what sort of animal would make that sound. My lungs seemed to be screaming nearly as loud, but I ignored them. I had to keep going. Mag was in trouble, and she was alone. That mattered more than any pain.

She is alone. She is alone, and I promised.

And in a bitter corner of my mind, a voice snarled, *But she promised, too.*

And then I came over the top of a hill. I was just in time to see Kaita plunge pace-long claws straight through Mag's chest and into the ground.

FORTY-TWO

I STOOD THERE FOR AN ETERNAL MOMENT, UNABLE TO UNDERSTAND, unwilling to believe. The only sound was the rain slamming into the muddy ground all around us.

I almost ran forwards. Oku wavered, looking between Mag and me, waiting for the command to attack.

But those claws . . . Mag's blood . . .

Never had I seen a weremage in their hellskin form, but I recognized it from the tales I had heard. And if Kaita could do this to Mag, I stood no chance. I hated myself for it, but something kept me from flinging myself into certain, pointless death by Mag's side.

I threw myself behind a nearby boulder, where I waited, panting from my desperate run. Oku darted into hiding beside me. Gritting my teeth and squeezing the stitch forming in my side, I edged out around the boulder far enough to see.

Kaita had Mag pinned to the ground. Blood flowed out of her, turning the mud into a dark slush. I could see it was not her first wound. Her lip had split, and a deep slice ran down the length of her arm.

None of it made sense. It was impossible. In more than two decades, I had never seen anyone so much as break her skin. And now she . . .

She is dying, I thought.

I did not want to believe it, but it was true. Any fool could see it. And Mag had to know it. But still her face was impassive, expressionless. She had her shield on her arm, and so she reached up to slam it into Kaita's twisted face.

It was like striking a mountain. Kaita did not even flinch. Her left hand was still plunged deep through Mag's body. Now, with her right, she snatched the shield in her massive claws and crushed it. The wood shattered to kindling. Shards of it plunged into Mag's flesh. Kaita's claws constricted further, and I watched them sink through Mag's skin, into the muscle, threatening to cut the arm off. Mag's blood flowed into the mud like a river.

The whole time, Kaita never stopped looking straight into Mag's face. She snarled and growled with every new cut. But Mag remained stone-faced. She did not flinch as the raindrops fell right in her eyes, as another blast of lightning tore the sky in half above her.

With her left arm in Kaita's claws, only her right arm was free—the mangled, sliced arm that had been wounded before. But one hand had been enough for the bear or the lion. So she formed her fingers into a knife, and she jabbed it towards Kaita's eye.

Kaita was too quick. She twisted her neck, and Mag's fingers struck her cheek instead. The bones snapped like twigs. Kaita's spikes gouged Mag's palm.

Kaita grinned, though it was more of a hateful snarl.

She released Mag's shield arm. All her fingers curled into a fist except the forefinger, leaving one great, razor-sharp claw extended to a point.

Slowly, ever so slowly, she drove the claw through Mag's throat.

Mag's lifeblood bubbled out, gushing around the claw. Her shield arm fell to the ground, and then her spear arm. Her feet slid through the mud as her legs relaxed. But her eyes never left Kaita, even as the light inside them dimmed.

Forever.

Kaita waited a long moment, as if to be sure. Then she straightened. She looked as though she could not believe it was over.

I had almost forgotten myself as I lay hiding behind that boulder. It was as if I was not even there, as if I had become disembodied, floating over the scene like a moon in the sky, observing but unable to intervene.

But now I had a horrible thought. What if Kaita sensed me? Smelled me? Heard me?

Yet as moments kept stretching, nothing happened. If she had been the lion or even the bear, she might already know I was here, despite the rain. This creature, this hellskin form, seemed to be built entirely for strength, speed, and invulnerability. Its senses were not keen enough to detect me.

Kaita stepped back and resumed her human shape. She turned and walked away. And now I saw that the brute woman stood nearby. I had been so focused on Mag that I had not noticed her at first.

The two of them embraced. Kaita took one last look back at Mag's fallen form. And then finally, they both turned and strode off west, to where I knew the rest of the Shades would be waiting.

Steady tears poured down my face, and I could not restrain my deep, sobbing breaths, though I tried to keep them quiet. Oku kept whining softly. I held a steady hand on his head, my fingers deep in his sodden fur, though I could not tell you whether it was for my comfort or his.

Finally, slowly, I stood from my hiding place and went to Mag. She still stared upwards, right where Kaita's horrid face had been. Oku trotted around to her other side.

I fell to my knees in the mud. Rainwater poured over me, soaking through my clothes, but I did not care. I could not deny what had happened, but neither could I believe it, and I would not accept it. Mag was never supposed to die. Eternal, Chausiku had called her, and he was right. She was too strong, too incredible—larger than life and certainly too remarkable for death. She was never supposed to go.

Especially if it meant leaving me here on my own.

I reached down and brushed her hair out of her eyes, and then I closed them. I fell forwards onto my elbows, my forehead planted in the mud, and my tears spilled to freeze on the ground.

Oku whined and edged forwards. With his muzzle, he prodded at her broken fingers. When she did not move, he pushed harder, lifting her hand to rest on her lap, like he was trying to get her up. When she still did not move, he licked her hand, cleaning off some of the blood.

"No, boy," I said, choking on the words. "She is gone. Sky save us. I should never have taken her from Northwood. I wish I had never left Strapa. I wish I had never met—" I stopped, for I could not quite bring myself to say it.

And then Mag's body jerked.

She gasped, the sound of her breath wet and bubbling through punctured lungs. Her back arched until I thought her spine would snap. Her head barely touched the ground. Every limb jerked and spasmed, her hand striking me in the chest. I could only stare at her in horror.

"Aaahhh!" she screamed from her ruined throat.

"Mag!" I cried.

Dark below. I had been sure she was already dead. This was even worse. Now I would have to sit with her through her agonizing last moments, and I would have to watch. It was Sten all over again.

And then I saw her fingers.

With sickening, wet cracks and pops, they bent back into shape. I saw the bones sliding beneath the skin, muscles and tendons tensing, squeezing, twisting. In a few moments, the hand had returned to normal, though it was still covered in blood and cuts from Kaita's bladed skin.

Then her slashed arm began to seal itself together. Fresh blood poured from every wound, but slowly the flow was stanched as the skin rejoined, covering them over.

I hovered my hands over her, wanting to help but not knowing how. My wondering gaze went from wound to wound, the gaping holes in her chest, the slit in her throat. All of them were healing. Her sealing wounds pushed out the splintered wood from her shield. Then the gaps closed to hide the blood and flesh beneath.

Finally, the wounds were gone, leaving nothing so much as a scar.

Nothing so much as a scar.

And then, all at once, many things made sense for the first time.

FORTY-THREE

We were in the mountains of Tokana, and Mag and I had found our first troll. Dark take her, she had taunted it, accusing it of working with the Shades. The troll roared and slammed its hands into the earth before storming towards her.

"No chance of peace, then," said Mag. "I suspected as much."

"Mag!" I cried, but too late. She crouched and leaped towards the thing.

It struck her a backhanded blow and sent her flying over a nearby house.

She landed where I could not see her, among the debris of another destroyed home. Her spine snapped. Broken, jagged beams from the wrecked house pierced her side and her leg.

Mag gritted her teeth and stifled her scream as best she could. Her arms were useless, and her spear and shield fell to the ground. For a short while, she sat there, heaving agonized breaths through her teeth.

Then her spine cracked and popped, pushing itself back into place. Mag cried out as she felt her bones rearranging themselves inside her, her nerves reconnecting to flood her mind with agony.

She could use her arms again. She reached up and seized the jagged end of the wooden spar. As she pulled herself off it, she whimpered at the feeling of the twisted wood ripping through her insides.

The wounds were already sealing when she fell to the ground on all fours. Soon there was no hole in her side. The slices along her palms vanished.

Shaking, she got to her feet and inspected herself. Scooping up some dirt from the ground, she scrubbed at the fresh bloodstains until they were dry. Then she snatched up her weapon and shield and ran back towards me and the troll. By the time she found me, there were no signs of injury. And in my panic at the troll, I did not notice the new bloodstains in her clothes.

We were in the mountains near Opara. Shades had ambushed Mag, Tuhin, and me. Mag had gone running off with Oku beside her, hunting the Shades in the dips and crags of the land. She had killed three already, and they were starting to figure out she was among them.

A Shade heard her coming and drew. Mag rounded the corner, and his arrow took her in the eye.

Her body went limp in an instant, like a puppet with cut strings. Oku howled in rage and leaped at the man. The Shade dropped his bow and drew a long dagger, trying to fend Oku off. They danced around each other, neither managing to land a blow. Oku paced around the Shade, growling, while the man tried to find a chance to plunge his blade home.

Behind him, Mag's body shuddered. Slowly, she got back to her feet. She gritted her teeth as she seized the arrow and pulled it out.

Her eye was still healing when the Shade turned, too late, and saw her. His face filled with horror as she plunged her spear into his heart.

She fell to her knees, shaking her head in a futile attempt to clear it of the pain. Tears poured from her remaining eye at the horrific feeling of her brain repairing itself inside her skull, and then of the bone growing back into place. As her mind started to clear, she probed the Shade's body with shaking hands. Her fingers found a waterskin.

"Thank the sky," she muttered, voice wobbling. She poured the water over her face and head, washing away the blood as best she could.

By the time she returned to me, I thought the blood covering her had spilled from the Shades she had killed. But Oku trotted by her side, looking up at her and whining, and I did not understand why.

We were in Lan Shui, and Mag was alone, fighting two vampires in the burning house that had once been a Shade hideout. We had named one Shoulders. The other was the largest, so Mag had dubbed it King.

She kicked Shoulders over a chair. Flames caught along its skin, and it screeched in pain as the fire consumed it. She followed up with her spear, impaling it against the wall.

Shoulders lashed out in its death throes. Its clawed hands and feet raked across Mag's arm, her shoulders, her neck. But Mag, secure in her battle-trance, did not flinch. She watched its body wither and die, vanishing in flames like parchment.

King smelled the passage down into the basement with the mage-stone blood. He knocked her aside, breaking one of her arms in the process. Mag fell to the ground, impassive, silent.

And by the time Yue and I found her, her wounds had sealed themselves, and her arm had returned to normal.

"One left," she said, pointing to the basement door. And we followed her down without question.

Mag was in the woods outside Shuiniu. She was naked and alone. She could not speak, for she knew no words. And she was hunting dinner.

A deer stood in the forest, a half-span ahead of her. In her hands was a sharpened stick—a poor substitute for the spontoon she would one day own, but still deadly in her grip.

She stalked as close as she dared. When she could not draw any closer without the deer hearing her, she threw the spear. The instant it left her hand, she was already sprinting forwards.

The spear plunged into the deer's flank. The animal screamed, even as Mag leaped through the air towards it. Landing feet first, she bowled it over and seized the spear. She yanked it out, shoved it into the deer's neck, and held the buck down while its body jerked in its final spasms.

She had crouched down, ready to feast, when she heard a snarl. She whirled faster than blinking, but not quite fast enough. Her fingers sank into fur as she clutched the throat of a panther.

It knocked her to the ground as she had done to the deer. But Mag was prey to no creature. Her hands became knives. She could not reach its eyes, but she struck it under the legs and in the jugular. It yowled in pain.

But before she could drive it off, its jaws clamped down on her throat. It gave a vicious jerk of its head, and her neck broke with a sickening *snap*. Mag's body went limp.

The panther held her for a moment. Then it dropped her and padded over to the deer. For a moment, it sniffed, inspecting the corpse, before digging its fangs into the hide and beginning to eat.

Mag's body jerked.

Her neck snapped back together, and she gave a strangled cry of agony. She closed her eyes, deep breaths forcing themselves in and out, while the wounds in her neck slowly sealed over.

She rose.

The panther turned. It stared up at her, its amber eyes glinting in the sunlight that broke between the tree trunks.

It must have known this was a fight it could not win, for it turned and fled deep into the woods.

Mag heaved a sigh and returned to her deer. Once again, she crouched, ready to eat. But this time, she kept a wary ear out for any other creature approaching her.

And then she heard something. Footsteps, coming closer.

She went to investigate. And she stumbled upon Duana, out for a walk.

It was the battle of Northwood, and the beginning of my long, long journey by Mag's side, seeking revenge against Kaita.

Sten had died. Mag had attacked Kaita with all her fury, but the weremage had escaped. Now the two of us stood against a fresh wave of Shades. But the people of Northwood had rallied around us, and there was a pitched battle in the streets.

I saw Mag surrounded by her enemies. I saw her kill, but I also saw them cut and pierce her with their blades.

A club struck me unconscious. And Mag saw me fall.

No, she thought, in the part of her mind behind the battle-trance. *Not Albern. Not him, too.*

She shoved through the crowd and scooped me up. Holding me under one arm, she carried me through the battle and to safety. Behind a building that hid us both from sight, she set me down and felt for a heartbeat.

It was there, and it was strong, thank the sky. Her battle-trance fell away, and she breathed a sigh of relief. But it turned to a hiss of pain as her wounds started to seal themselves.

When she was whole, she picked me up again. The battle was starting to wind down. She found Elsie and placed me in her charge, to be healed on the floor of the tavern's common room. When I awoke and saw her, I stared at her in wonder.

"Before I went down," I said, "I saw you surrounded. I thought I saw you wounded."

(I *had* seen her wounded.)

She stepped forwards and held out her arms. "They *did* surround me. I fought my way free. Do you see any wounds?"

(At least she did not lie to me. Not then, anyway.)

I did not see any wounds, and so I sighed. "You are frightening sometimes, Mag."

"Only sometimes?"

She smiled, and it hid every bit as much sadness as the mask of her battle-trance.

She was the Uncut Lady still. So far as any of us knew.

Sun stared blankly at Albern across the bar. Surreptitiously, she glanced down at her mug. How much of it had she had? Was this her second drink, or third? Was the ale the reason the old man had ceased to make any sense?

"What exactly are you saying?"

Albern's mouth twisted. And though he had revealed the tale's great secret to her, there was no joy in his expression, none of the restrained smile of a skald who enjoys the reaction of his audience. There was only a profound mournfulness.

"I am saying what you think I am saying, but you are reluctant to hear it. Do you begin to understand now, Sun? That was the moment I learned a lesson I have been trying to impart to you all this time—not just today, but since we met in that tavern.

"Mag's story, the legend that surrounded her, the impossibly grand tale of the Uncut Lady . . . it was never something we were meant to *believe.* It was a good story. It bolstered the spirits of all who knew her, and especially those who fought beside her. It made our lives grander to hear it, even if we doubted it was true. Because deep in our hearts, we knew it could not have been. And as you will see, the story itself was a protection of sorts. It hid a truth Mag did not wish to reveal."

Sun felt lost in wonder. There were a thousand things she wanted to ask, but all her questions seemed limp and useless in the face of this knowledge.

She was surprised to find that she believed him without question. Often before this, she had doubted Albern's tale, even though most of it seemed possible. This new revelation seemed entirely impossible, and yet she did not doubt it for an instant.

"Mag was never the person I thought she was," Albern went on. "In some ways, she was less than the legends, and in other ways, she was more. Yes, she was an incredible fighter, but not as great as the stories made her out to be. She *had* suffered wounds. She had even died before. Many times. But she always came back. And with every death, she learned, and she became faster, and stronger, and even better in the next fight."

"But . . . but *how?*" said Sun, finding her voice at last. "How is it possible? Where did she gain such power? And why?"

Albern fixed her with a look. "I know the answers to those questions. But I am not yet ready to give them. Can you accept that?"

Sun met his gaze for a long, silent moment.

"Yes."

"Good," said Albern. He sighed. "Then for now, let us return to that cold night in the rain."

FORTY-FOUR

"Mag?"

I could only stare at her in wonder. I had no idea what under the sky was going on. Mag's screams had subsided, but she still whimpered and groaned through clenched teeth. Her wounds were still stitching up, her body snapping itself back into shape. She was in agony. And what could I do about it? I could not even touch her without provoking a fresh cry of pain.

Her eyes focused for a moment, and then they found me. But she quickly turned away. "What are you doing here?" she gasped. The words were horribly mangled and garbled—her throat was not yet fully healed.

"What in the dark below do you mean?" I demanded. "I came after you, you absolute fool. What were you thinking, coming out here alone?"

"Why would I ask you to come?" she said. "Look at me. You would only have died."

"And you *should* be dead," I said. "Mag, what is—"

A horrible realization struck me. I seized Mag's shoulder and hauled her over to lie on her stomach. She tried to resist, tried to grip my wrist and render me helpless, as she had countless times before. But beneath her sealing skin, her muscles were still horribly mutilated, and she had no more strength than a toddler.

Once she was lying facedown, I seized her hair and shoved it up, pulling it side to side. I inspected the back of her neck, and then, when I found nothing, I tried higher up on the scalp.

"There is nothing," said Mag through gritted teeth. The muddy ground muffled her words. "Nothing, Albern, I swear."

I ignored her and looked carefully for myself. But she was right. There was nothing. I rolled her back over, and she glared at me as she came to rest on her back again.

"This magic," I said. "It is the enchantment of the Shades' master. How did you come by it? How long have you had it?"

"I do not know," she said, still clearly in pain, her teeth gritted.

"Do not lie to me, Mag!"

"I do not know, Albern!" she pleaded. "I have been . . . like this, since I could remember."

"But . . . but why?" I said. "How did it start?"

"I do not know," she said. "I have some . . . some vague, hazy memory of the middle of the woods, near that town called Shuiniu—the one I told you about, that was not far from Taitou. There I lived alone for many years, hunting for food in the forest. It was a long time before I met other people. I did not know how to speak when they found me. I only knew my name, and how to kill."

Another chill went through me. "Mag. How long ago was that?"

She took a deep breath and met my gaze. "Twenty years before we met."

Slowly I shook my head. "That is impossible. You were only twenty years old when we met, or around that age. Do not try to tell me you came out of the woods as an infant, already knowing how to fight."

"No, Albern," she said quietly. "I am telling you I came out of the woods like this. *Exactly* as I am now. In every way."

I suddenly felt dizzy, and I sank back onto my rear in the mud.

Chausiku had seen it. He had told me, but I had laughed him off. He said she was far younger than I was, and I told him she aged well.

She did not age well. She did not age at all. She looked exactly the same now as she had when we met. But for years, I had kept telling myself that was not true, because it could not be. I told myself I saw subtle differences, things only I could see because I knew her so well. But that was a lie, something to let my mind feel secure in the face of the inexplicable.

I had thought Chausiku could not see the truth because he was too removed. In fact, I could not see it because I was too close.

Mag had not aged since long before we had met. And in all the battles we had fought in our youth, and then in Northwood, and on the long road since . . .

It was not that Mag could not be touched. It was that she always came back. And she hid it from me. From everyone.

"You kept it a secret," I said. "Every time I thought I saw you injured, and you turned out to be fine. I was right. You *were* wounded, many times. But you healed, and I ascribed it to the chaos of battle. I told myself I had seen something that had not happened."

"Yes," she said. "Yes, you have the right of it." Mag's body was mostly together now. She pushed herself up to sitting, dangling her arms over her knees. She was avoiding my gaze again. The rain had died out somewhat, and now it merely trickled onto us.

I could not help a snort of laughter. "No wonder you always hated my nickname. You were never the Uncut Lady at all."

She shook her head. "No. I was not. Just a lonely wanderer with a curse, and no memory of how it came to me."

"And you are *sure* it has nothing to do with the Lord?" I pressed. "I told you of Trisken in the mountains. And you have seen the brute woman here. The way their bodies heal themselves, no matter the wound . . ."

"It is *not* the same," said Mag, her voice low but fervent. "You said nothing of Trisken's pain when you told me of his power. And I have seen the brute woman suffer wounds. When she shrugs them off, her body is not wracked with agony. And then there is that tattoo they have—sky above, Albern, you have seen me naked often enough to know I do not have one, not on my neck or anywhere else. This enchantment their Lord has given them, and what happens to me . . . they may be similar in effect, but they are nothing alike in nature."

"Mayhap," I said thoughtfully. "And yet there may be a link. But that is a matter for another time, I suppose."

"If you say so," said Mag. She sounded as defeated as she had that morning, when we sat despondent by the fire together. Oku nuzzled her hands with his head, as he had when she lay broken in the mud. Mag scratched him halfheartedly behind the ears.

I reached out and put a hand on her shoulder, shaking my head. "So, this is why you ran off on your own," I said. "This is why you *always* go off on your own, no matter the danger. You know you will not die."

"Yes," whispered Mag. "And if I was injured, I did not want you to see it. I have worked hard to keep everyone from discovering what I am, because I do not understand it myself."

I leaned back, looking up into the greying sky. The sun was gone in the west, and its last light was quickly vanishing. "I suppose that makes sense."

Her gaze flitted to me, and then away again. "You are likely angry with me."

I thought about that. "Did Sten know?"

Mag nodded. "And one other. My old master, Duana, who taught me brewing in Shuiniu. I . . . I am sorry, Albern. I have known you longer than I knew either of them. It is no defense, but I promise I did not mean to tell them. They found out."

At that, I finally had to laugh out loud. The look of shock it put on her face was priceless. "Mag, stop it. Dark below, you do not have to apologize to me that your *husband* knew more about you than I did."

Her eyes were wide now, and she blinked twice at me. "I . . . I suppose I am surprised that you are not more upset with me."

"I . . ." My voice trailed off. To be honest, I did not entirely understand it myself. "Mag, it is your life. It is not mine. But I do wonder—and please believe that this is only curiosity—why did you *not* tell me? What were you afraid of?"

She shrugged. "I am not exactly sure. But it . . . when does one bring up something like this? Certainly not when we first met."

"And how about all the time after, when we were fighting together?" I smiled to reassure her I was not angry. "It would have been nice not to be terrified every time you ran off and did something foolish."

To my surprise, Mag shook her head sharply. "No. Never that. I never wanted it to be known to anyone I fought beside. Even you. I never wanted it to become an expectation in anyone else's mind. Would you put it past some of our commanders to fling me into the thickest fighting, if they did not have to worry about me dying? You have seen what coming back does to me. Every injury is twice as painful. I suffer all the agony of the wound itself, and then the pain of my body putting itself back together." A frown crossed her face. "I think . . . I am not certain, but I think that is why I learned to fight so well. So that I could protect myself from suffering in battle."

I frowned. "You *think* that is why you learned?"

Her expression grew bleak. "I do not remember learning it, Albern. I mean it when I say that I have always been this way. Everything before that forest in Shuiniu is . . . empty. There is nothing. I told you yesterday that I wanted an after. Mayhap that is because I have never had a before."

I leaned back on my hands, staring at her. "Mag. You damn fool. I am sorry I found out this way."

Mag's eyes locked on mine. "You what?"

"You never meant to tell me," I said. "You should not have had to tell me if you did not wish to. I should have found out on your terms, or not at all."

"*That* is what upsets you?" said Mag. "Albern, that would never have happened. I did not want you to know. And it was never something I had to worry about when I was in Northwood and you were in Strapa. But ever since we set out on this long road together, I have been terrified you would discover the secret and be hurt that I had not told you decades ago."

I waved a hand vaguely. "You are speaking to the wrong person for that, Mag. I had no *right* to any of your secrets, least of all this. But still—why come out here alone? Did you think you could succeed against Kaita by yourself when we have failed together every time?"

She sighed, licking her lips. "I had to try. I thought that, if I had only gone alone, when we went to that Shade encampment in the cave, I could have ended her. I could have plunged into the thick of them, and who cared if I raised the alarm? They could not have killed me. So that is what I was going to try to do. And that is what I must try to do again." She started to push herself up. "Now that I know of her hellskin form, I can act quickly enough to—"

"Whoa now," I said, pushing her back down. I could never have done it if she were at full strength, but she was still weak from the healing. "You sit down, and you shush."

Mag's brows arched, and for a moment, she looked like her old self again. "Excuse me?"

"I will not." I thrust a finger at her. "You now find yourself in the same situation as everyone you have ever fought: you are facing a foe that you cannot hope to defeat in a fair fight. Instead you must be sneaky, as well as cunning. Now, to your detriment, you are terrible at both those things because they are skills you have never had to acquire. But fortunately for you, cunning is one thing I have in great abundance."

I looked off to the west, where Kaita and the brute woman had gone. Oku's ears perked up as he looked at me.

"Here is what we are going to do."

FORTY-FIVE

When Kaita and Tagata reached the Shade camp, Kaita returned to her tent. But it felt far too small to contain her. She emerged back into the open air and began to pace around a nearby campfire.

Her body felt weary, as if it had been somehow drained. She guessed it was from the effort of taking the hellskin form. She had never experienced this with any creature in her canon before, but of course, she had never commanded such immense power. Mayhap it taxed her body in some way with which she was not yet familiar.

But despite her underlying exhaustion, Kaita was also nearly bouncing with subdued energy. Her limbs would not stop moving, and any time she focused on her fingers, she found them drumming against her palms. Her eyes darted in all directions, seeking, searching, but she did not know for what.

Was this a heightened emotional state after finally killing Mag? It was possible. Or mayhap it was some aftereffect of the magestone. If so, it was far preferable to the weariness. But the two feelings combined made her feel an overwhelming desire to keep moving, while at the same time it seemed her body might give out at any moment.

Tagata had been watching her carefully ever since they had returned to the Shade camp. Kaita noticed it, and it did not entirely please her. But she tried to give a reassuring smile, and Tagata returned it.

"You did it," said Tagata quietly.

"I did," said Kaita. "I never need fear her again."

"Well done," said Tagata. "And now it would be good for you to rest. You are not used to the effects of the stones. You will feel better in the morning."

"I do not feel as if I *can* rest," said Kaita. She strode to Tagata, her gaze swinging back and forth, still seeking—seeking what? "I feel as though I can hardly stop moving. But that is fine. I can rest later, when we reach the Greatrocks." A smile twitched its way across her lips, and there it rested, quivering. She ran her fingers along the edges of Tagata's vest, tracing the lines of it. "Mayhap instead of resting, we should celebrate."

Tagata's smile dampened. "Not just now," she said. "But if you promise me you will sleep, I will happily accommodate you on the morrow."

Anger flared in Kaita's gut. She very nearly snarled before she could contain herself. Her hands leaped away from Tagata like she had been burned, and she turned to hide her ugly expression. Her sleeve rose to scrub at her forehead.

It was fine. Tagata did not understand what Kaita was feeling. How could she? And of course, if she did not wish to join Kaita in her bedroll, she did not have to.

And yet, why would she not want to? thought Kaita. *Why does she keep looking at me that way?*

She put a hand to her forehead. The weariness had begun to overpower the restlessness, weakening her limbs. It was a far cry from how she had felt when she ate the magestone.

The magestone. The rest of them were still in her cloak pocket. Mayhap another one would strengthen her. Before she could even decide to, her fingers began to steal towards them.

"Kaita."

She froze. Tagata was looking down at her, smile replaced with a stern scowl.

"What?" said Kaita, feeling her mood darken.

"You do not need another stone," said Tagata. "It will make things worse, not better."

Another flare of anger burned through Kaita's chest. "And what do you know about it?" she snapped. "You are no mage."

"Kaita," said Tagata again, and her voice was calm, "Rogan warned you of this, as he warned you not to go running after Mag on your own. The stones prey on your mind. You must remain aware of that, and you must resist them. Otherwise, you will be a danger to our kindred, not an asset."

A danger? Oh, yes, Kaita could be a danger. Her breath came faster, the fury rose in her mind until she could hear her heartbeat in her ears, and her hands clenched to—

No.

Kaita forced herself to be still. She took a long, slow breath, counting to ten, and then holding it for a moment before releasing it slowly.

Everything Tagata was saying was right. Kaita had known it since she was a child in the Academy, listening to fellow students whisper rumors. And Rogan *had* told her all this. And she had promised him, and through him, the Lord.

She would not prove too weak to keep her word. She could resist the stones.

"I am sorry," she said. She walked forwards and looked up into Tagata's face. When Tagata smiled at her, she laid her head against the woman's mighty chest. Tree-trunk arms enveloped her, and she lost herself in a deep sigh within them. "I have never felt this before. But the stones are not stronger than me. I will not succumb to their urges, and I will not disappoint you."

"I do not think you could ever do that," murmured Tagata. "Do you want me to hold them for you?"

Kaita's pulse quickened, and her breath came faster. "No," she said quickly. "At least . . . I do not want to give them to you. But when . . . when I fall asleep . . . would you take them from my pocket?"

"Of course, dear little one," said Tagata. "Now, let us get you in a bedroll. And no," she said with a smile, in response to Kaita's playfully raised eyebrow, "that does not mean anything more than it means."

"Fine," said Kaita with a snort. And for that brief moment, she felt almost like her old self again.

But then horns sounded at the camp's eastern end.

Both of them turned and froze, waiting for some further sign. But they could see nothing, and no sound came. The sun had long since vanished, and the moons were not quite high enough to illuminate anything.

"Come," rumbled Tagata. Together they ran for the eastern end of the camp.

They found a group of Shades already there, and more were gathering. But they were clustered behind tents, and they were all looking off to the east. Tagata and Kaita approached them at a low crouch, stooped to hide behind the tents.

"What is it?" said Tagata in a low voice. "The Mystics?"

"No redcloaks that I have seen," said a sergeant. "But mayhap one of their agents. Someone killed two of our sentries before he was spotted by a third. A man in a brown cloak."

Kaita's blood froze. She stood up in plain view, ignoring Tagata's panicked look.

There.

On a hill not far away, the twin moons silhouetted a figure. A bow was in his hand, and his brown cloak fluttered in the gentle night breeze. It was me, of course.

But the moment she saw me, I turned and vanished into the darkness.

"It is him!" she cried. She darted out from behind the tent, running east.

"Kaita!" cried Tagata. "Wait!"

"He is alone!" called Kaita over her shoulder. "I have kept my promise, Tagata. I will finish him off, and then I will return to you." She stopped for an instant, turning to meet Tagata's gaze. "I swear it, my love."

She turned and vanished into the same night that had taken me.

Tagata watched her go, feeling impotent and helpless despite all her vaunted strength. Almost she tried to run after Kaita, to keep her safe. But she looked around at her kindred, all of them looking confused, even frightened in the darkness. And she stayed put.

Mag was dead, after all. Any half-decent weremage should be more than a match for a normal man like me. And Tagata knew that Kaita was far more than half-decent, even before she had the magestones in her blood.

She sighed and kept her gaze on the shadows where Kaita had vanished. *Sky watch you, my love. Until life ends.*

FORTY-SIX

THE MOMENT KAITA LEFT THE SHADE CAMP, SHE TOOK HER HELLSKIN form. Her body swelled into the enormous white creature, and every thundering step drove her spikes and blades into the dirt. It left a trail across the land like a great plow pulled by a Dragon.

But soon she realized that hers were the only tracks. She had run in the direction she had seen me flee, but soon she reached hard, rocky ground. She had no footprints to follow. And the hellskin form had poor senses compared to the lion, or even the bear, and so she had no scent to go by.

She paused, looking back over her shoulder. But Tagata had remained with the rest of the Shades.

That is fine, Kaita told herself. *I did not even need her help to kill Mag. I will not need her to end Albern.*

Her gaze drifted upwards into the sky, where the moons rose ever higher. It was a clear night, perfect for flying. From the air, she would be able to see me more easily.

She hesitated a long moment, looking around to make sure I was not lurking nearby. When she felt she was safe, her eyes glowed black, and her body shrank, resuming her human form. For a heart-stopping moment, she stood there in the night, feeling exposed, before her eyes flashed black again, and she took the raven form. In a few moments, she launched into the air.

Now he will be simple to find, she thought.

But to her surprise, she still had trouble. I had, after all, been trained as a ranger, even if I had never officially become one. And in the long years since we both lived in Tokana, I had kept my skills sharper than Kaita had kept hers. Only here and there could she glimpse a few shallow footprints in the moonslight. Beside the tracks of my boots, there were the clear tracks of a dog. She had seen Oku often enough to recognize the sign of him. But the trail always vanished into rocks again. Kaita was forced to circle and wheel aimlessly until she stumbled upon a fresh set of tracks. Always she had to be aware of her height and avoid swooping too low where I could get a good shot.

He thinks to lure me into a simpleton's trap, she thought savagely. *He must think me an even greater fool than Mag was.*

But Kaita was drawing closer to the Mystic camp now. That put a quiver of fear into her heart. Was I planning on retreating to them? She could not follow me there.

But she *could.* Who cared how many of them there were? In her hellskin form, no blade could—

No.

It took a monumental effort to marshal her thoughts, but she did it. She had promised Rogan. And she believed in the Lord. If he had not wanted Kaita to plunge into the midst of her foes, there was a reason. She had said she would never doubt him again, and she meant it.

And then she caught a flash of brown cloth. There I was, still several spans away from the Mystic camp. And I was not running east towards them, but south, towards a familiar cluster of boulders set against the base of a hill. It was the tunnel entrance. The Shades had come out this way when they attacked the Mystic camp. As Kaita flapped her wings hard, powering towards me, Oku and I descended into the shadows beneath the hill.

Kaita laughed in her mind as I clambered over the boulders and disappeared into the earth. *If he thinks a cave will save him, he is a fool,* she thought. Best of all, I was still alone, save for my hound. She could hunt me down without breaking her word.

She landed atop the hill and shifted into hellskin form as quickly as she could. With a few lumbering steps, she dropped into the darkness of the tunnel beneath the earth.

Immediately she was faced with a new problem. With the hellskin form's limited senses, she could neither see me nor follow my scent.

But she was invulnerable. Who cared about seeing? It mattered little if she stumbled into the walls—they could do nothing to her iron-hard skin.

So she stumbled blindly down the tunnel, lumbering into the stone walls every few steps. It was irritating, but hardly debilitating. Things became slightly worse as the tunnel began to swing more sharply left and right so that she sometimes crashed face-first into the stone. It did not exactly hurt, but it was disorienting, and she had to take a moment to get her bearings. She growled each time, and each time the sound grew a little deeper, a little crueler.

Albern must have brought a torch, she thought, wishing she had had the presence of mind to do the same.

Suddenly her foot came down on empty air. She was at the top of the stone wall she had climbed during her escape from the tunnels. For a heartbeat, she teetered, trying to recover. But in the end, she plummeted five paces and slammed into the stone floor. This time it *did* hurt, her weight sending a crushing lance of pain through her shoulder.

A frustrated, growling roar burst out of her. And to her surprise, there were words in the sound.

"Dark take you, Albern!" she thundered. "Stand and face me!"

For a moment she lay there, blinking. So, the hellskin form could speak. It was the only beast in her canon that could, other than the troll.

Slowly she clambered to her feet. "Where are you, little ranger?" she growled. "But then, I suppose you never really became a ranger. Not like Romil and me. Not like Ditra." She bared her fangs in the inky black and began to stalk forwards again. "Ah, Ditra. You know, do you not, that she is doomed? Now nothing can stop me from ending her. She will die screaming on my claws, and then I will have your niece as well."

Still the tunnel ahead remained silent. Kaita growled, and the sound of it shook the stone beneath her clawed feet.

"Come, Albern!" she roared. "Have we both not waited enough? Let the long road come to an end. Mag did. She was happy to see it done, finally."

No reply came floating out of the shadows.

Kaita considered her options. She *could* take the mountain lion form. It would let her see in the darkness far better than I could.

Of course, the lion was more vulnerable. But vulnerable to what? To me? Surely not. The hellskin form was for Mag. The lion would be more than enough to deal with me.

Again she felt a moment's trepidation as her form shifted to human, and she braced herself for an arrow to come flying from the dark. But nothing came. And as the lion form took her, the tunnel became visible—still dim, but at least she would not go running into walls. And she could smell. My scent was there, and so was Oku's. And there were lingering whiffs of others—all the Shades who had come this way during their escape, and then Kun's small army that had followed them. Kaita could even faintly detect Tagata's scent, and her stomach fluttered.

She forced herself to focus as she proceeded down the tunnel, moving at a quick trot now. This felt much more comfortable. As powerful as the hellskin form was, it was still too new for her to feel fully in command of it. And with the magestones in her blood, even the lion was stronger, faster, more deadly than it had been before.

My scent told her I was some way off. And as she had guessed, I had a torch. She could even see the faintest reflections of its light far down the tunnel. And yet there was something . . . strange about the torch. An acrid scent drifted towards her, borne by the faint breeze that seemed always to fill this space. Her nose twitched, and then she loosed a tremendous sneeze.

She recognized the smell at last. It was burning pycnandra from the Greenfrost. It stung the nose and eyes, and with the lion's sense of smell, Kaita was particularly sensitive to it. She sneezed again.

But in her mind, she laughed. *Is this the best he can do?* she thought. *What a fool. I shall rip him limb from limb, and I shall take my time with it.*

She pressed on a little faster now. Every so often, she had to sneeze again. The burning masked my scent, but that did not matter. The pycnandra torch was like a glowing beacon in the darkness, and it drew her straight towards me.

Finally, she reached the entrance to the vast cavern where the Shades had made their camp. She stopped. In the center of the cavern was a flame—but it was a little campfire, not a torch. And I was nowhere to be seen.

Kaita crouched low to the ground, baring her teeth in a silent snarl. *Clever,* she thought. *But not nearly clever enough.*

With a source of light in view, she could now see the entire cavern as if it were day. I was nowhere to be found, which meant I was hiding somewhere in the rocks. Yet Kaita would be able to see me at a much greater distance than I would be able to see her.

She hugged the cavern wall, circling to the right. But she did not get even halfway there before she spotted me. I was leaning forwards between two rocks, squinting heavily in the dim light. All my attention was focused on the southern tunnel through which she had emerged. I had a cloth tied over my nose and mouth to protect me from the pycnandra smoke.

He missed me in the dark. She chuckled in her mind. *But I will not miss him.* She could not see Oku, but who cared about that? I would be dead before the dog even knew what had happened.

Silently she stalked forwards on her padded feet. Soon she was within fifty paces of me. Then thirty. She edged slightly around so that she was directly behind me.

Only ten paces now. It was an easy leap for the lion form. She tensed, her body coiling. The tip of her tail swished back and forth.

I whirled to face her.

"Hello," I said. And I fired the arrow I had nocked.

Kaita was too surprised to dodge. The arrow sank into her shoulder. She snarled and darted aside before I could loose another shot. Twisting her neck, she seized the arrow in her teeth and ripped it out with a yowl. Her eyes glowed black, and the wound began to seal itself shut.

Steer, she spat in her mind. *One arrow? Your whole quiver would not be enough to stop me.* She readied herself to rush me.

And then, scentable beneath the pycnandra, something filled her nostrils.

Familiar. Dangerous.

Kaita panicked. She tried to turn and flee. But from nowhere, a spear butt crashed into her temple. Even as Kaita reeled back, the spear came around again to crash into the other side of her head.

She fell on her side. Her magic slipped from her, and the mountain lion form melted away.

Mag stepped into view, Oku at her side.

FORTY-SEVEN

While I had drawn Kaita to the western tunnel, Mag had brought the pycnandra sticks through the eastern tunnel. With them she had lit the campfire as soon as she had arrived. The acrid smoke had kept Kaita from scenting Mag, and focusing on me had kept her from noticing any other signs of Mag's approach.

Until it was too late.

Now, together, we loomed over Kaita. Mag had her spear, and my bow was in my hand with another arrow nocked. To my right, Oku growled and bristled at her, his teeth bared.

Kaita glared up at us with hatred, her eyes flitting back and forth. There was some strange frenetic energy in her, more than fear or rage. I guessed it was the effects of the magestones. But they would have no chance to do to her what I had seen them do to Xain.

Her eyes went black, and the blackness spilled out of her in a strange glow that further darkened the already dim cave. But before she could shift, Mag slammed her in the temples again. Kaita cried out in pain.

"This is impossible," she hissed, glaring up at Mag. "You died. I killed you."

"You did not do a good enough job, it seems," said Mag lightly. Her voice was muffled, for—like me—she was wearing a bandana against the pycnandra smoke.

"No!" snarled Kaita. "I *saw* the life leave your eyes. This is a gift of the Lord, and you are not his."

"You are right about that."

"We do not plan to toy with you long, Kaita," I said. "Not like you did with Mag. But we did have a few things to say before your tale ends."

Kaita snarled and looked ready to lunge. But then the tip of Mag's spear was at her throat. She went very still.

"I am certain you think this is all my fault," I went on, "because of what happened in Tokana in our youth. Or mayhap you think it is Mag's fault, for joining me in the Upangan Blades. Dark below, you might even blame your Shade friends. But I want you to know, from the bottom of my heart, that that is not true. This is your fault, and yours alone."

I knelt, elbows on my knees, and made sure her withering glare was on me as I continued.

"You are a spiteful, hateful person, Kaita. I suspect you always have been. Your own choices are what brought you to this cave. It is true that you fell under the influence of cruel people. But so did I." There was no hiding the note of bitterness that had crept into my voice. "And I did not turn into the sort of detestable scum that you are. It was your choice to turn that hatred outwards, to let it become violence."

Kaita looked ready to rip my skin from my body if Mag's spear had not been poised to strike. "You are a useless whelp," she spat, "and you always have been. You abandoned everyone who could have made you into something great. And you think you are better than *me?*"

I arched an eyebrow. "Which of us has the arrow ready, and which is on her back?"

"You would be nothing without the sow at your side!"

The dizziness from Mag's strikes had passed. Kaita slapped Mag's spear away and rolled aside, her eyes filling with the dark glow. But Mag swung the spear around with the momentum of Kaita's blow, slamming the flat of the blade into her head.

Kaita fell facedown on the ground, gasping. Mag stepped up and put her foot on the back of her neck.

"You are wrong," said Mag simply. She was not in her battle-trance. She did not need it. And I suspect that she wanted to feel every emotion and sensation of this moment. "You could not be more wrong. Albern *is* better than you, in the only way that matters." Her gaze met mine. "In many ways, he is better than me. And he always has been. But as for you . . . you and I have been enemies since before I knew who you were. You have been trying to hurt the ones I love since the first day I saw you. You could have turned back whenever you wanted, gone on to find another path. But you chose each step you took, and every one brought you closer to this place, and this time. And once you took Sten from me . . ."

Her voice shook. And I saw the trance start to come into her eyes, sliding across her face. But it stopped, and she pushed the mask away, letting the tears flow.

"You should have slit your own throat that day. It would have saved us all a great deal of time. You could *never* have escaped me once I decided to kill you. And you would have served your Lord better as a corpse than alive. Then, at least, he would not have lost everything we have taken from him already. And he would not now be destined to lose everything we will take in the future."

Kaita screeched, *"I will rip you apart in the dark below, you—"*

Mag drove the spear through her heart.

Kaita spasmed beneath her boot, her fingers clawing at Mag's ankle. But she could find no purchase. She tried desperately to reach the spear, but Mag twisted it, and Kaita's arms fell to the ground. Her eyes were wide as she kept gasping like a fish flung onto the shore. Her form started to shift, her eyes glowing black. But Mag had struck her too hard, too many times. Shock and the Mystics' trick kept her from sealing her wounds, or from taking another form. And yet still she tried.

Mag squatted beside her. Kaita tried to strike, but Mag caught the wrist—just to hold it, not even squeezing. A pace away, Oku stopped growling and sat back on his haunches. He cocked his head as he looked down at Kaita's jerking form.

"Fare well," said Mag. "Sten is avenged. You may see him briefly in the darkness below, while he is resting, and before the evil ones take you. I am sure it will put him at peace. That is the only service you have left to render."

And Kaita died.

I will not lie to you, Sun. It felt good. Oh, I know it did not solve anything. It did not bring Sten back, nor did it lessen the pain of his absence. I understand why people say that revenge is not the answer.

But neither should they say that it does not feel good in the moment. Because it does.

And some people just need to die.

Mag, Oku, and I turned and left the cave. We did not look back at her. Not even once.

FORTY-EIGHT

Captain Kun was in what remained of his camp, holding council.

It was dawn. In the day and a half that had passed since the Shade attack, his force had rested, recovered, and reclaimed as much of their supplies and possessions as they were going to. Now he was discussing his plans with Tou and the remaining lieutenants. He was listening to them as they spoke. But mostly, he was thinking of Zhen, of his sister's eyes in his nephew's face, staring at an empty, uncaring sky.

Kun was torn. He knew it was his duty to lead the army to safety, to a place where they could resupply themselves and avoid starvation in the icy wilderness. But part of him wanted to go after Mag and I. He wanted to assemble a small group to hunt us down. And he wanted to lead the hunt himself, though that would endanger his forces.

It was not the right thing to do, but he wanted to do it all the same.

There came a hail from outside. One of Kun's guards had issued a challenge. The council all paused, looking towards the tent's large door. Tou glanced at Kun, and Kun met his gaze.

After a moment, the tent flap opened. In stepped Kun's guard, along with a tall archer of Feldemarian looks. Kun remembered his name as Chausiku. He had once been in my squadron.

Kun's jawline went rigid.

"Soldier," said Tou, frowning. "What is it?"

Chausiku lifted his hand. And now they could all see that it held an arrow, and to the arrow was tied a roll of parchment.

"This struck the ground near me, sir," said Chausiku. "It was only moments ago. The outside . . ."

"Let me see it, soldier," said Kun.

Chausiku swallowed hard. "Captain, mayhap I should give it to Lieutenant—"

"Yes, Captain, let me—" Tou began.

"Soldier," said Kun in a cold tone. "The arrow."

Chausiku hesitated a moment more, but finally, he handed it over. And on the outside of the parchment scrawled in ink, Kun could see a few hastily written words:

Chausiku. Give this to the lieutenant for the captain.

Kun's grip on the parchment tightened.

"Do you see?" he said lightly. "It is even addressed to me."

He forced his fingers to loosen, seize the string, and untie it. The parchment unfurled in his hands, and he began to read silently.

> *Honorable Captain Zhou,*
>
> *I, Sergeant Albern of the family Telfer, and Sergeant Mag, tender our resignations. Though she is not here to confirm this letter before it is sent, we feel qualified also to tender the resignation of Yue of the family Baolan. We regret the circumstances that necessitate we leave so abruptly. We regret, additionally and sincerely, the animosity between us at the parting.*
>
> *We never intended you or your forces any harm. We love Underrealm. We hope that one day, with enough service on our part, you will see fit to approve a petition of clemency for us.*
>
> *Speaking of service, we have spent the last day in pursuit of the enemy, and we have been successful. We have slain two sentries of the Shade army, and we can confirm that they are continuing*

their westward course towards the Greatrocks. We also have slain the weremage. You will find her corpse in the cave half a league to the northeast if you care to.

Captain, we are ashamed eternally for every detriment we were to your intention. We hope the squadrons we have trained are of great aid to you in the war. If you see fit to do so, give our love and our apologies to Tou and our units.

We hope to see you on the other side of the war, and we hope as well that you may think more kindly of us then.

Regretfully,
Albern of the family Telfer
Mag, the Wanderer

Kun read the letter. Then he read it again. Not once did he take his eyes from the parchment, but he curled the top and bottom ends of it, as though he was preparing to wrap it around the arrow again.

The letter solved nothing, of course. Mag and I had known what we were doing. We were criminals under the King's law, and Kun would punish us if he could. Slaying the weremage was good for the cause, but it did not undo what else we had done. Not really.

But for the first time since we had left him, his smile returned to him. It was not as strong as it once had been. It might never be that strong again. But it was back.

Tou saw it. "Sir?" he said.

Kun handed him the letter. "Had I known of his penmanship, I would have retained him as a secretary instead of a sergeant. Remarkable to fit so much on a single sheet. Read this. Show no one else. Relay the sentiments or not, as you will. But burn the letter when you are done."

Tou looked confused, but he took the letter. He started to read, and almost at once, a look of fury began to build on his face. When he finished, he looked up at Kun.

"We must go after them, Captain."

"No," said Kun with a heavy sigh. "We must not. For one thing, I doubt we could catch them without . . . without a tracker of our own. For another, we simply do not have the supplies for it. We must find somewhere to procure more. Then we must proceed west to the

Greatrocks with all possible speed, and find a way to send a message warning our comrades about the mountain passes."

"But Mag and Albern—"

Kun forestalled him with a raised hand. "My order is given, Lieutenant. Besides, while killing the weremage is far from deserving of a pardon, mayhap it has earned them a respite. Mayhap fate meant it to. Let them have a brief time, at least, where they need not fear us at their backs."

His eyes fell upon the empty tent door again. "It will not last forever. Their time will come, one day. I promise."

And then to himself, he thought, *I promise you, Zhen.*

FORTY-NINE

Some time later, we strode into the camp where Yue and Dryleaf were waiting. They were both awake, and they straightened when they heard us coming. Yue stood, and then she helped Dryleaf to his feet as well. Oku came running up to the old man, who reached down to scratch him behind the ears.

Mag gave me a look before we reached them. We had spoken already, and I knew she wanted me to say nothing of what I had learned. I gave her a quick, small nod to let her know I understood.

"Rest easy," Mag told them. "It is done."

"Truly?" said Dryleaf. He bowed his head. "After all this time."

"And all this long way," I agreed. "But yes. It is over."

"Well, I am glad," said Yue. "For the sake of avenging Lan Shui, if nothing else."

Mag went to Dryleaf and took his hand in hers, placing her other hand on his arm. "Come, my friend. Sit with me."

"Of course," said Dryleaf. He hobbled beside her and sat on the blankets when she helped him down, and then she took her place by his side. I was pleased to see that his head seemed to be getting better.

Yue had changed the bandages, and the new ones hardly showed any blood at all. I walked up beside Yue and put my arm around her waist. She did the same to me.

"I am sorry," said Mag. "I know I have said it before, but I say it again now. By my actions, I placed you in danger, and that is nothing a friend should do."

Dryleaf straightened where he sat. His hands released his walking stick, and he placed them on his knees instead. Suddenly he looked quite regal.

"Mag," he pronounced, "my darling girl. You really must deflate your head, at least a little bit."

Mag's brows arched. "I . . . what?"

"You are a remarkable person," said Dryleaf. "You always have been. And because of it, others naturally look to you for guidance and leadership. That is a heavy burden. It gives you a mighty responsibility, and you must take that seriously—but you should not let it become too familiar. Sometimes it leads you to take choices away from others. You rob them of the power—and, yes, the pain—of making their own decisions." He gestured vaguely with his hand towards me. "I think Albern was reminded today that he is your partner, not your sidekick. Yue and I are the same way. We are not your followers, and it is not solely within your power to determine our fate. Mag, it was *my* advice that you and Albern join Kun's army. That is what led us all down this dark road. You are allowed to make mistakes and to feel the burden of them. But so am I. And you are *not* allowed to take that from me or from any of the rest of us."

I could see the chagrin in Mag's eyes. She, like me, could hear the truth in his words. With Mag around, it was easy to feel yourself starting to revolve around her, the way the moons spun around the world.

"You are wiser than I will ever be," she said. "And I will heed your wisdom. In that case, let me rescind my apology." She planted her hands on her hips like a scolding mother. "What were you thinking, you old fool, suggesting we join up with the Mystics? You sent us all headfirst and heedless into danger. I may never recover. Albern certainly will not."

Dryleaf's solemn countenance broke into a wrinkle-ridden grin. "There. You understand, now."

Yue rolled her eyes. "Such pleasantries aside," she said loudly, "what is your plan now? We cannot exactly return to Kun."

"We cannot," I said, smiling. "Though we sent word to him that we hope may alleviate at least a bit of his ire towards us. But as for us, now we mean to find the children."

Mag's expression dampened, though I did not know why. Yue only looked confused.

"The children?" she asked.

"Our friends from Northwood," I said. "Four of them, and then there is the wizard, though he is grown. They were my companions on a long road. Last we knew, they were making for a stronghold in Feldemar."

"Fortunately, that kingdom is not far from us now," said Dryleaf.

"Yet they could have gone anywhere since," said Mag. "We should listen for rumors as we go. If they have turned in another direction, we may hear of it. You remember how Gem was spreading legends of Loren. Mayhap they have spread far by now."

"Mayhap," I said with a nod. It seemed plausible, but I was still confused by Mag's strange behavior. I did not know where these words came from.

"In any case," said Yue gruffly, "if your road to this point has been any indication, I am certain something else will come up along the way. A village that needs saving from wurts, mayhap, or a farmhouse infested with imps."

"Why, that sounds like a pleasant respite after the trials we have endured," said Dryleaf with a broad smile. "I would be grateful to lend my advice in such an endeavor."

"But not today," said Mag. "Today, I would like to rest, and then to sleep for the first good night's sleep I have had in a long time."

"A long time," I agreed softly.

And so we did. The day passed without incident, and then we bedded down for the night. I was too weary even to make life interesting for Yue, though of course, it would not be my last chance to do so. And the next day, we readied ourselves for another journey. Not a hunt this time, but a search for friends.

Mag and I had one last conversation that is worth recounting now. As we were strapping our saddlebags to our horses, she glanced over at me.

"We are in the after."

For a moment I did not know what she was saying. Then I recalled the desperate words she had spoken the last time we rested in Kun's camp. "We are. How does it feel?"

"Unfamiliar," said Mag. "I never had a beginning in Shuiniu. Then it seemed I was in the middle for a very long time. And then, after Sten died, Kaita felt like the ending. But now that end has come and gone, and a new story has started. My first beginning. I hope we make it a good one."

"I am sure we shall," I told her. "As long as we take care of each other. And of Dryleaf." I chuckled. "Especially now that we do not have Nikau and Orla to help us. I will miss them more than most."

Mag blinked at me. "Who?"

"The lovers. From Kun's camp. You remember them."

Her lips parted, and I could see the lost look in her eyes.

I frowned at her, exasperated. "Sky above, Mag, we ate with them often enough. Do not tell me you—"

"I lost them," she said, cutting me off as if she had not heard me speaking. "I lost them when Kaita . . ." Her voice trailed off, and she looked over her shoulder to make sure Yue and Dryleaf were not within earshot. "When I died. I lost them."

She strapped her last saddlebag in place and went to help Dryleaf.

A chill crept down my spine.

FIFTY

It was late in the day now, and the sun had set. Albern had lit a fire in the hearth sometime during the tale, but Sun could not remember him doing so. She had gone through another mug of ale, and though the taste was no less sour, it was beginning to turn her head fuzzy. At first, she thought she had misheard him.

"What did she mean, she lost them?" said Sun.

"That answer is a complicated one," said Albern. "But to put it simply—whenever Mag was badly injured, or when she died, some part of her memory vanished, never to be recovered. The worse the harm, the more she lost."

Sun shook her head. "Why?"

He gave her a sad smile. "That, too, is an answer I am not willing to give. At least not yet."

"Why am I not surprised?" said Sun. Then she had a sudden thought. "Is . . . is that why she forgot everything before the forest? Before Shuiniu?"

Albern looked mildly surprised. "Yes. That was remarkably quick of you."

“She forgot *everything?”* Sun felt a sudden chill creeping down her back, just as Albern had described in the story. “What happened to her? It must have been bad to make her forget *everything.”*

“It was bad,” said Albern softly. “But you shall learn. One day.”

Sun took a deep breath. But she did not argue. She had learned her lesson by now, that Albern chose the order of his story carefully. And this one would not have been nearly as captivating if he had mixed it up in the telling.

“I am sorry for my anger earlier,” she said. “You did not deserve that, and I was wrong. I thought you were lying to me. But everything you have told me so far . . . it was merely a beginning. The introduction to a larger tale.”

Albern smiled, but it looked a little guarded. “You are not wrong.”

Sun snorted. “I notice you do not say whether I am right. Very well. Can you give me your best guess of when we will reach the end of the story?”

“End?” said Albern. “Who said the story has ended?”

“I mean the end of *Mag’s* story, you twit,” said Sun. Then her eyes went wide. “Albern . . . *has* she died? I mean in truth, not the way she ‘died’ when Kaita killed her. Is she still—”

A knock came at the front door. Sun jumped, but Albern’s mouth twisted.

“There is my friend,” he said.

“No, wait!” cried Sun. “Answer me. You *must* tell me before you open that door.”

“It is too hard to answer,” said Albern.

“Say yes or no!” cried Sun. “Why is that hard to answer?”

“I suppose we shall have to see.”

He went to the door and peered through a viewing hole before turning and winking at Sun. “I am happy to report it is not your family’s guards. This is the tavern’s owner—or former owner, I should say. And, of course, our third partner in this venture.”

Third partner? thought Sun.

Albern swung open the door. Two people entered. First was a large woman, with as much fat as muscle on her body. She had a thick jaw and a missing finger on her right hand. But the second woman caught all of Sun’s attention. She was much slimmer, and the hood of her green cloak was cast back to reveal Dorsean features, hair cut a few fingers above the shoulders in a practical style.

Her skin was flawless, without a blemish or scar to be seen. She looked to be around twenty years old.

Sun froze.

Albern fixed her with a careful look. "Sun," he said, indicating the larger woman, "this is Zhaojia, the former owner of the tavern. And this here is Chao, a brewmaster who has graciously agreed to partner with me in purchasing and running this place."

Chao. Sun's wildly racing suspicions were confirmed in an instant. That was the false name Mag had used in the tales.

This was Mag. The Wanderer. The Uncut Lady . . . or at least, as far as anyone knew.

She could not speak. She could hardly breathe. This was not like meeting Albern in that tavern far away. This was like meeting an Elf, dangerous and extraordinary and entirely debilitating, for what could one do in the face of such incredible power?

Her mind began to work again, but slowly. If Mag was going by the name Chao, that meant she was pretending to be someone else. And she and Albern also seemed to be pretending not to know each other very well. Sun did not know why, but of course, she would not give away the scheme.

"I am very pleased to meet you, Chao," she said. "And you as well, Zhaojia."

"Pleased, I am sure," said Zhaojia with a nod. Then she turned to Albern. "You got my gift, I see."

Albern raised the mug of ale he had been in the middle of. "We did, and we thank you kindly for it. A fine concoction indeed."

Zhaojia scoffed. "You need not try to save my pride. I did not brew it, after all. It was what I could find that was fast and cheap, and that means it is not good, as a rule. We both know our mutual acquaintance here makes far better stuff than that swill. You have the rest of the money?"

"Of course." Albern reached to his belt and pulled out one of the thick purses he had received earlier. Then he paused and looked to Sun. "Sun, I mentioned before that you might find good use for your money by the end of the day. Would you like to join Chao and me in purchasing this tavern?"

An hour ago, this might have rendered Sun insensible, or mayhap caused her to faint straight away. But now, with Mag herself standing in the room, the absolute absurdity of the situation barely registered. "Why not?" she said. "I have no other plans."

"Wonderful," said Albern. "We shall sort out the details later, and I shall recover your portion of the payment."

Zhaojia and Mag both looked at Albern like he was sun-touched. But Zhaojia took the purse, opened it, counted the contents, and closed it up again.

"Very well," she said gruffly. "May you find better fortune here than I did. But then again, with her crafting your drink . . ." She tossed her head at Mag. "Well, I wish you good fortune, in any case. And I am off."

She strode out the door, and Albern went to close it behind her. The whole time, Sun could not stop staring at Mag. Once the door was closed and they were alone again, she finally tore her gaze away to look at Albern.

"What in the *dark* below—"

"Now, calm down," said Albern.

Mag, meanwhile, stood with her arms folded. At Sun's outburst, she arched a brow. "And who exactly is this?" she asked Albern.

"Chao," said Albern, "this is Sun of the family Valgun."

"Valgun?" said Mag. "That is a name of Dulmish nobility. What are you doing purchasing a tavern halfway across the world?"

Sun barely glanced at her, but kept her gaze locked on Albern, awaiting his answer. Albern gave Mag a weak smile.

"Though both of your manners seem to have fled, let me assure each of you that the other is pleased to make your acquaintance."

"Albern, *what is going on?*" said Sun, very nearly in a shriek.

Mag frowned at Albern. "I thought your name was Kanohari."

Sun waved a hand. "Of course, you are using your fake names. *Kanohari,* I need answers."

Albern's expression grew troubled. "Sun—"

Now Mag was looking stern. "A fake name? Why would you give me a fake name? If you are not Kanohari, then who are you?"

That froze Sun in place. Albern shook his head slowly.

"Chao," he said, "if you would give me a moment to speak with our new partner?"

Mag folded her arms. "I suppose," she said. "But make it quick. And you had better have a good explanation when you return. I do not take well to being swindled."

"Well do I know it," muttered Albern as he came and gently took Sun's arm. "Out back, if you do not mind."

"What in the dark below is going on?" hissed Sun as she allowed him to pull her out into the alley behind the tavern.

"A great many things," said Albern. He made sure the door shut behind them, and then he listened at it as if making sure Mag had not followed them. "But here is what you must know. Her name is Chao, so far as she, or you, or anyone else is concerned. And she knows me as Kanohari. Though I suppose I shall have to tell her my true name is Albern, now that you have said it, and it has not seemed to harm her."

Sun glanced at the door. "She does not know your real name?"

"She does not," said Albern. The sadness in his eyes was one she had seen often, every time he had spoken of Mag's darkest moments in the story.

"But why?" said Sun, shaking her head.

"There is a long tale behind it—" Albern began.

"You cannot mean to make me wait—"

He held up a hand. "Stop, and listen to me. There is a *long* tale behind it, which I shall tell you in full. But I will give you a *short* answer now because you deserve it, and you will need it. And it will help you help me, in the way we must treat her now. You know something, at least, of the end of Mag's story."

"I thought I did," said Sun. "Though now it seems it was not the end at all."

"But it was," said Albern, and he had never sounded more earnest. "Something terrible happened, more terrible than any tale could convey, though I will try. And when it did . . . that *was* the end of Mag's story. She lost who she had been, the person I met in my youth, who I followed from mercenary company to mercenary company, and through the Necromancer's War. I was with her when it happened, and I have been with her ever since, helping her as much as I know how."

"So she forgot you," said Sun slowly, piecing it together. "Just as she forgot Nikau and Orla because Kaita killed her. She remembers nothing at all now, because when she died . . . really died . . . it was bad enough that she forgot everything. Like in the woods near Shuiniu."

"Yes," said Albern.

"And that is why you told me this tale," said Sun. "So I would understand when I met her."

"It is one reason."

A horrible thought struck Sun. When she voiced it, she could not speak above a whisper.

"Does she remember Sten?"

Albern did not answer, but his eyes filled with tears. And Sun's own tears fell freely down her cheeks, and she tried vigorously to scrub them away.

"We have to tell her," she said. "You should have told her already!"

"Do you think I did not try?" said Albern. "Please, Sun. I have been with her for a long while since . . . since it happened. I have thought of nearly everything you could think of, and I have tried it. You must trust me in this. If I say you must not speak of something, or you must treat her a certain way, I beg you to believe me. When I have tried to tell her of her past life, it has caused her great harm. She becomes a wreck for days, and when the spell passes, she forgets it all anyway. Please, Sun."

Sun could hardly understand him. All she wanted to do was run inside and tell Mag everything that had happened in Albern's stories. But she mastered herself. And finally, she nodded.

"Very well. I believe you."

"Thank you," said Albern gently. "Now, let us return inside before she takes it into her head to come out here and trounce us both."

"So she can still fight?" said Sun.

"Like you would not believe," grumbled Albern, and he led her back in.

Mag—Chao—was waiting for them in the tavern's common room, her arms still folded across her chest. She looked expectantly at Albern, and he gave her a disarming smile.

"Now then," he said. "I should tell you something I was planning to reveal at a more opportune time. As Sun here has already revealed, my real name is Albern. I am of the family Telfer."

Chao's eyebrows rose. "Telfer? A noble as well, but this time of Calentin. What in the dark below is going on here?"

"Nothing nefarious," said Albern. "We are both somewhat . . . out of favor with our families. In fact, that is how Sun came to my attention, for she faced similar troubles to the ones I experienced when I was her age. Those troubles are what led me to take the name Kanohari long ago. But Sun met me by my real name, and I never told her another one."

He looked to Sun. "From now on, when we are in front of others, I will request that you call me Kanohari," he said, and then turned back to Chao. "And when it is the three of us, it would please me if you called me Albern."

A shadow passed over her expression, but it was soon gone. "Albern," she said. "Like the tales from Calentin history."

"Just so," said Albern with a pleased smile. "I chose the name after my wending."

Again a shadow came over Chao's face, and this time it stayed there. She placed a hand to her forehead, and it was trembling.

"Chao?" said Albern, worry in his voice. "What is it?"

"Nothing," said Chao. She smiled weakly at him. "A dizzy spell. It is so damnably hot outside. But very well. If Albern is your wending name, then I vow never to use anything else unless you ask me to."

"Thank you," said Albern, bowing his head. Sun could hear the relief in his voice. Whatever had come over Chao briefly, it seemed to have passed. Was this what he meant when he said she would have spells when he tried to tell her of her old life?

"Now, as for you," said Chao, nodding to Sun. "Albern here says you are to be a partner, and I trust him. But you seem a bit young to me. What do you know of running a tavern?"

Sun looked to Albern for guidance, but he merely held out an encouraging hand, as if to coax her. "Nothing," she said simply.

Chao's mouth twisted. "Honesty is an admirable trait, but you may need better qualifications."

"She is young," said Albern. "But she is not much younger than you. And in our wanderings together, I have found her more than capable."

Sun had to duck her head to hide a sudden flush in her cheeks.

"Very well," said Chao with a sigh. "Tell me, girl. What did you think of the ale here?"

Sun's lip curled. "It was awful."

"I agree," said Chao. "Would you like some of mine? I brought a wagon of it when I transported Zhaojia here."

Suddenly Sun's mouth was watering. "I would like that very much," she squeaked. From the corner of her eye, she saw Albern's amusement at her wonderstruck expression.

Chao led her outside, where there was indeed a wagon of ale casks waiting. Together the three of them got all of them down to the cellar, except for one barrel, which Albern set up behind the bar. Chao tapped it, and they poured three mugs. Chao set to right away, and Albern joined her, but Sun took a moment. She sniffed it, and the bubbles seemed to break in the exact right way to fly up her nose, tickling her and making her giggle. Finally, she tipped the mug back, taking a sip.

It . . .

It . . .

Sky above. Sun wanted to weep. Never had she tasted anything like it.

It was like honeyed sunlight poured from bouncing clouds of gossamer. Like the clearest river water kissed by ocean breezes, and smoked in the cleansing glow of a good campfire. And yet it was heady and intense, with the barest hint of . . . was it brandy? Some sort of fine, sweet liquor, and the taste of it weakened her knees.

A sip turned into a swallow, and then into a long, long draught. Before Sun knew it, the mug was empty. She stayed there for a moment, eyes closed, feeling every drop of it sliding down her throat and into her gut.

When at last she opened her eyes, Chao was looking at her expectantly.

"That . . ." whimpered Sun. "That is the most wondrous thing I have ever tasted. By a wide, *wide* margin. I had heard from Albern that you made fine ale, but this . . . this is so far beyond anything I could ever have imagined."

Chao turned to Albern with a wide grin. "I suppose she might work out, after all."

They shared a laugh. And then their talk fell to the tavern and its construction, and where they could get tables, and what sort of chairs they all preferred. Then they went upstairs and claimed their rooms—

Sun chose an excellent one on the front corner, with windows on two walls—and then back downstairs, where they talked of ale and wine and guests and ale and hiring help and ale again. Never did Albern or Chao talk over Sun, and they listened attentively whenever she gave ideas, even when she spoke hesitantly. And they argued for and against her ideas as vigorously as for their own plans.

Sun could not believe this was real. Here were two of the most significant figures of her favorite legends, and she was *working* with them. They were partners. No one could know how long it would last, of course, but Sun promised herself to cherish every moment of it.

At last, the night wound to a close. They had all had more than a few cups of ale, and their conversation had turned giddy and giggling. Finally, Chao rubbed at her eyes.

"I should sleep, or I will make even more of a fool of myself than I already have," she said.

"That is not possible," said Sun at once.

Chao arched an eyebrow. "Oh? Do you mean I could not appear more foolish?"

As Sun's cheeks flamed, Albern laughed aloud. "I think she meant you could not make a fool of yourself," he said. "This one's head is full of courtly graces, but she is new to tavern conversations. Forgive her."

Chao's mouth twisted in a wry smile. As she stepped around from behind the bar and towards the stairs, she paused. Slowly, she reached out a hand to Sun. Sun tentatively took it and found her wrist wrapped in a grip like iron.

"It is a pleasure to know you, Sun of the family Valgun," said Chao. "Forgive my doubtfulness before. I look forward to our partnership."

"As do I," said Sun, barely able to choke the words out.

Chao smiled, and then she gave Albern a nod. Finally, she turned and climbed the stairs towards her newly chosen room. Sun and Albern remained in the common room to clean up some of the mess they had all made. After a while, Sun looked over at him.

"Why all this, Albern? Why did you pick me? I thought it was for an adventure. Now you have me running a tavern. What is the purpose behind it all?"

Albern's lips puckered. He went behind the bar, took up a rag, and began to wipe off the small splashes of ale they had spilled.

"What I told you before is true," he said. "I saw a young child of nobility who seemed to hate her life, and I felt sympathy for your plight. But you are right. There is more behind it.

"I have told you that Mag was happiest in Northwood, with her inn, and with Sten. So many dark things happened after that. And I felt she deserved a return to that happiness. I thought this might be a way to give her such a gift."

He stopped wiping the bar and looked up at her. Sun met his gaze, but her breath caught in her throat.

"But that does not explain you, of course," said Albern. "I wanted to make sure you care about Chao. Because I wanted you to want to stay here with us and hear the rest of the story. I need someone else to know the whole truth of it. I cannot tell the whole world everything—that would be violating Mag's trust, and I vowed to her I would never do that. But one person should know everything, right down to the last. And I told you the story the way I did, jumping back and forth throughout Mag's life, so that when you met Chao, you would care enough about her to help me keep her secret."

Sun nodded. "I will," she said. "I swear it."

"Thank you," said Albern quietly. "At first, I thought the burden of this story was mine to bear alone. Then, when I learned the truth about Mag, I thought she would remember our deeds long after I had been laid beneath the dirt. But now . . ."

He gave a vague gesture towards the stairs. Sun nodded.

"Now, you are the only one," she said. "The only one who remembers everything."

"It is a heavier burden than I thought it would be," said Albern. "So I thank you, Sun, for the help you have been on the road so far, and for being willing to listen to an old man's story."

Sun lifted the broom and pointed it at him like a sword, frowning. "Willing? You would do better to call it *demanding.* I want you to resume the tale tomorrow, bright and early."

He eyed the stairs again. "I will not do so in Chao's presence. But whenever we have a moment alone, yes. I will continue the tale." He smiled at her. "And I will do so with pleasure."

Sun lowered the broom again and began to sweep. "You better had."

EPILOGUE

Sun had trouble falling asleep that night. Her mind was so full of thoughts from the day's incredible events that she could hardly close her eyes for a moment before opening them again, replaying the stories in her mind.

Eventually, she gave it up and went downstairs. She was not quite sure whether she wanted a drink or to walk around, but she certainly did not want to lie restless in bed, comfortable though it was.

She stood in the center of the common room and looked around. A tavern. And she was a one-third owner of it, along with Albern of the family Telfer, and Mag, the Wanderer. If she could have told herself even a month ago that all this would happen, she would have called herself a liar.

Footsteps sounded behind her. Sun turned to find Albern standing there, blinking at her in surprise.

"I cannot sleep," said Sun.

"Nor can I," said Albern.

"I keep thinking about the tavern, and about . . ." Sun glanced at the stairs. "About the story."

"Do not trouble yourself," said Albern. "She is asleep. I confess I do not face the same problem as you. My thoughts are still, but simple pain is what keeps me awake."

"I am sorry to hear that," said Sun. "Yet I suppose it is a good thing for me. I had a question. There is one answer you promised to give me earlier, but now I do not see how you can. You keep telling parts of the tale from Kaita's perspective. And you said you learned the details later. I thought you must have captured her, or interrogated her, or something. But Kaita died. So . . . how do you know what happened to her in such detail?"

Albern's expression grew dour. Instead of answering, he walked to the bar. Sun followed, plopping down on a stool. Albern pulled two large mugs of ale, and then he turned to hand one to Sun.

"Have a drink," he said solemnly.

Rogan approached the cave, the Lord at his side. Together they climbed over the boulders and stalked through the darkness of the tunnel. Though it was pitch-black, they walked unerringly, as though they knew exactly where they were going.

And in fact, they did. Rogan had already seen what he would find here, in this vast, empty cave. And he soon found it. Kaita's body lay facedown, twisted in pain. There was a hole through her back, and her blood covered the stone floor.

Weeping, Rogan fell to his knees beside her. He took up her hand, cradling it against his cheek, careless of the blood he spread on himself.

The Lord stepped up beside him, and then he felt his father's hand on his shoulder.

"Why?" said Rogan. "You said you knew why. I know our goals are worthy, more so than anyone else in the nine kingdoms. But this . . . this feels like too high a price."

The cave was silent for a long moment. When the Lord finally spoke, Rogan could hear the grief in his voice. "It *is* a high price. But no price would be too high to pay. The death of any one person—even Kaita, even Tagata, and yes, even you, my favored son—would be worth it in the end, if we achieve what we mean to. And yet now we may rejoice. Today, we need pay no price at all."

Rogan looked up at him in the darkness. "Father?"

"Lift her hair, my son."

As Rogan watched in wonder, the Lord pulled out a needle, ink, and a small hammer.

"Father," said Rogan. "I thought no wizard could receive your gift."

"So did I," said the Lord. "But now let us say, instead, that I never knew how to bestow it upon them. Not until I needed it most."

His hands were swift and deft as he tapped out a tattoo on the back of Kaita's neck. Rogan had seen it a dozen times before. But this tattoo was . . . different. It did not look like his own, like the design that all the shadeborn wore.

"Can you do this to anyone?" he asked in an awed voice. "Any other wizard, I mean?" His mind raced with the possibilities of what this could mean for the coming war.

"We shall see," said the Lord. "For now, put her on her back again."

Rogan did. The Lord placed his hand on Kaita's chest, where the spear had made its mark. And his eyes began to glow with a pure, unrelenting white light.

Her body began to convulse. She groaned, like a corpse expelling the last air from its lungs. Suddenly the groan erupted into a scream. Like Mag's when she had come back to life, Kaita's back arched, with only her head and pelvis still touching the ground. The scream bounced from the rocky walls and off itself again, becoming painful. Kaita's eyes were wide, and the blood vessels within them split, turning them red.

"Hold her, my son," said the Lord, his voice halting with effort.

Rogan seized Kaita and held her down. He wished to comfort her, but he knew that was impossible. Not until the ritual was complete.

And then, finally, her screams subsided. Her body sank back onto the ground, plopping wetly in the blood pooled beneath her. Her blood-red eyes spun, and then finally they focused on Rogan, on the Lord. Her expression held only anguish.

"Rogan?" she croaked.

He scooped her up into his arms, holding her and weeping anew, but this time with joy. And the Lord, though weary from his exertions, stood and placed his hands on them both. Rogan's heart filled with his warmth, with his love.

"My children," said the Lord gently.

You see, Sun, you have already realized that this was not the end of Mag's tale. It was merely the end of the beginning. What we did not know at the time was that another tale had begun as well.

ADDENDUM A

HISTORICAL ESSAYS FROM THE WORLD OF UNDERREALM

OF WEREMAGES, THEIR TECHNIQUES AND TRAINING

During the tumultuous days of the War of the Necromancer, several prominent weremages were of great importance.

(There are many who would insist we call them "therianthropes," in the manner of the proper speech of the Academy and of the nobility. But we shall here use the commoner's tongue for them, as well as for wizards of the other branches, for it renders greater understanding, and that is a nobler goal than lofty words.)

On the battlefield, a weremage's impact could be great. As powerful animals or terrible hellskin beasts, they could lay waste to entire squadrons of troops, or in the case of a powerful few, entire armies.

But more often, and far more potently, they were instrumental in many clandestine matters. Across the nine kingdoms, and on all sides of the conflict, they collected information, scouted out enemy movements, and even assassinated powerful foes. After all, who could be better for such espionage than a wizard capable of assuming any form?

Or at least, so most of the commonfolk believed. But as we shall see, they were rather misinformed.

To understand the many aspects of a weremage's power, it is best to start at the beginning of their training. One of the first things a weremage learns, whether from the Academy or from a private tutor, is the "creative" transformation of their own body. "Creative" transformation is differentiated from "acquired" transformation, which shall be discussed in detail later.

In creative transformation, imagination is paramount. But because imagination is the center of a weremage's ability, that ability is incredibly versatile in some respects, and heavily restricted in others.

The subject of color is a good example. In the mirror branch of alchemy, an alchemist must have powerful focus and mental strength to change an object's color. That is because an alchemist transforms the actual minute particles that *give* an object its color. But for a weremage, it is much easier to change the colors of their own body simply by thinking about it.

This is, in fact, how young weremages are tested for. The person administering the test only has to say to a child, rather sharply, "I did not know you had green eyes," or some other color the child's eyes do not in fact possess. If the child is a weremage, this will confuse them, and in their confusion, they will imagine their own eyes being the stated color. This causes them to change for a few moments, and so the tester knows they have a weremage on their hands.

The first two years of weremagic training in the Academy are entirely concerned with color. By the end of the second year, a weremage is expected to be able to change the color of any part of their body at will, and to any color demanded of them by their instructor. And while it is not a requirement, especially talented students will often delight in creating all sorts of patterns across their bodies, so that they appear to have artistic birthmarks, or intricate tattoos, or the like.

But as a weremage ventures into their third year, they study the techniques of transforming the shape and material of their body. This is much more difficult. It always begins with the simplest transformation: assuming another human's shape. Students are usually paired up and taught to "acquire" each other. "Acquire" is a term for learning another creature, memorizing the details and peculiarities of its form, and then practicing the transformation into the new shape until the weremage can do so at will.

To do this, the student will place a hand on their partner's body and focus all their thoughts upon the other person. Instructors command them to form a small picture of their partner in their mind, and then to "place" the picture between their temples. This technique is the foundation of acquiring a new type of creature, and it is one the weremage will use for the rest of their life. And while a skilled and experienced weremage can usually acquire a new creature in a matter of a few dozen hours, for the first acquisition, it usually takes the student months.

As an aside, the acquiring technique is why Mystic mage hunters are taught to disable weremages by striking hard at their temples. That part of the head is always a conduit for the weremage's magic, no matter what form they have assumed. Two hard blows, one on each temple, disrupts the magic's flow and keeps the weremage from being able to maintain concentration on a false form, and this causes them to revert to their own.

In any case, once they have acquired their target, the weremage will attempt a transformation. As one might expect, they usually have great initial success in changing colors to match the target, such as hair, eyes, and so forth. But they always struggle, at first, to change their size and shape to match their partner. Incorrectly done, changing one's shape can be incredibly painful. Not only must the weremage have a perfect image of the target, but they must also be able to envision a bridge, a transition between their current form and the new form. If they venture to change their shape before this is solid in their mind, then just as if they stepped out onto an unstable bridge in the physical world, they will plunge into a chasm of darkness. But these depths are composed of great pain, as their limbs and flesh twist and snap in agonizing ways.

Fortunately, such a botched transformation makes the weremage lose concentration. They will thus revert to their original form—hurt, and shaken, but not permanently damaged.

At the end of the process, and after many attempts, the student will finally have learned to acquire their study partner. This comprises the first entry in the weremage's "canon." The "canon" is the list of all creatures the weremage has acquired, and into which they may transform at will. Contrary to what many commonfolk believe, a weremage cannot simply turn into anything they want. They are restricted to the creatures in their canon.

Thus, in the Mystics (or any other organization specializing in battle or espionage), a commander must select weremages for certain tasks based on their abilities. A weremage with no bird in their canon, for example, will never be an optimal long-distance messenger. And a weremage with no large, dangerous beast in their canon will be no great help on a battlefield. Any weremage newly arrived to a fighting force will make their entire canon known to their commander, so that they may be utilized most effectively. And over the course of their lives, most weremages work to assemble as diverse a canon as possible, letting them cover a broad range of needs with the creatures they can transform into.

But acquiring, as has been stated, is a long and difficult process. As with all the branches of magic, it gets easier and easier the more often one does it. And of course, a weremage's innate skill and experience are also factors in the process. But this is only relative, and even a very seasoned weremage must still spend weeks studying a new species of creature to acquire it. Such study can of course be broken up, but weremages try not to do so. The more intensive the study, the more quickly the weremage can acquire the creature.

Therefore, even in the best possible case, acquiring a creature becomes very difficult if the target is dangerous, as is the case with bears, lions, or other large animals, and even for venomous beasts such as vipers. The weremage must spend a great deal of time in physical contact with the creature in order to acquire it. This usually means the target must be sedated or otherwise pacified, which can be both costly and difficult. The Academy maintains a menagerie of such beasts for their students to take advantage of, and the maintenance and upkeep of this facility is one of the school's greatest single expenses. Meanwhile, trained weremages from wealthy or noble families will often use their family's resources and influence to acquire more exotic animals, and each one added to their canon is a point of pride.

Once a creature has been acquired, other creatures of the same type are far easier to learn, and do not even require physical contact. If the weremage has acquired one bear, for example, and they can study another bear sufficiently and meditate on it long enough, they will eventually be able to effect a transformation that passes all but the most detailed inspection. This is, to some degree, a merging of creative transformation and acquired transformation.

Speaking of creative transformation, weremages are also able to apply this to any creature in their canon. This allows them to alter the coloring, shape, and sometimes even the substance of any acquired creature. There are many useful applications of such a technique. For example, weremages who specialize in combat will often increase the size, stature, and resilience of their favored battlefield forms. For example, Instructor Jia from the Academy favored the shape of a bear, but she increased its size until it stood twice as tall as an adult human, and she could turn its claws as hard as steel, so that they could turn enemy blades in battle. But by far the most common use of creative transformation is the assumption of a false identity. This is a talent shared almost universally by weremages across Underrealm, though some specialize in it almost exclusively—such as many spies among the Mystics, or the weremage Auntie in the city of Cabrus.

As has been said, a weremage must study and acquire another person to add humans to their canon. But once the first human has been acquired, creative transformation may be applied to the form in order to assume virtually any shape. It is best if a weremage can study a target and learn their habits and mannerisms, and thus form a more complete mental picture of the person. But if the weremage is very skilled, even an hour's study can be enough for a transformation that would fool all but close friends or family.

In Lan Shui, for example, Kaita was able to acquire the form of the boy Pantu after only a few brief meetings. And of course, much has been written elsewhere of the weremage Auntie, who acquired the shapes of not only Loren of the family Nelda, but also many Mystics who accompanied her, and who then used these forms to terrible effect.

When creative transformation is applied to acquired forms, it is sometimes referred to as "modified" transformation. This is a discrete subject of study, with most scholars being particularly interested in the limitations of modification. A common example for beginning students in this field is the problem of the blue jay and the cardinal.

Imagine that a weremage has acquired a blue jay. Then the weremage sets about modifying the transformation. First, they turn all their feathers red. That is a simple modification, and a casual observer might then mistake the modified blue jay for a cardinal. But anyone very familiar with birds would recognize the incorrect shape and size of the beak, the claws, and the overall build. The weremage might then try to modify the transformation further, compensating for these defects, but this would require an almost impossible level of concentration and focus.

This extreme height of power can become dangerous in some cases. Like all magic, a weremage's transformation requires concentration to maintain. The more the transformation is modified, the more concentration is required. If the weremage were distracted even slightly while flying in the modified form, they might suddenly revert back to their natural human form, and find themselves plummeting towards the ground from a dozen paces or more in the air.

The study of this property of weremagic has given the academia of Underrealm a great preoccupation with taxonomy, which as a result is a far more codified field than many other scientific pursuits. The concept of species differentiation, for example, is quite exactingly understood and constantly studied. It is well known that an animal may be easily modified within its own species, but it requires great effort to modify it to mimic another species entirely. This lends us further understanding of weremages' ability to assume other human forms so quickly, since all humans are, of course, the same species.

This particular detail is a greater problem to the wealthy and powerful of Underrealm than it is to the commonfolk. Impersonation of some wealthy merchant could be used to disastrous effect, at least as far as the merchant's coffers are concerned. A mimicked king, or even a lesser noble, could start a war. Though of course, only a particularly foolish (or desperate) weremage would impersonate a king. If such a scheme were ever discovered, they would suffer a long, slow death at Mystic hands—the same penalty leveled at any wizard attempting to sit a throne.

This is one reason that lords, monarchs, and other powerful figures of the nine kingdoms—particularly the High King herself—do their best to stay removed from all but their closest family and advisors. If a weremage cannot spend enough time with them to study their appearance, it becomes quite difficult to mimic them effectively.

As an extra precaution, most among the nobility, particularly kings, scarify or tattoo themselves with a distinguishing mark in a hidden place. Only a very small circle of trusted allies, always kept close by, are allowed to know of the mark's location and shape. A weremage would not, of course, know to create the mark. Therefore, even if they were otherwise able to assume the noble's form, the noble's inner circle would quickly be able to uncover the ploy.

The last subject of high import that should be discussed here is a weremage's transition from one form to another, without first reverting to their natural human form. This is a very powerful and difficult technique, and not every weremage is able to learn it.

When acquiring a creature, the weremage must envision a bridge between their body and the desired form. The same thing must be done to turn from one form to another: they must envision, and then craft in their mind, a bridge from the first form to the second. This requires immense concentration, focus, and also an exacting knowledge of both animal forms. For Kaita to turn from a raven to a lion, she had to know both creatures' bodies in as much detail as she knew her own. Then she had to craft the bridge between the bird and the cat, undergoing many,

many failed and painful transformations as she learned. And the same bridge that took her, for example, from the raven to the lion, would not let her turn from the raven to a serpent. Another bridge would have to be constructed.

In truth, Kaita was a highly accomplished weremage, and one of the greatest of her age. It is a shame that she was never allowed to feel that way—neither by Thada of the family Telfer, the Rangatira who scorned her, nor by Mag, who defeated her again and again no matter the strength of her animal forms.

Had Kaita ever been allowed to see just how powerful and valuable she was, one must wonder if she might not have turned to evil.

OF KAITA AND THE LAND OF TOKANA

There are two other important details concerning Kaita and her time in the mountainous region of Tokana, and they are worth discussing here.

When Kaita returned to her mountain homeland, hotly pursued by the Wanderer and Albern of the family Telfer, she became busily engaged in the activities of her fellow Shades. For the most part, this consisted of covert actions to further stoke ire between the Rangatira and the trolls, and this required a great deal of speedy travel through the peaks.

If it was possible, Kaita would of course take her raven form. But sometimes she had to remain grounded, and then she would use her mountain lion. When she did, she usually modified her transformation to hide the white tail of the lion she held in her canon. She did this because she had no wish for Ditra, the Rangatira, to hear of a lion with a white tail. Ditra would, of course, recognize the form at once, and she would know that Kaita had returned. Kaita feared that Ditra would be wrathful, and she would expend great effort to track Kaita down.

Albern and Mag, however, had already seen Kaita's lion in its natural form, including the white tail. They passed this information to Ditra, who received it much differently than Kaita thought she would. Not only did she keep the information from Mag and Albern, but she withheld it from even her most trusted advisors. She also assigned Maia, her lead ranger, to hunt for the weremage in secret. This greatly hampered the efforts of not only Maia, but Albern and Mag, and was a tremendous boon to Kaita's aims in the region—even if she was thwarted in the end.

The second interesting detail is the answer to a mystery that long plagued Albern: how did Kaita acquire her troll form, in which she named herself Gatak?

It is exceptionally rare for any weremage to acquire the shape of any of Underrealm's other sentient races, whether troll, satyr, imp, wurt, or what have you. There are old, old laws of the High King, nearly as old as Underrealm itself, that forbid the capture or enslavement of any of these creatures, which are sometimes referred to collectively as the "Awakened Folk" to differentiate them from beasts. Those who break this law may be put to death, along with any accomplices, and even any who knew of the violation but said nothing. It is not quite so strict as the King's harshest law, but it is not far off, either. And without the creature being so restrained, it is impossible to spend the necessary time in contact with them to acquire them.

Mysteriously, this law is one that the Shades also obeyed, just as they obeyed the ancient edicts protecting the Guild of Lovers, which saved Dryleaf's life in the hills north of the Greenfrost. And so indeed, it was not by unscrupulous means that Kaita acquired her troll form.

When she fled Tokana in her youth, driven out by Albern's mother, the Rangatira, Kaita spent a while in the wilderness. She was a ranger, after all. Living off the land was as easy as dwelling in a city or town, and more so when her magic made it a simple matter to hunt for food.

For some weeks she was alone. Now, this was deep in troll territory, but the trolls there were not numerous, and it was easy to avoid them. But after some time, she did encounter a troll—a elderly female named Sookar.

At first, Sookar behaved aggressively towards Kaita. But it happened that they met when Kaita was at her lowest point. She had given up any hope of recovering the life she had fled. She had been abandoned by her lover, Ditra, and disgraced in the eyes of her lord. Life seemed to have little purpose, and for days she had toyed with the idea of ending it.

Therefore when Sookar made as if to attack Kaita, Kaita did . . . nothing. She stood there, her eyes dead as if in Mag's battle-trance, and waited for the troll's great fists to smash her into a pulp.

And that is nearly what happened. But at the last second, Sookar stopped. She stared at Kaita in confusion and irritation. Why should this puny human not flee, or cower, or try hopelessly to fight? And because Sookar knew a little of the common tongue of Underrealm, she was able to give voice to her frustration.

"Why do you stand there?" she snarled. "Do you think I will not crush you?"

Kaita looked up into her eyes and said, quietly, "In fact, I hope you will."

It was one of the few things she could have said that would spare her life.

Sookar was an old, old troll at that time, but many years before, she had had a child. And that child had died after sneaking away from her and stumbling off a high cliff. For a long time aftewards, Sookar had been utterly listless. She would never have taken her own life, but she had often wanted something else to come along and end it, to end her pain and her sense of deep, mortal failure.

That feeling was still familiar to her, so many years later. And she saw it shining in Kaita's eyes now.

Her ears flapped in sympathy. Slowly, she lowered her boulder-sized fists, and she sat on her haunches in front of Kaita.

Sookar's pack had helped her survive the worst pain she had ever known. But this tiny human had no one.

And in that moment, Sookar resolved that she would be Kaita's pack, as long as she required one.

From that time on, she visited Kaita every day. She saw to it that Kaita had plenty to eat, and she did what she could to keep the area clear of predators that might threaten her. But for the most part, she spent time with Kaita, and she listened. And Kaita spoke, at first in a lifeless monotone, and then with tears, and then with increasing anger, of the wrongs done to her by Thada and the other humans of Tokana. Many of these matters were far beyond Sookar's understanding, but that does not always matter. Sometimes one need simply listen and share in another's grief.

And so for many months these two forged a deeper and deeper friendship, a tiny pack of two that treated each other like family. It was in that time that Kaita learned the troll tongue, which few humans have ever learned, and in exchange she taught Sookar to speak the human tongue with much greater skill. And in time, there came to be enough trust between the two of them that Sookar let Kaita acquire her form.

"Useful," she growled, "if you ever run into others of my kind out here in the mountains."

Of course, if she ever encountered a troll, Kaita could just as easily turn into a bird and flee. But she knew how rare it was for a weremage to have this chance, and she could hardly refuse. Over the course of weeks, Kaita took Sookar's shape into her canon, and she was able to become a troll whenever she desired.

After some months of this life, Kaita found herself growing restless. She had shed the desire for her own life to end. Now she wanted to go about building a new future. She did not know what such a future held, but she knew it was not to spend the rest of her days as a mountain witch, alone but for Sookar.

Yet at the same time, she had no desire to leave the old troll behind. Sookar was not closely associated with any pack, and if Kaita left, it would rob her of her last small semblance of family that remained. But Sookar eventually became aware of Kaita's hesitancy, and she urged her to go.

"You are meant to live your life," she said, when she and Kaita at last spoke openly of the matter. "This was part of it, but there is more to come. And if you sit here waiting until I have died, you will grow as grey and knobbly as the stones of the hills."

Kaita laughed at that, though the humor was bittersweet. And so she made ready to set forth from the mountains, and in time she left them. It was not long before the Shades found her, and the Lord lured her to his side with promises of power, and purpose, and revenge against those who had cast her out.

Many years later, Kaita returned to Tokana to further the Lord's intentions there. She went south at once to go and visit Sookar. Unfortunately, the old troll had passed away some years before. From that time on, whenever Kaita wore Sookar's form, she thought of it as honoring her memory. And she modified the transformation so that Sookar was young again, and hale, and hearty—the best version of the old troll that Kaita could imagine.

But the truth, which Kaita would never have been able to accept, was that Sookar's best days were those she spent with the weremage, alone together, deep in the mountains.

THE LEGEND OF MELDIN

Listen now, child, to a tale of Meldin, the Dragon, who lived thousands of years before Underrealm was first named.

Before the time before time, before even the beginning of our world, when the sky had not yet given humanity life upon the face of the earth, a Dragon mother laid five eggs. The sun sang at their arrival, and the darkness at the edge of the world cowered in fear before them. For in these five eggs were instilled the essences that would make possible the creation of all other creatures to live under the moons, and woven into their shells were threads of Fate.

The first and greatest of the eggs held the essence of fire; the second, water; the third, earth; the fourth, the wind; and the fifth held the love of all living beings for each other and for themselves. And all the Dragons knew that one day the sky would take these essences and weave from them all the creatures that flew within itself, and crawled beneath itself, and swam to hide from itself, as well as all the plants that would grow and flourish in the light of its sun. And never had these essences been glimpsed before in all the wide world, and the Dragons wondered to see them glowing within the veins and texture of the eggs' shells.

And one by one the Dragons came to visit the eggs, and to bow before them, paying respect and swearing fealty to these, the mightiest gifts bestowed upon them by the sky. And every Dragon loved the eggs, and they longed for the day when they would hatch and make possible the small creatures that would fill the earth with life, and movement, and joy. And every Dragon bent all their thought and wove threads of Fate to see to the eggs' safety, and to protect them from all harm and all evil.

But one Dragon among their number hated the eggs, and her name was Yendil. Yendil was jealous of the eggs and their power. Especially she hated, and yet desired, the essence of flame that shone in the first egg. The other Dragons spoke of how the flame would burn and twist everything before it, and yet when it had destroyed all it had touched, it would bring also the gift of life, turning destruction into rebirth. And Yendil desired this power, and she coveted the egg that held the essence of fire, and she desired to control the flame for herself.

Yet with all the Dragons protecting the eggs, and weaving threads of

Fate about them to protect them, Yendil could not destroy any of them, nor could she affect more than one. But by bending all her thought and intent, and weaving every string of Fate at her command, Yendil stole one of the eggs. She took it when the Dragons were bowed in worship of them, and she fled with the egg clutched in her claws, and it was the egg that held the essence of flame.

Then the Dragons wailed and gnashed their teeth, and those who had been set to guard the eggs quaked in fear, and the other Dragons fell upon them, and they were devoured. And then the Dragons who remained saw that Yendil was missing from their number, and they knew it was she who had stolen the egg that held the essence of fire. And they searched all of existence for the missing egg, and they never tired in their hunt.

But Yendil hid herself from them, and she entwined her own threads of Fate with those that had been used to protect the egg, so that the same woven Fate that protected the egg from destruction also protected it from discovery. And she entwined the weave of her own Fate with the egg that held the fire essence, so that she could not be destroyed unless the egg itself was also destroyed.

Thus Yendil hid with her stolen egg, until all the five eggs hatched on the same day. And then for five years more she hid, keeping prisoner the fire dragon that had emerged from the egg. And she forced it to use its flames to burn everything Yendil hated, which was everything in Creation, which at that time was all iron and steel, lifeless and hard. And the dragon's flame spread, and it melted the world, and the sky knew that the flame dragon had been born from the egg. And the Dragons knew it as well, but still they could not find the missing whelp, for they could not find Yendil through the shroud of her Fate.

As the flame dragon grew older, he was always in misery and in pain, for Yendil was a terrible taskmaster. Yendil named him Meldin, and he was her slave, and she made him use his flame over and over again, though Meldin wept to destroy the beautiful landscapes of Creation that lay before his sight.

At last, after five years, all the dragons were grown. And the four dragons who remained free gathered to each other. The dragon of the second egg was called Harish, and the essence of water was hers. And the dragon of the third egg was called Yorprax, and the essence of earth was his. And the dragon of the fourth egg was called Yarlos, and the essence of wind was his. But the dragon of the fifth egg had no name, for she would not claim one until her brother was found, and the essence of love was hers.

As they gathered together, Harish said to them, "Now we are grown, and we are ready to bring life to all of Creation beneath the sky."

And Yorprax said to them, "But we cannot, for still our brother is missing, and without his flame we cannot give life to all the things that will fly and crawl and swim."

And Yarlos said to them, "Then let us go and find our brother, for we who are his kin shall find him no matter where Yendil may hide him."

But the fifth dragon said nothing, and only wept for Meldin, for in her was the essence of love and that is a cousin to grief.

The four dragons thus set out into the world, and they could sense Meldin through all the weave of Fate that Yendil had wrapped about him. For the Fate that bound the five of them was stronger, and had connected them since first they were laid, and Yendil could not hide it from their sight. And the four young dragons found themselves at a mouth of a cave, and they knew it held their brother, as well as his captor, and so they entered it.

There they found Yendil lurking, and she was ready to meet them, for she had heard their approach. And there, too, they found Meldin, and he was trapped in a cage all of starsteel, the strongest of metals, and his flame could not melt it.

"Turn and flee," said Yendil. "This young one is mine, and his gift of flame also."

And Yarlos said to her, "He belongs to no one, unless it is to us by the bonds of the nest."

And Yorprax said to her, "You cannot hide him from us, nor can you keep him from us."

And Harish said to her, "We shall not flee from you, nor can you escape our wrath."

But the fifth dragon said nothing, and her grief had turned hot and furious, for in her was love and that is a cousin to wrath.

And Harish, Yorprax, and Yarlos did battle with Yendil. But they were not strong enough to defeat her, for they were still young and untested, and Yendil was ancient and large and cunning. And they thought they would fall before Yendil, and she would slay them, and devour them, taking their essence for herself.

But the fifth dragon did not fight Yendil. The essence of love was hers, and so she thought only of Meldin. And while her siblings battled Yendil, she tore at the cage of starsteel to free her brother. And though Mendil's flames had not been hot enough to melt the starsteel, the fifth dragon was able to tear them asunder with her claws. And she tore at the weave of Yendil's Fate, which had been combined with Meldin's, and separated them, so that their survival was no longer linked. And this was a mighty deed, for no Dragon before her had yet been able to separate strands of Fate once they were woven together.

But the essence of love was hers and that is a cousin to strength.

Thus the five dragons were united again, and together their strength was greater than Yendil's. And she was defeated, and was torn asunder and devoured. And now Meldin was free, and the five of them gave a great cry of exultation, and such was their joy that it reached every corner of Creation, and every Dragon heard it, and they joined their voices to the chorus.

And then the fifth dragon looked at her siblings, and she said to them, "I have never had a name, for Meldin was gone from us. But now that we are united once more, I shall take my name at last, and it shall be Rowan."

And together the five dragons made the long journey home.

ADDENDUM B

THE CALENDAR OF UNDERREALM AND A TIMELINE OF EVENTS

THE CALENDAR OF UNDERREALM

There are 363.5 days in an Underrealm year. In their calendar, these are divided into 12 months of 30 days each. To reconcile the extra days, at the end of each year there is a three-day holiday called, appropriately enough, Yearsend. It takes place in the middle of winter when the world is coldest, after which the world "comes to life" again. Yearsend is often a time of celebration, when people of all the nine kingdoms take to feasting and revelry, bidding farewell to the year that has ended and readying themselves to greet the year that approaches.

Even-numbered years have leap days, placed in the middle of Yearsend, so that it is four days long in those years.

For the sake of ease, the twelve months of the Underrealm calendar have been given their Latin names from the Gregorian calendar. However, they are arranged in the original *order* of the Gregorian calendar, with Martis being the first month of the year, as follows:

Martis — WINTER
Arilis — SPRING
Maius — SPRING
Yunis — SPRING
Yulis — SUMMER
Augis — SUMMER
Septis — SUMMER
Octis — AUTUMN
Novis — AUTUMN
Dektis — AUTUMN
Yanis — WINTER
Febris — WINTER
Yearsend* — WINTER

Martis comes just after Yearsend. As with any calendar, the "assignment" of seasons is arbitrary, and the people of Underrealm saw no reason to make them fit the calendar symmetrically. Therefore winter stretches from Yanis to Martis. Spring is Arilis to Yunis. Summer lasts from Yulis to Septis, and autumn is from Octis to Dektis.

In the strictest sense, then, the seasons do not fall where they are delineated on the Underrealm calendar. However, this assignment was seen as a neater solution than having the seasons begin and end in the middle of months, which would of course be chaotic and confusing to everyone involved.

** Yearsend is included for the purpose of showing its order in the calendar, though of course it is a three- or four-day period and not a month on its own.*

THE COUNT OF YEARS

"The Year of Underrealm 1" is the year in which Roth, the first High King of Underrealm, ruling from the city of Rothton on the island capital of Dulmun, declared the nine lands to be under his dominion. Though some scholars enjoy debating the exact count, it is generally accepted to have occurred 1,311 years before the Shades attacked Northwood.

(This is, however, an inaccurate counting, since Roth laid claim to Underrealm some eighty years before his granddaughter, Silvin, the third High King of Underrealm, would mark the start of the Underrealm calendar. But this truth has long been lost to history, another victim of the chaos of Underrealm's early civil wars.)

Years are notated as, e.g., *The Year of Underrealm 1312.*

WEEKS

Each of the twelve months of Underrealm is further divided into three weeks of ten days.

As we have done, the days were named for planets that the denizens of Underrealm could observe. But this presented a problem: only six planets were visible in the sky. These were named Taya, Yuna, Kina, Marama, Dal, and Kasay in the time before time, and gave Underrealm the day-names of Tasday, Yunsday, Kinsday, Marsday, Dalsday, and Kasday. Two more days were named for Underrealm's twin moons of Enalyn and Merida, giving them Lynday and Meriday. The Sun led to Sunday, as it did for us, and that was also the Underrealm day of rest.

It is said that before humans came to Underrealm, the tenth day (which always preceded Sunday) had various names among different peoples. And so, when the first High King of Underrealm, Roth, founded the nine lands, he named the tenth day after himself, calling it Rothsday.

Thus the days are, in order:

LYNDAY
MERIDAY
TASDAY
YUNSDAY
KINSDAY
MARSDAY
DALSDAY
KASDAY
ROTHSDAY
SUNDAY

A TIMELINE OF EVENTS

THE YEAR OF UNDERREALM 1312

OCTIS

7 Octis: The Shades begin their ritual in Lan Shui. Vampires are drawn to the town.

9 Octis: A peddler named Halfpace leaves Lan Shui heading north, carrying a weekly report from Constable Yue of the family Baolan. Yue's report contains mention of several folk outside the walls of the town who seem to have vanished. Vampires kill Halfpace in the night and leave his corpse by the side of the road.

10 Octis: Halfpace's corpse is discovered. Yue investigates and deduces that he was killed by a vampire.

11 Octis: Yue sends a messenger named Chen to Bertram to warn them of the vampire. That night he is killed on the road.

13 Octis: Chen's body is discovered by Yang of the family Ton, and Yue is notified.

14 Octis: Yue sends another messenger, Fen, this time to the south to try to avoid the vampire. That night, vampires kill her on the road.

15 Octis: Fen's corpse is found. Yue advises the nearby farmers to withdraw inside the town's walls. Many do so, leaving their farmhands out of work. One of these is a boy named Pantu.

17 Octis: Pantu is recruited by Dellek to run odd jobs. The vampire attacks continue for several weeks.

NOVIS

12 Novis: Albern of the family Telfer reaches Northwood, along with Loren, Gem, Annis, and Xain. They meet Mag and Sten and stay at the Leeward Shore.

Kaita, Rogan, and Tagata learn Trisken has been slain. They plan their attack on Northwood.

Near Lan Shui, a vampire kills a farmer named Zhanu.

13 Novis: Constable Yue investigates Zhanu's death.

19 Novis: Loren decides to leave Northwood.

20 Novis: Mag, Albern, and Sten help Loren prepare for her journey. They see Rogan. The Shades attack Northwood. Loren and her companions escape. Kaita kills Sten, and Mag nearly kills her in return. Albern is knocked unconscious, and Mag drags him out of the battle.

Rogan orders Kaita to lead Mag and Albern north to Tokana.

21 Novis: Albern awakens. He and Mag burn Sten's body. They pledge to hunt down Kaita. Mag recovers her spear, and they set off west.

DEKTIS

1 Dektis: Mag and Albern reach the Shade stronghold in the Greatrocks. They ambush a pack of satyrs and capture one named Greto. From her they learn that Kaita traveled into satyr territory.

2 Dektis: Mag and Albern ride west after Kaita.

Kaita reaches Lan Shui and reunites with Dellek.

4 Dektis: Mag and Albern find the trail of the Shade army moving north. They reach the foothills of the western mountains.

6 Dektis: Sergeant Ertu and his Shades return to satyr territory. Satyrs gather to hear their judgement.

7 Dektis: Mag and Albern come upon an abandoned satyr village. Albern names his horse Foolhoof.

A vampire kills most of the Ton family to the northwest of Lan Shui. Their youngest son, Liu, escapes with their wolfhound, Oku.

8 Dektis: Albern and Mag save the satyr elders and learn that Kaita has gone to Lan Shui.

13 Dektis: Mag and Albern reach Lan Shui. They meet Dryleaf.

Loren reaches the High King's Seat and warns High King Enalyn about the Shades in the Greatrocks. Enalyn does not immediately take her at her word, but she does send messengers to the nine kings warning them to be on the lookout for the threat.

14 Dektis: Mag and Albern slay the Shades in Lan Shui. They rescue Liu and Oku from the Ton homestead. They kill the vampire that slew the Tons. Pantu adds more magestones to the ritual flame. Kaita kills Pantu. In Pantu's form, she tells Mag she has gone to Opara. Mag, Albern, and Dryleaf discover the Shade ritual. Six more vampires attack Lan Shui, and Mag kills one.

15 Dektis: The people of Lan Shui lure the vampires in and do battle with them. All of the creatures are slain, and the Shades' ritual is destroyed. Mag is injured in the fighting, but she hides it from Albern. Yue is also injured, and she must rest to recover.

16 Dektis: Mag and Albern ride for Opara. Dryleaf and Oku come with them.

28 Dektis: Word reaches King Taka in Calentin of the Shades' reappearance. They send word to all the Rangatira warning them to be on the alert.

YANIS

1 Yanis: Word of the Shades reaches Rangatira Conrus of the family Matara in Opara.

2 Yanis: Word of the Shades reaches Rangatira Ditra of the family Telfer in Tokana.

3 Yanis: Kaita reaches the Shades in the stronghold of Maunwa near Opara.

5 Yanis: Trolls first attack a human settlement in Tokana. It is a small village well within the trolls' lands as described in the pact. Over the following weeks, trolls continue to attack human settlements with greater frequency, moving closer and closer to human lands.

6 Yanis: Dryleaf falls ill in the town of Shainlu in northwestern Dorsea. Mag and Albern pause their travels.

10 Yanis: Dryleaf fully recovers. Mag and Albern resume their journey.

16 Yanis: Mag and Albern reach Opara and stay at the Ugly Squirrel. Word of them reaches Kaita. Riri refuses to act against them. Kaita advises the other Shades to flee to Tokana.

17 Yanis: Mag and Albern visit Victon.

18 Yanis: Victon brings Mag and Albern to Rangatira Matara. The Rangatira assigns Tuhin to help them find Kaita. Dryleaf finds out that Mag and Albern are Loren's friends.

Trolls attack a village north of Tokana. It is the first village they have attacked that is unquestionably within human territory, according to their pact with the family Telfer.

19 Yanis: Mag, Albern, and Tuhin slay the Shades in Maunwa. Mag is injured in the fight but hides it from Albern. They learn Kaita has traveled north to Tokana.

20 Yanis: Mag and Albern set out from Opara for the land of Tokana.

21 Yanis: Word reaches Ditra of the trolls' latest attack on one of her villages.

24 Yanis: Dotag slays Chok and takes command of the troll pack. He demands the Shades bring back Gatak.

Shades and the kingdom of Dulmun attack the High King's Seat. Enalyn and Loren survive the attack. Enalyn sends word to the nine kings to inform them what has happened.

Two sellswords and a Mystic reach the High King's Seat only to find it burning.

FEBRIS

4 Febris: Kaita reaches the Shades operating in Tokana.

5 Febris: Yue's healers declare her convalescence at an end.

9 Febris: Word reaches King Taka in Calentin of the Shades' attack on the Seat. They immediately send word to all the Rangatira.

11 Febris: Trolls attack the town of Ahuroa, close to Kahuanga.

12 Febris: Word of the attack on the Seat reaches Rangatira Matara in Opara.

13 Febris: Word of the attack on the Seat reaches Ditra in Tokana.

14 Febris: Mag and Albern reach the city of Kahuanga in the land of Tokana. Kaita receives word of their arrival.

15 Febris: Mag and Albern ride out from Kahuanga for the town of Ahuroa. They discover Kaita stalking them in the wild but fail to capture her. Rangers arrest them and bring them to Ditra. Albern learns his mother died. Ditra gives them permission to hunt Kaita, but secretly assigns Maia to find her first.

16 Febris: Mag and Albern set out to hunt for Kaita in the wilderness.

Kaita, as the troll Gatak, persuades Dotag to increase his attacks on Tokana.

20 Febris: Mag and Albern return to Kahuanga to learn more villages have been attacked, and the trolls are now killing villagers.

21 Febris: Mag and Albern resume their hunt.

30 Febris: Mag and Albern face their first troll in the wilderness. Mag is horribly injured, but she conceals it. Maia saves them from the troll. Albern learns the weremage's name is Kaita and recognizes her. He confronts Ditra. She imprisons Mag, Albern, and Dryleaf. She and Albern have their first conversation in her chamber, where she learns Albern knew about Romil's death. She sends him back to his cell.

Kaita and Dotag plan their final assault on Kahuanga.

YEARSEND

1 Yearsend: The trolls attack Kahuanga. Kaita's Shades attack Ditra in her keep and kill Maia. Ditra's troops repel the trolls at the wall before being driven back to the keep. Kaita's deception is discovered by the trolls. Apok kills Dotag and takes command of the troll pack. Kaita escapes from Mag and Albern.

2 Yearsend: Apok and Ditra begin to rebuild the pact between the trolls and the family Telfer.

3 Yearsend: Dryleaf and Oku return to Kahuanga.

THE YEAR OF UNDERREALM 1313

MARTIS

1 Martis: Yue, confident Lan Shui will remain safe, decides to give up her post as constable to seek out Mag and Albern. She spends nearly a week turning over her duties to Ashta.

5 Martis: Albern sings his song about Jordel to Dryleaf for the first time.

9 Martis: Shades dressed as Dorsean soldiers attack Feldemarian homesteads in the forests west of Dahab. Word takes three days to reach the city, whereupon messengers are sent to the Feldemarian king.

10 Martis: Yue rides out of Lan Shui, making for Opara.

11 Martis: Mag and Albern leave Kahuanga for Opara.

18 Martis: King Alim of Feldemar dispatches diplomats to King Jun of Dorsea, demanding reparations and a cessation of attacks by Dorsean troops along the Skytongue River.

21 Martis: King Alim's messengers reach King Jun in Danfon. Negotiations between the two kings begin, with King Jun denying any involvement in the continuing raids along Feldemar's southern border. King Alim threatens to bring the matter before the High King, who has forbidden any Dorsean aggression while the threat of the Shades persists.

28 Martis: Shades dressed as Dorsean soldiers attack the Feldemarian town of Kuni across the Skytongue River from Dorsea.

29 Martis: Mag and Albern reach Opara and stay with Victon.

30 Martis: Mag and Albern speak with Rangatira Matara, seeking information about Kaita. Rangatira Matara suspects the Shades are hiding in northeastern Dorsea.

ARILIS

1 Arilis: In the traditional annual ceremony of the Spring Turning, the throne of Calentin passes from Taka of the family Tapu to Amahu of the family Emere.

2 Arilis: Mag and Albern leave Opara, heading for northeastern Dorsea.

4 Arilis: Yue reaches Opara. At the constabulary, she inquires after Mag and Albern and learns they left the city only two days ago.

5 Arilis: Yue leaves Opara before dawn, riding hard to catch Mag and Albern.

7 Arilis: Mag and Albern enter the Sunmane Pass.

9 Arilis: A landslide blocks their progress through the pass, requiring them to find another way around.

Yue enters the Sunmane Pass.

12 Arilis: Mag and Albern come down out of the Sunmane Pass into northeastern Dorsea.

Shades dressed as Dorsean soldiers attack farmers near Tombi in Feldemar.

14 Arilis: Yue comes down out of the Sunmane Pass and begins to search for Mag and Albern in northeastern Dorsea.

15 Arilis: Kaita reaches the Shade encampment near Dunfen Lake to find Tagata has just left. The Lord speaks with Rogan. Rogan sends word for Kaita to join him. He also issues orders for Wojin to proceed with their planned rebellion.

22 Arilis: Mag and Albern reach the town of Taitou and meet Kun.

MAIUS

5 Maius: Wojin stages a coup to steal the throne from his nephew, Dorsea's King Jun.

6 Maius: Word of Wojin's coup reaches Taitou. Kun orders his Mystics to be on high alert, and he begins to recruit a force of militia.

7 Maius: Troops loyal to Wojin accost Yue on the road, but she escapes their grasp. Word of Wojin's coup reaches the town of Huzen.

8 Maius: Mag and Albern reach Huzen. Fighting breaks out in the town between Wojin's troops and Jun's loyalists. Mag and Albern flee the town. Dryleaf advises them to ally themselves with Kun.

Rogan's summons reaches Kaita, and she sets off to find him.

9 Maius: Mag and Albern ride for Taitou to join Kun.

Yue reaches Taitou and learns that Mag and Albern were there. It is her first solid lead in weeks. She leaves the town and begins to search for word of them in nearby towns and villages.

10 Maius: Mag and Albern reach Taitou. They make their wager with Kun to train his troops.

11 Maius: Kun introduces Mag and Albern to Tou and assigns them to their squadrons.

13 Maius: Kaita reunites with Rogan. He gives her the magestones and tells her to join Tagata.

17 Maius: Kaita finds Tagata. Together with their troops, they begin a long march west for the Sunmane Pass.

18 Maius: Loren of the family Nelda deposes Wojin of the family Fei from the throne of Dorsea. The capital city of Danfon is thrown into chaos. Word of this development is slow to spread through the kingdom.

19 Maius: Yue encounters the Shades in the Brackenbough Wood. She sets off south to warn the Mystics in Taitou.

21 Maius: Kun's trial. Dibu defeats Tou. Kun announces they will march north the next day.

22 Maius: Kun's force marches north from Taitou. Yue finds them and reunites with Mag, Albern, and Dryleaf.

23 Maius: On Yue's counsel, Kun turns his march northwest to skirt around the Carrweld Forest.

25 Maius: Kaita's force reaches the River Marsden. They lose a day's time sneaking across the river in order to avoid the town of Kuan Shui.

26 Maius: Kun turns his march due west.

28 Maius: Kun's march reaches the town of Kuan Shui on the banks of the River Marsden. He learns that Wojin has been removed from the throne and deliberates traveling to Danfon, but decides to continue his pursuit of the Shades.

29 Maius: Kun finds signs of the Shades' westward march.

30 Maius: Mag and Albern guess the Shades are making for the Sunmane Pass. They devise a plan to catch them in the Greenfrost, and Kun approves it. Tou's company splits off from the main force and marches hard to catch the Shades.

YUNIS

3 Yunis: Kaita and Tagata first catch sight of Kun's army pursuing them.

4 Yunis: Tou's company ambushes the Shades in the Greenfrost. The Shades retreat north to the hills.

5 Yunis: The bulk of Kun's force catches up to Tou's company before dawn. Mag and Albern scout the hills to find the Shades. Second battle between the Shades and Kun's army. The Shades retreat into the tunnels beneath the hills. Mag and Albern disobey orders and find the Shades. They return to tell Kun.

6 Yunis: Kun leads his force into the tunnels after the Shades. The Shades circle around underground and attack the Mystic camp. Zhen, Kun's nephew, is killed. The Shades retreat west. Mag, Albern, Dryleaf, and Yue flee the Mystics. Mag is killed by Kaita but rises again, and Albern learns her secret. Mag and Albern kill Kaita together.

7 Yunis: Mag, Albern, Dryleaf, and Yue set out to find Loren.

The Lord resurrects Kaita as a shadeborn.

ADDENDUM C

FAMILY TREES OF SOME NOTABLE FAMILIES OF UNDERREALM

THE FAMILY TELFER

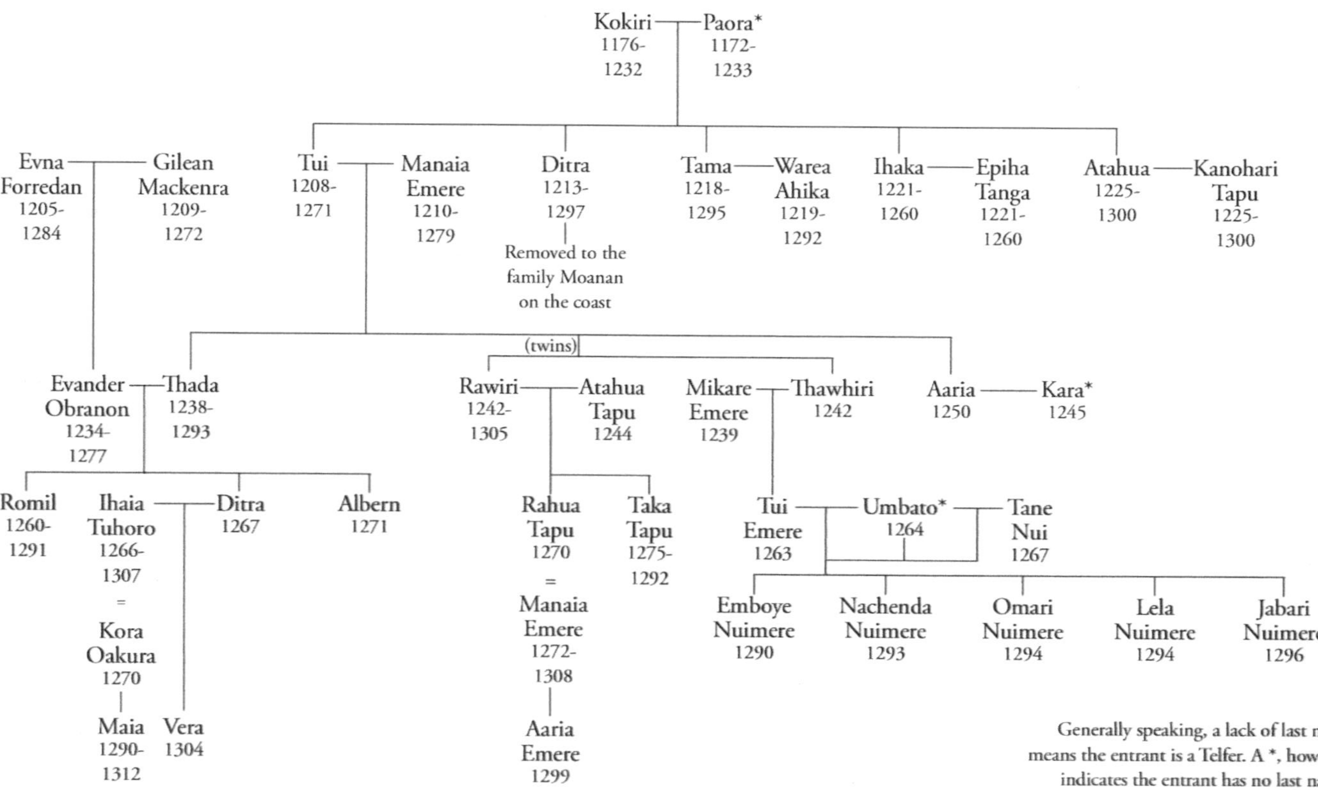

THE FAMILY ADAIR

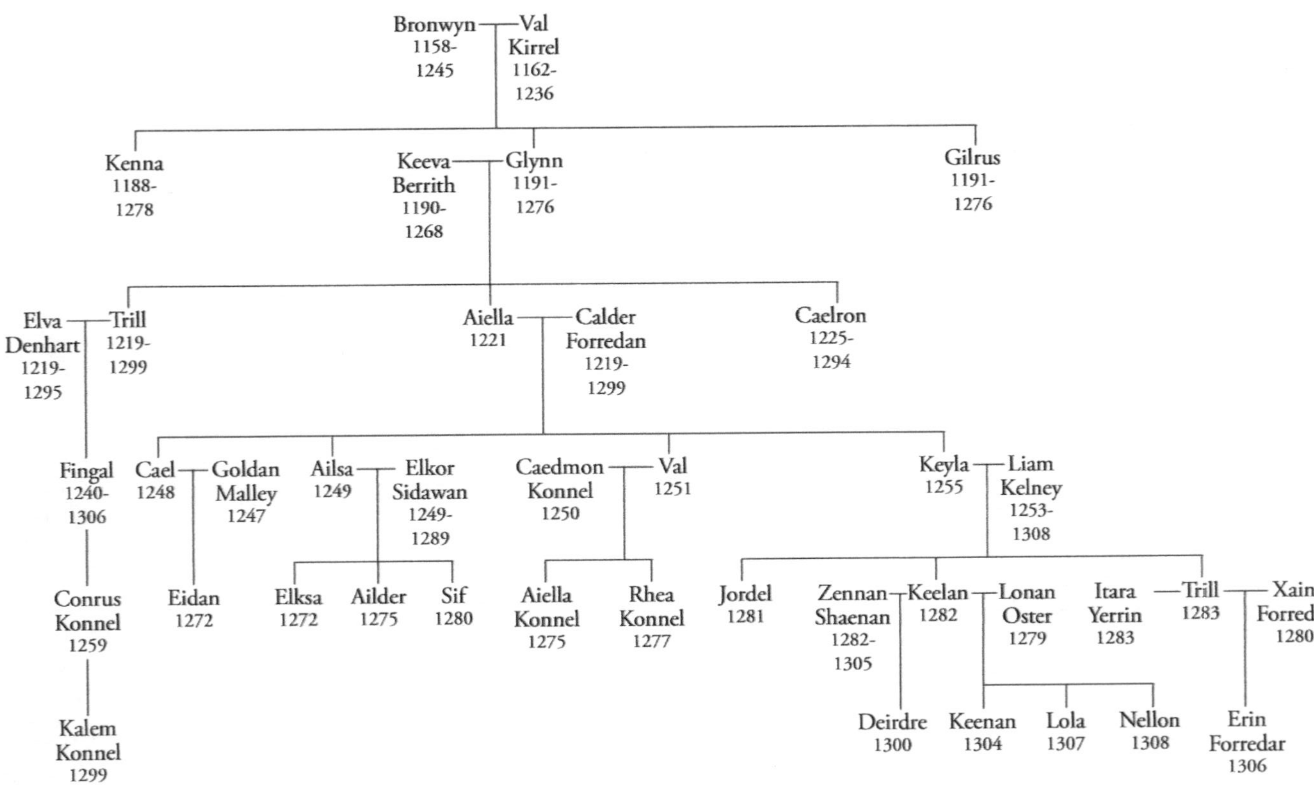

THE FAMILY LEMSTAD

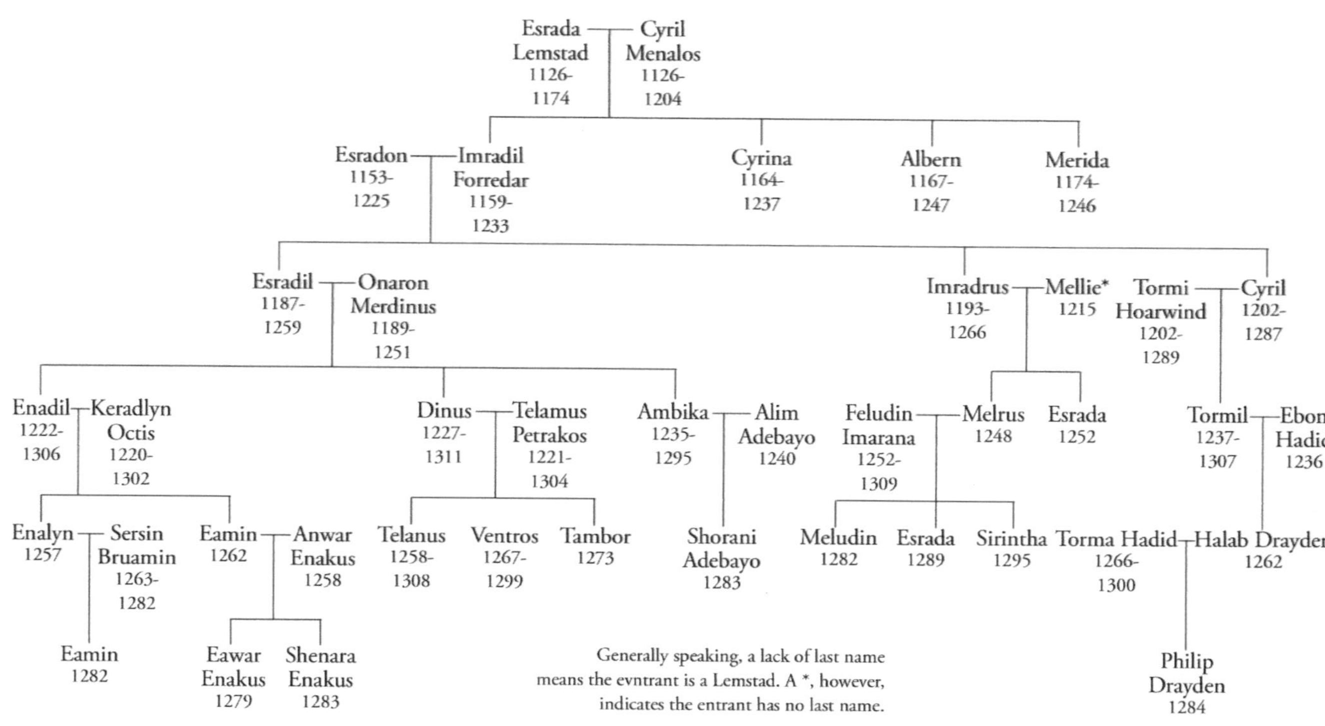

ADDENDUM D

A SELECTION OF
DOCUMENTS OF NOTE

NOTES FROM THE SHADE HIDEOUT IN LAN SHUI

Being a selection of some of the notes kept by Dellek, the Shade captain, in the Dorsean town of Lan Shui during their experiment to summon vampires to attack the town.

* * *

2 Septis

1. I have reached Lan Shui. Preparations have begun ahead of my coming, but things are slightly behind schedule. My first order of business shall be to get things back on track so that we are ready to begin our real work the instant Father gives us the order.

9 Septis

1. The cauldron has been procured. That constable, Sinshi, nearly ruined everything as we were smuggling it into the town. He came stumping about, asking what was in our wagon. Fortunately, he was witless enough to believe the driver when she said it was only a stack of empty barrels. The people of this town are lazy and careless. They will not be for long.

The cauldron's arrival is ahead of schedule, but we are still understocked on blood. What we have now will not even fill it halfway. I have had an idea I wish to explore further. In the lands outside this town, there are many farms and homesteads. They are well away from the walls and inhabited by solitary folk. Often they do not see anyone else for days. With careful study and planning, some of them could be harvested. There is the matter of storage and transport, but we still have our alchemists who created the ritual chamber.

The main problem is quantity. Together with the shipments that are reported to be arriving soon, we would need some dozens more. I am not sure so many can be found in this area.

I will pursue this matter further.

14 Septis

1. I may have found our first candidate. An old man named Grist, who lives some hours southwest of Lan Shui. He has no family nearby, and he is of an independent kind. His farm is enough to feed him with little left over, and so he rarely comes to town for anything. I am leaving an agent to monitor him and ensure there will be no surprises, while I and some others will look for more.

After reflecting on this for some days, I believe I may need to start harvesting soon. I cannot be sure when the Lord will give his order, but I suspect the time is imminent. Strange disturbances and disappearances in the area may be suspicious, but we do not have an eternity to wait. With the Shades at my disposal, we can harvest only a few people each night. It may take as long as a week to collect all the blood necessary to begin the ritual in earnest.

I will think upon this further. For now I will simply continue to identify future candidates, and learn as much about them as possible. When we do strike, there will be no surprises.

15 Septis

1. I am going to kill that idiot, Aldo.

He has been the one in charge of determining the right amount of magestone to use in the cauldron's cooking fire. We are, of course, rather desperately short on magestones, and I impressed this fact upon him very thoroughly. The Lord has sent word that we should be receiving a new (and plentiful) shipment of them soon, but for now there are only a precious few dozen. It has been Aldo's job to investigate their properties as they pertain to the ritual. The stones are, of course, exceedingly flammable, but their use for our current purpose is hardly codified.

Well, Aldo overdid it, as is his wont.

Apparently he was unsatisfied with the size of the darkfire flames he had built, for he added two more magestones. They burned straight through the bottom of the cauldron. Thank the sky it only had a pint or two of blood in it, or I really would kill him.

But more important than the lost blood is the cauldron itself. It is completely ruined now. Libet acted quickly and used her magic to shear off the bottom section of the cauldron before the darkfire could spread to the top—and badly singed two of her fingers doing it. Thank the sky the darkfire did not catch in her skin. I would not enjoy explaining to Trisken how I lost one of his alchemists.

Even though Libet acted quickly, however, it was mostly a useless gesture. The top half of a cauldron is useless if the bottom is missing. And if Askila and Libet tried to reshape the remainder into a new cauldron, it would be far too small for our purpose.

And we went through such pains to get the cauldron in the first place. Now we shall have to fetch another, and hope we are as lucky with the constables a second time.

At least Aldo seems to know how drastic his error was. I doubt he will be so foolish again.

16 Septis

1. We have thirteen potential candidates for harvesting now.

I hope Father sends his order soon. I am anxious to begin. This ritual will work. I can feel it. And if it can be used in the war . . . the sheer number of cities that could be laid low by such a technique! Danfon, Opara, the entirety of western Selvan—to say nothing of Hedgemond. Weeks, mayhap even months of terror, and then the beleaguered citizens will welcome us as their rightful saviors.

If only I had a dark-damned cauldron.

18 Septis

1. Sky bless Aldo and his foolish, foolish face. I was right before. He knew just how grave was his error, and he has been working tirelessly to correct it. He went out exploring in the town and bought a great quantity of wrought iron. This he brought to Libet and Askila, and with enough of it to use for raw material, they were able to replace the bottom of the cauldron. They warned me that the material would eventually degrade over time, but we should have at least six months. That should give us plenty of time to conclude our business here in Lan Shui, and then to procure another cauldron for use somewhere else.

Aldo is still a fool, of course, but even great foolishness can be overcome by an earnest heart and enough dedication.

Now that we have a workable cauldron again, I am going to have the alchemists dig us a much deeper hole beneath it. I will not risk losing it again.

20 Septis

1. I have decided to start the harvest. Tonight. I am worried that the order will come, and that we will be woefully underprepared.

We can only hope that I am not too early, and that suspicion is not raised before we are ready.

I shall split my squadron into two groups, each of which can harvest two candidates each night. One alchemist with each group shall form the containers to keep the blood from spoiling.

It will take us a week and a half to collect what we need. I only hope the order comes soon after that.

22 Septis

1. I can hardly believe it. Word has come from the Lord. We are to begin the ritual. It seems I began the harvest at just the right time.

Father is lenient. He understands I may not have all of the necessary materials to begin the ritual immediately, and so he has merely asked us to begin as soon as we are ready—before the ides of Octis, if we can manage it.

The harvest goes well. I have laid my plans carefully. The Lord has placed great faith in me, and I will not fail him.

4 Octis

1. We do not quite have as much blood as I would like. There are many more candidates to be harvested. But I grow anxious to begin the ritual. Each night brings greater risk of discovery. Askila's target nearly escaped her grasp last night, and that would have been a disaster.

Yet at the same time, I do not wish to start with insufficient blood, and cause the ritual to fail because we did not collect enough. It is a quandary.

Three more days. I shall give it three more days, and then I shall begin, no matter our supplies.

7 Octis

1. It is time. I would rather we had another dozen bodies' worth of blood, but this shall have to do. We can continue to add to the cauldron after it is already boiling, after all. And I cannot risk any more delay. Of the candidates who remain, all are far more risky than the ones we have collected so far. Most of them have regular contact with the townsfolk, and it will not be long before their absence is noted.

At midday, we begin the burn.

2. The burn has begun. I started with a single stone. Caution is warranted in the beginning, I think. Certainly I do not want to repeat Aldo's mistake.

The heat is considerable, even from a pace or two away. But the cauldron remains cold to the touch. I will give it more time.

3. It is nearly sundown. The cauldron has warmed slightly, but the blood is still cool, though we have been stirring it constantly.

I am adding another stone and then retiring for the evening. There will be no harvest tonight. Everyone deserves at least one day's rest after the grueling pace of things recently.

8 Octis

1. I woke this morning to find the cauldron too hot to touch, and the blood bubbling. This is it. This must be it. I have sent agents into the town to see if there were any disturbances in the night. I feel certain there must have been.

The harvest will continue this evening. The only thing that can stop us now is a lack of sufficient blood. Therefore I will cast as much into the cauldron as I can manage.

2. Curse this town. There were no vampires in the night, but something else has happened. Our activities have at last begun to draw notice. The constable captain, that Yue, is asking about after some of the folk beyond the walls who have disappeared. From what my agents could discover, she does not know what exactly has happened. There is no suspicion of murder, at least not yet. Hopefully she thinks it is merely some wild animal preying on the helpless.

Of course, very soon she will have a new thing to blame for the disappearances. That is, if the ritual works.

Which it will. It must.

3. Evening is here again. If there is no sign of success during the night, I will add another stone in the morning. Mayhap the subjects are simply too far away in the mountains, and they need further incentive.

9 Octis

1. I sent out some agents to gather word in the town. Nothing. It becomes difficult not to despair.

As soon as they returned, I added another stone to the flames. The darkfire is still a good distance away from the cauldron, but I cannot stop worrying that I will overdo it. The heat in the chamber is bad enough, but the oppressive air the ritual creates is far worse. I do not know if I imagine it, but I feel I can even sense it when I leave the building, and for several spans around.

This setback would be more tolerable if I knew why it has happened. It is possible, I know, that there are no vampires close enough in the mountains to sense the ritual's presence. But all our best research indicated that Lan Shui would be the ideal setting for such an endeavor. Were we wrong in that? Or is this some other failing of mine? Did I not do enough to codify the specifics of the ritual? Did I let the blood sit for too long? Is the degraded cauldron interfering somehow?

I cannot know the answer, and so I can only sit here and wonder, helplessly.

Nothing else to do today but wait, and burn, and pray for some further guidance from the Lord.

10 Octis

1. I sent out my agents again just after sunup. They returned with nothing, again. No one in the town seems to have been attacked. There have been no sightings of vampires in the area.

The nighttime hours plagued me with thoughts and wonderings of where I could have gone wrong. And I believe I have it. I did not have enough blood. I pushed too hard. The Lord urged me to begin before the ides of Octis, but I acted in rash pride. I thought to impress him by beginning early, when I should have trusted in his infallible judgement.

Father forgives, but I do not want his forgiveness in this. I want only to please him, and to serve him. And I have failed at both. He deserves a better officer than I.

2. I scribble this with shaking fingers.

It has worked.

I despaired because the agents I sent out this morning discovered nothing. What a fool I was. Of course the vampires would not have attacked the town straight away. Instead they attacked a messenger, one sent by the constables to deliver their weekly report to Bertram. The old man was leagues away from the walls when the vampires found him.

Early this morning his body was discovered, and it was some hours before Captain Baolan could go and investigate. When she came back to town she was apparently reticent, but rumor has it that the body was completely drained of blood.

A vampire has come. More than one, if we are lucky.

I will again call off the harvest. The wilds are no longer safe.

This morning I despaired of my service to Father. Now I am vindicated, but I care little for being proven right. I care only that I have not failed him.

11 Octis

1. Word has spread through the town that the constables have sent another messenger to Bertram. If he should reach the city and warn them of the vampire attack, that would be frustrating, but hardly debilitating. Now we know the ritual works for certain. As long as we are safe here in this town, we will take every opportunity to experiment. The height of the cauldron, the number of magestones, every factor will be weighed, adjusted, and observed to gather more information for use in the coming conflict.

Thus if the redbacks of Bertram should find us here, we will lose nothing, but only be slightly delayed in our discoveries.

For the first time in a very long while, I am nothing but eager for tomorrow.

12 Octis

1. I write this near the end of the day. There were no reports of an attack in the night. But if there are only one or two vampires in the area, their victims simply might not have been discovered yet. Sky above, it took the constables long enough to discover the folk we were harvesting under their very noses.

13 Octis

1. The operation is more successful than I could have hoped. Someone discovered the body of the constables' messenger. He never reached Bertram. He and his horse were slain at night on the road.

No help is coming to Lan Shui. No one shall come to rescue them. We can wait here until the whole town has been wiped free of life, and then retreat into the Greatrocks, leaving the cauldron behind to keep the vampires in place.

The fires dropped somewhat low, and so I added another magestone. Our supply is short—I have only a dozen and a half left—and there is no sign of the fresh shipment the Lord mentioned. I have sent a messenger into the Greatrocks to find out about the shipment and see if it can be expedited.

Speaking of which, I imagine the constable captain will try again to send word to Bertram. I await the results of such an attempt with bated breath.

15 Octis

1. A second messenger was indeed sent, and she was killed. They found her body this afternoon. The constable captain seems to have come to her senses and advised all nearby farmers to withdraw within the walls—something she should have done days ago.

This does bring to mind another concern, however. I am somewhat disgruntled that the vampires have not yet attacked the town itself. Are there too few of them? Is that even something that would concern them?

I am tempted to throw another stone into the fire. After all, it was a three-stone burn that attracted the vampires in the first place. But I worry about going through our supply too quickly. And besides, the answer may be simple. Mayhap the vampires do not strike the town simply because there are so many other, easier targets outside the walls.

For now, it is best to wait and see. Hopefully the farmers heed the constables' advice, leaving the vampires nowhere to feed but Lan Shui itself.

17 Octis

1. I have hired on a local boy to run errands for us in town. He was a farmhand until his master retreated behind the walls in order to escape the vampires. His name is Pantu, and he is as ugly as a troll. Still, his help will be valuable. The constables are ever watchful now, and we cannot move about Lan Shui as freely as we once did. Thank the Lord that we do not need to try to sneak in a replacement cauldron in under these circumstances!

14 Novis

1. A fresh shipment of magestones has arrived! Thank the sky. I was down to my last five. Now we have two full packets, more than enough to sustain the ritual for several months. And according to the messenger, there are even more in the mountains. A delivery has come to Commander Trisken in our Greatrocks stronghold, a gift of the family Yerrin, just one week ago.

Still no messengers have been able to escape Lan Shui. With more magestones, I feel confident that our aims here shall soon be achieved.

Strangely, however, the messenger brought another instruction: I am not to build a fire from more than two magestones at a time. The Lord dictated that I let things play out as they have been. I do not understand the instructions, but I do not need to. I will obey. The flames will be kept to two magestones, with a new stone added to the fire every two days.

20 Novis

1. Messengers to and from the Greatrocks have now begun to travel at regular intervals. Today they brought terrible news.

Trisken has fallen.

It is hard to imagine. I cannot picture a world without him in it. All of the shadeborn I have met . . . Rogan, Enfil, Odobe, Tagata, Poruk, and poor Trisken . . . they all seemed so invincible. Sky above, they are supposed to be *invincible. Yet here we are.*

He was always so kind to me. As kind as he was unforgiving to the Lord's enemies.

I should not linger overmuch on this. My kindred need me.

25 Novis

1. An unexpected delight in a bleak time. Kaita will be coming here soon. The messenger's reasons were vague, but apparently the Lord wishes her to oversee operations here for a time before she moves on.

If it were most anyone else, I might be worried that the Lord was displeased with me for some reason. But I think he knows that sending Kaita to me could never be a burden. Happily will I share with her all the progress we have made here, and then we shall have time to catch up. I forget when last I saw her, but it must be at least three years ago now.

Meanwhile, the town grows more frightened every day. There is at least one new death every night, though for now the vampires have stayed far enough away from the town that no one within the walls has seen them. However, there is no doubt in my mind that there are more than one of them out there, though no one in the town has been clever enough to notice yet.

I am glad I had Libet and Askila reinforce the protective seals on the ritual chamber before they left. It cannot be long now before the beasts are within the walls.

2 Dektis

1. Kaita reached Lan Shui today, and I confess her behavior worries me.

She has always been passionate and driven, but her demeanor now borders on that of a zealot. I do not know that I have ever seen her this consumed with a singular focus, and I worry that it might lead her to lose sight of the larger tapestry of our doings in the nine lands.

But then, mayhap I should be more understanding. Two old foes pursue her, and she has come to me for help.

I shall assist her in sending these two wanderers on their way. Then, hopefully, Kaita will be able to rest.

WOJIN'S DECLARATION OF INDEPENDENCE

The First Year of the Age of Fei
From the hand of Wojin the Mournful, of the family Fei, King of Dorsea

No occasion is more suited to cast one into grief than the loss of family. The grief grows sharper the nearer the kinship, is yet worse when those one loses are younger than oneself, and becomes manifold when more than one person falls to time's brutal sway.

By such measures may you understand the sorrow in my heart when I inform you of the death of my nephew, Jun of the family Fei, who was your king as well as mine. Too must I write you of the death of his son, Senlin of the family Fei, rightful heir after his father.

One would understand if the reader now required a moment to compose themself before continuing. Indeed, one would encourage the reader to do so. For stern and uncompromising action is now required, and a weeping heart may poorly rise to such challenge. Therefore give yourself the time you require to dry your tears and steel your spine before you read on, and learn the manner of this bereavement, which is the kingdom's as much as it is my own.

With misery fresh cast aside, let us now examine eagle-eyed the cause of our loss, and the action demanded in turn.

I do inform you now:

That the High King Enalyn of the family Lemstad has grown jealous and anxious at the rise of the star of King Jun of the family Fei.

That she did covet the riches of our kingdom even beyond that which we paid her in just and fair tax, which taxes she raised highly until they were no longer just, and which then required we make righteous war to earn the coin to pay.

That she did then object to our wars and spoke perfidiously against them in her court, out of fear of decrying our king openly.

That she was further incensed by the riches stolen from the southern reaches of the kingdom of Selvan, which she hails from, though the taking of such riches was necessitated by her own unjust and covetous taxes.

That she did barbarously and cruelly order the assassination of King Jun and dispatched her agents to enact the same.

There is now no other choice. I, Wojin of the family Fei, being the eldest living brother of the father of King Jun, and thus the most eligible living heir to the throne, do now take up his seat upon the throne.

I shall never touch his crown. That shall now be a hallowed relic of the royal family of Dorsea until time ends, and it shall be placed on prominent display in the royal palace. A new crown shall I have forged for myself, silver in pale imitation of Jun's golden light, which shall forever humble me in its shadow.

Here, too, do I declare the kingdom of Dorsea an independent kingdom. Free are we of the bonds that once tied us to the nation of Underrealm, and especially of the bonds that held us to Enalyn, the so-called High King. Any person who would so deviously and evilly beguile and ensnare one of her own most loyal servants deserves neither loyalty nor fealty, but only scorn and war.

I declare this now on the 5th day of Maius in the First Year of the age of Fei.

I so decree, even as my tears of mourning stain this page.
Wojin the Mournful, of the family Fei
First Independent King of Dorsea

KEEP READING

Kaita is gone. Mag's wanderings have just begun. But this is not the end of the tale.

War has come to Underrealm. Mag and Albern will need the help of other heroes to survive it. Join them as they unite with other great figures of Underrealm in *Quest,* the first book in the saga of the Necromancer's rise.

Get it NOW:

Underrealm.net/Quest

THANK YOU TO MY PATRONS

A number of you contribute to my Patreon. Your unswerving support means the world to me, and many times it's kept me going when I would otherwise have had to quit. Each and every one of you has my sincere gratitude.

If you'd like to become a supporter, you can find my Patreon at:

Patreon.com/GarrettBRobinson

(Patrons are listed in order of lifetime support).

STUDIO EXECUTIVES

Sybil R. Case, Hayley Marsden, Kris Nieder, A Howard, Mark Monroe, Dakota Heath, Sara Scimone, Mysery, Joshua Kluender

PRODUCERS

Erik Gross, Eric, Val Ritz, John Maryn

ABOVE THE LINE

Hank Green, Kai Chochinov, Kelsey Nolen, Eric Ugland, Felix, LupineKing, Jesse S, Sarah, Predawn, Dia Chappell, Renae Brown, Gin Hollan, Gerald Hornsby, Mike C, Lia Marie, Lauren Brender, Thoth Process, Katy Schneider, Juniper, William Johnson, Meri, Dwight Kuhl, Dorothy Holzman, CherryFlight, Tim Beauchamp, Maeve Shea, Tammi Labrecque, Spinnerlynne, Aidn White

PATRONS

Michael O'Neal, Jack F Erikson, Kakirtog, the Charr in gold, Logan Rutherford, Rosie Reast, Brenna Gawain, Donovan Scherer, Mr. C, Kyle Hamman, Chad Kukahiko, Kj Caston, Nicholas Rem, Lady Bee Games, Amber Morant, Salgood Sam, Cathleen Mitchell, Alicia Garner, ExactoBeau, Melanie Shukost, Kimberly Grube, Wicketbird, Steven Geyer, Stephanie Glinski, Sean Cheasley, Peter Bromage, Paul Tressler, Nancy Pillot, Matthew McCray, Mary Paulk Powers, Jenny

Kira Franke, Jeff Barrows, Game Programming Academy, Eric Cerini, Edwin Wallum, David Blaskovich, Ashton Sanders, Ailysha, Annalise Moore, Michael Bishop, Kris, Ian J Middleton, Brett Kane, CJ Edmunds, Summer Wilson

THE BOOKS OF UNDERREALM

THE NIGHTBLADE EPIC

NIGHTBLADE
MYSTIC
DARKFIRE
SHADEBORN
WEREMAGE
YERRIN

THE ACADEMY JOURNALS

THE ALCHEMIST'S TOUCH
THE MINDMAGE'S WRATH
THE FIREMAGE'S VENGEANCE

THE TALES OF THE WANDERER

BLOOD LUST
STONE HEART
HELL SKIN

THE TENTH KINGDOM

A CLOAK OF RED

RISE OF THE NECROMANCER

QUEST

THE CHRONICLES OF UNDERREALM COLLECTION ONE

THE BOOKS OF UNDERREALM

CHRONOLOGICAL ORDER

NIGHTBLADE
MYSTIC
DARKFIRE
SHADEBORN
BLOOD LUST
THE ALCHEMIST'S TOUCH
WEREMAGE
THE MINDMAGE'S WRATH
STONE HEART
THE FIREMAGE'S VENGEANCE
HELL SKIN
YERRIN
QUEST
A CLOAK OF RED
THE CHRONICLES OF UNDERREALM

CONNECT ONLINE

DISCORD

Discord is a free voice and text chat engine for gamers, geeks—and for readers like you.

Legacy Books has a Discord server that we think is pretty awesome. You can chat with Garrett Robinson and ALL the authors of Underrealm, as well as many other readers just like you:

Underrealm.net/Discord

Garrett can also be found on the following social media:
Twitter: @GarrettAuthor
Facebook: GarrettBRobinson
Tumblr: GarrettAuthor

ABOUT THE AUTHOR

Garrett Robinson was born and raised in Los Angeles. The son of an author/painter father and a violinist/singer mother, no one was surprised when he grew up to be an artist.

After blooding himself in the independent film industry, he self-published his first book in 2012 and swiftly followed it with a stream of others, publishing more than two million words by 2014. Within months he topped numerous Amazon bestseller lists. Now he spends his time writing books and directing films.

A passionate fantasy author, his most popular books are the novels of Underrealm, including The Nightblade Epic, The Academy Journals, and The Tales of the Wanderer series.

However, he has delved into many other genres. Some works are for adult audiences only, such as *Non Zombie* and *Hit Girls,* but he has also published popular books for younger readers, including The Realm Keepers series and *The Ninjabread Man*, co-authored with Z.C. Bolger.

Garrett lives in Oregon with his wife Meghan, his children Dawn, Luke, and Desmond, and his dog Chewbacca.

Garrett can be found on:

EMAIL: garrett@garrettbrobinson.com
TWITTER: twitter.com/garrettauthor
FACEBOOK: facebook.com/garrettbrobinson

www.ingramcontent.com/pod-product-compliance
Lightning Source LLC
Chambersburg PA
CBHW030828310726
48980CB00006B/684/J

* 9 7 8 1 9 4 1 0 7 6 7 9 8 *